I0657458

A SOLDIER'S LIFE

BOOK 5: The Boutan Caliphate

First Edition

Written by AlwaysRollsAOne

Erick Thiemke

Editor: Ceileigh Mangalam

Cover Art and Images: Generated by Night Café

– Edited by Illustrator Diana Roche

Acknowledgments:

My parents for supporting me through the writing process and helping me pursue my storytelling dreams.

My supporters on Patreon, thank you for supporting me, motivating me, and helping shape the story.

The community of Royalroad.com for help in editing and feedback on the story as it has progressed.

The story is self-published by the author from his web serial story: A Soldier's Life

The cover and images were generated using AI and edited by a professional graphic artist, but no text within the story contains AI-generated content.

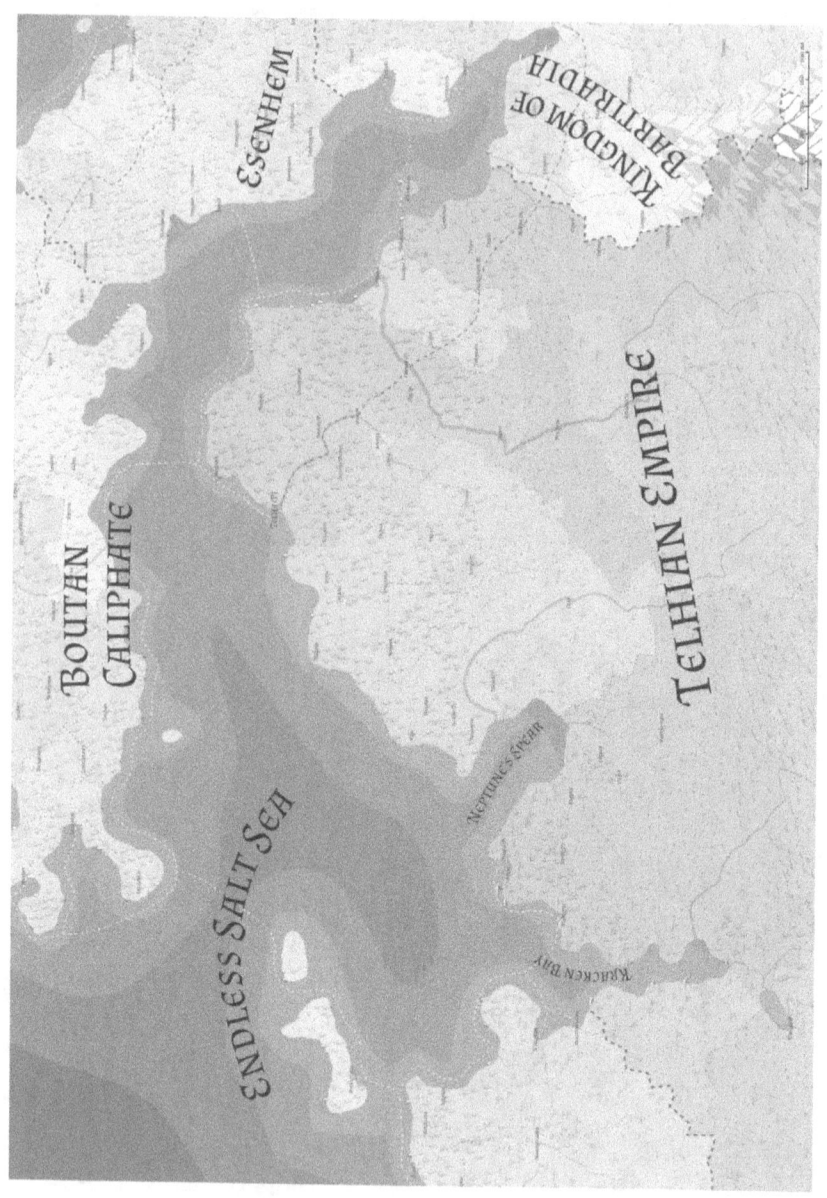

Table of Contents

CHAPTER 244: PROLOGUE 8

CHAPTER 245: GOLIATH CREED 14

CHAPTER 246: THE ROAD LESS TRAVELED 20

CHAPTER 247: THICK-SKINNED......................................25

CHAPTER 248: VIGILANTE JUSTICE 30

CHAPTER 249: GNOLL PARTY 36

CHAPTER 250: RETURN TO TELHA 43

CHAPTER 251: CAPTAIN DESDEMONA............................48

CHAPTER 252: ANCHORS AWEIGH 55

CHAPTER 253: CAPTAIN ON DECK 62

CHAPTER 254: YOU CAN'T KEEP AN OLD HOUND DOWN.......69

CHAPTER 255: DINNER DISCOURSE 75

CHAPTER 256: SAW HULA GIN?....................................81

CHAPTER 257: I NEVER REALLY LIKED SUSHI...................87

CHAPTER 258: TIME IS OF THE ESSENCE 93

CHAPTER 259: ELVEN CUSTOMS 99

CHAPTER 260: GUILD REWARDS...................................105

CHAPTER 261: BREAD, BATH, AND BEYOND 112

CHAPTER 262: GUILDMASTER PREJUDICE 118

CHAPTER 263: MISTAKES WERE MADE...........................125

CHAPTER 264: HARD LESSON 131

CHAPTER 265: FORGING BONDS 137

CHAPTER 266: GREASING THE WHEELS OF JUSTICE 144

CHAPTER 267: INVESTMENT OPPORTUNITIES 150

CHAPTER 268: SECRET DEPTHS REVEALED......................161

CHAPTER 269: BURDEN OF LEADERSHIP.........................169

CHAPTER 270: KONSTANTIN 177

CHAPTER 271: DINNER PLANS.....................................193

CHAPTER 272: CARAVAN GUARD DUTY..........................199

CHAPTER 273: DINNER DISCOURSE 206

CHAPTER 274: PARTY CRASHER..215

CHAPTER 275: FINAL PREPARATIONS 220

CHAPTER 276: GUARD DUTY 228

CHAPTER 277: HOWL YOU DOING? 235

CHAPTER 278: HANDLE WITH CARE..243

CHAPTER 279: SHOW ME THE MONEY 249

CHAPTER 280: FAKE IT TILL YOU MAKE IT..255

CHAPTER 281: FORTUNA'S CHOSEN 261

CHAPTER 282: SKELETONS IN THE CLOSET......................................268

CHAPTER 283: THE CHRONICLER 276

CHAPTER 284: REVELATIONS..283

CHAPTER 285: BUTTON UP 290

CHAPTER 286: MISUNDERSTANDINGS 296

CHAPTER 287: THE VAULT OF THE SPIRIT ARACHNID....................303

CHAPTER 288: SPEED RUN 310

CHAPTER 289: SHE LOOKS FAMILIAR..316

CHAPTER 290: MYNASHA..323

CHAPTER 291: STRENGTH OF GIANTS..330

CHAPTER 292: EXILED ELDER..338

CHAPTER 293: VICTORY IN DEFEAT 345

CHAPTER 294: ORC SUBTERFUGE 353

CHAPTER 295: WHEN IT RAINS ... .360

CHAPTER 296: TROLLS TO THE LEFT OF ME, OGRES TO THE RIGHT ... HERE I AM, STUCK IN THE MIDDLE WITH YOU 366

CHAPTER 297: MASTER BAITER AGAIN..375

CHAPTER 298: FISH IN A BARREL..382

CHAPTER 299: CASTILE VERSUS KONSTANTIN 390

CHAPTER 300: HONOR, GUTS, AND OGRE FUNK............................403

CHAPTER 301: KONSTANTIN CRASHES THE PARTY 411

CHAPTER 302: THE STUDENT BECOMES THE MASTER..................................416

CHAPTER 303: THE COMPETITION..................................423

CHAPTER 304: HOW TO WIN FRIENDS AND INFLUENCE WARLORDS..................429

CHAPTER 305: PIXIE PROBLEMS 436

CHAPTER 306: THE PIXIE GAMBIT 443

CHAPTER 307: CATCH AND RELEASE..................................449

CHAPTER 308: RACE TO THE SPIRE 458

CHAPTER 309: CLOUDY WITH A CHANCE OF TITANS..................464

CHAPTER 310: KHRUSOS 469

CHAPTER 311: HUMBLED HOARDER..................................476

CHAPTER 312: CHANGING FORTUNES 481

CHAPTER 313: THE THIRD TRIAL..................................487

CHAPTER 314: THE DEMONIC DEPTHS..................................497

CHAPTER 315: HOUND VERSUS HOUND 504

CHAPTER 316: CAUGHT BETWEEN A ROCK AND A HARD PLACE 509

CHAPTER 317: WHY DO THEY ALWAYS RUN? 517

CHAPTER 318: YOU'RE GOING TO NEED A BIGGER BOAT..................524

CHAPTER 319: EPILOGUE 534

Raelia was prepared for the worst-case scenario. With her fate in the legionnaire's hands, anything was possible. She truly thought he would turn her over to his mage commander, making her a prisoner of the Telhians. She was surprised when she appeared in a dark forest in the light of a single glowstone held by the legionnaire. Eryk hadn't betrayed her.

She slowly relaxed, not sensing any danger. Her breath clouded in front of her in the still, cold air. "We are out of the dungeon?" she asked Eryk. She resisted wincing at the stupidity of the question.

Dispassionately, Eryk responded. "We are. We are about twenty miles west of Parvas. Do you know where that is?"

Raelia took his flat, unemotional tone to mean that Maveith had not made it. Taking in her surroundings, she asked with a note of sorrow, "I know where Parvas is. Did Maveith not make it?"

Eryk looked annoyed at her question. "Maveith is sleeping." He gestured behind him. "My company and my mage commander aren't far off. You should get going. I suggest traveling south, crossing the river, and then making your way home." Her pack appeared in his outstretched hand. "Food and some fragile items are inside, so treat the pack with care. You should make haste." He gestured behind him again at the unseen danger of his mage commander.

Raelia ground her teeth a little. After two weeks of fighting together in the most dangerous dungeon she had ever heard of, now he was tossing her away with no parting words—not even a thank you. She then realized that for her, it had only been a heartbeat since he had placed her in his space.

Eryk looked exhausted and maybe in pain. What had he been through in the days, weeks, or months she had been imprisoned? At least he had kept his promise. Not that she liked him, though he wasn't terrible-looking for a human. Well—as long as he wasn't wearing the red Legion armor. What was she thinking? He had killed Vaeril. She hardened her resolve.

She sheathed her blades and took a few steps forward to take her pack. The weight surprised her and she fumbled it briefly. Eryk winced when she almost dropped it. She shouldered the pack and was about to turn, but paused. Whether she wanted to admit it or not, he hadn't killed her the two times they had fought—and he was not a terrible human. A bit of an ogre's ass, but not a bad human.

"If you are ever captured …" She paused, considering her words. "Ask for General Clalyn Glavien. I will tell my brother you helped me, and he will ensure you end up in a work camp instead of being strung up with the other legionnaires."

"What a generous offer," he said with a mocking undertone. Raelia winced as she realized what she had said. Of course, she would free him from the work camp if she learned he had been captured. She hadn't said that aloud but thought it was implied. She rolled her eyes at him rather than clarify, since she doubted she would ever see this legionnaire again.

She waited to see if he would say anything else. When he didn't, she checked the position of the moon and tramped off into the snow. Strangely, she didn't feel like she was turning her back on an enemy. The snow crunched under her feet as she made her way south. She increased her pace, needing to gain distance from his mage commander. It was too easy to be tracked in the snow.

Raelia pushed herself hard for hours till she reached the river. Crossing the icy flow was going to be unpleasant. She hoped he had given her at least two waterskins she could empty and use as floats. She started to unpack and froze. *That stupid bastard!* She cradled the griffin egg and pulsed aether into it.

The faint stirrings were still there. Whatever reason he had for keeping a griffin egg was secondary. He had wrapped it carefully, but still, the freezing temperature could have killed the unhatched chick. She came up with a thousand things to say when she saw Eryk again, none of them pleasant.

Then she reeled herself in, realizing she was looking forward to interacting with him again. Not just to yell at him for his lack of knowledge, but to banter with him. How could someone be so irritating?!

She spent the next hour securing the egg inside a Ranger's cloak, another priceless gift the infuriating legionnaire had given her like an old pair of socks. She made a cradle to carry the egg in front of her. She could only guess at the age of the egg, and estimated it would hatch in two or three months. At least there were three Legion canteens in her pack.

Two canteens were full of water. When she poured out the third, the distinct odor of alcohol filled the air. Rather than waste it, she sipped it and frowned. *Where did he get Elven Ambrosia? And he stored it in a soldier's canteen?* The idiot was wasting priceless ambrosia that took a century to age. She bit her tongue and cursed him inwardly as she dumped the contents into the snow. It would make floating across much less dangerous and right now, her life was more important than elven whiskey.

9

When black spheres with orange and red swirls rolled out of a cloth bag, Raelia's jaw dropped. An apex and major affinity fire essences. Had Eryk put these in her bag? No, it must have been Maveith. No, Eryk controlled all the essences, and Maveith always deferred to him. For some reason, the priceless essences enraged her further. That bastard had tilted their relationship in his favor even further. *Who gives affinity essences away like candy? An idiot, that is who.*

She still had the charm essences from the harpies, but she was waiting to consume them. Unlocking a new affinity was not going to be pleasant and it might be better to sell them. She was not going to raise her charm affinity high enough to learn a spell form anyway.

When night arrived, Raelia stripped naked, packed everything in her pack, and wrapped it tightly with a tarp tent. She attached the canteens as floats and walked hesitantly into the water, pushing the pack before her as the icy water sapped the heat from her body. She needed to get across the river before cramps set in and she drowned. She kicked furiously among the floating chunks of ice as she crossed the river, pushing her precious package. She pushed any thoughts of the horrors that might be lurking in the river's depths to the back of her mind. Best to just cross quickly.

Exhausted from reaching the far side, she dragged her naked body from the water up the bank. Ice was already forming on her body and she cursed Eryk for taking her thermal stone. Her spell form to heat the air around her was weak, acting too slowly to warm her body as she shivered. Her numb fingers retrieved the apex fire essence and placed it in her mouth. Heat surged through her body, forcing away the cold. She hadn't been sure that would work, but thankfully it did. If the legionnaire had been there, she would have acted like she knew it would happen.

She fumbled through her pack, happy everything had remained dry. Once she was dressed, she wrapped the griffin egg securely in her cloak. The artifact should keep the egg warm, but she would check every hour. She was already growing attached to the unhatched chick.

As she moved carefully through the woods toward Bartiradian lands, she found herself looking forward to training a griffin again. She even came up with a name for the unhatched griffin: Baldo. It was a Telhian word for a foolish person. So what if she was naming her griffin after the legionnaire who had given her the egg.

Her journey through the Telhian wilds over the next week went relatively well. It had gotten so cold one night that she had risked a fire and attracted a gnoll hunting party. She had used a fireball to disperse the gnolls, killing three, and

10

had run for the rest of the night, worried the burnt survivors would return with more of their pack. At least there was no snow on the ground this far east.

The effort of constantly avoiding Telhian towns and patrols had Raelia on edge. Twice, she had covered her ears and pretended to be a malnourished civilian to walk the roads. She used the griffin egg to bulge her belly, as even in the Telhian Empire pregnant women should be able to travel relatively unmolested. It was a risk, but the road saved her valuable time and the Hounds would be patrolling the woodlands this far east. The most stressful moment was when two mage companies passed her on the road. That convinced her that perhaps she was taking too much of a risk.

She knew she was only about two hundred miles from the border when she left the road. She used the Ranger's call as she approached: a short, common-bird sound repeated at specific intervals. After half a day, it allowed the Rangers to find her. Her knees nearly gave out from relief when two tall elven Rangers revealed themselves.

"Little woman, what are you doing in my woods?" one of the Rangers asked with a good-natured smirk. She missed elven humor; it was refreshing after dealing with the human.

Raelia drew on her elven fortitude and stood tall. "I fell off my griffin and had to walk," she replied snarkily. She bowed formally and introduced herself: "Raelia Glavien. Trained Griffin Rider and Ranger. I request an escort to my brother, General Clalyn Glavien." The two elves looked doubtful, even when she revealed her elven features.

It was another week until she was back in a Bartiradian city. The Telhians had captured the city of Guiracas and the war was in full bloom. She learned the Bartiradians and Esenhem elves were entering a loose alliance to capture a valuable target. She was not told what it was, but she learned it was outside the city of Macha, that accursed city where she had lost Moonclaw and nearly died—and where Eryk had spared her life.

Her brother finally debriefed her. She was glad it was him and not the Ranger commander. Clalyn entered the room where she was under guard and they hugged each other fiercely. "Raelia, when I heard the Rangers were bringing you from the wilds, I couldn't believe it. Where have you been for the last three months?"

"Trapped in the elven city of Caelora. There is an ancient dungeon there, larger and more powerful than any dungeon I have ever seen," Raelia responded. She knew she needed to give something valuable to the Bartiradian command after failing to protect Vaeril.

Clalyn frowned. "You were in a dungeon? We know Vaeril is dead. The Rangers I sent found his body two months ago near a decaying wyvern and Telhian drake. Do you know what happened to Traeliorn? The mages at the college have not been able to contact him for six weeks."

She was surprised that it was her brother questioning her and not an Inquisitor. She was glad it was him, but still, she was surprised. "I haven't seen Traeliorn since he brought me to Vaeril. I have recovered enough to rejoin the Rangers. But I have also procured my own griffin egg."

"From the dungeon?" Clalyn asked. He had clearly been made aware of all her possessions already, judging by his lack of surprise. The egg and all her gear were in the next room. The charm essences were there as well, but she had consumed the second fire essence.

"No," she said before thinking it through. She actually didn't know where Eryk had obtained the egg. Clalyn nodded heavily and Raelia read his body language. He was about to give her some bad news. Was he going to take the egg from her? The breeding program should be producing enough griffins unless the war was going much worse than she assumed.

"You are not returning to the Rangers. Father has arranged for you to be sent to live with an aunt in Artiria." As soon as Raelia heard the news, her eyes widened.

"The capital of Esenhem? Why?" she asked, confused but quickly angering.

"To protect you. With your prior failures and now Traeliorn missing, people want answers. Powerful people, Raelia. An Inquisitor will question you and then you will be sent to Artiria to be a liaison for House Glavien," Clalyn informed her. He gestured at the egg. "I will see if you can keep that, but I cannot guarantee it. The charm essences will most assuredly be appropriated, though."

It was like Raelia had just crashed her griffin into a cliff face. Her family had left Esenhem hundreds of years ago because the Esenhem Regents had refused to fight the Telhians. Now, she was being sent there for her protection. "Why?" she asked numbly.

"Esenhem and Bartiradia are allies—at least for now. We have even managed to coordinate with the Supreme Cleric of the Boutan Caliphate to stretch the resources of the Telhians as his orc warlords attack the western Telhian Empire. The Telhian Empire will crumble in the coming years." As Clalyn said this, Raelia wondered why she was worrying about the stupid legionnaire's fate.

When Clalyn left, she spoke with the Inquisitors. There were two: a pleasant old human woman named Kiara and a young, dark-haired dwarf named Braer. They were just as interested in the Shimmering Labyrinth as they were in clues to the whereabouts of Traeliorn Kelran and the human legionnaire.

She couldn't keep the legionnaire's powerful space affinity secret from them. They already knew about it, but still, both the dwarf's and human's questions indicated they doubted her words. Raelia could only tell the truth, but surprisingly, she kept some of his secrets: the powerful essence collector and his other spell forms. She didn't hide the fact that he was not a Telhian and, in fact, an otherworlder, conscripted into the Legion. Maybe that would help him gain some leniency if he were captured.

Kiara seemed to think that Eryk being an otherworlder explained a lot, but Raelia had never heard of an otherworlder with such a strong affinity. After two days of intense questioning, she was finally allowed to walk freely in the city. Her rank had been stripped, and she would never serve as a Griffin Rider or Ranger again in the Kingdom of Bartiradia.

Clalyn did not see her off to Artiria. He was training a detachment for the spring assault on Macha. Everything was very secret, and she had no inroads to the alliance or the goals of the assault. She only knew this was the largest offensive the Bartiradians had amassed in decades. They were determined to keep something from Telhian hands, and it was not the Shimmering Labyrinth. Numerous scholars eagerly came to find her to ask her more questions about the dungeon before she left.

When she was ordered to depart for Esenhem, she was directed to a horse-drawn carriage. A wizened old elf sat in the sturdy coach. The woman's immaculate dress and brilliant jewelry reminded Raelia of the nobles in the Bartiradian courts. She looked at Raelia and ordered impatiently, "Get up, girl. I am eager to finish my business and be on my way back to Artiria."

After Raelia sat, she noticed her Ranger's cloak wrapping an ovoid object on the seat. Her worn pack was on the floor. Maybe her other possessions were there. "Yes, your brother made sure it traveled with you. I am Maeralya Glavien, your aunt. You will be staying with me while we try to repair the relations between our fractured families. During the trip home, we need to make sure you are presentable to the other Esenhem Regents."

I started to help Maveith secure his homestead so we could depart and search for his sister in orc lands. Outside, Maveith was pulling down the stretched weasel pelts and relaying the battle of how he and Lyonis had hunted the two creatures down. "They were the young ones that had formed a mated pair and recently laired nearby. I didn't want to worry about a litter of giant weasels in a few months, so we trapped one and killed the second one when it came to free its mate." I could hear the anxiousness in his voice, which was highlighted by the speed at which he was working.

I still had the two weasel pelts I had purchased from Maveith with Legion ration bars. They were still my favorite sleeping accompaniment with the griffin-down pillow under my head—not that I had much time for restful sleep recently. Maveith wasn't taking the pelts and I didn't offer to store them. In fact, I was considering clearing out my dimensional space for Ginger. It was going to be hard enough traveling the Empire with a goliath. A healthy war horse was even more conspicuous.

"Who did you imprison in your space this time, Eryk?" The goliath's deep voice bellowed in admonishment as he secured the giant weasel pelts in a stone chest to protect them from vermin and the elements.

Ginger neighed at me, and I chose to think she was supporting me and not Maveith, even though it sounded like she was agreeing with him. "A young girl, her brother, their mother, and a First Citizen mage," I replied casually.

"You forced women and children into your space! Eryk, I thought better of you," Maveith chided me. This time, I was sure Ginger was siding with Maveith as she nudged me hard in the side with her head.

I was a bit exasperated with his viewpoint. I was doing the best I could. "It was either that or kill them. I need to get them outside the Empire. I doubt anyone would come searching for them, but if I release them in the Empire, it might cause me problems. None of them can identify me, but if they are interrogated, it will most certainly lead back to me since I was tasked with killing them." Maveith nodded slowly, accepting my explanation.

It didn't take us long to secure Maveith's stone cabin and prepare a massive pack for him. Maveith wedged some stones into the wooden door and nodded that he was ready, eagerness and trepidation in his eyes. I led Ginger as we started walking. Maveith seemed to calm and asked, "What of the goliaths who told you my sister lives?"

"I sent them here. They might not have made it. The wilds are dangerous and many towns and cities are along the road. I told them to use Duchess Veronica's name if they were captured." When I finished talking, Maveith's brow furrowed in thought.

"Then I should talk with Duchess Veronica before we leave." Maveith nodded firmly. "We play checkers when I report to her, so I am sure she would tell me if there is word of goliaths."

I slowed my steps and Ginger took it to mean that it was time for an apple. She nudged my back to make an apple appear. "You can't reveal I am alive, Maveith. The Hounds think I am dead, so the Empire thinks I am dead. I prefer that it remains that way," I told the goliath, handing greedy Ginger an apple.

"I would not betray you, Eryk." Maveith's eyes brightened with a plan. "The Duchess knows I am waiting for you to travel home. I will tell her the news of your death came to me."

My left eyebrow rose in doubt. "Who told you I was dead then?"

Maveith acknowledged his mistake and continued formulating a plan. The news of his sister had clearly rattled him, as he normally thought things out. "I can see the problem. I will not tell her I am leaving, as I would not have been informed of your unfortunate death. But I must know if she is aware of the goliaths. If they need aid, we should give it to them before finding Zorana. You can wait for me with Ginger while I talk with Veronica." I nodded. I wanted to know what the Duchess knew as well. Was she aware of the plot and that the backup Archives had been destroyed?

We traveled south toward Sobral. Maveith asked, "How are we going to get into the Boutan Caliphate?" His hand rested on his runic hammer as he scanned the woods. He had been smart and rubbed charcoal into the head, obfuscating its brilliant polish.

I had given this a lot of thought and had devised a plan. "Unless we are going to shapeshift into orcs, we need to enter as members of the Adventurers Guild. Just like in the Telhian Empire, adventurers from outside the territory are allowed to delve into their dungeons."

"Goliaths don't become adventurers, Eryk," Maveith said tersely, already putting holes in my plan.

I stopped walking and looked at the goliath. "Why not?" Maveith stopped with me, appearing introspective.

"I actually don't know. It is just frowned upon by my people. If I had to consider it, then I think it is because adventurers only care about one thing: gold. Goliaths care more about family, friendship, and only killing for a purpose."

I didn't know what to say, so we walked in silence for a while. Finally, Maveith spoke again after much consideration. "I don't see why I couldn't join the Adventurers Guild. If it is what is required of me to save my sister, I will do it. Other goliaths will not look at me favorably, though. We cannot take any assignments that I disagree with." Maveith had to think out a path to rationalize his decision to join the Adventurers Guild.

Relieved, I didn't hesitate. "Agreed." The weight of Maveith's trust in me made me worried that we might not find his sister, or worse, that we might find out she was dead. Still, I was leaving the Empire and felt it was a worthy cause. Risking my life for a friend was better than dying for an empire that cared nothing for me, nor I for it.

"After you talk with the Duchess, we will travel up the old trade road to the capital and seek passage on one of the Adventurers Guild ships. If we are lucky, a ship captain I am familiar with will be there. Her name is Desdemona. Although I don't think she likes me very much."

Maveith grunted, "Did you store Desdemona in your space without her permission as well?"

"No. Adventurers just don't like legionnaires," I retorted, but Maveith was already grinning at his joke. I was glad he was slowly relaxing after learning his sister might be alive.

I grunted at his poor humor and walked into a clearing. "I will wait here. There are some early spring plants I can harvest for my alchemy. And yes, I am sort of an alchemist now. Hurry and talk to the Duchess so we can head east and make the trade road before dark."

Maveith dropped his pack and I stored it in my dimensional space as he walked toward the city. I let Ginger wander and eat grass while I collected valuable spring flora. Maveith returned late in the evening at a light jog. I went on alert, but he put me at ease. "I am sorry it took so long. I learned my friend Eryk was killed by the Boutan orcs and needed to show an appropriate amount of grief at the news. The Duchess even hugged me and soothed me personally."

"How much soothing did she do?" I asked teasingly, trying to needle him after he had ribbed me about my relationship with Desdemona. "And did she have news of the other goliaths?"

Catching his breath, Maveith reflected on his encounter with the Duchess. "She hugged me for a few minutes and rubbed my back, but her arms barely encircled my chest."

"A few minutes?" I chided, surprised.

I think Maveith flushed, but it was hard to tell with his gray skin. "Over the last month, I have counted her as a friend. She confides in me about her troubles of running the duchy while we play checkers and I tell her about my past adventures," Maveith said thoughtfully.

"And yes, the goliaths are being escorted to her. Two were injured in their travels but are healthy now. They were captured five days ago in Freira. She just learned of them two days ago and was waiting for my visit to tell me about them. She is now arranging for them to be ported to Parvas and then escorted here. She will care for them and help them get home," Maveith said, relief evident in his voice.

My jaw was slack. Did the Duchess have a crush on Maveith? Was he too oblivious to realize it? I wasn't the best at reading the body language and cues of the opposite sex but it certainly sounded like the Duchess was sweet on the big bald gray man. "Is she happy when she sees you?" I probed as we started moving east. Ginger was requesting another apple but I ignored her; four was her limit today.

"She said our meetings are the only time she feels happy enough to smile and laugh openly. Her brother went to the capital, but her mother remains a guest and a source of her angst. Veronica even mentioned I could stay in the Citadel if I wanted to," Maveith said cheerfully. I shook my head but didn't pry further. Sometimes ignorance was best. Maveith might never return to Sobral, and the Duchess might not survive the war.

When we reached the white marble markers indicating the border of the Duchess's lands, we followed them to the old trade road. "Are you sure we shouldn't just follow the river, Eryk?" asked Maveith, voicing his reluctance at the path I had chosen.

"We can handle a few dire wolves. Or are you worried about passing the Ruins of Caelora?" I asked while slapping a spring fly on my neck.

Maveith voiced his concerns. "Both. Dire wolves will have just had their spring litters and will be looking to feed their pups. I am not ashamed to say that I hoped never to see Caelora again. Do you plan to raid the library when we pass?" Some fear seeped into his tone.

"This is the fastest way. If we followed the river, it would add sixty miles to our trek." I reassured him, "I don't plan for us to go anywhere near the ruins, Maveith." Maveith nodded in relief. As if in response, his stomach rumbled in hunger. It took me a moment to puzzle out why that didn't make sense to me. "Where is your ring of sustenance?"

Maveith pulled a leather cord out from under his shirt, the shiny ring dangling from it. "I wore it for two months but found I preferred feeling hungry and the joy of eating." He put on a wide smile.

I shook my head, but I had to agree with him. The ring did kill your appetite and make you feel full much quicker. Sometimes, food even tasted bland if you were already satiated. I produced a burrito and handed it to him. "Put it on, Maveith. We may not be at risk of starving, but with just two of us, the reduced sleep the ring requires will be invaluable in our journey."

Maveith finished the burrito in three bites, moaning in delight at the unfamiliar blending of flavors, and I handed him a second. "If I must," he said, sighing sadly. He worked the ring onto his large finger as he ate the second burrito, chewing a little more slowly, needing four bites this time. It would still take a week for the ring to acclimate to him. But when it did, we would need only two hours of sleep and one meal a day to sustain our bodies.

With night coming soon, we started to look for somewhere to camp. Maveith asked, "Are you not going to ride Ginger?"

"I don't have a saddle, and I wouldn't be able to use my new spell form if I did. I learned my earth affinity spell form; it is called earth speak. I have been checking our surroundings as we travel." I tried to act like it was no big deal.

Maveith frowned and said, sounding hurt, "You didn't learn shape stone?" That was Maveith's spell form, and I think he wanted us to match.

"No. This spell form allows me to send out an aetheric pulse of earth-laced aether to get an instant image of my surroundings," I informed him, expecting him to be impressed. He was not.

"I know what it does. A few goliath hunters use it to find burrows in my village. It has a limited range," Maveith said apprehensively.

"Yeah, I know being able to see out only sixty feet is a limitation, but I still manage," I said smugly. I kept walking as Maveith stopped, stunned.

It took a moment for Maveith to recover and catch up. "Sixty feet! What is your earth affinity?" he bellowed loud enough for everyone within half a mile to hear him.

I spent the next three hours proving to Maveith that my range was over fifty feet. I found small animals and even told him where he could find a silver coin twenty paces off the road. As night quickly closed in, we moved off the road, Maveith still in disbelief.

"You see so much with each earth pulse. How do you interpret what you see so quickly?" he said, cleaning off the silver coin he had dug up. Maveith didn't care about coins, but this one was ancient and he wanted to see the stamped images for their historical value. It appeared to be a Telhian coin featuring an image of a lion on one side and a portrait of a strong-looking man on the other. The script had worn away.

I motioned my distracted friend into some heavy thickets that would be defensible as a camp. Maveith had been awfully vocal today, and I think he missed talking to me, but we were getting closer to dire wolf territory. As we set up camp, I finally answered him. "Lots of practice."

Maveith looked confused. "How do you not get overwhelmed? From my understanding, earth speak shows you everything."

I thought about how I was doing it as I handed Maveith his pack from my dimensional space. "Before I send out the pulse, I have already focused on where I am looking. I hold the image and study it. If I see something interesting, I refocus and pulse again. With earth speak inscribed on my core, I can pulse two or three times a second now and even pick up movement."

For the first time since I had met Maveith, he looked jealous. As he set up his bedroll, I set trip alarms outside our campsite and sprinkled myconid powder in a wide arc. After I was done, I found Maveith already eating. I hitched Ginger's lead line to a thick bush and wondered how she would react to being placed in my dimensional space. I got myself comfortable on the ground next to Maveith, a rock supporting my back as I took watch.

"Do you want this?" I held up the dreamscape amulet for Maveith.

He considered for a long moment before nodding slightly. "Yes. I will practice against the orcs and tell my sister we are coming for her."

"Maveith, that is not how it works," I said, concerned. Was I setting him up for major disappointment?

Maveith mumbled softly, "I know, Eryk. I just need to talk to her." I didn't say anything else and let him sleep. In a few days, the ring would cut his sleep down, but moving in the dark of night was dangerous for the two of us in this region. I missed my Hound goggles.

The night went by quickly, with only insects and owls speaking to me. My earth speak allowed me to see the nightly foragers emerge. Maveith came out of the dreamscape twice to check on me, and both times, I sent him back. I needed to plan our next steps. Getting out of the Empire was not going to be easy.

"You shouldn't have let me sleep the whole night," Maveith grumbled as light, misty fog rolled in with the morning. I waved off his concern. The fog felt a little unnatural for this time of year, but a lot of mornings had felt that way recently.

"I am fine, Maveith. I am going to walk Ginger and pick up my alarms." Maveith dug into his pack for breakfast as I moved away. Ginger was probing me for an apple. "Just grass this morning," I told her, and she immediately looked indignant. As I worked, she eventually took to grazing. I sent out earth speak pulses, only detecting two deer bedded down in a small gully nearby.

Back on the road, Maveith was chipper from his great night of sleep and, thankfully, talking in a whisper as we walked—well, a whisper for him. The mist cleared and the azure sky showed itself. Birdsong filled the woods as we walked. Maveith had the right side and I had the left, but I occasionally focused my earth speak pulse on his side of the road.

Before midday, we encountered our first dire wolf tracks. "Over two days old," I said, standing. Maveith nodded in agreement. "But there were four of them," I added unhappily.

Maveith, a little distressed, added, "If the females had their litters, the males will be hunting day and night to feed them while they nurse." He looked back at Ginger. "Dire wolves have a fixation on horsemeat." Ginger huffed indignantly. I couldn't tell if she understood Maveith's words or his body language and tone.

"Griffins like horsemeat too, but don't worry, girl. I won't let them get to you." I pulled my black spear from my dimensional space to carry with me before we continued.

The dire wolf tracks crossed the road frequently and we even found a blood trail. Maveith stooped and pressed the large splotch. "We are lucky. It is still tacky. They got some prey last night and probably won't be hunting again so soon. We should increase our pace." I agreed, and all three of us broke into a jog. The echoing of Ginger's shoes on the ancient pavers had me on edge, but haste was our ally.

We covered over fifteen miles in the afternoon and hadn't seen any tracks for the last few miles. We were approaching the site of the abandoned wagons where the company had discovered the lockbox, and I had Maveith hold Ginger's reins while I looked upon the site again.

It looked the same as I approached and sent out earth speak. Rusting metal items and bones were littered a few inches under the soft earth around the site. Scavengers had disrupted whole skeletons, but I located nine different skulls as I fine-tuned my feedback from the spell.

Castile seemed to think there was something extremely odd about this scene, but I didn't find anything noteworthy. I searched for something besides some clusters of coins—probably coin purses of the dead. I dug a little and retrieved six gold, nine large silver, seventy-six silver, and dozens of copper coins, large and small. I didn't need the coin, but it never hurt to have more. The mystery of what had ambushed and killed these traders still remained.

I returned and let Maveith clean the coins while I scouted ahead. Two hours later, I yanked on Maveith's leathers and pulled him off the road. He shoved the coppers he had been cleaning into his rough linen pants. "What?" he hissed.

"Two men about fifty feet ahead, just off the road," I stated as I tied an easy-pull halter hitch for Ginger.

"Bandits?" Maveith asked, confused. I was also confused, as we hadn't seen any wagons, horses, or human tracks.

"Maybe Hounds or Bartiradian Rangers. Both figures are prone. Give me a moment. My earth speak doesn't work well through flora and fauna." I focused and pulsed multiple times before I started to relax. "One of them is dead, and the other is close to it. I can't discern their races. Wait here."

I walked cautiously up the road while Maveith prepared his bow in support. Ginger seemed confused as she didn't sense or see any danger. The two bodies were concealed off the road, but I could easily follow their tracks and dried blood, days old. They had come south from the Ruins of Caelora. Maybe they were men who had thought to raid the city.

I walked over to them and lowered my spear to the one who still lived. He had a runic sword clutched in his hand that was caked in dried blood. He smelled of rot as well, and I could see a larva moving in a massive chest wound. He was not going to live much longer.

I poked him with the spear and his eyes flashed open. He coughed painfully and weakly. He was middle-aged with graying hair. His dead companion was very young and didn't look like a warrior. Maybe a servant. He was missing his right arm and had been dead for days, judging by the smell and maggots.

The man rasped. I stepped on his sword and knelt, tilting a canteen into his mouth. He struggled to swallow and most of the water was wasted. Once he could swallow, I dribbled an orc healing potion into his mouth. He was too far gone to realize the foul taste. It wasn't going to save his life but prolong it so I could get answers and decide if he needed saving. He was fairly delirious at the moment, and I did not recognize him.

Maveith appeared behind me while I tended to the man, waiting for him to speak. I waved Maveith back as I didn't want the man to see the goliath. I was dressed in common clothes and fairly plain-looking. Maveith understood I didn't want him to be seen and led Ginger a short distance down the road. "Why are you here?" I asked softly.

His eyes couldn't focus and he kept trying to wet his throat and tongue, so I gave him more water till he spoke in a soft rasp. "Our camp was attacked by a wyvern."

"Why were you on this road?" I asked. I realized the wyvern must be left over from the summoner and the Empire had not gotten around to removing it with the war escalating. I had seen one flying in the distance when Maveith and I had escaped the city, and there had been two wyverns that decimated the building we found near the dungeon entrance.

"We were looting the ruins," the man managed to say after more water. "The First Citizen was leading us."

"Which First Citizen, and why isn't he off fighting the elves and Bartiradians?" I asked, now with more curiosity.

"Boris Angella. He hired us to raid the Ruins of Caelora before the Emperor could send an expedition." His voice was sounding better and the orc's lesser healing potion had stabilized him. I doubted Duchess Veronica had sent her brother here. More likely he was here of his own accord, trying to plunder the ruins without anyone knowing.

"How were you dealing with the specters?" I pressed the dying man. Maybe they had brought the kettle of souls with them.

"He said most of the specters were banished, but we had a necromancer with us and he had a soul prison. We made slow progress. There were not many specters near the western gate," the man stated, clearly exhausted from talking. "Is my boy dead?" he asked while I thought.

I looked at the younger man. "Yes, I am sorry." I didn't want to have to deal with a wyvern—or two—again. "Is the First Citizen alive? Was Justin Cicero with him? Were there any other First Citizens?" The man appeared to be giving up his weak hold on life after I told him his son was dead. He didn't answer me, so I shook him a little and repeated my question.

He answered weakly, "No. Only Boris, but Count Cato sponsored the expedition. There were eleven of us when the wyvern attacked. Not sure if any others made it." The man was straining to look at his son, and I helped him. I looked at his wounds. I could give him four or five of the orc healing potions to possibly save him, but then he would return and tell someone else about seeing me. He hadn't seen Maveith, at least. Still, the risk was too great.

"I have oblivion pills," I said softly to the man. "Do you want them? Do you want us to bury you with your son? Or burn your bodies?" His mind was not working well, but he slowly nodded and mouthed, "Burn." I gave him four oblivion pills and let him drift off and pass away. I didn't feel right taking his essence after helping him die when I could have saved him.

I worked with Maveith to make a funeral pyre. We waited till night to start the fire so the smoke wouldn't draw the wyvern. Once lit, we moved away quickly to where we had prepared our accommodations for the evening.

I sent the man's runic blade to my dimensional space, but it was unremarkable and poorly forged compared to others of its kind. It was still worth good gold, and he no longer needed it. Our accommodation was a shallow cave on a hill a good mile from the pyre. It smelled of urine and had small animal bones, so we must have displaced a modest predator.

I told Maveith everything the man had told me. "Are we going to search for the First Citizen?" he asked as he ate some jerky with a sour face. I could tell he was upset that the ring of sustenance was working and that he no longer felt hungry.

"No, we are not going to search for him. If we do come across him, we have to kill him. I prefer to avoid the wyvern's hunting grounds completely. We will move off the road and travel parallel to the river under the trees and pick up the old road north of here," I explained. If we came across First Citizen Boris, I would kill him. I couldn't risk him recognizing me, and to tell the truth, I welcomed his death at my hand.

Chapter 247: Thick-Skinned

Traveling the path along the river the next day made for much slower moving than if we had remained on the ancient trade road. Still, I didn't want to risk being spotted by the wyvern. Maveith didn't complain about our route. At least the wyvern would have kept lesser predators from violating its hunting grounds. The only threat my earth pulse returned was a cluster of giant trapdoor spiders. They were not even that large, just the size of large house cats.

After a few hours, Maveith relaxed and started cleaning the coins we found by the wagons. We were both moving fairly silently; my earth pulse was very effective, and Maveith needed something to occupy his time. "Most of these coins are from the Endless Dark," Maveith said softly, keeping his voice as low as possible.

"What? Are they goblin coins, then?" I asked, half-interested. My knowledge of the Endless Dark was limited. My current focus was on scanning the banks of the river with earth pulses.

"A few are goblin coins, but most of them have dark elf scripts and images." Maveith handed me one of the silver coins. He had cleaned most of the dirt off it. He was right: it was Elvish. One side had a date stamped on it, as well as the words Ishaena Esari, which translated to City of Pure Blue Stone. On the other side was the face of a female elf. Time had flattened the relief, and I was not familiar with the elven calendar.

"How do you know they are dark elves? The elven language is the same as the surface elves," I asked, handing him the coin back.

Maveith took the coin and rubbed it a little more with a cloth before answering. "The elf matriarch pictured on the coin is Novaneae Dralahidoe. She rules a dark elf city on the other continent in the Endless Dark, Ishaena Esari. When I left my home, I picked up a lot of threads of knowledge. One of the human cities I passed through traded with the dark elves, who only trade in their coin because the humans mix impurities into theirs." He held up the coin. "I recognize this coin."

Maveith hadn't seen the coins we got in the wagon lockbox, and I never saw them after they had been cleaned. Most of the coins in the Telhian Empire were either Telhian coins or blank dungeon coins found in reward chests. There was some consistency with other empires in coin denominations, but the Telhian Imperial Reserve collected foreign coins and reminted them with Telhian images.

I only knew this because merchants preferred dungeon coins due to their high purity over Telhian-minted coins, similar to what Maveith had indicated with the dark elves' preference for their own coins.

"Are the dark elves evil?" I asked Maveith, continuing the conversation as a distraction.

Maveith let out a long exhale, which told me he was thinking about how to answer. "I know very little of them and have only seen a few in my travels. Actually, the dark elves are not dark. Their skin is mostly pale to alabaster in hue. They are called dark elves because they live in the Endless Dark. Their hair is as white as their skin, but the ones I have seen dye their hair various colors as a status symbol. Their warriors always dye their hair black." He paused as he reached for old knowledge. "They are not friendly to the elves on the surface, but I do not know the reason. Maybe Raelia would know." Perhaps Maveith said the last part as a hint that he wanted to see her again.

"We are not going to visit Raelia. If I can avoid it, I will never enter Bartiradian lands. We have to be thirty miles north of Caelora by now. Let's move back to the trade road," I said as I started angling us back. Orienting was not easy without landmarks and the Aganterao River was my only reference. The trade road ran parallel to the river all the way to Telha.

As we stepped onto the ancient road, I immediately frowned as I kneeled and studied the road. Konstantin had mentioned one evening that the stone pavers were spelled so no vegetation would grow on them. Still, the canopy had encroached above, and the road was heavily shaded and covered in most places in soft soil, likely from decades of composting leaves.

Maveith was kneeling with me. "Most tracks are headed south." He voiced what I had already seen written in the soft layer of dirt. "These wagon, horse, and human prints must be from the First Citizen's expedition." I nodded in agreement.

My eyes studied the tracks that were not heading south—three sets of prints, probably all men. One man was dragging his right leg. Maveith was patient while I studied and walked the tracks heading north toward the capital. "They abandoned everything; they do not appear encumbered. Two of the men are injured. One has a serious leg injury and the other has an upper-body injury."

Maveith cocked his eyebrow in question. I pointed. "This set of prints shows the man dragging his right leg, and this set has uneven steps favoring the right side." I demonstrated how I pictured the men walking based on how the tracks spoke to me.

"You have gotten more skilled at reading tracks than I," Maveith said in appreciation. I nodded absently at his praise. In the Hounds, I had learned to track people so I could hunt them.

"The tracks are probably just over a day old. We are going to catch them before they reach the capital," I said, digesting the idea that I might have to kill the men. Maveith remained quiet, waiting for me to make a decision on the fate of the men on the road. I removed the blood compass and channeled aether into it. Castile's sample was still pulling southeast toward Caranhagan. I had more samples for Castile that I could use, but I hated resetting the blood compass to see if Boris was alive.

I sat on a log and opened the compass. Maveith stood over me and remained alert while I meticulously cleaned the artifact, heated it, and retrieved a new sample. Maveith hovered, interested in what I was doing but not interrupting me. A half-hour later, I closed the compass and channeled my aether into the device. The compass pulled modestly north, and I judged the pull. "First Citizen Boris is one of the men ahead of us."

Maveith looked appreciatively at the compass and then up the road. "What do you want to do?"

"I am only getting one pull on the compass, and he is less than thirty miles ahead of us according to the strength of the pull. They can't see a goliath and live." I focused on Maveith to see if he objected to me killing Boris. I had no love for Boris and would probably be doing Duchess Veronica a favor if I killed her brother.

Maveith didn't object but had a pertinent question. "What are we going to do when we get the capital, then?" Maveith asked. "I do not wish to be sent into your space, Eryk."

I sighed. "No time would pass for you, but I understand." I explained my loose plan: "We will cross the Aganterao River, and you can wait with Ginger on the northern coast. We will pick you up once I have chartered an Adventurers Guild ship."

Maveith looked at Ginger, who cocked her head in question, hearing her name. I could tell Maveith didn't like my plan, but we had few options to get out of Telhian lands without passing warring armies.

I looked at the tracks, the sky, and the road behind us, coming to a decision. "Stay back a quarter mile, Maveith. I will walk Ginger forward and confront the men." Maveith's face pinched in displeasure at being left behind. "I can handle myself, Maveith. I have an aether shield amulet and my bag of tricks," I assured him. I showed him the aether shield amulet to prove my point and started walking ahead. Maveith waited unhappily and Ginger looked back at him as we opened up the distance, confused.

I handed Ginger an apple to soothe her. "Don't worry, Maveith will catch up, girl." I moved at a fast walk, checking the tracks every hour. It appeared the men were resting frequently. As night approached, I halted and waited for Maveith to catch up. Ginger was excited to have our pack back together, nudging Maveith like she was scolding him for being slow.

"They are not far ahead, Maveith. The last urine stain on the tree was still wet and pungent. I just wanted to let you know." Maveith nodded and I walked away again with a confused Ginger.

Two miles later, in the deep twilight, my earth speak pulse found the three men thirty feet off the road. I walked slowly and waited for them to reveal themselves. Boris's crass voice cut the air: "We have bows trained on you, traveler. Leave your horse and head back the way you came." Although my pulse gave me a fuzzy image of them, I knew none of them had bows.

I was chewing on some tough jerky as I spoke. "Bandits? On this road?" I asked, amused. I had deepened my voice and he had not recognized me.

"I am not a bandit," Boris barked, raspy with pain. "I am First Citizen Boris Angella and I am commandeering your mount."

I stood and waited for the three men to make their way onto the road. One man had his leg splinted and had an empty scabbard on his hip—his sword was another lesser runic weapon in the moonlight. Boris held his dungeon-forged weapon but had his ribs wrapped. The third man looked uninjured but frail, definitely not a warrior. No weapons and no shoulder musculature—maybe this was the necromancer.

In my deep voice, I sought information: "Duchess Veronica did say her brother was stealing from the Emperor. She asked me to go keep an eye on him and report."

The three men looked at each other, a bit confused, and Boris spoke for them. "How did my sister find out about my expedition?" Boris said, vitriolic.

This was interesting information, and I was glad I had taken the time to talk. "She has her own spies in Count Cato's household," I said dismissively. I balled up the chewed jerky in my mouth and spit out the salty glob on the ground. I could sense it was getting close to the time to dance.

Boris sounded a little desperate. "One hundred gold for your horse and your silence." Boris stepped closer and the uninjured man started to form a spell form in his hands, indicating their intentions. Magebane appeared in my hands and I released Ginger's reins. Boris was a good swordsman but he must have broken his ribs, as I easily deflected his blade and slashed above his knee, cutting deeply into his quad. Even his hardened skin couldn't stop the magebane.

The mage's spell splashed across my aetheric shield as the amulet worked. The blue flash of the shield lit up the surroundings briefly and highlighted my face. My disguise included a deep reddish brown rubbed into my hair and beard, and my face had some dark shadows that made me look older. Still, recognition flashed on Boris's face.

"You!" He stumbled back as if he had seen a ghost. "Kill him!" The mage was confused by the aether shield, and their third companion could barely stand. Boris's stoneskin spell form was already dissipating from the aether poison of the blade. I didn't hesitate to move past Boris to reach the mage. I slashed his arm as he tried ineptly to block it. I then turned on the third man, who was limping backward. I moved into him, blocking a feeble strike with an air shield and then delivering a lightning stab to his throat.

I turned to face the crippled Boris and incapacitated mage while pulling out a glowstone. That should alert Maveith to come forward. "What did you do to me?" Boris rasped angrily as he struggled both to use his aether and remain standing.

I ignored his plea and asked the mage, "Are you the necromancer?" He nodded fearfully.

"Tell me, what is a soul prison?" I asked calmly.

Chapter 248: Vigilante Justice

Under the light of the glowstone, the mage cringed away from me. Boris had dropped to one knee, supporting his body with the runic sword. "Don't tell him anything," he spat angrily at the mage.

I looked down the road and could see the large, shadowy shape of Maveith coming. I raised my sword and addressed Boris. "I didn't ask you, Boris."

"Your friend betrayed you. I know your secrets," Boris said obnoxiously.

"My only true friend is about to join me," I said without looking away, thinking it was a trick.

"Brutus." Boris searched for his last name. "Brutus Salacia. He told me all your secrets!" I really was not up for a villain's monologue.

"And where is Brutus? Did you kill him?" I said impatiently.

"He slowed the wyvern for our escape. He is dead! But he told me …" I raised my sword, not caring what Brutus had told him. I was already dead to the Empire.

Boris made to defend himself from his knees, but I batted aside the runic blade easily and came back with a rapid slash across his throat. Boris was stunned at my act and his eyes widened in disbelief at what I had just done. Did he think his status as a First Citizen or whatever secret Brutus had told him would shield him? My anger from all my interactions with the First Citizen and his minions had boiled over.

Boris wasn't going to be walking away tonight. I watched as his hand went to his throat to try to stem the bleeding. The terror in his dark eyes from knowing he was going to die didn't affect me. "For Brutus then," I whispered. In my mind, I had avenged another legionnaire's death due to a First Citizen's greed.

Boris slowly fell forward, collapsing before Maveith reached us. I watched him bleed out and die, then turned to the dumbfounded mage. Under the glowstone's luminescence, I probably looked like a callous murderer. I licked my lips slowly to find my voice. "What is a soul prison?"

The mage fumbled in his pockets and produced a large crystal. "A … a … a necromancy vessel," he stuttered out. "Weak necromancers require a soul to animate the dead." I walked forward and took the offered crystal. It was twice as thick as my finger, and the rich purple color reminded me of an amethyst.

"This helped you clear the ruins?" I asked the terrified necromancer.

"Yes," he squeaked out, cowering in fear as Maveith arrived and took in the scene. Maveith didn't look shocked or disappointed, which helped me accept my act. I think the fact that I didn't feel any remorse was what unsettled me. Killing was feeling too normal for me.

I turned back to the necromancer. "What were you trying to get from the ruins?"

Even though he hadn't moved, he was out of breath. "The library. We were trying to reach the library. The ancient tomes are worth hundreds of gold each," he stated, his eyes fixed on Maveith. I had to agree that the shadows of the glowstone made the large goliath look more menacing, especially with his impassive visage.

"Did you succeed?" I asked, then snapped my fingers to get his attention when he didn't answer.

"No. We were only camped for five days before the wyvern came at dusk. Brutus told us there might be a wyvern in the area. Boris didn't believe him," he said spitefully, and eyed the dead Boris.

I looked at him doubtfully. "Five days? The snow is gone and the library is only four hundred yards from the western gate."

He nodded emphatically. "The soul crystal can only hold one soul. After each specter was captured, I had to empty it. It takes time to use a soul to power a simple ritual."

My mind raced back to what he said earlier about the soul crystal. "Wait, were you creating an army of undead?"

He put up his hand in capitulation and panic. "No. I didn't break the Empire's laws! I burned the soul with lesser necromancy spells to empty the crystal!" He was breathing heavily in worry and sweating visibly. I wasn't familiar with the necromancy laws, but I assumed raising the dead was probably frowned upon. There were special mage companies that hunted necromancers, but the Hounds frequently tracked them. Hearne's lectures in Hound training had never focused on the undead, as we had been in abbreviated training.

"You were not trying to enter the dungeon?" I asked after a long pause to think.

The necromancer seemed to be relaxing, thinking I might let him live because of my calm tone and rational questions. "Count Cato wanted us to find the path to the dungeon entrance, but we had no plans to enter. We were just supposed to load the wagons with the elven books and return for this expedition. We didn't realize there were still so many specters left in the city. Brutus said his mage company cleared most of the specters around the library and western gate. He said it would be easy." His tone was a bit angry now.

"How many specters did you kill with this?" I held up the soul prison.

I could see his mind racing. He must have thought I wanted an accurate count. "More than forty, less than fifty."

I couldn't help but laugh, and it might have sounded a little maniacal as he cringed. "Less than fifty in five days?" I said, a little mocking. Castile could do that many with the kettle of souls in an hour. In my last days using the kettle of souls, I could have done about a hundred in a day. It wouldn't have been a pleasant experience, but it was possible for me.

The necromancer straightened. "Draining a soul is taxing work! The Count wasn't able to obtain the artifact that the mage company used. It was moved to the Imperial Archives until an expedition could be assembled. But then the Emperor left to fight the invaders ..." He trailed off, thinking he had defended himself sufficiently.

Maveith's deep voice from behind me asked, "What are we going to do with him?" The necromancer looked just as interested in my answer as Maveith.

"How does this work?" I held the slightly chilly purple crystal in my hand.

The necromancer took my question as a lifeline. "When the undead is killed, you place it where the creature dissipated. It pulls in the soul after a minute or so."

"Would it work on him?" I asked, indicating Boris.

He got a little nervous. "Uh, yes, but it would take much longer, maybe an hour, as he was living, not dead. The crystal would be fighting his corporeal body for the soul. There are stronger soul prisons that work quicker, but this one is not very strong and really only good for the undead." From the tension and uncertainty in his voice, I thought using this device on people, even recently dead people, was also against Telhian law.

I nodded in thanks, as he had been very helpful in answering my questions. I took a slow, deep breath. "I can't let you live. Do you want to take some oblivion pills before I remove your head?" The color drained from the necromancer's face, and he turned and ran. I would have run in his shoes too.

"Do you want me?" Maveith's voice asked softly behind me.

"No. It is my burden." I pulled a bow from my space, fixed a paralytic arrow to the string, drew, and released. Even though night had fallen, the necromancer ran straight down the old road. He only got thirty yards before my arrow pierced his back. He let out a scream and stumbled for ten yards before falling to the ground and floundering like a fish out of water.

I walked up to him. He wasn't even aware of my approach. The arrow had missed his heart by a few inches, but his lungs were rapidly filling with blood, judging by how much blood he was spewing. Magebane came down on his neck to end his suffering. My conscience felt a little heavier, but I was starting to become numb to the killing.

I dragged the body back to Maveith, who hadn't moved for the entire time, but held Ginger's reins. "Can you hold this while I search the bodies?" Maveith took the glowstone as I searched. The most valuable item by far was Boris's dungeon-forged blade. The pommel had an intricate pattern carved into it and was probably easily recognizable in the Empire. I sent the blade to my space with the magebane.

Boris also had a heavy coin pouch, a gold signet ring, and some papers signed by Count Cato. A wax stamp was attached, too. The papers were for passage on the Count's business, and the bearer was not to be detained. The letter was likely how Boris and his group avoided the press gangs.

The necromancer didn't have anything useful on him, and the guard just had the lesser runic weapon. I searched the bushes where they had bedded down and frowned. There was nothing but two heavy cloaks. They must have fled the wyvern and left everything behind.

I returned to the road and took out the collector, not making eye contact with Maveith as I worked. The necromancer produced a milky-gray minor essence. Affinity essences were usually multicolored, so I did not think this was the necromancy affinity. It took me some time to recall the attribute the essence fortified—aether shaping. I didn't hesitate and consumed it. I might be able to successfully write out spell forms with a few dozen more of these shaping essences.

Boris's body yielded a minor constitution essence, which I offered to Maveith. He only considered for a breath before accepting it. The guard produced a minor strength essence, which I also offered to Maveith. He briefly argued that I had done all the killing, but for some reason, these last two days had made me nauseous. I knew I had crossed a point past which I had no remorse for killing people.

"We will stack the bodies and burn them," I told Maveith, and he worked with me. I had some alchemy accelerants, and we left the bodies burning behind us.

I pulsed earth speak as we walked in silence—well, not complete silence, as Ginger's hooves thudded softly on the earth and occasionally clicked on an ancient paver.

"We should move off the road," Maveith intoned after we had gained some distance from the burning bodies.

The night was not overly dark, and Neptune's Tear gave us decent light, but I agreed. I used a few pulses of earth speak to find an old structure just off the road, not quite claimed by nature. Only two crumbling stone walls remained, but they gave us some shelter and were modestly defensible. With Ginger along, we didn't have a lot of options.

We spent some time clearing the debris and setting trip alarms before settling in. I needed some sleep, even with the ring. I made sure the aether shield amulet was charged before letting Maveith stand watch while he had an early breakfast. I found I couldn't use the dreamscape amulet with the aether shield amulet on. They were like opposing aether magnets. When I tried to activate the dreamscape amulet, it tried to jump from my grip.

Grumbling, I stored the dreamscape amulet and just tried to get a few hours of rest. The nightmares came quickly, but I did not shy away from them tonight. They started with the Hounds chasing me because I had killed a First Citizen. I quickly turned from prey to hunter and eliminated the Hounds one by one. The last man I killed gave me pause because it was Konstantin. I was woken by a soft bell being tripped on one of the alarms.

My eyes were open and I was instantly on alert. "Maveith?" I asked the darkness as my eyes adjusted. I sent out an earth pulse.

A short distance away, Maveith replied, "I don't know what is out there."

When the image came back, I swore, causing Maveith to look back at me. I changed my focus and sent out more pulses. "Gnolls. A lot of gnolls." A large pack had surrounded our campsite.

Maveith had his bow out as shadowy shapes moved through the trees. I tried to count, but not all the gnolls were within range of my earth speak pulses. They were not just passing by. They were clearly preparing to attack. Maveith had his bow drawn and Ginger was getting anxious. "At least thirteen, Maveith," I hissed. "They all have spears."

The gnolls were not too skilled at remaining silent. Branches snapped in the night, and their soft, cackling speech drifted on the air as they prepared. We were in the corner of two ancient walls, with thick trunks covering a third side. I pulled some pellets out of my belt pouch while tracking the gnolls. "Maveith, I have some blindness and sneezing pellets. It should slow them and make them vulnerable." I imagined Maveith nodding in the dark as his back was to me. My last pulse showed the first gnolls rushing our position. "They come!" I hissed.

Chapter 249: Gnoll Party

The gnolls' cackling language erupted from all around us. In Hound training, Hearne had told us this was an intimidation tactic by gnolls when they hunted. We didn't have to wait long as a trio of large gnolls rushed the only wide opening. With just three enemies, I considered holding the pellets. Maveith's bow twanged and one of the gnoll shadows jerked from the impact of his heavy arrow and spun to the ground, accompanied by a piercing yip. I knew gnolls had excellent night sight. We were at a disadvantage in the low light of the blue moon and severely outnumbered.

I sent one last earth pulse, and then I slammed two sneezing and blindness pellets on the stones near the entrance. There was no wind tonight, so we shouldn't have to deal with the spores blowing back on us.

The pellets shattered on the ground and the air ignited their payload with a pop. A ten-foot-wide cloud burst in the moonlight. Since those four pellets had no smoke variants, we could still make out the gnoll shadows as they rushed us with their spears.

"Seven heartbeats before the spores become inert," I warned Maveith about entering the cloud. "Five are about to scale the wall to our left. Can you handle the two remaining in front?"

"Easily," Maveith rumbled as he released a second arrow into a confused gnoll coming through the cloud. He tossed aside his bow to pull his hammer from its belt loop. The black spear appeared in my hands, extending my reach to strike the climbing gnolls. With a quick flick of the spear, the head of the first gnoll was separated from its body. Unexpectedly, the weight of the five gnolls scaling the wall affected its stability. The old stone base popped, and the ten-foot wall started falling slowly toward us.

"Maveith! Move right!" Maveith looked over and understood my urgency. I slapped Ginger's flank. "Run!" She understood the command and bolted past Maveith, trampling the last blinded gnoll as she exited the structure, rushing into the night. It wasn't ideal, but it would have taken too long to coax Ginger to move out of the corner in the confusion.

The ground shook as the stones making up the wall broke apart like shattered glass. The gnolls who rode the wall to the ground were stunned, and some appeared injured as they yipped in dismay. I took the opportunity to use the black spear to stab two of them in vital locations—the heart and head. Maveith's hammer cracked a third's head, and I heard him cursing the loss of his bow under the collapsed wall.

The gnolls were not done with us. We didn't see the thrown spears in the moon's low light. One spear pierced Maveith's abdomen, and he grunted in displeasure. My aether shield flashed, draining its charge as a spear targeting me was deflected. The flash of light from the shield blinded us for a moment.

I pulsed earth speak and detected five more gnolls rushing us. "Handle the last one in here," I ordered Maveith, who was carefully pulling the spear out of his torso. If we stayed in the structure, they would be free to attack us from range with spears.

As I rushed the oncoming gnolls, I was worried for Ginger. But first, we needed to eliminate the gnolls. As I ran into the open, the temperature of the air suddenly dropped unnaturally. Gnoll mages were rarer than an ogre that didn't reek. It appeared Fortuna was taking the night off from watching over me.

Frost appeared on the ground as I ran, but more deadly was the unnatural fog materializing around me and filling the woods, rising to the canopy. The gnoll shaman … mage … Whatever you called it, it was smart. The fog was thick and rising, and soon, the woods would descend into complete darkness, giving the advantage to the gnolls' dark vision. Gnolls hunted at night but usually in packs no larger than six. If I ever had a chance to talk with Hearne again, I was going to bitch about this encounter, as it was far from what he taught us.

Just before I clashed with the lead gnoll, I sent out an earth pulse and cursed. The flash image returned more than ten gnolls in range, some of which were half the size of the warriors. Focusing on my opponent, my air shield deflected a spear, and my spear tore out his guts. I pivoted and swung the black spear in an arc, slashing two more gnolls, one critically, just below the neck. The remaining two uninjured gnolls backed off and defended instead of attacking.

I couldn't waste time as the darkness was rapidly encroaching. I cut one of their spears in half in a quick exchange, the black spear easily cutting the shaft. These gnolls were strong but very unskilled with their weapons. The most experienced hunters in the pack would have attacked first, but they were now all dead. I pressed forward, as I doubted it would be long before I was in complete darkness.

I started to form an idea of what these gnolls were doing. These gnolls must be migrating their entire pack—maybe away from the war front. The distant gnolls were smaller, so likely younger, and running away from the combat, and their high numbers matched my conjecture.

Before I could engage the remaining gnolls, an unseen arrow pierced my thigh, and I struggled to remain standing. I grasped the arrow and it snapped in my grasp and crumbled. I concluded it was an ice shard and not an arrow from the gnoll spellcaster nearby. I was hobbled and soon fending off the four resurgent gnolls as they got confident from my injury.

I wanted to pulse earth speak and search for the caster but couldn't find the time to divert my attention from the fight as they attempted to surround me. Without my aether shield amulet available, one of these ice arrows could strike me in a vital region. As I worked on healing, I shuffled to put my opponents between me and the mage's likely direction.

The ice arrow had penetrated deeply, and it must have had a freezing effect tied to it, as the surrounding muscle was damaged as well. I pushed aether blindly toward the wound. When I was sufficiently healed, I surprised the gnolls, lunging on my bloody, injured leg that I had been favoring.

I grunted in mild pain since the wound was not quite healed. The spear pierced the surprised gnoll's sternum. I extracted the tip at an angle, widening the wound and causing a spray of blood. The other young gnolls backed off in fear. They didn't realize my vision was almost gone as darkness quickly descended. I broke away and raced toward the gnoll I suspected was casting spells. If I could eliminate him, I hoped, it would break the gnolls' spirit and lift the darkness.

Unfortunately, my guess was correct, and another unseen ice arrow pierced my chest. It had been too dark to see the attack, and I collapsed behind a tree, wheezing as cold blood filled my lungs. It hurt to breathe as I quickly and carefully worked the ice shard out to speed up the healing. As I healed the injury and spat congealed blood, I switched the spear for magebane to deal with the caster. The thick fog covered the canopy and the darkness was almost complete. My earth pulse told me the gnolls were retreating, no longer interested in the fight.

I released a long breath of relief. If I had to continue the fight, I would have had to use a glowstone and be a marked target with attacks coming from the darkness. I focused my senses on listening to the woods. Maveith was still in the structure, but I didn't hear any sound of Ginger. After a few moments, I heard Maveith's voice cut the night air fifty yards away. "Eryk, where are you?"

"Stay there, Maveith. I will come to you. The gnolls are retreating. They are a large migrating pack," I yelled back. My chest injury had healed sufficiently for my breathing to return to normal. The metallic taste of blood lingered in my mouth. I kept spitting to clear it.

The gnolls were fleeing, already out of the range of my pulses, and my aether core was pretty depleted. I was content with letting them retreat, as the darkness was not receding.

As my racing, adrenaline-fueled heart calmed, I spent time recharging the aether shield amulet and then stood from my cover. I moved back toward Maveith, but no attack was forthcoming. In the light of a glowstone, Maveith was leaning against the wall, his abdominal wound mostly healed. "Do you need more of the orc healing potions?"

"My mouth may never recover if I consume another," Maveith whined in good humor. "I have just some lingering soreness but will be fine. Where is Ginger?" His tone changed to concern.

I listened to the quiet night and didn't hear anything. "I will go look for her with earth speak. She probably didn't wander far away," I replied with hope.

"I will go with you," Maveith stated, not taking no for an answer. I didn't object, and we moved into the dark woods. I pulsed infrequently to conserve aether and wondered why the dense fog overhead hadn't dissipated with the departure of the gnoll spellcaster and his pack. Maybe it was because there was no wind tonight. We were forced to use a glowstone to light our way.

A pained equine cry cut the night a distance away. Maveith was already lumbering ahead to Ginger's rescue. If it was strange to put our lives in danger for a horse, neither of us mentioned it. I paced myself with Maveith, holding the glowstone and magebane. The horse's second cry had us both shifting into a sprint. My earth pulses increased in frequency as we closed in on the combat.

I got some rough feedback on what was happening. One of the gnolls had roped Ginger and secured her to a tree. She was fighting back as they tried to take her down with spears. "They are killing her!" I snarled as I began to outpace Maveith.

Maveith's war cry echoed in the night behind me, drawing the gnoll's attention away from Ginger. I reached them first and slashed into the nearest gnoll, deflecting his spear with magebane while tossing the glowstone on the ground to light the area. My second slash was to free Ginger, who was bleeding from multiple stab wounds. Instead of running, she reared and came down on a gnoll, crushing its skull in retribution.

I only detected six gnolls in the clearing. One was dead and one was wounded. Maveith's hammer crushed a third, and then things went dark. I guessed a gnoll had covered the glowstone, so I produced another, but its light only lasted a few breaths before being snuffed out like a candle. Maveith was blinded as well. "I can't see," he said, his deep voice echoing nearby.

I pulsed earth speak again and saw the three young gnolls grouped together. Their cackling language echoed in the woods, and I guessed our loss of sight was due to the gnoll mage somehow. More cackling conversations occurred around us in the deeper woods, and it angered me. Ginger was huffing angrily nearby, bleeding as I tried to call her to me. "Ginger! Come! Apple!"

It didn't work, as she was also blind and heavily injured, but at least her training kept her from running from the battle. A thud sounded, and Maveith grunted, "An arrow has struck me."

"Is it an ice shard?" I asked as I continued to pulse earth speak to fight the fog of war. I was now fairly certain which of the distant gnolls was the caster.

"Yes," Maveith's voice returned angrily as I heard ice crunching in his grasp.

"I am going to rush the caster. He only has two guards," I informed Maveith. Not being able to see in the dark was becoming an annoyance. I was so accustomed to the night vision goggles of the Hounds that losing that ability needled me. Perhaps I should have searched the Archives for Hound gear or tried to locate more Hound caches in the western Empire.

As I raced toward the trio of gnolls, my aether shield flashed as an ice shard shattered on the defensive magic. The flash and confusion allowed me to close the distance, and the gnoll guards interposed themselves to protect their caster. I had overestimated myself. In the dark, I took a spear to the shoulder and one to the chest and had to step back and recover. It was too hard to fight in the dark, even with earth pulses, when my opponents could see and I could not. I could tell their general location and their rough movements, but their bodies were not clear enough to defend myself from their attacks.

I retrieved the blindness pellets and cast them into the ground, but I knew they were prepared for the trick from the cackling warning from the mage. I started to retreat, backstepping toward Maveith and Ginger, and produced my third glowstone. It too soon winked out, and I shoved it agitatedly into my pouch since my aether wouldn't charge it. I only had one glowstone left in my dimensional space.

The two gnolls with spears were now getting bolder, stalking me as I retreated. I had stopped the bleeding from the spear wound, but defending against the mage and his guards was too difficult if I couldn't see. My aether was dangerously low from the night's combat as well. Fuck, I swore to myself. I needed to see in the dark. And then I could.

I was stunned as my vision suddenly crystallized. My vision was like twilight, heavily gray in color, but high in contrast. I understood what had happened. I had just imprinted a spell form to see in the dark. I was channeling aether into the new spell form on my aether core, and it was affecting my eyes, similar to the Hound goggles.

My vision was only clear to about twenty-five feet, but that was good enough to handle the overconfident gnolls. A grin slowly formed on my lips, and the gnolls sensed the change in my demeanor. Before they could back away, I rushed the pair.

They didn't stand a chance; their brains were still processing my change in confidence. Magebane made short work of the pair, and I chased down the mage after his guards fell. The mage tried to flee, necklaces of bone rattling as he stumbled away in fear. I cut him down from behind and realized he looked ancient for a gnoll. I pulsed earth speak, but no more gnolls were in range.

There were still more gnolls out there, but they were mostly females and pups, unlikely to bother us. I returned to Maveith, who was still in the dark but guarding Ginger with the remaining gnolls all dead. "It's over, Maveith; the caster is dead." I produced the last glowstone to shed light on us. Maveith blinked until his vision cleared. My eyes didn't need to adjust to the light until I dropped my new spell form.

I hadn't planned to hunt down the remaining gnolls, but after seeing Ginger's wounds in the light, I changed my mind as my anger surged.

Ginger was in bad shape, but at least the artificial clouds faded with the death of the gnoll mage. She was so upset she wouldn't even take an offered apple. While Maveith stood watch, I calmed her and talked to her as I used healing salve to close nine puncture wounds. "Don't worry, Ginger. Revenge is coming."

I checked her over one more time, wiping the blood away to make sure I didn't miss anything. The deep punctures would require a healing potion, but I didn't think Ginger would consume the orc Pathfinder brew, so I gave her one of my few Hound lesser healing potions. She still didn't like it, foaming more than swallowing, but I think she got most of it down.

"Maveith, how are you doing?" I asked, Ginger finally appearing recovered. I relaxed. At least her appetite was back, as she ate three apples noisily from my hand.

"It is difficult fighting in the dark," he complained in a flat tone. "I have some abdominal pain, but I think it is from the orc potions and not a lingering injury." Maveith released a sharp flatulence, and then another, his digestive system agreeing with his assessment. "Yes. That helped relieve some of the cramping." Maveith was completely serious and not making a fart joke, but I laughed anyway. After the night's ordeal, I needed the laugh.

I turned inward toward my aether core to try to feel out the change. I channeled aether through the new spell form and my vision sharpened again. It was a weak spell form, and I guessed it must be my illusion affinity. Night vision had not been in the spell form book I had studied, so it was a mild surprise, but it made sense. The night vision was significantly weaker than the Hound goggles, lacking color, but it compensated for a weakness. The spell form also felt more primal than the other intricate spell forms I had learned. The only time I could recall studying night vision spell forms was when I briefly examined the night vision goggles with my earth speak.

This was actually the second time I had imprinted a spell form through willpower and need. The first time was when I created a spell form to pull as much out of an essence as possible. I was in Legion training and had just won my first essence from placing in the spear competition.

I patted Ginger reassuringly and retrieved the collector. Under the light of my last glowstone, Ginger and Maveith followed me to the gnoll mage. The other glowstones were darkened and useless. Whatever the gnoll mage had done to them had destroyed their ability to absorb aether and give off light. The fact that he did that from over fifty feet away was impressive and indicated he had been powerful.

Under the glowstone, the gnoll mage had wrinkled skin and bristly, thin white fur. He—no, it was a she—appeared ancient and had loops of bone necklaces hanging around her body. Maveith grunted, "A soothsayer."

"A what?" I asked as I placed the collector over the strangely citrus-smelling body.

"A soothsayer. The bone necklaces are for divining the future. A soothsayer would cut the thread, toss the bones, and then read them. I have never heard of a gnoll being a soothsayer before, though. I wonder who trained it," Maveith said, intrigued. Thick aetheric smoke was drawn into the collector. A major essence quickly formed, but I thought enough smoke had been drawn to form an apex, from my experience. I had never seen a clairvoyance/divination essence before. The sphere appeared oily as I turned it, and images in the oil came and went before I could focus on them.

I moved to her two guards next and then the rest of the gnolls. The collector formed two minor quickness essences, two minor dexterity essences, and one major strength essence. The strength essence was from the largest gnoll who had led the rushing group. Maveith had put one of his large arrows near its heart, and it bled out from the injury.

"Do you want the major strength essence or the four minor essences?" I asked Maveith as I stood from the last young gnoll, who had yielded nothing. The morning sky was graying, and I was eager to track down the rest of the gnolls.

Maveith was cleaning his retrieved arrows with leaves. He looked up and considered. "The quickness essences are good enough for me." I deposited all four minor essences into his hand and consumed the strength essence myself. I didn't even ask if he wanted the soothsayer's essence; it would improve my ability to maximize gains from essences.

"The gnolls are heading west. I want to try and hunt them down," I stated while rubbing Ginger's neck.

Maveith sucked his teeth. "Shouldn't we continue? We will lose a day hunting down the gnolls." He indicated the eight dead gnolls around the structure in which we had camped. "We killed their best hunters and their powerful soothsayer. If we were to remain in the Empire, I would agree it is in our best interest to hunt them, but we are leaving, are we not?" Maveith stressed the last a little.

I could hear the underlying urgency to get to his sister in his voice. I pulled out Ginger's grooming kit to remove the dried blood and sighed. "Okay, I agree. We will continue on to the capital. We will cross the river tomorrow and approach on the far shore." Maveith nodded in appreciation that his advice was taken.

We moved at a fast pace up the old trade road for the rest of the day as we closed in on Telha. We crossed the river as planned. I put everything I could in storage and Maveith and I swam across in our underclothes while Ginger made her way across with me holding her lead line. She was actually pretty excited to swim and danced around on the opposite shore, excitedly shaking the water off. My horse liked swimming and wanted to go back in.

We dried off in the spring sun and then dressed. After last night, I was tempted to don armor for protection. It could have blocked those two ice arrows, and not wearing a helm meant I was one lucky blow from being knocked out or killed. The aether shield was a remarkable artifact, but it only worked once before requiring a short cooldown, and needed to be fed aether to recharge.

As we walked through the woods on the opposite shore, I informed Maveith of my plan. "Maveith, you are going to take Ginger north to the coast. I will charter a ship from the Adventurers Guild and we will pick you up."

Maveith didn't like my plan. "I don't think we should separate, Eryk."

"Goliaths are rare. If I am seen with you, it will be easy to figure out that I am alive." I rubbed Ginger's neck, "Ginger would also be seized for the war effort." Maveith grunted unhappily but didn't offer an alternate plan.

We found more signs of gnolls, goblins, and something that looked like the tracks of a troll to me, but they were weeks old. There were more than a few boot prints as well, belonging to a civilized race. It looked like the rain had been sparse the last week, leaving old tracks intact. When we reached the location of the Gnoll Garden, the tower where the Mage College trained their mages and where the Hounds used to train, I scouted ahead alone.

The tower was abandoned, with no fresh tracks nearby. Still, being cautious, I led Maveith and Ginger on a wide loop around it. After traveling a few miles north, I stopped us. "Maveith, continue northeast from here." I handed him Corvus's Hound medallion from my hand. "If you get in trouble with someone who isn't a Hound, tell them you are on Hound's business. Don't show that to a Hound, as the man it belonged to is now dead."

Maveith took the amulet. "I don't like being separated. How long will you be?"

I had to consider the question. "Don't wait longer than a week. If I can't get a ship in two days, I will join you here. Watch for a ship flying the Adventurers

Guild flag near shore. You see that, then show yourself. This is an artificed spyglass." I handed him my Hound spyglass. "Just channel aether into it; turn these to change the magnification. I will be on the bow." I then asked a difficult question. "Do you want to give a blood sample?" I had explained the blood compass to him but hadn't broached the subject. It would make it easier to find him.

"I think that is wise." He tore a scrap of cloth, cut his arm unflinchingly, soaked the cloth, and handed it to me. I nodded at his trust and sent it to my space.

Maveith played with the spyglass while I pulled out his pack and prepared supplies for him and Ginger. When we parted, I was optimistic. Even if I couldn't charter a ship for us, I hoped to learn enough in the Adventurers Guild Hall about how we could safely enter the Boutan Caliphate.

I moved through the night, practicing with my new spell form. Seeing everything in grayscale was disappointing, but it was better than not having the ability to see in the dark. I pulsed earth speak as I moved along the river. I arrived at a fishing village a few miles upriver of the capital. It was dangerous living on this side of the river, but I guessed it was also much cheaper for the people. Most of the houses looked like they were of rough construction, and I guessed that fewer than a hundred people lived there.

When the sun rose, I walked with a limp into the town. Only a single watchman was on the wooden palisade. It didn't take long to barter for passage across the river for five large coppers. The old man and his grandson happily paddled me to the docks of the capital. The old man politely answered my questions during the entire two-hour trip to the capital. He didn't ask me questions in return, which I appreciated.

He didn't know much about the war other than that barges loaded with men and supplies frequently went upriver. He delivered fish every other day to the docks in Telha and usually made half a silver for the effort. Taking half the day to bring me to the capital for five large coppers was a welcome break from casting nets all day.

When we reached the dock, I tipped him a dirty, small silver and stepped off. The lower docks smelled like a mix of salt water, fish, and unwashed bodies. I was happy to note that a ship flying the Adventurers Guild crest was in the larger docks. It had the same symbol as my guild medallion: a tree with leaf-covered branches and mirroring roots. I just had to hope they were not still locked down and could sail.

There was a lot of activity as laborers rushed about the small watercraft. The village I had come from was not the only fishing village that supplied the capital. A city guardsman intercepted me before I took three hobbled steps. "Name and business in Telha," he rasped with a dry throat and foul breath.

"Lucien Beatrix. Just doing some shopping for the family." My disguise had rough clothes and a worn cloak. My hair and beard had streaks of gray, and I walked with a heavy limp and a slightly hunched back.

The guardsman seemed to consider me for a long moment. "The cost to enter the city is a large copper." I didn't actually know if that was true or not. I had never had to pay as a legionnaire before. Instead of arguing, I angrily dug into my pockets and produced a large, dirty copper.

Maveith had cleaned the coins, but it was hard to erase the length of time it had been buried. The guardsman studied the foreign dark elf coin for a long time before pocketing it and walking away. Dozens of different coins passed through the city. Sometimes a vendor would refuse one, but it was not overly suspicious to pay with foreign coins or dungeon coins. The coins would eventually find themselves melted down and stamped into proper Telhian coins.

I walked through the city, maintaining my limp and looking longingly at the bathhouses I passed. When I reached the thoroughfare, I gazed right for a long time. That way led to the Mage College, where Renna should be. I was tempted to confirm her health and perhaps convince her to come with me and desert the Empire. Eventually, I walked to the Adventurers Guild, not risking a visit.

Entering, there were a lot fewer people here than the last time. The air smelled of stale beer and sweat. I assumed the diminished population was due to the war. Seated at a table were five people playing cards. I recognized Guildmaster Icarus smiling and playing cards. He looked up at me, interested in my entrance, but didn't move. Desdemona had her back to me but I recognized her dark, sun-beaten black hair. She was talking animatedly to someone, accusing them of cheating in a friendly tone.

I hobbled to the table, drawing everyone's attention. Desdemona craned her neck, but no look of recognition flashed on her face. Guildmaster Icarus spoiled my disguise. "What brings you back to our Guild Hall, legionnaire?" Desdemona squinted her eyes a few times before recognition finally flashed on her face. She didn't look happy to see me, so this might be harder than I had planned.

I was not happy that I was recognized, and that I was openly being called a legionnaire. I put on my best smile and took a seat at the table. "Today, I am a member of the Adventurers Guild." I placed my bronze guild medallion on the table, showing my name and number: 13-393919.

"Looking to use the tablet reader again," Icarus said, arching his eyebrow and looking suspiciously at my leg. I thought my limp was convincing, but maybe not to him.

"I was hoping to talk with Desdemona privately and spend some coin with Tarvon in the back," I replied to Icarus, eyeing Desdemona for a reply.

"What could you possibly want with me?" Desdemona barked in an exasperated voice. Why did this woman hate me?

"Are you still a ship captain?" I asked softly.

The table was suddenly quiet. Icarus looked at the others playing cards, who stood and walked away, leaving just Icarus, Desdemona, and me at the table. Icarus rested his hands on the table and leaned forward. "You are looking to get smuggled out of the Empire."

"I am that obvious?" I chuckled, hopefully hiding my nervousness. I knew the Adventurers Guild hated the Empire, so I assumed I was safe in approaching them. Whether I could get what I wanted from them was another question. "Myself, four others, and my horse," I requested with open hands toward Desdemona.

Desdemona's eyes widened and she shook her head. "Five legionnaires would draw too much attention. My ship is already being watched closely." She waved me off, dismissing my request. Icarus looked just as doubtful.

"Actually, I am the only legionnaire. The others will be picked up along the coast east of here with my horse." The revelation did not convince them but made them more skeptical. Of course, they probably thought that if the others couldn't even enter the city, transporting them would be just as illicit.

Icarus spoke slowly and carefully. "Just because you are a Guild member, legionnaire, doesn't mean we will accommodate your requests."

I nodded. "I understand. Would this be proper remuneration?" I placed the major essence of clairvoyance on the table in front of Desdemona. Just seeing her shocked look made it more than worth it.

It was an essence I would likely never use, so using it as barter was an acceptable loss. Desdemona picked it up and stared at it like it was the most precious diamond in the world. It was worth somewhere in the range of fifty to five hundred gold. Being an affinity essence, it would be toward the upper range, I guessed.

While Desdemona was enthralled, Icarus spoke. "A valuable essence for sure. Still, what you are asking is dangerous. We are supposed to report any First Citizen or legionnaire attempting to leave under suspicious circumstances." He broke into a friendly smile. "Then again, such a situation has never happened in my tenure as the Master of this Guild Hall."

"Well, there is more. I am actually looking to adventure under the Guild in the Boutan Caliphate, but am trying to get to the Grand Duchy of Manch first." I had a lopsided smile on my face at their incredulous looks. I could read maps and knew the difficulties of my route. Desdemona even put down the essence.

Desdemona appeared incredulous. "Grand Duchy of Manch? I have a sea ship, not a flying ship. To reach Manch I would have to sail around the Boutan Caliphate. A month and a week if the winds are with us. This would not cover my costs and crew for such a journey." She reluctantly held out the essence to return.

"There are flying ships?" I questioned longingly.

Desdemona laughed at me. "No. Maybe during the Golden Age of the Titans, if you believe in the legends. Now, the only things that dominate the skies are dragons, and they don't like competition."

I sighed, disappointed. "I was hoping to use a portal to reach Manch," I revealed.

Icarus was nodding and thinking. "You could sail to Sanco in Esenhem, then. The elves don't have portals, but there are displacement mages who can teleport your group for a significant fee." He nodded to the essence, giving me an estimate of the price to expect.

"From Sanco, you can port to the Esenhem capital of Artiria. Then you can portal from Artiria to Gramney. It won't be cheap for five people and a horse, though. The elves are also fairly strict about who they agree to port." He was clearly referencing the fact that I was a legionnaire and Esenhem and the Telhian Empire were at war.

He continued, "The Caliphate doesn't have any portals. And anyway, all non-orc adventurers need to register at the Guild Halls in either Khoura, Harcif, Imararal, or their capital of Becar."

I mentally stored that information, as I had planned to ask about how adventurers crossed borders during war. Desdemona studied me, trying to puzzle me out. "There are plenty of dungeons elsewhere on the continent, but if you are hiding from the Empire, the Boutan Caliphate is probably a good choice." That actually seemed like a good reason, so I just gave her a slight nod, letting her think she had figured me out.

Icarus considered me and then gave me some advice. "If that is the path you have chosen, then I suggest you register at an Adventurers Guild Hall in Esenhem. While guild members are more accepted in the Boutan Caliphate than in the Telhian Empire, there is some … culture shock. A number of orc adventurers operate within Esenhem. It might be prudent to convince one to join you to help you navigate to the Boutan Caliphate and avoid upsetting a warlord or cleric." While his advice was wise, I couldn't see Maveith working well with an orc. I nodded appreciatively at his advice anyway.

My long shot exit strategy seemed like it was going to work out. "Would you be willing to take me?" I said, smiling at Desdemona.

"Not that simple." Desdemona smirked roguishly. "I need to put in a request to sail, and then my ship would be searched on the morning we pull anchor. Sometimes they send some Truthseekers to question the passengers, but with your guild medallion, you shouldn't be questioned—but no guarantees."

"How long till we sail, and how long to Sanco? My companions are waiting," I asked Captain Desdemona coolly.

"Two days to ensure the appropriate people approve our departure and seven to eight days to reach Sanco," Desdemona said professionally. She had switched from mocking glares to something akin to respect. At least, that was how I was interpreting her body language.

"Excellent. Can I get a room here tonight?" I asked Icarus.

He nodded. "No additional charge." He stood and left Desdemona and me at the table.

Desdemona studied me intently and started to make me feel uncomfortable. "I think I will go and talk with Tarvon."

"I will join you to get this appraised." She rolled the essence deftly across the backs of her fingers and over to her palm. Was it just me, or was she trying to impress me?

The halfling was filling out some paperwork at his counter and looked up with his merchant's smile. It took him a moment before recognition flashed in his eyes. Was my disguise really not as great as I had thought? I attributed it to the fact that I was making eye contact. Desdemona pushed past me. "Tarvon, got an essence for appraisal."

She placed the sphere down and spun it on the counter. Tarvon snatched it with deft hands. "Where did you come across a divination essence, girl?"

Desdemona gave me no credit as the essence's original owner. "Barter for passage. I might consume it if the cost is reasonable," she said with a hint of hope in her voice. If she had the clairvoyance/divination affinity, then her infatuation with the sphere made sense.

Tarvon seemed indignant. "I log all transactions honestly." He reached under the counter and produced a scale, and I was immediately confused.

"Isn't it just a major essence?"

Tarvon scoffed, "Boy, every essence is different. Although essence spheres come in three sizes, their density and purity can vary greatly. It doesn't affect lesser essences much, but it can affect the price of major and apex essences by as much as fifty percent."

I watched, fascinated, as he carefully weighed, measured, and used some type of aetheric probe on the sphere over the next few minutes. Satisfied, he opened a logbook and scribbled in it. Desdemona had lost her patience. "And?"

Tarvon was holding back a smile. "One point three. Let me check the current exchange rates." He opened another book to reference, but Desdemona beat him to it.

"Four hundred gold … so, five hundred and twenty gold?" She spat unhappily.

Tarvon didn't acknowledge her while he did his own math. Finished, he stated, "Five hundred thirty-six gold and eighteen silver." Desdemona frowned and exited the back room. Tarvon turned to me. "While Desdemona is the *Shorebreaker's* captain, the Guild owns the vessel. This is probably five years' pay for her." I had the distinct feeling I might have overpaid a little. Tarvon put his smile back on. "What can I do for you, legionnaire?"

"Just an adventurer now. Any healing potions?" I asked.

"Not with the wars. If I did, there would be almost a fifty percent premium as well. Desdemona is only running her …" He paused and looked me over. "Where is she taking you? To the other continent?"

I didn't particularly appreciate how easily everyone was figuring out my intentions, but maybe my request was not so rare. The further you got from the Empire, the safer you were. "Just away from the war." I stuck with the deserter theme. "Oblivion pills?"

Tarvon reached under the counter and retrieved a large jar of the pills. I purchased the entire jar of one hundred. With the transaction complete, he asked, "Anything else?"

"Some adventurer's armor and one item for a scroll of revelation." Tarvon's eyes immediately brightened. He hopped off his stool, which brought him level with the counter, and quickly walked into his office, expecting me to follow.

I had a number of items that still needed to be identified. I didn't want to put them all out there, as I was worried it might make me a target. Since I was getting some adventurer leathers, I thought getting the earth drake bracers assessed would be advisable. As Tarvon sat at his desk and set up the revelation scroll, I placed the bracers on the desk with a gold coin. He was already aware of my dimensional space, so he was not surprised.

"Where do you find all your artifacts, Eryk?" He asked in a friendly tone as he took the pristine leather bracers and the gold coin payment.

"Here and there," I hedged. The Adventurers Guild supposedly supervised all the dungeons in the Telhian Empire in return for a noninterference policy with the Empire's affairs. The halfling looked at me but then shrugged and continued his work.

Tarvon activated the scroll, the runes glowed, and he read the results with his mastery of the runic language. Although I couldn't activate the scroll, I could make out parts of the runic script that flashed in the air. Finished, Tarvon picked up the bracers and licked them. It wasn't a gross lick, just a little taste. "Earth drake bracers. They disperse impacts across your entire body. Excellent defense against bludgeoning weapons. But if the bracers become too damaged from slashing attacks, the runes running through them will be disrupted and they will become useless."

"Thank you." I took the bracers back, satisfied. "The adventurer's armor?"

"The armory is in the cellar. Talk to Draymond down there," Tarvon said helpfully. He seemed to be expecting me to ask for more, but I just stood and found the stairs down.

The air smelled of oil and leather and had a metallic taste to it. Could you actually taste the air? The room opened up into a wide space. Weapon racks lined the walls, but there were actually very few weapons on the racks. A wiry man was hunched over a table and was stitching a leather pack. He looked up, his eyes too big for his face. He reached for a glass and took a long pull before speaking. "Whatcha need?" His accent was thick and I couldn't place it.

"Adventuring leathers," I responded, seeing an assortment of armor behind him.

He pointed his thumb behind him. "Find whatcha want and I will add it up." Draymond ignored me and returned to his work.

I started sorting through the leather armor on stands, tables, and chests. I started to appreciate my fitted Legion armor much more as I tried to piece together a set of leathers. The leggings were easy to find, and also a decent metal helm with padding. The boiled leather chest piece was much harder to fit. The selection was very limited. It wasn't even hardened with resin, like Legion armor.

Maybe if we had time, I could be fitted for a new suit on our journey. I knew Maveith was going to want to move as quickly as possible to find his sister. The detour to Gramney was already going to delay us more than a week, but I wanted to leave word for Castile and the company and drop off my passengers.

I ended up getting a chest piece that was closer to hide armor, as it was the only thing that fit well enough. When I placed everything on the table, Draymond muttered, "Three gold, seventeen silver." I produced the coins as I considered it a fair price.

Wearing slightly mismatched armor was going to gnaw on my soldier discipline. I scooped everything up and carried it upstairs. Icarus helped me check into a room on the third floor with the innkeeper. It was a small room, and the smell reminded me of Murphy's Oil soap. The mattress was stuffed with feathers. It was a bit musty, but comfortable. I spent some time securing the room and coming up with a quick egress strategy through the lone window. I could use two air shields and cross the alley to the adjacent building's roof.

I wasn't going to sleep well, knowing where I was. Before settling in for a short nap, I cleaned the blood compass and put another sample of Castile's blood into it. I was relieved to feel a weak pull, letting me know that she and the company were still alive.

After resting in my room, I spent most of the night fitting the new leathers to my frame and breaking them in by practicing sword and spear forms. I remained in the room the entire day and was surprised when Desdemona came and checked on me.

"Just checking to make sure you hadn't run off and I still have to sail your legionnaire ass out of the Empire. We can sail the morning after tomorrow," she said with a smirk.

She was clearly flirting with me. Her abrupt change in disposition left me confused. I managed to quip back, "Feel free to check on my legionnaire ass anytime."

Instead of replying, her smirk grew, and she turned and strutted down the hallway. Judging by the sway of her hips, she was definitely flirting, or maybe she was indicating I should follow her? I slowly closed the door, trying to decipher the captain's intentions. Would it be cheating on Renna? Was I even in a relationship with Renna? There would be time to figure it out on the ship, as Maveith was my priority.

Reluctantly, I took the blood compass out, cleaned it again, and added Renna's blood sample. Maybe if she was in the city, I could risk going to see her, even though it would be a terrible idea. I was surprised but not shocked when her sample pulled in the same direction as Castile and had similar strength. They were together on the Empire's borders. Renna was a war mage now.

I stayed in the room all day. Late in the evening, the city bells started to ring. Of course the city would be attacked when I was about to leave! I dressed in my armor and rushed down to the common room. If I was correct, the Adventurers Guild was the safest place in the city. The invaders would leave it untouched as long as no adventurers joined the defense.

Icarus was in the common room and looked over at me. "The city is not under attack. The word is spreading through the city that the Emperor is dead."

Was the Emperor dead? I stood stunned but impassive. My hand drifted to my pocket and I activated the compass. It still had a faint pull, so Castile was alive—or recently dead. My mind raced, and Icarus studied my reaction.

"You don't look surprised, legionnaire," he stated appraisingly. "The news is likely days old," he probed. He probably thought my flight was due to the Emperor's death.

It felt like everything was snowballing and spinning out of my control. "I am just stunned. What does this mean?"

Icarus eyed me again before speaking. "It is just a rumor right now, spreading like fire through the city. If true, they will lock down the city to maintain order."

Our conversation was cut short as Desdemona slammed the heavy entry door open, and before it slammed shut, I could see the chaos starting in the street. She had a tense energy and an angry tone. "There is smoke coming from the palace." Her eyes locked on me. "Is this your doing, legionnaire?"

I could see why this woman was single. One moment she was hinting at a tryst, and the next moment, she was accusing me of killing the Emperor and burning down the palace. I bit my tongue, holding back a nasty retort. "No, I had nothing to do with it. Is this going to affect us sailing tomorrow?"

Desdemona barked a laugh. "Are you daft? The palace is burning! I doubt they are going to let anyone leave the city now. At least not until a new Emperor sits in the palace." She collapsed heavily into a chair and put her feet up on the table, tilting precariously back in the chair. She locked her fingers behind her head. "All we can do is wait."

Maveith and Ginger couldn't wait. I quickly came up with a plan in my head. "That doesn't work for me. Would this help?" I produced Count Cato's writ of unfettered passage and handed it to Icarus. I could have handed it to Desdemona, but she was currently rubbing me the wrong way.

Icarus eyed the seal and read the parchment, surprise blossoming on his face. After a moment, he said, "It might." Desdemona, irritated that no one was telling her what was written on the parchment, leaped to her feet, let the chair crash to the floor, and stomped across the room, taking the writ.

She read it, confused, and looked at me. "Where did you get this? Are you are working for Count Cato?" she said accusingly. By her tone, I surmised Count Cato had a poor reputation with the Adventurers Guild.

I decided to reveal more than I should, but I needed to get out of the city and pick up Maveith soon. "No. I took it off the dead bodies of his men who were exploring the Ruins of Caelora. They apparently ran afoul of a wyvern." Icarus and Desdemona made eye contact, and unspoken words passed between them.

Icarus addressed me cautiously. "What were they doing in Caelora? Last time you utilized our hall, you alluded to the rumors that a dungeon was found in Caelora. Are they true?"

At this point, I didn't see any harm in telling them the truth. "Yes, there is a dungeon inside the city of specters. Almost impossible to reach safely, as the specters respawn."

"Respawn?" Icarus echoed. He pursed his lips. He nodded, deciphering the odd word. "I see, and the Emperor was aware of this dungeon. That is a violation of the Guild's agreement with the Empire," he said tersely.

The air suddenly felt heavy, and I felt out of place. In a tight tone, Desdemona offered to Icarus, "If I move now, I might be able to use this to get out of the harbor. I can carry a message for you, father."

"That is best. Most likely, if we use any of the message senders, word would get out that we know for certain," Icarus said in agreement.

It seemed whatever I did, I always seemed to stir shit up. "What are the implications of the Shimmering Labyrinth Dungeon being revealed?"

Icarus considered me before explaining. "Our Telhian charter grants us administration of all dungeons within the Empire. The First Citizens have a right to purchase retrieved artifacts that our members intend to sell. By keeping a new dungeon secret, we are entitled to a lessening of certain restrictions upon our Guild operations. Unfortunately, I am not in a strong position to negotiate." He patted his small beer belly with a smirk. "Desdemona will get word to our assembly, and they will send someone with a stronger hand." I could tell he was hinting at someone more powerful. "Do you object?" he asked directly.

"No, my bridges are already burned with the Empire," I replied candidly. This got an approving look from Desdemona. I had already decided to abandon the Empire, so this did not affect me. It looked like it would only negatively affect the new Emperor and First Citizens, which was fine with me. "Are we leaving now?" I asked Desdemona with a crooked smile.

She rolled her eyes and barked an order at me. "Yes, grab your things, legionnaire. We will head to the *Shorebreaker* immediately."

"I am ready to go now." I held my smile. I was wearing my new adventurer's armor, and the magebane blade hung on my hip. Although the hilt was intricate, I figured all the other blades I owned could be recognized.

Desdemona huffed and rushed into her room, returning with a leather pack that I assumed was her go bag. She was about to shoulder it but instead tossed it hard at me to carry, not hiding her teasing smirk. "Follow me, legionnaire."

"You know if you keep calling me legionnaire, someone might believe you and detain me," I voiced humorously.

Desdemona stopped and spun, walking to get face-to-face. In a challenging tone, she snapped at me, "Do you think I am an idiot?"

Say no, Eryk, say no. "Well, I don't know you well enough to make that judgment."

Icarus coughed, amused. Desdemona's bronzed face started to darken as she flushed in a torrent of emotions. She had to look up as she was more than a head shorter than me. Her eyes were ablaze as she scowled up at me. Her finger stabbed into my armor repeatedly as she talked. "The only stupid one here is you." She then spun and stormed out.

I whispered so only Icarus could hear. "That was not a very good comeback."

Icarus laughed again. "Don't let her get too far ahead, Eryk. She has a tough exterior, but I think she actually likes you." He winked and indicated I should go with a gesture. Did he just give me permission to seduce his daughter, or tell me that his daughter was seducing me? I adjusted the straps on her pack before shouldering it as I moved to catch up to her.

She had slowed, and I was soon walking next to her. She walked confidently and didn't speak as we wove through the city streets toward the docks. It looked like every city guard had emptied into the streets to keep order. In the distance, I could see a line of blue-gray smoke rising from the palace. I wondered if that was the Archives burning. Maybe the blood sample was being burned at this very moment. I rechecked the compass in my pocket, reassuring myself that Castile was alive. If she was dead, I probably would not head to Gramney. My course was set for the moment anyway.

As we stepped onto the timeworn, salt-crusted stone piers, dozens of large ships were actively trying to make ready to sail, but soldiers, legionnaires, magistrates, and city guards were barking warnings to stand down. It was complete chaos. Desdemona stormed up the gangplank of her modest ship. "Isaak, prepare to sail!" she barked at a sailor. He nodded and started yelling orders, spurring a flurry of sailors to action.

A desperate man in white magistrate robes barked at Desdemona from the pier, "Captain! All ships are being held for three days. Please …"

Desdemona spun and marched heavily down the ramp to the magistrate. His two city guardsmen reached for their weapons. "Magistrate Jochen, Count Cassius Cato has chartered my ship for an urgent mission. We are to get to his estate and secure it."

The magistrate took the writ she slapped in his hand and read it. His mind seemed to be working. "How are you going to get to Count Cato's estate by ship?" he asked skeptically after reading the writ and confirming the Count's crest.

Desdemona caught herself but snatched back the writ. "We are getting more men to guard his Citadel. Most of his men were sent to the war front." She obviously had no idea which city housed Cato's Citadel, and neither did I.

The magistrate seemed to weigh his options. "If you can wait four hours, we can have a message sent to the Count to confirm."

"You have thirty minutes!" she said confidently. She turned her back on the magistrate and jogged back up the ramp. I cocked my eyebrow as she passed, and her eyes gave me a fiery warning not to question her intelligence after the poorly thought out ploy. I heard her whisper to Isaak, who I assumed was her first mate, "Cast lines in ten minutes."

I moved to the center of the deck as men raced about in a dance, preparing the rigging. Magistrate Jochen was left stunned. He looked young to be a magistrate, maybe in his early twenties. After getting over his shock, he sent one of his guards off at a run.

Desdemona joined Isaak in giving orders, and as she passed me, she said, "I hope Cato is not in the city and easily found, or this could be a very short trip."

I kept having to move out of the way and eventually found an unobtrusive spot all the way in the stern. The ship was not large, maybe sixty feet bow to stern and twenty feet in width. I watched the stone docks as the magistrate fumbled with what to do. It was clear we were not waiting on him. He raced to talk with other magistrates, but everyone was occupied arguing with other captains in the chaos. When we cast lines, we were not the first; others were trying to get past the breakers into the mouth of the river to join the current.

Tall towers guarded the harbor with massive ballistae on top. All were manned, but none of them fired as the small parade of daring ships left the harbor. Desdemona came to me, breathless, sweat glistening on her brow from having worked with her crew to make sail as quickly as possible. "If we had waited till night, they probably would have stationed men on the decks of every ship. You got lucky; I don't take no for an answer," she said with a flirtatious smirk.

I could see why Desdemona was a captain. There was something attractive about a woman with a commanding aura and confidence in her element. She didn't stay near me as she walked the deck and navigated around the other ships fleeing the capital. It was still over a mile in brackish water to reach the sea.

Desdemona tossed her jacket away, revealing her muscular, tan frame under a thin blouse and leather vest. She moved with a practiced grace across the deck, giving sharp orders. When she passed close to me, I asked, "Can I help?"

She took a moment to look me up and down doubtfully. "You should remove your armor. If you fall overboard, you will likely drown trying to swim in that. Have you ever sailed before?"

"No. This is actually my first time on a sailing ship," I replied. "But I am willing to learn."

"First time? I will be sure to break you slowly. Wait till we hit the open water and see if you still want to help then." She grinned mischievously at me as she prepared the Shorebreaker to raise full sail.

As soon as the river pulled the ship into the sea, it began to rock with the waves. Desdemona kept eyeing me, but I never stumbled once. My stomach did churn a bit, but I bit down and contracted my abs to counter the seasickness. Every time she looked at me, I just smiled back.

The ship was being tossed roughly, and I think the course's purpose was to try and get me nauseous. Desdemona finally gave up and gave a string of commands. "Hoist the sails! Pickle, to the nest! Lasho, calm the waters! Vodoma, funnel the wind to the sails!"

A choreographed action took place, and the sails dropped and snapped to attention in the wind. A man scrambled up to the crow's nest. Two sailors, who I hadn't realized were mages, started weaving spell forms. The water immediately around the ship calmed, and the mast strained under a stronger wind as the *Shorebreaker* started cutting through the water much faster, leaving behind the other ships escaping the capital.

With the deck steady and the ship under speed, I complimented Desdemona. "A fine ship and crew."

She brushed it off, but I think she blushed. It was hard to see under her tanned skin. "They are. Where are we picking up the others?"

"Stay close to the coast. He has a spyglass, and when he sees the Adventurers Guild flag on your ship, he will reveal himself on shore," I explained.

She shrugged. "My cabin is the first door through there," she said, pointing.

"Is that where I am staying?" I asked innocently.

"No, put my pack in there," she ordered. Even though her voice was harsh, I could see the twinkle in her eye.

I entered the foredeck and found her captain's cabin. It had the sickly-sweet scent of perfume and just one large hammock. I tossed the pack on the large, polished table with two fixed benches, which provided comfortable seating for four. It was spartan except for the closets, which I couldn't resist and peeked into. They were packed with clothes, and it was from there that the sickly-sweet smell was coming.

Returning to the deck, I had someone show me my cabin. My tiny cabin was simple: a hammock, a desk, and a single chest. I sat at the desk on a chair fixed to the floor. I cleaned the compass, sterilized it, and added Maveith's sample. I took a deep breath and activated it. We had only been separated for two days, but the wilds were dangerous. A steady pull eased my mind, and I returned to the deck.

I leaned on the rail and watched the shore for Maveith. I tried to count the crew as a distraction, and there were either nineteen or twenty above deck, not including Desdemona. There were more belowdecks because I could smell dinner being prepared and hear frequent, varied shouts from below. We sailed for nearly seven hours, and I was getting worried the sun might set and make it hard to spot Maveith as the compass pull grew stronger.

Fortunately, before dusk, Pickle called down from the crow's nest, "Big bloke on shore with a horse!"

Desdemona looked at me, and I nodded. "Thought you said there were five passengers besides yourself?"

Everything had been so rushed that I hadn't had time to prepare for my passengers to be removed. Now, I decided it was best to hold them until we reached Gramney. "Yeah." I pretended to look at the shore and thought I could make out Maveith. "It doesn't look like they will be joining us."

Desdemona shrugged. "No refunds."

The ship made anchor just fifty yards offshore, and the waves were being calmed by aetheric magic. Lasho went with us in the rowboat to calm the waters. Maveith had a huge grin on his face as I jumped off the bow of the small boat into the breakers, and we clasped each other's wrists. I asked, "Any trouble?" He shook his head no.

Getting Ginger into the boat only took a pair of apples to bribe her. I had been worried about getting her on deck, but didn't need to worry, as there was a ramp on winches that led to the ship's hold on the port side. The *Shorebreaker* frequently took on all different types of cargo, including livestock. The rear hold had a slight ammonia scent, coarse floorboards, and eight individual stalls.

I spent some time getting Ginger comfortable and settled, but she seemed familiar with water transport. Maveith had fed her already, and two young deckhands assured me they would take exceptional care of her. I handed them each a silver to make sure.

When I finally got back on deck, Desdemona already had the *Shorebreaker* under sail and was talking animatedly with Maveith, her bright white teeth in a constant smile. They seemed to be getting along, and I just hoped Maveith didn't say too much.

Seeing me, Maveith said, "Eryk, Captain Desdemona is an avid fan of checkers. She thinks she can best me three out of five games after dinner while we discuss my travels from Stone Mountain Island."

I had thought Desdemona was flirting with me, but maybe that was just her way of being friendly. Perhaps I had misread the situation entirely, as I was often prone to do with women. I was probably never going to see Renna again, but I had some hope we might reunite.

"I'm going to get some rest." I waved to my friend, wishing him the best of luck with Desdemona. As I turned, did she look disappointed? I returned to my cabin, secured the door, and took out the dreamscape amulet. Setting it loosely in my grasp, I entered the dreamscape.

Chapter 253: Captain on Deck

As I settled into the dreamscape, Konstantin rushed to me. "Ready to resume your training?" I wasn't sure if this was my subconscious missing the old man or him being his regular annoying self. A slight pain of loss lingered, as I didn't know if he still lived. How involved had he been in the plot? I wish I had taken a sample of his blood during Hound training; not knowing would nag at me and make me anxious at every shadow, expecting him to step out.

"Not tonight, Konstantin; I have to study some Elvish." I pointed at Scholar Favian.

Konstantin had a sour expression on his face. "What good do you think it will do to talk with your enemies if you can't defend yourself from their blades?" he spat on the ground and walked away.

Scholar Favian smiled. "Don't worry. He will cool down after a time. You need my instruction?" I rarely conversed with Favian in the dreamscape but he seemed eager to help.

Unfortunately, the extent of Scholar Favian's knowledge was limited to my own. The good news was that during my time with him, we spent hours reviewing the Elvish language and script. I had spent long sessions with the scholar working on my pronunciation and practicing with verb tenses in Caelora.

I exited the dreamscape every two hours to check on our ship, but only pitch-black night and the rush of water greeted me when I looked through the small porthole. From the height of the porthole, I thought it was made to piss out of. At least, that was what I used it for.

While working on Elvish pronunciation, I walked the deck during the day. The *Shorebreaker* was rolling a bit with the waves, and I assumed the mage had exhausted his aether. Only a handful of crew dressed in thin, loose garments were on the deck, and they ignored me after giving me curt nods. I spent an hour with Ginger, and she seemed to be doing well—well, after an apple she was doing well. I suspected this was not her first time on a ship, as legionnaires frequently used barges in the Empire.

When I returned above deck, Desdemona had taken the helm. She didn't even acknowledge me, so I stripped down to work bare-chested on my sword forms with the black blade. My blade whistled through the air as I chained multiple movements together.

I was preening a bit and pushing myself to work up a good sweat in the cool morning sea air. There were two middle-aged female members of the crew who appreciated the show—and more than a few of the male sailors as well. I caught Desdemona sneak her own glances and then pull the mage who calmed the waters to her to talk.

Shortly after their conversation, the ship seemed to be surging and falling with the waves. It was a childish attempt to disrupt my practice, but I was more concerned for Ginger. I checked on her before continuing and used the unstable deck to train.

The ship riding the swells had roused Maveith as well. "Late night?" I asked my friend.

"Very," he huffed, licking his lips. "Desdemona pushed me hard and taught me some things." Maveith started to strip as well to join me in my practice before continuing. "She won five of our thirteen games and then taught me how to play backgammon." It took a little explanation before I understood the unfamiliar word they used for backgammon.

Maveith started to stretch, and I was happy to see the *Shorebreaker* had returned to cutting evenly through the water instead of riding the waves. "Do you want to practice, Maveith?" I asked, thinking we could give the crew a good show.

Maveith sucked his teeth, thinking. "No air discs?" he questioned softly. It never took me long to win when I used them.

"Agreed," I said immediately, and began wrapping my blade. Maveith went to retrieve his hammer, and soon, we were sparring on the deck. Maveith was faster than I remembered, but it didn't matter, as my own speed gains had far surpassed his increases. With my small buckler, I could deflect his hammer before it built up speed and get inside his guard. I was even ready for his off-hand punches and low kicks.

We got lost in the physical exercise, and soon, both of us were coated in sweat. My mop of black hair was plastered to my scalp while Maveith's profuse sweat rained down on the deck with each impact. We both understood this was practice and exercise more than a test of our skills. Still, I used a few openings to slap Maveith's ass with the flat of my blade. I was trying to impress Desdemona and caught her watching more than once, but maybe she had eyes for Maveith.

When I deflected a heavy swing of the runic hammer into the deck, the boards cracked before the hammer rebounded. Desdemona barked angrily, "Don't destroy my ship, legionnaire!"

Maveith immediately defended me. "It was my hammer that did the damage, Dee." He was breathing heavily and bowed slightly toward the fast-approaching captain. "I will compensate you for any damage."

"The legionnaire was the one who forced your hammer into the deck with a clumsy parry," she said hotly as she finally reached us. "All brute strength and no finesse!"

"Do you think you are a better match for me?" I said with a wide grin. The truth was that I had switched my style to forceful and direct combat with Maveith. I was looking for exercise and trying to match the goliath's strength. I was a much better swordsman than I appeared to the crew and Desdemona should have realized that if she had paid attention when I practiced my sword forms.

"You are probably too exhausted from your practice with Maveith, legionnaire," she remarked, stepping back to assess me. The thing was, I might have been sweating profusely but I was not winded, nor did I feel tired.

"Eryk actually has amazing endurance and can go forever. I don't think I have ever met his match," Maveith noted as his breathing started to settle. Desdemona cocked her eyebrow.

"Thanks, Maveith, but I can speak for myself. I would gladly give you a lesson if you want some exercise and to sharpen your skills." My tone was playful, and her eyes understood the implication. The crew around us had paused to watch our interaction, clearly hoping to see their captain in action. I think she was weighing her chances.

She finally said, "First to three strikes wins?"

"Agreed. Maveith can officiate." Maveith vehemently shook his head no. "Fine. Your first mate Isaak, then?" Isaak turned over the helm to another and eagerly joined the entertainment on the main deck.

Desdemona drew her long, thin blade—a rapier with a smaller guard than normal. With her off hand, she drew a stiletto. She hadn't struck me as a two-weapon fighter, but her eyes brimmed with confidence. She started to limber up and asked, "Spell forms?"

I smirked. "I am not telling you what my spell forms are."

"No, you dolt. Are they allowed in our contest?" I could see her crew starting to make wagers on the outcome, eager for some good amusement.

"It wouldn't be a fair contest then. You wouldn't stand a chance," I replied confidently. "Are you going to wrap your weapons?"

"Spell forms are allowed then." She beamed widely. "Don't worry if I stab you a little; Vodoma can heal you." Instead of playing into her overconfidence, I smiled, pulled the tacky wrapping off my black blade, and made Corvus's runic dagger appear in my off hand. I was sure Tarvon had already told Desdemona about my dimensional space, but judging by her surprised look, maybe not.

She stepped back, reassessing my two blades and me. "That is a different blade than the one you carried on deck in Telha." Her eyes were focused on the runic, dungeon-forged dagger. I probably should have had it identified before using it in combat. It had no remarkable effect during my fight with Corvus, but then again, I didn't give him much of a chance.

"Maveith was carrying it for me," I replied unflinchingly. His pack had certainly been large enough to conceal the blade. She narrowed her eyes but didn't contradict me. I was interested to see what her spell forms were. It would be excellent practice for me to react to an unknown factor.

Desdemona didn't wait for an announcement to start and instead rushed me. I had trouble following her movement as she seemed to blur, and I guessed it was her spell form. As she closed in, I focused and reacted to her movements, but she seemed to have four arms instead of two. Maybe it was an illusion, but it did not matter. I managed to block all four attacks and separate. Steel clanged twice in the air as she moved past me.

She turned to face me quickly, clearly angry that her attack had not connected. Her chest was heaving from the effort, and I almost told her she needed to work on her conditioning, but I bit my tongue. Her crew was also visibly shocked that their captain had missed all her strikes. Maveith was the only one clapping at the performance, impressed by what he had just seen. The seeds of doubt had been planted in her mind. "Interesting spell form. What was it?" I asked, grinning. "Perhaps you have something else you want to try?"

I relaxed my stance a little as I studied her. I guessed that she was slightly older than me and had grown up in the Adventurers Guild, so she had to have a lot of experience. "Illusionary feint," she finally said. "It projects multiple attacks, and I can watch my opponent and then choose which one to utilize."

"Impressive," Maveith said aloud.

"If I had not blocked all four, you would have adjusted to the two successful attacks?" She nodded slowly. "I agree with Maveith. Impressive. What else can you do? Or if that is all you have, you keep using it."

I caught Isaak and Vodoma smirking out of the corner of my eye. Desdemona's chest heaved with adrenaline and she didn't respond. Her jaw tightened and she rushed me again. This time, I was forced back after blocking four attacks twice in a row as she chained her ability in an attempt to catch me off guard. It was taxing even for my quickness, and I retreated four steps as I dealt with all her attacks.

It was curious how heavily she was breathing after the attack, and I pieced it together. She was, in fact, making all four attacks somehow. Or at least, she was using the energy to make all four attacks. The small woman didn't look happy. I hadn't even used a single spell form.

Before consuming all the quickness essences, I probably wouldn't have been able to keep up with her. And if she were a little faster, things could be playing out very differently.

After she caught her breath, she made another attempt and then another. This was actually excellent training for me, and I was going to let her continue, but she scored a cut on my thigh on the third sequence. She had extended her illusion on larger vectors, and I couldn't get the runic dagger to block the fourth attack in one sequence.

A sweaty mess, she grinned like a Cheshire cat. Isaak, realizing his captain had scored, announced it: "Dee one, Eryk zero." At least he was using my name and not calling me legionnaire.

Having some pride, I didn't plan to lose. The next rush found Desdemona tripping over the invisible air shield and her ass receiving the flat of my black blade like Maveith had earlier. She gave me a satisfying yip at the strike and quickly rolled away. She was on her feet in a blink, trying to puzzle out what the hell just happened. Exasperated, I turned to Isaak and raised my hands questioningly. He finally announced, "Dee one, Eryk one." I nodded my thanks.

Desdemona looked to Maveith for help, as she hadn't been able to figure out what I had done. Maveith started to speak. "It was a—" but my harsh look silenced him.

The captain was clearly tired from using her spell form. It wasn't aether exhaustion but physical exhaustion. In the next exchange, I didn't even have to use an air shield to leave a cut on her bicep with the runic dagger. Isaak reluctantly announced, "Dee one, Eryk two." I could tell who among the crew had bet on me by their happy faces, but most looked downcast, about to lose their coin.

"You are no longer bleeding," Desdemona noted. She was clearly stalling for time to recover.

I looked down at my bloody leggings. "Yeah, it looks like it. You did ruin these pants. If I win, will you sew them for me?" The look in her eyes told me she knew she was overmatched. My brutish, direct attacks against Maveith were gone, and I was now agile and defensive. If I were fighting myself, I would have my doubts as well.

My third point was an elbow to Desdemona's head. I had actually been trying to grapple with her, but she was like a slippery eel in close quarters. It was either an elbow to her head or her stiletto in my kidney. Note to self: do not try to subdue a woman to impress her when she can stab you with a twelve-inch blade.

Isaak called me the victor and Maveith clapped loudly. The crew exchanged coins and slowly returned to work.

"Maveith, lunch and a game of backgammon?" Desdemona asked the goliath, clearly exhausted. Her sweaty clothes clung to her short frame. By the look in her eyes, I could tell she was going to press my friend for all my secrets in the hope of coming out on top next time. As Maveith happily followed Desdemona to her cabin, I thought to myself that she didn't have to try this hard to be on top.

Chapter 254: You Can't Keep an Old Hound Down

Konstantin sat cleaning his weapons deep in the rocky crevice where they had set their lookout. It was unnecessary, but it gave him something to do while he waited and mourned. He was still reeling from when Cornelius had revealed Eryk's death to him. The blood compass had no pull on Cornelius's sample.

The foolish boy had gotten himself killed, and it hurt more than it should have. He had mentored dozens of young men who had died, so why did this feel different—more painful? He compartmentalized his feelings and focused on his responsibilities.

He had been pulled from Castile's company to assist the greatly undermanned Hounds. The Emperor planned to portal behind the Bartiradian Army and launch an attack from the rear. He had been among the first men through the portal and was paired with Western Hound, one of Centurion Sergius's immediate subordinates, Gracilis. This assignment suited him. If Antonia's plan was enacted, he would prefer to be as far away from the Emperor as possible when betrayal occurred.

Looking over at Gracilis, he shook his head. He hadn't wanted to be paired with anyone but had no choice. At least Gracilis was competent. After exiting the portal, they moved undetected four miles southwest into the hills overlooking the Bartiradian army. Now, they watched the edge of the enemy camp from a mile away, ready to report any change. Gracilis was currently watching with the spyglass they shared.

"Any change?" Konstantin asked in a bored tone.

"Just two mages sneaking off into the woods for a quick romp. The woman isn't too bad-looking if you want to watch." Gracilis turned and offered the spyglass to Konstantin.

"How far outside of camp? Could we catch them unawares?" Konstantin asked, sheathing his blade. It had been months since he had slain an undead with his weapon, and its hunger gnawed on him after its gluttonous time in Caelora.

"No, there are sentries. Two, in fact, and they are enjoying the show from a large beech tree," Gracilis said with a chuckle. "Shouldn't be long now; dawn is coming."

Konstantin grunted and stood. Hopefully, the army would all be through the portal by now. He wondered if Zyna would make her attempt on the Emperor's life during the battle. He might depart the field and return to the safety of his palace if this battle was won. Konstantin moved to lie with Gracilis on the ground. In front of him was the message book, and Konstantin read the last few messages.

Centurion Sergius relied too heavily on these artifacts. The last two pages had dozens of shorthand notes. Most appeared to be the positioning of various Hounds and the progress of the Emperor's army. He had to admit that knowing events in essentially real time was useful. He was about to ask for a translation of the shorthand when Gracilis hissed, "The alarm just sounded." As if to echo his statement, short horn bursts echoed in the hills. Griffins took flight, one at a time, and raced in the direction of the Telhian portal.

"This is going to get messy," Konstantin rasped, worried about his companions. He might work for Antonia, but his loyalty was to Castile as much as it could be. She was as close to a genuine leader as you could get among the mage ranks and more dependable than any First Citizen he had known.

The pair remained prone on their bellies as they watched the army stir over the next hours and begin to march. It was an impressive sight and very orderly for the amalgamation of different troops. Konstantin quickly needed clarification on what he was seeing. "Why are they committing all their forces to engage the Emperor?"

Gracilis checked his book before answering. "Tiberius has not marched yet. They probably think the army appearing behind them is Tiberius's and Octavian's forces."

"Why are Octavian's provincial forces with Tiberius?" Konstantin asked, confused. He was sensing something in the air. A danger, and not that of the Bartiradian army about to be crushed between the Emperor's and Tiberius's armies.

Gracilis's slow response was suspicious. "Don't know. I am just reading what my Centurion is writing."

Konstantin was already on guard as Gracilis rolled into him and attempted to stab him. Konstantin's viselike grip held the Hound's wrist at bay, but he was not prepared for the short skinning knife that stabbed a half dozen times into his abdomen before he could distance himself and get on his feet deeper in the crevice. The wounds were not mortal, but a familiar paralysis started to spread from Konstantin's gut. Gracilis didn't give Konstantin a chance to draw his blade and tackled him.

Gracilis just needed to restrain him long enough for the poison to paralyze Konstantin. "Just let it go, old man," Gracilis hissed. "Events are in motion, and you are not going to be part of them. Don't make your trip to Pluto's realm more painful than it needs to be."

"You are fucking dead," Konstantin said with spittle spraying from his mouth as he pushed the pain aside. Gracilis was not aware that Konstantin had dosed himself with the paralytic for years. He wasn't immune but could remain somewhat functional. He slowly felt Gracilis overpowering him. He pushed all his aether into flinging a stone into Gracilis's wide-open eye.

The impact surprised Gracilis, damaging his eye, and he briefly relaxed his hold on Konstantin. Konstantin took full advantage, pulling Gracilis toward him and biting hard on his nose; his teeth sank deep and metallic blood filled his mouth as he yanked his head back and forth. The crunching cartilage gave way, and Konstantin spat the bloody nose into Gracilis's good eye.

Gracilis kicked away and drew his sword in one motion. His ruined nose gushed blood and it sprayed on his strong exhales. Konstantin was quicker, and his runic blade drove up into his opponent's sternum. Unfortunately, Konstantin was still vulnerable even though his enemy was as good as dead. Gracilis's blade bit deep into Konstantin's arm, cutting through the armor to the bone. The bone was probably broken as well.

The violent exchange only lasted ten heartbeats, but it took its toll on both men. Konstantin grunted, ignoring the pain as life flowed out of the Hound down his blade. The blood rushed down the blade's length and soaked his hand. The weight of Gracilis slowly became too much, and Konstantin collapsed to his right.

Konstantin tried to suck oxygen, but the paralytic only allowed for short, forced breaths. He worked his only lesser healing potion to his lips, cursing Gracilis and Centurion Sergius. He calmed as best he could and fumbled to wrap his arm so he would not bleed out, as the potion would not be enough for his extensive injuries.

He had lost a lot of blood and could barely move under the effects of the poison. Konstantin painfully dug out his canteen and searched Gracilis for a lesser healing potion. He forced the water down, angry that Gracilis only had a pair of lesser stamina potions in his belt and nothing in his small pack. The paralytic was making movement too difficult, so he crawled deep into the crevice. Morning had arrived, and the army in the distance was marching. All he could do was watch. Soon, his fatigue and blood loss caused him to fade into unwanted sleep.

When he woke, it was midday and the army was gone. He focused the spyglass and saw the camp was overrun with Telhian soldiers cutting down the camp followers. A few Bartiradians were being raped, and the screams drifted to him even a mile away.

Konstantin sucked his canteen dry and then drank the one in Gracilis's pack. The effects of the paralytic had passed, but he was still groggy. He turned to studying the message book. Dozens of messages had been written since Gracilis had tried to kill him, but he couldn't puzzle out the shorthand cipher.

He started to pack what he could and staged the body to appear as though Gracilis had been surprised by the Bartiradians. It might not make a difference if there was a civil war among the Hounds. He sensed this was more than a power play by Centurion Sergius, though.

He couldn't use his left arm as the healing was incomplete and the bone was still broken. What treachery was happening? What had happened in the hours he had been passed out? Where should he go? He had ten days of food. He painfully shouldered his Hound pack with one arm and moved toward the battle.

Three hours later, Konstantin was on a bluff overlooking hundreds of dead as carrion raptors feasted. If he had been in charge, this was where he would have observed the battle. He was kneeling over the headless body of Cornelius. "You taught us always to be prepared for anyone to betray us, Cornelius. Looks like you got too old and forgot your own advice." The body had been stripped, but Konstantin searched him anyway.

The tracks in the earth told him two Hounds had killed Cornelius and taken his head. Dragon shit. It meant he would be subjected to a necromancer, and all the conspirators would be revealed. It looked like Centurion Sergius had figured out the conspiracy and sided with the Emperor. Most likely, Antonia was dead, but should he try to confirm? He had no love for the scheming woman. Antonia was likely in the capital, but getting there was going to be a chore with a broken arm.

He sighed, realizing that Castile and Zyna must also be dead by now. He tried to convince himself that he would be dead too if he had stayed with Castile, but that didn't ease his guilt. He shambled down to the battlefield and slowly exchanged his Hound gear for legionnaire gear. At least with this he could get his arm healed without drawing the attention of the traitorous Hounds.

He found an exhausted healing mage further into the bloody field. "I am close to burnt, legionnaire." The man held up his hands in capitulation.

"Can you get the bone set and healed at least?" Konstantin winced as he moved his arm in the sling. The man sighed but gave a short nod, and he sweated through the healing. The pain eroded away and Konstantin flexed his arm.

"Most of the muscle is repaired as well," the mage rasped, collapsing to the ground. Konstantin didn't even thank him as he moved in the direction the battle had gone. He found an Imperial legionnaire waiting for healing on a rock. His left arm was missing from the elbow down. It would take a tremendous amount of aether to regenerate the limb.

Konstantin sat heavily next to him. "What news of the victory and the Emperor?"

The man coughed a laugh and spat blood. His injuries extended beyond the arm, apparently. "Victory, yes. The Emperor took all the cavalry he could muster to run down the remnants of the Bartiradian forces."

Konstantin nodded but didn't know how to ask if the Emperor had been betrayed or if it was common knowledge that the East and West Hounds were warring behind the scenes. Instead, he handed the Imperial legionnaire a canteen he had looted. The man took it as they watched a few soldiers run around the field to find the living and keep them so. When the legionnaire passed out, Konstantin made him comfortable, as he was likely to die without healing.

Konstantin eventually joined the search for the living as he looked for men he knew. He recognized a few faces among the dead but only recalled a handful of names. When he found Kolm's body, he knelt, closed the man's eyes, and said a short blessing on the body. He couldn't find any other members of the company among the dead, but it was a massive battlefield that had shifted during the fight.

A rider wearing Octavian's colors came racing on horseback through the field. He repeated the same message over and over: "The Bartiradians have killed the Emperor; Duke Octavian has avenged him!"

The few men around were stunned by the news. Konstantin didn't buy it for one second. The Emperor had too many powerful mages and Imperial legionnaires guarding his person. He started to move in the direction the rider had come from, but slipped into the woodlands for cover. It took time to reach the site of the second battle. He observed from a safe distance.

It was clearly a mage battle. The scent of ozone was strong and many trees were still burning. Octavian's men were stripping the bodies of Imperial legionnaires and mages. One Imperial legionnaire started to stand, and two of Octavian's men cut him down. Then he saw Hercule and Sergius walking among the dead and cataloging them. Sergius had betrayed both Antonia and the Emperor. Konstantin ground his teeth, but he was in no position for revenge. He faded back into the woods, the fate of his company unknown.

He waited until night, when the men cleared the field. Then he walked among the dead. With the Hound goggles, it was not difficult to find High Mage Zyna's red hair and stripped body. A hole was burned through her eye socket. She had moved on the Emperor, and maybe she was the one who had succeeded in killing him.

He needed to satisfy his curiosity as he searched the bodies. When he found Adrian, he felt the pain of loss. Adrian was like an estranged brother to Konstantin. There was no time to bury him. He couldn't find Castile or a number of others in the company. Had they gotten away? Or did Octavian have them in chains?

With no allies and few places to go, Konstantin made his way north toward the capital to get the answers he wanted and the revenge he needed.

Chapter 255: Dinner Discourse

I rested in my gently rocking hammock for the rest of the day with the porthole open. The rushing water drowned the crew's calls on deck as the *Shorebreaker* moved through the sea, getting further from the Telhian Empire. I only had a few books remaining in my dimensional space, but I took the opportunity to read them.

My primary reading material was an interesting Elvish book on medicinal herbs. It was one of the few books I had remaining from Caelora and it gave me the chance to work on my Elvish and study rarer flora and their uses. Even after fifteen hundred years, the text and pictures had not faded at all.

Toward evening, a loud knock came at my door, and I was fairly certain it was Maveith before I even opened it. Maveith's head almost touched the ceiling when I answered the door. He leaned inside my room and looked around. "Very small. My cabin is larger and my hammock is almost as big as Dee's."

"Have you tried out the captain's hammock?" I asked with a smirk.

"Not yet, but she offered. The one in my cabin fits me well enough, though." I lost my tongue momentarily, as I was not privy to the conversation where Desdemona offered her hammock to Maveith. My large friend seemed oblivious to flirtatious or suggestive comments by the opposite sex.

"Did she press you for information about me?" I asked my friend conspiratorially.

Maveith beamed brightly. "She tried to get me drunk and tell her your spell form. Don't worry. I have not revealed any of your secrets." He bit his lip, reconsidering. He admitted, "Except that you are dead. Well, that the Telhian Empire thinks you are dead. She asked if anyone would come looking for you, and I let it slip."

I waved off the goliath's error. If that was all he revealed, then I would be fine with his slip of the tongue. "How are you doing, Maveith?" I asked as he squeezed into my small room.

"I am well. I just checked on dinner and came to inform you that you are welcome to join us in the captain's mess when the bell sounds." He squatted on a stool. "I decided I prefer checkers over backgammon."

He said it like it was a major revelation, so I had to ask, "And why is that?"

"There is too much chance involved with the dice." He leaned in and whispered conspiratorially, "And I think Dee cheats. No one can roll as many double sixes as she does every game." I released a chuckle. No doubt our Adventurers Guild captain was using loaded dice, or her spell form that gave her two chances with every roll.

"What's for dinner?" I asked, considering the offer. It was not like Maveith and I needed to eat, but I would go for the social aspect.

"Marinated lamb, roasted vegetables, fresh bread, and a few other scents I could not identify," Maveith said, licking his lips, clearly salivating. I found that with my own ring, I was rarely hungry or salivating.

"You didn't reset your ring, did you?" I narrowed my eyes accusatorially.

Maveith looked away, not making eye contact. "I might have accidentally taken it off for a moment," he admitted.

I just shook my head in disappointment. "I will join you two for dinner." I was tempted to remove my own ring, but the secondary benefit of only needing two hours of deep sleep was too valuable to lose.

"Excellent!" Maveith beamed. "Dee was hoping you would. I will go inform her of your impending company."

Maveith escaped my cabin, probably thinking I would scold him for resetting his ring of sustenance if he remained. An hour later, the ship's evening bell rang for dinner. I found the small captain's dining room on the port side. It was not luxurious. A long, worn table with seating for ten dominated the room.

Only Maveith and Desdemona were seated, and there were three place settings. It appeared this was a family-style meal, with six large bowls in the center of the table. Three were steaming with rice, cubed grilled lamb, and vegetables. The other three bowls had bread, fruit, and olive paste.

My attention was drawn to a smiling Desdemona after surveying the food. She had braided her hair, washed her face, and wore a dark-blue, V-necked tunic that hugged her torso and accentuated her bust. She had a silver chain that perfectly overlapped her tan lines. She was seated at the head of the table with Maveith to her right. The third place setting was to her left, and I considered sitting opposite her at the other end of the table before taking the seat prepared for me.

Desdemona's perfume overpowered the delicious scent of the food. As soon as I sat down, Maveith started to help himself. I waited patiently and asked Desdemona, "How is our speed? Are there any dangers?"

She spooned some rice and vegetables onto her plate and mixed them with her fork before responding. "Six days to Sanco. We are flying the Adventurers Guild flag. No one on the seas should challenge us. Krakens rarely attack ships, as there is enough for them to feast on below the waves. There are no known merfolk settlements on our route either. My weather mages are excellent, and we will not have to fear storms or rough waters." I nodded, suitably impressed.

"What of the Telhian Navy?" I asked, taking some warm bread and spreading the olive paste on it.

She said thoughtfully, "Telhian Navy? I think the elves sank two of their six known warships. The other four are probably hiding in a harbor somewhere. Other than that, they have a few dozen shore runners, nothing that will venture as far offshore as we are."

She speared and chewed on a piece of lamb while maintaining eye contact with me. "The Telhians have not had a strong navy in over two hundred years. The Emperor decided it was too costly to maintain warships. From my understanding, back then there were krakens, sea serpents, and even a leviathan terrorizing the local seas. The Emperor invested heavily in his portal network instead."

Maveith was already filling his plate for a second helping. "Portals are rare elsewhere in the world. I didn't even know they existed before I came to the Telhian Empire. I assume being able to find enough mages with a high enough displacement affinity willing to do the daily spellcraft is difficult."

Desdemona pointed her fork in Maveith's direction and said, "You know, building those permanent portal stones really cost the Empire a lot of gold. I won't lie; it was a solid investment. It's actually one of the things that other kingdoms envy about the Telhian Empire." She let out a frustrated huff. "Maybe the only thing they admire. Plenty have tried to replicate their portal network, but they can never quite get it right."

My stomach lurched for a moment as the ship fell. Desdemona's attention turned sharply. She was ready to leave to check on it, but a moment later, Isaak's head popped in the door. "Just an unnaturally large swell. We came down the other side of it fast." Desdemona settled but seemed on edge while dinner continued.

I tried the lamb before asking about the Adventurers Guild. "When we get to Esenhem, I just check into the Guild Hall and Maveith can register as a member?"

Desdemona arched her brow and smirked. "Not that easy. There is an immigration and customs office in the port. They will search you, check you for diseases, and question you on your business. With your guild medallion, it shouldn't be too painful."

She tapped her chin in a teasing manner. "But probably, with the war, there may be Inquisitors to question you as well. If that is the case, I suggest you tell them the truth. Just tell them you are a legionnaire deserter."

I nodded but wasn't too concerned with my bone inscriptions. Maveith was working on his third plate and slowing down a bit. "What questions will the Inquisitors ask me?" he asked, concerned. "Will it be hard to join the Guild?"

"Goliaths are generally welcomed in all countries. I doubt their Inquisitors will question you." She patted his hand to alleviate his worry and eyed me, indicating I was not likely to be as lucky. "Not many goliath adventurers, though. You won't have any trouble registering. The fee varies between the different Guild Halls. It probably costs more in Esenhem than the Empire, but I can write you a recommendation and have the fee waived." She smiled at him. I couldn't decide if she was trying to make me jealous or if she was really interested in Maveith.

I decided to act indifferent to her teasing. I assumed she had dressed up for me, but you know what they say about assumptions. I focused on getting as much information as I could. "Will we have trouble using the portals as adventurers?"

"Getting teleported from Sanco to Artiria will be difficult. The elves are cautious about who is traveling to their capital. Being ported from Artiria to Gramney, less so. You will be searched in Gramney upon arrival, but the Grand Duchy relies heavily on trade and doesn't like to upset travelers unless they are suspicious." She winked at me and smirked.

Desdemona finished her plate and reclined in her chair, stretching. She had excellent posture, her chest straining against the fabric. She was definitely eyeing me—enticing me, and not Maveith, but I was enjoying the game of ignoring her now.

Maveith, thinking ahead to entering orc lands, interrupted our little game. "What do adventurers do in orc lands?"

"Same as in any land. Clearing dungeons, guarding caravans, serving as bodyguards, hunting monsters, and investigating crimes. The orcs take dungeon delving very seriously. Dungeons unattended for too long release their monstrosities into the Endless Dark, and they eventually find their way to the surface. The Boutan Caliphate guards all the exits from the Endless Dark fiercely. There is probably no safer kingdom on this continent when it comes to roaming creatures."

I thought Maveith was smart to ask. Maybe we could get a head start on understanding the challenges of looking for his sister. "What about orcs themselves? The books I read were old and not very detailed."

Desdemona's face split into a grin. "You are going to the Boutan Caliphate and don't know about their culture?" My sour face made her raise her hands. "Fine. The Boutan orcs are divided into three classes: the clerics, the warlords, and the people. The clerics are orcs who can cast true magic. They rule the Caliphate, and their leader is called the Supreme, or Supreme Cleric. They govern all the politics and laws. The warlords train and lead all the warriors. A warlord might be the captain of a warship, a general overseeing a barracks in a city, or the head of a family of Pathfinders. Warlords are the only orcs who can own slaves in the Caliphate."

"The clerics cannot own slaves?" I asked, confused about the hierarchy. Usually, those with power did what they wanted.

Desdemona shrugged. "You would have to ask an orc why they can't. My guess is that it is some power balance. Only warlords can own land as well. The people are the citizens, farmers, craftsmen, merchants, and children. They can own buildings but not the land under it."

It sounded like a confusing caste system. "Is there a way to purchase a slave from a warlord?" Maveith asked eagerly. Desdemona seemed confused by his enthusiasm, and I guessed Maveith had not told her the true reason we were venturing into the Caliphate. She still thought I was fleeing the Telhian Empire and planning to hide among the orcs.

Desdemona took a moment to organize her thoughts. "I am not an expert on the Boutan orcs. I have dealt with orc pirates outside the Caliphate and orc mercenaries before, but in general, I have taken the philosophy that when I see a Boutan warship, if it doesn't bother me, I won't bother it. I know the warlords live by six tenets."

"Do you know what they are?" I asked when she didn't offer them.

"Ugh. You are asking about things I learned as a child. Loyalty to family is the first," she stated, quickly getting into a groove. "Might to rule over those beneath you. Honor the people you rule. Respect the land. Courage in the face of your enemy."

Maveith had leaned forward. "And the sixth?"

Desdemona thought hard, not wanting to disappoint. "Ugh, it translates into something like their version of righteousness. Basically, it means to be honest with yourself and your enemy and to have a purpose in your killing."

From my interactions with and observations of the Boutan orcs to date, this seemed to fit. The table was silent for a time before I spoke. "Thank you for the dinner and conversation."

Desdemona looked surprised that I was standing to leave. "Do you want some kava? Perhaps a game or two of backgammon." Kava was coffee from Tsinga, and that had me tempted to stay. I never got the coffee beans from the dungeon roasted to make my own.

I paused, acting as if I was considering before saying, "Not tonight." I winked at her. "Besides, Maveith says you cheat." Maveith was caught off guard and coughed so hard he choked. I made my exit after taking in Desdemona's incredulous expression. Yeah, it was totally worth it, and from her lack of denial, I guessed she did cheat.

I checked on Ginger before heading to my cabin. It wasn't long before I was in the dreamscape, working on my Elvish.

Chapter 256: Saw Hula Gin?

I thought my Elvish was getting better. I even ventured to have Raelia join Favian and myself as I practiced in the dreamscape. Raelia had another opinion of my proficiency, and gave it with her sharp tongue. "You are insulting a language that has been spoken the same for ten millennia. You are better off sticking to Telhian."

"I think he is much improved," Favian said, defending me.

I pointed at Favian, but Raelia just rolled her eyes, which was a habit I had taught her in the dungeon. The truth was that my Elvish was decent compared to before. Just like studying spell forms or practicing with my weapons, it was easier to take what I learned in the dreamscape to the real world.

Xavier and Konstantin were sparring on the far side of the scorpion chamber. They were tossing good-natured insults back and forth, which seemed to revolve around me and not their contest. It gave me the thought that practicing with the blade and learning Elvish didn't need to be mutually exclusive.

Thinking that I might have to practice against Desdemona again, I created her likeness and entered practice with her while Konstantin and Xavier paused to give me feedback.

I exited the dreamscape in the middle of the night. The water rushing along the hull outside my porthole was strangely soothing, along with the slow swinging of the hammock. I pulled out my last glowstone and the light-purple major essence I had gotten from Corvus. I turned the intellect essence in my hand, considering where it had come from, how it could improve me, and what it might be worth to someone else.

I held the glowstone behind it and watched the swirling colors play within, inspecting it from every angle I could. It was odd to imagine the power held in the small sphere. Maybe not this sphere, but the magic affinity spheres. Once we got to the safety of a city, maybe I would have the courage to unlock the water affinity. I had a pair of apex water essences in my dimensional space. I stopped debating, pushing aside my reluctance, and consumed the intellect essence.

A slight feeling of vertigo, and then my thoughts crystallized. My recent Elvish lessons played at high speed in my mind before the rush faded as rapidly as it had come on. My vertigo fled and a slight headache took its place.

I pulled a burrito from my space as the hunger pangs from consuming the essence gnawed at my stomach. As I nibbled on it, I questioned our course of action. Maybe the intellect essence was having an effect. The smart thing to do would be to pay an experienced adventuring group to extract Zorana for us. I would only need to sell one of the artifacts in my dimensional space to hire them.

No. Maveith wouldn't agree to anything other than going himself. Still, the odds seemed oppressive, as it was us against a nation of orcs. I was hoping Castile and the company were in Gramney. But then again, why would they join us? I hated thinking so much. I swung out of the hammock and went on deck. A stiff, cold breeze was keeping the sails taut without the aid of the mages. A handful of glowstone lanterns swung with the waves at vital locations.

A few of the sailors tiredly walked the deck. "Need help, Eryk?" Isaak asked, walking toward me.

"I don't need much sleep." A thought occurred to me. "Do any of the crew speak Elvish?"

"Aye, a few. I have a grasp of it, but Leoch grew up with Elvish parents. He is our boatswain." He switched to Elvish. "Looking to learn a few words so the elves don't string you up by your balls? Or maybe you hope to seduce an elf and take her maidenhood?"

I replied in Elvish, "They don't have string strong enough, and elf maidens are overrated."

Laughing, Isaak switched back to Telhian. "Not too bad. I could always use the practice, too. Leoch would expect a few large coppers for his time, but like I said, he grew up with the elves. His mastery of the tongue far surpasses mine. It is a good language to know as it is the only tongue spoken the same in every corner of Desia."

I spent the rest of the night talking with Isaak by the helm, adding dozens of words to my vocabulary and getting comfortable in conversational Elvish. When the sun rose, I was handed off to Leoch. The boatswain repaired the ship and kept it seaworthy. Most of his job was scraping the barnacles off the hull when they were in port. But today he was replacing a recently damaged deck plank so that no one would trip on it.

"You don't mind helping me with my Elvish?" I asked in Elvish as I served as his assistant with the task.

"Not at all. Keep your coin; Isaak was just trying to do me a favor." The middle-aged man smiled. "But I wouldn't be opposed to you helping with my duties while we practice."

"Not a problem," I replied in Elvish. We talked as we worked. He corrected me when needed and filled in the gaps in my knowledge. We started by repairing the damage to the deck that Maveith had caused and then moved on to inspect the rigging on the sails, grease the pulleys, check all the anchor pins, and wax them. We finished all his work shortly after midday.

My Elvish was a work in progress. The language had not changed in millennia, and I learned there was a formal form of the language reserved for court and royalty. It was unlikely that I would ever need the formal tongue of Elvish, but Leoch's adoptive parents were actually part of the elven court, so I got a crash course in formal Elvish.

While we worked, I had learned Leoch's life story as well, as we needed to keep the conversation going and I wasn't going to volunteer much beyond my time in the Legion. "I grew up in Esenhem. My parents adopted me from an orphanage. They were too old, even for elves, to have children, so they liked to visit other cities and adopt children. I don't know why they adopted a human, but I was a cute kid." He smirked. "I think it made them feel young to have children constantly around. They were good to us, and I have a dozen brothers and sisters across Esenhem. I will never want for a place to stay."

"Are humans accepted in Esenhem then?" I asked.

He nodded. "I wasn't bullied growing up, if that is what you are asking. Elves generally treat every race with respect if it is given in return." He chewed his tongue before continuing, "The only exceptions are half-elves. Human and elf coupling is uncommon, so resulting half-elves are rare and very few exist. I am ashamed to say it, but I joined in the harassment of two half-elves growing up. Stupid kids do stupid things." He huffed and went silent for a time after that.

To revive our conversation, I changed the topic. "Why are you on an Adventurers Guild ship?" I asked with genuine curiosity.

He explained with a grin, "Getting my shipwright license in Esenhem takes a fifty-year apprenticeship! By the time that happened, I would be retiring. Instead, I joined the Adventurers Guild and signed on as the boatswain to the *Shorebreaker*."

With our day's work finished, I handed Leoch an apple, which he happily munched on. "These are out of season, easily worth a silver in Esenhem and well worth my time." Since it was a fresh dungeon apple, it was probably worth more, but I didn't tell him. I had no want for coin, and Ginger might object to me selling my stock of apples. Ginger had settled in, and the deckhands were taking excellent care of her as promised.

"Any advice for traveling in Esenhem?" I waved Maveith over, planning to take a break, but I would be back tomorrow to practice again.

"The cities of Esenhem are ruled by a Regent. A council votes on the Regent to serve a twenty-year term of service, which is usually renewed. My mother was an advisor to the Regent, and my father cared for the Regent's estate. My advice is: don't piss off the Regents. Check the local laws in the Guild Hall." He reached out and we shook wrists.

"Can I help again tomorrow? I still need a lot of work on verb tenses."

Leoch nodded happily. "And proper names. You can insult someone if you address their station as too low in relation to yourself." He was making it sound more complex than it actually was. Every elf was at a higher station than me, so I hadn't been practicing addressing those of lower station. Maybe Leoch had a bad experience growing up.

I practiced on deck with Maveith in the afternoon. I found myself uninvited to the captain's dinner that evening. Apparently, calling the captain of the ship you were sailing on a cheater was frowned upon. I had thought she would find a way to tease me back, but instead, she was giving me the cold shoulder. I really needed to work on my flirting skills. At least Maveith was enjoying his time with Desdemona.

Four days into our voyage, I was helping Leoch repair the port railing while he helped me struggle through obscure Elvish vocabulary. A call rang down from the crow's nest. "Sighting, port aft!" The bell rang immediately after, and the ship became a flurry of activity.

I rushed to the stern to find Desdemona there with her spyglass out. "What is it?" I asked, thinking it was another ship.

She didn't answer me, and instead yelled to Isaak at the helm, "Come starboard half a turn!"

Maveith joined us at the stern and I asked for my spyglass back since Desdemona had not answered me. I smugly put my larger spyglass to my eye. After a few well-practiced adjustments, I could see the disturbance in the water. An array of dorsal fins cut the surface. "Cool, dolphins," I noted.

"Not dolphins, sharks," Desdemona retorted irritably.

Confused, I reacted defensively to my error. "I didn't know sharks swam together like that."

"They don't unless they are being controlled." She looked at me and then back and forth between her small spyglass and my larger one. She reached for my artificed spyglass and I released it. I knew Pickle up in the crow's nest had a lesser artificed spyglass, but it was weaker than my Hound one. Desdemona's current brass one was not artificed at all. She put my spyglass to her eye and cursed, "Circe's tits. They are changing to match our course."

"They are just sharks. They shouldn't be able to do anything to the *Shorebreaker*." I knew she had to be concerned for a reason, so I was hoping my statement would prompt an explanation.

Looking through my spyglass, she responded, "I said they were being controlled." A long hiss escaped her lips, and she yelled to her crew, "Sahuagin!" This caused another flurry of activity as the crew made to repel boarders.

"What is a saw-hula-gin?" I asked as Desdemona rushed away to prepare. We didn't cover many sea creatures in Hearne's lectures.

Thankfully, Leoch was close to me and informed us, "It is pronounced sah-hah-gwin. They are fishmen, more commonly called sea devils. They are controlling the sharks. They are swarming, either to relocate their queen or establish a new queen. If you know anything about ants or bees, it is the same thing."

The masts groaned as the mages increased the wind to maximize our speed at Desdemona's calm but loud order. I could hear a flurry of activity below the deck as well: the deckhands securing all the portholes. The crew was strapping on hardened leather armor pieces, and those with bows and crossbows sought a position to fire from. The crew was practiced in their preparation, but you could sense a very somber mood.

"They are merfolk?" I asked Leoch as I observed the bustling activity and began to retrieve my adventurer armor from my dimensional space to put it on. I had learned a great deal about the dangers on land in my new world. I even witnessed some young merfolk harvesting on the night shore while I was a sentry for a Hound, but my overall understanding of the threats in the oceans was limited.

Leoch coughed a laugh as he checked his knives on his person. "No. If you call a merfolk a sahuagin, the insult can only be repaid with your death. They are mortal enemies of the seas. At least merfolk can be reasoned with. Sahuagin will consume anything and everything in their path. They are the locust plague of the sea and have earned the name sea devils."

85

Desdemona returned to our position to check on the swarm. Using my spyglass, she noted in a detached tone, "They are closer. Maybe two hours before they overtake us." She handed back my spyglass, giving me a slight nod in thanks for its use.

"How deep in the shit are we?" I asked, after looking at the swarm for myself. All I could see were over a hundred shark dorsal fins, but it was too difficult to count accurately.

"The orc warships generally keep the sahuagin populations in check in the Endless Salt Sea. Their fight with the Telhians must have distracted them from their task," she said, looking at me and speaking in an accusatory tone—like it was somehow my fault. "The best we can hope for is that they tire of the pursuit and go look for slower prey. We were lucky we did not cross their path during the night. By the number of sharks, I am guessing over a hundred warriors."

I remained on the stern and watched with Desdemona, Maveith, and Isaak as the foamy water in the distance got closer and closer. When Desdemona was certain we were going to be overtaken, she barked an order at her two mages: "Conserve your aether for the fight."

It wasn't time to hide my aces, as it was clear our lives hung in the balance. I summoned a bow and quiver to my hand. Desdemona's eyebrows arched in surprise. "Any advice on how to fight them?" I asked.

She took a moment to reply, trying to grasp the size of the bow I held. Her eyes flitted to my rings, probably thinking one was a storage device. I wasn't wearing my gloves, as I had been working on my tan.

She responded seriously, "I have never fought more than a raiding party of thirty or so before. They give no quarter, so fight till you are dead. Don't let them drag you into the water. The warriors will try to get on deck, net you, and pull you overboard for the sharks to finish you."

I digested her words. That sounded awfully unpleasant.

A large shark appeared four hundred yards away with a strange fish-like humanoid riding on its back. It emitted a challenging sound, revealing sharp teeth beneath its unsettling lips. Its blue- and olive-skinned body was dominated by webbed appendages. As I prepared to take action, all I could think was, *They certainly are ugly.*

Chapter 257: I Never Really Liked Sushi

The churning water at the stern split as the school of sharks moved to encircle the *Shorebreaker*. The mages had stopped calming the water, and our ship now rose and fell as it crashed through the waves after our failed attempt to outrun the swarm. Maveith lamented having lost his bow as I released my first arrow. The large dorsal fin was fifty yards away, but I misjudged the ship's movement and overshot my target. By chance, the arrow thudded into the fin of another shark.

Desdemona hissed at me, "Don't waste your arrows on the sharks! Save them for the fishmen." I was about to say I couldn't see the fishmen when I noticed the light reflecting oddly on the swelling water. Just below the churning surface, the drab green humanoids swam en masse. Fuck, there were a lot of them, and more sharks were interspersed among them just below the surface.

A foolish sahuagin was almost breaking the surface near the ship, and I quickly put an arrow into it. It spun away quickly, disappearing into the dark depths of the sea. Both the arrows I had released had the Hound bleeding toxin on them, which should kill their targets in time. Maybe it was too much to hope that the sharks would go into a feeding frenzy as well due to the bleeding.

Other archers and crossbowmen started to release their arrows and bolts. Once they started boarding, the bows would be useless. My next two arrows failed to land. One went high, missing a shark, and the other missed because I misjudged how deep beneath the surface one of the sahuagin was.

Maveith's voice cut through my concentration. "Why haven't they attacked?"

"They are either planning to sink us or, more likely, waiting for all their warriors to get in position to rush us at once from all sides. They may be feral creatures, but they are not stupid," Desdemona said angrily as she watched the sea devils taunting us from below the waves. Desdemona walked the deck to encourage her crew while I continued to consume my supply of arrows.

When I was out of both my Hound and Pathfinder arrows, I produced the two lesser runic swords I had taken from First Citizen Boris's mercenaries, handing one to Isaak and the other to Leoch. They took the blades with surprised nods of thanks, but the grimness on their faces told me they doubted that we would live. Another sailor I didn't know barked a warning: "If they are not trying to sink us, they will attack the sails first."

His warning manifested moments later. The large sahuagin riding the shark behind us raised a trident coated in flames in the air and flung it at our sails. The trident flashed over one hundred yards in a blink. It tore through our primary sail, splashing unnatural fire across it. The magical fire quickly spread before slowing, leaving a sizable hole in the sail.

The sail rippled and whipped loudly, signaling the loss of speed. I soon felt it as the deck lurched beneath my feet and we slowed. Dozens of bone grappling hooks started to appear along our rails. As the crew moved to hack the grappling lines, the sahuagin surfaced and flung spears from the water at those braving the railings. Very few crew had arrows left to attack the exposed targets.

A focused Desdemona screamed an order. "Now, Lasho!"

Lasho was the mage who specialized in calming the waters around the *Shorebreaker*. He wove a complex spell form a few feet from me. Loud cracking sounds erupted around the ship, giving me hope, but the ship rapidly slowed further. I went to the edge of the railing and dodged a spear, but I still managed to peek overboard. Ice was spreading from the hull outward. Some fishmen were trapped in the ice, and others had lost the lines attached to the grappling hooks.

"Lasho, get below deck!" Desdemona yelled as she made to cut a grappling line. Lasho was weak on his feet from the massive aether expenditure. Looking at him, I wondered if he had burned his channels.

I moved along the stern, flicking my wrist and cutting the grappling lines with my dimensional space. Since I was performing this from almost ten feet away, my gesture was intended to conceal exactly how I was accomplishing the feat. A fish head appeared over the railing and I raced forward to decapitate it with the black blade. The head rolled onto the deck and the body fell back into the water, but another head appeared to my right. Maveith's hammer came down with a grunt. The head of the sahuagin burst like a watermelon, covering us in fishy-smelling shrapnel. I spit something out of my mouth. "I really don't like sushi."

"What is sushi?" Maveith questioned the unfamiliar word as his hammer came down again. This time, I used his body as a shield before I was splattered again.

"Raw fish, Maveith," I answered as I reached out and cut two more grappling lines in quick succession with my dimensional space.

"I agree. Raw fish is too chewy. But why are we talking about food in the middle of a fight?" Maveith said as he dodged a net from below. The net was intended to entangle the victim, allowing them to be pulled back over the railing. As the net started to drag across the deck, I cut the attached line with my dimensional space so Maveith didn't get tripped or entangled.

Cries of battle were all around us, and the chaos only escalated. The pitched battle for the ship was confusing, and I was cutting fishmen down, slicing nets, and cutting grappling lines as fast as I could. The reassuring presence of Maveith at my side moved with me. I cast an air shield to intercept a net targeting me and looked at the rest of the ship.

The ice ring was working. Only a few fish creatures managed to board and were quickly dispatched. Although they were bipedal, their webbed appendages hampered their movement. More and more of the nets were being cast blindly in hopes of snaring the crew.

One crewman had his arm tangled and was being dragged across the deck. I leaped off the sterncastle to the lower deck and cut the line at the railing with my blade. I continued my momentum to cut another fishman climbing aboard. The deck briefly shook as Maveith landed nearby. My tall shadow wasn't going to be separated from me.

Together, we made our way down the port side, clearing sahuagin and grappling lines. Although they were not coming fast, there seemed to be an endless supply of the fishy creatures. I could tell Desdemona's crew was slowly losing. At least four had fallen to spears, and another four were too injured to fight. The injured crew moved to the center of the deck to be defended by others. The ship's healing mage was unable to attend to them.

I shouted, "Healing potions!" I slid a handful of the Pathfinder potions across the deck toward the injured and then turned back to the fight.

Desdemona had remained on the stern and was fighting alongside her first mate, Isaak, and three other crew. We had bought ourselves a little breathing room, as the grapples stopped coming and the sea devils were forced to climb the hull. It was a much slower process for them than climbing with the aid of the grappling line.

Our wind mage, Vodoma, was using something like my air discs to help defend her crewmates, and Maveith and I briefly protected her rear while the injured crew recovered with my potions. Someone shouted, "Help in the bow!"

"Got it!" I grunted after gutting a fishman. I moved off the port side toward the bow as two larger sahuagin, each with four arms, had just climbed aboard. The pair quickly overwhelmed the lone crewman, and one held their victim while the other bit into the hapless man's neck. The needle teeth cut easily into the flesh, and blood sprayed as the sahuagin tore the sailor open.

Maveith's deep and winded voice yelled behind me, "If they have eight arms between them, does that make them an octopus?" I didn't have time to shake my head as I reached the pair, Maveith's heavy steps resounding reassuringly behind me in support. My target was the one feasting on the now-dead crewman.

Its partner tried to protect my target, imposing itself in my path. The abomination stood as tall as Maveith and raised two spears in its upper arms while the lower pair prepared for me with bone daggers. If it hadn't been so windy, I would have been able to use my pellets. My air shield deflected its first spear attack, and my blade the other. I remained out of reach of the daggers as I removed one of its spear arms in an upward slash.

As the arm flew away, the sahuagin's sharp scream drew its brethren's attention to our fight. Its pained, foul cry ended as Maveith's hammer descended on its chest, sinking in with a squelch.

My aether shield flashed as a trident deflected away from me in a flash of fire. The same sahuagin who had ignited the primary sail had thrown it from the water and was riding his mammoth shark below the bow. Even now, the sail still burned above as ash floated in the air around us.

The four-armed fishman used the leader's distraction to attack my side. Maveith barked a warning but couldn't help me in time. My black blade got around to deflect the first spear while my hand slapped away the other. An air shield blocked one of the daggers, but the bastard got its fourth arm around my defense. The dagger punched into my rib cage. My leather adventurer's armor offered only brief resistance, but my spider-silk shirt underneath aided in minimizing penetration.

"Argh!" Maveith yelled as the head of his hammer thrust straight out over my shoulder, shattering the bloody, sharp teeth of the creature and continuing out the back of its head.

These two four-armed devils were clearly the strongest of the sahuagin swarm, and we had taken them out easily enough. They had probably waited for us to soften up before joining the assault. The scream of rage from the large, shark-riding sahuagin made me pause to take everything in.

Another trident was being handed to him from the water. Dozens of bodies of the fishmen and crew were strewn across the deck while fighting still raged. I activated an air shield as the fiery trident approached, stopping it and causing a wave of heat and flame to pass over me. I gave the fishman leader the finger even though he didn't know what it meant.

I looked for where I could help the most. Back in the stern, Desdemona was fighting alone and looked about to be overwhelmed. "Maveith, hold the bow!" I didn't wait for him to respond as I raced down the length of the ship to help Desdemona. The deck was coated with a thick layer of blood, and I slid more than ran to the captain's aid. My side was almost healed as I cut a net to free a crew member on the way.

Three large nets appeared over the stern, two of them catching Desdemona. They immediately went taut and started dragging her to the railing. She ditched her sword for two daggers on her belt and furiously tried to cut herself free, but she had no chance of succeeding in time. I vaulted off a crate up to the sterncastle and slammed into the railing to stop my momentum. My blade came down, cutting the two lines attached to the nets.

I winked at Desdemona as a spear pierced my back. *Damn it, no good deed goes unpunished.* I moved away from the stern and fell to my knees. I looked down. The spear had punched through my gut. Isaak was holding a massive gash closed as blood coated his hands. I reached for my belt and tossed him some Pathfinder healing potions. "Healing potions," I muttered, my throat parched.

"What about you?" he rasped as he fumbled for the vials on the blood-slick deck.

"Just a flesh wound," I rasped, in some pain. I cut the back of the spear with my dimensional space and gritted my teeth as I pulled the remains of the spear out through my chest. My sense of humor was lost on Isaak as he looked on in shock. Annoyingly, the adventurer's armor wasn't cooperating, making the process more difficult. I wish it had made the process of going in more difficult than coming out. I took a Hound healing potion as I tried to stand, but I was very shaky from blood loss. Both the potion and my healing spell form worked on closing the injury.

I leaned on the mast for support as I looked over the carnage. Desdemona had not freed herself from the two nets yet, and a sahuagin was about to reach her. She was too far away to help her in time, and I didn't know where my black blade was. The black spear appeared in my hand, and I flung it weakly at the fishman. It had been instinctual, and I thought at the last moment, *Shit, I better not miss.*

The spear pierced the creature and it fell onto the struggling captain. Her head jerked toward me, and I gave her a slight nod as I focused on healing. That spear had done a significant amount of damage. The sahuagin looked to have exhausted themselves now, as very few were climbing on deck. At least a dozen crew members were still fighting. Maveith stood defiantly in the bow with a half dozen bodies around him, including the large sahuagin who had been tossing the flaming tridents.

I took a step, testing myself before I moved to help Desdemona free herself. She was covered in blood and gore from rolling around on the deck. "Need a healing potion? Are you wounded?" I asked as I assisted her.

She looked me in the eyes and then gazed down at the bloody hole in my armor. "Nothing urgent," she said, respect and gratitude in her eyes.

Isaak was now standing. "Maveith took down the prince. It has broken their spirit, and the rest are moving away to protect their queen." He was pointing at the shark-infested water, where the fins were moving away from the ship.

I retrieved my black spear and made it disappear, to Desdemona's wide-eyed shock. I found my black blade among the bodies and body parts, and I took the stairs instead of jumping off the stern deck this time. I went to help clean up the mess. Only a few sahuagin were alive, but they were suffocating out of the water, making gurgling sounds. They were all heavily injured, and I moved about the deck, silencing them.

Maveith came over to me. He had a half dozen minor injuries and was covered in sahuagin guts and his own blood. He had a massive grin on his blood-speckled face. "I get it now. You don't like sushi."

Chapter 258: Time Is of the Essence

The sun was already making the deck sticky with drying blood. The first calls were to stabilize the injured. Pickle, his right arm in a sling, climbed laboriously up to the crow's nest to resume his watch, but I thought the sahuagin had been bloodied enough that they would not return. Still, Desdemona was eager to get the ship moving and gain distance.

I overheard Isaak talking: "It is unlikely they will return, but they could always decide to be vengeful and sink us. The ice coating on the underside of the hull won't last much longer." I hadn't been aware that the ice had encased the underside of the hull.

As I looked over the dozens of bodies and parts, the fish smell was already rising to a dangerously high level of nauseating. "Desdemona, do you have a collector?"

She had been facing away from me, talking to Isaak and her mages. She looked exhausted and pained, having lost over half her crew. "Collector? Essence collector? Do I look like a wealthy captain to you?" she said, a little exasperated at the question and her despairing situation.

"Then you don't mind if I use mine?" I asked, eyeing the sahuagin Isaak had called a prince. Shocked looks passed between her mages and Isaak. They started whispering to each other quietly. "Time is of the essence?" I said as they talked. I was disappointed that my clever play on words was missed.

Desdemona turned and announced hopefully, "None of my crew and half the essences to the ship."

I thought that was greedy on her part, seeing she would have gotten nothing if I hadn't had the collector. But I was just as tired as they were and didn't care to argue. "Fine, but I choose which half Maveith and I keep." Desdemona waved me off to return to her crew, which I assumed meant she agreed. The battle had lasted almost an hour in my estimation, so many of the slain fishmen would likely yield nothing anyway.

I moved to the foul-smelling, messy bow. The fiery trident prince had a shattered leg and his chest was caved in. Maveith was standing over me as I produced the collector. "You did a number on him," I said appreciatively.

"Number? I only struck him twice. He was a tough fight. Stabbed me thrice in return with his oversized fork," he said in a gravelly tone laced with resentment.

I shook my head, unsure if Maveith was trying to be funny or serious. The collector started pulling thick blue aetheric smoke. From my past experience, I could already tell this was going to be an apex essence. An apex water essence formed, and I thought it odd, since the prince had imbued his tridents with fire. The essence disappeared into my space, and I looked down at the deck to see if anyone had seen it. Desdemona was facing me, giving orders, but she couldn't have seen what essence had formed.

"Are you upset I asked you to remain in the bow?" I asked Maveith as I moved on to one of the four-armed sahuagin.

Maveith considered the question longer than I thought he needed to as I got a major coordination essence from the fishman. "Yes. I couldn't protect you from so far away, but I understood the necessity of defending the bow."

"I can take care of myself," I said casually, and regretted my words as he frowned. "But I count you as a friend, Maveith, and appreciate your concern for my well-being." That seemed to satisfy him, and he nodded curtly with a grin. The other four-armed creature yielded a lesser dexterity essence. It was a bit disappointing, as it was one of the three strongest sahuagin.

Desdemona and Isaak came up to the bow with a few crewmen. "We are laying out the bodies to expedite the use of your collector. I want to get them overboard as quickly as possible. My ship is already starting to carry their foul scent. Are you done with these?" I nodded and she ordered, "Search 'em and toss 'em!" I hadn't thought about searching them. They looked naked except for their metal-and-bone bracelets and belts. I shrugged, not concerned about the loot. I moved to the main deck and continued my harvesting.

In the end, I tried the collector on sixty-seven of the sahuagin warriors and gained one major strength essence, two lesser quickness essences, six lesser strength essences, four lesser constitution essences, three lesser dexterity essences, and one lesser perception essence. Seventeen of the sixty-seven had yielded an essence. Although my collector was near-perfect in dungeons, it was less effective outside of them.

The crew was in rough shape, both physically and mentally, and were moving lethargically. I helped toss the sahuagin bodies overboard after finishing with the collector.

The ruined sail was taken down and cut up. The dead crew were tightly wrapped and weighted and would be buried at sea after a brief ceremony. There was still a lot of work to do before honoring them. Fourteen of Desdemona's crew had been killed on deck, and two more had been pulled overboard. Of the fifteen still living, three were maimed and unable to work the sails, and another six needed time to have their injuries healed after the mage recovered her aether.

Most of the crew worked to retrieve the spare sail in the hold and raise it. While all this was going on, I checked on Ginger. She had clearly panicked and kicked her stall during the fight, splintering the wood. She was excited to see me and forced her head into my chest, butting my head. "It's alright, girl. It's going to take a lot more than a bunch of fish to take me out. But I think we will avoid traveling by boat in the future." With the crew busy, I tended to Ginger and gave her two apples with her feed.

Returning to the deck, I saw a steady stream of water flowing across the deck from the bow. Lasho was pulling seawater up to the deck with his spell form. On their hands and knees, the crew scrubbed to wash away the blood, scales, and gore. Maveith was working diligently with them, but I passed on aiding this task.

I walked to the still-filthy Desdemona at the helm as the fresh sail was being stretched in the wind, the creases slowly disappearing. I produced all twenty essences I had collected in a bowl. Desdemona's eyes betrayed her surprise and covetousness at the sight of the essences. "Twenty? More than I expected. Where did you get your collector?"

I ignored her question about the collector. "This is everything I collected. Your share is the six lesser strength essences and four lesser dexterity essences." I pulled the spheres out of the bowl and handed them to her. The muscles in her jaw twitched slightly at seeing the apex water affinity essence remain.

Desdemona relaxed as she pocketed the essences. "Isaak is separating the half share of the jewelry for you and Maveith." I raised my eyebrows, slightly surprised. Maveith and I had accounted for about one third of the dead sahuagin, but I hadn't expected her generosity. Then again, without our participation, the ship would definitely have been overrun. Perhaps this was an unspoken trade for half of the essences I gathered with my collector. I nodded in thanks.

"Leoch has cleaned your runic swords and put them in your room. Thank you for the loan. They helped." Her statement was laced with an unasked question. When I only nodded, she pressed a little more. "Your runic spear was an impressive weapon, too. If there is time, I would like to look at it more closely."

Unfortunately, there was no innuendo in her tone or on her face. I think she was mostly curious about where I was storing something so large. Still, I couldn't resist responding, "Maybe I will show you my spear after we clean up and are somewhere more comfortable." My grin and tone were full of innuendo, and maybe it was not the right time after she had lost half her crew. But the adrenaline and violence of combat can do strange things to you.

"Yes, maybe after cleaning up a bit," she responded, licking her lips and then spitting, regretting her action; her face still had dried fishman blood on it. "My crew and friends call me Dee, by the way. If you are not going to help with the cleaning effort, talk with Lasho about a shower."

Although her body language was responding to my sensual overtones, her tone was meant to guilt me into helping scrub the deck. It didn't work. As I walked to the bow, I handed Maveith the major strength essence and the two quickness essences. He only wanted the quickness essences, but I insisted he take the strength essence as well.

In the bow, Lasho pulled a stream of seawater higher to fall on the deck in a makeshift shower. With a respectful nod, he noted, "When you're ready to rinse, let me know, and I'll remove the salt from the water." I quickly shed my damaged adventurer's armor and all my clothes to make full use of his efforts. The annoying part was removing all the crusty blood and fleshy bits from my hair.

I didn't even bother to note if Desdemona was watching. However, Vodoma, the female wind mage, had taken the opportunity to move closer to talk with Lasho. Judging by their broken and nonsensical conversation, it was clear what the middle-aged wind mage was after a closer view. With respect to Lasho's efforts, I washed as quickly as possible before requesting fresh water to rinse.

I packed up my fouled clothes and stored them, cleaned my hands, and then produced clean clothes and sandals, to both mages' surprise and envy. There was no point in hiding my space after what I had displayed in the battle, but I wasn't going to pull any people out or reveal just how large it was.

The deck-cleaning effort was nearly complete, but the lingering smell of rotting fish was going to persist for a very long time. I patted Maveith on the back on my way by, nodded in the direction of Desdemona, who had her eyes on me, and headed to my cabin.

I found the two runic blades cleaned and on my hammock, and stored them. I swung in my hammock, trying to sleep, but the fishy scent hung in the air even here. I used the dreamscape amulet to escape the smell. My manifestation of Scholar Favian was much more helpful after I poured all the knowledge of Elvish from Isaak and Leoch into him. I spent four hours practicing Elvish before being pulled out of the dreamscape. Instantly on alert, I was out of the hammock and on my feet.

I hadn't secured the door in case we were attacked again, but I had attached a line to it to pull the amulet from my grasp if someone opened my door. That person was Maveith. "Is there an issue?"

He had a guilty look on his face at disturbing me. "No. I knocked and when you didn't answer, I tried the door."

"It is fine, Maveith." I bent over to retrieve the amulet and untied the string.

Maveith was mostly clean as he squeezed into the cabin. "Dee has asked for you to join her for a late dinner." He paused and stressed, "Alone. I think she wants to thank you for your help during the attack." My eyes widened in surprise. I couldn't hold back a smirk, although I had already come down a bit after my combat high.

Desdemona had her captain's cabin door open as I reached it. She was dressed in a thin, mustard-colored blouse, and her hair was still wet from washing. Her bright smile creased her tanned face as I entered, and she motioned that I should close the door. I complied. She was sitting at the table, and I sat across from her. The table had a spread of dried fruit, jerky, and nuts. Her smile faded. "I apologize for the meal, but Cook was killed in the engagement."

"The food is fine. I am sorry you lost so many of your crew," I said consolingly. She nodded sharply, and I could tell she was in a bit of pain from the loss. "There is nothing you could have done differently, Dee." She winced like I had stabbed her, and I liked that she felt guilt over losing her crew. It meant she cared about them—just like Castile cared about the men of the company.

I was modestly hungry from all the healing, so I poured myself a glass of wine and helped myself.

"You always second-guess yourself after the battle," she said heavily after regaining herself. She nibbled on some fruit, and there was silence as we both ate slowly. Before long she asked with a silly grin, "You said you would show me your impressive spear?"

I produced the runic black spear I had used in the fight in my right hand. Her eyes immediately traveled to the golden ring on that hand before her eyes took in the weapon. She clearly assumed the ring was a storage device of some sort. She placed her hand on the black shaft and stroked it some. "Treant obsidian, if I am not mistaken." She eyed the black leaf pattern on the spearhead. "Elvish?" she asked.

"Dungeon-artificed," I responded while watching her admire it. There was still some blood drying on the tip. She nodded as her hands ran along the spiraled grain reverently. "What is treant obsidian?" I asked, watching her intently.

"Wood from an ancient treant. When a treant's age surpasses its life, it will fall into an eternal slumber, and its wood will blacken, like so. It is the strongest wood known to man and treasured by the elves. I have never seen anything like the spiraling grain pattern, though. You can almost feel the power bound within." I let her admire the weapon before returning it to my storage.

Desdemona exhaled like she had been holding her breath. "I cannot thank you enough for saving my ship and crew. Your prowess in battle reminds me of fabled heroes." She cracked a smile, which I returned. "You are full of surprises." Her bare foot intentionally brushed my leg under the table. "I bet you have another spear hidden away somewhere?" Her foot slowly climbed my leg

...

As Maveith had mentioned, Dee's hammock really was palatial. The massive hammock was far more comfortable than my own. Currently, the short woman was sprawled across my body, sleeping. She was much heavier than I would have thought. Her intense body heat was causing us both to sweat under her heavy blankets, but the alternative was exposure to the cold night air of the sea. Her head rested on my chest, and she drooled slightly as she slept. Well, at least she didn't snore.

I had recently used my amulet and didn't need sleep, so I lay awake while she rested after a grueling day. Her perfumed wardrobe held the fishy scent at bay. I lay awake the entire night, playing complex Elvish phrases in my head. Before the sun rose, a short, hard knock came at the door. "Captain Dee. First light is coming, and we are ready for honors."

Dee licked her lips, coming awake quickly. She pushed off me and barked at the door, "Thank you, Isaak. I will be on deck in moments." Dee slid out of the hammock, ignoring me completely while she dressed. I lay on my side and watched her.

When she was almost dressed, she addressed me. "You said you wanted to help. We will need help with the sails if we are going to reach port. I am sure Maveith will help." She wasn't very good at guilt-tripping me.

I thought I was the paying passenger here. But I understood the necessity. With an affable smile, I asked, "Do I get to keep my cabin upgrade?"

Her eyes traveled over me quickly while she fought to hide a lecherous smile. "Perhaps we can negotiate a suitable payment for such an upgrade." Before we could start negotiations, she was out the door. I rolled out as well, planning to attend the burial services for the dead crew.

Bowls of nuts and jerky were tossed carelessly on the floor. Last night, we started by testing the structural integrity of her table before moving to the hammock, and the food had been victimized. I started dressing, shaking out bits of food from my clothes before donning them. I walked on deck as the entire crew moved somberly. The sails were ordered to be luffed so everyone could attend the ceremony.

We all gathered near the stern deck, a few crew members eyeing me and nodding in gratitude. Maveith came and stood behind me as we waited. "Did you play backgammon all night?" he asked quietly. "You never came out of Dee's cabin."

A little confused, I turned to see a massive grin on Maveith's face. He knew what we had been doing, and we had not been doing it too quietly, either. I was coming up with a reply when Captain Dee stepped forward. Dee had a sorrowful look on her face and made eye contact with each of her remaining crew. She then stood over the canvas-wrapped bodies and spoke reverently.

"A bounty given by the seas can be a bounty taken by the waves.

"The sea is a harsh mistress, but her salt runs in our veins and is hers to reclaim.

"We give our friends and companions eternal rest in the deep, dark depths of her embrace.

"We hope they may watch over us until we can join them below the surface."

A few men nodded at her words, and two moved to the first body. Isaak came to stand where Desdemona had stood. He took a deep breath. "Cook joined the crew in the port of Ishmael three years ago. He was the finest cook I served with on any ship, and his stuffed crab cabbage will be missed. Whatever god rules the sea will now be blessed with his services."

The two men pulled the wrapped body to the edge and dropped it in the water. The ship had slowed enough that the splash was easily heard. The men moved to the next body, and someone else came to speak in memory of them.

I watched the wrapped body float behind the *Shorebreaker*. With the backdrop of the rising sun, it quickly sank in the ship's wash. I stood and listened to someone tell a short story of each crew member before they were sent into the water. When all the bodies were cleared, the two crew who had been pulled overboard by nets were honored with words as well.

Without further ceremony, Dee ordered the ship back to full sail, and the ship lurched under our feet as the wind caught the primary sail once again. Vodoma was still using her aether to heal the crew, but Lasho was calming the waters since his aether had recovered.

The rest of my day was spent with Maveith learning how to be a sailor. Truthfully, most of the time, it was just Isaak or another of the crew yelling at us what to untie, pull, loosen, or retie on the cleats. Without Vodoma creating our wind directly behind the sails, we needed to constantly work on angling the sails ourselves.

Most of the time, I had no idea why we were doing things and just followed the commands that were yelled at me. At midday, Isaak asked, "I thought you would need a break by now. How are the hands?"

"I heal fast." I held them up to show they were completely healed. Earlier, I had untied the wrong line, causing a boom to shift. Foolishly, I grabbed the line and was dragged across the deck before bracing my feet. The hemp rope had been pulled through my hands as I fought the wind, tearing them up. "I can go as long as you need me to," I said confidently.

He patted me on the back, smiling. "Well, save some of your energy for the captain." He walked away, smirking to himself. I shouldn't have been surprised that the crew had put the deaths behind them so quickly. It was something I had learned in my Legion company. It hurt, but you found a way to compartmentalize until you could lift a pint of ale in memory.

Maveith's gray skin was sun- and windburned, and he had left for his cabin to rest and eat. I stayed and worked the entire day, finding the work satisfying as I puzzled out what effects my actions had on the sails.

That was how I spent my next two days: slowly learning to sail during the day and resting in Desdemona's company at night. Maveith would join us for the evening meal, play a game of checkers, and leave. There was nothing romantic about our time together, and I understood I was a distraction from her loss. On the third day, an elven cutter was spotted, and soon, the coast.

The cutter was half the size of our ship and didn't even have lower decks, but it surfed the waves effortlessly. It sailed parallel to us for over an hour before it moved alongside, and Desdemona conversed with their captain. I thought my Elvish was actually better than Desdemona's but was wise enough to keep that to myself. From the exchange, I learned we were only twenty miles south of Sanco and they would shadow us there.

The shoreline was sandy but turned into thick woodlands after a few dozen yards up the beach. I watched the shore with my spyglass when I was able, and monstrous crabs scuttled across the beach. There were very few signs of civilization until we approached Sanco. The first hint that we were getting close was a large number of fishing boats. Dee was standing next to me. "Elves don't like the water much, but they love to eat fish."

"That is just the high elves," Isaak said from behind us. "Eryk, your loot crate is ready for you when we dock, but you can pick it up at the Adventurers Hall. They will use it to confirm our sahuagin kills."

Isaak left and Desdemona faced me. "I will help you through customs. If they do have an Inquisitor, tell them you are fleeing the Telhian Empire. Try to avoid saying you were a legionnaire if you can." Our purely physical relationship was over. She turned away from me to bring her ship to port with her message about the dungeon.

We approached the massive stone wall, which formed an artificial bay. Our sails were stowed and Vodoma and Lasho guided the ship with their magic. Tower fortifications dotted the wall, and ballistae and bowmen were visible as we sailed past. The water in the bay was eerily calm, with only small waves created by ships underway by magic.

It was hard to take everything in at once. The city was built entirely out of stone, and the buildings had no sharp corners; everything was rounded and flowing like water.

Since elves lived for centuries, I didn't know what to expect for my first time in one of their cities. The buildings had numerous garden terraces, but no structure exceeded five stories to my eye. With magic and time, I expected something more—grandiose. We crossed the bay to some long wooden piers. Four other ships were here, three flying the Bartiradian flag. The other ship's flag was unfamiliar.

Burly elven shoremen help tie off the *Shorebreaker* before extending a ramp to our deck. Desdemona had changed into more formal clothes and walked down the ramp alone to wait on the pier. There were elven guards—probably the city watch—in dull-green garb along the length of the pier, but they seemed surprisingly unconcerned about our arrival.

A figure in red marched down the pier. When his flowing robes reached Desdemona, he stopped, and they got into a lengthy conversation. The language was not Telhian or Elvish, so even though I could hear them talk, I had no idea what was being said. All I could do was wait.

"It doesn't smell." Maveith's deep voice sounded behind me. I inhaled deeply, and he was right. The familiar salty air was gone, and the persistent fishy smell had vanished from the *Shorebreaker*.

Isaak's voice chuckled from behind us. "It's not gone, but sort of purified by some ancient magic. I told you the high elves don't like the smell of fish. Like most elven cities, this city sits in a ley line nexus but doesn't have a dungeon. Once we leave the harbor, the fishman stink will resume." He groaned in realization.

Desdemona waved us down the ramp to talk with the port authority. Maveith tramped behind me and we approached the tall elf. His silvery red robes pooled around him as he assessed us with his eyes. He seemed more interested in Maveith than me, and I assumed goliaths were rare in Esenhem. "Planning to port to Artiria?" he finally said in Elvish.

I nodded. "And then on to Gramney."

"Your guild medallion?" He held out his hand and I pretended to retrieve my belt, pulling it from my storage. "Fifty silver for each of you and five gold for your horse." He pointed. "Pay at the white stone building at the end of the pier. It is the registration office. You need to be screened by the mages to confirm you are in good health."

Desdemona interrupted, "The goliath still needs to enroll in the Guild."

The elf sighed impatiently. "He can return to have his medallion stamped. For now, I wish to make certain he will not bring any disease into the city." I now realized that we had moored at the docks for foreign ships. We couldn't enter the city without passing the white building he indicated.

After Ginger was unloaded, two city guards in pea-green uniforms walked us down the docks to make sure we didn't pass the white building without entering it. I looked curiously up at the other ships as we passed them. The Bartiradian ships were bulky merchants with mostly human crews on deck. I did see a chatty halfling and a hairy dwarf sunning himself.

One remarkable thing about Sanco was how clean the city was. There was no filth on the smooth cobblestone walkways, and all the buildings looked as if they had been recently washed, the ancient stone looking almost new. Ginger was interested as well, and I just hoped she wouldn't do her business while we were being inspected.

For such a large city, there were surprisingly few foreign ships here. I surmised that was probably due to the war. I hitched Ginger to a post outside the white stone building and entered with Maveith. A silvery-haired elf offered us a big smile. "New arrivals on the Guild ship from the Telhian Empire?" he asked in Telhian.

Apparently, the idea of slow-moving customs was not unique to Earth. Maveith and I had to endure an hour of questions while the old elf slowly scribed our answers. I got off more lightly than Maveith, maybe because I had the guild medallion or because I was human. The questions for Maveith never seemed to end. Maybe the administrator was satisfying his own curiosity.

We ran into our first hurdle when we were asked to declare our artifacts. Maveith readily volunteered, "Two rings, one hammer, and a skinning knife." Fortunately, he wasn't required to note what the artifacts did, but the old elf was impressed by the count, judging from his reaction.

When my turn came, I crafted my words to be the truth. "On my person, I have two rings, an amulet, bracers, one blade, and one dagger." I was wearing one of the simple runic blades from Boris's men as well as Corvus's dagger. My paranoid inner self was screaming at me for revealing so much. Maveith was acting unconcerned, but I felt my anxiety rising. I had trusted so few people for so long, this declaration was not easy.

After he wrote out what I had said, he looked up. "The belt?" His question hung in the air, and I was somewhat shocked. Did he have a way of seeing artifacts—some type of aether sight? I didn't panic and put on an act, pretending I had just forgotten about the belt—which was true.

"Yes. I overlooked that. It has a few potions in it, too. Do you need to log them as well?" He studied me and slowly shook his head.

"No. Potions are fine for adventurers. That will be six gold for you two and the horse. The healing mage will be by this evening. You can wait in that room, and Mikhael can order food for you from the tavern." I placed six gold dungeon coins on his desk and he nodded appreciatively. I checked on and fed Ginger before moving to the waiting room with Maveith. Maveith ordered a ton of food, and from his appetite I guessed he had "accidentally" removed his ring of sustenance again.

It was more than two hours before a vibrant, black-haired, blue-eyed elf arrived. He was full of energy and beaming happily. "Your mount has been cleared to enter Esenhem. I healed her cracked hoof." He looked us over, beaming. "It is true! An actual goliath!" Maveith didn't speak Elvish, so I worked as a translator.

The medical exam was quick, but like the old elf, the healing mage was curious about Maveith, and it took him over an hour to finish with us. We were still not finished, though. There was another customs room with two disinterested guards. My anxiety rose when the older elf said, "Please empty your packs and anything you have in magical storage for us to examine." *Well, dragon shit.*

Chapter 260: Guild Rewards

Although my appearance remained calm, my heart raced. The guards waited expectantly as Maveith complied with their request, emptying everything in his pockets, which was not much. Did they find it odd that we were not carrying large packs—only entering the country with the clothes on our backs? Maveith's pack was in my dimensional space, as well as both our sets of armor.

My biggest uncertainty was whether they were aware I had a dimensional space. If they could detect it somehow, would I be denied entrance to Esenhem if I didn't empty it of everything? I thought it was improbable that they knew about it, but the uncertainty nagged at me. And if they did know, they must have no idea how large it was, judging by this pair of average-appearing guards. I concluded I would have been detained immediately if they knew I was carrying four people inside my dimensional space.

Dee had advised me that customs was just a formality for adventurers, but this seemed anything but. I waited while the guards inspected everything Maveith placed on the table. They held their hands over the items but did not touch them. They were curious about the major strength essence, but they didn't confiscate it. Instead, they talked to each other in Elvish, hypothesizing about what creature or dungeon it might have come from. When they finished, they indicated it was my turn.

I started by emptying my belt pouches, and they immediately had me pause. "What are these?" asked one of them. He pointed at a pile of pellets his hand had just passed over.

"Blindness pellets," I replied, unfazed. I assumed they would not be unusual for adventurers to have.

The elf guard chewed the inside of his cheek. "Made from myconid spores?" he finally asked. I nodded, and he indicated that I should proceed. Then he questioned me about the smoke and sneezing pellets, since their shells were different colors. I skipped over the blood compass for now, as it was an artifact I had not declared.

Instead, I moved it into my dimensional space. I started stacking large amounts of silver coins on the table, and with each handful, their eyes widened. The guard held his hand up to stop me. "First time? We just need to check for poison, parasites, insects, and diseases you could be carrying."

Now it made more sense why the myconid pellets caused them some consternation. These guards must have a spell form similar to Konstantin's. The nature of my expansive belt pouches had been revealed, so I didn't backtrack. There were several surprises for them as I continued with the orc Pathfinder potions, two dungeon potions of levitation and one of fire resistance that I kept in my belt, a jar of oblivion pills, and a jar of minty mouthwash.

My manticore pouch was also produced, and it had two lesser constitution essences in it. I had consumed the other minor essences in my possession, and besides these two constitution essences, all I had remaining were the three apex water essences, but they were in my dimensional space. Maveith, who had been watching from beside me, proudly noted the origin of the pouch. "I made that for him from the scrotum of a massive manticore bull that we slew together. It was easily over a thousand pounds." The two elves nodded in appreciation. From the size of the pouch, it was clear that it was not a lie.

"Is that all?" the guard asked, as I seemed to have concluded pulling endless things from my magical belt. Even I was surprised at how much junk I was carrying around on my waist. I could only imagine their reaction if I started pulling things out of thin air from my dimensional space. The pair were much more alert than when we had started; I had been good entertainment.

"Just a crate of dungeon apples," I replied offhandedly.

"Are they still on your ship? Nothing else was delivered for inspection," the elf asked, confused. It was the response I had hoped for. Their response hinted that they were unaware of my dimensional space. Still, a crate of apples appeared on the table, causing both guards to step back.

"I was told they were out of season and I could get a few silvers for each," I replied to the dumbfounded guards.

After a moment of shock, one of the guards stepped forward and passed his hands over the crate. I had only volunteered the apples because I had placed them in the old crate I used for my legion supplies. The guard squinted a little as he inspected the contents. "You said dungeon apples?"

"Yes, I was considering selling them in your capital," I repeated.

The other guard, who had remained quiet for most of the inspection, spoke. "Don't take less than ten silver each. Don't know of any dungeons that produce apples, and the wealthy nobles will pay that or more in Artiria." The other guard nodded in agreement with his partner's advice.

"See Master Daesac on your way out to have your guild medallion emblazoned." The two guards left me to put everything back into my belt. The fact that I had volunteered the existence of my dimensional space rankled me a little, but I had already revealed its existence on the *Shorebreaker*, and there was a risk the crew might talk, so it was for the best.

"Are all customs that extreme?" I asked Maveith as I tried to remember where everything went.

Maveith thought on the question before responding. "Some are more severe. I have seen artifacts identified and confiscated with no remuneration, men arrested after being questioned, and men stripped of their wealth for debts they had in other lands. The elves here seem to rely on people volunteering what they are bringing into the country." I guess I just didn't like my secrets being in the open after working for so long to hide them.

The old elf was still seated in the entry room even though it was late in the night. "I trust all is well?" He smiled at us and held out his hand. I retrieved my medallion and handed it over. He turned it over in his hand and pressed his thumb on the tree. A brief metallic scent stung my nose, and when he removed his thumb, a silver bird reaching for the sun was left behind. "As long as you obey our laws, this will get you quickly past future customs."

He turned to the goliath. "Friend goliath, return with your adventurer's medallion in the morning, and I will press our seal upon it. Now, it is late, and my ancient bones need some time on a softer surface."

The aged elf rose and walked gingerly out a back door. A much younger elf entered to take his place and asked, "Do you require me to summon someone to escort you in the city?"

"Thank you. We are looking to find our way to the Adventurers Guild Hall," I replied.

"Your Elvish is surprisingly good. I will return in a moment." He left and came back with a guard in the drab green uniform of the city guard. It was a fairly long walk through the city and the streets were lit with soft white glowstones. Elves had better low-light vision than humans and goliaths, so they did not require much light. I tried to use my new night vision, but the overall effect was only a mild improvement due to the short range of the spell form and the filtering of most of the color.

Even in the lower city, elves moved about the meticulously cleaned streets without fear or trepidation. At such a late hour, doing so in a Telhian city would be putting yourself at risk from unscrupulous people. Maveith's focus was elsewhere. "All the stonework was completed with the shape stone spell form. Much more detailed work than I could have done."

"I would still take your cozy abode over city life, Maveith. All it takes is practice to improve if you want to mimic these buildings," I reassured my friend as Ginger's hooves echoed behind us.

"I don't have the aether for such creations. It took me years to hollow out the stone for my cabin." His hand brushed a curved corner on a building. "The stone here even resists my effort to shape it. It takes a skilled stoneshaper to do that. Someone who has learned over hundreds of years. I don't have that kind of time," he said resignedly.

His statement pained me, as I did have that kind of time. How was I going to spend my centuries upon centuries? My thoughts were interrupted as our guide paused outside a building. The weathered sign had the Adventurers Guild symbol, a tree with branches covered in leaves mirrored by a root system below. The interior was bright, and soft music played within. I thanked the guard with a silver, which surprised him.

There were stables around the back of the Guild Hall, and we got Ginger settled before entering. I also ordered one month of hay and grain to be delivered in the morning. The young elf woman must have thought we were staying in the city long term and would probably be surprised when it disappeared when we left.

The large, ornate common room of the Guild Hall felt quite somber and was extremely warm. I noted that Desdemona's remaining crew occupied a few tables and were well on their way to drunkenness. A number of elves, a few humans, and a pair of halflings I didn't recognize were scattered throughout the room. Just like at the elven customs office, Maveith drew the most attention. Isaak held up a mug to salute us. "Join us to remember our fallen!" He was clearly drunk and his speech was slurred. Two of the crew stumbled to another table to give us their seats.

As we sat, an elven waitress placed two frothy mugs in front of us. She was rail thin, and her almond-colored hair was plastered to her face with sweat. I guessed she was the only one working tonight and was being kept busy by the unexpected crowd of heavy drinkers. "Already paid for by the captain," Leoch said, saluting me from another table.

I sipped the elven ale and found it cold, strong, aromatic, and mildly sweet. The cold beverage made taking large sips all too easy. Maveith drained his own mug, and the serving woman quickly refilled it. "Where is Desdemona?" I asked as I nursed my drink, enjoying the taste more than the alcohol's effects.

"She should be back soon," Isaak slurred. "Dee, Vodoma, and the local Guildmaster were off to send a message about the sahuagin attack and the new dungeon in the Telhian Empire. Some of the locals are watching the

Shorebreaker so we can properly mourn our comrades." He filled his mug from a pitcher before the waitress could, spilling surprisingly little.

"Some of us mourn faster than others." Leoch indicated Isaak, who seemed the most drunk of the group.

"Do we have to wait for the Guildmaster to return to get Maveith his guild medallion?" I asked as the overworked server placed food in front of us. I dropped a silver on her tray even though the food was already paid for as well.

"Dee took care of it. Maveith needs to fill out the paperwork in the morning," Isaak said as he hiccupped. He tried to stand and nearly fell over. He had trouble searching his pockets but eventually found two keys and stared at them, trying to remember. He then handed one to Maveith and the other to me. "With the compliments of Guildmaster Theodas. He even offered to purchase your sahuagin prizes." He leaned on the table to get close, his breath heavy with the sweet alcohol. "You should accept it. He is paying more than what you would get as a thank you. Dee talked up your battle prowess."

At the other table, Leoch laughed, "If I wasn't there, I would have thought Eryk single-handedly held back a sahuagin hive by the way she told it."

Another of the *Shorebreaker*'s sailors interjected, "Oh!? She was talking about the battle! I thought she had been describing what happened in her cabin after the battle!" Everyone was so drunk that they broke into raucous laughter at my expense.

Maveith, who was on his third mug, joined in the ribbing with his boisterous, deep voice, "I was concerned for Dee's safety and almost went to check on her the first night."

Rather than be the target of the night's jokes, I took my room key and found my room. The room smelled of lavender and sweet citrus oil. The mattress was firm but slightly spongy. I pulled out my griffin pillow and stripped before lying down. I killed my light buzz with my purify self spell form, removing my intoxication completely.

The blood compass appeared in my hand and I was hesitant to use it. If Castile had died fighting the Emperor, then her blood would have decayed by now, and I would feel nothing. I pulsed aether into the device, and there was a slight pull. I released a relieved sigh. It took time to orient myself, but I think the compass was pulling almost straight south—toward Bartiradian lands. Was she captured or making her way to Gramney through enemy territory?

I slept a little restlessly that night. I didn't use the amulet or an oblivion pill even as guilt gnawed at me for not trying to help Castile and the others escape. I was up extremely early and checked on Ginger. The stable hand apparently slept in the loft and came down to help me. She hadn't gone out for the hay and grain yet, so I tasked her with getting me a saddle and tack for Ginger. I didn't want a new saddle to break in, just a quality used saddle so Ginger could start earning her keep.

Maveith came down to the common room in severe discomfort from a splitting headache, and I almost wanted him to suffer. Instead, I handed him a morning glory stem to alleviate his hangover. He was unfamiliar with the remedy so I explained that he was to crush the stem and suck the sap out.

His deep voice rumbled across the common room. "Ugh. I never consumed such tasty ale before. I thought it would be disrespectful not to drink with them. But I did get this last night!" Maveith proudly produced his bronze guild medallion and handed it to me. It had a shiny luster to it and displayed his name, Maveith of the Stoneskin Clan. Underneath his name was his guild number, 49-6954.

"Nice, Maveith. Do you want me to head to the customs office with you?" I asked, handing it back.

"I can manage. I think Dee wanted to talk to you before we left." He leaned in conspiratorially. "She came into my room last night thinking I was you." I cursed in my head. *Damn it, Isaak, you gave me the wrong key!* I had missed her parting farewell.

After Maveith got a large breakfast, he left with a guide to get his medallion inscribed. Desdemona came down and sat at my table. Her hair was askew, and I thought there was some dried vomit on her shirt, so maybe it was a good thing she hadn't found me last night. I handed her the morning glory, and she immediately knew what it was. Crushing it in her hand, she sucked loudly and let out a satisfied sigh.

"You are more useful than you look, legionnaire," she said with a smile.

"Did you enjoy Maveith's company last night?" I returned.

She laughed, "No. Isaak was passed out, and I couldn't remember the other room's number." She got a little more serious. "The Guild has decided to reward you for your efforts. You are being promoted to the silver rank for saving the *Shorebreaker*." She produced a silver guild medallion with my name and guild number. My surprise made her smirk. "Well, it was either this or pay you three hundred gold. This was cheaper for the Guild." She gestured for my bronze amulet. I handed it to her and it disappeared into her pocket.

"I didn't have a say?" I asked, but I didn't know how valuable a silver guild rank was either. It also already had the Esenhem bird on it.

"You still get your gold, legionnaire. Guildmaster Theodas has purchased your sahuagin treasures for seventy-six gold, almost twice what they are worth." She dropped a heavy pouch on the table with a thud. "He is also negotiating on your behalf for passage through the portals as we speak. You should be leaving for Artiria and then Gramney to carry this Guild missive." She placed a scroll on the table. "It just details the sahuagin attack and is more of an excuse for him to pay your way to Gramney."

"Will it include Maveith and Ginger?" I asked, taking the pouch and scroll.

"Yes, the goliath and horse are included." She said irritably, probably expecting a thank you.

"I have half a day before I have to leave. Maybe there are private baths in the city?" I said suggestively.

Her expression changed to disappointment. "Maybe next time we meet, legionnaire. I need to recruit replacement crew and provision my ship. I have been ordered to sail as soon as possible to retrieve guild negotiators and deliver them to the Telhian Capital." Desdemona stood, locked eyes with me for a moment, and said, "Thank you." She then spun and left the Guild Hall. It felt more like a *Goodbye* than an *I hope to see you again.*

I waited for Maveith to return. He smiled, showing off his stamped medallion. He didn't need to see my new silver medallion. "What now, Eryk?"

"We leave for the elven capital this evening, but first we find a bathhouse!" I patted my friend on the shoulder and led the way out of the Guild Hall.

As we wandered the streets in the daylight, we took in the fascinating sights. I saw something I never thought possible: a fat elf. It was almost unfathomable to me. There were a number of slightly pudgy elves, but this merchant, selling an array of bread, had a gut that would make Santa proud. I couldn't resist and stopped at his street stall.

The smell of his fresh bread was wonderful, and maybe he partook of his own wares too much. Maveith bought six long loaves with nuts and cheese baked into the top. I shook my head as Maveith paid the exorbitant sum of six silver for the bread.

I chastised him for his weakness. "Maveith, you really need to keep the ring on." Instead of responding with his mouth full, he handed me a loaf. I was tempted and tried the still-warm bread. The crunchy exterior was rich, sweet, and savory. The fluffy interior nearly melted in my mouth. This was definitely not normal flour.

"What is this made of?" I asked as I quickly took another bite. This was closer to a dessert than a bread.

The fat elf winked at me. "It is my personal secret mix of three different flours and my family's yeast. But the real secret is basting the loaves with goat butter when they are close to finished to give it the crunchy shell." The baker then went into a ten-minute speech on the intricacies of his craft. It went way over my head, but we listened while we ate our loaves. I guessed that when you had centuries to master a craft, even something as simple as baking, you made it as complex as possible to challenge yourself. I couldn't argue with the end product.

At Maveith's insistence, I purchased and stored a dozen loaves in my dimensional space so they would remain fresh. The fat elf didn't look overly surprised at my use of a dimensional space and even kindly directed us to a bathhouse.

The bathhouse was not as ornate as its Telhian counterparts, and it cost two silver coins for each of us. I had accumulated a lot of filthy clothes in my dimensional space, and it was time for a reckoning. Unfortunately for the elven bath attendants, they would be dealing with my fouled laundry. I didn't include the clothes that were soaked in blood and paid extra for a double wash.

Although many elves in the city were dressed in thin fabrics that left little to the imagination, open nudity appeared taboo in elven culture. The bathrooms were private, and we didn't see any other patrons. Large individual brass tubs were filled with heated, scented water, and we were able to remove the screens between two of these tubs. Still, the elven attendants seemed to shy away from looking at our naked bodies. I sighed as I sank into the scented water, Maveith following directly after in his tub.

Even though the tubs seemed large, Maveith's knees still jutted high over the rim and his hips were snug, making it difficult for him to scrub himself. The water was laced with a fragrant oil that was absorbed into my skin. Smelling like fragrant flowers was not ideal for trackers and hunters like Maveith and me, but it was a welcome vanity after being among sailors for a week.

I shared some mouthwash with Maveith and trimmed my hair and black beard. I was growing accustomed to having a beard, but grooming it and shaving my cheeks was a chore with the straight razor. When our clothes were returned clean and dry, we left the bathhouse, leaving a sizable tip for the workers who would have to scrub our filth from the copper tubs.

Maveith was studying his fingernails and sniffing his hand as we walked the city. "I can see why you are always talking about getting clean. I can't remember the last time my hands didn't smell. Even my fingernails are clean." He held out his left hand for me to inspect, but I batted it away, unsure if he was serious.

We circled the city just to explore a little and to satisfy my Hound training. Walking the walled perimeter was too suspicious, but seeming to wander the streets shouldn't draw more attention than we already did. We were being watched; I didn't know if it was because Maveith was a curiosity. We did find Sanco's portal stone, so we returned to the Adventurers Hall.

I went to collect Ginger. The stable hand had gotten me a large, worn, dark-brown leather saddle for her, and it was hanging in her stall. Upon inspection, I found it to be of fine quality and well worth the gold coins I had given her to procure it. The saddle blanket was new, dark gray, and very soft, which would prevent chafing.

A large delivery of hay and grain was nearby, and I assumed it was what I had ordered. It was also of the highest quality and something I wouldn't have expected to receive in the Empire. I confirmed no one was around before moving it all to my dimensional space.

As I saddled Ginger, I found the stable hand had already adjusted the cinches for Ginger and for my size, so the process went quickly. I just needed to lengthen the reins a notch and set the stirrup length. Ginger was patient throughout. Maybe she was looking forward to carrying me around again as long as I paid her apple tax.

Maveith nodded appreciatively. "Ginger looks good." He walked over and rubbed her neck as she preened a little in her new saddle and tack.

"Let's head to the portal before the stable hand returns." I left two silver coins for her excellent work. I had discovered that tipping was not unusual in Esenhem, but it was not expected. I mostly wanted to leave before she returned and inquired as to where all the grain and hay had gone.

As we walked toward the upper city, Maveith still drew a lot of stares. He was a minor celebrity, with children rushing into the street to catch a glimpse of him as he passed. For all Maveith's humility, he wasn't fazed by the attention and waved to the elven children, who returned the gesture. When we reached the gates of a walled-in courtyard, four elven guards halted us until we announced ourselves. They did a cursory inspection of what we were carrying, checked our guild medallions against their log, and then allowed us inside.

An array of individuals and carts was milling about the courtyard. Ginger yanked on the reins briefly as she wanted to go meet a large white stallion on the far side. Her warhorse training caused her to calm down after I gave her reins a single pull.

Most of the people here were elves dressed in a variety of styles. A few humans huddled together around a large cart and I assumed they were merchants. There was a lone halfling sitting atop an isolated cart, struggling to stay awake. Maveith interrupted my people watching. "Where is the portal?" he asked in Telhian.

A dwarf, or maybe a large halfling, huffed nearby and was clearly irritated, needing to vent. He spoke Elvish as he ranted, "Elves don't use portals, friend goliath. Look at the stones. There is a teleportation spell form anchor embedded there. Elves don't have enough good displacement mages to make a portal network possible. Had to wait six days for this transport, and then they only gave me a day's warning to get ready!"

A blond elf woman in drab gray clothes nearby felt the need to join the conversation and her pale-blue eyes sparkled. "I hear the elven mages succeed most of the time. Always a risk that the mage sends the group too far—or too high." The elf was practically laughing at making the dwarf uncomfortable.

I noted two city guards standing just a few feet from the elven woman and quickly deduced she was our mage. "And how proficient are you with your teleportation magic, Master Mage?" I used the elven honorifics for someone of a higher station than me, even though this was not a formal occasion.

She smiled and tapped her chin in thought as the dwarf made to disappear into the crowd, realizing he had insulted the elf who was sending us to Artiria. "Hmm, this will be my ninety-seventh sending from Sanco to Artiria. I have only failed twice."

"The odds are pretty good then," I replied respectfully in Elvish with a smile, sensing she was teasing us.

"Here, I thought you would be more fun to tease, adventurer—my two failed attempts were during my centering training. Only one pig was killed, but that was a decade ago." She walked up to Ginger, her guards following, and stroked the horse's neck appreciatively. "Are you the adventurers Guildmaster Theodas bartered passage for?" she asked conversationally.

"Is there more than one goliath in Sanco?" I asked, being a bit cheeky.

The elven mage was not embarrassed. "I suppose not," she said in broken Telhian. I think she was trying to demonstrate she knew of our origins.

I was not concerned yet and kept speaking Elvish. "What is different in teleportation, compared to using a portal stone?"

As with anyone proud of their work, the elf gave a lengthy explanation. "A portal creates a gate between two points. It costs a lot of aether to keep open, but it is much safer than teleportation magic since both points are linked. The issue is that it requires a displacement mage at each end of the gate with sufficient aether to keep the gate open. I lock onto an anchor stone I am familiar with and shift everything inside the spell form to that anchor stone, hundreds of miles away. If I hit my target, the air around the spell form in Artiria will be pushed away instantly, causing a booming sound. If anyone is inside the target area when I teleport us, they will likely be killed."

I nodded. "Impressive. Sounds like an easy way to assassinate someone."

"Perhaps. However, defenses against teleporting are simple, and if there is too much mass to displace on the other end, I will get a massive backlash and risk burning my channels. Also, the teleporting mage must be intimately familiar with the destination and needs to include themself in the teleportation. The disgruntled dwarf mentioned that there are not many displacement mages in Esenhem—the magic affinity is rare in elves, and many of my specialty have killed themselves during a relocation."

She finished with Ginger and stepped back. "A fine warhorse. I need to finish my preparations. After the stories I heard about you, I thought you would be— different." I didn't have a chance to ask what stories she had heard about me, as her guards shielded her while she prepared.

115

Maveith moved off to talk to the halfling on the wagon, and I mounted Ginger to walk her a little and feel out my new saddle. Before I knew it, one of the elven guards asked everyone to move inside the spell form. Another guard walked the perimeter and barked, "If you want to get there in one piece, make sure all your body parts are inside the outer circle!"

The golden-haired elf mage remained in the center of the formation with four guards keeping people at a distance while she worked. I had enough experience now to feel the aether saturating the metal spell form we were standing on. I could feel the aether coming from deep in the earth, not from the mage. Just as I was puzzling out that she was tapping into a ley line, the air gained a strong scent of ozone, and there was brief darkness before the sky and surrounding walls shifted.

Lazy clouds moved above us, and the sun had jumped to a new location in the sky. The courtyard walls were much higher and made of a darker stone. Large trees extended high in the sky, reminding me of the hearth tree in Caelora. The trees were not alone, as stone structures challenged some of the trees for dominance in the skyline.

The ozone scent dissipated and the familiar scent of salt air replaced it. We had moved four hundred miles across Esenhem, all the way to the opposite coast. The mage returned to my side as the others started moving toward guards dressed in off-yellow uniforms. As she moved past me, she said, "I will see you in the morning, adventurer. I am your ride to Gramney."

Before Maveith and I could move for the exit ourselves, a tall man in plate armor approached us. The armor was polished, but there was almost no sound as he moved. His confident gait, chiseled jaw, and hard eyes told me he had seen his fair share of combat. Maveith moved to my side, sensing a confrontation. I thought I could see the top of a guild medallion hanging around the man's neck.

He gave me something like a salute, his sword arm touching his opposite shoulder in deference. "Eryk Marko and Maveith Stoneskin. I am Knight-Banner Cordin Lucusta of the Duchy of Manch. I am here to escort you to the Adventurers Hall."

"Why do we need an escort?" I asked, somewhat concerned.

"The Artiria Guildmaster would like to speak with you and has rooms ready for you. I will accompany you to Gramney in the morning to make sure you deliver your message," the warrior stated flatly. There was clearly more going on here than I was privy to. I looked up to Maveith, who shrugged. The others who had come with us had almost cleared the courtyard now. Not wanting to create a scene, I followed Cordin out of the courtyard.

Chapter 262: Guildmaster Prejudice

Our armored escort walked briskly through the city, not giving us much time to take in the sights. Just like Sanco, the Esenhem capital of Artiria was meticulously clean. There was a greater grandeur to the buildings as well, but the architecture still mirrored the other elven city with its graceful curvature and lack of sharp angles on all the structures. Dark, glossy wood panels adorned the roofs of most buildings.

A number of the buildings also extended high into the sky, competing with four hearth trees that I guessed marked the corners of the city. These hearth trees, however, could not compete with the grandeur of the one in Caelora. Perhaps these trees were younger, or their growth had been controlled.

Maveith still received his fair share of stares, but they were more in passing than intense study. I guessed this was since he was not as unique here. Elves dominated the streets, but humans, halflings, dwarves, and even the occasional orc and catkin walked among them. I tried not to gawk, but still, my head could not help turning to watch the unfamiliar races pass. Two local city guards escorted a large reptilian man matching Maveith in height. These city guards had off-yellow uniforms, differing from the pea-green uniforms in Sanco. Each of the elven cities was ruled by a Regent and maintained its own martial force.

From what I had learned about Esenhem customs, the long-lived soldiers and guards were trained individually, not as a unit. This meant they did poorly when forming large armies, which put them at a disadvantage against organized armies like the Telhians.

"Are there any goliaths in the city?" Maveith's deep voice asked our escort.

"There is a delegation in the Court of Regents. Maybe four goliaths if I recall. I have only been to court once, and there are delegations from most nations in Desia," the knight said helpfully.

"From Stone Mountain Island?" Maveith asked hopefully.

The knight slowed for a few steps, thinking. "No. The Blackwood, I think." Maveith's excitement quickly diminished.

Maveith turned to me to explain, "There is a small city of goliaths on the other continent. The Stone Mountain Island clans have little contact with them even though they are just a day's sail away. They have different values from those of the clans." The knight turned slightly, clearly interested in learning more, but held his tongue when Maveith didn't elaborate further.

We soon found ourselves at the Adventurers Hall, but I would have been content to explore the city. It was a modest structure, two stories and mostly of dark granite. It stood in the shade of one of the hearth trees. The entrance was a massive tace wood door that was engraved with the Guild's branching tree symbol.

Cordin led us around back to the stables, and I handed off Ginger's care. Cordin's impatience led us immediately through a back door. The smell of food and ale mingled with the sound of stringed instruments and a melodic voice. It was one of the few doors I had seen that Maveith was not required to duck under since I had met him.

A standard-looking inn's common room greeted us. Tables were filled with elves, humans, and one pair of dwarves. Two elves strummed instruments while a third crooned a soft melody in Elvish. Maveith got some curious glances, but no one openly stared. I could tell from experience that these men and women were combat-seasoned. Cordin didn't hesitate as he walked across the room, passing a long bar lined with shelves of colorful bottles and staffed by a young-looking, female elven barkeep, who smiled in welcome as we passed. The knight was headed toward the back room, and we followed.

It felt like we were being dragged along. I wanted to relax and take in the sights of this unfamiliar city. Also, my Hound training was screaming at me to be better prepared for these impromptu encounters. There was no choice now but to find out what the Guildmaster wanted. We followed Cordin to a large, spacious office where an elf with long, gray-streaked black hair sat behind a desk that was far too big for him. Dozens of orderly stacks of paper covered the desk as he worked on a folder in front of him, not looking up.

Cordin, having completed his task, announced us: "The two from Sanco are here." When the Guildmaster waved his hand in acknowledgment, Cordin left, closing the door behind him. The Guildmaster didn't look up as he read and then put a quill to paper. He wrote for almost ten minutes before putting down the implement. I sensed that he was testing our patience on purpose, so I waited.

When he looked up, I could read his eyes. He was not happy to see us. He studied Maveith first before studying me. "You are the Telhian?" It was an accusation, and it was easy to tell he did not like the Empire.

"I am not Telhian. I came from the Empire, but I am not a citizen." A flash of surprise crossed his face and quickly disappeared. I assumed it was due to my proficiency in Elvish rather than my statement. Maveith stirred uncomfortably next to me as tension hung in the air.

His eyes narrowed. "But you were of the Legion?" I began to see where his anger was rooted. I shouldn't be surprised that he had learned I was a legionnaire. Desdemona probably included it in a report to the Guild.

I responded carefully. "I was conscripted, yes. I took the opportunity to flee in the confusion of the war."

He shook his head negatively, still discontented with my presence. "And Guildmaster Theodas raised you to silver for a single battle." It was more a statement than a question. His voice remained hard. "I have dealt with your ilk before—ex-legionnaires who say they are abandoning the Empire and seeking sanctuary in the Guild." His hard eyes looked through me. I sensed some aether in the air, but my bone inscriptions didn't react.

He continued, "Most of you are spies. If I find your loyalty to your First Citizen masters has not been broken, I will see you excised from the Guild and have a bounty placed on your head." His threat was stated in a cold, flat tone that sent a chill through me. Not so much from the words, but from the power I sensed from this elf. It reminded me of Traeliorn, the summoner.

Maveith didn't like his tone and defended me. "Eryk is no spy."

"Friend goliath, you should keep better company. Life is too short to be caught in the Empire's web," the Guildmaster replied coolly. "You are not to leave the Guild Hall while you are in Artiria. You are not to speak to anyone until you leave in the morning. That is an order, as you are on an official Guild assignment. You are dismissed." He pulled another stack of paper toward him to continue his work, ignoring us.

I was worried about the Guildmaster because we would have to pass through Artiria again on our way to the Boutan Caliphate, but I didn't think it was the right time to use my minuscule powers of persuasion to change his opinion of me.

When we exited the office, a young elf awaited us to escort us to our room. The plain room had two beds, and the only positive aspect of our confinement was that they were big enough for Maveith. There was no window or hearth. After talking with the Guildmaster, this felt more like a cell.

Since we had not been given a meal, I handed Maveith a burrito as I prepared to get some sleep. He was clearly still reacclimating to his ring as he munched away loudly. The beds were not uncomfortable, but an acidic scent hung in the air. Maybe the lingering scent of a cleaning solution. Maveith was asleep before me, and I utilized the dreamscape amulet to review the little information I had about the Duchy of Manch.

In the morning, we were escorted by Knight Cordin back to the courtyard for the teleportation to Gramney. The elven displacement mage smirked knowingly when we arrived. She definitely knew more about me than she had let on and was probably aware of the frosty reception I had received.

She didn't seem to share the Guildmaster's antipathy toward me. It made me concerned that perhaps her interest in me was based on the number of artifacts Maveith and I declared at customs, or maybe the existence of my dimensional space.

I couldn't resist not knowing and walked up to her, her guards becoming alert and their hands resting on their sheathed weapons. I produced and handed her an apple, which she took after a moment. "A dungeon apple," I explained. Ginger neighed in dismay while Maveith held her reins. I was giving away her apples, so her distress was understandable.

I assumed the mage had been informed about the crate of apples I had shown at customs, but judging from her surprise, maybe not. She inspected it for a while before taking a bite. Her eyes quickly widened, and she lost some decorum as she devoured the offering. I could tell that just like Zyna, the elven mage had received some euphoric effect from the dungeon aether saturating the apple. She regained some composure. "Where?" was all she asked as she licked the juice from her lips.

"A dungeon in the Empire," I hedged, not telling her more. "How difficult will it be to port back from Gramney to Artiria?" I figured I had gained enough goodwill from the apple to exchange it for some information.

"The Duchy does not have displacement mages capable. Myself and one other share the duties among the Esenhem cities. Between us, we usually port to Gramney once a month, but … we have been off schedule. I will return to Esenhem with my guards immediately after arriving. Another return trip may be some time away," the elf woman explained.

Maveith became uneasy. I had told him we would only spend a few days in Gramney to drop off my passengers and search for Castile. He announced his concerns. "The halfling trader said the Esenhem war effort was interfering with the schedule."

"The war is of Telhian machinations. We warned the Emperor to leave what was buried, buried. He did not listen," the golden-haired mage said tersely. "We reclaimed the Isle of Amatalhos peaceably. No one was killed, and we allowed those who wished to leave to do so. We only stepped foot on Telhian soil when he did not heed our warnings."

"What warning? Why is unearthing Atlantium, the city of the Titans, bad?" I asked politely.

The mage was more shocked than I thought a centuries-old woman should be. Her jaw flapped for a moment. "You are remarkably—well informed." Still, her words had difficulty coming, and I assumed it was because she did not know the answer to my question. "Humans live brief lives. They forget the ancient histories."

When she did not go on, I asked, "Will you enlighten me, then?"

She gathered her thoughts. "The Titans destroyed the world once with their magics. Whatever is buried there might do so again. No man, elf, dwarf, or orc should possess such power," she said vehemently. "Telhians have long abused their power and cannot be trusted with more."

"And the elves have never abused their power?" I questioned her, but her face immediately darkened. I thought this would lead to a cordial discussion, but she ended the conversation there.

"I need to have message sendings sent to make sure our arrival zone is clear." Her guards interposed themselves between us, and I felt I had angered her. I was certain elven history had its share of tyrants, but she wouldn't listen to me. Personally, I guessed the elves just wanted the power buried in Atlantium for themselves— otherwise, the timing of their annexation of the Isle of Amatalhos didn't make sense.

When we were alone, Maveith asked worriedly, "We are not going to wait a month in Gramney for the elven displacement mage, are we?"

He had been very patient with our progress toward the Boutan Caliphate. This trip to Gramney was the first part of our journey that would take us in the wrong direction. I made him a promise. "No. If we cannot find transport after a week, we will make our way on foot." He nodded thankfully and relaxed. I would not have shown the same patience if it had been one of my sisters.

The circle was even more crowded than it had been the last time. Most people looked like traders, with oversized packs or densely-packed carts. The elven mage worked as the group pressed together, her eyes darting to me more than once. I felt the aether in the metal runes beneath our feet build to a crescendo as they drew from the ley line, and after a brief period of darkness, we were standing hundreds of miles away.

Gramney was not what I expected. Our arrival was heralded with horns and soldiers surrounding the runic stonework upon which we arrived. They wore dark-blue uniforms and tabards emblazoned with a rearing golden unicorn. Knight Cordin's impatience and recognition had us quickly past the guards. We fell in step with him, and I asked, "Are we heading to the Adventurers Guild?"

"Where else would we be headed? You have your missive to be delivered, and it will complete my escort," he replied somewhat impatiently.

"We are a Guild assignment for you?" Maveith asked, interested.

"Yes. Guildmaster Theodas contacted me. I am to ensure you don't cause trouble and get you safely to the Guild Hall in Gramney." He paused and pointed at a large wooden building. "The Guild Hall. I have to check in with my baron, but I will be in the Guild Hall later tonight to collect my payment. Perhaps we can share a drink then." He saluted with his fist and walked away. I secured Ginger in the stables before entering.

The Guild Hall reminded me of the one in Telha, albeit with many more adventurers. My eyes passed over the crowd, looking for an orc, but I was disappointed. Maveith drew some curious stares, but no one moved to engage us. I walked slowly past the posting board and noted many of the postings centered around the dungeon outside the city. Mostly, local restaurants wanted meat, fungi, or flora found within.

As we reached the counter, an older woman with creased smile lines on her face asked our business. "We have a missive from Guildmaster Theodas in Sanco." I placed the sealed and rolled document on the counter, expecting to be brought before the Guildmaster.

"Very good. If it is tied to a posting, please present your guild medallions," she said politely while maintaining her smile. Her language was close to Telhian—Latin, but she had a strong accent and I needed to focus to understand her.

"Do I not need to hand it to him in person?" I asked.

"You could wait. He is currently training in the dungeon and will be back late tomorrow," she replied patiently.

"I see. You can hold it then." I had already received my reward in the form of transport to Gramney. Even if something extra was attached to completing this delivery, I doubted it was substantial.

I turned away from the counter and looked through the postings with Maveith. Maveith asked me questions as we read. "Are we going to take an assignment?"

"No, just trying to act normal. We are not even going to stay in the Guild Hall." I checked to make sure we were not being overheard. "It is time to unload my passengers." Maveith nodded a little too excitedly for my liking.

Gramney was less clean than the elven cities. The fetid sewer under the streets was noticeable in the air near the street grates, and the alleys were filled with vagrants and debris. Still, the city felt safe enough with cheerful pairs of guards walking the streets.

It took us half a day to find acceptable accommodations in a wealthy district. The inn was called Crescent Crossroads. I thought it might be the most luxurious inn in all of Gramney. I rented an entire floor suite with five rooms and a massive common room connecting them. There was also a private bath with running water—which may have been why I selected this particular inn. It was time to consume the apex water essence and unlock the affinity. Having a bath nearby would be welcome.

Maveith and I were in one of the rooms with two large beds. Maveith sat on the bed across from me, bouncing and shaking the frame, as he had never seen springs on a bed before. I could only imagine what the people on the floor below us were thinking. "It's too soft and bouncy. I don't think I could sleep." His large mass was sinking into the soft mattress every time he landed. If he lay down, it would probably swallow him.

"You can always sleep on the floor, Maveith," I said, irritated. I had paid a large gold coin for four nights, and that was supposedly a two-gold discount, according to the innkeeper. At least Ginger's stabling was included in the cost. With a thud, I dropped his pack onto the floor from my dimensional space. He bounced a few more times, considering, before kneeling and starting to unpack his large bedroll.

While Maveith set up his sleeping accommodations on the floor, I considered how I would release my passengers. I had four people to extract—a mother and her two children, and a First Citizen mage. The wisest choice was to bring the mother out first and get her acclimated so she could calm her children when they came out next. The mage was probably going to be trouble, but at least she was dosed with magebane poison.

"Maveith, why don't you see if there are any orc adventurers in the Guild Hall." Even though he knew the plan was to add an orc to our group to serve as a guide, he ground his teeth a little. "I don't need help with the mother and children. You can meet them when you come back." The truth was I didn't want them to be frightened by Maveith. If you didn't know goliaths were honorable people, Maveith was rather intimidating.

He finally let out a long sigh of disappointment. "Okay, I will inquire. I will bring back dinner for us and them." He had been drooling at all the food carts as we searched for an inn.

After Maveith left, I went to the most opulent room in the suite. This was clearly for a lord. The large window offered a marvelous view overlooking the square, which featured a massive statue of a pegasus in flight with an armored knight on its back.

From Hearne, I knew that was impossible. Pegasi were rare creatures, but they were more gliders than flyers and couldn't get aloft with any significantly weighted rider. As far as aerial steeds, griffins were larger and more powerful, but still required slight riders to avoid fatigue. I briefly wondered how Raelia was doing. Her griffin egg should have hatched by now—or at least I hoped it had hatched. It would have been cruel to give her an egg with a dead embryo.

I pulled the window's blinds closed, lit the room's three oil lamps, and produced my glowstone. I placed clothes for the three on the bed with the jewelry the mother had packed herself. When she appeared, she crumpled to the floor. I had given her two oblivion pills, and to her, that had happened just moments ago.

I placed her body on the bed and untied her. She was quite beautiful, with silky blond hair, vibrant skin, and delicate facial features. At that moment, I realized I had never learned her name. Centurion Sergius never mentioned it, and she never told me. I remembered that her children's names were Marius and Clara.

I watched her sleeping, her chest rising and falling, then turned away, suddenly feeling creepy. Maybe I could wake her? I shook her shoulder strongly until her groggy eyelids fluttered. She was going to have to fight off the effects. She had difficulty speaking and her eyes wouldn't focus on my face, but she had some recollection of what had happened. "Where?" she asked, confused.

"You and your children are in Gramney in the Duchy of Manch," I said softly.

She was slow to process what I said, but memories suddenly came back to her. She tried to stand but failed to do so, falling to the floor in a heap. She was drowsy and fighting the effects of the oblivion pills. It was stupid for me to wake her. I should have had patience and let her wake up on her own. As I helped her onto the bed, she pushed me away. "Don't touch me!" She then remembered I had her children, so she needed to be polite to me. "I can manage," she said more civilly.

I let her get on the bed, and I could tell she was fighting off sleep. Two oblivion pills were a lot for her slight frame. "Just rest for now. You are safe, as are your children, I promise." Her eyes told me she didn't believe me, but sleep soon took her.

Maveith knocked a few hours later while I watched over my victim. I waved him in, and he brought a feast in numerous canvas bags. He must have hit every vendor stall in the city: mini pies baked on formed wax leaves, different types of skewered meat and vegetables, three different kinds of bread, and a bag of cookies with jam baked into them. The crumbs on his clothes showed that he had done a lot of sampling on his expedition.

After unloading his haul, he stood over the woman, studying her and then looking at me. "She is pretty. The children?"

"Not yet. She is working through the effects of two oblivion pills." Maveith nodded in understanding and looked at all the food he had brought. I asked, "Any luck with an orc guide?"

He chewed his cheek unhappily. "There are three orc adventurers in the city. I have two addresses. The third is guarding a trade caravan and will return in a month. It would be best if you interviewed them," he stated with a note of pleading.

Maveith did not talk quietly. The woman fluttered her eyes and Maveith leaned over her, smiling. She screamed as her eyes focused on his gray, beaming face. It was just as I feared. I pulled away the confused Maveith and soothed her. "It is fine. Maveith is a goliath. A good goliath."

Seeing me, her scream died. "I … I … I am sorry." She was still disoriented and slightly terrified. I motioned Maveith to the door in case someone came to investigate, but it was a short, piercing scream, so maybe it went unnoticed.

"What is your name?" I asked with a friendly smile.

"You don't know my name?" She suddenly sounded exasperated and exhausted. "Viridia Janus, wife of Milo Janus. Are you not the one who kidnapped me? Are my children here?" She had not seen my face, evidently, but she should have recognized my voice. She sat up, taking in the luxurious room. She was shaking but hiding her fear well.

"Give me a moment and I will check on Clara. You can change out of your nightwear." I pointed at the pile of clothes. "The jewelry you packed is there as well." Viridia blinked her vision clear, fighting off the fading effects of the oblivion pills. I moved into the common room, closing the door behind me. I went into the smallest room, probably for servants, and pulled the girl onto the bed. She had been sleeping peacefully when I pulled her into my dimensional space months ago.

Parts of her mattress, sheets, and blankets appeared with her. If I had placed her into my space by touching her, I might have been able to differentiate the various fabrics from the girl. The girl was a miniature version of her mother and sleeping heavily, oblivious to her fate. I removed the cut fabric gently to hide the evidence of my powerful spell form. I was going to get her mother, but didn't need to.

Viridia Janus came through the door, ran to her daughter, and started crying into her chest. Clara stirred and asked her mother what was wrong. The mother just wrapped her arms around her daughter and hugged her to her body while standing.

I guessed the girl's age to be ten, not past accepting affection from her mother. Viridia had clearly doubted my sincerity in guaranteeing the safety of her children. The young girl hugged her mother back, confused and on the verge of tears herself because she didn't know what was going on.

"Where are we? Where is Marius? Is father home?" the girl asked her mother, who cradled her to her chest. Viridia looked to me for answers as she continued to hold her child against her chest.

"Marius is well. I do not know the fate of Milo Janus," I told them truthfully.

Maveith stood in the doorway, taking up the entire doorframe. Clara noticed him for the first time, her eyes widening in shock. She was not afraid, though. After Viridia's reaction, Maveith was more hesitant. "I have some food in the other room," he offered, pointing awkwardly.

"Mommy, is that a giant? Did you get me a giant for my birthday?" the young girl asked excitedly.

"Of course, because they were all out of unicorns," Viridia said sarcastically. The young girl didn't catch the sarcasm and pushed away from her mother's hold to approach Maveith. Viridia calmed down and whispered, "How did we get to Gramney, and where is my son?"

I would do my best to keep my secrets, and I tried to distract her with past events. "I smuggled you here through a portal. The Emperor is dead, and the Telhian Empire is besieged from four sides. I suggest you and your family make a new life here with your wealth."

"If I had known you were telling me the truth, I would have opened the secret vault in the villa." She sighed resignedly. "Still, we have trade assets and agents in the Duchy of Manch that were out of the Emperor's reach, and the olive fields should be fruiting in a year or two. Milo can build his network again." The way she was talking, she still thought her husband was alive, but knowing Centurion Sergius, that was unlikely.

"Can you control your son when I wake him? Almost no time will have passed for him," I asked her, wanting to finish the reunion. Her emerald eyes slowly gained life and sparkled with hope. She was accepting her fate and slowly formulating a way to survive.

Getting her son out was slightly trickier. When I stashed him away, he had been awake and walking onto the villa's balcony. I was in another small room when Marius appeared. He was sweaty, barefoot, and shirtless. His confusion quickly turned into an attack as he lunged at me. I sidestepped his tackle attempt and called for his mother as I threw a wet towel at him. Viridia rushed into the room and didn't cry this time as she wrapped up her confused son. She was calming him as I stepped out.

I checked on Maveith and the girl. They were in the lord's suite having something akin to a tea party on the floor. Clara was asking Maveith a stream of questions while she plated food for him. He seemed happy, and I noticed the checkers board Desdemona had given him to his right, so I left him to his fate. Did I do the right thing? Yes. Would this goodwill come back to bite me in the ass eventually? Probably.

I still had one passenger, but this had taken a lot out of me. The First Citizen was a mage and much more dangerous than the mother and children. I entered our room and rested on the bed while I ran the apex water essence across the back of my knuckles. It was a fascinating essence with the appearance of shifting water inside.

Maveith arrived in our room late at night. "I hope you let her win a game or two," I said, smirking.

"I let her win them all," he said loudly, then quieted, worried the girl might have heard.

"I am going to use this tonight," I said, tossing the sphere lightly in my hand. "Can you watch over me and help me clean up after?"

"Of course!" Maveith said agreeably. "Let me first make something to cover my mouth and nose."

Maveith stayed in the bathroom with me as I prepared to take the essence to unlock the water affinity. He had watched over me in the Shimmering Labyrinth when I unlocked a new affinity, so he knew how painful, messy, and foul it would be. We had wet blankets, and the modest tub was filled with water for me to scrub right after.

Maveith had prepared everything but looked concerned and reluctant. "Eryk, are you sure you want to do this?"

I held up the apex water essence to him. "All you, big guy. I don't need any more." He shook his head and backed away as he held up his hands. I shrugged, stripped down to just my loincloth, and lay down on the wet towels. If I had the urge to vomit, a bucket was nearby. We were as prepared as we could be.

"Bottoms up," I saluted Maveith and deposited the essence in my mouth. It tasted like sugar water as it dissolved, and I quickly swigged some water from a canteen. Maybe that wasn't very smart, as I would probably throw it up, but my mouth was already cottony.

I focused inward and felt the aether spread through my body from my stomach. When it found my aether core, all the water aether flowing through me raced toward it like magnets attracting each other. That was as long as I could focus inward, as every muscle in my body contracted, contorting my body into weird poses. I forced myself into a protective fetal position, thinking I just needed to ride it out for a minute or so. Anyone can deal with intense pain for a minute.

My skin burned as a slimy, foul-smelling substance was pushed out my pores. My loincloth was suddenly full of shit and urine, but I didn't remember releasing it. My heart raced and I panted to catch my breath. This was by far my worst experience. It sounded like I was underwater as Maveith's voice tried to reach me.

"Eryk, what's wrong!?" He sounded a bit panicked.

Through clenched teeth, I rasped out, "Should be fine in a minute."

"It has been almost half an hour!" Maveith said worriedly. *Ah, shit. Well, that sucks.* Then I passed out.

When I woke, my suffering had not ended. My muscles would not work; having been seized for too long, the ligaments had been strained, and my muscles were brutalized. I still tried to move, but all I could do was shudder. I moved my head with great difficulty and couldn't see Maveith. Had he abandoned me? No, he wouldn't do that. Crusty, acidic salt caked my lips as I tried to speak. My vocal cords were sore and would not work—had I been screaming?

I tried to channel my healing spell form, but I couldn't control the aether. It felt like sand running through my fingers. Panic welled up inside me as I feared I might have permanently damaged my ability to channel aether. However, it wasn't like the fire in my aether channels when I had burned them.

Instead, it was my abused aether core that was not directing the aether as I willed it. I couldn't even focus inward to study the problem, as the pain was too distracting. I fumbled for the lip of the tub, planning to pull myself inside, but stopped. That would be stupid; I might drown if I passed out again.

I released the tub, grunting as the floor greeted my face. The door creaked open. "Maveith?" I tried to say, but it just came out as a hiss of air.

Viridia stood in the doorway, her hand covering her nose and mouth with a wet cloth. Her voice was slightly muffled. "He left to get help. I said I would watch you, but the smell was too foul. I have been waiting just outside the door." I could see her daughter just beyond her. Clara got a whiff of the odor and vomited in the common room. Viridia hissed at her son to help his sister clean the mess. She came in and closed the door behind her.

I pointed weakly at the canteen, and she retrieved it and fed the contents to me. I greedily drank it down, coughing because it was so hard to swallow, but realizing I needed the fluids. "How long?" I said with a sore larynx after finishing the remainder of the canteen.

"Maveith left perhaps two hours ago. Before that … I think he said you passed out an hour ago, or you took something an hour ago. He was frantic. Are you poisoned?" she asked as she took some towels and started rubbing away the crusty film on my skin.

"Something like that," I said painfully. I could barely move. I thought the apex water essence had finished its work and my body had been tempered, or at least my aether core had been. I tried thrice to look inward at my aether core, failing each time.

"Whatever you are doing, stop. Your skin is burning up, Eryk," Viridia said in a scolding tone only mothers had. *Had I even told her my name?* Maveith must have given it to her. To her credit, Viridia did not shy away from my foulness as she worked to clean me.

"Into the tub," she ordered with a huff after she had fouled a half dozen towels. I almost laughed, as the simple act was too much for me. She helped me to my feet, and I fell into the cool water, almost pulling Viridia with me. Water rushed over the side, soaking the woman. It had been warm when I consumed the essence hours ago, but now it was cold and it numbed my aching body.

"We will work from the head down," she announced determinedly. She worked on my hair and face, making coughing sounds as she scrubbed. "It would be easier to just shave your head." I looked at her and was about to agree, but she added with a weak smile, "I was kidding. Eventually, we will get it all out."

The water had turned to a murky brown by the time she finished scrubbing my hair and face. She helped me out of the tub to drain and clean it. I lay on the wooden floor and fell asleep from exhaustion. She roused me softly. "It's clean with fresh water. Back into the tub," she ordered. We repeated this a third time before the water finally stayed clear. I heard the door to the suite open, and Maveith's heavy footfalls sounded as he rapidly crossed to the bathroom.

The door slammed open, and he coughed as he inhaled. "You're awake!" He said, relieved. "I found a healer of mages! Took most of the night and some convincing to get him to come." His head whipped around, looking behind him, and he thundered out the door and down the stairs, returning with a man in a nightshirt who was sweating heavily. The healer had age lines on his face, which was surprising given his pointed ears. Maveith introduced him awkwardly: "This is Elaro Morlamin. He is the best healer in the city."

"Not the best. But the best for a mage in distress." The healer caught his breath in the doorway, putting his hand over his mouth as he took in the scene. "How many did you consume, boy?" he asked with his hand over his nose. "No time to lie. I have never seen an emergence this extreme in all my considerable years."

"Just an apex water essence," I said with a dry throat.

"Apex?" He sounded impressed but frowned. "How many apex essences, and were they *all* water? You didn't try to emerge more than one affinity at once? If so, you are lucky to be alive," he said as he moved into the room. Maveith and the healer squeezed out Viridia due to the size of the bathroom, but she was probably glad for some fresher air. Maveith had apparently given the mage healer some background about what I had done. I didn't blame him, as convincing the mage to come here must have been difficult in the middle of the night.

"Just one," I said, but the look on his face told me he didn't believe me. The elf knelt at the edge of the tub, a spell forming between his hands as he studied me. The faint aetheric lines were traced too quickly for me to follow. His brow furrowed as the spell form completed, and his eyes stared blankly ahead. I could feel my body being violated by the spell form and reflexively tried to resist. The more I tried, the more the pain flared.

The elf shook his head, disappointed. "Your aether core is a mess, boy. It is leaking aether like a sieve." He muttered to himself in Elvish, "Just one, and I'm the son of a dragon." His hand roamed over my chest, around my heart where my aether core resided. "You are fortunate. Nothing that cannot heal itself in time."

"Why does it still hurt so much?" I asked with some relief, knowing I would heal and beyond caring that Viridia was hovering just beyond the door.

"You created a new facet on your aether core to create water aether." He switched to Elvish. "Waste of good apex essences if you ask me." He continued in the local language, "This filth"—he indicated the soiled towels—"is your body removing anything antithetical to water aether in your body." He looked over the bathroom and sighed. "When you first create an affinity aspect on your aether core, it is usually quite bad. Each successive essence is less—impactful. By the fifth or sixth essence, it calms quite a bit, and you don't even stink." He chuckled, then coughed after breathing in too much. I figured I had completed the entire purification process with one essence due to my convergence spell form.

"It wasn't this bad before," I said defensively. I didn't want him to think I was an idiot. I was sliding lower in the tub and forced myself to sit up, wincing at the effort.

The elf was shocked. "How many affinities have you unlocked? What fool taught you it was worth unlocking a new affinity, boy? You would need a hundred apex essences to learn the simplest spell form. An utter waste for a warrior." He reverted to Elvish to curse me: "The foolishness of youth to grasp at what he cannot have."

"This is my third," I replied in Elvish. He was momentarily shocked by my words, either because they were Elvish or that I had unlocked two other essences, or both.

"Third?" he said in mild surprise. After regaining his tongue, he was now speaking only in Elvish and ignoring the fact that he had insulted me twice. He created a more complex spell form and entered his examination again. My body still resisted his probing, but I could not stop him. "Your core is—complex. How many affinities do you have?" he asked as he continued to inspect me with interest.

I weighed the importance of telling him the truth. He was clearly a skilled and probably powerful mage who I knew almost nothing about. But he was my best chance to recover my magic. "Thirteen," I replied in Elvish.

The elf mage stopped and sat back on his heels away from the tub, stunned. "Are you lying to me, boy?" At least the mage couldn't decipher what affinities I had by his intrusive efforts.

I looked him in the eye. "Yes, I am lying. It is actually fourteen now if I just added the water affinity. When can I channel aether again?" I asked impatiently. Maybe the elf could heal my injuries, and this folly could be put behind me.

He studied me for a long time before responding. "Let me explain. Your core is small. Twenty-five on the scale maybe." He didn't wait for me to reply. "Your core didn't have enough space to add the water affinity, so it distorted your aether core, fracturing it to make space. Right now, it cannot hold aether with the damage, and it is leaking aether as fast as it is pulling it in." He sighed, looking even older. "The good news is that it will heal like any physical injury. I just need to seal your core away for a time. It will be unpleasant not to have access to your aether, but find me in two weeks, and I will inspect it. If it has recovered enough, I will remove the seal." He shrugged. "Or you can let your aether core leak and eventually collapse and never use magic again. It is, of course, your choice."

I had a dozen questions, but Elaro didn't wait and once again invaded my body with his spell knowing what my choice would be. This time, it felt like he was squeezing my chest, and I couldn't breathe. Then, a great emptiness filled me. It was as if my heart was missing, but that organ thudded steadily in my chest. I realized the empty feeling was because I couldn't sense any aether in my body. Either there was none, or my aether sensing required my aether core.

The elf mage looked exhausted and stood unsteadily. His nightshirt was soaked in sweat and bathwater. "Your goliath friend knows where I live. Do not try to use aether. I have sealed your core, and the protective shell may shatter if you try. Avoid all potions that restore aether as well. Normal healing potions are fine, but use them in moderation."

That was why I couldn't heal. My aether core had no aether to funnel through the spell form. "Do we owe you gold?" I asked as I tried to rise.

"You can pay me when I see you again. If you encounter—difficulties, you can call on me before then," he said as he continued out the door. I was slightly worried. Was there a healer's confidentiality code? Would he figure out what I had done and keep my secret? Maveith helped me to my bed.

Over the next week of bed rest, my body healed fast with the help of three orc Pathfinder potions, but I thought my taste buds had melted off my tongue. After four more days, I was walking gingerly outside to get some sun. Maveith was always at my side, watching over me. It was frustrating to be unable to heal away all my aches and pains with just a focused thought.

Viridia had been incredibly helpful over the past two weeks, but as soon as I could walk and care for myself, she took her children in the morning and left. Her husband's trading company had a small office in the city. Viridia had been trying to prove her identity and, during a Truthseeker's interrogation, had finally established that she was not dead and that she was Milo Janus's wife.

Once confirmed, she learned that her husband was dead and that she had inherited everything—offices and investments in seven cities in four different nations, a plantation with five hundred acres of young olive trees, and three merchant ships. There had been five ships, but one was missing at sea and the other had been sold to pay debts.

The woman was not at all helpless and planned to run the trading company, and to get revenge against the Telhian Empire for having her husband killed. We had gotten close while she cared for me, but nothing physical developed between us, as she was more concerned with protecting her children.

During my recovery, Maveith had been disappointed that I could not retrieve the dreamscape amulet for him to use, but he shared in Viridia's caretaker duties. Healing mostly naturally had not been fun. Even with my impressive constitution, it had been a week before I could move without pain. Then, over the following days, I gradually began physical training.

At first, Viridia's son Marius had hated me. He blamed me for his abduction to a foreign country and for his father's death. I couldn't blame him. Even his mother explaining that I had actually saved them didn't help. Then, as I worked on my sword forms in the suite, he practically begged me to teach him. Once I agreed, he wouldn't shut up.

Marius had wanted to be a legionnaire before the Emperor had targeted his family. Now, he just wanted to fight to defend his mother and sister. It was admirable, and we developed a mentor-mentee friendship. Toward the end of my recovery, he had even started pushing his mother toward me, but I was not a good choice for a surrogate father, and Viridia was grieving the loss of her husband.

After almost two weeks I was getting stir-crazy being in the suite, so I walked the streets with Maveith. We had no destination or plan in mind. It was just a chance to get some fresh air. We were also looking for signs of Castile and the company. It had been three weeks since I had heard of the death of the Emperor, but I couldn't access the blood compass to see if Castile was closer.

Maveith had finally kept his ring on and grumbled about how the smells of the carts did not elicit a reaction from his stomach. We still stopped at most stalls to sample the wares and spend some coppers. Fortunately, I had plenty of coins in the many pouches on the artifact belt.

We had just turned down a crafter street where woodwrights and metalsmiths worked. The sound of saws and hammers echoed in the air as we walked. Maveith was drawing a fair amount of attention, so I gave him some space to be admired, searching the small shops for something interesting to inspect.

At one of the forges, I paused as two smiths yelled back and forth. "You are a fool! Just listen to me. You need to fold it and hammer it back to length before folding it again!" The familiar woman's voice was unmistakable.

"Old woman, out of my forge! I do not need to be instructed by you!" a hoarse, angry male voice barked.

I stepped into the forge to confirm my guess. A much thinner Ignis stood there, confronting a smith. She was in dirty, baggy clothes. "Let me at it and I will show you how it is done," Ignis said, arguing with the sooty, thick-armed smith.

"It is my forge! Out! Or I will call the guard. Go harass another smith!" he bellowed at her.

Ignis growled but turned away and took one step toward me. Even though it had only been a few months, she looked years older with new lines on her face. Recognition flashed on her face when she saw me. I crafted a smirk. "Hey, Ignis. Are you available to make me a new suit of armor?"

Ignis cracked a smile. Her front tooth was chipped. "The old fire witch made it then? Where is she? She better have another bottle of that elven wine you gave her. I need to forget some things."

I moved closer to keep our conversation private. "She didn't make it. At least, I couldn't locate her with my blood compass." Ignis's expression fell at my words. I was curious about how she was tied to the plot to kill the Emperor, so I decided to invite her to join us. "We have a suite at an inn. Plenty of extra rooms if you are interested." She had gotten close enough that her body odor offended me. "We have a bath," I added as more incentive. She decided to trust me and nodded, but she might not have been in a position to decline my offer given her wretched state.

Ignis had a slight limp as she walked back with me. "Why is the goliath following us?" she asked, jerking her thumb at the looming Maveith two steps behind us.

"There is a goliath following us?" Maveith said jokingly, turning around to look, chuckling. I was glad he was in a good mood. He had been anxious about being delayed in our quest for the last two weeks while I healed, but he never complained.

I looked back at Maveith, offering him a smirk. "Maveith is a friend. His sense of humor is still in development. We fled the Empire together and joined the Adventurers Guild. We can talk more after you clean up."

I explained to Maveith who Ignis was. "Ignis was the best armorer for the Imperial Legion. High Mage Zyna recruited her and she was part of the conspiracy." I handed Maveith a few large silver coins. "Get Ignis some clean clothes, and whatever else she might need." Ignis took a minute to gratefully give Maveith a short list.

When we arrived at the suite, Ignis was impressed. "You have done well for yourself. Do you know anyone else who made it?"

I answered helplessly. "I don't know who else should be here. I am looking for Castile, but I have been recovering from an injury. How much did you know about the plot?" I asked seriously.

She let out a long, tired sigh. "Enough. I knew enough. I had my own part to play. Zyna warned me to run if things turned to dragon shit after news of the Emperor's death reached Telha. When I learned Antonia was dead, I left immediately. Zyna set up an account for me here at the Grand Duchy Depository, but I was waylaid on the road in Bartiradia, and they took my account marker. Now I can't claim a copper of it. I was looking for work when you found me." Ignis didn't continue and excused herself to enter the bathroom. She was a shadow of her former self. I thought the old armorer needed to mourn Zyna and the others who were lost alone.

Maveith returned before Ignis emerged. He had a large bundle of clean used clothes, packages of items Ignis had requested, and some food from the street vendors. I knocked and placed the clothes just inside the door. Ignis was still in the tub of heated water and waved me out. "Thank you, but give me another hour. This heated water is doing wonders for my old muscles and joints."

Ignis took only half that time before she emerged, looking invigorated. Maveith eagerly offered her the food he had laid out, and we sat in the common room while she stuffed herself. She was clearly hungry and barely chewed her food. She told her tale between bites.

"I didn't play a large role. I just supplied a few sets of the Imperial Armor for those infiltrating the Archives. After the news came, the palace grounds were in disarray and there weren't enough legionnaires to keep order. I left the moment I heard about Antonia's death, but the barons were already positioning themselves to grab as much power as possible. I barely made it through the portal to Macha." She had moved from meats to potatoes and finished off her meal with grilled vegetables.

She pulled her wet gray hair behind her and tied it. "I feel most sorry for the children. There must have been four hundred in classes at the Imperial Palace. Some of them have since found themselves kidnapped for leverage." Ignis sat back, finally satiated. "You need some armor? I need a place to work, and the materials." She smiled tiredly, showing her chipped tooth again.

"There probably isn't time. We are headed to the Boutan Caliphate in a few days. Maveith's sister is being held there."

"By a warlord?" she guessed. "I would go with you if I were ten years younger." She barked a contrived laugh that told me she wouldn't go even if she was ten years younger.

"Do you know anything about the Caliphate?" I asked, but Ignis was already shaking her head.

"Nothing. I talked to an orc ambassador's aide once, but he kept asking me questions about the Imperial Legion. He thought I was an ignorant, hammer-swinging bitch and would give up details of our strength." All pretense of joviality was gone. She inhaled and made a request. "If you can spare some coins so I can get some used hammers and tongs and find a place to stay, I would appreciate it."

I liked her direct, no-nonsense personality. I laughed, causing her to frown as if she thought I would say no. "Ignis, you can stay here. There are plenty of rooms. How much are your smith's tools?" Most of my coins were inaccessible in the dimensional space, but I had a lot of silver and a few gold coins in my belt.

Ignis visibly relaxed. "Twenty gold for good quality new. Twelve gold for used. But I am sure I can haggle them down to ten or less."

"And how much to rent or own a smithy?" I asked, and her eyebrow rose. She started doing some calculations in her head.

"In this city, I don't know the property cost. But in the Empire, a new forge would be a few hundred gold—five hundred on the low end. To use a smith's shop—a gold a day if he can still work at the same time. If not, two gold or more."

I dug deep into my pouch, pulling out a handful of large silver coins. I spread them on the low table between us and counted them out. Thirty-nine coins, just short of four gold. I repeated the process and her eyes narrowed as she deduced the belt pouches were more than they seemed. After I was done, two gold coins and stacks of silver coins totaling an additional ten gold coins were on the table.

"Get your tools tomorrow. We can figure out a place where you can ply your craft afterward." I nodded at her with a reassuring smile. "Get some sleep. You look better, but you need to rest."

"Too generous," Ignis whispered, but it didn't stop her from gathering the coins. "I will consider this a loan. Give me a month, and I will have your coin returned to you twofold."

I heard Ignis leave at first light. I was fairly certain she would return. I walked with Maveith to the healer's residence later in the morning. I wasn't surprised when Maveith brought us to a villa in the wealthiest district. A massive ironwood door dominated the entrance. Maveith knocked, and the door was opened by a youthful elf in formal dress. He nodded. "You return, goliath. The ambassador has been expecting you and your friend."

I looked at Maveith, irritated, as he had not told me the mage was an ambassador. I looked up at the flag over the door, and it was not the flag of Esenhem. The flag had a maroon background with an hourglass and sword clutched in the claws of an eagle. I didn't recall the flag from my studies, but there were many kingdoms in the world.

Maveith had told me the story of finding Elaro Morlamin. When I passed out, he ran to the Adventurers Guild Hall for help. At the Guild Hall, they sent him to a healer in the city. When Maveith found the healer and explained what happened, the healer said he couldn't do anything for me, but there was an elven mage healer who might. Maveith had gotten lost finding Elaro's residence, but when he found the place, he pounded on the door.

Two city guards drew swords on Maveith, but fortunately, Elaro was woken by the disturbance. It had taken Maveith some time to explain what had happened, as he was simultaneously trying to keep my secrets. Elaro, to his credit, agreed to come immediately.

The elf servant escorted us up a flight of wooden stairs to a library with floor-to-ceiling shelves. Elaro was sitting in a chair, reading. He closed the book and rose to greet us with a smile. We shook wrists, and the servant excused himself. Elaro was in fine robes, and his hair was pulled back into a braid. "Please sit! I will inspect your aether core shortly." He seemed excited. "I admit it took me nearly two days to puzzle it out. And I only figured it out after I decided you were being truthful with me!"

I sat slowly, suddenly on guard. "What did you figure out?" I asked cautiously.

"Why you had such a strong emergence with a single apex water essence." His eyes twinkled as he opened his arms, indicating his revelation. "You inscribed a convergence spell form for maximizing essences!" He seemed proud of himself. I wasn't sure if his knowing was a good or bad thing.

"Yes. You guessed correctly," I affirmed. I wasn't going to go into detail about just how strong the spell form was, though.

He clapped his hands happily. "Amazing. You are only the third person I have met in my centuries who has inscribed that spell form! Is that why you became an adventurer? Do you have one of those essence collectors?" he asked in an excited rush of words.

I wasn't sure how to respond. My pause made him wave off his questions, thinking that he had overstepped. "It is no matter. Come closer and I will inspect your core, and then we can have lunch." This was why we were here, so I rose and went to him.

His spell form violated me again, and he hemmed and hawed like he was searching for something. Maveith looked on nervously. "Is there a problem?" I asked after a few minutes.

"No. No problem. I was trying to trace out the affinities on your core. Since you have so many, it is good practice. Your aether core has restored itself enough that it shouldn't leak. When I release the constraints I placed on it, you will feel dizzy from the rush." I felt him working inside me, and then there was a euphoric rush. It was as if a part of me was being restored, and I could feel my spell forms once again. I itched to use them.

Elaro backed away. "Good. You should limit the amount of aether you push through your affinities for a month or so, but you will be fine. Lunch should be prepared." He led us to a dining room set with formal-looking dishes. Elaro had two other servants working for him, one elf woman and one human, and they helped us sit. I decided to test my access to my dimensional space and thank Elaro at the same time.

"Here, this is for you." I placed one of the dark elf red wines I had carried with me from Caelora on the table. It was still coated in a little bit of dust. He took the bottle and his eyes widened as he studied it. Each bottle had an artistic relief on the glass. I reactivated my slow aging spell form and felt no discomfort or difficulty.

"I must say, you are the most interesting person I have met in some time. Consider this sufficient payment for your treatment." That shocked me, as I had been prepared to hand over a hundred gold for his fee. He handed the bottle to the servant. "Caelorian wine, if I am not mistaken. I heard rumors that the Telhians had sent an expedition. You have explored the cursed, haunted ruins then?" he asked politely.

I was surprised, and it briefly showed on my face. I nodded at his question. "You are well connected to have knowledge of Caelora. I didn't recognize the flag above your archway ..." I left the question hanging. His servant returned with a cup of red wine, which he sniffed and sipped. He had a thoughtful but satisfied expression on his face before responding.

"You wouldn't recognize my homeland. Milvanoris fell over two hundred years ago on the other continent. The Grand Duchy is famous for taking in refugees if you have a large enough purse," he said considerately. "The Grand Duke graciously still recognizes Milvanoris as a sovereign power even though my people are scattered to the winds and our cities are buried by the sands."

Maveith only nibbled at the food and asked, "What happened to your nation?"

A pained look came over his face as he told his tale. "We were not a large elven nation by any means. Less than a hundred thousand citizens. The human Coalition of Cities played with magics beyond their control. No rain fell in our lands for three years, and we..." He paused, reconsidering his words. "I went to treat with them. They refused my overtures to end their meddling with the weather. Most of my people dispersed to find lives elsewhere as our land turned to dust and sand. Our mages tried to reverse the effects, but a weather battle between our hundred mages and a thousand human mages was not a winnable endeavor."

Maveith was listening carefully and asked, "You were the king?"

Elaro laughed. "No. My father was on the council, and I served at their will like many others. Maybe your people would consider me similar to a prince in my role. I play that part here, helping any of my people who find their way to Gramney and representing a lost kingdom in the local courts." I could tell he was unhappy talking about it, so I steered the conversation away.

I was trying something that reminded me of couscous with plenty of herbs. "Will I be able to consume any more affinity essences?"

He considered the question. "I suggest you do not try to emerge any new affinities without a mage specialist healer close by. But as for your existing affinities, yes, you can consume their affinity essences. I would still let your core rest for a month." He added, "Fourteen affinities. If I were still a researcher, I would want to study how you managed it with such a small aether core."

I felt comfortable with Elaro and asked, "Is being born with eleven affinities rare?"

"Extremely. More so, considering your core size. Most elven mages have five to seven affinities, but usually only two or three are strong enough for inscription and spellcraft," he replied with a professorial tone.

I nodded thankfully. My development was temporarily stalled, but I could continue in time. I listened as Maveith and Elaro struck up a conversation about Milvanoris. Stone Mountain Island was off the coast of the other continent, but the desert that was Milvanoris was still thousands of miles away from Maveith's home island.

Later, while we were leaving, Elaro invited us back. "Please visit again. The courts in the Grand Duchy are tedious, and I enjoy conversing with unique individuals." I was unsure if he was referring to Maveith or me.

I checked on Ginger before we returned to our suite. Ignis had not returned yet. I informed Maveith that we would be leaving in two days for the Boutan Caliphate. He eagerly left to get supplies for our trip, which seemed like it was going to be by land and not by teleportation.

In the common room, I pulled out a number of things from my dimensional space. The two lesser runic blades from Boris's men, a lesser runic short sword that Ignis gifted me, six elven daggers, and the legionnaire armor Duchess Veronica had made for me.

When Ignis returned, she looked excited about her heavy burden. It looked like her expedition had been successful. The old woman was nearly bursting with happiness but stopped, confused at the items I had placed on the table. "What is all this?"

"I was thinking you could sell this to open your smithy." Her confused look made me ask, "Is it not enough? There are three runic weapons here. Not dungeon-forged, but good enough to get a hundred or more gold."

Her eyes drifted to the new, polished legionnaire armor. I could tell she was trying to figure out how I had gotten it here. "Why would you do this?" she asked with healthy skepticism.

"I am going to consider it an investment. I will own half of your smithing business. I will come by every few years to collect my profits. And to commission work for myself." I smirked as I saw her eyes begin tearing up. She rubbed her eyes before they released any tears.

"Half? That is ridiculous! I will be the one doing all the work." Her negotiation was half-hearted.

"What is fair then?" I asked. I didn't consider anything I had laid out useful.

She shook her head, irritated. "Fine. You drive a hard bargain. Half it is, but only of the profits!" She walked over to study the items more closely. "Did you even wear it?" She was talking about the armor.

"Once, for a few minutes. A duchess had it crafted for me after I did her a service," I replied, and Ignis raised her eyebrow before giving me a lascivious smirk.

She jolted suddenly, remembering something, and faced me. "I rushed back here. Do you know a legionnaire named Mateo? He was just arrested for fighting. I think he was defending the honor of a waitress, but I didn't see the whole incident. He was wearing pieces of common legionnaire armor painted black."

"Where?" I asked, my heart racing. If it was Mateo, maybe others made it too.

"It was in the trade district. There is a jail along the west wall near there. That is probably where he is being held," Ignis informed me.

"Are there any others? How was he wearing legion armor in the city?" I asked anxiously, preparing to leave. I wouldn't wait for Maveith, but Ignis could tell him where I had gone.

"He just had legion vambraces and greaves, and they were stained black. I didn't see any others, but I arrived as he was being taken away." Ignis was examining one of the swords. "Don't do anything rash, Eryk. He assaulted a citizen of the Grand Duchy. Even if he was in the right, he will have to pay a price."

I pulled the blood compass to my hand and activated it with Castile's sample inside. The pull was strong but not close. Maybe three miles west or slightly less, by my estimate. I smiled. Castile and Mateo were alive. Maybe the rest of the company was waiting outside the city and Mateo had just gotten into a little trouble. "Tell Maveith where I went." I belted on a regular sword and elven dagger, not wanting to risk my runic weapons if things escalated.

My adventurer's medallion was hanging outside my tunic. I learned that if I was going to walk around the city with weapons, it made the guards less suspicious of me. I was not wearing armor because it was not needed; at least, I hoped it would not be needed. The city of Gramney was large and it was a long walk to the western side from the upper district.

As I got closer, I stared off a few pickpockets, their movements much too obvious. The jail was not difficult to find and was fairly massive, nearly two hundred feet long, tucked along the western wall. Numerous guards walked outside it and on the wall above the structure. I could see the small windows denoting the cells.

I put on a friendly smile when I spoke to one of the guards. "One of my friends has recently been incarcerated. Where can I go to see about getting him free?" The guard assessed me, judging my appearance. My clothes were decent and should have signaled that I was a man of wealth, though I favored darker colors over the brighter hues that nobility everywhere seemed to prefer.

It didn't take him more than a glance to direct me. "The arbiters' office is at the end." He pointed.

I thanked him with a large copper. "Thanks for your help. Enjoy an ale after your shift." He nodded happily, and I made eye contact to ensure he remembered me. It was always best to let the local guards know you were friendly.

As I approached the offices, a familiar voice was talking loudly. "I don't understand! The woman said he was protecting her, and the man was still alive, just a few bumps on his head. Why can't we pay damages and be on our way?" I peeked into the office to see an exasperated Benito arguing with a man in royal-blue robes.

The arbiter seemed to be losing his patience. "His case will be handled in the order it was received. You can return tomorrow evening. It should come up by then. The arbiter on duty will review the arrest and decide on the damages due, and if the sentence will include time on the work crews."

I walked in and stood behind Benito, towering over him by a head. I was disappointed there were no other legionnaires here. Benito's clothes were worn and not Legion issue. As Ignis had said, Benito also had legionnaire greaves and vambraces painted a dark, flat black. He didn't smell too great, either. "What kind of trouble did Mateo get into now?" I asked Benito conversationally.

Benito looked back for a second. "Eryk, we were drinking all peaceable-like, and I went to take a piss. When I came back, Mateo had knocked out some grizzled laborer. He swears the …" Benito's brain finally caught up to what his eyes were seeing and he slowly turned. "Eryk?!" He reached out and touched me to make sure he wasn't hallucinating. He moved in and gave me a half-hug. "I told them Pluto wouldn't take you. You were just gonna pop up somewhere. And here you are!"

He squeezed me for an awkward amount of time. "Good to see you too, Benito. People are going to talk if you don't release me." The arbiter smirked and Benito stepped back.

A pained expression came over his face. "Damn it, Eryk. Why couldn't you have shown up two weeks ago? Castile used my betting pool money for food. You owe me seven silver!" Although he didn't mean it, he sounded offended.

I chuckled softly and he smiled, realizing his own joke a little late. "Did everyone make it?" I asked more seriously.

Benito's expression changed to despair. "No. Konstantin wasn't with us for the"—he looked at the arbiter—"battle." He thought for a bit, bringing up the memories. As he did, I moved us outside, out of earshot of the arbiter. Benito continued, "Firth lost his hand. The healing mages hadn't gotten to him to reattach it by the time we rode with the Emperor. Linus, as well. He took an arrow to the neck and was mostly healed, but not enough to ride."

"This was at the battle against the Emperor?" I asked.

"No, before. We crushed the Bartiradians between two armies." Blood drained from his face at the memory. "Bloodiest fight I have ever been part of. We won, but some of the Bartiradians fled, and the Emperor ordered pursuit. Everyone who was able grabbed a horse. Mine was a big black brute who kept wanting to turn around, like it was scared and knew what it was riding into."

"The battle," I prompted, before his mind got too far sidetracked.

Benito nodded. "We rode up on the Bartiradians, dismounted, and the Emperor cast his black lightning. The day was clearly won, and then …" He paused. "I didn't really see what triggered it, but soon we were fighting the Imperial Legion. It was crazy, even though Castile told me it might happen." He shivered. "I don't want to think about it. More spells than arrows in the air." His voice got heavy. "Adrian, Kolm, and Malory fell in the fight."

After a pause, he leaned in conspiratorially. "It was Blaze. Blaze put an arrow in the Emperor's eye at fifty paces! After that, the Duke pulled his army away, and Castile ordered us into the woods. It's been weeks crossing Bartiradia to get here. The first few days were rough, but after we disguised ourselves as mercenary caravan guards it was easier."

"Who is with you now? And where are they?" I pressed.

"They are in a hamlet outside the city to save coin," Benito said. "Castile, Blaze, and Lirkin. Wylie was with us but disappeared on the second night. Castile said to let him go. Oh! And Mateo is locked up." He gestured profanely at the arbiters' office.

My heart got heavier with each name he listed. There was a chance Konstantin, Linus, and Firth were alive, but the only ones who had made it to Gramney were Castile, Mateo, Blaze, Benito, and Lirkin. "Well, at least you had a cook," I said softly, remembering Benito's quip on entering the Shimmering Labyrinth.

Benito took a moment to figure out what I meant. "Lirkin is in a bad state. He has an infection in his leg from a gnoll spear that he received five nights ago. Blaze wrenched his knee and is laid up too. Mateo and I were here to find work to make some coin for healing poultices."

"Why doesn't Castile use her magic? Surely she could make good coin with it," I asked.

Benito was saddened again. "She is burnt, Eryk. During our first few days in Bartiradia, we only traveled at night. She was using her shadows to conceal us from the enemy." That shocked me. Castile always seemed so unassailable. She also knew when she had reached her limit. My best guess was that she knew being caught would be a death sentence.

I patted Benito on the back. "Okay, let me see if I can grease the wheels of justice for Mateo."

"Grease the wheels? Are you going to cook for them?" Benito said, confused.

"Just wait here." I returned inside to confront the arbiter. He exhaled and nodded at two guards nearby to be on alert. I stepped close to him and whispered, "I have been told there is a special fee to expedite a case review?" He motioned the guards back, a good sign.

"The friend of your acquaintance?" he asked politely, seeing my hand covering a gold coin. I nodded. "Let me take a look. We *do* need to clear some cells today." He went to a folder and started paging through it till he found the sheet he was looking for near the back. "Hmm. Looks like a simple tavern fight." He acted like he was considering the case as he readied a stamp. "Two large silver or fourteen days on a work detail is the normal fine," he announced loudly so the guards could hear him. "But it looks like both parties were equally at fault here. I think one large silver or a week laying quarry stone."

"He will pay the fine," I said, adding a large dungeon silver to the counter with a clink. The arbiter took the silver, scratched out the verdict, and stamped it. I moved my hand away from the gold coin, and the paper covered it. "Sign here. Next time he is caught fighting in the city it will be forty silver." The gold coin disappeared with the paper. He turned to a guard. "Pull the Telhian from cell nineteen. He is free to go."

I went outside to bring Benito in, but he had been close enough to see. "Since you are giving out coin so freely, do you have the seven silver you owe me?"

"No, Benito. Getting Mateo out just cost me one hundred and ten silver. I am going to stand in the corner to see if Mateo recognizes me." I smirked, anticipating his reaction.

It was a good twenty minutes before Mateo was marched out of the long hallway. Two guards walked behind him as he limped toward us. His right eye was swollen shut and his lip was crusty with blood. Benito turned to me and said, "The city guards did that to him for resisting." I wanted to slap Benito. The guards could clearly hear him, and it was ruining my surprise.

Mateo was missing his greaves and vambraces, and it didn't look like he was getting them back. "What's the damage?" Mateo asked Benito.

"I found a friend who paid to get you out," Benito said happily.

"A friend? Did Castile come into town?" Mateo said, confused.

I was leaning against the wall, and Benito gestured toward me. I should have been more explicit in my instructions to him. Mateo squinted with his one good eye. I was standing in the shadows, as there was only a single window in the room. "What the—?" He stepped closer, not believing it. Like Benito, he needed to touch me to confirm. "Eryk? But you are dead. Castile said …" He moved in for a full hug, getting a little choked up.

When we separated, I said, "Yeah, it seems to happen a lot. You two can go get the others. Try to avoid getting into any fights on the way. We are at the Crescent Crossroads inn in the trade district. Third-floor suite. Don't tell Castile. I want to surprise her." I looked pointedly at Benito. "Mateo, why don't you do all the talking."

"We? Who is with you?" Mateo asked, staring at my adventurer's medallion.

"Maveith is with me, and we are headed to the Boutan Caliphate. But we can talk about that later."

Benito's eyes widened. "You're going into orc lands? Why would you do that?"

Mateo shook his head at Benito. "He said he would explain later. Let's go get Castile and the others. We are renting a small house far outside the city. It is a half-hour walk, so it will be some time with my leg." We spent a few minutes talking. Their journey getting here was obviously quite the story.

As I walked back alone, I couldn't believe Adrian, Kolm, and Malory were dead. Castile had lost two-thirds of the company's legionnaires since I joined. When I entered the suite, Maveith rushed to me. "Is the company in the city?"

I nodded. "Where's Ignis?"

"She took one of the swords to sell. Where are they?" Maveith rumbled excitedly, looking at the door.

"They were staying outside the city. There are only five of them, Maveith." Maveith's excitement faded at my words.

We waited for an hour before the thunder of multiple people could be heard coming up the steps. There were some whispers in the hallway before a short, sharp knock. Maveith and I rose to greet them. I opened the door to see Castile standing in the hallway, the company men behind her.

Castile didn't look healthy and was speechless at seeing me, her jaw trying to work. We stared at each other for a long time before Benito asked, "Are we going in? Do they have any food?"

Benito, not waiting for the stunned Castile to move, gently pushed her aside and stepped past her, entering the common room. "Nice place! I don't see any food. Can you order some from the tavern below? The stew smelled good on the way." Benito dropped his pack and sat heavily on the sofa. His pungent scent from being on the road for so long filled the room.

Castile finally regained herself and asked, "How are you here? How are you even alive? Cornelius told Konstantin you were dead." She said the last word with finality.

"It's Eryk. He is like crotch crickets. Always surprising you when you least expect it," Lirkin said from behind Castile. He squeezed past her, too. His leg was bandaged and he walked gingerly.

"Drink this, and don't complain about the taste," I said, handing him an orc healing potion as he passed me.

Realizing what it was, he patted me on the back affectionately before sitting down with a groan and a sigh. His pack joined Benito's on the floor, along with his sword belt. "Castile, if you are not going to enter, may I?" Mateo asked politely, unlike Benito and Lirkin. Castile numbly moved aside again, still processing my appearance. Maveith was greeting the men and pouring them cups of water.

"There is a bath," I announced to those in the room. "You could all use it," I hinted. They smelled of the road and horses. Blaze was the last one behind Castile, but he waited patiently, using the wall for support, his knee in a brace.

Castile finally stepped forward into the suite. Blaze entered behind her, and we briefly clapped each other's backs in a brief hug. I handed him a Pathfinder potion as well. Lirkin warned him, "Ugh, Blaze, you might want to keep your limp instead of risking losing your ability to taste." Lirkin was trying to clean his tongue on his shirt and spitting into it. "What foulness are you poisoning us with?"

"Pathfinder potions. I killed a few dozen orcs for them. I will remember that you are not interested in consuming them in the future," I said with a roguish grin.

Lirkin immediately reconsidered and said, "I am sure they just take getting used to. Either that or eventually, I won't be able to taste anything anyway and it won't matter."

Castile, looking at the men lounging as a beaming Maveith served them, turned to me. "Can we talk?"

"Let me feed the rabble first," I said, smiling. I walked to the low table in the seating area and produced my last twelve burritos, along with two canteens filled with elven ambrosia.

Benito was already biting into the first one. His mouth full, he said, "This makes the walk here worth it." Blaze reached for the canteen to wash the taste of the Pathfinder potion from his mouth. A loud conversation erupted as they ate and drank, and I moved away to talk with Castile in one of the rooms.

Castile immediately sat on the bed as I closed the door. Her feet and body were weary. "How did you get here?" I asked her quietly.

She exhaled in a long breath. Her tone was heavy. "Me first, then you. Zyna enacted the attack on the Emperor. He should have been spent but had a reserve of aether. It didn't go well, and many were lost. The Empire was crippled by the number of mages killed in the rebellion." I handed her some cold blood orange juice. Her eyes widened as she sipped it, and she licked her lips clean of the sweet, acidic drink.

"We slunk away after the battle and made our way east. There were fewer of us than planned, but it made it easier to move in stealth. We only traveled at night but were found by a mounted patrol. I overextended in the fight to make sure none of them escaped, and we took their horses." She winced, and I assumed that was where she had burned her aether channels. "That night, Wylie rode back to the Empire. Probably to report to Firth."

"The horses were a blessing. We rode them hard during the night for a week before they failed us, and we abandoned them. A few days later, we abandoned everything that marked us as Legion and served as merchant guards for a small, fast-moving caravan for a week. After that, we made our way to Gramney on foot. We arrived three days ago, weary, poor, but whole." Castile finished with her very brief summary. She hadn't even mentioned that a gnoll had wounded Lirkin.

It was my turn, so I began at the beginning. "After Hound training, I got a lookout position in Kraken Bay. Other than the loneliness, it was serene and peaceful. The Caliphate fleet sailed down the bay, and I was ordered to shadow them." I eliminated most of my adventures and skipped over capturing the First Citizen Mage.

"The Caliphate put ashore a group of Pathfinders, and I noticed goliaths were moving the cargo. I wasn't going to intervene, but was spotted. I was forced to

151

eliminate the Pathfinders and free the goliaths." Castile arched her eyebrow at how casually I talked about eliminating a Pathfinder squad. "One of the goliaths had news of Maveith's sister. The news was ten years old, but gave me hope she was alive. I followed the largest part of the fleet until they spotted me again. I fled and managed to locate the Archives."

Castile got excited, but it quickly faded. "You found the Archives? I suppose it is too late to return and destroy the samples."

I produced Castile's jar in my hand and handed it to her like a prize. "I destroyed the Archives—everything in it. I only took this to find you and the company."

Castile reached for the inscribed jar but pulled her hand back before reaching for it again. She turned the jar over, looking at the square pieces of bloody fabric within. She was mesmerized by the tumbling fabric for a time before asking, "The Archives at the palace?"

"I don't know. There was a fire at the palace when I left. Ignis supplied Imperial Legion armor to infiltrate them. Maybe she knows more," I said uncertainly.

She looked me in the eyes. "How did you get here?" She stressed the question.

"After the Archives, I found Maveith in Sobral, and we went to the capital from there. We took an Adventurers Guild ship to Esenhem and teleported here from the elven kingdom. We have been here about two weeks," I said, skipping the details. She didn't need to know about the gnoll migration, First Citizen Boris, or the sahuagin swarm.

"Two weeks!" she said in disbelief. She almost dropped the jar. She laughed a little hysterically, like I had told a bad joke. "We spent nearly a month getting here. Every day was perilous and could have ended our flight." She shook her head in disbelief, thinking I had taken a boat ride and gotten here relatively unscathed.

After she calmed down, I asked, "Benito said you were burnt? How bad is it?"

A pained look on her face made me want to comfort her, knowing how debilitating it was. "Twice I burned my channels. Once for the Bartiradian mounted patrol and once to hide us from a cyclops venturing out from a cave from the Endless Dark. I won't know how bad it is until I can access a tablet reader, though."

"Oh, you need a tablet reader? I have an elven one, but it is so old that it is configured for humans. It was one of the first built by elves, from my understanding. Do you wish to use it?" She cocked her head at my statement, and I knew I was showing off a little since I didn't need to hold my secrets as tight any longer. She slowly nodded, and I produced the tablet. It barely made a sound as it settled on the floor.

Castile stood immediately, marveling at it in amazement. She looked at me and then back at the tablet in disbelief. *Yes, Castile, I really am that big*, I said in my head. Castile couldn't read Elvish, but all the attributes and affinities were in the same order. She traced her hands along the tablet, hesitant to activate it. "Did you get this from Caelora?" she finally asked.

There was no reason to deny it. "Yes. Are you going to use it?"

Castile took a deep breath, reluctant to know the bad news, but she activated it anyway. My eyes immediately traveled to her affinities to satisfy my curiosity.

Elemental Magics (Common)	
Fire	0
Air	26
Water	0
Earth	0
Lightning (Energy)	49
Spirit (Healing)	0
Nature (Plant)	0
Unaffiliated Magics (Uncommon)	
Charm (Mind)	5
Illusion	62
Clairvoyance	46
Protection (Guardian)	0
Necromancy	19

Celestial (buff)	0
Abyssal (debuff)	28
Rare Magics	
Space	0
Time	0
Displacement	0
Materialism	0
Worlds	0
Void	0
Convergence	0

I was underwhelmed by her affinity strength. But she was one of the most effective mages in Empire because she was adept at using what she had. Still, Renna was much more powerful when it came to affinities. Castile interrupted me. "Can you read me my magic attributes? I don't know Elvish." My eyes moved across the tablet and I read them to her.

Magical	
Aether Pool	*58/60*
Channeling	*44/50*
Aether Shaping	*64/68*
Aether Tolerance	*35/37*
Aether Resistance	*27/30*
Prime Aether Affinity	*Illusion*
Minor Aether Affinity	*Energy*

When I read out the channeling rating, she nearly collapsed. I stopped reading. "How bad is it?" I asked, concerned.

"I lost three potential points," she said numbly. "I will never recover." She realized that she would be in pain for the rest of her life, every time she used her magic. I wished I could console her, but it would likely take a dozen or more apex channeling essences to restore her channels. They were just too rare. I sat beside her on the bed while she stared blankly ahead.

I waved at the tablet, "Your magic attributes put mine to shame, Castile. I will try to provide whatever you need to live a comfortable life here before I leave with Maveith." She nodded numbly. A knock came at the door.

Mateo had slurred speech as he spoke. "Castile, we decided you should use the tub first. If you don't want to, then we are going to draw straws."

Castile hesitated before she stood. "I am going."

After she left, I looked at the tablet. I could give it to her. It would be a very profitable venture for her. I was charged gold to use one in a Telhian city before I discovered the one in the Adventurers Guild. I cleared Castile's reading, squeezed the tablet, and sent a pulse of aether to activate it.

Elemental Magics (Common)	
Fire	0
Air	0
Water	4
Earth	42
Lightning (Energy)	8
Spirit (Healing)	23
Nature (Plant)	0
Unaffiliated Magics (Uncommon)	
Charm (Mind)	5

Illusion	13
Clairvoyance	0
Protection (Guardian)	30
Necromancy	0
Celestial (buff)	0
Abyssal (debuff)	0
Rare Magics	
Space	101
Time	90
Displacement	80
Materialism	9
Worlds	88
Void	22
Convergence	74

Relief flooded me. I had been worried the damage to my aether core might have affected my affinities. Would Castile be envious of my scores? There were some secrets that I was not willing to share. My eyes drifted to my displacement affinity. Worlds and displacement were the only two affinities for which I could inscribe a spell form. Maybe it was time to start focusing on a displacement spell form, even though I lacked the aether to use it effectively.

I looked over at my attributes.

Physical	
Strength (+5/+2)	67/84

Power (+5/+1)	62/88
Quickness (+1/+0)	54/62
Dexterity (+1/+0)	64/75
Endurance (+3/+0)	79/98
Constitution (+2/+1)	61/73
Coordination (+2/+1)	57/69
Mental	
Intellect (+3/+2)	38/58
Reasoning (+2/+1)	53/62
Perception (+1/+2)	57/64
Insight (+0/+0)	37/52
Resilience (+2/+0)	56/71
Empathy (+3/+2)	22/26
Fortitude (+3/+0)	63/90
Magical	
Aether Pool (+0/+0)	24/26
Channeling (+3/+0)	39/61
Aether Shaping (+1/+1)	9/9
Aether Tolerance (+0/+0)	50/56
Aether Resistance (+1/+0)	16/19
Prime Aether Affinity	Space

Minor Aether Affinity	Time

My potentials had not changed significantly due to my limited access to essences. My physical attributes had only seen modest improvement in the past few months. I was fortunate that the essence had prevented me from losing points during periods of laziness or illness, such as when I had needed to heal naturally for two weeks. I reset the reader and returned it to my dimensional space.

I walked back into the common room to a quartet of drunk legionnaires. No, they were no longer legionnaires, even if they still wore pieces of black-stained armor. "Do you have any more of this?" Lirkin asked, waving the empty canteen in front of him.

I produced the black jade chalice from the dungeon, which they were familiar with. I transmuted a quart of water into elven whiskey—called ambrosia. Benito snagged the canteen after I filled it from the chalice.

Mateo looked me in the eyes. "Maveith told us about his sister. If you can wait, once we get Castile settled, we will go with you."

Blaze added, "I always wondered what it would be like to be an adventurer. Killing monsters, rescuing citizens, always on the road to the next fight." He was grinning madly at the thought of doing the same things he did as a member of the Legion.

Benito finished his pull on the canteen and handed it to Lirkin. "But we get paid more, right? Adventurers are rich?"

The door opened and Ignis walked in, causing the group to go silent. "You found them. The mage didn't make it?" I pointed at the bathroom and she nodded. Ignis looked at me. "I sold one of the weapons and found a forge on the outskirts of the trade district. The smith is moving to be with his aging parents in the village where he was raised."

"How much?" I asked, getting to the point.

"Eight hundred gold, but I will talk him down to seven hundred tomorrow and explore getting a loan," Ignis said as she moved to sit with the stunned men.

I introduced her, as she wasn't making an effort to do so. "Everyone, this is Ignis, Master Imperial Blacksmith."

"Master Armorsmith," Ignis returned coolly. As they introduced themselves, I added six loaves of the delectable elven bread to the table. The hungry piranhas made short work of it.

I got into a conversation with Ignis. She had gotten ninety-seven gold for the sword, and it was the best of the three. The non-artifact armor would only fetch fifteen gold if sold to a collector, in her estimation. Since she was going to be about five hundred gold short, I handed her the silver earrings shaped like leaves from the Shimmering Labyrinth. Maybe they had some artistic value.

"Are these valuable?" I asked, placing them in her free hand. The other was occupied by a loaf of the elven bread.

Ignis took the earrings and tossed them lightly in her hand. She studied them closely, then looked at me. "You are full of surprises. Where did you get platinum earrings?"

"Caelora," I responded, not mentioning that I thought they were silver. I should have realized they were platinum by their weight.

Ignis seemed to consider the two swords and the earrings, nodding to herself. "About five hundred gold. I can make it work."

"You said you needed seven?" Twenty large gold coins appeared on the table as I placed my hand on it. All eyes looked at the stack and then at me.

Mateo's eyes widened at the stack of gold. "Oh, mighty djinn! I wish for one thousand gold coins!" He bowed to me and nearly stumbled to the floor. The ambrosia was a powerful drink.

Benito chirped, "You still owe me seven silver!"

I was trying to gradually introduce them to my dimensional space. I waved my hands again and they followed them intently, but all that appeared was a bright-red apple that I bit into casually. Castile remained in the bathroom while we celebrated, and we only checked on her once. She exited shortly after and went into one of the rooms instead of joining us.

As everyone moved to find sleeping accommodations, Lirkin came to talk with me. "Someone should stay with Castile. It feels like we are abandoning her here. If it's okay with you and Maveith, I will stay with her. I can find work at an eatery in the city and watch over her. I heard many mages have trouble dealing with the burn."

I patted Lirkin on the back. "We don't mind at all. Have you ever thought about running your own tavern?"

Chapter 268: Secret Depths Revealed

I let the men deal with their surprisingly mild hangovers in the morning. I had sampled the ambrosia on a few occasions as a sentry at Kraken Bay. It was a little sweet for my palate, but if you could get it cold, it was better than the best ale. It didn't take much to get buzzed, and I had never experienced a hangover the following day. I would have to remember to refill the pair of canteens from the black chalice since my companions had drained them.

Ignis gathered the swords and earrings and prepared to make an offer on the smithy. Castile looked much better after a long rest, but her face was still filled with uncertainty. Leaving no room for argument, I told her, "Castile, you and I are going to visit a mage healer this morning. He is an elf and specializes in mages."

Castile looked skeptical, but changed into her cleanest clothes and joined me. The rest of the men were going to spend the morning on laundry and then register at the Adventurers Guild, Maveith eager to show them the sights. Last night, I had offered to come up with funds for Lirkin to purchase a small tavern or inn in the city, and he was going to scout his options. I guessed the cost would be similar to the smithy, so I would need at least another seven hundred gold.

I shouldered a heavy pack I had prepared for visiting Elaro and left with Castile. As we walked through the city, Castile's eyes and mind wandered. The myriad of races is what primarily drew her attention. I broke her daze by asking a question. "What do you plan to do now that you are free?"

"Free at a cost," she murmured testily. She composed herself. "I can still channel aether. It is difficult to focus on casting true spells through the pain, but the spell forms on my core are more manageable. I will find solace as a tutor of magic or perhaps as a bodyguard." She spoke of the latter profession with derision. Her ability to unweave aether to prevent others from casting spells was one of the spell forms she had inscribed on her core. I assumed that was why she was considering being a bodyguard. Maybe she had planned for the others to join her in the enterprise.

"Why not the Adventurers Guild?" I inquired.

In a tired voice, Castile responded, "I am spent. Not just from being burnt. As a woman mage commander, I could not have a family until after my service was completed. Maybe now …" Her voice faded. We walked for a while before she spoke again. Her throat was a little tight. "Adrian and I … he always said … after we had both escaped the Legion."

That was shocking news, as I had never seen them be affectionate with each other. Castile chuckled, seeing my bewilderment. "Not with Adrian. We just planned to start families after the Legion. He was always more of a paternal protector than a lover." I nodded but didn't want to discuss our dead comrades. We had reached Elaro's villa, and I spent a moment explaining the flag and the nation of Milvanoris before we knocked.

It wasn't long before we were seated in his study. Castile marveled at the private library. "I see you have brought a lovely friend with you. Are you experiencing more symptoms, or is this a social visit?"

"My recovery is going well," I said, as Castile's questioning look shifted from me to the elf. "We are not here for me today, but for my friend here. Castile has burned her aether channels, and I was hoping you knew of a remedy."

The elven noble reclined and his lips tightened. "Aether burn. There is only one cure: apex channeling essences." Castile tensed as hope fled her. "If she doesn't want to use her aether, I can shield her core as I did for you. It will remove her ability to cast spells, but she will no longer feel any pain. It is a fragile containment, and attempting to use any aether will shatter it."

"That is not an option," Castile hissed moodily.

Elaro shrugged. The old elf looked sympathetic, but not invested in Castile's decision. "The only other thing I can offer is a draft that will numb your pain some. I don't suggest it, since it is addictive and also numbs your other senses as well. But if you are having trouble sleeping, it can give immense relief."

"Thank you for your time," Castile said, ready to leave.

"You are not alone," Elaro consoled Castile. "I have seen dozens of mages in my time with burnt channels. If it is recent, know that you will adapt in time. The body is amazingly resilient, and you can overcome the pain with some mental training to push aside the effects and form spell forms normally." I had only lost one point of potential and had managed to acclimate to the burn, but I didn't mention it. I didn't want to reveal that my aether burn was cured.

"Can you teach her?" I asked for Castile, who wore a mask of despair.

Elaro exhaled slowly. "While I have knowledge of techniques, I am not a teacher."

Ignoring his hesitance, I pulled a bottle of elven red wine from my pack and placed it on the table to my right. "How many lessons would this procure?" I had planned to use the wine as payment for a cure, but since no cure was available, the lessons would do.

Elaro licked his lips instinctively, and I could tell he had enjoyed the last bottle, weakening his negotiating position. "For you, my friend, three dozen."

"Excellent," I said, smirking as I added five more bottles, one at a time, from the pack. "That is 216 lessons. Is that enough to learn the techniques?"

Elaro laughed at my bravado. Castile quickly figured out where the bottles had come from by the dust coating them. "I figured I could instruct her successfully in thirty lessons, which is why I offered thirty-six." He gestured at the bottles. "Do you even know the value of what you have dancing on the edge of the table?"

"I suppose this is where you tell me I overpaid," I said, laughing softly but not really concerned.

"Quite so," Elaro said, smiling. He rose from his oversized reading chair and walked to the small table, starting to clean the dust off the bottles. "Each bottle is worth a few dozen gold on its own for the artwork and the preservation runes woven into the glass."

He worked through the bottles as he talked. "The Caelorian elves were master craftsmen, and the artwork reflects the wine's deeper meaning—not that I can discern it without some research. The wine itself …" He paused, considering. "I couldn't place a value on it. To a drunkard—a silver. To a human king or wealthy merchant, for the prestige of drinking wine over a thousand years old— maybe a hundred gold. A few-fold of that to the right elf who can truly appreciate it—and afford it."

Castile was looking on, somewhat numb to the sums being mentioned. I could see her thinking and read her thoughts. We had left behind thousands of these bottles in Caelora. "What would you pay for a bottle?" I asked.

Elaro sighed. "While I am not destitute by any means, I do not have extensive funds. My income is minimal, and as I informed you on your last visit, I frequently assist refugees from my defunct kingdom."

It didn't take me long to make an offer. "Are there those in Gramney that could pay the price? Would you be willing to serve as a broker for four bottles and keep the fifth as your fee?" The sixth bottle was for Castile's lessons. I added quickly, "Of course, leaving the true origin of the wine out of the equation."

Elaro's eyebrows danced in amused thought. "Perhaps. The ambassador from Esenhem, for one, would pay." He started to nod. "I agree to your offer." We shook wrists on it.

"You can give the gold to Castile," I said, stepping back after we shook. Elaro seemed eager to peddle the wine, and I assumed it was a way for him to gain some prestige in the court.

As we were walking back, Castile said, "You didn't have to do that." I didn't know which part she was referring to—the lessons or selling the wine.

I shrugged as we walked. "It's fine. I still have fifty bottles in my space. I will leave a dozen more with you." I didn't notice that she had stopped walking for a few steps. I walked back and collected her. "Lirkin is staying behind to watch over you, Castile. He is looking to purchase a tavern or inn. You can facilitate its purchase with the coin Elaro gets for you."

"What else are you hiding in your space?" she said, trying to hide a smile at my loyalty and generosity. I may not have been able to solve her aether burn, but she was being put in a comfortable position. I didn't want to give her false hope, but Maveith's homeland was supposedly flush with manticores, and those creatures had yielded channeling essences for me. I had no idea if I could gather the amount required to heal Castile, or if my path would even take me there, so I didn't mention it.

I handed her a hot meat bun, which she juggled for a moment before biting into it. Even though no one was near us, I sent an earth pulse out to confirm we were alone and to reveal anyone invisible. Satisfied, I continued talking. "I have collected quite a few odds and ends. One of them I was hoping for your help with."

"This is good," she said, about the meat bun. "What do you need help with?" Her mood had changed drastically since she had gained some hope for the future. I wasn't sure about revealing the full power of my dimensional space to Castile, but she could keep my secrets. She already knew I was an otherworlder.

"A First Citizen Mage," I said as we walked.

She thought about it for a moment. "It shouldn't be hard to dispose of the body. Just bury it in the woods. Why do you need my help?"

"The problem is, she is still alive. I just don't want Benito and the others to know. I am not sure if they can keep it a secret." Castile had stopped walking again, the meat bun hovering in front of her mouth. I had to walk back and collect her again. Since she was paralyzed, I continued talking normally. "Her name is Selene Greco. I was tasked with killing her by Centurion Sergius when I was a Hound. I don't think she will be happy or cooperative when I bring her out."

I waited for Castile to process this. The street was fairly empty, but I sent out another earth pulse to ease my paranoia. It would be best to move the conversation inside. I ushered her into a small tavern and got a private booth. It was still early morning, and the place only had one other customer. I ordered drinks and food for us and waited for Castile's disbelief to catch up with the conversation. She eventually spoke. "You have a mage in your dimensional pocket—alive?"

"Yes. She is bound, poisoned, and sedated, so she can't use her magic, but yes, I do." Some crispy fried bread was placed in front of us. It was a bit too greasy, but I took a bite, and it reminded me of garlic bread.

Castile was slowly processing the implications. "Then ..." I nodded before she finished. "And when ..." I nodded again. "Why did you stay in the Legion?"

I shrugged, keeping my voice low. "I am just an ignorant otherworlder, Castile. If I thought I could have run, I would have. Konstantin kept telling me it was a death sentence, and I believed him. Now, what are we going to do about the mage?" I didn't want to discuss my dimensional space further, which she understood by my tone.

Castile ate numbly for a time before returning to the topic of the mage. "The Grecos? I heard something about the orcs killing Baron Greco," Castile said. "They had a daughter, but I don't know if I ever met her. My company cleared one of their deep silver mine shafts of kobolds four or five years ago. The Baron was a reasonable First Citizen for the power he wielded and even entertained the company for two days at his estate to thank us."

"Duke Octavian and Centurion Sergius had them killed to get their silver and gold mines. You have something in common. You both hate Duke Octavian." Castile was staring at me like she didn't know me. I just sipped on my sour ale and waited for her to catch up.

"If you can ... then did you kill creatures with it?" Castile guessed. I was surprised she had made the connection so fast.

"Yes. The bulette, manticore, and wyvern. It is also how Maveith and I survived the dungeon, but we had to bloody our weapons many times as well. Yes, he knows." It sounded like I was boasting, so I felt the need to add my failure too: "The summoner was too strong and resisted, so I had to kill him the hard way. I killed his ice drake that way." It felt good getting the secret off my chest.

I could see Castile had an avalanche of questions. I tried to answer them as quickly as I could. I wasn't surprised when she asked if I had kept any food from the company in the Ruins of Caelora. I admitted I had the summoner's apprentice pack and that there had been a few days of food in it, but I hadn't known about it until after I entered the dungeon.

Castile slowly acclimated to the new reality of what a monster I truly was. Her disposition had changed greatly in the last few hours. "I will take care of your mage problem," she affirmed after I answered her bevy of questions.

"Great. I will leave her with you when we leave. She has a pack of gold and silver trinkets that should placate her when she finds herself alive and gets them back. Her ring and amulet were given to Centurion Sergius if she asks about them." I had taken the aether shield amulet from Corvus, but I was not returning it—I considered it a transportation fee.

Another thought occurred to me. "Her two legionnaires may come looking for her. Helena and Sylph. I gave them a clue she might be here, but I don't know if they will puzzle it out."

I let Castile finish her meal, as she needed the calories. "Are you ready to return to the others?" I asked. Castile still looked at me like she didn't know me, but at least the initial shock had worn off.

When we got back to the suite, it smelled foul. The men had laid out all the gear in their packs and were repacking with new gear and rations they had purchased at the Adventurers Guild. Drying clothes hung from cordage strung across the room, adding to the unpleasant odor.

Guild medallions hung proudly from their necks as they worked. "Look, Eryk." Benito held up his token. "They let me join! Mateo thought they might not because there was a height requirement, but there were three dwarves in the common room there, so I knew I was tall enough!" Mateo hid his amused snicker.

Maveith's deep voice cut through everyone's conversations. "We got everything we need. Do you want us to get horses as well? I don't know how to ride." I considered the question. There were large mounts for someone of Maveith's bulk, but I was uncertain of the cost and availability.

"I will check with the portal office this afternoon. If there are no scheduled portals to Artiria, we will get everyone a mount," I announced. It appeared I was going to be in charge of our little band—or at least I was going to be the one paying our way.

Ignis returned a short time later. She had liquidated the platinum earrings and runic weapons. She had a tentative agreement for the smithy she wanted in place. I thought about waiting for her to craft everyone armor, but I knew

Maveith had waited long enough. He had been patient, but I could see the delay weighing on him.

Everyone had piecemeal leather armor to go with their black legionnaire greaves and vambraces. It made us look like proper mercenary adventurers. It looked like they still had their runic weapons from Caelora, but they had wrapped their hilts to hide their true natures.

When Lirkin returned, I took the opportunity to leave and check the portal office. I left some silver for them to get food from the tavern below. Maveith joined me as I left the inn. "We are leaving soon?" he asked as we walked, handing me a pouch. I took the pouch and checked it, curious. It contained several gold coins. "Your half of the payment for delivering the message from Sanco to the Guildmaster here."

"You can keep it." I handed it back to him. There were about twenty gold in the pouch. "We will leave as soon as we can. We still need to find an orc guide, but we can do that tomorrow. If we can't find one here, we can get one in the Caliphate."

Maveith talked as we walked, telling me about his morning and their time in the Guild Hall. Maveith had paid for the others to register, and there had been no issues other than a few people recognizing their accents as Telhian. He got the impression that Telhians were not well liked.

When we reached the portal office, Fortuna was smiling on us. A tentative portal to Artiria was scheduled for four days later. The cost was five gold per person and ten gold for a horse. We were definitely not getting any mounts, and it was time for Ginger to get used to my dimensional space.

Maveith was confused when I only paid for passage for six people. "Is Ginger staying with Castile? Who is the sixth person?" he asked as we walked back to the inn.

"I cleared some space for Ginger. The sixth person is the orc guide if we find one. I didn't want to risk the portal getting sold out," I explained. The number of people was limited for each teleport, but we had gotten lucky, as the portal registry had recently opened. There was a chance the portal would not occur if the elven displacement mage didn't arrive, though.

"Ginger will fit? Will I fit too?" Maveith asked, more as speculation than practicality.

"Maybe one day we will find out," I said, laughing menacingly.

"You will not cage me, foul mage," Maveith said in mock worry, moving to the other side of the road in jest.

When we returned to the suite, Lirkin and Castile took me aside. Lirkin seemed eager to talk about his options in the city. "I found a few places. Some I thought were out of reach." He looked at Castile, who nodded. "One is nestled between the trade district and the river dock district. An older proprietor has a lovely little inn that hasn't seen much business since the new docks were built further upriver, with two new luxury inns opening there. He wants to retire with his wife and move away from the city."

"How much?" I asked.

Lirkin looked to Castile again for support before saying, "Twelve hundred gold, but the furnishings for the eighteen rooms will be included, as well as a fully stocked kitchen." His voice had changed to hopeful. "He showed me his books. They do about three hundred gold in business annually, but it used to be closer to four hundred."

I looked to Castile and back to Lirkin. "And one of the rooms will be for Castile?"

"There is actually a small house attached to the stables in the back courtyard," Lirkin said eagerly. "It has three additional bedrooms."

"And that is fine with you?" I asked Castile.

Castile laughed softly, a sign she was adjusting. "I slept on the ground among filthy men most nights these last twenty years. A private room with a bed is a luxury."

"You can handle Elaro's brokering the sale of the wine then," I said, as I made the twelve promised bottles appear on the table. As far as I was concerned, the company men were entitled to the bottles as a share of the loot. I was just doing my job as the company porter. It was also some penance for not revealing my capabilities to the company.

Lirkin huffed, "You had some left, huh? Didn't think I would see another bottle in my lifetime. Maybe we have a chance to enjoy it now."

Castile started cleaning the bottles and had other ideas. "These bottles are your inn, Lirkin." Castile turned to me. "Ignis said you own half of her smithy. Are you doing the same for Lirkin's inn?"

"Why don't you and Lirkin split ownership?" I replied indifferently. The truth was, it was very doubtful I would ever return to Gramney in their lifetimes. Even if we failed to find Zorana, I had still promised to travel with Maveith to confront his father. Stone Mountain Island was on the other side of the world.

"I don't think that is equitable," Castile rebuked me with a shake of her head, and Lirkin nodded in agreement. "A three-way split for ownership?" she offered. Lirkin was already nodding, so I guessed they had planned this.

Mateo was moving across the room, his eyes locked on the bottles of Caelorian wine, not having heard our conversation. Castile barked in her command voice for everyone to hear, "Mateo, those bottles are worth more than the Primus's sword you carry." That caused him to pause and look down at the weapon on his hip in confusion.

"Primus Scorpio?" I asked, slightly confused.

Mateo grinned. "Yeah, he didn't need it anymore."

I held out my hand and he drew the blade, handing it to me. He had disguised the hilt, but the silvery metal along the blade and the runes clearly marked it as dungeon-forged. I tested the blade with a few swings, sensing a power in it. Unfortunately for Mateo, that power needed to be unlocked. I could feel the sword thirsting for my aether like the magebane.

"It is a fine weapon, Mateo." I handed it back to him. "Be careful where you draw it."

"We have had a lot of practice hiding the nature of our weapons over the last few months. I have Delmar's dungeon blade, but it is yours if you wish to carry it," Lirkin said as he retrieved his sheathed weapon from his room.

"No need." I stopped him. "I am well equipped." I fingered Orc's Torment on my hip. I would have to switch it for a different blade before we entered the Caliphate, maybe even before I interviewed the orc guides. "We have a portal to Artiria, Esenhem's capital, in four days. It should save us a lot of walking."

Benito's eyes went wide with excitement. But it was Mateo who asked a question. "I always wondered if there were brothels in the elven kingdom." Castile gave him a sharp, disapproving look. "Not that I would partake, but I just heard that elves know things … Never mind. I will shut up now." Benito looked confused, and I doubted Mateo would restrain himself if there were brothels in Artiria. It would be fine as long as he didn't get himself into too much trouble.

I moved to sit with Blaze, who I hadn't talked to for some time. He was inspecting some new arrows he had purchased and was regluing some fletchings. "Why did you decide to join Castile?" I asked him privately.

He put down the arrow he was working on. "It just felt right. Every time I draw my bow and release, I get a feeling that my aim is right. I got that feeling with Castile."

"Then why are you not staying with her here?" I questioned further.

"Same reason. It just feels like the right direction for me. It is a noble act to help Maveith and his sister. Maybe I was always destined to be an adventurer and defend those who couldn't defend themselves with my bow." Blaze spoke plainly, but there was something deeper in his words.

"Did Castile tell you that you use aether when you release an arrow?"

"She mentioned it, but I have never been able to feel the aether, no matter how hard I try," Blaze said, smirking. "My aether shaping is just five. I will never be a mage."

I opened my hand to reveal the pink hair ring. Elven hunters chased elk around the workings. "This artifact will help you with your bow." I placed it in his hand and he inspected it. "It needs to be worn in the hair. If you don't like the color, you can paint it." Blaze's hair had grown some, but it would be a challenge to wear the ring at the moment.

"Thank you. How does it work?" he asked, turning the pretty hair clip over.

"Figure it out with Castile. Once your hair lengthens, it should hold it comfortably." Next, I pulled out my Hound poison kit and showed him how to treat his arrows. I then gifted him the poison kit, including the lesser thermal stone. He would need to channel aether if he wanted to use it, so hopefully it would motivate him.

Ignis returned, beaming as she announced to the room, "I am now the proud owner of the smallest blacksmith forge in the city!" We all clapped and would shortly use the news as an excuse to drink.

"We leave in four days. Can you get this sorry lot fitted and suited?" I asked, grinning at her.

She surveyed the eager expressions, each wearing mismatched armor they had collected during their difficult journey. A few sported pieces of armor they had recently bought at the Adventurers Hall. We looked like true vagabond mercenaries. "I might be able to make you look decent, but as for new armor, I have no jigs, stamps, or stencils prepared. It would be from scratch, and maybe I could get one of you properly suited."

All eyes turned to me. It appeared I was the one making the decisions from here on out—the burden of leadership. "Do your best with Maveith, Mateo, Blaze, and Benito. You can sell this for supplies." I tossed her a ring.

She caught the gold ring and inspected it. "The Angella Crest?"

"First Citizen Boris Angella's ring. He no longer has use of it," I said snarkily. "Boris was trying to loot Caelora. Maveith and I ran into his exploration party on the old road. A wyvern had killed most, and the rest were limping back to Telha."

Castile snapped, "The First Citizen pixie prick deserved his fate. It doesn't leave this room, though. The Empire may be a thousand miles away, but its ears are not. If Boris's mother lives, she will seek vengeance." Everyone nodded in understanding. I doubted Duchess Veronica cared about her brother's death, but Castile had spent more time with the family and knew them much better than I did.

We had food sent up and started feasting and drinking late into the night. My thoughts turned to Ginger, and I left the group to feed her an apple. She was happy to see me and nudged me for a second right after. "Ginger. An opportunity has come up. Lirkin is buying an inn in this city. You could stay here with him and Castile, or you can come with me. If you come with me, strange things will happen and it will be dangerous. Do you want to stay here in safety or come with me?"

I thought it was my serious tone, but Ginger seemed to be listening intently. She cocked her head to the side and nudged me in the chest. I produced an apple and she didn't take it right away, nudging me again—and then she chomped on the apple. I was going to take that as *Yes, I will come*. I sent out an earth pulse to make sure no one was close, and then Ginger disappeared. This spooked some of the horses, and the stable boy came running. I explained that I had traded Ginger away.

Over the next three days, I helped Lirkin and Castile purchase the inn, signing papers and negotiating with the current owners. The others helped Ignis set up her smithy. Every night, they came back filthy from cleaning and doing repairs. Ignis balanced her efforts between equipping them and getting her smithy ready. She removed the stones from the ring and melted the metal down before selling it, heeding Castile's warning.

Even though they were tired from the hard days, I had us all start training together in the small courtyard behind the Crescent Crossroads before the evening meal. They complained tenfold the amount they used to when Delmar or Adrian had enforced their training. But they were seasoned men and knew the value of it. For all their whining, they worked hard to win the prize of being the first to use the bath that night—I always won. I used the dreamscape amulet at night to sort out their weaknesses and prepare for the next day's session.

The tavern Lirkin had selected was old but well maintained. It had a small basement larder with no connection to the city's sewers, which, after Macha, we all agreed was a good thing. However, it didn't have running water like the Crescent Crossroads, so he would have to hire staff to haul it from the city's aqueduct.

Elaro was doing his best with the wine, but the process of selling such luxury items took time, which included everything from verifying the authenticity to negotiating a price. The first two bottles he sold were to the Esenhem ambassador for roughly three hundred gold each. The aged ambassador was able to decipher the meaning of the relief art and took the two most valuable bottles out of the four. The other bottles were sold to an ambassador from Keisinia and a merchant prince from Linshania for just over two hundred gold each.

The nine hundred gold started the transfer of the inn. There was a balance due of two hundred and ninety gold at the closing in the City Deeds Hall. Lirkin sold an elven runic dagger from Caelora, and Castile sold something of her own. Annoyingly, they had me sign the ownership documents as well.

It was still going to be a few days before the current innkeeper and his aged wife could move out, but the structure and all the headaches that came with it were now Lirkin's. Castile had the dozen bottles of wine to sell in an emergency. She didn't think revealing more to Elaro at this time was prudent.

The search for an orc guide did not go well. The orc caravan guard, Bragaran Agher, had returned but was not interested in joining us. He made good coin doing two trade loops with a local merchant. The next candidate, Synrathe Glimmerborn, was actually a criminal in the Caliphate and laughed at me when I asked him to join us. He said he would be strung up by the testicles if the warlord he stole from caught him, and he was being literal, not figurative. The last potential guide was Folmar Crimsonhand.

Folmar was large for an orc and had tattoos that marked him as one of their elite warriors. I was not familiar enough with orc society to know if he had belonged to either faction. He was haughty beyond compare, looking down on me and demanding half of all the coin we made. By his tone, I also guessed he assumed he was the one who would make the decisions. With this failure, I decided to try again in Artiria, but was worried about the local guildmaster interfering, since he did not like ex-Telhian legionnaires.

I managed to get some time in Elaro's library. All the books were in Elvish and from the fallen Empire of Milvanoris. Although the Elvish writing was consistent, the calligraphy was slightly different, making it harder to read.

He let me page through all his volumes on spell forms. He lacked volumes on materialism and worlds, but had tomes on all the other affinities. He thought I was just searching for something to imprint, and was not aware of the dreamscape amulet.

On a night in the dreamscape, I took the time to try to figure out my night vision spell form from the illusion affinity. I had imprinted it during the fight with the gnolls, but it was imperfect, with limited range and mostly shades of gray. I quickly found the reason why that was.

I had not imprinted night vision, but something similar to a spell form called mage sight. Mage sight allowed a mage to see aether clearly and to differentiate objects by their aether density. It was extremely valuable to mages learning how to write out spell forms in the air, or see the framework of other casters' spells. My spell form was just a weaker version of mage sight called aether sight.

If I had imprinted night vision using the spell form within the books, my vision would have had color and significantly greater range. If I had imprinted mage sight, I would have been able to see aether and its flows clearly.

There were some benefits to aether sight, namely that it did not require your eyes to see. If my eyes were removed or I was blinded, aether sight would still give me the ability to see. I could also increase the distance I could see with a higher affinity, but I would never be able to see color. Unfortunately, there was less clarity in seeing with aether than with true mage sight. I counted it a blessing anyway, no matter the limitations.

It had been a great few days of working, eating, drinking, and joking with everyone again. Castile's sternness had started to slip as she started to get accustomed to her new life. We all moved to Lirkin's inn. Although the old innkeeper was still in the house by his stables, the inn was temporarily empty of patrons.

I was in the largest room on the third floor with Castile, dawn just getting ready to show itself. The teleport to Artiria was at high noon. The others had already suited up and said their goodbyes. Castile looked me over. I was wearing my black manticore cloak, earth drake boots, and bracers. My adventurer's armor had been cleaned, repaired, and properly fitted by Ignis, even though she noted that she despised working with leather and inferior armor.

"Are you going to leave her on the bed?" Castile asked to break the silence.

"Yes." But I was thinking of what else I could do to help Castile. I had been seriously considering leaving the elven tablet reader for her. She could have run a very profitable business with it. But it was worth thousands of gold and might make her a target. I didn't have many books left in my space, but they should be easy to sell and wouldn't draw much attention. All of them had been copied into the amulet anyway. A stack of twenty-five books appeared on the table, one or two at a time. "You can sell these and give this one to Ignis."

She shook her head in wonderment at the assortment. I didn't have the heart to tell her about the stash in the chancellor's suite at the Telhian Mage College. Over five hundred books were hidden there. I only had seven books remaining in my space now: two Caelorian herbalism books, a spellbook reward from the Shimmering Labyrinth, an elven spell form book for the energy affinity, and the three-volume set for the displacement affinity.

"I have copies in the amulet," I explained, then went silent.

Castile looked hard at me. "Well, this doesn't have to be an awkward farewell. Somehow, I expect to see you again. You always turn up eventually. I hope you find Maveith's sister."

I nodded, moved to the bed, and deposited the heavy pack of trinkets and coins Selene had fled with. "If she asks where the rest of it is, tell her I gave it to her legionnaires."

Mage Selene Greco appeared on the bed. The clean room suddenly filled with pungent odors, including urine and body odor. Castile inhaled sharply, showing her shock at seeing the body and the mage's chest slowly rising and falling. She moved to the woman. She was bound tightly and had a bandage on her leg from where I cut her with the magebane. I had told Castile about the poison and the oblivion pills I had force-fed her. I had treated her fairly roughly, and it would be best if I was gone when she regained consciousness.

"Fortuna watch over you," I said softly to her back, and left the room.

Castile muttered to herself, "Like she has time to take her eyes off of you."

The others were all dressed up and wore mostly matching armor when I joined them outside on the street. Ignis had even made Maveith's armor mostly match the style of the others'. We looked more like a proper fighting force, except that Benito was blowing snot rockets, Blaze was leaning against a building trying to get a few more winks, and Mateo's eyes were wandering to every woman walking the streets.

I gathered my company and headed to the courtyard for the teleport while Maveith explained to the others how it worked. On arrival, the golden-haired elven displacement mage noticed me immediately. My group tensed as she approached with a grin on her face. "How was your stay in Gramney?"

"It was fine," I replied cautiously.

"You know, there was a very disheartened young elf in Artiria who was upset when you and the goliath didn't come and seek her out," the mage said slyly. "I hate to ruin a surprise, but she may be waiting for you when we arrive." The mage retreated and her guards encircled her while she recovered, leaving me stunned. *What elf?*

Mateo was instantly at my side, staring at the beautiful elven mage walking away. "Eryk, you sure get around. How are elves?"

"I wouldn't know," I said numbly, dismissing Mateo's assumptions. I was more concerned about the elf waiting in Artiria. Shit, there was only one elf that knew me and Maveith. How could she be in Artiria? Why wasn't she in Bartiradia? I looked at my currently happy companions, wondering how I would explain this.

Konstantin's journey to the capital took a grueling two weeks on foot, steering clear of the main roads teeming with soldiers and legionnaires. With the death of the Emperor, it was surprising that the Esenhem elves hadn't made a move toward the capital or the Atlantium ruins to the south. Konstantin speculated that their ultimate goal would be the Atlantium ruins, but their recent losses had made them exercise caution.

Under the cover of night, he carefully concealed his armor and weapons amidst the dense foliage of the woods before assuming the guise of a rugged woodsman. Venturing into small farming towns, he sought out whispers and rumors, only to find a bewildering lack of consensus among the townsfolk.

One claimed that the orcs had triumphed in the western Empire, while another vehemently argued that the Legion had successfully repelled the orc fleet, sinking their ships at sea. The disagreement was a bitter reminder of his lost connection to the Empire's information network. Konstantin could only listen impassively, wary of being recognized when he ventured into the bustling inns of larger towns.

He was glad to finally be at the capital's gates, and it looked like news of the Emperor's death had arrived before him. Konstantin entered Telha in beggar clothes, white chalk aging his facial hair and a brace on his foot, giving him a believable limp. Loose, tattered clothes covered his muscular frame. The fresh-faced guards searched him roughly, taking his purse of coppers but letting him pass. That minor theft alone told him things had deteriorated.

Moving into the city, he felt a lot of tension in the city streets, and people were hyper-alert as they moved. Konstantin paused at a street vendor and paid three times what the skewered meat should have cost. The vendor even gave him the gristly portion, thinking him a crippled beggar.

Konstantin walked past the eastern Legion Hall, surprised to find the gates locked and no movement inside the compound. That was a shock in itself. Never had the Hall been closed in his memory, and he could only surmise there were no legionnaires available to be quartered there.

He slowly made his way to a dimly lit alley nearby, settling in among the discarded debris that should have long ago been cleared away and hauled far outside the city to a refuse pit. As he waited for the cover of night, he took brief, restless naps, swatting away bold rats that ventured too close.

With the ethereal glow of Neptune's Tear illuminating the night sky, Konstantin stealthily scaled the wall of the eastern Legion Hall, landing softly in the courtyard. The city housed two other Legion Halls: the Imperial Legion Hall within the palace and the western Legion Hall, which trained men who volunteered to serve in the Legion. However, the Hall he entered tonight was designated for conscripted legionnaires, a somber reminder of his own involuntary service.

The Hall was completely quiet as he searched the extensive structure in the dark, confirming it was empty. He found the armory and equipment rooms locked and bolted. It took him a few attempts with his spell form to open the lock. He stepped inside and saw the room looked ransacked, most of the equipment and weapons gone. After closing the door, he used a glowstone to pick through the remnants and get proper clothes and weapons. He had hated burying his precious sword outside the city, but knew a runic weapon would have given him away.

"What do you think you are doing, old man?" A voice cut through the air behind him.

Konstantin whirled and crouched, cursing his failure at stealth. A portly woman stood in the doorway. She had not only opened it without him noticing but had also entered the room. A testy Konstantin replied, "You are older than me, Gilda." The woman was Antonia's master poisoner and, despite her bulk, was quieter than a cat on the prowl. She had been working in the kitchens when he had last seen her.

"Some of us age better than others." She shrugged. He moved the glowstone to get a better view of her. She had dried blood on her cook's apron and looked pretty haggard.

He studied her expression as he spoke, ready to react to any provocation. "Duke Octavian betrayed us. Sergius and the Western Hounds have allied with him and have probably killed all of Cornelius's loyal Hounds."

She nodded slowly, her eyes heavy with lack of sleep and her voice flat, without emotion. "I thought as much. Antonia is dead, her headless corpse resides in her villa, two weeks past."

"Sergius took Cornelius's head as well. A necromancer will ferret out all their secrets in a short time. Why are you still here then?" Konstantin pretended to relax but shifted his position to gain easier access to a spear leaning against the wall. If Gilda had sided with Octavian, he wanted to be ready.

178

Gilda moved into the room and shut the door behind her, which sent alarms through Konstantin, as there was no other exit. "I took care of the two Imperial necromancers." She sat heavily on a bench, a clear slash opening up on her apron, showing naked flesh. It was her blood that had stained it, but the wound was now healed.

Testily, she said, "I did my part in this dragon-shitstorm of a plan. Two Dukes, a High Mage, and five barons are dead. The strongest opponents to Octavian's bid to take the throne are gone." She exhaled. "For all my work, what did it get me? Knifed when I went to report my success to Antonia."

Konstantin allowed himself to truly relax. He had always admired Gilda's unwavering commitment to honesty, even if it was always a carefully curated version of the truth. "Then why are you still here? It has been two weeks," he asked, genuinely curious about her continued presence.

"The same as you, I assume. I seek revenge. It's not just the necromancers I've been targeting these past two weeks. I'll do whatever it takes to frustrate that goblin-fucking bastard," Gilda's smile took on a distinctly malicious edge, a stark contrast to her typically grandmotherly demeanor.

This woman always made Konstantin uncomfortable. Not only was she a master poisoner, but he knew she had spell forms that allowed her to move relatively unseen and unheard. He had not pieced out what spell forms, but knew they existed. Even Cornelius had been wary of this woman. How Antonia had tamed her was a mystery he was likely never to unravel.

Still, there was a chance for some information. "The palace Archives?" Konstantin asked. The blood samples were kept there, under the palace.

Gilda shrugged. "There was a fire, so they are partially or completely destroyed. I don't know or care. I was never part of the Archives. The three agents sent in never came out after the fire." Konstantin winced internally at that. He had helped train those three young men: Omar, Albertus, and Pellion. They were all intentionally failed out of Hound training many years ago to seek refuge in Antonia's service, as planned.

He began questioning why he was even here. If Antonia was dead, he should just run—but they would find out he was still alive after the Hound he had been paired with did not report in. He began packing a small bag in earnest. "What are you planning, old man?"

He weighed telling her the truth. If he approached this the right way, he might recruit her much-needed aid. "The Archives. I want to make sure there is nothing left."

"You want to gain entrance to the palace?" She tsked at him. "Foolish man, prune the branches like me if you want vengeance for the betrayal. A tree cannot grow if all the leaves are gone."

"I don't want vengeance. I want my freedom." Damn, that was probably the wrong way to appeal to her. Gilda didn't say anything as Konstantin dug through the chaotic piles for supplies. How was he going to get into the palace? It was unfamiliar terrain to him. He really wished he had his runic weapon instead of the steel gladius he now wore, but he would make do. Maybe he could liberate an upgrade. The Imperial legionnaires had many fine runic blades among their number.

"You will never get in without someone competent holding your hand," Gilda finally said flatly, and Konstantin smiled to himself.

"I will manage unless you know someone dependable." He shouldered his pack, ignoring her, and took a step toward the door. Gilda stood and blocked him, and he waited for the inevitable.

"The palace holds someone important to me," she said with some false sincerity. He could tell she was looking for a reason to join him. At that moment, he gained a deeper understanding of the woman before him. She seemed to crave purpose, yearning to be guided and utilized like a tool. Had Antonia recognized this need and harnessed it? It was as if she was a weapon seeking a master. He had encountered soldiers and legionnaires with similar traits. The problem lay in their tendency to act without empathy, a good trait for a poisoner, but not for someone you needed to rely on in a fight.

"Who do you need in the palace?" Konstantin said, pulling the baited hook.

Gilda hesitated before replying. "The Imperial prison has been overflowing in recent days. There is someone I would like freed instead of beheaded," she said calmly. That did not seem like this woman. Under her smiling demeanor was just cold shallowness.

"One of Antonia's?" he asked, digging.

Gilda considered her next words before revealing, "No, a nephew of mine. He was in classes at the palace." She said it plainly, but it left Konstantin shocked. Only children and bastards of the First Citizens were educated on the palace grounds. Never would he have guessed the woman in front of him was from that stock. He briefly wondered which family she had been attached to.

Gilda continued with a fabricated smile, "It is decided, then?" Her face slowly morphed from that of an aged fat woman to a younger, leaner version of the same woman. Konstantin stepped back, to her amusement. His hand drifted to his gladius. *Shit*, he thought, *it isn't a silver or runic weapon.* "Intimidated by a young woman, old man?" Gilda said, bemused at his angst.

She started stripping off her now-oversized clothes and began searching through the piles for something to wear. As she worked, Konstantin couldn't help but ask, "Which is your true body?"

This slightly younger version still had the same features, so it was likely a spell, but you could never be certain with shape changers. He guessed the spell she was using could only change her age and body shape. "A lady never tells," Gilda said with a counterfeit smile.

"You are no lady," Konstantin retorted. He had known her long enough to feel safe in saying that.

"Agreed," Gilda said dismissively. She then removed her underclothes and dressed in the legionnaire clothes she had found in the mess. He noted this body appeared much fitter than the prior one. The problem Konstantin was grappling with was that when she was nearly naked, her body appeared too perfect. He needed her help now, but he would press a silver coin to her flesh if he had the chance.

They left together under the waning glow of Neptune's Tear. The shadows seemed to swallow Gilda as she moved, her footfalls nonexistent. Konstantin wore Hound boots that did the same for him, but her silence was clearly an aetheric working. They moved together like they had practiced it for a lifetime. Whenever a guard approached, the shadows seemed to shield Konstantin as well. It was a useful spell form, whatever it was.

Gilda was familiar with the city and quickly led them to the Mage College. They used the chancellor's secret entryway for access. The College was disturbingly quiet as they moved to the courtyard. Two Imperial legionnaires guarded the entrance to the palace grounds. Gilda finally hesitated as they stood in the shadow of the walls.

"Is there a problem?" Konstantin asked in the softest whisper.

"I am trying to decide if killing them will be to our benefit or not," she whispered back.

A mage in white robes approached the pair boldly. They were too far away to discern the words, but the conversation was very animated. The irate mage was eventually turned away, denied entrance. They slithered along the wall, approaching the guards, and Konstantin assumed she had decided to kill them. When they were within ten feet, a black hawk squawked and landed on a tree.

Gilda slipped past the guards while their attention was diverted. Konstantin almost missed his chance to follow.

Inside the palace grounds, they quickly moved away. "Not bad for an old man," Gilda whispered as they moved toward the immense palace structure.

"You could have informed me of your intentions. What if I had attacked them?" he grumbled. He disliked not being the one in control.

Infiltrating the palace was much easier than expected. The patrols were thin on the grounds, with most of the Imperial legionnaires either dead or still in the field. The palace halls were also empty. Gilda was not appreciative of the numerous sconces holding glowstones in the wide hallways. Without shadows, it was challenging to remain unseen.

Fortunately, Gilda knew the palace well, and the pair descended into the bowels of the structure. "That went better than anticipated," she finally rasped. "We only crossed three runes. Don't look worried, old man. None of them were triggered." A chill went up Konstantin's spine. Was Gilda also a skilled mage?

"We will check the Archives first." She turned and led them through a maze of passages. Konstantin fought to remember each turn and distance as they went. Just how many times had Gilda been in the palace to be this intimately familiar with it? Maybe she had been educated here as well.

The smell of soot and fire started to grow in his senses. Gilda slowed and peered around a corner before boldly walking out. Two large wooden doors were charred and hanging crookedly on their hinges. The large room beyond was dark, and fumes in the air stung Konstantin's eyes as they entered. "I will watch the door. Do what you must."

Konstantin produced his glowstone to reveal piles of charcoal, shattered glass, and outlines of fire-consumed bodies in blackened legionnaire armor, eleven bodies at his first count.

The fire had burned hot and fast. The smoke inhalation had likely killed the legionnaires. In the distance, there were still rows of untouched shelves, and he walked quickly toward them. On reaching them, he saw the bottles were coated in a thick layer of dust, topped with a fresh layer of soot. He continued to check more bottles to confirm his suspicions. The newer samples had burned, and these older samples had not been touched. Unfortunately, only a simple catalog number was on each runic jar, and he didn't have a reference.

He returned to the entry doors, pocketing his glowstone and half-expecting Gilda to have left. Her voice came from the shadows. "Satisfied?"

"Never," he shot back. "But we can look for your nephew now."

Gilda tilted her head and cracked her neck. "The holding cells are at the opposite end of the palace. I expect there will be a greater number of sentries since there is actually something to guard there." Konstantin decided she knew the palace far too well to not have lived there for a time.

They started moving down the brightly lit subterranean corridors. The sound of metal Imperial armor resounded around the corner. Gilda didn't shy away, nodding to Konstantin and holding up one finger to denote one guard. He moved ahead of her. He listened and waited. At the right time, he stepped out, his gladius's tip going right into the throat of the surprised legionnaire. He lunged, shifting the angle of the blade so it traveled up into the brain.

Quickly, he grabbed the legionnaire as he fell so he wouldn't bleed on the floor and pulled him away from the exposed corridor. Gilda checked to make sure no one had noticed, and they pulled the body into a storeroom—no blood had stained the marble floor. Konstantin left his blade where it was and unbuckled the man's sword belt. It was not a runic weapon, but it was better than what he was carrying. They were about to leave the room when two paired footfalls sounded outside, their owners in the middle of a conversation.

"… he wants all the inventory checked against the books again. Thirty-nine artifacts are missing."

"Someone probably escaped with them in the confusion."

"We will probably have to question all the prisoners again for the Centurion."

"Sergius should come down and check them himself. He spends most of his time eating and writing in his notebooks." The footfalls faded away.

"Don't even think about it," Gilda hissed. "We have another objective. After we free him, you can run off and confront Centurion Sergius on your own."

He supposed he shouldn't be surprised Sergius was here, as it was far from the fighting. It was much safer than the war front, and he probably wanted to review the Imperial treasury before Duke Octavian was elevated to Emperor. His desire to confront Sergius raged within him, but he nodded to Gilda. They tailed far behind the two Imperial legionnaires, heading in the same direction.

At one point, the pair of soldiers stopped, turned around, and listened for a time before continuing. While Konstantin's footfalls were silent, his armor and clothes were not. Fortunately, they did not come back to investigate. The two legionnaires eventually unlocked a large door and entered, closing it behind them.

"That must be the artifact repository," Konstantin voiced softly.

Gilda spoke, and the tension in the air was easy to feel. "It is, but there are two more guards inside, if not more. Are you capable of taking on four legionnaires without the benefit of surprise?" She quickly raised her hand, signaling for silence. "No, don't answer that. We still have a ways to go before we reach the cells." Konstantin shrugged and followed.

The remainder of their journey was surprisingly uneventful. They encountered no further guards or palace staff. However, upon reaching the cells, they were taken aback to find that the security was lax there as well. A lone, sleepy legionnaire and a pair of men in servant clothing stood by the entrance.

Gilda motioned Konstantin to remain behind as she walked out into the open. Her confident walk drew the eyes of the three watchers. "I was sent down to get your order for breakfast. Oats and buttered bread or hard-boiled eggs with biscuits and gravy?"

The legionnaire started to tense as something gave her away, and Gilda pounced. A dagger appeared in her hand and she slashed the throat of one of the servants, causing blood to spray across her body. The legionnaire was not slow in drawing his blade, but he never completed the act as Gilda's blade punched into his eye, and she rode him to the ground. The third man was running and screaming silently. Gilda caught him in four steps, tackling him.

She was weaponless and struggling to choke her victim. Konstantin rushed forward to assist, kicking the downed man in the head. Even though he was unconscious, Gilda turned his neck sharply, causing a pop. She must have released the silence spell form. She stood, searching the legionnaire for the keys. They both knew they didn't have much time before they were discovered.

The iron-banded door the legionnaire had been guarding opened into a corridor lined with more iron-banded doors, each featuring a small barred window. Gilda began searching each one quickly. Konstantin peered into the first, discovering a half dozen young boys in a miserable state. They were likely children of the First Citizens being held hostage, but apparently not who Gilda was looking for.

He started checking the cells after Gilda had peered in. Each cell held no less than four people, adults and children. Some were dressed in finery, others in undergarments, and others in legionnaire underclothes. The last group was probably made up of legionnaires who could not be trusted in the transition of power. He didn't recognize any faces, though. He paused to question one legionnaire: "Who are you?"

The five men looked up, fatigue evident in their eyes. "Legionnaires in service to Duke Vito."

"Where is your Duke?" Konstantin asked, formulating a plan.

"Held in quarters above," the eldest man said, standing. "Octavian needs his support for the throne."

"Are you willing to rescue him?" Konstantin asked. The men immediately shifted and focused alertly on Konstantin. They had killed the guards silently, and none of the prisoners were aware of it. The eldest and apparent leader nodded but seemed suspicious. Konstantin worked his spell form to open the simple lock, since Gilda had the keys. When it clicked, he slid the deadbolt aside and swung the door open cautiously.

Stepping back, he allowed the men into the corridor. They seemed to think it was a trap until they saw the dead bodies outside the entryway. They took one tentative step and then rushed to loot the bodies for weapons to rescue their Duke. He doubted that the men were familiar with the palace or that they would find their Duke, but any confusion was good confusion. If he could free more legionnaires, it could only help their escape.

Nine more legionnaires were freed, including two women. One of the women paused to ask Konstantin a question before leaving. "Is Duke Octavian or Centurion Sergius in the palace?"

From the vitriol in her voice, he knew why she was asking. Female legionnaires were rare, and he didn't know many. "Do they hold your mage commander or First Citizen?" Konstantin asked her.

"They had her killed for her family's silver mines," the woman spat. Konstantin searched his memory; there were only two silver mines in the Empire. Barons managed both.

"The Grecos?" he guessed. The other mine was far in the the southwestern Empire and probably under orc control by now. The Greco mine had even produced some gold, if he recalled correctly. When he was with Castile's company, they had cleared some kobolds from its depths.

"The Greco line is dead, and we are sentenced to the axeman. I would rather spend what remains of my life watching them bleed on the end of my spear." The muscular woman had spirit and fiery eyes, and Konstantin liked that.

Her younger companion was cradling her arm. "What is wrong with her?"

She spoke for herself, her pale blue eyes locking with Konstantin's. "My hand was severed and reattached but never healed properly. I still have one good arm and that is all I need." She didn't possess the same energy as the other woman, but any help was welcome.

"Only Sergius is in the palace. Once my companion finds her relative, we can search for him, as I wish his death as well," Konstantin said, hoping they would wait for him. They were weaponless and dressed only in underclothes, but they were trained legionnaires. They were anxious but hovered in the entryway to the cells, keeping watch.

It was still a time before Gilda returned with an unremarkable teenage boy behind her. They looked nothing alike. "Found what you were looking for?" Konstantin asked while studying the boy.

Gilda looked at the boy behind her. "I think so. He looks like him and answers to his name, but the last time I saw him was six years ago." The boy looked terrified.

"What of the others in his cell?"

"I left them there," Gilda said, nonplussed. Konstantin nodded, as that was probably the safest place for them.

"Are we good then?" Konstantin inquired, really asking whether their joint endeavor was at an end.

"If you leave with us, I can get you out of the palace grounds safely," Gilda offered.

Konstantin exhaled. "No. Sergius killed my friends and tried to kill me. It is time he paid, or time for me to visit Pluto's Realm." Gilda shook her head, disappointed. Konstantin held out his hand to shake, which she considered before extending her own. As their hands touched, she withdrew sharply. "Thought so," Konstantin muttered. "Be safe, Gilda." He turned his back on her and put the silver coin he had palmed into his pocket. It appeared Antonia had collected a shape changer into her service.

Reaching the entryway, he collected the two legionnaires. Without a guide, they were exploring blindly, but Konstantin led them back toward the artifact repository. On the way, they encountered one of the freed prisoners and two Imperial legionnaires twisted together in bloody death. Weapons and some armor pieces had been stripped, but the women still procured greaves and daggers for themselves. Konstantin waited while they worked on fitting the straps of the leg guards. The blood pools from the bodies continued to grow, indicating the fight had been very recent.

"Why are you two still alive?" he asked the pair, curious.

"We were captured in the city of Loule. We were portaled here a week ago to be questioned by the Truthseekers. That happened four days ago. They just haven't gotten around to removing our heads since the last two axemen died in their sleep." The older woman barked a dark laugh. Konstantin grunted, assuming it was Gilda's work.

He knelt to help the woman with the limp hand, who was frustrated with the straps holding the metal greaves. "Lose your hand defending your mistress?" Almost all female legionnaires ended up guarding a First Citizen woman.

"A cursed Hound took it before killing Selene Greco. He tormented me by reattaching it to highlight my failure," she said angrily. As he finished with the greaves, she introduced herself. "My name is Sylvia, but my friends call me Sylph."

Konstantin nodded at the introduction but didn't give his name. He also needed clarification. "A Hound left you alive? Count yourself blessed by Fortuna's kiss, then. Their orders are always to leave no witnesses."

"He knew Helena," the younger woman jested at her partner.

Helena spoke. "He left us alive and with enough coin to flee. We got recognized in Loule when we tried to get Sylph's hand healed." Konstantin frowned at the pair's ineptness. It was not difficult to remain unobserved.

"Which Hound pack left you alive?" He actually doubted their story now. Left alive and with coin? Not even the sentimental Hounds he knew would do that.

The older woman sensed his doubt and told him the truth. "It was just one. No Hound hunting pack, and he took most of the wealth Selene had packed. His name was Eryk. We were in legionnaire training together, and I kept his head above water."

Konstantin couldn't help but laugh, putting the two on guard. "Okay, that I can believe. Eryk would be foolish enough to do that."

The one named Helena asked with some aggressive anticipation, "Then he still lives?"

With a tired voice, Konstantin informed them, "If you seek vengeance against him, then I am sorry. He dines with Pluto already." The two women looked at each other, unspoken words passing between them. "His blood is also on Sergius's hands, and I look to repay him for it."

The three spoke no further as they moved deeper into the complex. As they approached the artifact depository, Konstantin said, "The Imperial residence should be above us. That is most likely where we will find Centurion Sergius guarded by the loyal Imperial legionnaires. If you flee now, there is still a chance you may escape."

Helena just walked past Konstantin, taking the stairs up. Sylph followed, shrugging. Echoes of fighting could be heard when they reached a black and white marble hallway at the top. The dozen men Konstantin had freed would be dealt with before long. Even now, a warning chime was echoing in the halls.

The problem was that he needed to figure out where to search, and the element of surprise was gone. Helena tried a nearby door and, finding it locked, shouldered it open. The loud snapping of wood echoed through the hall as the three entered the room.

A dim glowstone lit the room. The furnishings indicated that it was one of the many sitting rooms in the palace. Helena was marching to the far wall, where several ornamental weapons were on display. They looked exotic, and she took down a polearm, an infantry glaive. She tested the shaft before nodding to herself. Sylph helped herself to a scimitar with a gold pommel decorated with sapphires. She checked the blade before nodding, and Konstantin assumed the weapons had been gifts to Emperors over the ages. This would not be the only such display room in the palace.

Now better armed, they returned to the hallway. It appeared they were a distance from the conflict, and Konstantin knew they were on borrowed time. He paused at a door that had strong light emitting from underneath the bottom edge. It was also locked, and Helena was about to force it open when Konstantin held up his hand. He was desperately low on aether but was familiar with the style of lock. A push of the aether, and the door released, swinging free. He stepped in to see an array of servants huddled on the far side of the room, all petrified.

Konstantin couldn't believe his luck. Helena was prepared to leave, disgusted. "Where is Centurion Sergius?" Konstantin bellowed authoritatively. No one answered, so he tried a threat: "If one of you brings us to Centurion Sergius, you all can live."

"Are you going to kill him?" A meek young woman asked from the back of the group. There was a thread of hope in her voice, and Konstantin knew he had found a guide.

It was not long before the three were following the woman through the servant passages, up stairs and down unused hallways. The girl was practically running, fearing that one of the others would send a warning or that an Imperial legionnaire would intercept them. She abruptly stopped, out of breath. "A left here and then the doorway at the end of the corridor is the Supreme Chancellor's chamber. He has been staying there, but I do not know if he is there now. There are usually two legionnaires standing guard."

"Is there anywhere else he might be?" Konstantin pressed. The young servant's eyes were wild with fear as she shook her head. "Go hide, and don't come out for a long time."

Konstantin looked at his two companions and nodded. He peeked around the corner and saw a legionnaire and a Hound standing guard. They noticed him, too. The Hound turned and entered the room, leaving the legionnaire alone. Konstantin didn't hesitate and charged. Helena was on his left and Sylph on his right, but much slower. The legionnaire braced his body shield on the ground and readied his blade. The man was a fool.

Konstantin ran full force at the legionnaire. Their blades rebounded off each other, and then Konstantin's body weight hit the shield, forcing the soldier back into the door. With his shield pinning him, Helena's glaive had an unobstructed path to the man's face. He managed to turn his head in time so that the glaive skidded off his helm and into the door. But now he was facing the other direction, and Sylph's blade finished him.

Konstantin got a spurt of blood on his face as she extracted the scimitar. Konstantin pushed the body away and went for the door. It wasn't locked, and he pulled it open, expecting to have to roll away, but no attack came.

The ornate room's walls were filled with paintings. A movement to his right caused him to dodge in that direction. He recognized the Hound, Hercule, as one of Sergius's trusted seconds. A foul man if there ever was one. Konstantin had heard rumors that he tortured and raped his victims when sent on assassination missions. He would be doing the Empire a service by removing him.

The door behind him swung open, revealing their target. The pudgy Centurion Sergius stood ready with a runic shield and blade. Recognition and surprise flickered across his features. "Konstantin! You should have stayed under whatever rock was hiding you." Sergius's eyes drifted to the barely armored woman beside him as he assessed his odds.

Sergius flexed his grip on the sword. Konstantin doubted he practiced much anymore. He had consumed his share of essences in his time, but you still needed to practice regularly for the muscle memory to come naturally. Realizing who the women were, Sergius spat. "I see you were responsible for the prisoners escaping. It won't matter; they are probably all dead by now."

"As you will be shortly." Konstantin grinned maliciously.

In a more placating tone, Sergius replied, "I am sure Octavian can find a place for you. Perhaps you want to take command of the Western Hounds?"

His hollow offer was met with Konstantin sprinting forward. Hercule moved to intercept him but was engaged by Helena's glaive, which gave Konstantin room to circle and engage Sergius. Konstantin's sword rang off the shield, his arm instantly going numb. He backpedaled furiously to avoid the swing of Sergius's blade.

He switched his blade to his other hand and cursed. Of course Sergius would be wielding artifacts from the repository. If he lost the use of his other hand, he was dead. At least the two legionnaires were keeping Hercule occupied. He circled Sergius, one arm almost useless from the rebound spell on the shield.

The dungeon-forged blade Sergius wielded was likely special too. Konstantin knew he was not going to win this fight. After a full circle, he turned and dove at Hercule's back, targeting the hamstring. Sergius rushed to intervene, but it was too late. Konstantin didn't do much damage, but even a minor injury to a hamstring in a fight could tilt the odds. Sylph and Helena pressed their advantage while Konstantin threw his sword at the charging Sergius.

The sword bounced violently off his shield, shattering on its impact with the wall. The shield worked more than once. Konstantin drew a knife and took up a defensive stance. Hercule screamed and then gurgled, but Konstantin's eyes were locked on Sergius. The scrape of boots told Konstantin the women were circling wide. Sergius was backing up, probably wishing he had kept more men to guard his chamber.

He chanced a glance at his companions. Sylph was bleeding from a long cut on her bad arm, and Helena had a minor slash above her knee. She handed him Hercule's sword. Together, they encircled the sweating Sergius. "Do you want the treasury? Thousands of gold coins? Or maybe all the artifacts you can carry?"

He backed toward the room he had exited. Konstantin circled and blocked his escape. Feeling began to return to his numb arm, so maybe he hadn't lost it after all. This day just kept getting better.

Sergius tried to convince Helena or Sylph to turn on Konstantin, but the words were dead on their utterance. Konstantin pressed Sergius, giving Helena an opening with her glaive's long reach. They discovered the dungeon-forged blade emitted an arc of lightning on landing a strike. The crack of thunder forced

Helena to drop her weapon as her hands smoked, and she was momentarily stunned.

They shielded Helena while she recovered. Sergius became panicked and tried to break their circle, but couldn't without exposing himself. It was Konstantin who got the first blow on Sergius's shoulder, causing an aether shield to flare. This also gave Sergius a chance to rush to the exit.

Gilda was just outside the door, back in her plump older body and dressed in servant clothes. Sergius didn't think the fat old woman was a threat and never saw the blow coming. A stiletto pierced his eye and he grasped at it momentarily before his brain realized he was dead. Seeing Sergius dead, Gilda gave a satisfied nod to Konstantin.

"You came back for me?" Konstantin asked in surprise.

"My relation is free of the palace, and I thought I would check on you. I can help you out of the palace if you wish, but the sun is coming, so we need to move soon," she offered with a practiced, matronly smile. Konstantin considered the offer before nodding.

Konstantin quickly searched Sergius's body, taking the small coin pouch and handing healing potions to each woman. He pocketed two others for himself. Sylph picked up the runic shield and inspected it. "You need to be able to control your aether to use that," Konstantin advised.

"I can charge a glowstone," Sylph said, and Konstantin shrugged. He had already sheathed the dungeon-forged blade on his hip as his prize.

In the inner room of the chambers there was a study, and a number of large artifacts lay on the table. All were too big to carry, but he recognized one. The bronze kettle of souls rested apart from them, sitting innocuously on a shelf of books. If he was going to take anything it would be this, to prevent Octavian from looting Caelora. It had many dents from their exploration of the city and the Shimmering Labyrinth. Dozens of books lay open. Some were texts and some were message-sending books for Sergius's Hounds. He still didn't know the cipher and didn't care to carry them out of the palace.

He addressed the women. "Take whatever you want, but we should leave the grounds before sunrise. Our guide outside is anxious. Where do you plan to go?" Konstantin asked offhandedly as they prepared to leave the chancellor's chambers.

The women looked at each other, and Helena spoke. "When we got captured, we were on our way to Tegairosia. But Eryk said Gramney in the Grand Duchy of Manch was nice this time of year."

Konstantin paused and murmured to himself, "Did he now?"

I found my way to Maveith's side, leaning into him. In a harsh whisper to make myself heard over the ambient noise, I warned him, "Raelia might be in Artiria. If you can talk to her privately, try to convince her not to tell the others that she was with us in the dungeon."

Maveith's eyes were lively, a grin spreading on his face. He had befriended the Griffin Rider in the dungeon and missed her. At first, I thought he had an interest in her as a lover, but I believe she served as his surrogate sister. Protecting her from me was penance for abandoning his own sister. "Really? Raelia?" His deep voice was laced with excitement.

I was annoyed at his excitement and his failure to realize the implications. "The displacement mage hinted at it." I nodded over at our companions. "They can't know she was in the dungeon with us." I had planned to reveal my capabilities to my comrades gradually, but this would be too much, too soon. Even if Castile already knew what I could do, she didn't know about the elf.

"Raelia won't tell them if you ask her not to," Maveith grumbled softly.

"Why don't you tell her not to tell them for both of us?" I patted Maveith on the back, confident she would listen to Maveith more than to me. The guards were starting to call for everyone to bunch together if they didn't want to leave anything behind—whether that was luggage or a piece of their body.

Benito and Blaze came near me while Mateo grinned madly, talking with a plain-looking young woman. I guessed she was a merchant's daughter by the deep frown of the older man nearby, intently watching the interaction. Then again, maybe it was his wife. Mateo was definitely one of those men who needed the discipline of the Legion.

The human guards backed away, circling their charge as the elven displacement mage started her working. From my understanding, all she was doing was setting the destination and pulling aether with the assistance of the runes running beneath our feet.

The teleport felt a bit different this time. There was a momentary bout of vertigo that made me stumble, and I was not the only one. Several merchants vomited or stumbled to the ground. The elven displacement mage even fell to her knees, and I sensed something had gone very wrong. The courtyard around us felt familiar, and the mustard-uniformed guards nearby confirmed we were in Artiria.

To my right, Benito whined, "I feel like I just got kicked between the legs. It's not the first time, so I know what it feels like." Blaze was using his bow for support, and Maveith was helping Mateo to a seated position as he wavered on his feet.

I moved to the displacement mage as her guards screened her. "What happened?" I asked in Elvish, trying to get her attention as she recovered. This was a bad time to ask. Her response was to vomit on the worn, rune-scribed stones, and her guards drew their weapons on me.

She spat furiously to clear her mouth. "Don't let anyone leave! Someone is carrying an anchor stone!" The Artirian guards surrounding the courtyard trained bows on us, and others leveled spears. My group looked to me for direction, and I signaled to stand down. Like proper soldiers, they did, but remained ready to defend themselves by clustering together.

Two elven mages in shiny black robes walked briskly into the courtyard a moment later. Each had a pair of guards. My fellow travelers parted to let them reach our displacement mage. I moved as close as I could and strained to listen. "We were almost pulled back to Gramney. Somewhere among the travelers is an anchor stone that harmonized with the runes. I was barely able to hold the link and force us through."

A black-haired mage spat on the ground, clearly angry. "We will find the offender, Maerlyn." Soon, the mages were directing the city guards to search everyone. No one looked panicked; most were confused or recovering from the rough teleport.

I moved to stand with my companions and watched as they worked through the group. Blaze asked seriously, "Is there going to be a problem, Eryk?"

The guards were not aggressive but didn't take no for an answer as they moved through the passengers. I watched before I responded to Blaze's question. "No, not for us. From what I understand, the teleport almost failed because there is an anchor stone among the passengers. We are probably lucky to be alive."

Benito whined a little. "It did feel like dying. My stomach still feels like it's in my throat."

They never got to us, finding the offending object in a merchant's hand-pushed cart. One of the mages found it with a wand capped with a soft-glowing green stone. Four city guards moved in to cuff the cart's owner as he proclaimed his innocence. The middle-aged human was defensive as they cornered him. "I didn't know! It was among crates of curiosities I purchased in Gesedmuria!"

Two guards hauled away the merchant's cart, but inspections didn't stop there. Mateo was the first of our number to be inspected, and he did not like it. He was not accustomed to being a suspect after being a respected legionnaire for so long.

One mage stood back while the other asked questions, starting by recording Mateo's medallion number. The mage proceeded to hold the wand over the runic sword he had claimed from the Primus. The wand's light intensified with its proximity to the weapon. It was clearly a device for detecting artifacts.

Surprisingly, the mage didn't ask for the weapon, but his companion noted the weapon in his books. This was similar to our customs inspection in Sanco, except it was conducted in the open. That was all the runic equipment Mateo had, and they moved on to Blaze. Blaze was calm as the black-robed mages worked. They had him empty his pockets on a table as the device responded to something on his hip. Blaze complied, and the mage quickly pulled out the pink hair ring from the pile.

The wand-wielding mage inspected the artifact for much too long for my liking before putting it back with the other things. The relief work was beautiful, depicting an elven hunting party pursuing elk. He also took an interest in Blaze's sword, a blade forged by the Caelorian runic smiths. When it was drawn, the highly reflective steel caught the attention of the merchants and guards. The Caelorian artifact was just as much a piece of art as it was a weapon. Handing the blade back respectfully, the mage moved on to Benito.

Benito was all smiles as he was inspected, enjoying the attention. The only artifact on his person was his sword, and Benito was upset when all the mage did was log its existence. Benito's blade was a runic weapon most likely forged by the hands of men. Maveith only had to show his adventurer's medallion. They didn't confirm if he had added any new runic equipment. My turn went just as fast, but the inspector looked at me dubiously after recording my medallion number.

With the inspection completed, we were allowed to leave the courtyard and enter the city. The walkway was lined with local guards in their mustard uniforms. I didn't know if this was normal, or due to the issue we had with our teleport. Exiting into the street, the others were gawking at the architecture and all the different elves. That was fortunate, as they didn't notice the young elven woman among the throng leaning against a building across the street.

Raelia was barely recognizable in a long green dress with a tasteful silver chain. Her hair was pulled back, highlighting her sharp facial features. Her clean appearance added beauty to her youthful elven face. We made eye contact and I could see the corner of her mouth rise into either a smile or a smirk. I didn't see a griffin, so maybe the egg had not been viable, as it should have hatched by now. Or perhaps griffins were not allowed to roam in the city.

"Let's get to the Adventurers Guild," I announced to everyone with some forced excitement. "We can tour the city later. Maveith, why don't you get us lunch?" Maveith was already beaming and anxious to go to Raelia. I ushered my companions away, Mateo and Benito in a deep conversation comparing elven women to human women. The shock on Raelia's face as I ignored her and walked away was memorable, and I suspected I would hear about it later.

I escorted Blaze, Mateo, and Benito to the Adventurers Hall and got us a few rooms. Fortunately, the local Guildmaster did not show himself when I checked us in. I inquired at the desk, and a helpful elf informed me that two orcs were in the city and neither was attached to a group. I got their information and found Maveith entering the Hall.

Blaze was browsing postings while Mateo sat at the table sipping an elven ale and conversing with three elves, two of whom were female. He only spoke Telhian, so he was revealing our origins. Benito played a solitary game resembling darts, dropping them upon seeing Maveith. "Where's the food?" Benito looked crestfallen, disappointed that Maveith had failed in his assignment.

"You can order something here, Benito." I handed him a silver coin. The Adventurers common room was more of a bar than an eatery, but they did have a kitchen. The coin got Benito away from us so I could talk with Maveith.

"How is Raelia? Will she keep our secret?" I whispered to my friend.

"She is outside." He exhaled slowly. "She is not happy with you for ignoring her, but I tried to explain." I motioned for him to continue. Helplessly, he went on, "I don't think I did a very good job of it."

I sighed. "Stay here and keep the others inside. I will go talk with her." Maybe sending Maveith had been a mistake.

I stepped out into the street to find Raelia in her fine dress with one of the city guards behind her. I reevaluated the young, muscular elf in city colors. No, not a city guard: a bodyguard. His sharp eyes studied me like I was a villain. I approached them cautiously. "Raelia, long time no see."

Confusion passed on her face at my turn of phrase. She shook her head, clearing her thoughts, "Your Elvish has improved. It no longer hurts my ears to hear you speak."

Was she teasing me, or was she genuinely angry? I proceeded cautiously as it appeared she held some sway here, judging by her dress and bodyguard. I kept my tone conversational, not playing into her provocation. "I see you made it to safety. How did you end up here and not in Bartiradia?"

Raelia hesitated before answering, and her tone had hints of sorrow. "I was exiled from Bartiradia. Well, I was not exactly exiled, just sent away so my failures wouldn't stain my family. I am actually the Bartiradian ambassador to Esenhem. Or at least one of them." I was confused, since I assumed that an ambassador role was a step up from Ranger.

I switched to addressing someone with a higher station in Elvish. "Well, you do look the part, and you're quite breathtaking in your dress. It accentuates your figure nicely." Her cheeks flushed a little. I thought I had caught her off guard with the compliment and formal Elvish address. When she didn't respond immediately, I continued, "Did Maveith talk to you about my companions?" I indicated the Guild Hall and eyed the elf behind her. I assumed she had already reported everything from our time in the dungeon, and no one was arresting me, which was good.

"That you don't want me telling them I helped you escape the dungeon?" she said teasingly, smirking.

I didn't care to debate how much help she actually gave. I also wasn't going to let her have leverage over me. "If you are going to tell them, then I can always just do it myself. We are all traitors to the Empire and can never return. I am sorry about the griffin egg." I thought changing the subject might help my case. Maybe I could interview the orcs tomorrow. We could get horses and ride out to get away from any trouble she might stir up.

"What about the griffin egg? Baldo is doing well and nearly fifty pounds already." Her eyes suddenly flared in annoyance. "You should have told me it was in the pack! If I hadn't checked, the cold weather would have killed him. Are you such a fool that you have no idea how to care properly for an egg!?" Her teasing had turned to anger in defense of the griffin, and I could already tell she was attached to it.

"Yes," I said flatly, agreeing with her rather than arguing. That left her speechless, as she had clearly expected some verbal sparring. Maybe she was even looking forward to it, judging from her disappointment. "Baldo? That is a Telhian word. Why would you give an elven griffin a Telhian name?" Baldo meant something like a foolish man. *Wait, did she name the griffin after me?*

"It just felt right," she finally whispered to herself. "I can't change it now. He has already imprinted the name." There was an awkward silence between us before she finally asked, "Do you want to meet Baldo?"

"I am sure Maveith would. I did promise to find him a griffin big enough for him to ride." I was steering the conversation away from me, but her eyes looked so hurt at my words that guilt forced me to change my mind. "But I have always wondered what baby griffins look like."

She latched onto my concession. "It is settled then. We are at Regent Maeralya Glavien's residence. We will expect you and your entire party."

"I don't think my friends can handle a dinner with someone of such high standing," I said sincerely.

"You would reject the invitation of a Regent of Esenhem?" Raelia said, grinning playfully. This elf changed her emotions from sentence to sentence. She sighed, "Fine, I promise not to tell them about our time in the dungeon together."

"Why don't we just not include them?" I said, a little pleadingly.

Her eyes narrowed slightly, studying me. "Maveith said they were your friends. Besides, my aunt has always wanted to talk with legionnaires." The onset of a headache signaled my growing unease as I imagined Benito and Mateo engaging in conversation with an elven Regent. As I envisioned a potential disaster, Raelia turned to me and said, "One of the Regent's servants will come and collect you at sunset here." With those words, she walked briskly away, the bodyguard trailing her, leaving me to consider the impending dinner.

I walked inside, a little numb, to find the group eating at a table. I moved and sat down with them, smiling weakly. "Good news. I have made dinner plans."

I absent-mindedly poured myself a drink, taking an empty but probably used mug. Benito was excited at the mention of food. "What is for dinner? I bet the elves have some amazing cooks! These sandwiches were pretty good. I bet they spent thousands of years learning how to cook well, right?"

Maveith rumbled a laugh. "Elves can live to a thousand, yes. But few ever complete a second millennium." Our conversation caught the ears of the elven adventurers seated around us. I thought it best to steer the conversation away from elves.

I looked over my happy companions and dampened their mood a bit. "You can't wear your armor or weapons to the dinner. We are dining with an elven Regent," I announced. Maybe I should not have told them about the dinner. I could have shown up only with Maveith and made excuses about their absence.

"Elven Regent? What's that?" Mateo asked, snacking on breadsticks with a noticeable crunch.

"The elves elect Regents to their cities and large towns. They rule for a period of time before another vote is cast. All the Regents gather here in the capital in the Assembly to discuss policy and enact laws," Maveith explained to Benito. Hopefully he had simplified it enough.

Benito was thinking really hard and his response wasn't surprising. "The food should be really good then, right?"

Blaze was more thoughtful and curious. "How do they cast votes? Does everyone get a vote, even the children? How do you know who to vote for?"

An elven adventurer with jet-black hair had been listening in. She leaned her chair back so it was dangerously close to tipping and craned her neck to look at our table before speaking. Her Telhian was decent, but slightly accented. "The towns hold a festival. Those wishing to be Regent give a speech and everyone over twenty summers votes. The top two vote recipients then debate in front of the crowd. At the conclusion, another vote is cast to determine the winner. It takes an entire day, but only happens once every eight years. Larger cities are divided into districts to elect a proxy to cast their vote in the city's court or petition for Regent." She went back to her table to resume a game of Go.

Mateo, noticing the elven beauty interested in our table, stood up awkwardly and introduced himself, to our amusement. "I'm Mateo, and I find what you said extremely—fascinating. Could I buy you a drink, and you explain your …?"

The elf turned back slowly, her sharp features studying a grinning Mateo intently. "No," she said flatly, and turned back to her game. Mateo looked a little hurt, and we held in our laughter at his being shot down.

"Don't worry, Mateo. There are a lot of fish in the sea," I said to cheer him up. The elven woman turned and briefly arched her eyebrow at me, but her two male companions had sour looks as they locked threatening gazes on me. I happily returned a challenging stare until they looked away. The elf woman took my measure and turned away last.

Maveith's face was scrunched in thought as he puzzled over my analogy about fish. Blaze thankfully whispered to him to explain it. I looked at my rough-looking group; they couldn't go to the Regent's residence in their armor underclothes. The problem was that clothing was expensive, and my group was poor. I leaned over and tapped the raven-haired elf on the shoulder. She looked over at me questioningly. "Can you escort my companions to a place where they can get some decent clothes?"

"Which Regent are you looking to impress?" She was clearly interested and posed her question with a grin. Her interest in my offer had her male companions staring with disapproval again.

I didn't know if Regent Maeralya wanted it spread she was associating with Telhians, so I didn't mention her name. "I am not looking to impress her, just to have my companions in clean clothes that won't embarrass us. A large silver for an hour of your time to take them?" I offered her a large silver, making it appear with a soft snap of my fingers. The trick didn't impress her, and she probably thought it was sleight of hand.

"Enyara, don't help the Telhians," her companion said testily. He was the one opposite her, playing the board game.

"I can make my own decisions," she barked back, annoyed. She surprised me, snagging the silver coin like a viper. She nodded at me. "A large silver for being a tour guide for an hour, no longer."

Mateo was happy, but paled when he realized he didn't have any coins for the shopping trip. As the emotions played on his face, I saved him again. "Maveith, go with them and pay for their clothes. See what you can get for yourself as well." His massive hand encompassed mine in unspoken understanding, and I palmed Maveith eight gold coins from my dimensional space. Maveith had additional coin, and I hoped the gold would buy each of them something presentable. Being the leader was getting very expensive.

With my team headed out into the city, I had a chance to look at the jobs on the wall. I got some stares as I walked the length of the postings on the board. What I needed was something that would take us into the Caliphate.

The nearest thing I could find was a merchant escort from Artiria to Khoura. Khoura was an orc city on the border with Esenhem. By fortuitous coincidence, it was also one of the places I was told we could register as adventurers in the Caliphate. I needed to work on my written Elvish, as it took me time to puzzle out the posting, to the amusement of the elves watching me.

Wanted: Mounted Guards for Three Wagons. Minimum six, maximum eight. Two silver pieces per day, per guard. Food and feed included.

The distance was five hundred miles, I estimated, but I was not certain what the merchant's pace would be. I pulled the tack out of the heavy paper and brought it to the desk. The elven attendant took it and held out his hand patiently. I quickly figured out it was for my medallion.

He was a little surprised that my medallion was silver as he recorded the information. "I actually wanted to ask the merchant a few questions before accepting," I said before he proceeded further.

The elf appeared moody and went into some files in the back. When he returned, he stated flatly, "The Stumble Inn, down the street to the left. Rolf Sheadings, room six." I wasn't sure if my treatment was due to the Guildmaster or just that humans were generally not well liked—or maybe it was my Telhian accent.

The inn was easy to find. A quick inquiry and I found Rolf drinking at a table and reviewing stacks of paper while an elf bard crooned a melody by the hearth. Rolf had a manicured beard halfway to his waist and a thick head of rusty brown hair to match it. I moved to stand across from the dwarf, my adventurer's medallion displayed outside my armor. "Rolf? I am Eryk Marko, and I am interested in your posting in the Guild Hall."

The dwarf looked up, studying me. He nodded slowly, coming to an opinion of my capability by my appearance alone. "Human and silver adventurer to boot. Don't care about the color of your medallion, the rate is still two silver per guard per day," he stated firmly.

"How long will the trip take, and will you be traveling further into the Caliphate?" I asked, helping myself to a seat opposite him. His large, crystal-blue eyes studied me more intently, and he put down his fountain pen. Most of the documents appeared to be ledgers.

His beard swayed as his jaw worked. "We make thirty miles a day and have planned stays in towns every night. Your party will all need to be mounted, no exceptions. Had too many a guard who said they could walk thirty a day, and their feet always failed them. The wagons and horses will be stabled in a barn in town, and I expect at least half your men to sleep in the loft there to watch the wagons. The trip takes twenty days; sometimes bad weather adds a day or three," Rolf finished, and waited for my response.

"What dangers are typically on the road that you need guards? You also didn't say if you would venture further into the Caliphate," I said in consideration.

He clasped his hands. "Most trips, I have had no trouble. But along this road in the last twenty years, the most serious confrontations we have had were with a forest drake, giant spiders, meddlesome sprites, and a banshee." He watched me as he listed off the dangers, and I didn't flinch. He nodded approvingly. "I will not venture into orc lands. I will spend a month selling and buying from the orcs in Khoura and then return to Artiria. Usually, we have a train of two other merchants, but this time, it is just me."

"No bandits? Do you usually have more guards?" I asked, thinking this job was a possibility.

The dwarf laughed at me. "Bandits in Esenhem? Maybe close to one of their borders, but elves don't tolerate thieves and cutthroats." He finished his chuckle. "Aye, you are right. We normally have a dozen adventurers guarding the train, but eight is the most I can afford without denting my profits too much. My regulars took off with a caravan to the south," he added, some bitterness to his words.

"There are five of us, but I am looking for a sixth at the moment. A goliath and four men," I informed him.

His eyes widened. "Heard there was a goliath walking about. That is him, and he is an adventurer. I can't wait to see the beast he rides," he said, slapping the table in amusement.

"Yeah, me too," I added, thinking it might be hard to find a horse big enough for Maveith. And Maveith didn't even know how to ride yet. Thinking back on my own riding lessons, I knew Maveith would be in for a rough time of it.

"I think we can accept. If I don't find a sixth, will five be good enough? And when would we depart?" I asked. There was always the possibility of just riding out on our own, but I wanted the appearance of true adventurers, especially before we headed into the Caliphate.

"Five? Are you the only silver?" I nodded. "With a silver and a goliath I could agree to that. Should charge you extra for how much I hear a goliath can eat." His smile showed through his beard. If Maveith could keep his ring on, he was going to be surprised. "Three mornings from now. You can meet me here, Eryk."

We shook wrists on it, and he completed a letter of acceptance to the Adventurers Guild. I returned to the Hall and spent nearly an hour filing the paperwork for accepting the posting. The funds for payment would be held by the Guild and paid in the Khoura Adventurers Hall when we delivered the merchant safely. When I asked what would happen to the funds if we didn't arrive or failed, the elf scoffed a little and said they would revert to the Guild after a year if neither party claimed them.

The others had not returned, so I left to purchase mounts. After asking around, I was finally directed outside the city. A good mile's walk brought me to a stable. I had only seen a few horses in Esenhem, so this was either going to be cheap or very expensive. A half dozen corrals had a few horses each, and the stalls in a large building were full. A tall, lean elf woman in tight leather saw me watching the horses and approached. She had a strong scent of horse about her and was almost as tall as me.

"Do you need help?" she asked in a deep, resonant voice with a businesslike tone.

"Do you have a horse big enough for a goliath?" Her eyebrows shot up in surprise at my unusual question.

"A plow horse?" she hedged.

"No, a riding horse for the road" I returned, and her brow furrowed.

"How big of a goliath?" she asked.

"Seven and a half feet and maybe three hundred and fifty pounds—but could be as high as four hundred with gear." She slowly nodded as she thought about it.

"I only have two that might work for him. A black from the Caliphate. Spirited but listens well. Or a painted-brown from the south. A bit old but still serviceable. If you are not in a rush, I have a few that I can finish breaking over the next two months."

"We are departing in three days. I will look at the black," I said, and I followed her into the stables. The black was huge, standing taller than Maveith.

"He has been studded a few times, but none of his progeny have matched his size and temperament," the woman said unhappily. I walked into the stall. He was spirited and could be dangerous to an untrained rider. But after an apple, he cooperated with my inspection, and I spent a good fifteen minutes checking him out. I was impressed. I was surprised the elf was parting with him.

"He is not battle-trained, but he will do. How much?" I finally asked, satisfied.

"Seventy-five," she said, causing me to cough. That was the price of a prized warhorse in the Empire. I could see horses were not as common in Esenhem, but that was ridiculous. I had also been told this was the only horse dealer in Artiria. Seeing my consternation, she explained, "He is a good stud when the mare can hold him, and I hate to lose him."

"How much for a good riding horse for me?" I asked regaining my composure, still stunned by the exorbitant cost.

"Between ten and twenty-five," she said, undeterred by my shock. Damn, I hated being the leader.

I sighed. "Show me your stock, I need three." She beamed and her face dimpled. She called in two other stable hands to help as I went through their stock.

I spent three hours looking at over thirty horses. Their scent rubbed off on me as I worked. I was looking primarily for temperament and fitness. I was not able to afford warhorses—not that I saw any in the stables. At least I learned why horses were so costly in Esenhem. The elves did not maintain a cavalry, and horses were considered a foolish investment due to their short life spans of about thirty years.

The three I selected for Benito, Mateo, and Blaze were large and well fitted, but didn't come close to the black in size and strength. I almost thought about getting Benito a pony as a joke, but then I would have had to buy him another horse later, so I shelved the idea.

Haggling was not part of Esenhem culture, so I wouldn't be able to lower the cost. Still, I tried to get a little more. "Can I at least get saddles and tack thrown in?"

The horsewoman looked amused, her dimples showing again, but she was looking to close the sale. "Used and refurbished. We even have something that should suit the goliath." Relieved, I produced the 142 gold. It was painful; the price took a massive bite out of my coin reserves.

It was late in the day and close to sunset, so I needed to get back. I arranged for the mounts to be brought to the Adventurers Hall stables before returning. I found my companions in the common room drinking with the raven-haired elf. Benito was telling the tale of how he became a legionnaire, and she was laughing hysterically. I didn't know elves had a sense of humor. I scanned the room but didn't see her original companions.

My men were dressed in suitable, simple, dark-green and brown outfits, and their wet hair indicated they had bathed. Maveith handed me the leftover coins: two gold and a dozen silver. Blaze looked at me questioningly, as I still wore my adventurer's armor.

"I will go change," I announced to the table. Back in my room, I changed into my best clothes, donning my manticore cloak. My outfit was mostly black, and looking in the mirror, I thought I appeared more sinister than my companions. Maybe I should have joined them on their shopping trip. It was too late now, as the sun was already on the horizon. I still smelled of the horses, but at least my beard and hair were trimmed.

I returned to the common room to find two city guards in their pressed mustard uniforms standing at my companion's table. A brief pit of worry opened in me, but it turned out that they were our escort and not here to arrest my companions. It was time to meet the Regent, and I just hoped the men hadn't drunk too much beforehand.

Chapter 273: Dinner Discourse

As I stepped outside, my companions followed, and I was relieved to observe that none of them seemed overly intoxicated. Mateo began sharing intriguing details about our guide, Enyara.

He emphasized that she was a skilled tracker and had a long affiliation with the Guild. She often operated independently and was currently available for hire.

Her skill set bore a resemblance to that of a Hound of the Empire, but her expertise lay in tracking monsters rather than people.

Mateo's evident fascination with the elf concerned me, and I hoped that his infatuation would not complicate matters. I made it clear that I was not keen on adding her to our group, as I was already struggling to keep my own secrets.

"Why are we going to see a Regent? Maveith wasn't too forthcoming," Blaze said conversationally as he walked by my side, drawing my attention.

I gave as little information as possible, but could already see the inevitability of Raelia revealing too much. Maybe I was going along because I wanted my friends to know. "The Regent was curious about the famed legionnaires of the Telhian Empire. The young elf woman who invited us is an acquaintance of Maveith's."

Thankfully, Maveith backed me up. "Her name is Raelia. She is nice, and you will like her. She was once a Griffin Rider, and she promised to show us her new young griffin." I gave him a look that suggested he was disclosing too much information, and Maveith stopped speaking.

"She is an ambassador from Bartiradia. Best not to talk about any of our fights with the Bartiradians," I said, my headache growing as I cut off Maveith. The Empire was currently at war with Esenhem and Bartiradia, so this shouldn't alarm them, as we had forsaken our oaths.

"If she has a griffin, is she still a Griffin Rider?" Mateo asked perceptively.

Maveith remained quiet, so I answered vaguely, "I think she used to be one." Yes, this was not going to go well. Blaze was the one who had shot Raelia out of the sky in Macha during the siege.

"I always wanted to know what it would be like to fly. Is it like falling upwards?" Benito asked, more to himself than the group. His slight lisp said he had drunk more than the others.

A catkin entourage passed us on our left, causing the conversation to stop. The feline men and women had large yellow eyes and wore royal-purple robes with royal-blue sashes. Since we were in the wealthier part of the city, I assumed they were ambassadors. Perhaps even from Tsinga, where most of the catkin on the continent originated.

We arrived at a blue-gray granite manor. Like all the architecture in the city, curves dominated its aesthetic, with not a single sharp angle showing. It was modest-looking from the street, and I guessed our Regent was not as prominent when compared to the other estates. Our escort halted at the entrance to stand guard. Attendants ushered us inside, wearing pristine white uniforms adorned with small embroidered crests of a falcon in flight.

I led the way, following the attendants. The building appeared to be made from polished granite, and the hallways were decorated with mosaics made from hundreds of thousands of tiny semiprecious stones. The mosaic images were mostly nature scenes and extended from the floor to the high ceiling. It must have taken years to complete even one. My companions admired the images in awe, understanding the time required to construct them.

Curious, I sent out an earth pulse to get a layout of the entire structure. It was larger than it seemed from the street and extended far back, with many rooms and private gardens outside that were not visible from the street. It was three stories with organic, curved corridors that reminded me of branches on a tree. The basement was only a single level below us and was connected to a water and sewer system.

There were nineteen people in my range besides our escorts. Most people were scattered through the satellite rooms, four looked like guards, and three were seated at our likely destination, which appeared to be a dining hall.

Mateo walked into my back. I had stopped to examine the spell form's feedback. "Is everything alright?" he asked alertly, thinking I had stopped due to danger.

"Yes. I just got lost in the mosaic mural." I gestured to the waterfall mural on our right with naked elves swimming in the pool underneath it.

Our attendants paused, waiting on us patiently. Mateo studied the image intently as I continued. The dining room was oval-shaped, with one sizable circular window looking out onto a colorful garden. The night was settling, and soon it would be dark.

An oval table matching the room's shape dominated its center, capable of seating over twenty. But the only place settings were at one end of the table. Raelia sat tall next to a matronly-looking elf woman with streaks of gray in her auburn hair. On the other side of her was an older male elf with nearly white hair. The pair was immaculately dressed to match Raelia. Even with their fresh clothes, my companions were considerably underdressed.

Raelia stood, looking regal in her emerald dress with decorative bracers. My companions, especially Mateo, were captivated by the young elf woman. I had seen her covered in blood and smelling like two-month-old underwear, so I wasn't as enamored. She did look even better than she did on the street this morning, though.

In her poor Telhian, she introduced us. "May I present the adventurers: Maveith of the Stoneskin Clan. Eryk Marko. Blaze Neptune. Mateo Evander. Benito Vesta." She smirked at me when she introduced Maveith first, but I was okay with being second as it fit my narrative. On the other hand, how she knew the names of my companions concerned me. I hadn't even known their last names before this moment.

"Blaze Neptune?" I heard Benito whisper to Blaze.

"I am bastard born under the full glory of Neptune's Tear," he whispered back.

Raelia ignored the lack of etiquette from my whispering companions and introduced the Regent. "My aunt, Regent Maeralya Glavien of Bragoas. And her consort, Mage Laeroth Araro."

Not knowing what to do, I bowed in both their directions respectively and addressed them in formal Elvish. "We kindly thank you for the invitation and the warmth of your home. We look forward to a wonderful dinner. Please accept this as a token of our appreciation for your hospitality." I produced a bottle from underneath my manticore cloak.

"What did he say?" Benito asked a little too loudly. Blaze elbowed him to shut up.

An attendant came forward, took the bottle of Caelorian wine from my hand, and brought it to the Regent. She studied the relief work, her consort looking just as interested. Raelia was dumbstruck by her aunt's whispers, and her eyes snapped back to mine, her surprise clearly evident. I had never shared any of the wine with her in the Shimmering Labyrinth.

The Regent spoke in Telhian much more practiced than Raelia's speech. "Remarkable. A truly monumental gift. I hope our offerings at dinner can match the generosity you have shown, Adventurer Eryk Marko. Please sit next to my consort and have your companions sit as well."

We moved to take our seats, Maveith to my right in a seat specially prepared for his girth. When everyone was seated, the first food was brought out: some white fish with an aromatic red dipping sauce. There were only four squares of fish each, and my men consumed the small portion in seconds, washing it down with sweet water. I ate more slowly, on guard for the forthcoming conversation. At least Maveith had been given a double portion.

Laeroth opened with a question after watching us eat. "You were legionnaires of the Empire? Did you fight the army of Esenhem?"

Maeralya was more diplomatic, giving her consort a harsh glare. "I apologize for Laeroth's rudeness. We lost many fine young men and women in the war. Some were his students."

Lareoth's tone turned sharp, "The failure was that only half the Regents sent support for the occupation. If the Assembly had voted for a joint resolution to …"

Maeralya put her hand on his arm to stop his rant. "He is upset with our tortuously slow political workings. The Assembly of Regents was not keen on invading the Telhian Empire. Only a few Regents pulled their city's forces together to address the—threat. I sent three hundred soldiers and mages from Bragoas, half of whom have been killed." The woman was talking conversationally, but I could see her own underlying anger at the loss. What had Raelia dragged us here for? Some type of verbal abuse?

"No. It is understandable. We have not been well received when your people hear our accent, for good reason," I replied, almost switching to Elvish but keeping the conversation in Telhian for my companions.

The Regent nodded, finding my response fitting. "Are you referring to Artiria's Guildmaster in particular? He lost a brother and has petitioned the Assembly to ban any Telhian-born adventurer from Esenhem for the next hundred years."

I looked at Raelia. She shifted uncomfortably, clearly caught off guard by the direction of the conversation. Maybe she hadn't known her aunt and consort would condemn us for the actions of the Empire.

Blaze gave me a hand sign, and I nodded, permitting him to speak. "Eryk and Maveith were not part of our company for the battle." He indicated Mateo and Benito. "We did engage the soldiers from Esenhem under the Emperor's banner. At the time, we were guarding the northern flank, and we never saw combat against your people. After the Emperor was slain, we took it as an opportunity to shed the shackles of the Empire." Blaze was surprisingly—very—diplomatic. I almost expected him to reveal that it was he who had slain the Emperor, but he didn't go that far.

Laeroth did not look placated. His neck veins were bulging and he clearly wanted to say more. Maeralya ignored his seething and calmly asked, "Why did you become adventurers?"

Benito, not realizing he shouldn't be talking, spoke. "We became adventurers because we are going to rescue Maveith's sister in the Boutan Caliphate." It was not like it was a huge secret, but the entire table froze. Judging from Raelia's expression, Maveith hadn't told her.

Regent Maeralya broke the awkward silence. "That is certainly a noble endeavor." Her tone showed that she doubted our chance of success. "Are you planning to delve into any more dungeons in the future?" The realization of why we were here suddenly struck me. They wanted information about the Shimmering Labyrinth. I could piece it together now with their interest in the wine and the fact that Raelia must have told them a lot about the dungeon, but she had never seen the entrance.

"Perhaps. We have to cross nearly the entire length of the Caliphate to look for Zorana. Do you know anything about the dungeons of the Caliphate?" Out of the corner of my eye, I caught Blaze stopping Benito from talking with a soft elbow jab.

The Regent was smiling, but I could see past the mask. There was a hidden purpose to our being here. The next dish had been placed before us. A white meat with green sauce for dipping. "The orcs believe the dungeons are sacred. A way of testing true warriors. A warrior must complete seven of the eleven dungeons in the Caliphate to be tattooed by the clerics. A warlord must complete all eleven plus a twelfth alone."

"We could all become orc warlords?" Mateo asked. His plate was already clean, but his eyes had been wandering to Raelia for most of the meal.

"No. The twelfth dungeon is not accessible to outsiders, and the Supreme Cleric is the only one who grants entry. Even orcs who have completed the first eleven dungeons are sometimes denied an attempt. Just like every other nation, there are politics at play in the Caliphate."

"Does that include the Pathfinders?" I asked.

The Regent shook her head. "No, the Pathfinders are special family units that train together. Their tattoos are focused on stealth. The elite warriors of the Caliphate are few, but they are some of the strongest warriors on the continent. Their tattoos enhance their speed, strength, and endurance," Maeralya informed us patiently.

I nodded, realizing that the orcs I had seen fighting in the Coliseum were the elite fighters of the Caliphate. Recalling the fight, I surmised they would have defeated the Imperial legionnaires if they hadn't been drained of aether and had been given equal arms and armor.

Laeroth stood and feigned discomfort. "I think the meal has disagreed with me. I think I will retire for the evening." It was clear why he was leaving. He hated that Regent Maeralya was being civil with ex-Telhian legionnaires. I was surprised Raelia had been so quiet this evening. She was sitting dutifully and had not participated in the conversation.

The conversation remained centered on the Caliphate, and Regent Maeralya was eager to share the social structure of the orcs with me. I had read some books, but words could never do justice to actual experience, and the Regent had traveled extensively in the Caliphate.

"The orcs have a tiered class system. The best way to think of the Caliphate is as a flock of sheep," she started. "The sheep are the citizens that need to be protected by the shepherds, who are the clerics. The warlords, elite warriors, and Pathfinders are guard dogs directed by the shepherds. The sheep are docile and expected to always obey. You will find the orc citizens to be nonconfrontational for the most part. Their warrior caste, however, is always seeking to validate themselves." I couldn't tell if the Regent respected or looked down on the orc society.

"How does one go from being a sheep to a guard dog?" Blaze asked inquisitively.

The Regent put on a thin smile. "By proving oneself in a dungeon. But most commoner orcs who test a dungeon never exit," the regent said with finality. She directed a question at me: "And your dungeon experiences? Are they extensive?"

I looked to Raelia, who had lost some of her regalness in the evening. She didn't make eye contact with me and no longer sat nobly. She was realizing she had led us into an ambush. I decided to give the Regent a taste of what she wanted. "We all spent time in the Shimmering Labyrinth in Caelora." I indicated my companions. The Regent let a smile escape, briefly revealing her true purpose for the dinner.

"All of you? We have some ancient texts that reference the famed dungeon. Is it as extensive as they indicate?" the elf woman said, trying to contain her eagerness.

"Over one hundred rooms," I replied unflinchingly. Blaze arched his eyebrow at me as I revealed the details of the dungeon, but he didn't know Raelia had probably already told them. And if she had, then they knew about my impressive dimensional space.

"Amazing. That is the largest dungeon I have heard of. The merfolk have large dungeons beneath the seas, and there is the Black Sands dungeon on the other continent, but to my knowledge, none have more than forty rooms. We foolishly destroyed most of the dungeons in Esenhem centuries ago. It reduced monster scourges on the surface, but now just three remain." She smiled. "Let me be forthright with you. We are negotiating a truce with the Telhian Empire. I want to know everything about the Shimmering Labyrinth you can tell me."

"I thought you wanted Atlantium." I responded evenly.

Regent Maeralya's face slipped into a shocked expression. She would have been even more shocked if she had known I had been there when it was discovered. She slowly spoke. "We are already working on a pact to share what is uncovered there, but your people are still embattled about who will take the Emperor's seat. If you have truly forsaken the Empire, knowledge of the Shimmering Labyrinth will be useful, as well as something I can bring to the Assembly for inclusion in the treaty."

Raelia spoke for the first time. "Perhaps you can question these three about their time in the Shimmering Labyrinth, and I can show Baldo to Maveith and Eryk."

"I want to see the griffin, too," Benito voiced loudly.

I sensed Raelia wanted to talk with Maveith and me privately. "After you answer the Regent's questions," I told him. Benito looked disappointed that he would have to wait, but he would get over it.

We followed Raelia up the stairs. I sent out an earth pulse and located the griffin curled into a ball in a room on the third floor. Due to the brevity of my first pulse and its small size, I had mistaken it for a dog. Raelia opened the door with a click, and the creature snapped awake, its eagle eyes focusing on us. Seeing Raelia, it bounded over to her, clearly excited.

As we entered the room behind her, it chirped and hissed at us, its feathers standing up. It puffed itself up to confront the biggest threat—Maveith. "Baldo. Calm. Friend," Raelia said the command words in Elvish. The young griffin disagreed, keeping itself puffed up, but it stopped hissing at Maveith. "Griffins need a lot of familiarity to form trust in their first few months."

I had carried this one's egg for over a year. Maybe it had imprinted on me. I reached out my hand to pet it. Raelia looked like she was about to warn me before its head darted forward and it bit my hand. I winced and restrained myself from killing it immediately—the ungrateful little bastard.

"Baldo. No. Release!" Raelia barked, more annoyed at the griffin than worried about my hand. She knew I could heal myself and did not seem worried that her pet had pierced my hand. When it released me, its tongue cleaned my blood off its beak, and it appeared to savor the taste.

The little monster had almost pierced my hand through and had fractured a bone with its powerful bite. I funneled aether to heal the wound, and the bleeding stopped. Raelia looked a little concerned until the wound closed. She was stroking his feathers. "He needs time to acclimate to new people. We will have time on the road."

"The road?" I asked, feeling confused.

"The road to the Caliphate. I am going to help rescue Maveith's sister."

"Excuse me? Who invited you?" I rasped in disbelief.

Raelia's posture got defensive. "I can make my own decisions. And if Maveith needs help, I am helping him," Raelia said haughtily to me. Baldo hissed at me as if reinforcing her assertion.

I put my foot down. I wouldn't let the elf dictate to me. "I am in charge of my adventurer team." I looked to Maveith, who nodded in support. "I choose who we take on. Besides, you can't take the griffin." I pointed at Baldo and he lunged to bite my finger. I snatched my hand back and he got only air, confused that he had missed.

"Baldo is already flying and hunting small animals," Raelia retorted as she stood in front of me defiantly. Baldo chirped in support and eyed my digits.

"And what if an orc warlord thinks he would make a good trophy or tasty jerky?" I countered smugly and maybe a bit harshly.

She puffed up her chest in her green dress. It didn't really work well, as she was a head shorter than me and had to look up. "The Esenhem treaty with the Caliphate would prevent them from doing anything to Baldo. Orcs have honor, unlike the Telhians!"

My mind was surprisingly clear during this argument. I pressed on her fallacies. "You are a Bartiradian and not of Esenhem. You are just an ambassador to Esenhem."

Raelia's eyes showed her mind working as she thought up a response. Her words still came out heated, and Maveith got uncomfortable with the yelling but did not intervene. "I am an elf, and they won't know the difference." A little more conciliatorily, she continued, "Besides, I am more of an ambassador in training and do not have the true support of Bartiradia. I am just a pawn to bring my estranged Glavien family branch back into the fold of the Esenhem greater family." Her anger evaporated as she finished, and I could see the frustration on her face. Why was I always a sucker for a pretty face in distress?

I tried a new tactic to get her to change her mind and see reason. "They aren't going to let you leave. They need you for that purpose."

She exhaled hotly. "I can't go back to Bartiradia because I am a disgrace there—I lost my griffin over Macha and then my charge, Vaeril. Now they are trying to blame Traeliorn's disappearance on me." I played a role in all three of those things. Did the Bartiradians think Traeliorn was still alive?

"I don't want to spend the next two decades under the thumb of my aunt, playing dress-up in the courts and pretending to be interested in what everyone is saying." She had calmed considerably, and I could tell she was trying a different tactic with me—pity. Her eyes widened and her hands trembled slightly. "Please, may I join your adventuring team?" Even Baldo seemed to be mimicking her deferential disposition, no longer trying to snack on my fingers.

Maveith looked over at me, and his face was easy to read. He wanted Raelia to come with us despite the danger. I tried to fuel her anger to bring it back. Could I even rely on her not to betray us? "You hate Telhians. You despise me." I searched her eyes for her genuine emotions as she responded.

Her eyes locked on mine. "You are not Telhian. And I don't despise you." She paused. "I just find you infuriating." *Is there a difference?*

"You are trying to use me to escape a life of luxury and safety?" I countered.

Our eyes still locked on each other, she continued, "I am a skilled Ranger. I can speak and read the language of the orcs. I have been schooled in their customs and traditions. I can aid Maveith and you in your quest to find Maveith's sister." I got an inkling that she was stretching the truth.

"You are not an adventurer," I hedged, but I felt myself giving in, trying to rationalize her joining us. *How am I conceding so easily?*

She made a dismissive gesture. "Ten minutes in the Guild Hall and I will have my medallion."

I heard Blaze talking to Mateo as they climbed the stairs. "I will consider your offer," I said before the others reached us. An elf attendant entered the room, my companions following.

"Look, it is the miniature griffin!" Benito shouted, causing Baldo to hiss at him. Benito didn't care, approaching dangerously close and not doing a proper threat assessment. "Can we ride it? I mean, when will it be big enough to ride?"

"Benito, stand back. Even that small, its beak can break bone," I warned him. He reluctantly stepped back.

Raelia moved to protect Baldo, stroking his crown feathers to calm him as he grew antsy with all the people crowding around him. "Griffins rarely take more than one rider in their lifetime. Baldo has chosen me," Raelia stated with finality.

Benito looked disappointed, and I could see the griffin was overwhelmed by all the people. I produced a shred of bloody dungeon bear meat and tossed it at

Baldo. He instinctively snatched it out of the air, and his beak worked the meat into a paste to swallow. I wasn't good at reading griffin body language, but I definitely think he liked it. His eyes were focused on me, not as a snack but as a dispenser of tasty snacks.

"What did you feed him?" Raelia said accusingly. "He is on a strict diet, Eryk," she added, concerned.

"Dungeon bear meat. It was fresh." I said unconcernedly.

Baldo clearly liked it, and his taloned feet were carrying him closer to me, looking for more. "Baldo, sit," I commanded in Elvish, holding up another sliver of the meat. Baldo followed the hand holding the morsel, and I repeated the command. He sat and puffed out his chest obediently. "Good, Baldo." I tossed him the meat while Raelia was processing that her griffin had just obeyed me, abject horror on her face. Food is a powerful motivator. I noticed Blaze intently studying my and Raelia's interaction, trying to puzzle out our familiarity.

"We are heading back to the Adventurers Hall," I told my companions abruptly. I no longer felt the need to answer Regent Maeralya's questions about the Shimmering Labyrinth. The others' answers should have been more than sufficient to detail the location of the dungeon. Maybe the elves had another way to dispose of the specters guarding Caelora. Anything that made Octavian's life more difficult was a bonus for me. As we walked, I confirmed with Blaze that the Regent had gotten what she wanted.

"We told her the location of the dungeon, but didn't reveal the library or how we approached through the undercity. Is that what you wanted? You didn't leave us with instructions," Blaze said as we walked the glowstone-lit streets.

I realized I had left them hanging and would need to be a better leader in the future. "Yes, you did the right thing. The Adventurers Guild is already aware of the dungeon. With Esenhem and Bartiradia knowing, Octavian should have a massive headache to deal with."

Blaze seemed reluctant to speak for a moment but finally asked, "You said Maveith knew the elf girl Raelia, but you seem to have a lot of—familiarity with her as well."

Why did Blaze have to be so damn observant? Raelia and I had certainly looked at each other with familiarity during the meal. Maveith was trying to keep the secret, but by doing so was making it more obvious. Thankfully, Benito was oblivious, and Mateo was focused on every pretty woman—and some not-so-pretty ones he saw. I was unsure what to tell Blaze. We were trailing the group and out of earshot.

I wasn't going to lie to him, and came clean. "She was the Bartiradian Ranger with the summoner. The first summoner Konstantin and I killed. Master Mage Sebastian attacked her with his drake and nearly killed her. Maveith and I healed her." Blaze remained quiet while we walked, and it concerned me.

"I have let more than one enemy go who was in the sights of my bow," Blaze said quietly to me.

I exhaled slowly. "She was the Griffin Rider you grounded in Macha." Seeing the shock on Blaze's face was worth telling him. "Twisted fate seems to keep putting her in my path."

"How did she escape Macha?" Blaze questioned. *Of course he would want to know that.*

I switched to one of Konstantin's favorite tones he spoke with when he didn't want to talk about something any longer. "I left her for dead, but their healers got to her. It is best not to mention Macha around her. She is still bitter about losing her griffin, Moonclaw." Thankfully, Blaze nodded.

Halfway back to the Adventurers Hall, I added, "She has asked to go with us." Truthfully, I was planning to sneak out of Artiria with our merchant caravan in a few days and not look back.

Blaze didn't respond for a long time, and I thought my decision was correct. But he eventually formulated a response. "Without Konstantin, we do need a good scout. I am sure with your Hound training you could do the job, but it is hard to lead us and be the scout. The Bartiradian Rangers are some of the best forerunners on the continent."

He did make a good point. We did need a scout for our little group. Maveith was capable but also very large. Being a good hunter was much different from being a good scout. One of the orcs I planned to interview could do the job. We arrived at the Adventurers Hall, and I paused at the entrance, my companions doing likewise, all of us confused. Raelia was at the counter in commoner's clothes, clearly registering to become an adventurer.

"How did she get here before us?" Mateo asked dumbly.

I was grinding my teeth, and Blaze may have noticed. I had a strong feeling that Raelia was not going to take no for an answer. She glanced back at us with a slightly mischievous smirk on her face. "Did she just smile at me?" Mateo asked hopefully.

Blaze patted Mateo on the back, holding in a laugh. "No, Mateo. I think she was declaring victory."

"Victory in what?" Benito asked, a puzzled expression on his face.

Blaze somehow understood I needed him to serve as the group's intermediary. He explained to the others, "I think she plans to join us and help Maveith retrieve his sister."

As we talked, I saw Raelia pointing at our group, which was still clustered near the entryway. After a discussion with the elven clerk, she sauntered up to us. "Looks like you already accepted an assignment as a merchant guard. You need to add me to the job's registry," she said confidently, as if the matter had already been decided.

I controlled my temper and looked her up and down with a stern gaze. "I don't think Baldo can carry your weight. You will have to purchase your own horse," I said flatly, and walked away. It was such a small victory after being cornered into accepting her, but I would take it.

With her new bronze adventurer's medallion in hand and an impish smile on her face, Raelia offered to buy everyone ale. "All the ale you can drink, on me," she said, placing a worn gold piece on the table.

I took her to the side for a moment to remind her not to tell them that she had been in the Shimmering Labyrinth with Maveith and me. "It is fine that you are trying to ingratiate yourself with my companions, but you cannot tell them you fought with us in the Labyrinth. At least not for a time."

She gave me a look like I was an idiot, but to my annoyance, she didn't confirm that she wouldn't reveal this truth. Raelia grinned. "You mean *our* companions. Now I have to go and get to know them a little better." I had a round with everyone and tried to relax, half-listening to the conversations as Raelia, Blaze, Benito, Maveith, and Mateo spilled their life stories. Suddenly, Raelia drained her mug and said she needed to return to care for Baldo.

She was slightly unsteady on her feet. Watching her leave, I noted she did not have an escort. I assumed she had snuck out to join the Guild. I just hoped we would not be chased down by an irate Regent claiming we were abducting her ward. I excused myself, as I had some nighttime duties of my own to attend to.

I relaxed in my room, taking brief trips into the dreamscape to train with my companions. I was working on identifying their weaknesses to help eliminate them the next time we practiced. The manifestations of Konstantin and Xavier were a great help in offering advice, and I found I missed Konstantin's constant berating.

Well past midnight, I slipped out the window. I moved to the stables behind the Hall and found my mounts had been delivered. I checked them thoroughly and, happy, gave them a late-night snack. After confirming no one was around with an earth pulse, I placed Ginger in an empty stall. She immediately panicked at the sudden change in her environment.

Holding her reins tight, I rubbed her neck. "Ginger, it's me. Calm down, and I will give you an apple." She calmed quickly, but the damage was done.

Her angst stirred up the other horses, and soon, the elf stable hand appeared, bleary-eyed. He looked at me with a questioning expression. "I just brought my mount in to stay with the others that were delivered," I informed him as I rubbed Ginger's neck and fed her another apple with my other hand. He looked skeptical but was apparently too tired to argue and left. I settled Ginger in over the next hour, constantly talking to her soothingly. I wish I had done this a few more times to help her acclimate to being moved in and out of my dimensional space.

After Ginger was comfortable, I snuck back into my room. I was immediately on alert when I climbed through the window. The building was mostly stone, so my earth pulse told me someone was in the hallway, clearly waiting outside my door. It was not one of my companions, as they were all accounted for. The person seemed to be waiting for me and knocked as I stepped into the center of the room. I calmed myself and opened the door.

Guildmaster Jhaartael was standing there, clearly unhappy. His voice was gruff and abrasive. "Regent Maeralya told me to apologize to you. I would have waited till morning, but apparently you were busy sneaking around the stables and climbing through your window, so I knew you were awake." He looked smug, having revealed that he had been watching me.

Since I had been in the presence of powerful mages before, I could sense that this man had great depth of power. He had been spying on me, but did he see me release Ginger? No, otherwise he wouldn't have been so calm and smug. "I was checking on my horses. I wanted to make sure they were delivered safely."

He narrowed his eyes and grunted. From his light reaction, I was positive he had not seen me remove Ginger. He continued with a slight warning in his voice. "I am told you took a posting with Rolf Sheadings. I will be watching to make sure it is completed and that he makes it safely to Khoura."

He stared at me for a heartbeat before he turned on his heel and marched down the hallway. He clearly still did not like me or trust me, even with the endorsement of a Regent. Good thing I would not be in his city much longer. Maybe the Regent would reconsider her goodwill toward me when Raelia disappeared. No, that would create too many problems. If Raelia wanted to travel with us, her aunt would need to be told.

I didn't sleep that night, sending out frequent pulses to check on the others in my mild paranoia. There was also some interesting and exciting action going on in other rooms in the Guild Hall. After over forty pulses, I suddenly stopped. Someone was wandering the halls, and I thought he was trying to find the origin of the pulses. It was the first time anyone had been able to sense the earth speak pulses.

I was the first one in the common room in the morning. I had to order food for everyone from across the street, as the kitchens in the Adventurers Hall were only open for lunch and dinner. I got an impressive spread for everyone, and Benito was the first to arrive. His eyes were a little bloodshot and vacant, but that didn't slow his consumption of the offerings on the table. The short man's stomach seemed bottomless.

Mateo arrived with Maveith, and Blaze was last. As everyone was eating, I talked. "Your horses are in the stables. Take them out for some exercise, break in your bodies, and familiarize yourself with them. Teach Maveith how to ride, and tonight, we practice in the yard out back. We leave in two days as an escort for a dwarven merchant to Khoura, a southern city in the Caliphate."

"Will Raelia be joining us for practice?" Mateo asked, too eagerly.

A little annoyed, I answered him. "Maybe. I don't know. It wasn't my turn to keep track of the elf." Blaze arched his eyebrow in amusement. Was he seeing something I wasn't?

"What are you going to be doing today?" Blaze asked as he slowly stacked his plate.

"Doing leader things. I am going to interview the two orc adventurers and see if they are a fit for us," I replied.

Mateo talked with his mouth full. "If we need another, Enyara is still available. She has reasonable rates, and I think she already has a horse."

"With Raelia, we don't need another scout," I said tiredly. "Or another elf," I muttered to myself. After last night's visit from the Guildmaster, I now assumed Enyara was working for him to keep an eye on us. Her group had seated themselves next to us in the common room and listened to our conversation, but maybe I was too paranoid.

I left the group to finish breakfast and headed to the port district. The first orc was named Glamrar Understone. He lived by the docks because most of his jobs were on ships. I was fortunate that he was not currently at sea. His residence was in an apartment building that overlooked the harbor. I knocked, and it didn't take long for a scantily clad elf woman to open the door. Her angular features showed amusement at my shock. "Looking for Glamrar?" she asked, grinning. I nodded like an idiot because her shift was translucent, leaving little to the imagination.

She opened the door to let me in, exposing me to a musky scent and cooking bacon. Deep in the apartment, a large, bare-chested orc was cooking breakfast. He was not tattooed but was almost seven feet tall and thickly muscled. After explaining the mission to the brutish-looking orc, he shook his head. "No. My wife would kill me if I returned to the Caliphate for any reason."

"Yes, I would!" the elf woman yelled from the bedroom with levity.

He pointed his cooking spatula at me. "Yes, I married an elf. Do you have a problem with it?"

"No. Sorry for interrupting your morning." He nodded good-naturedly, and I retreated out of the apartment. Why was it so hard to find an orc for my party?

According to the elf clerk at the Guild, the only other candidate in Artiria was a healing mage. The healer, Tarek Blackjaw, was easy to find and was a dedicated delver. There were only three dungeons in Esenhem, but he was determined to complete all of them and was not interested in returning to the Caliphate until he did.

He explained his reasoning: "I seek to one day be named a warlord of the Caliphate. Though my skills could have me named a cleric, my blood runs hot for combat. When I am truly confident in my delving, I will return and claim the mantle of a warlord."

He was surprisingly amiable, considering the other orcs I had met, and I found myself engrossed in a lengthy conversation with Tarek as he meticulously divulged details about the dungeons within the Caliphate. My time with him offered a rare glimpse into their culture, but recruiting him eventually proved to be a fruitless pursuit. I wondered if my search would yield better results in the Caliphate or if it was a hopeless endeavor.

I returned to the Hall to find a groaning Maveith laid out on the common room floor. The others sat a bit uncomfortably around a table. I took a seat next to Blaze. "Any fortune in your search?" he asked as he shifted uneasily in his seat, showing some soreness from riding again.

"None. It appears all the orcs who have left the Caliphate do not wish to return." I indicated Maveith. "Riding lessons?"

Blaze nodded. "We did twenty miles. You selected fine mounts for us, and they like to run. Maveith lost his saddle four times and has yet to find the rhythm. He is constantly trying to force his will upon the large black." A small smirk appeared on his lips. "I see you found a mount with the same coloring as your first."

"No, it is Ginger." I stopped talking, as I saw Blaze was not being serious. "Any sign of Raelia?" I asked half-heartedly.

"No, she has not shown herself," Blaze replied. "Are we going to train in the yard?" I could tell Blaze was hoping I would say no. After so long out of the saddle, a twenty-mile ride had to be difficult on all of them.

"Just two hours," I announced loud enough for everyone to hear. Benito groaned the loudest.

Mateo made to stand but stumbled as he got to his feet. "I miss Adrian," he muttered at my lack of sympathy for their injuries.

Blaze had my back. "Adrian would have you practicing for two hours before turning you over to Delmar to dig defenses for the camp. Eryk has been paying your way since we left and got you a fine mount." I gave Blaze a slight nod of thanks.

In my mollifying command voice, I addressed the group. "We need to work on our communication; being such a small band, teamwork is paramount in a fight. Blaze, you are going to have to put down your bow for a while and swing your sword." Blaze joined the others in a mock groan at my betrayal after he supported me.

During the extended session, I served more as an instructor. I was using what I learned in the dreamscape to ferret out their weaknesses and help them improve.

Our tactics were simple. Maveith, for all his size and strength, would still best serve as a ranged threat with Blaze. Mateo and I would serve as our front line, with the speedy Benito filling in on the flanks as needed. Maveith, with his runic hammer, could always come from the back in support.

We worked up a good lather and drew more than a few eyes because of our training intensity. Mateo was working twice as hard because Enyara was one of the spectators. When I called an end to the practice, we sat on benches drinking from our canteens.

Enyara approached to stand over our group. "You fight well for Telhians. Are you any good with that? Care for a wager?" She was indicating Blaze's bow and arrows. Blaze looked at me for approval to accept. I knew what this was. She was trying to show her aptitude with the bow to impress me. She was trying to worm her way into the group. It made me even more suspicious that the Guildmaster was involved.

"Show her how to shoot, Blaze." I tossed an apple to Blaze, who deftly caught it. He nodded and took a bite, masking his discomfort as he stood. After swinging a sword and holding a shield for the last two hours, he was at a significant disadvantage in the contest.

The contest drew considerable attention from the elven adventurers, and bets were being placed. Benito fought past his soreness to be part of the betting action. He sought Maveith to back his wagers, as he had almost no coin. He should have evaluated Blaze more closely before placing his bets on him, as Blaze had difficulty stringing his bow.

Blaze placed his apple core at the furthest distance the training yard allowed, fifty paces. He raised his bow, aimed, and lowered it three times before releasing it. He was trying to find that feeling he told me about—maybe some type of clairvoyance spell form. The arrow crossed the distance, knocking off the apple core sitting atop the archery target. He got appreciative nods from the spectators and a uncomfortable fist pump from Benito.

Enyara frowned slightly, not expecting Blaze's success or maybe the small target. She walked to the apple core, which had been split in two. "What's going on?" A familiar voice to my side asked. I hadn't noticed Raelia arrive.

"A contest of archery skill," I replied without looking at her. "Did you receive permission from your aunt to join us?"

Raelia was suspiciously quiet as we watched Enyara stick the halves together and set the apple core atop the target again. As she walked back, Raelia said, "I got a horse and a special saddle for Baldo and me."

"That is not what I asked," I said, finally looking over at her. She was dressed in adventurer clothes and leather, wearing the Ranger's cloak from the dungeon. It looked like a normal cloak, but I knew better. With it, she would be an excellent scout for us.

"She can't stop me. I am an adult." Her petulant tone almost made me laugh. Realizing how she sounded, she spoke more confidently. "Yes, she is aware I plan to leave her household."

"Will it cause me trouble?" I asked seriously as Enyara took aim. She didn't take nearly as long as Blaze before she released her arrow. Her arrow thudded into the target, an inch below the apple core. The impact was enough to knock the apple core off. A groan of dismay and despair echoed through the elves. Benito cheered madly as he tried to figure out who owed him coin.

"No, Regent Maeralya will not interfere." After a pause, she added, "She is not happy with me, though. And I expect she will be informing my parents and brother back in Bartiradia that I am running off with some Telhians."

Raelia's brother was a general in their army. I almost asked if he was still alive, but instead, I accepted her word that we would be unmolested when we left. "We leave the morning after next. Be outside the Hall an hour before sunrise. Where is Baldo now?" I asked.

"In my room upstairs," she informed me, relieved. She must have thought her position with us was not guaranteed. I just assumed she was not going to take no for an answer. Personally, I was a little surprised at how quickly the elf woman was joining us, and she didn't seem nervous at all to be adventuring with ex-legionnaires. She was placing a tremendous amount of trust in us.

I grunted because that seemed like the thing Konstantin would do at this moment. "We are going for a ride in the morning. You can join us." Raelia let loose a satisfied smile that made her look beautiful in the evening light.

Maveith, who had been listening from a bench nearby, groaned. Enyara was receiving some ribbing from the adventurers as they broke up to get an evening meal. I caught her looking at Blaze with a respectful and perhaps covetous stare. She clearly had not thought she would lose to him. Benito was giving Blaze a share of the silver he had collected from the elves.

I arranged for a meal for everyone before checking on the horses. Ginger was upset with me for some reason, and I thought it was because we had not gone for a ride with the others this morning. It was easy to find Raelia's horse from its unique saddle hanging outside the stall. It was long and looked like there was a special pillion seat behind it for Baldo. It was more of a basket than a seat. Raelia weighed maybe a hundred pounds, and Baldo fifty, so her gray mount would be carrying less weight than Ginger. There were grips inside the griffin's basket for Baldo to hold onto if Raelia broke into a gallop.

I handed out half-apples before returning to eat. Raelia was eating contentedly with the others, already feeling like she had been accepted into the fold. They were all laughing at something Benito was saying. Looking around the room, it seemed like we were more accepted here today than yesterday, our Telhian stigma fading. After enjoying a meal of baked chicken and roasted veggies, everyone retired early to rest their abused bodies. I lamented not being able to convince the orc healer to join us.

I was up first in the morning. Ginger was saddled and eager for the ride. The others wandered into the stables one by one. Maveith was a bit gimpy as he walked to his black stallion. I was proud the goliath had not utilized a potion to wash away his injuries. Raelia arrived last, Baldo in tow. The dog-sized griffin looked around curiously as he stayed glued to Raelia's side.

When we all mounted, we walked our horses out of the city. Baldo was sitting regally in his little nest in the saddle. "Don't griffins eat horses?" Mateo asked.

I nodded. "It is their favorite type of meat." I patted Ginger's neck. "Don't worry, girl. I won't let the big bad Baldo eat you."

Raelia defended her griffin. "Baldo is smart and listens to commands. He will only eat horses if I allow him to." Baldo hissed and chirped at hearing his name. I decided, as a leader, I wouldn't tease Raelia or Baldo. How long I kept that promise to myself remained to be seen.

Outside the city, we rode together, never breaking into a trot even though I sensed Ginger's eagerness to do so. Ginger was also setting the pecking order among the horses, even bossing Maveith's massive black mount with a nip when Maveith started to have trouble controlling him.

As we rode, we discussed how we would protect the three wagons, who would be positioned where, and how we would engage a threat. It was more of an open discussion than me dictating tactics. I made it clear that Blaze was second in command after me.

We returned after midday and rubbed down the mounts. Baldo took to hunting rats in the hay, even catching one, to Raelia's delight and praise. I thought Raelia was meshing well with the others. Mateo certainly enjoyed talking with her, although he was doing most of the talking.

Although the merchant was providing food and feed, I sent Mateo and Blaze to obtain additional supplies for the horses. Everyone was expecting another training session tonight, but I let them off, to their relief. I told them to be ready two hours before sunrise to meet the merchant. It was time to make our way toward the Boutan Caliphate.

I was the first one to the stables, but it was four hours before sunrise. Ginger was happy to see me even though I was disturbing her beauty rest, and the other mounts knew I was the human with the apples. After giving Ginger a rubdown, I inspected Raelia's gray.

It was a young stallion in excellent condition, and he responded well to my hands as I checked his hooves, musculature, and teeth. Ginger was getting a bit jealous in her stall, but I wanted to be certain the gray wouldn't be a hindrance in our travels. It was difficult to tell if he was battle-trained, but he was definitely not skittish. "What are you doing to Stormcloud?" Raelia's voice cut across the stables.

"Just making sure he is healthy," I replied as I exited the stall.

"I know how to select and care for my mount," she said defensively. Baldo chirped in agreement but plodded up to me, looking for a treat. I held up a shred of bear meat, and he sat instantly, his tongue hanging out in anticipation. If griffins could drool, Baldo would be at this moment. I tossed the meat and he snatched it out of the air, to Raelia's disapproval.

She moved into her stall to saddle Stormcloud. "I like his name, did you choose it? Generally, legionnaires don't name their mounts, so they don't get too attached. But this is Ginger." I indicated my red-brown mare, who was not happy that my attention was directed at the gray and the griffin. I produced an apple to counter her jealousy.

Raelia considered my words as she worked, getting Stormcloud ready. "We were always taught that forming a bond with your mount was imperative to success. There is an intrinsic partnership between the rider and the mount. Without cooperation and understanding, you put both of you at risk."

I nodded and decided to praise her opinion. "Wonderful advice. How good of a mount will Baldo be? Will he always have black feathers?" I tossed him another piece of meat when Raelia's back was turned.

Raelia turned to look at Baldo, whose eyes were locked on me as he ground up my latest offering. Raelia exhaled in frustration. "Yes, he will be mostly black. He is a mix of a western species that are night hunters and usually midnight black in color. Baldo will still have lighter gray coloring on his legs and head from one of his parents."

We didn't have more time to talk, as Blaze and Mateo entered the stables with their heavy packs. Maveith, still walking gingerly, was next, followed by a catatonic Benito. We all worked to get our mounts ready, snippets of conversation passing between us. Soon, we were leaving the stables. I noticed the Guildmaster standing on a small balcony, watching us leave. If I could read his mind, I bet I would hear, "Good riddance."

Although we were early, Rolf Sheadings had all three of his wagons lined up in the street, each with a pair of stout ponies. "Good sign, you being early!" he said happily. "The first wagon is mine. My wife, Lola, will drive the second. My brother is late, but he will be guiding the third." He looked at our group in the glowstone-lit streets. "Never thought I would see a goliath on a horse. But I'm not sure if that monster could be called a horse." He chuckled to himself. He noticed Baldo sitting tall on the back of Raelia's mount.

He walked up to the griffin and Raelia gave Baldo the command word to remain calm. "An eagle," he guessed as he approached. "No, a griffin? What do you need a midget griffin for?"

Raelia pursed her lips. "He is a hatchling, just a few months old but already hunting and learning to scout. In a year, he will be nearly full-grown; a year after that, I will be riding him."

Rolf huffed in surprise. "Well, I'll not be paying extra for him. Feeding the goliath and his mount is going to be painful enough. Hopefully, your feathered scout can supply his own dinner." Rolf turned away from Raelia's indignant expression and went to finish his preparations.

As soon as Rolf's brother arrived, we were out of the city and heading north. There was no need to send a scout ahead, as there was an elven village on the road or within sight of the road every few miles. Unlike the Empire, which had a vast expanse of hostile wilderness, Esenhem was well settled. Maybe that had to do with the elves being so long-lived.

I had a pair of us lead and a pair of us trail the wagons. The third pair flanked the central wagon, but as Rolf had said, it appeared it would be a fairly boring trip. The road itself was packed with smooth clay. Blaze, ever curious, asked Rolf, "Who maintains such a fine road?"

"The Highway Guild sends out their mages regularly. We may pass one on our trip. Their mages summon an earth elemental to follow them and repair the road as they go. This is Esenhem's main trade road, which is serviced twice a month. Lesser roads might see a mage and his elemental once a month or less, depending." Rolf chewed on sugarcane and spat it out. "It is one of the reasons I settled in Esenhem. It is safe and has the best roads on the continent, making travel much faster."

"Telhian roads are paved," Blaze noted.

Rolf spat some more chewed sugarcane. "Dwarves are not welcome in the Empire, and besides, after the Telhians built their portals, I heard a lot of the roads went into disrepair," he responded bitterly. Blaze didn't respond, and the conversation died. I had to agree that these roads allowed the wagons to move quickly. The horses didn't even churn up the hard-packed clay as we walked. The traffic we passed on the road was mostly on foot, and horses were rare.

We stopped at a small farm in late morning, and Rolf picked up some large bags of flour to add to his goods. Although we were not expected to help, I had my companions help load the flour. Rolf muttered something about not paying extra for the help, but didn't tell us to stop. Rolf paid for the farmer to feed us, and soon after, we were back on the road. I had to hide my smirk at Rolf's reaction when Maveith only ate a quarter loaf smothered in butter and jam.

I had my group rotate positions to change who we rode with. It helped the conversation avoid becoming stale. Rather than talk to Raelia when she was riding next to me, I made a game of sneaking strips of meat to Baldo. I rarely succeeded in my stealth, but it was fun to try. "Baldo. Hunt," Raelia ordered, finally exasperated with my efforts. Baldo looked at me, but Raelia chastised the griffin. "Baldo. Hunt," she said more forcefully. The griffin took to the air in a *whoosh*.

Raelia eyed me, took a deep breath, and patiently explained, "I am trying to teach him to hunt on his own. If you overfeed him, he will have no motivation to hunt."

Her patient explanation made me feel slightly guilty for interfering with his training. While we waited for Baldo to return, I asked a question to satisfy my curiosity. "Aren't you afraid he might fly off or be attacked by something more dangerous?"

"Griffins bond to their parents on hatching and typically do not leave the nest until around nine months. During those first nine months, the trainer substitutes for the parent, having the griffin rely on them for survival, and teaching them. If Baldo encountered a dangerous predator, he would return to me for protection." She held a small fireball in her palm to reinforce that she was ready to protect her griffin.

Benito's surprised voice rang behind us. "The elf girl is a mage, too!"

Raelia spun in her saddle and barked at Benito, "I am not a girl! I am forty-seven summers!" Benito cringed as the micro-fireball in her hand tripled in size, and she looked ready to throw it.

"Calm down, Raelia. They have never had elf companions before. Also, Benito hit his head a few too many times while growing up," I advised her. The fireball vanished; this time, she was the guilty one for overreacting.

Baldo returned, clutching a fat raccoon in his talons. His landing startled the horse teams pulling the wagons, causing Rolf to curse and wrestle with them to calm them. Baldo ignored the commotion he had created and proudly walked up with his kill, dropping it in Ginger's path. Raelia turned bright red in either anger or embarrassment.

I chose to defuse the situation. "It is dungeon bear meat," I told her. "He appears to really like it." I pulled out a wet bag filled with strips I had cut and handed it to her. She looked at the bag and then at me as I turned to ride with Mateo, sending Benito to ride next to Raelia. My hope was that she would apologize to him. Being a leader is difficult when you are trying to incorporate such varied temperaments. Still, I admitted to myself that having Raelia's mage abilities and knowledge with us was a boon.

Soon, Baldo was back in the saddle with Raelia feeding him from the bag I had given her and talking to Benito. They were too far ahead of us to hear the conversation, but Raelia was smiling at something Benito was saying as he talked with his hands as much as his mouth. Mateo was talking to me about how it was funny that Raelia was older than his mother, yet she looked younger than his sister. I just let him talk and nodded along.

We reached our destination early, which gave us plenty of daylight to settle into the large merchant's barn. Half my team had to remain in the loft of the barn for security. The massive barn had room for over twenty wagons, and Rolf's wagons joined the seven wagons already here. I learned that these merchant barns were standard along the roads of Esenhem and free to use. I could see why merchants preferred to trade in Esenhem.

Although it was not required, I had my companions rub down the six horses pulling the wagons with ours. Rolf grumbled that he was not paying extra, but didn't object after his wife slapped him on the side of his head.

I was having us do all this work not to earn extra coin, but in the hope that Rolf would give a glowing evaluation of our job. A positive review would be marked on our adventurer records, and we needed to build our reputation. Besides, the extra work we were doing was minimal compared to what legionnaires usually had to do. I chose Benito, Blaze, and Maveith to sleep with the wagons the first night.

We encountered an issue when Baldo was not allowed in the merchant's inn. The elf proprietor didn't believe Raelia when she asserted that Baldo was trained and wouldn't soil the room. This would probably be a regular occurrence, so it looked like Raelia and Baldo would stay with the wagons for the next three weeks. Maveith and Mateo foolishly agreed to stay with them each time, leaving the rooms for Benito, Blaze, and myself.

Maveith had been abnormally quiet due to his pain from riding, stoically holding back his groans. When I had learned to ride, I had been less—manly. Even with his saddle pain, he was still in good spirits because we were getting closer to his sister. For evening weapons practice, I had everyone go through the sword forms in slow motion with weighted blades, correcting movement errors I had noted in the dreamscape. Maveith practiced a little with his hammer, but I let him off easy, seeing him masking his pain.

Rolf had a few trades with the townsfolk, some selling and some buying. His margins couldn't have been that big, as I only noticed silver being exchanged. Maybe these evening stops were essential for Rolf to turn a profit on the trip.

We only got a single room in the merchant's inn. Two bunk beds with clean linens and a privy shared with guards from other caravans. The merchants had fancier rooms and private privies. After making Blaze aware of how to wake me, I spent my early evening in the dreamscape, practicing with my companions there. I also gave Oscar a fair amount of attention in the dreamscape, realizing why I wanted the griffin to like me. I missed having a loyal companion. It was also probably why I had invested so much in Ginger.

We had breakfast with the other guards in an outbuilding. The food was plentiful but somewhat bland. Most merchants only traveled with a couple of guards, but since Rolf was heading into the Caliphate, he chose to bring more. From brief conversations with the young elf guards, we learned that the last hundred miles of our journey would be the most perilous. Breakfast was brief, as Rolf informed us that we needed to prepare to leave for the next leg.

That was how the next eleven days went. The caravan stopped once or twice during the day, with Rolf selling or picking up goods in the smaller towns. In the larger towns with the merchant barns, we practiced in the evening with everyone's riding legs firmly restored. Maveith was slowly becoming a competent horseman. He even named his mount Nightshade and spoke to him as he would to Ginger, much to the chagrin of Blaze and Mateo.

Although I kept Raelia supplied with bear meat, I still managed to find Baldo begging for more. Once, he tried nipping me to get more, and I berated him in Elvish, then turned my back on him. He crept cautiously behind me a few moments later, pressing the top of his head into my palm. "He is apologizing. Gently rub his ear holes to accept it," Raelia said encouragingly. I did as she advised, and the griffin clucked softly in contentment as I found the sweet spot.

"They are kind of cute when they are not trying to kill you," Blaze noted with a smirk. I nodded in agreement, but what I liked most about the young griffin was that his feathers smelled like the outdoors, just like my pillow. Of course, the feathers in that pillow were from Baldo's parent, so maybe it was best to keep it hidden from him.

We had settled into our travel routine as we rode into another town the evening of the thirteenth day on the road. The large merchant barn was close to the road, but Rolf had us hold before heading to the barn. The town square had a large commotion, and as we approached, he explained, "If there is a problem, I don't want to have stabled the horses and wagons just to have to move out later."

The square was filled with elves and two humans, from my initial appraisal. Most had common-looking sheathed blades or bows in hand. Rolf asked loudly of the elven mob, "Good folk of Esanor, what is at issue?"

We had mostly been ignored up to this point, but now we drew the attention of the thirty-plus people gathered. One of the elves spoke for the group. "A child was killed and another is missing. We are preparing a hunt."

Rolf nodded slowly. "Do you know what monster killed them?"

I slid off of Ginger as Rolf was talking to the local elves. "Our local Ranger thinks it was a werewolf and went to Nirimporti to get more Rangers and adventurers to hunt it down. We are not going to wait four days for him to return if there is a chance Naedia's daughter is alive."

It was easy to pick out the mother in the mob from the other women consoling her. I could see Blaze, Maveith, Benito, and Mateo dismounting and getting ready, sensing danger but not understanding the conversation. We all had runic weapons and could harm the shape changer. I didn't notice a single such weapon among these simple elven townsfolk, but there could be silvered weapons among them.

Raelia was still mounted as I spoke loud enough for the community to hear: "You lack the tools and expertise to hunt such a creature. We will stable our horses and hunt your werewolf on foot. If the child lives, we will bring it back to you." The mobs hopeful eyes turned to us.

233

Chapter 277: Howl You Doing?

From Rolf's expression, I realized that I had exceeded my authority. Rolf was not the only one in shock; Raelia was still seated on Stormcloud, looking at me strangely. The elven townsfolk began murmuring excitedly among themselves as the leader told me what happened. "This morning, the beast broke into the house. We think her brother tried to protect her, and the werewolf killed him and took her. She was hauled away screaming before dawn. By the time our men had roused, her screams were fading into the woods."

I frowned, as it was just a few hours to sunset. The werewolf had nearly a half-day head start. I considered taking Ginger for faster pursuit, but I needed to use my earth speak spell form, so it would be better if she remained behind. Finally, Rolf regained himself and reminded me, "You are contracted to me."

I chewed on my response for a moment. Maybe my Hound training had taken over a bit, or maybe it was the young elf girl who was in trouble. A pack of Hounds could hunt a single werewolf. Werewolves were usually solitary creatures, but not always. Still, I had a lot of confidence in my skills. "Do I have your permission to hunt the werewolf?"

"What are your chances?" Rolf asked, stroking his beard thoughtfully. I could tell he was feeling the pressure from the townsfolk. I had given them hope, and he didn't want to snatch it away.

"Of killing the beast? One hundred percent if I can catch it. Of saving the child …" Hearne's lessons on werewolves were extensive, and I had also read about them in the dreamscape. I spoke more quietly. "Depends if it took her to infect or as a meal. Werewolves are intelligent creatures. It can hunt plenty of food in the wild, so it doesn't need to hunt people and draw attention to itself. I am guessing it plans to infect her and use her as a mate eventually. Lycanthropy becomes permanent after thirty days, and once it does, it cannot be cured by any means."

Rolf looked a bit uncomfortable as he wrestled under the gaze of the townsfolk. There was a hopefulness in their eyes. "That confident?" he said skeptically. A bit exasperated, he consented. "I can wait a day in town, but in case you do not come back, you need to leave at least two of your companions behind so I can finish my trip."

Blaze had a questioning look on his face, as we had been speaking in Elvish. I switched to Telhian to address my companions. "A werewolf took a child just before dawn. I am going to hunt it alone. You are all staying here."

"Harpies' tits, Eryk. We are going with you," Mateo said angrily, resting his hand on his sword.

Maveith's face clouded as well. "You can't stop us from coming with you."

"No. You will all stay here and go with Rolf if I don't return in time. We have an obligation to him and also to Maveith. Besides, I am the only one here immune to the effects of lycanthropy," I said stoically.

"Your healing cannot prevent the disease," Raelia snapped angrily.

"My protection is from a different spell form," I admitted. Her jaw didn't seem to work. She had both questions and doubt on her face—and maybe some concern.

Raelia, still mounted, questioned my decision. "There is nothing to gain with this hunt. These people have nothing to reward you with, the child is likely dead, and werewolves are incredibly powerful adversaries. They are also highly magical creatures with strong innate resistance."

I paused. Raelia was hinting that my dimensional space might not work on the fiend. I was not worried about being bitten, as my spell form could purify my blood. I dismissed her arguments. "I will be fine."

Blaze approached and spoke privately with me in one last effort to sway me. "Eryk, is this a wise course of action? Night will fall in the next hour, and the werewolf has a sizable lead." He was trying to make me see reason, but he didn't know the extent of my abilities.

I revealed another of my secrets to him. "I have a spell form that allows me to see in the dark. My Hound training prepared me to hunt these creatures. I am the one with the advantage here. But if I don't return, finish escorting Rolf and help Maveith find his sister." I patted him on the shoulder. I nearly decided to hand out a few things from my dimensional space, but that would send the message that I doubted myself.

I handed Ginger's reins and a bag of apples for her to Maveith. "I should go with you," Maveith said, but I shook my head.

Mateo offered me the Primus's blade in its sheath. "Eryk, do you want to exchange blades? I think the stronger the runic blade, the more effective they are against werewolves."

"No need, my friend. I have Boris's dungeon blade." I walked past him. Baldo, not understanding I was leaving, hopped after me, chirping for bear meat. Raelia called him back and whispered something in Elvish under her breath that sounded like, "You cannot convince a fool to stray from his desired path." It was loud enough for me to hear.

I followed the town leader to the house the werewolf had attacked. The window had been torn away, and claw marks gouged the hardwood. Through the window, I could see dried pools of blood where the brother must have been killed. Studying the ground, I easily found the clawed prints. They were massive and resembled bear tracks more than wolf's. Wolves have four toes, while bears and werewolves have five. These impressions were nearly as big as Maveith's.

"Did anyone see the werewolf?" I asked my guide.

The elf shook his head, confused. "No, our Ranger was certain it was a werewolf, and he has three centuries of experience." I scowled and stood. That was a jab at my short-lived human race.

"If it is a werewolf, it is likely an alpha," I confirmed.

"That is what Ranger Taegan said. 'Most likely an Alpha.' It was why he went to seek help. Will you not attempt it then?" the elf asked, distressed and fidgety.

"I will still go," I noted, and started to walk toward the woods. When I reached the edge of the woods, I sent out my first earth pulse and began to jog. There were three types of werewolves. The most common were the infected. They were men and women infected with the lycanthropy disease. These werewolves could appear as normal people but could transform into monstrous humanoid wolves, greatly enhancing their speed and strength.

The second type of werewolf was the true werewolf, which was what I was expecting to face. This creature's natural form was a large humanoid wolf. They could transform into a large wolf at will but would never pass for human. They were more feral than the infected but still highly intelligent. The third and most dangerous type were alphas.

Alphas were larger, stronger, and faster than normal true werewolves. They were similar to dire creatures, who were mutated from aether saturation. I had fought dire boars and a dire owlbear in the Shimmering Labyrinth, but I would have no idea how dangerous this foe was until I faced him.

As I distanced myself from the town, I switched my blade to the magebane. Being struck by this weapon should prevent the creature from transforming, but that was more of an educated guess. I left the sword sheathed on my hip as I increased my pace. By the next heartbeat, the black spear was in my hand. It was my strongest weapon and would give me greater range than the werewolf's claws.

Disturbingly, the trail was relatively easy to follow. I expected more caution from an intelligent creature. Four miles from the town, my fears were assuaged. The trail completely disappeared. The sun was setting and the shadows were extending. The clouds above indicated that it would be a dark night.

It took a few earth pulses to find the trail again. The werewolf had climbed a tree, swung to a few others, and then resumed running on rocks. His heavy mass had disturbed the rocks and let me pick up his trail again. It was still many hours old, so I increased my pace.

I funneled aether through my night vision spell form and continued my pursuit as night fell. The child was alive! I found signs where the werewolf had rested and put her down while he drank from a stream. She had barely moved during these rest periods, and I could only imagine her fear.

The Esenhem woodlands were teeming with wildlife, big and small. They scattered before me as I pursued my quarry. The most dangerous creature I encountered was a lone centaur who had bedded down. It was a female, and she endeavored to remain hidden as I passed. I had no time to deal with her and passed quickly.

After hours of pursuit, I paused to drink some water. I took the break to reset my blood compass using Maveith's blood. Not because I was concerned that he was following me, but so I could locate the caravan after confronting the werewolf. I activated it and sensed Maveith was over twenty miles away. I couldn't believe I had traveled so far. Dawn was still hours away.

I knew I was getting closer to my quarry as the tracks became fresher. The werewolf lair was probably not much farther, and I could smell hints of pungent urine in the air. Just like wolves, werewolves marked their territory by peeing around the perimeter. I decided to withdraw till sunrise to see if I could locate them with the spyglass.

I found a modest, mostly grassy hill and settled among the rocks. I was not alone for long as a creature approached me from behind. My earth pulse identified it as a werewolf, though it was smaller than I expected my target to be. I surmised it was a sentry I hadn't noticed.

Either way, it was stalking me and planned to attack. When it cleared the rise and rushed my back, I was ready. The black spear easily pierced its hairy chest, holding it at bay. I drew the magebane and beheaded it in one swift motion. The werewolf hadn't had time to emit a warning howl, but in the aftermath, I increased the frequency of my earth pulses.

The corpse was that of a mature, elven, female werewolf. It was clearly infected, but it was not a true werewolf. Maybe the alpha was building a harem for himself. After waiting for a few minutes to be sure I had not been discovered by more, I retrieved and used the collector. The aetheric smoke coalesced into a minor dexterity essence. I stored the collector and essence and turned to studying my sight lines with the spyglass.

A small finger of smoke told me they were cooking a distance away, just over a mile in my estimation. My jaw tightened. I hoped that they were not cooking the girl. I needed to know how many more of the creatures there were. I was confident against one or two, but three or more?

While I was looking for movement, another werewolf moved into the range of my earth speak pulses. The creature moved cautiously, following the path of the last one. I guessed it was tracking by smell—possibly how the first one found me. This time, I was not going to let it get close. I moved to engage before it crested the rise, swinging the black spear in a tight arc.

The werewolf was more agile than I had predicted, and it leaped back out of range, emitting a warning howl as it did so. Others quickly returned the call, and I cursed Fortuna for abandoning me. Why had I thought it would be a good idea to hunt these creatures alone? My own foolishness was to blame for thinking there would only be one.

Although the wolf avoided my first swing, it was unsuccessful the second time. I pulled the spear back and extended it in a quick thrust into its abdomen. The spear's leaf tip cut through hairy hide and muscle, and I pressed down, opening it up. Its intestines spilled onto the ground. In shock, it was unable to defend itself as I swung the spear again, this time across its throat, silencing it.

I moved to the best defensible position on the hill and waited to see what fate had in store for me. The werewolves circled the base of the hill and I did my best to count their number. I thought there were four more plus the larger alpha, and I hoped there would not be any more uninvited guests—my dance card was definitely full. The alpha was massive. It stalked between the trees below, sniffing the air for my scent and the blood I had spilled from its pack mates.

There was only one smart way they could attack. They would space themselves around the hill and all rush me simultaneously to overwhelm my position. It would only take one successful bite to immobilize my arm or leg, and from there, I would be finished. Calmness overcame my simmering fear. All I needed to do was kill them one at a time.

Kneeling with one hand on my spear and the other holding a fistful of pellets, I waited calmly for the attack. There was no running at this point. It was the alpha who signaled the assault with a snarl and a barked command. I was surprised when he didn't join the four females in the rush. I decided he was just delaying his rush, but I didn't have time to worry about it.

I smashed smoke and blindness pellets on stones near two of the werewolves and the alpha's likely path of ascent. I faced the other direction and the black spear flashed, removing the hand of a werewolf. A thrust penetrated the throat of another as I danced among them. I cursed as the spear tip burst out of the back of its neck as the werewolf fell toward me, trapping the shaft.

I was not going to have time to extract the spear before the others reached me. I released the spear and drew the magebane. A splatter of blood from the werewolf with the missing hand hit my face. She spat spittle and blood from her mouth as she tried to tackle me for her pack mates.

The beast was a clumsy fighter, relying on her strength and speed but being far too direct in her attacks. I retreated and sidestepped her claw swipe before hacking the back of her neck. I was surprised at the minimal penetration magebane achieved against the thick hide of her form. Her one good hand went to the cut as it flowed freely. She lost a few fingers as magebane descended again, this time cutting deep enough to crush her spine. She fell limply. If she was not dead, she would bleed out quickly.

I turned to face the final three threats, believing I was in good shape. My blindness pellets had done their job, and the other two smaller wolves were awkwardly rubbing their eyes as they emerged from the dissipating cloud.

These females were thinner and leaner, and most likely more recently infected. The alpha roared from inside the cloud before bursting through in anger. Although his eyes were squinted and caked with dried tears, he looked less affected than the others.

I needed to even the odds quickly. I rushed the blinded female on my left. The hulking, eight-foot alpha had enough vision to intercede. He barreled into me in a flash of movement, caring nothing for my blade. I managed to get magebane angled under his ribs as he tackled me. The magebane slid easily up into his heart, but his surprising willingness to give up his life meant that his arms wrapped around me. He took my forearm in his jaws as he tried to take me with him in his death throes.

We crashed to the ground, his mass forcing the air out of my lungs as he landed on top of me. I fought to hold him at bay. The earth drake runic bracers were holding up under his powerful jaws, but his neck was jerking my arm hard as his saliva sprayed over me. I was pinned to the ground and ready to remove the alpha's head when something bit into my leg and yanked hard.

The alpha would die shortly, so I redirected my dimensional space to the one using my leg as a chew toy. I removed a portion of its head, killing it instantly, but bottoming out my aether. The alpha was weakened enough that I was able to roll him, switching to the top position. Magebane was buried deep in the alpha's chest, the hilt covered in hot, slick blood. I grabbed the hilt and yanked on it, doing more damage until the alpha finally seemed to concede its life.

I wrenched my arm out of its slackened jaws and stood, looking for the last werewolf. It was fleeing, stumbling blindly down the hill.

There was damage to my shoulder, forearm, and shin. I hobbled to retrieve the black spear and fumbled for a Pathfinder healing potion in my belt. My hands were coated in blood, and I consumed as much blood as potion. The werewolf blood actually made the foul potion more bearable to drink. Soothing relief flooded my injuries as it worked, and I made to pursue the last werewolf. I caught her before she made it halfway back to the camp. She appeared to be moving by smell and not sight. She hadn't been aware of my approach from behind, and in two quick slashes I severed her spine and then removed her head.

My adrenaline from the fight was still surging, as I didn't know if there were more enemies. I climbed back up the hill to take in the carnage. The soil was soaked with blood, some of it mine. The female werewolves were mangy-looking creatures in their current forms. I thought only the alpha was a true werewolf, with a denser pelt and a massive, menacing, fanged maw. I retrieved the magebane from the alpha's chest and let my aether recover as my heart settled.

First, I used an earth pulse to ensure no others were coming. Then, as I recovered aether, I fully healed my injuries. I knew I had been infected, and my purify self spell form showed me the foreign infection propagating in my blood. It was more difficult to remove than a normal disease, taking more aether and focus, but I slowly eradicated its presence inside me. At least I would not be howling at the next full moon.

When I felt mostly whole and pure again, I looked around. It was time to harvest what I could and see if the elf child was still alive. I hoped all this effort was not for nothing.

While I worked, I pulsed earth speak regularly to ensure I had no more unwanted guests. The first thing I did was collect essences from the corpses. The alpha yielded an apex essence of aether resistance, while four of the remaining five she-wolves yielded lesser essences. Two of the females had been pregnant, and they yielded empathy and perception essences. The other one yielded a minor essence of strength. I felt no guilt, as those babes would have been true-blood werewolves.

Flies were already starting to lay eggs in the bodies. I was soaked in blood, so the flies found me a viable target as well. I considered walking to a stream to remove as much blood as possible, but thought to wait until after I confirmed the elf child was alive. I might have another fight ahead of me.

Before leaving the hill, I cut the heads off all the bodies and stacked them together. Werewolves wouldn't regenerate like trolls, but it just felt like a smart move. That alpha's willingness to impale itself on my sword worried me.

I wasn't sure if I should return with all the heads as proof of my kills. Raelia had said there wasn't a reward from the village, but maybe the Guild would pay me for my efforts. All the werewolves had been nearly naked, so there was nothing to loot. Their camp, however, might have something worth scavenging.

It was midday, and the sun's heat was quickly drying my blood-soaked clothes into a crusty mess. I circled around and approached the werewolf camp from the far side. My earth pulses informed me there were only two small persons, probably children, in one of the three lean-to shelters. Still, I was cautious, and even discovered a stash of coins buried under one lean-to as I looked for traps with my pulses.

When I entered the camp, I smelled the strong scent of urine. Curing meat hung inside one of the shelters, being smoked by a fire. The meat appeared to be mostly deer, but there were also parts of at least one skinned humanoid.

Before confronting the two victims, I returned my spear to my space and sheathed magebane. I walked into the open, and the children recoiled at the sight of me. I admitted, I did look a fright.

The children had torn and tattered clothing and wore heavy iron collars around their necks. Chains attached the collars to weights to keep them from running. One girl had a bite mark on her shoulder; the puncture marks showed evidence of recently dried blood.

The other young elf girl had a bite on her forearm that looked infected with yellow puss. She must have been picking the scabs regularly. The alpha was probably waiting for them to be fully infected before releasing them to join his pack.

I found and tossed them both blankets that had been out of their reach, but they made no move to cover themselves. It was easy to tell which of the two had been recently abducted. One of the girls was filthy with tangled brown hair while the other child was still relatively clean with hair that was straight and shiny.

"The werewolf and the others are dead," I told them in Elvish. They barely reacted, clearly petrified and wary. "I am with the Adventurers Guild and am here to rescue you." Still no response. "Do you know where the key is for your collars?" I hadn't found anything on the bodies. Finally, the cleaner girl shook her head nervously.

I turned away to search the other two lean-to shelters for the key. One was being used for provisions and for smoking the meat, while the other was for sleeping, full of nasty piles of blankets and clothes. In the provisions shelter, I pulled the stubborn floorboards up to access the coins I had detected, thinking the key might be with the coins.

The worn chest was buried in sandy soil and filled with silver and gold jewelry, some simple, some ornate. The coins were mostly silver, and I found it strange that the werewolf kept them, given that silver was anathema to them. Three large gold coins and a dozen regular gold coins rounded out the collection.

The jewelry and coins should be enough reward for me if the village or Guild didn't recognize my efforts. I sifted through the jewelry but didn't notice any artifacts. I sent the entire chest to my dimensional space and looked up to see the two young elven girls staring at me.

"Do you want to leave?" I asked in as friendly a tone as I could muster. The newer victim nodded uncertainly, like I might be tricking her. The filthy one just stared at me, and I could see a feral quality in her eyes. How close was she to being fully infected?

I approached them cautiously and held out four red pills. "Each of you needs to consume two of these. They will help you relax." The cleaner of the two reached out tentatively, delicately taking two of the oblivion pills. The other was not so gentle, her hard, yellow nails digging into my spider-silk gloves. She had been trying to hurt me intentionally, but didn't penetrate the gloves. She had bruised the skin underneath with her unnatural strength, but I quickly healed. Maybe she was beyond saving, but it was not my decision.

"Water?" the first elf girl asked pitifully. Her voice was dry and cracked. I could see from where they had chained her that she didn't have access to any water. I went to the provisions shelter and found a waterskin for them. I watched carefully as the two consumed the oblivion pills and collapsed into a deep sleep. I was suspicious of the dirty one and searched the rest of the camp before dealing with the two.

There was a store of weapons, but they were starting to rust. Werewolves preferred to claw and bite in a fight. I sent seven swords, a dozen daggers, two bows, and forty-odd arrows to storage. There were no runic weapons, but they were all of good quality and could be sold for a few gold each.

Walking back to the two elves, I found I had been right to be wary of the dirty one. A slurry of red-brown saliva had dribbled out of her mouth. She hadn't swallowed the oblivion pills, but they had eventually worked on her anyway. I took some cordage and tied both girls' legs together and then their arms behind their backs. I carefully used my dimensional space to cut the iron collars free. I stored the first elf, and while I waited for my aether to recover, I scavenged up a large sack. It was actually a waterproof sleeping bedroll.

When the second young elf joined the first in my dimensional space, I returned to the hill. All the heads went into the bedroll, which then went into my space. Looking at the bodies, I thought to burn them, as I was not sure if scavengers could spread the infection. I transported all the bodies in my space to the shelter with the smoking meat.

It didn't take long for the fire to spread and burn down the small structure. I moved out of range of the smell of burning flesh and hair. I judged the fire wouldn't spread and then consumed the apex aether resistance essence. It was one of my weaker magical attributes, and I couldn't recall consuming one before, but I had now consumed over a hundred essences.

As the essence spread from my abdomen out to my aether channels, I felt a chill come over me, as if I was freezing from the inside out. It passed as quickly as it had come, but it was one of my more unpleasant essence experiences.

It was early afternoon when I began my light run back to the elven town of Esanor. I was relying on the blood compass, as there was no way to follow my trail in a timely fashion. It was good practice for moving silently and using my earth speak. Still, I knew it was over twenty miles and would take me five to six hours.

I stopped when I found a suitable pool in a shallow, wide stream. I wish I had someone to watch my back when I cleaned my clothes and gear, but I would just pulse earth speak more frequently. Stripping, I put on fresh underclothes but scrubbed my armor and rinsed the bloody clothes. The spider gloves and shirt were easy to clean, but the leggings and other clothes were going to be permanently stained. At least I would be able to get the smell out of them. In damp clothes, I continued my trek back. I assumed my clothes would be dry by the time I arrived.

At sunset, the woods shifted from birdsong to an orchestra of insects. I wasn't as fortunate tonight as I was when I tracked the werewolf last night. A predator either picked up on my movement or I was not being as quiet as I thought. The thunderous crash of tree branches being snapped alerted me long before my night vision located the creature.

It was faster than I was, but it had the advantage of having four legs. I focused on running while I tried to identify what beast it was. As it closed in, I became fairly certain it was an earth drake, based on the feedback from my pulses. Unlike ordinary creatures, this one was clearly outlined, indicating that it resonated with the earth affinity. It was not nearly as large as the one I had encountered in the Shimmering Labyrinth. I knew they were territorial, so I must have passed through its domain.

Hearne's advice on encountering one was to learn how to run faster. They had thick-scaled hide, and the larger they were, the harder the hide was to penetrate. They were probably the dumbest of the drake species, but you didn't need a lot of smarts when your enemy couldn't injure you.

I moved into a denser thicket of ancient trees. Although the trunks were spaced farther apart, this should slow the drake, as it would have to weave around them instead of charging through. It would likely halt its pursuit if I could escape its territory. If it continued and got close enough, its life was forfeit.

The thundering pursuit scared anything in front of us out of our path. It was stubborn and still closing in on me, so I decided to confront the creature. I sheltered behind a massive oak, expecting it to snake around to one side. Instead, it used the tree to stop its momentum, shaking the ground and causing debris to fall from the tree all around us. Maybe it had thought I was trying to climb the tree to escape it and hoped to knock me down. It would have worked if that was what I had been doing.

The draconic head snaked around the tree, ready to snag its prey. I almost felt sorry for it when I saw the look of confusion in its eyes as its head fell to the ground. I had only removed a thin slice of its neck, beheading the creature. The ground shook as the body settled to the forest floor a moment later. I watched the life leave the majestic creature's eyes before it slid down to rest against the tree. It had certainly been an eventful day, and I deserved a rest.

I patted the snout of the drake. "Sorry, but I gave you a chance to let me go, big guy. Don't worry, I won't let your body go to waste. Earth drake hide makes great boots and armor." A spray of blood from its nostrils seemed to disagree with me. It wasn't alive, just expelling the air trapped in a cavity. I sighed, now speckled in blood. "That was not very nice. I just took a bath."

I used the collector as soon as I had recovered enough aether. The drake was not large, just over thirty feet tail to snout, but it still yielded a major earth essence, which I consumed immediately. I washed it down with some water, as the essence had a grainy texture when it dissolved. The aftertaste reminded me of dirt.

I could tell the essence's effects were minor, but even minor improvements to the affinity extended the range of my earth speak. I then proceeded to skin the drake. I used a mix of dimensional cutting and Boris's dungeon-forged blade. I got nineteen squares of the hide, scales still attached. The scales would have to be removed to treat and prepare the hide, but it was enough for a few future sets of armor.

The chance encounter had stalled me for two hours. I arrived back in the village a little after midnight. Torches were lit around the town, probably in fear of the werewolf returning. I could see Maveith sitting outside the merchant's barn. He was sewing something, clearly waiting for me to return.

I circled the village to approach the barn from the far side. There were torches here as well, but no sentries that I could detect. I placed the two elven children and the bag of heads on the ground. I started thinking I should only turn in the alpha's head. Appearing to have carried the large sack and the two girls might appear conspicuous. The horses stirred in the barn. I guessed it was the smell of drake blood on me.

Benito opened the door, glowstone in one hand, sword in the other. Mateo and Blaze followed behind him, but relaxed at seeing me standing there. Raelia and Baldo stirred atop the roof, gawking at me. They must have been sleeping, but had she been waiting for me up there? Baldo chirped, confused, his nostrils flaring at the unfamiliar bloody scents in the air. Maveith walked around the barn, grinning as he noticed me.

Blaze was the first to speak. "Is that your blood or the werewolf's blood?"

"Let's go with the werewolf's blood." I huffed a chuckle. I pointed behind me. "I got a pair of kids if you want to tell the elves. Don't untie them; they are both infected, and one is feral. I think I am going to clean up." I had heard Ginger get antsy in her stall when she heard my voice, so I went to check in with her before heading to a nearby stream. My companions were speechless as I walked past them, but I heard Benito mutter something about some elves that owed him some silver.

Chapter 279: Show Me the Money

When I returned from washing my armor and rinsing my clothes—*again*, the children were gone and my companions were standing around the seven heads on the ground. Maveith looked up at me, his voice full of concern. "There were seven of them."

I moved in close to the group so we couldn't be easily overheard. I assumed the townsfolk were focused on the children at the moment, and my night vision told me no one was hiding nearby. I slowly and coyly counted aloud. "Yes, seven. The big one there, I think, was an alpha, and he was kidnapping and infecting women to start a pack," I said dismissively. My companions were still stunned that I had fought seven werewolves alone. I should have only brought back the alpha's head.

I produced the three essences to distract them. Benito's eyes caught the glint of the spheres in the light of the glowstone. "They had essences on them! You got really lucky!" Benito said with admiration.

"No, I used a collector on them," I replied casually. This bit of information would come up sooner or later, and now seemed like a good time. Maveith and Raelia already knew about the collector from the Shimmering Labyrinth.

With his eyes on the essence, Mateo asked, "Where did you get a collector? Did Castile give it to you?"

"No, it belonged to Durandus. But don't talk about it in public. Collectors are even more valuable outside of the Empire," I informed him, and eyed my companions to make sure they understood. The shock on Mateo's face was priceless.

"Hey, I think Flavius was looking for that collector," Benito said, breaking in the silence.

Blaze was more thoughtful. "You've had it since Macha? Suppose it makes sense since your space is larger than Castile assumed. Was that where the extra food in the Caelorian Library came from?"

I almost wished for the quiet, reserved Blaze over this introspective Blaze. I admitted it. "Yes."

Mateo laughed. "Lirkin and Adrian told us all to shut up and be grateful we had it." I hadn't realized the men had talked about the miraculous appearance of food in the library. I had been exhausted from using the kettle on specters and hadn't paid much attention to anything else going on. I should have known the men would have been wise to the miracle of food suddenly appearing, as meals were something everyone had fixated on.

"I prefer not to talk about our time in Caelora," I said sorrowfully. We had suffered and lost a lot of friends. I snatched back my hand from Baldo, who had lunged for the essences.

Raelia yelled at him, "Baldo. No!" She looked at me with shame, "Sorry. I purchased him a minor essence of constitution two months ago. He really enjoyed it."

"Griffins can consume essences?" Mateo asked in a shocked tone.

Raelia pursed her lips and lectured the group in a tone I knew well from the Labyrinth. "Any creature besides the unliving, to my knowledge, can. Constitution essences are prized for mounts as they can slightly lengthen their lives and make them viable mounts for longer. For Baldo, that essence should make him airworthy for me for about four decades, and he should live almost fifty years."

Out of Baldo's reach, I handed Benito the empathy essence, Blaze the dexterity essence, and Mateo the strength essence. "What is this for? We didn't do anything," Mateo said, holding up his dark-purple sphere with the glowstone behind it.

I hesitated for a breath before I replied. Was I being like Castile and trying to buy the loyalty of my companions? Maybe. Their gains would be so small they wouldn't matter—but still, they had chosen to support Maveith and me.

"You are part of the adventuring team. An equal split of the bounty we find." I said that now, but Castile always kept most of the mental essences for herself, and probably all the magic ones as well. She was generous, not stupid.

Benito had already popped his empathy essence into his mouth. Mateo and Blaze followed suit shortly after. Baldo let out a sorrowful crooning sound, disappointed that he got nothing. I tossed him a cube of bear meat to quiet him. "Did you all practice this afternoon?" I asked, and suddenly, no one made eye contact with me.

Raelia, grinning, spoke for the group. "We went for long walks in the woods." She quickly added, "Not far from the town. Maveith and I tried to teach the others how to move quietly. Mateo is a lost cause, but Blaze and Benito did well enough." The truth was clear: they were venturing out in hopes of finding me, but I had traveled far from town. If they had come with me, one or more might have been injured or infected.

Someone was coming, and Raelia let us know who it was with her superior night sight. "Rolf is coming from the merchant's inn. That is where they brought the afflicted."

We waited as the dwarf merchant walked purposely toward us. His thick beard hid his expression in the shadows of the night. He barked happily, "Well, you stirred things up a bit. They will be leaving to bring the children to a healing mage in the city in an hour. Sadly, one looks too far gone. The good people collected a reward for you." Rolf fished out a small but heavy-looking pouch. "North of seven gold in small coins if my eyes worked properly when they were filling the bowl."

"Tell them they can keep it," I said, waving off the reward. Benito started coughing, and Rolf's eyes showed shock. "I found some coins in the werewolf camp. Plenty of compensation. They will need that gold to pay for a cure." From my Hound lessons, I knew it took a powerful healer to eliminate lycanthropy from the blood.

"The Healers Guild won't charge for a lycanthropy purge," Rolf said. Seeing that I was not going to take it, he lowered the bag to his side, Benito's eyes following it. "Plan to collect a bounty on those?" He indicated the werewolf heads.

"There is a bounty?" I asked, intrigued. It had been on my mind, but mostly, I wanted to demonstrate that the threat had been eliminated.

Raelia shook her head, disappointed in me. Her body language reminded me of our time in the dungeon when she had lorded her superior knowledge over me. At least now, she wore a smirk. "The Adventurers Guild has bounties on all dangerous creatures. You need to bring proof. I thought that was why you brought the heads."

"How much?" Benito asked for me, his eyes still following the sack as it disappeared into Rolf's pocket.

"It differs by the kingdom, since they are the ones who ultimately pay the bounty. In Bartiradia, a werewolf head was a large gold. I don't know if an alpha was more. In Esenhem? I don't know. I just joined the Adventurers Guild recently," Raelia explained purposefully.

"They are Eryk's kills. It is his gold," Blaze stated, like it was decided by all of them.

"Well, tie them tight in a bag. I don't want the wagons stinking. There is a branch of the Adventurers Guild in Kaelsilo. We will be there in two days." Rolf looked back at me. "You sure?" he confirmed, meaning the town's reward, and I nodded. He sighed like he disagreed with me. "I will explain it to them, then. Don't want it seeming like you are spitting at their generosity."

"Tell them to prepare a sendoff feast to show their gratitude," I told him before he retreated. He walked away, muttering something about stupid mercenaries. The others were in conversation, speculating about how much the bounty for the heads would be, and I followed Rolf to get a few hours' sleep in the guard rooms adjacent to the merchant's inn.

In the morning, there was a feast for the ages—at least for this modest town. There was more food than we could ever hope to eat, but Benito and Mateo tried. We invited the other guards to share, and it was not lost on me that Rolf let us leave a few hours late. Apparently, most of Benito's bets were with the other guards, as silver was exchanged at breakfast. We even got a rousing send-off from the elven villagers. It was nice to be appreciated.

Even in the waterproof sleeping roll, the heads baked in the sun and began to stink during the day. We tied the bag to the back of the last wagon, and no one guarded the rear. At night, we buried it in sand to mask the smell.

A day later, I was presenting the heads to a Guild clerk while the others tended the horses. She was wearing a mask as she pulled the maggot-infested heads from the bag with a practiced hand. She was not squeamish as she examined each nasty, monstrous head. "Where did your team encounter the werewolf pack?" she asked, trying not to breathe in after she finished.

"About twenty-two miles southwest of Esanor. The werewolves had three open-faced log shelters. I found two infected children, and they are being brought to Nirimporti to be healed," I replied helpfully.

"Was there a posting for their rescue?" she asked as she signaled for a lean elf in an apron to approach. "Burn these, please." She muttered to herself, loud enough for me to hear, "My job would be much easier if all adventurers could be trusted to always tell the truth."

"No, there was no posting. We arrived in the afternoon, the child was taken before dawn, and the local Ranger went to get help," I replied.

"No reward then. Pity. It couldn't have been easy to handle so many, even though these females were probably small. It's been seven or eight years since we had werewolves in the region, never a good omen." She pulled out a sheet and began to write out what I assumed was a voucher. I was never good at reading upside-down. She asked for my and the others' medallion numbers. Even though they had not assisted, I gave her everyone's registration numbers.

She completed the sheet and turned it around for me to confirm what she had written. It was a relatively simple bureaucratic form, as things went. It listed the location and details of the kills. I didn't see the amount of the bounty anywhere on the sheet. "Was there no bounty for the werewolves?"

"I don't have the gold here to pay out. This will be filed in Artiria," she indicated the report she had created. "It will take a week or two to get there; I will hold a copy in case it doesn't. Then, at any large Guild Hall in the world, you can use a message to confirm it with Artiria and pay yourself or anyone in your group the bounty. The gold actually comes from the Esenhem coffers, not the Guild."

"And how much is that bounty?" I asked, not thinking it was large due to her nonchalance. I also did not have a great relationship with Guildmaster Jhaartael.

"Alphas are a scourge. One hundred gold for him. The lessers, ten gold each. But I am being generous, since they were a pack. Normally, it is five gold for a recently infected." She might have been smiling under her mask, but I couldn't see it. "That leaves you 144 gold." Seeing my confusion, she explained. "Ten percent to the Guild, ninety percent to you." She spent fifteen minutes stamping out a bronze voucher for me with the amount owed and the corresponding number on the report she filed. "Don't fret; once it is approved in the Artiria Guild, payment will be quick." With this snail-paced bureaucracy, I doubted it would be quick.

Maybe I should be angry about a ten percent tax, but it was much more egregious back on Earth, where taxes ate half my income. "Is there a bounty book?" I asked before leaving.

"I have an older copy here. It is updated annually by the kingdoms where the Guild is allowed to operate. Mostly, it is utilized to generate job postings for subjugations of threats." She retrieved a book from the shelf and handed it to me. It was basically an indexed system for Esenhem bounties. She helped me by turning to the werewolf index. As she had said, the alpha was listed at a hundred gold, but there were other add-ons listed. For instance, one additional gold for each person the creature had killed or one silver for each livestock.

Also as she had mentioned, a lesser werewolf was five gold, but if they were in a pack of four or more, each bounty was raised to ten each. As I was engrossed in the details, she said, "Most bounties are pretty standard kingdom to kingdom. When a monster crisis arises, we mostly use these books to create job postings in the Adventurers Halls. The kingdom coffers will cover the reward." I nodded, thinking it was a semi-efficient reward system.

I paged to the earth drake to see what the bounty might have been. It was based on the size of the drake and a few other factors. The size of the one I had killed meant it was just thirty gold. Seeing where I was looking, the clerk explained, "Some dangerous creatures that have a lot of harvestable materials are listed for less than you would expect. An earth drake this size could be harvested by a skilled skinner, generating one to two hundred gold. Most kingdoms account for that when rewarding kills."

After I paged through the entire book, I thanked the clerk and went to find my companions at the merchant's barn in town. They had all finished with the horses and were joking around while Baldo hunted rats in the loft. I showed them the bronze voucher. "It was 144 gold. That is twenty-four gold each, but the wheels of bureaucracy turn slowly. Maybe in two or three weeks." Blaze looked about to speak. "I don't want to hear it. Equal split on the bounty." There was probably a similar amount in the dirty chest I had found. I would hold those for company funds.

The rest of the trip was mostly uneventful. We ended up traveling with two other merchant caravans from the elven city of Pevora to the orc city of Khoura. Rolf grumbled as he paid our wages: forty-four silver to each of us with a twenty-six silver bonus. Shocked at his generosity, I asked him why.

Grumpily, he told me. "Word spread of your deeds in Esanor. I did better than an average run. But there might have been some misunderstanding that is I who sent you to rescue the child. I didn't correct that assumption." He chuckled wryly, and I joined him. "If you have given up your foolish notion of going deeper into the Caliphate, I would be willing to pay you ten silver a day and your companions five. Your group is certainly more competent than most the Guild sends to me. I would even pay for the griffin's nourishment."

I looked at my companions nearby. Benito was looking around in awe at all the orcs. His purse was heavy with silver that needed to be spent. Blaze was holding the reins of all the horses, waiting on me. It looked like Raelia was having second thoughts about bringing Baldo along because of all the attention he was getting from passing orcs. Maveith was grinding his teeth as four goliaths carried a carriage further down the street. Mateo—Mateo was eyeing an orc brothel down the street. At least I assumed that was what it was, judging by the women loitering outside.

"No. We have a plan in mind. May Fortuna bless you with large profits." I shook wrists with the dwarf and joined my companions on our walk to Khoura's Adventurers Hall.

Chapter 280: Fake It till You Make It

Khoura was a sprawling city nestled among fields being cultivated for planting. The outer walls were a dark stone, but most of the buildings within were made of wood. It almost felt like we were in an alien world, with nearly every citizen being an orc. Orc skin was mostly tones of gray, but there were occasional orcs whose skin had greenish or reddish tints.

I caught Maveith's attention as he focused on the goliaths carrying a carriage. "Now is not the time. We are here for your sister, not to free every goliath in the Caliphate."

Maveith ground his teeth. "It is not right. Too many goliaths have been taken by the orc pirate slavers over the years."

Raelia offered unhelpfully, "It is because the warlords see controlling larger men as a sign of their power. The slavers only sell to the Caliphate; they are not part of the Caliphate."

Raelia didn't appease Maveith, and I could see his veins beginning to bulge in his neck. I moved us out of sight of the goliaths. "Let's go see about registering our guild medallions in the Caliphate." I took Ginger's reins and led my companions down the street, searching for the Guild emblem. The Adventurer's Hall should be somewhere along the main road.

The city was very clean and the citizens were well dressed. The architecture was crude but sound, relying on large beams. Since it was a border city, I didn't think we would draw much attention, but I was wrong. Curious eyes followed us as we led our mounts down the main street. Raelia's mount released a load as he walked, and a young, light-gray orc emerged from the alley nearby to clean the mess immediately. One thing the city lacked was orc guard patrols.

I questioned Raelia since she was close. "Where are all the city guards?"

Raelia lectured everyone in a scholarly tone that could be considered condescending. "There are none needed in the streets. Orcs do not commit crimes against one another. The warlords bicker among themselves like old human housewives, but citizens of the Caliphate believe they should live their lives to serve the good of all the people. The elves believe it has made their craftsmen somewhat uninspired during their relatively short lifespan."

Blaze asked curiously, "How long do orcs live?"

Raelia paused, sifting through her memories. "For the warlords and elite warriors, dying in battle is considered the highest honor. As their strength begins to wane, they deliberately seek out more dangerous fights. Reaching fifty summers is seen as a full life for them. The Boutan clerics live twice that, and the common citizens fall somewhere in between. But I should say—I'm no expert. Most of what I know came from my aunt's lessons."

"I thought that was why we brought you along—because you were the expert?" I said, casting Raelia an amused glance. She didn't answer, just frowned, clearly irritated. I could see the tension in her shoulders as every orc eye stayed fixed on Baldo, who was perched like royalty in his pillion seat atop Stormcloud. The griffin seemed to bask in the attention, but the attention paid to her griffin was making Raelia nervous.

We soon found the Guild symbol, a tree with hundreds of branches mirrored by roots, on a sign over a building that looked more like an inn than an Adventurers Hall. The young orc stable hand did not speak Telhian or Elvish, and we had to rely on Raelia to converse with him. After a lengthy back-and-forth, it was two coppers a day for each mount and an extra copper if we wanted grain mixed with the hay.

I decided to pay three days in advance, just in case we had to delay our departure. I gave the young orc a silver, which included a tip of twenty-eight coppers. Raelia relayed my expectation that he change the water in the stalls three times a day for each horse and that he only give them the best hay and grain. I knew from Lucien that if sand got mixed into the hay, it could cause problems in the future that would require a healer.

Ginger didn't like the unfamiliar smells or the strange orc stable hand, but settled down after an apple and some comforting words. With our mounts stabled, we headed into the Hall from the rear entrance.

As we stepped inside, a thick haze of sickly-sweet smoke clung to our clothes, hanging in the air and curling around the dim glowstones overhead. The scent was cloying—part spice, part rot, like overripe fruit left too long in the sun. Dozens of low tables filled the room, each surrounded by adventurers lounging and drinking, with a few puffing lazily on ornate pipes shaped like serpents and beasts. The coals inside a large fireplace glowed a vibrant red, casting strange shadows.

A long, scarred, stained bar stretched across one side of the room, where a few hefty orc adventurers nursed heavy mugs and muttered in low voices. Behind the bar, mismatched bottles neatly lined shelves, their contents an array of colors.

Across the chamber, the standard assignment board stood against the far wall—faded, scratched, and covered in a patchwork of curled parchment. A pair of armored orcs strode along its length, scanning the notices with bored expressions, their weapons clinking softly at their sides.

Surprisingly, we did not draw much attention until Baldo chirped loudly and hissed. A server had stepped too close to Raelia, and Baldo was warning the cautious young orc away. A dozen heads turned our way to study our group and the griffin. Under the hard gazes, Baldo puffed up to appear bigger, but after traveling with him for three weeks, I knew he was actually afraid.

Ignoring the attention, I headed for the clerk's desk, my group following. A gray-haired orc was reviewing some paperwork and looked up, mildly annoyed. "We are here to register our guild medallions to work within the Caliphate. Six rooms for two nights if available." I spoke in Elvish and he pursed his lips, his short lower tusks showing.

"How many and where will you be traveling?" he asked in rough Elvish, but his sharp eyes were examining my group. He was clearly eyeing our weapons and making a judgment of our skill. Our runic weapons were disguised as best as we could manage. Only Benito stood lazily in our party, straining his neck to make out a card game being played by a halfling, two orcs, and a human.

"We will be looking over the job posting board, but we hope to delve into The Vault of the Spirit Arachnid and The Whispering Grotto." He looked surprised at the dungeons I had mentioned.

"That is quite the trek," he said, focusing on me suspiciously.

My talk with the orc healer had been very productive. The Vault of the Spirit Arachnid was in the middle of the Boutan Caliphate, and The Whispering Grotto was on the northern coast, not far from the warlord who had purchased Maveith's sister, Zorana. "We have a contract with an arcane weaver in Esenhem who wants the ethereal silk from the Spirit Arachnid and an alchemist who wants troll blood from The Whispering Grotto."

"The blood is only viable for a few days after harvest," he said, doubting me.

"A member of my party has a small dimensional space," I replied. He slowly nodded in appreciation, accepting my explanation.

"Medallions," he finally requested. I was the first to hand mine over. His eyes were briefly shocked by the silver coating, and then he noticed my number. "Thirteen?" he said, annoyed. "Your membership originated in the Telhian Empire?" My guild number was 13-393919. The thirteen indicated at which

Adventurers Hall I became a member, while the second number was my membership number at that location.

"Is that going to be a problem?" I asked flatly.

He tapped his quill on his ink pot. "No," he said curtly, but I could tell it was an issue for him. Just another kingdom that disliked Telhians.

He wrote down my information. As he handed me the medallion back, I informed him, "I am only registered in Telha. I am from Tsinga. I have no loyalty to the Empire." I don't know if he believed me, but he seemed somewhat appeased.

Now a little more helpful, the clerk offered advice. "There is a backlog for entry into the dungeons you are interested in—three weeks or more. You could sign up for the queue here if you wish. One gold for each dungeon."

"What if I miss my delve date?" I asked suspiciously.

He waved his hand dismissively. "You are just placed at the end of the queue. Miss ten dates and you relinquish your fee."

After witnessing his hesitant reaction to my origin from the Empire, I couldn't shake off suspicion about his true intentions. However, considering he was a Guild clerk and expected to assist, I reluctantly handed over two gold coins to maintain the expensive facade.

I'd made it clear to my companions that we weren't here to delve into dungeons—just to pass through the city. After a brief flurry of paperwork and a few exchanged nods, the clerk handed me two bronze tokens etched with orcish runes, their surfaces worn from frequent use. A message sending would be dispatched in the morning to officially register the tokens in the dungeon queue.

Everyone was anxious about how long I had taken to register. Fortunately, the rest of my group's medallions were from Esenhem guilds, and the clerk proceeded to log them quickly. We were told there was a ten percent Caliphate tax on all completed jobs, but other than that, we were now allowed to review the job board.

I paid for six rooms, each costing a silver, which included breakfast and all the light ale we could drink. Each room had two beds, but I thought we could all use a little privacy after that long trip. The good news was that Baldo was allowed in the Hall and could stay in Raelia's room. In fact, two large war dogs were lying in the corner of the room behind a large tattooed orc in leather armor who was drinking and talking with others. The dogs' eyes were following Baldo with anticipation.

"Get settled, and I will review the board," I told everyone as they scattered and headed up the thick wooden stairs to find their rooms. My job was futile, as the postings were all in Orcish. I found Raelia, and she locked Baldo in her room and returned to the board with me.

"What are we looking for?" she asked as she studied the very first posting. I could see she was struggling with the orc script but wasn't going to admit it.

"Anything that takes our path toward the center of the Caliphate and the Spirit Arachnid Dungeon." I said it loud enough for nearby adventurers to hear. Raelia studied each slip for a few minutes before moving onto the next one.

"This one is a monster subjugation job." She slowly read, "Village of Vormaz, ankhegs nesting near the fields." We walked to a large map at the end of the postings and found the village more northeast than northwest, like I wanted. We began to go through other possible jobs one at a time.

Locate an escaped bull in the wild.

Find and eliminate green goblins raiding a chicken egg farm.

Basilisk eggs for an alchemist.

Sword trainer for twin sons of a merchant in Khedeilal.

This last one was a possibility because it was a hundred miles east of Grila, where the Spirit Arachnid Dungeon was located. The problem was that the tenure for the instruction was thirty days and was subject to renewal. We found two postings for merchant escorts, but I didn't want to take any of them because caravans moved so slowly. We could make twice the distance daily without being slowed by a merchant.

"Any delivery jobs? The Caliphate doesn't have a portal network, so there must be a lot of transportation jobs," I asked Raelia, whose eyes were strained from translating.

"I think the merchant caravans handle those," Raelia replied tiredly. "This one requires a silver adventurer." She tapped a paper as she continued to read it. "I don't think it suits us, though. It is for an earth mage to search for what they believe is an ancient battlefield. The orc cleric is looking for buried artifacts to confirm her guess."

"Where is it, and how much does it pay?" I asked, intrigued.

"North of Adorechi—about fifteen miles according to the posting. Twenty gold if successful in recovering artifacts; otherwise, one gold per day of searching, up to ten days," Raelia read slowly. I took the posting and pulled it down to bring to the clerk. The city of Adorechi was about three hundred miles from here but not too far from the main trade road. More importantly, it was in the direction we wanted to travel.

"But we don't have an earth mage!" Raelia, said, exasperated. "If we take a job we are not equipped to handle, we will be penalized by the Guild." I ignored her and walked to the clerk. Raelia followed me helplessly.

The clerk looked at the posting and then at me. He already knew I was a silver adventurer but maybe had heard Raelia announce that we didn't have the skills for the job. "A member of my group has the earth speak spell form," I informed the skeptical clerk. Raelia looked a little shocked.

The orc chewed the inside of his cheek for a minute and sucked his tusks. He slowly started the paperwork to enroll us in the job. "You have eight and a half days to report to Cleric Glasha in the city of Adorechi." I nodded, as that was less than forty miles a day, manageable on the main trade road. After the paperwork was complete, I headed back to our rooms with Raelia. "Tell the others we will leave midmorning tomorrow. I would have liked to give them more of a rest from the saddle, but circumstances do not permit it."

"Who has earth speak among us?" she asked in a harsh whisper. "Maveith has a stone shape and isn't capable of true spells."

"I do," I said, opening the door to my room and closing it behind me before Raelia could ask more questions. I left her stunned in the hallway, where she stayed for a few minutes before I heard her head to her room. Baldo was clearly excited to see her return, clucking for attention through the thin walls.

This trip would take us a third of the way across the Caliphate and bring us that much closer to the warlord who had purchased Zorana ten years ago. I decided to forgo searching for an orc guide among the adventurers. Raelia was somewhat suited to the task, and I didn't want to risk having too many unfamiliar eyes watching me.

I didn't use the amulet or sleep much that night since I was restless. There was a lot of uncertainty ahead of us in the Caliphate lands, and everyone was looking to me to be the confident rock, even though underneath, I felt just as uncertain as they did.

As the leader, my mistakes could get my friends killed, and I was feeling more pressure now that we had entered the Caliphate. There was an old saying my music teacher in high school used to say—fake it till you make it.

It was the first time I had felt exhausted in a while. My ring of sustenance and essence-fortified attributes could not overcome my lack of sleep and the stress of leadership. I dressed in my adventurer's armor and then rubbed down Ginger before breakfast. When I told the stable hand we were leaving today, he went to get the coppers I had paid for the remaining days. I refused the refund, to his confusion.

There was a small outfitter in the Guild Hall who had detailed maps of the Caliphate, far better than what I had in my dreamscape. I bought the four maps that covered the northern Caliphate. The southern Caliphate lay across the Endless Salt Sea and bordered the Telhian Empire. I studied the maps while sampling the offered buffet.

The Adventurers Hall breakfast was poorly attended, based on the number of adventurers drinking last night. I had read a cookbook from the Caliphate, but didn't recognize anything being offered. I went with thinly sliced, cured meat on a doughy pita, slathered in some green paste. The paste was a pungent garlic pesto, and the only thing that gave the improvised pocket sandwich flavor.

Raelia sat with me as I consumed my small sandwich, judging me. "Still wearing the ring?" she said as she sorted through her plate, which was stacked high with the offerings of the buffet. I had taken the ring of sustenance from her in the dungeon and never returned it, even after we came to an accord.

"If you want it back, you can give me the cloak back," I said with a smirk, knowing she wouldn't accept. She wore an artifact called a Ranger's cloak, which allowed her to blend into her surroundings. At night, she was nearly invisible. During the day, if she didn't move, she remained the same. The cloak had been in a reward chest from one of the creatures I had killed in the Shimmering Labyrinth. It also held special meaning for wood elves.

"It was a fair exchange," she said hastily. Baldo chirped at not being fed, and Raelia gave him a chunk of meat from her plate after he obeyed two commands. The griffin was growing rapidly and had added half its weight in the last three weeks. Before too long, he wouldn't be able to ride on Stormcloud. Raelia picked at the plate while Baldo got the majority; clearly, something was on her mind.

I waited patiently as I sipped some bitter wine. I thought she would ask about my earth speak ability, but her mind was elsewhere. "Could you place Baldo in your dimensional pocket if I asked?" I was a bit shocked at the request. She was aware of my space's power, having spent a lot of time in there herself.

"Possibly. Why?" I asked, but I already knew the answer.

She sighed with relief. "I should be training him ten hours a day, but it is hard to do so, being constantly on the move." I looked at her dubiously. She had been training the griffin constantly in the saddle. It would be more difficult as we increased our pace from escorting merchant wagons, but it would still be feasible.

"Fine! It was a mistake to bring him!" She hissed in a concession. "He is too vulnerable, and there is too much interest in him." Baldo chirped, hearing his name, and Raelia gave him more meat. I could needle her about how she had thought she knew better than me and had insisted he wouldn't be a liability—but I didn't.

Instead, I considered how to explain Baldo's disappearance to the others. Was it the right time to reveal that I could move live creatures and people into my dimensional space? Benito and Mateo talked too freely, and they could let it slip after a few rounds at a tavern.

In a compassionate tone, I replied, "I understand your concern. Do your best to care for him for now. If there is no other recourse, I will do as you wish. I don't want to explain his disappearance to the others at the moment." Relief flooded her face, a burden lifted. Her face brightened into a smile directed at me.

"Thank you," she said softly. She touched my arm and then withdrew it quickly, acting like it was unintended.

Maveith's voice rumbled down the stairs, guiding the others. As they helped themselves, Mateo complained that the food wasn't to his taste. Blaze reminded him of our time starving in Caelora, and he quieted. I took the time to explain the job we had taken in simple terms. "One of the orc clerics is looking for an ancient battlefield. We will escort her and assist her in finding evidence buried with time."

"Ugh, I thought I wouldn't have to dig again after leaving the Legion," Mateo groaned as he consumed pickled duck eggs.

"Don't worry; it will be a quick assignment but a long ride, slightly over three hundred miles on the road. It will get us much closer to our true objective." That got a hearty nod from Maveith.

"That is a long way to travel for a job. Is there nothing else we can do along the way?" Blaze inquired, sampling a number of the offerings on his plate. In my opinion, the meat was a bit salty but not terrible. Apparently, it was not to his taste, and he only ate something that was boiled in rolled cabbage leaves.

Blaze was being pragmatic, even though I was more focused on haste than making coin. However, it might be best to maintain the appearance of trying to earn as much coin as possible, like normal adventurers. "You can examine the job board with Raelia to see if anything is along the trade road on our way to the city of Adorechi," I decided. Raelia looked pained. I could tell her mastery of the written orc language was limited.

Benito didn't have the same reservations about the food and was working on his second plate. Once everyone was finished, we would saddle up and depart. My goal was to cover forty miles today and then sixty miles each successive day. Blaze returned with a posting an hour later and handed it to me. "Someone wants their parents' farm checked on. They haven't heard from them in four months. It is near Adorechi."

I looked to Raelia so she could explain it more clearly. "The local baker has parents on a farm about twenty miles east of Adorechi. We would pass within a few miles of it. Shouldn't take us long to tell them their son is worried about them." I guess even orc children cared about their parents.

"Unless monsters have eaten them," Mateo noted offhandedly.

"Then all we have to do is return the letter to the local Guild with a note on what we found," Blaze said glibly. "We will still get paid." On the posting, the noted payout was small, just ten silver pieces, but that might be a substantial sum for a baker.

"Fine, it will only be a few hours' detour. Blaze, since you wanted more work so badly, you can saddle Ginger for me while I accept the job." As my companions left, I approached the desk. It was much quicker to accept this quest than the last one. I received a folded letter with a black wax seal, which I sent to my dimensional space as I walked to the stables. Soon, our group was on the road.

The main trade road of Esenhem continued into the Boutan Caliphate. As we rode, farmlands sprawled deep into the plains on either side of us. This differed from the Telhian Empire, where farms were clustered together for protection from the dangers of the wild. There were fewer roaming creatures in the Caliphate than in the Empire.

We rode in pairs, with the lead pair responsible for scouting and the rear pair scanning our backs. The middle pair was allowed to relax and not be on constant alert. Not that there was much of a threat. The road was wide but rougher than in Esenhem, and we mostly saw orc farmers driving ox carts toward larger towns and cities. We didn't see a single mounted patrol that would be commonplace in the Empire.

Raelia used the time to have Baldo hunt large birds when she spotted them flying. The griffin was still clumsy in the air against the smaller and more agile hawks and eagles. But Raelia explained that the aerial pursuit was training his fitness and agility. When he got too frustrated, he would abandon his prey and dive down onto an unsuspecting rabbit, fox, or fawn. He still liked to exchange the kill with me for dungeon meat. I thought he could sense the aether in the flesh instinctively. Maybe if he consumed enough he could become a dire griffin, but I didn't know for sure.

During the ride, I explained my earth speak spell form to my companions. Benito needed a bit more explanation than the others, as it was hard for him to conceptualize. I also told them not to discuss my ability or its range with anyone, as it was an indicator of my earth affinity. Raelia knew enough about the spell form to be stunned when I admitted my range. She stared at me for most of the day after that revelation.

We made excellent time, the only issue being small clouds of spring blackflies hazing us. Raelia demonstrated her usefulness with micro fireballs she used to incinerate the offenders. Even though Raelia warned the group, the first such explosion spooked Maveith's horse, causing him to tumble backward off his saddle and land in a tangle of limbs on the ground. It gave us all a good laugh, and I worked with Maveith to train his mount not to be spooked. It was largely about the mount trusting the rider to inform it when real danger was present.

There were no large merchant barns for us to stay in along the trade road. Our options were to camp, pay for an inn, or negotiate with a farmer for space in an outbuilding. However, most of the farms we passed lacked stables or barns. Truthfully, life in the Caliphate did not seem so bad.

When Benito cycled back to ride with me on the third day, he had a giddy look on his face, which I knew couldn't be good. "Eryk, I was thinking."

Mateo, behind us, laughed aloud. "Thinking? Who are you and what have you done with my friend Benito?!"

I looked back at Mateo, "There is a person among us who speaks before they think at all." Mateo knew I was talking about him but pretended to inspect the others like he was trying to figure out who I was indicating. "Go ahead, Benito. Tell me what epiphany you have reached."

"Epiphany?" He tested the unfamiliar word before giving up on it and rambling excitedly, "Growing up, we had a bard visit during the holidays. He used to tell and sing us stories about all the great heroes and their companions. Well, a lot of the hero companies had names. We should come up with one for ourselves to be sung about in the taverns long after we are gone."

Blaze supported Benito's idea immediately, albeit with self-aggrandizement. "I like it! We should be Diana's Chosen." Diana was the goddess of the hunt and master of the bow.

Mateo offered his own vision of our company: "How about Handsome Fiends?"

Benito offered up, "Castile's Castoffs!"

The suggestions continued over the next two hours before one finally struck me as fitting. It was one of Benito's many suggestions and probably had to do with the fact that he practically worshipped the goddess Fortuna. "I like it," I said aloud, stopping the shouts of ideas. "We will be called Fortuna's Chosen."

"Personally, I liked Blaze's Misfits better," Blaze said in jest. "But I suppose that will do. It flows off the tongue."

It took five days to reach the branch off the main road that led to Adorechi. Raelia interpreted the inscription on the large stone marker for us. She needed to convert the distances the orcs used to Esenhem measurements, so she took a moment. "Adorechi is thirty-four miles. The town of Dewmire is about twenty miles away. We need to head north from there to find the baker's family."

It took half a day of riding to reach Dewmire. "Town" was generous, as it was just a collection of twenty wooden buildings. The entire town looked like an industrial area for processing massive bovines called aurochs. Half the buildings appeared to be for smoking and salting meat. There were dozens of racks lining a field for treating and prepping hides. That was where Maveith's attention was drawn as we approached.

When the wind shifted, the odor churned my stomach: death mixed with curing hides and aging meat. The slaughter grounds must have been nearby, as some of the horses got antsy. Baldo's head was up and his nostrils were flaring. A filthy stream of water was coming from the buildings to join the wide stream that passed the town.

"Raelia, take Maveith and Blaze to ask the locals for directions." Being a leader had to have some privileges, and one of them was not having to get closer to the foulness. "We will wait upwind, north of the town." The three dismounted and walked into town while we led all the mounts around, while keeping our companions in sight.

It wasn't long before the three returned. Raelia told us what they learned. "They found the old orc couple dead in their beds four months ago. Thinking it was a disease, they burned the farmhouse down to avoid the spread. Nothing is left, according to the town's steward. I have directions if you want to confirm."

"How far is it?" I asked, not too keen on the unnecessary delay. I was wondering if orcs would murder each other and cover it up by burning down a house.

Raelia pointed north. "We follow the path along the stream for about two miles. There will be a wooden bridge to cross to the other side. We continue following the stream on the other side for two miles."

It was getting late in the day, and we would probably have to camp at the farm after investigating. We would not make Adorechi before nightfall. All eyes were looking at me, even Baldo's. I sighed. "Let's go confirm so we can add the details to the report." I swung up into Ginger's saddle and led the group.

We passed two wheat farms before crossing the narrow wooden bridge over the wide stream that fed the town. There were farms on the banks, along with a few large pastures that contained the aurochs. For some reason, Benito didn't seem to like the big bovines.

The farm appeared just as it had been described. Nature was slowly reclaiming the fields surrounding the charred remains of the farmhouse, with wild vegetation beginning to encroach upon the landscape. The only remnant of the once-standing farmhouse was the partially collapsed, soot-covered chimney. Two large open-sided shelters stood near the burnt remains. One was filled with farming tools, while the other housed firewood.

As I carefully made my way through the ashes, I sent out earth pulses. I discovered a root cellar under the debris, but to my surprise, there were no signs of any bones. It crossed my mind that perhaps the neighbors had already taken the remains and given them a proper burial. "Do orcs bury their dead?"

Raelia thought a moment. "I don't know. There is a big party for their friends to celebrate their lives, but I don't know what they do with the bodies. We have not passed any cemeteries."

A collection of copper and silver coins was secreted in the root cellar, but accessing them would have required too much effort, and they were out of reach of my dimensional space. I walked the perimeter of the charred remains, but my earth speak revealed nothing else. The others waited patiently. It was already dark when I was finished.

I didn't find anything unsettling that could have caused the fire, but I decided it was safer to head back and camp by the stream. "We will camp by the stream and finish the trip to Adorechi tomorrow."

The stream was only a few hundred yards from the burned farmhouse. Maveith cooked for everyone, and the others set tents while I walked the campsite perimeter with Raelia, setting simple tripwires. Raelia was talkative this evening.

"I think you did the right thing coming here to check. It will give peace of mind to the baker," she said while setting a tripwire.

"Every delay is a burden on Maveith's conscience. He has not asked anyone to play checkers once," I disclosed.

"I talk to Maveith every day. You are doing a good job, and he knows it. He trusts you more than you know. He knows caution is the best course of action and has the patience to endure it," Raelia said supportively.

Neptune's Tear had been bright when we set camp, but now clouds concealed its light. Drops started to hit the ground and our tarp tents, rapidly growing larger and larger. Lightning flashed and thunder rumbled in the distance. "Lets get to the camp. It feels like a heavy rain, and nothing should disturb us." I packed up my snare kit and hurried back to stay as dry as possible.

We had gone a whole week without rain. It figured that the first time I decided we should sleep outside we would get a rainstorm. It wasn't long before the storm was upon us, with strong winds, constant flashes of lightning, and heavier rain. With no sign of the storm letting up, I roused everyone to move to the farmhouse shelters in case the stream overflowed. Drenched, we trudged through the mud toward the higher ground of the farm.

Chapter 282: Skeletons in the Closet

Getting to higher ground made sense, and the burned-out farm was on top of a hill. We didn't need the glowstones with the rapidly flashing lightning, but had them out anyway. Only Mateo's horse was giving us trouble, as the constant waves of thunder spooked him. He even bolted and dragged Mateo through the mud for fifty feet at one particularly close strike.

When we returned to the farm, we were caked up to our knees in mud. We all huddled into the open shelter made from split logs. It was used for farming tools and for keeping the harvest dry, but the tools looked to have been scavenged, as there were only broken and rusty ones remaining. The pounding rain only seemed to increase as we settled in. It was cramped but manageable with the six horses.

"Is this natural?" Blaze yelled over the rain as he stripped to wring out his underclothes. We had been in magical weather before, and it had never turned out well.

Raelia answered him. "Usually, there are flash storms in the plains closer to Khoura, but I don't think it is the season. Maybe it is magically induced." She hesitated. "It does feel that way." Raelia was completely dry under her Ranger's cloak, to my surprise. Was it the cloak or a spell? With rain as heavy as it was, not even Legion cloaks could keep you completely dry. Raelia averted her eyes as Mateo and Benito also began to remove their armor and wring out their underclothes.

Maveith bellowed over the loud rain, "That bridge is going to be underwater in the morning. We will have to stay on this side of the river all the way back to Dewmire." I nodded, recalling some challenging terrain for the horses on that side.

I spoke loudly so everyone could hear. "Rub down the horses and find a dry spot to get some sleep. Actually, maybe we should leave the horses here and sleep in the firewood shelter. There should be enough room for all of us. I will stand watch half the night and Maveith the other." By now, the others knew we both had rings that allowed us to get less sleep and food. No one objected to getting a full night's rest. We hastily unsaddled the mounts and hung everything we could to drip dry. Heavy, wet gear was always a miserable experience the next day. The others quickly leveled the piles of wood to create beds off the ground.

The rain continued to fall for the next hour as we once again got ready for the night. I didn't remove my armor or make an attempt to dry off as I stood watch. The others were hanging up everything they could to dry. The lightning and thunder had abated some, but the flashes played tricks on the eyes, making shadows in the trees. Fortunately, my aether sight seemed unaffected by the lightning flashes.

My earth speak was muted with the waterlogged ground, but I still got fuzzy feedback. A large number of mice, snakes, and other small critters had been drowned in their burrows. The rain had come too fast for them to flee. I gave the group my thermal stone to set their bedrolls around while I kept watch. The heavy rain acted like white noise, and soon, my exhausted companions were asleep.

The rain didn't abate for nearly four hours, and then it stopped instantly like someone had shut it off. The only sound I heard was water dripping from trees, pattering on the ground and our roof. Even that settled after thirty minutes, giving way to an eerie quiet.

Raelia stirred, rolling closer to the thermal stone. With the air stilled, I could tell that someone in our enclosure had passed wind, but it had been silent flatulence and I didn't know who the perpetrator was.

I saw Maveith's eyes open, and he stared at the ceiling. Four hours was more than enough rest for him with his ring. He rose silently and crossed his legs underneath him. He nodded to me, indicating he was ready to take the watch.

For me, the woods surrounding the farm seemed too eerie, and I was going to remain awake. Maveith stood and quietly put his armor back on. He wasn't successful, and a grumpy Mateo ducked deeper inside his bedroll. Maveith moved to stand where I was.

I whispered, "I will stay up with you as long as I can see in the dark." Suddenly, Neptune's Tear revealed itself, casting a blue glow over our surroundings, but I remained with my friend. We sat silently, not wanting to disturb the others. Maveith's arm extended, pointing into the woods, and I focused. My aether sight didn't reach very far, but I did see the strange shadow he was pointing at.

"A deer or large wolf," Maveith guessed in a flat whisper. "Probably got active after the rain finished and is hungry."

I tried to follow the creature in the low light, but it was over a hundred yards away in the woods, and I kept losing it. The spyglass appeared in my hands, and I adjusted it. Finding the creature in the distance took me a while, as it was flitting between the trees for cover. It was definitely aware of our camp. "Rouse the others quietly. It is bipedal and circling the camp."

Maveith grunted softly and woke Raelia first. I was impressed; she was out of her bedroll and on alert in a breath, her Ranger training taking hold. Baldo, on the other hand, was still curled into a ball and sleeping. Worried there might be more, I scanned across the fields and around the farmhouse with the spyglass. I didn't see any other movement. Blaze, with his amazing eyesight, helped me locate the interloper.

"I might be able to hit it," Blaze stated, his bow ready.

"No, we should know what we are attacking and if it is a threat. It could have been out there in the storm the entire night watching us." I kept a focus on it as everyone prepared. "Mateo and Benito, stay with the horses. Blaze and Raelia, trail Maveith and me."

Moving silently in wet clothes was much harder than you would think. I headed into the woods. Even more frustrating was our feet sinking into the mud with each step. I heard Raelia tell Baldo to stay, and he let out a long, whining chirp—the one he often makes when he's hungry. He didn't want Raelia to leave him without feeding him breakfast first. The creature in the woods was spooked and disappeared from our line of sight among the trunks.

"Do we follow it?" Maveith grumbled to keep his voice low.

Raelia was hissing at a repentant Baldo, who curled up on himself. He knew that when he was bad, he wouldn't get any food. I weighed the pros and cons before responding. "I don't like something out there watching us. We will still go investigate."

I had Maveith stay five paces behind me and Raelia and Blaze twenty paces further back with their bows. "Don't enter the tree line," I told Raelia and Blaze. "I don't want you to lose sight of Mateo and Benito in case there is another threat or this one circles around." Ginger neighed as I entered the tree line, but quieted quickly at Mateo's urging.

Entering the woods was actually a relief. The forest carpet was thick with leaves and pine needles covering dense roots. It was not muddy, even with all the rain. Either the ground had absorbed the rainfall, or the runoff was enough to make movement easier and quieter.

I kept checking with earth pulses and looking back at my companions as I ventured into the woods. I finally found something: two skeletons, recently and haphazardly buried. They were mostly covered by waterlogged leaves and churned earth. This must be where the baker's parents had been put to rest.

I caught movement to my right, but didn't see what caused it. Maveith couldn't see under the denser canopy, so I hissed at him, "Retreat to Raelia's position in case it runs."

I walked past the buried skeletons and approached the area where I had seen the movement. It was only by the grace of earth speak that I detected the two skeletons rising behind me. My blood chilled as I alerted the others. "Undead!" I whirled to face the skeletons rising from the earth, while continuing to search for the humanoid with earth speak.

The grinding of bone on bone echoed as the two skeletons rose, wet clumps of leaves sliding off them. Faint blue light illuminated their joints, apparently welding the bones together. In a macabre sight, some bits of charred flesh and desiccated organs hung on their frames.

During Hound training, Hearne had said that the only times we were likely to encounter undead skeletons were if we were foolish enough to venture into a dungeon that created them, or if we were in pursuit of a necromancer. The blue aether binding them needed to be sustained by someone or something. Destroying the spine was how we were taught to fight them.

I switched Boris's dungeon blade for the black spear. The skeletons had no weapons and were charred black from the fire. They advanced clumsily toward me and I swung the spear in an arc, trying to catch both of them. I was surprised when the ribs and spines shattered under the blow. Both skeletons collapsed to the ground in a pile of bones. The upper torsos still had some fight, both pulling themselves free and starting to crawl toward me.

I shattered one skull and then the other with quick stabs of the spear. The remaining aether holding them together sank into the ground. The bones must have been brittle from the fire, judging by how easily they fractured, or maybe it was the spear's magic. One of these days, I would have to get a revelation scroll on the artifact. My worry was that whoever performed the reading would know how powerful the artifact was, and that would make me a target.

Maveith came rushing to help, a glowstone in one hand and his hammer in the other, ready to smash. He ended up skidding past me on muddy leaves and tripping over tree roots. As he tumbled to the ground, the figure broke and ran. I chased after what I assumed was a necromancer. Maveith got to his feet behind me as I ran and skidded to catch the fleeing person.

I surged ahead, boots pounding against the damp forest floor, and closed the distance between us. With a swift downward thrust, my blade sank into the back of his thigh, damaging his hamstring. The orc let out a strangled cry as his leg gave out beneath him. He stumbled blindly through the darkness, crashing shoulder-first into a tree with a sickening thud before collapsing into the underbrush.

He lay there, whimpering, clutching the back of his leg with trembling fingers. Maveith arrived moments later, holding the glowstone aloft. Its pale blue light spilled over the scene, casting long shadows and illuminating the fallen figure. The orc was caked in mud from head to toe, the muck clinging to him like a second skin. Beneath the grime, his features looked unexpectedly youthful—smooth cheeks and wide eyes—while fear and pain highlighted his innocent appearance.

"Were those your skeletons?" I asked in Elvish. He was too distracted by his pain to answer me, or maybe he didn't understand Elvish. "Go get Raelia," I told Maveith, and waited for them to return. After sending out an earth pulse, I returned my spear to my dimensional space and replaced it with Boris's blade.

Even through the pain, he noticed my weapon swap. His eyes were wide as I tossed him a bandage for his leg out of thin air.

Maveith returned with Raelia at a jog, and I stood back and let her interrogate the young orc. Raelia had boasted she was fluent in the orc language, but she struggled to keep the injured orc's attention and stumbled through the conversation. After a time, she turned to us. "He said he is the son of the farmers."

I was immediately confused. "Did the baker have a brother? We were not asked to check in on a brother." The answer took some back-and-forth before Raelia turned to me again.

"He was adopted a year ago," Raelia informed me, though she sounded uncertain. "He says the old farmers never told either of their sons. One is a baker and the other a pig farmer." We all looked at each other, but eventually they turned to me to decide.

"Ask him if he created those skeletons," I said seriously. I already knew he had to be the necromancer. When I had approached his hiding position, the skeletons had clearly risen to defend him. Instead of answering Raelia's inquiry, he just started sobbing uncontrollably.

I grimaced, seeing where this was going. "How does the Boutan Caliphate deal with necromancers?" I asked Raelia.

Her tone was heavy, and maybe she felt pity for the young orc. "I believe outside of talking to the deceased, it is outlawed." Raelia looked back at the bones in the distance. "We would be doing him a favor to kill him now. Bringing undead into existence is punishable by death in most kingdoms."

I winced. We had three choices before us. Leave him, turn him in, or kill him. Even with his orcish features, I guessed him to be no older than fourteen. "Ask him how the farmers died." Maybe his answer would make my decision easier. I waited while Raelia worked to get it out of him. The pain was still distracting him. She also got more comfortable with the orc tongue as the conversation progressed.

When she finished, she looked grim. "They died in their sleep. Probably from something they ate. He got really sick as well, but lived. He didn't know he had magic and, while mourning them, raised them as ghouls. When neighbors came to check on them, he got scared and ordered them to remain in bed and not move. The neighbors burned the house after looting it."

"He then raised them again, but this time as skeletons," I finished. I believed he had the necromancy spell form for raising the dead. "What do you think we should do?" I asked Maveith and Raelia while the orc whimpered.

Maveith leaned on his hammer in thought while Raelia answered with some fervor. "Death. If he created zombies, his necromancy must be very powerful. The dead and living cannot coexist. In Bartiradia, he would be publicly executed for creating ghouls."

"We are not in Bartiradia," I reminded her.

Maveith clearly pitied the orc boy. With a sigh, he agreed with Raelia. "Powerful necromancers have caused more wars and death across the world than any single nation. If he can raise the dead at such a young age, I am afraid of what he might become." Raelia nodded in agreement. "But there are always the Death Hunters," Maveith added.

I looked quizzically at Maveith, but it was Raelia who answered with an uncertain nod. "The Death Hunters might be a possibility. They accept necromancers into their ranks and teach them to hunt and destroy the undead. But their Citadel is all the way in Nausis."

Maveith shook his head. "They have a stronghold in Esenhem."

"A stronghold, yes, but they train their members in Nausis. Are we going to turn around and escort him four thousand miles there?" Raelia said a little heatedly, and Maveith winced. I could see the goliath realizing that it would delay us by many months to do so.

"I can try something …" I said, turning to the boy, and he winced as I focused on him. He couldn't run, and was at our mercy.

I made to place him in my space and sort it out later. I got immediate backlash as my aether bottomed out. An instant migraine formed and I was unsteady for a moment. His aether resistance was too strong for me as he instinctively resisted my attempt to send him to my dimensional space. He didn't even realize he had done it, judging from the confusion on his face. Only Traeliorn had been able to resist me, and since then, I had increased my affinity. How strong was this child?

I briefly considered adding the orc to our group as a guide, but if he was found to be a necromancer, it could cause us problems in our quest. He was obviously alone, and no one knew he was out here. What would be the harm in letting him go?

"Are you all right, Eryk?" Maveith asked worriedly. He had hefted his hammer and was ready to strike the young orc. Raelia had stepped back from the orc as well, not understanding what was happening.

"He is strong," I explained, and Maveith understood what I had tried to do.

"I will do it," Raelia said, drawing a blade.

"No!" I stopped her with a gesture. "He cannot come with us, but he can decide his own fate. Tell him about the stronghold in Esenhem and how to get to it."

"You cannot let him go!" Raelia said heatedly. "Necromancers must be ..."

"Tell him, Raelia!" I said angrily.

It took some time for Raelia to explain to the boy. We found out his name was Tovin. He didn't know who his real parents were and professed to have worked hard before they had been poisoned. His filthy, calloused hands made me believe his story. I gave him one of the Pathfinder potions to heal his thigh, and he drank it happily. I guessed orcs had different tastes.

When he was able to walk, I gave him some food in an old Legion pack. As he shuffled off into the trees, he looked back a few times, thinking it was all a trick. Raelia looked disappointed in my decision and Maveith looked indifferent.

I tried to explain myself to her. "Choices, Raelia. Everyone is capable of evil— or good. He deserves the chance to make that choice."

Her eyes bored into me and it reminded me of when I had released her in the dungeon. "You just didn't want to kill a boy. If he does join the Death Hunters, then you did good. If he raises an army of undead, then you contributed to his evil," Raelia said tersely, turning her back on me and walking back to the others.

I explained what had happened in the woods. Benito, Blaze, and Mateo had no particular opinion on necromancers, viewing them as the same as any other mage. Raelia just huffed, saying they had never seen an undead horde tear through a village, but she admitted on further questioning that neither had she. As we mounted to leave, Blaze leaned into me. "Next time I want to take on an extra job, just remind me what a clusterfuck this was."

I huffed in agreement, and we headed out on the muddy, four-mile trek back to Adorechi.

The mud hadn't firmed up by the morning, and the horses struggled to walk. I ordered everyone to dismount and walk them, and we fared little better than the horses, sinking to mid-calf. Baldo sat upright in his seat, confused as to why the stupid people were walking in the mud. Raelia was still disappointed in me for letting the orc boy go, not talking to me at all.

As we had feared, the bridge was gone—swept away in the night. The broad stream we'd crossed two days before had swollen with fast-moving, muddy water. We were forced to remain on this side, picking our way along a treacherous slope of wet stone and tangled roots.

That's when Mateo's horse lost its footing. The creature slipped with a sharp cry, hooves scrambling in the slick mud before it triggered a small landslide. Rocks and soil cascaded down, taking the horse with it and vanishing into the brown waters below. For a long moment, I thought the horse would be lost—but it surfaced downstream, flailing, and managed to haul itself onto a gravel bank. It stood trembling, drenched and smeared with river silt, but alive.

We scrambled down to it as quickly as we dared. The horse was favoring its front leg badly. I knelt beside it, hands checking along the joint and tendons. "A sprain," I muttered. "Deep, but no bones broken. It won't carry weight like this." Mateo swore under his breath.

We had a choice: burn one of our few healing potions or let the horse limp the last miles to the city and hope there was a healer with skill enough to set it right. Either way, we were slowed.

From there, it was a cautious and miserable trek back to town. The orc auroch-processing town of Dewmire had not escaped the effects of the torrential rain. A large section of the town had been washed away, and it appeared that much of their production capabilities had been impacted. We didn't stop to help clean up the mess, instead moving onto the muddy road toward Adorechi.

A few miles down the road, the surface began to improve. With Mateo's horse lame, we couldn't ride fast enough to cover the last twenty miles. It turned into a long, slow journey, but late in the evening, the walls of Adorechi came into view. Square stone towers dotted the walls, but the city didn't seem particularly impressive to me. The map stated the population was ten thousand, but the halo of farms surrounding the walls might comprise a significant portion of the city, or perhaps the Caliphate was just being generous with its census.

I knew this city had sprouted up because a dungeon was not far from the walls. If I remembered my conversation with the orc healer correctly, it was called the Silent Tunnels. It was a four-room dungeon with an interesting quirk: there was no sound anywhere. You needed to communicate effectively with your delve team without talking for success. It allowed four people to enter and was reasonably tame as far as dungeon monsters went. We were not planning to detour to it.

As we approached the gatehouse, a tall, tattooed orc walked out to meet us. His black hair was braided into a long ponytail. He wore soft leather armor but made sure his arms and neck prominently displayed his tattoos. His dark-gray eyes narrowed at our group, and he asked something in Orcish. Raelia translated, "He wants to know if we are here for the dungeon and wants to check our adventurer's medallions."

"Is that normal? Checking the identity of adventurers?" I asked.

"I just became an adventurer recently," Raelia said tersely. She turned back to the orc. A brief conversation between Raelia and the elite orc continued before she informed us, "He checks all adventurers entering the city. This is Warlord Drutha, and he rules Adorechi." While making eye contact, I bowed my head slightly, a sign of respect but not deference in the Caliphate. Best not to anger the local warlord.

"Tell him we are here to escort Cleric Glasha on her expedition to look for an ancient battlefield," I told Raelia in Elvish, but she didn't need to translate. The warlord barked a laugh and spat on the ground.

"Wasting her time, that one. Been ten years, and she hasn't found a trace of the Last Battle." He waved dismissively at us, his curiosity satisfied without even confirming our identities. He turned his back on us as he entered the gates and climbed the stone steps to a tower. Two guards approached us to check and log our medallions before we were allowed to enter the city.

Blaze whispered, "Why was the city lord out here to greet us?" He had caught enough of the conversation to pick up that Warlord Drutha ruled Adorechi.

"Maybe he can't stand his wife and kids and is just trying to get away for a bit," Mateo offered, in good humor. "That is what my dad would do when he had a spat with my mother, or when I was being particularly difficult."

I ignored Mateo's comment, and my thoughts shifted to the cleric and the job. "We will see if the cleric can heal Mateo's mount. If not, we'll see to getting him healed. Raelia, get directions to the Adventurers Guild." After a brief conversation with the guards, Raelia obtained directions through the small city.

As we walked through the city, I thought it felt much simpler and smaller than other cities. The absence of a sewer system left the city with a lingering scent of waste. The buildings were predominantly wooden but varied in condition from poor to new. Several structures were undergoing renovation. The most disconcerting aspect was that only orcs walked the streets. We didn't see humans or other races about. The orcs considered themselves superior to other races, yet they allowed free trade in the Caliphate. Was there something different about this city?

The Adventurers Hall was one of the rare stone buildings in the city, and once we had the horses settled and they had received their apple bonus for getting us here safely, we entered. A pungent scent assaulted us, a strong skunk smell. Benito started sneezing uncontrollably. "Ugh, what is that! It reminds me of the time I tried to capture a skunk. I smelled like that for a month."

I recalled the orc cleric saying something about the dungeon taking away your hearing and assaulting your other senses with its creatures. I tried to remember the dozens of rooms in various dungeons we had talked about. "I think it is from a dungeon creature—a type of giant stink beetle." Benito grunted and got his sneezing fit under control.

We received many curious looks from the occupants of the hall, most of which were directed at Baldo. Almost everyone in the common room was an orc, except for two humans playing a card game at one table and a lone elf brooding alone in a dark cloak at another. I nodded at Raelia, indicating she should go talk to the elf while I approached the clerk. She frowned, but moved to obey with Baldo happily following her.

The wrinkly old orc clerk was missing a tusk, but there was a hint of her past athleticism in her movements. She didn't speak Elvish or Telhian, so I handed her the job posting. She read it and called over a younger orc, who rushed out of the hall. I thought he was going to get the cleric for us.

I then spent a few minutes miming that we had finished the other task and wrote a note for the baker about the fate of his parents. I only mentioned that they had succumbed to disease or poison in their food, and the locals had burned their bodies. Finished, the old clerk dismissed me with a wave of her hand. I went to sit with Raelia and the elf to wait.

Raelia introduced the demure elf, some of her annoyance gone. He was wearing loose clothes under his cloak and clearly resting. "This is Kaeryn Chaeven. He has been delving into the dungeon with his group over there." Raelia indicated the two humans and three orcs playing cards.

"Eryk Marko of Fortuna's Chosen," I introduced myself, offering to shake wrists, which he did. His forearm was thin and his hand lacked grip strength, so I assumed he was a mage.

He arched his eyebrow at Raelia. "Traveling with a Telhian?" There was a lot of implication in his words.

Raelia narrowed her eyes at the elf, her voice sharp with conviction. "He's no Telhian—and he's one of the finest warriors this continent has seen. More than that, he's a good man. His principles run deeper than most, and overshadow his ignorance."

I think she just defended me. She flushed when I made eye contact with her.

After the awkward eye contact with Raelia, I questioned the elf. "Why are there so few non-orcs in the city?"

Kaeryn grinned. "Because there is nothing here but a shitty little dungeon. And I mean that literally. The floor of the third room is covered in bat shit." He toasted me with his mug and drank.

"Then why are you here?" I asked.

"We are escorting him." He pointed at one of the orcs playing cards. "Torgan Baneshield, son of some warlord, trying to prove his worth to his father. We are taking him through the twelve dungeons in the Caliphate so he can petition the Supreme Cleric to delve into the Warlord Dungeon."

"I heard the local dungeon is not that difficult. Why are you still here?" My tone was inquisitive. The elf drank and seemed to decide he liked me well enough to answer.

"We have completed it three times. Torgan needs some seasoning, and we are working on our teamwork." He grinned. "Also, the final chamber usually gives a major essence in the reward chest. It is about the only thing worthwhile in this city."

I nodded, pretending to be impressed. I had to remember essences were rare, and collectors were even rarer outside the Telhian Empire. The messenger the old clerk sent had returned, and following him was a light-green-skinned orc with brilliant red hair. I guessed it had to be dyed, as I had not seen any other orcs with hair matching the flaming color.

"Our charge has arrived," I said, excusing Raelia and myself from the elf's company.

I caught the cleric's attention and motioned her to a large table in the corner. I got Blaze's attention and he rounded up the others, who were playing darts with two orcs—or a version of darts, as the target was not what I knew. I thought Benito had money on the game, as he grudgingly handed over a large copper when he was called away.

As we sat around the table, I studied Glasha. She was on the younger side, but maybe she kept herself young with magic. The warlord had mentioned she had been searching for a decade. Her fiery hair was messily braided, with strands sticking out, and she wore worn leather clothes, reminiscent of pre-colonial Native Americans from Earth. "Are you Glasha?" I asked in Elvish to confirm.

"I can speak Telhian," she responded in amusement as she looked our group over. "I can speak nineteen different tongues and read most of them. Yes, I am Cleric Glasha Mistborn. Which one of you has the earth magic?" she continued eagerly.

"That would be me," I admitted.

She looked surprised. "What spells? And what range can you sense?" she asked, but her expression showed doubt, perhaps because I dressed more like a warrior than a mage.

"Earth speak. And out to about twenty-five feet," I responded. Her face lit up, and her eyes showed she was excited and deep in thought. I had shortened the distance to someone with an earth affinity around thirty-three, rather than revealing my true ability.

"Much better than I expected," she mumbled to herself. To our group, she said, "The contract begins when we leave Adorechi. I would like to leave tomorrow."

I hedged her enthusiasm. "We have a lame horse that needs tending, and we are curious about what exactly you are looking for and what dangers we might need to prepare for."

She waved her hands unconcernedly. "I have some minor healing spells if the injury isn't grave. As for dangers, there are a few: wild bull aurochs are aggressive, and then there are giant vultures, but they wouldn't attack a large group, and there have been reports of a basilisk from the nomads traveling through the area."

"Is that all?" I replied sarcastically. Basilisks were eight-legged lizards. Surprisingly, they were not fast with their eight legs, and relied on their magical gaze to petrify man and beast alike. Once frozen in the gaze of a basilisk, you were as good as dead, turning to stone in ten heartbeats. The basilisk would consume their sculpture, turning the statue back into flesh within its stomach.

The only way to return a companion to their flesh was an alchemical potion brewed from the beast's stomach acid. I did not have the alchemy recipe for that brew.

The cleric dismissed my concerns with a shake of her head, her red braids swaying with the motion, "The area we are searching is mostly grassland. We will be able to see anything coming long before it reaches us."

I didn't like her nonchalance about danger. "You still have not told me what we are looking for and why you have found no trace in ten years of searching."

Excitement lit up her eyes again. "The final battle between the orcs and Titans. Although, between you and me, the orcs were joined by humans, elves, and dwarves alike. It broke the chains of our oppressors and pushed the Titans into hiding. They never recovered."

"How do you know the battle was fought here? It is a big planet," Blaze questioned the cleric.

She sat up straight as she lectured us animatedly. "True, true. And the battle was fought over five thousand years ago as well. I have traveled to the libraries in Esenhem, Keisinia, and Tegairosia, reviewing ancient scrolls and tomes. Unfortunately, only the elves preserved their books well against time. I am certain the battle took place on this peninsula. I am gradually narrowing down likely terrain features that match vague accounts in books and songs. Now I am looking for ancient weapons of the Titans buried with time."

I could have inquired if she was aware of the Atlantium ruins being uncovered near Macha, but I didn't want to stir that pot at the moment. "To what end? What good will finding the location of the Last Battle serve?" I asked. Blaze nodded at my question.

"I am a chronicler. I record the history of the Boutan Caliphate for those who come after me. But what of what came before? What can we learn from past heroes and fallen kingdoms? Maybe one day we will be in the place of the Titans, fighting for our survival."

"If you don't learn from history, you are doomed to repeat it," I replied.

"Oh! I like that! Can I use it in my next writing?" Glasha said excitedly.

"Fine," I shook my head disinterestedly. Another scholar out for knowledge's sake. Maybe I could put her in contact with Favian? I wondered how the old man was doing after Caelora. "Mateo, show her your horse. If Glasha can heal it, we will depart in the morning." I paid for everyone's rooms and secured my own before getting a few hours of practice in the dreamscape.

The following morning, we gathered outside the Adventurers Hall. Glasha was riding a stout white pony bareback. I noticed Adorechi's warlord watching our departure from one of the gate towers. His scrutiny was disconcerting, but at least we had no plans to ever return to this city. The place we were searching was fifteen miles north over wild terrain, and I hoped this would be a quick and uneventful expedition.

It wasn't long before our group had ventured beyond the surrounding farmland and headed into shrub and bushlands. At midmorning, I was riding next to Glasha, whose excitement was contagious. She had Benito and Mateo talking energetically about finding some ancient weapons of the giants and wielding them in battle.

It passed over both their heads that they would have no way to lift them, much less wield them. I had seen a storm giant's blade firsthand, and it was longer than both of them end to end. I also didn't know how well artifacts would hold up over five thousand years. Normal weapons would be a pile of rust by now.

I thought I would use the riding time productively. "Glasha, can you teach me your language?" I asked. Raelia turned around in her saddle, her face clearly annoyed, before turning away.

She laughed. "The orc tongue is an amalgamation of a dozen different tongues. Unlike the elves or Telhians, we have no formal education across the Caliphate. With how much the language has morphed, I am sure I would have difficulty talking to a Boutan orc from five thousand years ago."

"Still, I would like to pick up a little just so I know when I am being insulted, at least," I replied seriously.

She laughed again. "There are more ways to insult your opponent than praise them in my language." Seeing that I was still serious, she shrugged. "Fine. Be warned, I have been told by other humans that our language will corrupt and rot your mind." We began with a basic vocabulary and then progressed to verbs.

The only dangers around us were prairie dogs, and that was more for the horses, since they could accidentally step into one of the burrows and break a leg. By her frequent glances, I could tell Raelia was upset with me for not asking her to teach me the orc language. But learning from a native and a linguist was too good an opportunity to pass up. Baldo even picked up on Raelia's mood and was eyeing me with disapproval—that was easily assuaged with a tossed piece of raw bear meat.

Around midday, we stopped to eat in the middle of a sea of knee-high grass. At least it was early in the season and the grass was not high enough to hide serious threats. Dismounting, I sent out an earth pulse and found nothing of interest.

Glasha was orienting herself as Maveith prepared food for everyone. He had slid into the role of the group's cook, and he enjoyed doing it even though he ate very little of what he prepared. He lacked the skill of Lirkin, but it was good fare, and he was good at balancing his seasoning. In return, I gave him the thermal stone to carry.

Glasha closed her eyes, and I could tell she was using a spell form. Maybe something similar to Castile's all-seeing eye. When she opened her eyes again, she nodded and smiled. "We will start our search two miles northeast of here and move due north for ten miles, then turn northeast for ten, and then repeat for a few days." We were going to zigzag northeast then. I just nodded. The length of each leg we traveled would be imprecise, but this job was just for ten days, and we were moving in the right direction.

The rest of the day was pretty monotonous. We would walk the horses one hundred yards; I would pulse earth speak, wait for Glasha to confirm which direction she wanted to head, and then do it again. We generally followed her original plan, moving mainly northeast, but she seemed to have gut feelings that she tried to follow. As we moved, I continued my language lessons, and the others formed a perimeter to watch for danger.

We had no luck that first day and camped in the open plains. Glasha only had a bedroll and no tent, but was accustomed to sleeping under the stars. I paired with Mateo for the first half of the night watch, and Raelia paired with Maveith for the second half. Raelia was the only other person in our group who had good low-light vision besides me.

I spent my time in the dreamscape practicing my Orcish, but I infused my manifestation of Raelia with the orc language I was learning from Glasha. Truthfully, Glasha was a much better teacher, encouraging and patient, while my manifestation of Raelia was arrogant and mocking whenever I made a mistake—not that I made many in the dreamscape.

When I woke, Maveith cooked a feast for everyone, and we resumed our search. Glasha was suitably impressed with my overnight improvement in the orc language, which still sounded like French to me. There were even some words derived from Latin. I found my first buried treasure midmorning of the second day of searching: a rusty scimitar buried a few inches deep. It broke apart as Benito excavated it.

"No, not old enough," Glasha said, disappointed. "And not deep enough either. Ancient structures of the Titans are usually buried a few feet below the surface in similar terrain."

My next discovery was a partial skeleton alongside some coins. The skeleton bore no discernible marks or weapons but could have been dragged here by a predator. When I informed Benito about the coins, he became enthusiastic in his digging, unearthing twenty-two copper coins and eighteen silver ones.

Glasha took the coins and cleaned one of the silver ones, as the copper was too corroded to clean easily. The mostly black coin revealed its secrets to Glasha. "Stamped with Supreme Cleric Khavgu's mark. He guided the Caliphate some two hundred years ago. Not what we are searching for." She handed the coins back to an eager Benito.

Mateo and Benito worked together to clean the coins and split them as we continued. It wasn't long before Mateo had a proposition. "Eryk, you can find these coins so easily out here. There have to be dozens of abandoned villages and towns in the world with thousands of coins lost."

"No, Mateo. I am not interested in becoming a treasure hunter," I replied dismissively.

"But we will do all the digging!" Benito offered in a pleading tone.

Trying not to dampen their enthusiasm, I offered a compromise and reminded them that our goal was Maveith's sister's rescue. "I will consider it. We have other goals currently." I nodded to Maveith, who had been getting anxious at our slow pace. To distract him, we were all playing checkers with him at night. He was not showing his normal enthusiasm for winning, and I reassured him that we would get to his sister soon. I did not mention the possibility that she might not be alive. If that was the case, then vengeance was on the table.

My next discovery had me somewhat in awe. I circled a long area of the plains, pulsing my earth speak. Everyone was mounted, following my movements and anxiously awaiting my pronouncement. "There is a tunnel at the extreme range of my ability, but I don't know where it leads," I finally said. This was only a partial truth, because at the extreme range of my earth speak was a skeleton of a dragon.

I was tracing rodent tunnels that wove through the bones. The grave stretched more than two hundred feet, and the tail appeared to curl around the body. Scattered among the remains were great scales—unmistakably draconic. If dragon bones truly never decayed, then these remains could be unimaginably old. Artifacts from a battle five thousand years past were found just a few feet beneath the surface—so how ancient must something be to lie fifty feet below the plains? That was the dilemma: they were fifty feet down. And getting to them was going to be difficult.

I planned to research dragons when I had the chance to see if an expedition to recover the bones or scales would be worth the effort. As we left the site, Raelia eyed me curiously while we followed the orc cleric to the next site. I might have shown too much awe in mapping the extent of the skeleton. I looked for landmarks and mentally cataloged them in case I returned.

Late in the day, the sun was particularly hot. We were sweating as we looked for a place to camp for the night. Glasha suddenly spoke. "There is water that way, about two miles. A small gully with some aurochs. The horses need the water, no?"

"How many aurochs?" I asked, knowing the wild bulls were ornery beasts.

"I saw six, one bull," she said. I nodded, thinking it was manageable.

"Raelia, if it charges, fireball the head to blind it. I will take down the bull quickly, and the heifers will flee," I said.

"Heifers?" Blaze asked, unfamiliar with the term.

"Females," I corrected. I had worked on a dairy farm one summer. Before coming here, it was the hardest work I had done in my life.

We didn't need to worry about the aurochs, as they spilled out of the gully as we approached, trotting off into the plains, being urged on by the bull. The water wasn't running clear, but it was the best we had for the horses. Glasha had healing magic, so I was not overly concerned. A few young trees lined the stream, cutting across the plains, and we set camp under one of them. I walked the camp with earth speak, but did not find anything worrying beneath us.

After our dinner, Blaze asked Glasha some pointed questions. "If you are a chronicler, why did you have to hire adventurers?"

Glasha was chewing on some fatty bacon as she talked. "The orcs only record the history of the present. My sect does not care about the past or the future. I save my coin and search for the past on my own when time permits. My pursuits are frowned upon by others in my sect as a waste of my time."

"Do you know about the Titan city near Macha?" Benito asked. I rolled my eyes at Benito. I had asked him not to talk about it. He winced under my stare, having suddenly remembered.

"The excavation of Atlantium?" Glasha replied, unfazed. "I am aware. If it is Atlantium, and I have my doubts that it is, it will draw more than the elves to it in time. It served as a good distraction for the Supreme to call for a crusade and reclaim lost land."

"I heard the Caliphate lost a great warlord riding a roc in the conquest," I said offhandedly.

"How do you ride a stone?" Benito asked.

Raelia laughed. "A roc is a dragon-sized raptor. The second-deadliest beast in the air."

Glasha was nodding, studying me. "Warlord Trakor was killed in the campaign. He stole the egg from Talon Fang Peak far to the north before his Warlord Trial. He raised the beast from a hatchling and used its strength to become one of the four strongest warlords in the Caliphate. He used that influence to assume command of the crusade to reclaim the lost lands of his ancestors."

Glasha smirked. "He crashed his roc, aptly named Chaostail, on the expedition and died. The clerics with him managed to heal Chaostail, but without Warlord Trakor to handle him, Chaostail attacked the fleet, throwing the crusade into, well, chaos." Glasha smiled at her description of the events, clearly not fond of the slain warlord.

"Was that the only roc in the Caliphate?" I asked. It was I who had caused the massive avian to crash by removing part of its wing when it attacked in a dive.

"There are none that I am aware of, but there could be one being raised in secret. A hundred young warriors head to Talon Fang Peak every winter to try and repeat the feat of Trakor. The few that I know to have returned have come back empty-handed."

I was curious about the ripples my actions had caused but too worried to inquire further, in case I accidentally revealed my participation. In the end, the orcs had captured Varvao despite my actions, and the western part of the Telhian Empire had been annexed by the Caliphate. We settled into our bedrolls soon after, with our watches remaining the same. Raelia seemed to have forgiven me for letting the boy necromancer go, but she was focused on keeping Maveith in good spirits.

Although Neptune's Tear was absent tonight, the stars were bright and gave the landscape an eerie glow. I slept restlessly after my watch, waking every twenty minutes. I thought it was the running water nearby that had me on edge. Mercifully, dawn came without incident. Benito had come up with a thousand questions for Glasha about rocs by breakfast, almost none of which she could answer. It appeared the young Benito fancied himself riding atop a dragon-sized eagle one day.

We followed the water source at Glasha's direction, and I pulsed earth speak when told. I had thought this was going to be a quick and easy assignment, but if we never found anything, it was going to take the entire ten days. Blaze whistled twice from the front, and everyone immediately went on alert. Blaze hissed back, "I don't know what it is, but it hasn't moved."

I rode up next to him, producing my spyglass. By the water's edge was an odd quadruped. Its large body looked feline, but the torso of a woman rose from the beast's frame. Glasha motioned for the spyglass, and I handed it to her. She studied the distant creature for a few minutes before handing it back. "It is a lamia. Malicious creatures of deceit and guile, but it looks like the basilisk already got to it. We should head east. Hopefully, that will keep us out of the basilisk's territory."

Mateo, not understanding the danger, said, "How do we even know it is still around?"

"Basilisks don't abandon their victims. It will be back to snack on that one," I stated for her. Glasha nodded in confirmation. At least we hadn't wandered near the burrow of the basilisk.

We took a wide route around the statue of the lamia. I didn't know much about lamias other than that they were shape changers and not native to this continent. I recalled from the bestiary I had copied from the Mage College that they were from the Scorching Waste and preferred the taste of human flesh.

"How is there a lamia here?" I asked Glasha after I felt we had safely distanced ourselves.

"Warlord Karnak tried to breed them a decade ago. Don't ask me why but the rumor was he had a fetish for the creatures. Karnak was killed by his lamia slaves, and a dozen of the vile creatures escaped; all were thought slain over the years. And yes, that statue could be a decade old. But I do not feel the need to investigate." I nodded at her explanation. I also did not feel a need to investigate.

Three days and a hundred miles later, I finally found something worthwhile. It was like a bright beacon reflecting my earth pulse. The artifact clearly had synergy with the earth affinity. Mateo and Benito eagerly went about digging up the artifact, which was buried beneath thick sod. It was a few feet down and it took them some time to reach it, but Mateo proudly held up the metallic pauldrons, sized for a large man or orc.

They were easily cleaned, and the steel matched that of the dungeon-forged blades. Glasha was reverently running her hands over them. Even if they were not what Glasha was seeking, the artifact should be enough to fund dozens of future expeditions.

All our eyes focused on Glasha as she studied and completely cleaned the artifact. "Is that prize enough for you to return triumphant?" I asked hopefully after letting her admire the piece.

"Yes, it is proof. This is from a powerful extinct dungeon. It is over five thousand years old," she said happily. "A great orc warrior probably wore it on the battlefield here."

"How do you know that?" Blaze asked, confused but interested.

"I just cast the revelation spell on it," she said with a tusky smile. I knew there was a spell that mimicked the revelation scroll used by the Adventurers Guild Halls. This unassuming orc cleric had apparently learned it. There were several things in my dimensional space whose functions I still had no idea about. Maybe I could get a little more out of this job …

Glasha carefully packed the runic pauldrons. They could probably fit Mateo or me, but they needed padding fitted to them. Of course, their bright-silver appearance was a beacon on the battlefield. The cleric was grinning the entire time, and I was happy we would be done with the job. "We can escort you to Grila," I offered. A confused look came over the cleric's face, and I guessed she didn't see the job as done.

"Why would I want to travel to Grila? We still haven't found any artifacts of the Titans," she mumbled. "While this piece ages to the Last Battle, it is not enough evidence the battle was fought here."

I looked apologetically at Maveith. I didn't want to ruin our adventurer reputation, as it was our cover for moving through the Caliphate. I exhaled slowly. "Very well. Where do you wish to search next?"

Glasha nodded slowly, probably thinking we might have had thoughts of treachery. The pauldrons were extremely valuable as an artifact. "We will spiral out from this location."

"If that is your wish." I nodded in assent.

We began spiraling outward from where we had uncovered the pauldrons. The battlefield had likely been picked clean of most runic artifacts over the millennia, so stumbling upon them was a stroke of absurd luck. Maybe they weren't from the final battle at all. Maybe some warlord fell off his flying mount and died out here alone five thousand years ago. I kept that thought to myself. Glasha was in a good mood, and I didn't want to ruin it.

The next day, about two miles from the pauldrons, I found three buried shields relatively close together. They were a bit deeper down, almost twelve feet, but I was guessing they were artifacts since they had stood the test of time. "Benito, it's time for your skill at digging again."

Benito eagerly dismounted with Mateo and Maveith to start digging. Glasha had healed their hands from digging up the pauldrons. Raelia sent Baldo into the sky to scout, and Blaze took up the watch with her. It was going to be a long dig this time as the shovels Glasha had brought were not very large. I could have accelerated our progress with my dimensional space, but I didn't want to reveal my true capabilities to Glasha.

"What did you find?" Glasha said anxiously as she watched my companions toss earth.

"A trio of shields. They are all for a normal man, though, not Titan artifacts." My revelation made her deflate. She started chewing on the end of her scarlet ponytail in nervousness as we waited. It was three hours before the Maveith struck the first shield and handed it up to us.

Not caring about her clothes, Glasha eagerly started clearing the decorative shield. I could already tell it was not a dungeon artifact. It was far too ornate and lacked the persistent silvery appearance. It was also much more challenging to clean than the pauldrons. The cleric went through all the waterskins and ended up caked in mud herself.

Benito blessed Fortuna as his shovel clanked against the next shield. "The other one is just a few inches below that one," I yelled down into the hole. Soon, my three companions climbed out of the pit, their hands torn apart from blood blisters. I interrupted Glasha, and she took a break from her efforts to heal them.

Benito's eyes were wide as the ancient artifacts were slowly cleaned. "Are they made of gold?"

Glasha shook her head. "No, bronze. And they are not shields," she said triumphantly. I was confused. They were a bit small for shields, but their round shape and shank for the forearm strap indicated they were shields. "They are buttons!" she proudly declared.

Benito's face twisted in confusion, unable to puzzle it out. "What type of Titan would have buttons that size?" Blaze asked.

"Stone giant craftsmen probably did the relief work, but this was probably worn by a storm giant, the largest of all giants," Glasha said distractedly. "Give me time, and I will delve into its secrets."

I sent Maveith and Mateo to get Glasha more water, since Benito had done most of the digging, and we set up camp by our hole in the ground. I figured the cleric would not move until she had used her revelation spell on all the shields— buttons.

As I prepared food for Maveith to cook, I asked her, "How does your spell work? What does it tell you?"

The filthy cleric cocked her head. "It is more of a lore spell. Not only can I see the runes buried deep in the artifact, but I get flashes of the artifact's history."

"What did you see with the pauldrons?" Blaze asked, intrigued.

"I didn't invest enough aether to see far enough back. The only impression the artifact gave me was that a powerful warrior once wore them, and the runes are designed to resist lightning," Glasha replied. Her eyes were following the returning Maveith.

"Magical lightning?" Raelia asked.

"All lightning," Glasha confirmed with a tusky grin.

I left her to her work as we set the perimeter for the camp and settled in. I was hoping that with the excavation of the Titan artifacts, we could end this job early. Glasha continued to work well into the evening while we hobbled, watered, and fed the horses, and Maveith cooked a small feast. Mateo and Benito were famished from their shoveling, and Maveith had a larger portion than normal as well.

Glasha shouted late into the night, "I found it! These *were* worn in the Last Battle!"

Everyone came out of their tents at the commotion. Glasha was even filthier than before. "We found the site of the Last Battle?" I asked hopefully.

The orc cleric hesitated for a moment. "The last time these were worn, a storm giant wore them during the Last Battle. This one magnifies your voice. This one keeps you constantly clean. This one serves as a guard against poison. There were six buttons in the complete set, judging from the image flashes I got from my revelation spell, but I don't know if the others were artifacts."

Under all the filth, I could see the orc cleric was exhausted. She had expended a lot of aether, and it showed in her deep-set eyes. "You found your proof. Rest, and we will escort you to Grila tomorrow," I said with finality. Her look reminded me of a kid upset that it was time to stop playing. When did I become the adult? "Go to your bedroll!" I ordered. Glasha jumped at my tone but obeyed.

In the morning, we stopped at a stream so everyone who needed it could clean themselves. Glasha oriented us toward the city of Grila. I thought her all-seeing eye was more powerful than Castile's.

As we rode, I debated whether to ask for her help in using her lore spell on some of my artifacts. I was most curious to learn more about the black spear and magebane. I also had a few unidentified artifacts: a large sapphire necklace from the Shimmering Labyrinth, Boris's dungeon blade, and Corvus's dungeon dagger.

It might be too early to trust the odd orc cleric. If she could see flashes of the artifact's history, she would know how I obtained them and would figure out what I could do. Glasha spent all her time in the saddle examining the titan buttons. I hoped she didn't burn her aether channels with all the spellcraft she was using on them. I tried to distract her by insisting we continue with my language lessons. She acquiesced and stored the large bronze buttons in her saddlebags.

A day's ride from Grila, Blaze emitted two sharp whistles of warning. He was riding at the vanguard, twenty yards ahead. I rode up next to him. "What do you see?" He pointed to some half-buried bodies a quarter mile away. The spyglass was soon out, and I examined the site. The bodies had not decomposed, and the skin clearly marked them as orcs. The others approached as I dismounted and sent out an earth pulse, finding nothing.

"We should ride around," Raelia offered after handing me back the spyglass.

Glasha, still fatigued from using so much aether on the buttons, used her scrying spell to examine the site. She had a distant look on her face, and she informed us, "I don't see any warriors among the dead. Two oxen. It looks like the earth just swallowed them. Probably ankhegs. It is mating season, and the corpses were probably left there to feed the young when they hatch." Glasha's eyes focused as she released the spell. "We need to take care of them or find a warlord immediately who can."

I had fought ankhegs many times in the dreamscape. They had a tough shell but turned slowly. Their acid spit was troublesome, but you could dodge it easily enough if you recognized their thorax undulating just before they sprayed. "I will go confirm it is a nest. Blaze, Raelia, and Maveith, cover me with your bows. Mateo and Benito, protect the cleric."

I drew Boris's dungeon blade and walked confidently forward. I was pulsing earth speak as I went and soon found the underground tunnel network. My footfalls attracted the ankheg, and I waited for it to erupt from the earth. The ground trembled under my feet, and I dodged by pushing off an air shield for leverage. The air shield also had the added benefit of slowing the creature, as it was confused by the brief resistance to its emergence.

I went to a two-handed overhead swing and removed one clawed appendage. I circled behind, targeting the six support legs to immobilize the monstrosity. It was not as large as the ones in the amulet, and I quickly had the creature flailing on the ground. Without its legs, it could not pull itself back underground to escape.

During the brief fight, the archers barraged the head with arrows, scoring a number of hits. It wasn't long before the beast succumbed to its wounds. After pulsing earth speak, I yelled, "All clear!" I walked to the mostly buried bodies and found the corpse of another ankheg a few feet below. If this was the male, then the female would have laid eggs within it after mating.

The others rode up, and Mateo's jaw was already jabbering, "Are you sure you need us along?! Killing a pack of werewolves and taking down this giant roach in moments!"

"The arrows killed it, I just immobilized it," I replied indifferently. The dreamscape ankhegs were much larger and stronger than this one. Still, I could see the awe and worship in Mateo's and Benito's eyes.

"You slew a pack of werewolves by yourself?" Glasha asked, interested.

"Not all at the same time," I said, dismissing the claim. "There are likely fertilized eggs under the bodies. Should we handle them?" I wasn't going to reveal the collector to Glasha. I was sure the ankheg would only yield a minor essence anyway, judging by its size.

That was how we spent our afternoon, digging down and destroying a dozen ankheg eggs laid inside the male specimen. Well, that was Benito and Mateo's afternoon anyway. The rest of us supervised. In return, Glasha was going to certify the eggs' destruction at the Adventurers Guild. Each egg would earn Mateo and Benito a large silver as bounty. The ankheg itself was worth another gold on top.

Covered in yolk and mud and starting to attract flies, Benito and Mateo rode as the rear guard. Still, both were happy they had earned 120 silver for an afternoon's work. I thought Blaze looked slightly regretful he hadn't joined them.

Grila was a large city, and soon, we approached the surrounding farmlands. Glasha paused to tell the first orc farmer we met about the bodies and the dead ankheg. They would reclaim the bodies and harvest the beasts. The majestic walls soon loomed larger as we approached our destination.

Outside the stone walls of Grila we prepared to part ways with Glasha. Still atop her pony with her treasure secured in the saddlebags, she thanked us. "You performed beyond expectations. I will report the job complete to the Guild and leave a bonus. You can claim your bounty for the ankhegs as well." She paused, and I could tell there was something else she wanted from us.

After an awkward pause, she continued, "The clerics of the Boutan Caliphate are going to elect a new Supreme. The death of the last Supreme has not been made public. If you are interested, one of the candidates requires—an escort."

Raelia interrupted Glasha. "Escort? That should be the responsibility of the elites. Why would a candidate require outside adventurers?"

Glasha winced. "She has no allies and refused my advice to withdraw her candidacy. So far, no one has taken up her sigil, so she has no escort."

"While that is a tempting offer," I said, trying to sound gracious, "we have other plans and have booked queues for two dungeons. The one outside of Grila, for one."

Glasha looked surprised. "You plan to delve into the Vault of the Spirit Arachnid?"

The plan was just to check on our space in the queue and then head north toward our true destination. "Yes, but if the wait is too long, we will continue to the Whispering Grotto."

A devilish grin appeared on her face. "Yes, it is a popular dungeon. I will make sure you are placed at the top of the queue." Before I could object, she turned her pony and entered the gates of Grila. Dragon shit, I didn't consider that the cleric would have sway with the Adventurers Guild. My companions looked over at me questioningly.

His face a little paler, Benito asked innocently, "We are going into the dungeon then?" Benito had a hard time in the Shimmering Labyrinth. Not only had he been injured and almost died, but we had all lost a lot of companions and friends.

"There is a limit of five for this dungeon; you do not have to enter," I replied, to his relief. If we had to delve into the dungeon to keep up appearances, I would make it quick. "Maveith, don't worry. This dungeon run will only take a few hours, and we will be riding north toward our true goal."

The gray man nodded in acceptance. "I understand the necessity and I am ready to enter with you."

I had read a little about the city we were entering. The city of Grila was in the heart of the Caliphate, and as such, it was a crossroads for travel and trade. It was on a small plateau that allowed sewers to be easily incorporated into its design. Water was raised from deep wells by Archimedes' screw. Well, the text didn't call it that, but I managed to figure out what it was called on Earth in the dreamscape. It was an ingenious use of technology and not something I would have expected to see in orc culture.

Passing through the gates on horseback, I observed that the orcs flaunted the abundance of the city's water, with fountains, trees, and small herb gardens outside of homes. The orcs themselves were dressed in mostly gray and off-white colors, not favoring the brighter colors of the Telhians.

I wouldn't call the city beautiful by any stretch, but it definitely had a more natural feel than most cities in the Telhian Empire. I asked for directions in my limited Orcish, getting a sneer from the orc laborer at my battery of the language, or maybe it was because I was human. He directed us toward a throng of people, pointing in their general direction. I suppose we should have followed Glasha if the Guild Hall was her destination.

The press of orcs and people lessened as we moved farther away from the gates. The simple structures were made mostly of black stone and aged red oak, both resources found in the dungeon. The Adventurers Hall was entirely made of this black stone and located near the center of Grila. It towered over the other buildings nearby, even the manor of the warlord who ruled the city. Tattooed orcs loitered outside the hall, and we found the stables across the street instead of behind the structure. After some exchange of coin with the stable hands and dispensing a few apples to the horses for jobs well done, we entered the Adventurers Hall.

An orc minstrel played the lute while another thudded on some soft, deep, bass drums. The rhythm was repetitive but therapeutic in its simplicity. A light hint of tobacco hung in the air, adding an earthy richness to the atmosphere. The room was well lit with glowstones to offset the dark, black stone walls that seemed to absorb the light rather than reflect it. There were multiple desk clerks. It was the largest guild hall I had seen.

Was this all because of the popular dungeon? Blaze nudged me, interrupting my assessment of the room. "Glasha is over there. Maybe you can stop whatever she is doing in regard to getting us into the dungeon."

Blaze sounded anxious and obviously didn't want to enter the dungeon either. I moved up behind Glasha while the others made their way to get food and drink after nearly two weeks in the wild. Hopefully, with the abundance of water, this guild hall had baths.

Glasha was engaged in a lively conversation with the orc clerk, her gestures animated and words spilling forth in a rapid cadence. I strained to keep up with the discussion, but the pace was too quick for me to grasp more than a few scattered phrases. Thankfully, it looked like we had gotten here shortly after her.

Glasha turned, following the eyes of the clerk. "Here he is! I will sign both contracts as completed, and the Guild can send someone to confirm the ankheg nest's destruction." Glasha turned to me. "My payment will be brought to you shortly. Forty gold," she said, smiling. It was twice what we were owed, but still a small fraction of the value of the artifacts.

"Thank you. There is no need for additional compensation with the dungeon queue. It wouldn't be fair to bump the others who have been waiting," I stated with an appropriate note of gratitude for her efforts.

"It is already done. I used my privilege to get us the next delve in the morning," Glasha said, happily beaming in a tusky smile.

I was confused as I parsed out her words in Orcish. "Are you planning to come with us?"

"Well, that is the only way you can jump the queue, with a cleric of the Caliphate. You don't have a healer, and I feel I owe you a debt. I will not require a share of whatever you harvest. Besides, after seeing your fighting prowess, I doubt there will be any challenge for you in the dungeon of the Spirit Arachnid."

I clenched my jaw, trying to hide my frustration and anger. If Glasha was with us, it would limit what I could do or risk exposing my secrets. A dungeon would have been a good place to reveal more of my abilities to my companions, especially if Benito was not coming.

Another orc dropped a heavy bag on the desk with a clinking of coins. "Forty gold," the orc clerk said, picking up and extending the bag to me. "Just a moment for the ankheg bounty. That will be another three gold, five silver, and eighty-eight coppers." A second bag was passed to me a moment later.

My confusion at the higher bounty made Glasha explain, "There is a slight increase during the mating season for eggs. Also, there were thirteen dead farmers, so there is a vengeance bonus."

Glasha looked pleased with herself as I took the coin. Not seeing a graceful way out of the delve, I asked, "How does a delve work in the Vault of the Spirit Arachnid?"

The clerk answered my question in Orcish. I asked him to slow down his speech, and he started over: "At sunrise, the guardians will let you through the entrance as long as the previous party has vacated. If you fail to exit after a day, all harvests and prizes are seized on your exit and taxed at fifty percent."

Glasha quickly put her mark on some documents from the clerk and excused herself. "I need to file a report of my find and log the items with my superiors, but I will return soon." She wore a devilish smile that made me think she was up to no good. But she was gone in a rush of energy—yep, definitely up to no good.

I joined my companions at the table; they were sharing a massive haunch of roasted meat in the center of the table, cutting off strips for their plates. Bowls of yellow mashed potato and boiled red beets were also being shared. A flagon of dark, fragrant, rich gravy was being passed around. I sat next to Raelia, who was feeding Baldo chunks of meat as he obediently followed simple commands.

I shaved off a few thin slices of the pink meat, scooped a generous helping of potatoes, and ladled the thick gravy over both. The gravy was easily the best part—rich, savory, and clinging to everything it touched—while the potatoes had an earthy, almost nutty flavor—maybe puréed mushrooms. Raelia handed me a full mug without a word.

The ale hit hard, stronger than I had expected and bitter enough to curl the tongue. With such poor taste, I could see why the Pathfinder potions tasted so bad. We ate in a noisy sort of silence—clanking utensils, low muttering from nearby tables—broken only by Baldo's insistent chirping whenever he felt overlooked.

Blaze was the first to sit back, rubbing his stomach. "Where are we going next, Eryk?"

"The dungeon in the morning. The cleric wormed her way into the delve, but it will be good to have a healer with us. We will run the six rooms quickly." Everyone was looking at me expectantly. "Maveith, Blaze, and Mateo will join us." Benito was relieved and Mateo seemed indifferent, but Blaze had some angst.

Raelia, maybe seeing his reluctance, offered, "I will go in Blaze's place." I looked at her, about to ask about Baldo.

Relieved, Blaze said, "I would much rather watch Baldo than delve."

"I am sending him back to Esenhem," Raelia said sharply, which surprised everyone.

"He understands directions?" Benito asked in awe. "I used to get lost walking in the woods outside of town."

Raelia's eyes seemed to be searching for an explanation. To me it was clear she was going to ask me to move Baldo to my dimensional space. "Griffins can return to the place they were hatched. It is instinct." I almost wanted to call bullshit, but it wouldn't help the situation. Instead, the others took the statement as fact, nodding in appreciation. After all, she was a Griffin Rider.

Maveith belched out a question, his breath laced with alcohol. "What do we know about the dungeon?" I looked at my friend, slightly worried. He had never drunk to intoxication before, and I guessed he was coping with our slow pace in his own way. I promised myself we would move faster after this diversion.

I told them what I knew from my lengthy talk with the healer in Artiria. "Six rooms. A safe room on entering and another after the third room. Only five can delve at a time. The first room is the easiest, with giant black stalagmites jutting from the floor. Myconids—fungus men—are the creatures in the room. The second room is a bridge across a green, algae-ridden lake. There are giant snapping turtles lurking in the water. The third room …" I had to pause to recall my conversation with the orc healer.

"I believe it is a rocky expanse of black boulders. It is the room where they primarily harvest the black stone you see around town in the buildings. The creature inside is called a lurker." Knowing they were unfamiliar with the creature, I explained further. "They are large, winged creatures that drop from the ceiling and encompass their prey in their leathery wings, constricting them while their jaws gnaw away at their flesh."

"Sounds pleasant," Mateo grumbled. He clearly was having second thoughts about coming on the delve. I paused to toss the reward sack for the ankhegs between him and Benito.

"The ankheg reward. Also, here are six gold coins for Glasha's job." I passed around the gold sack, and each happily took their coin out. We attracted some looks from the other tables. I did not know if six gold was a lot for an adventurer here. I made a note to myself not to pass out pay in the open again. It was my fault, as we were frequently paid in Legion Halls, and we had openly been paid over seventy gold each for the dungeon discovery in Telha. I didn't consider six gold coins a large sum anymore, but it was.

When the gold sack came back to me, it had ten small golds remaining. The extra four golds were for Fortuna's Chosen expenses. I assumed I would be paying for everyone's rooms and meals again. Benito and Mateo were whispering to each other, probably discussing how they planned to spend their coin. Maveith was more interested in the challenge of the dungeon. "What of the last three rooms?"

I nodded, returning to the briefing. "The fourth room has a most foul pair of beasts. Rust monsters. They can instantly corrode any metal that contacts their antennae. And these are even more foul, as they can destroy runic weapons. The good news is that they can be dispatched at range.

"The fifth room is Mateo's favorite, a single ogre. It fights with a club and is pretty stupid, from what I was told. The final room is a large forest chamber. There is a single ghost spider hiding there. A ghost spider can turn itself invisible and move silently. Its body is just about the size of a horse." I tried to sound reassuring about the spider, but I hated spiders. "There are also numerous webs in the forest that are easy to get entangled in, so you need to be careful with your movement."

I had talked with a nonchalant tone so as not to scare the others. Truthfully, since this dungeon was delved daily, the creatures shouldn't be overly strong for their species. There were also a number of valuable creature harvests we could get out of this delve.

I took care of everyone's rooms and paid for their drinks for the evening. As our state of inebriation climbed, Glasha returned to the Adventurers Hall. She joined our table, having trouble hiding a smirk, and I wondered just what she had been up to. She didn't seem the type to hire mercenaries to ambush and kill us for our runic gear. It had to be something else, and I would be glad to ride away from her orbit after the dungeon.

Mateo was so drunk that he was having trouble talking coherently while asking Glasha personal questions, which she seemed more than willing to answer in her accented Telhian. That was my cue to excuse myself. A short time later, I found my room and lay down in the lumpy bed. The good thing about the building being mostly black stone was that my earth speak resonated well with it.

I actually felt less safe in the Adventurers Hall room than I did in the wild surrounded by my companions. There were just too many unknowns here. I paid extra for a room with a private copper tub and running water, but the water was not hot, so I retrieved the thermal stone from Maveith for a hot bath. Once I was finally clean, and much later in the night, my earth pulse detected Mateo and Glasha entering the same room. Both of them were extremely intoxicated, judging by their movements, and I thought it best to let them make their own mistakes and regret them later.

I decided to avoid using the dreamscape amulet while I was in the Adventurers Guild Hall, not knowing if mystical eyes were spying on me. After a few short naps, I practiced with the spear, magebane, and Boris's blade. I was topless and working up a good sweat. I was considering a second bath when a knock at the door made me pause.

My earth speak confirmed it was Raelia and Baldo. I was expecting them. It was a few hours before sunrise. Letting them in, I could see the indecision in Raelia's face as Baldo sat without prompting, expecting a meaty treat from me. Her eyes traveled over my sweaty body momentarily before she looked away, her face slightly flushed.

Knowing why she was here, I tried to reassure her. "It will be fine. He will not know any time has passed. It is also better this way."

"It's still hard. He's my responsibility," she said, her voice tight with distress. Baldo's head flicked back and forth between us, his sharp eyes tracking the tone more than the words. I tossed him a strip of bear meat to distract him—griffins, I had learned, had an uncanny ability to sense emotion. Right now, Raelia was radiating despair.

"This is going to keep him much safer than if he traveled with us," I reassured her. "Baldo, do you want to go where all the bear meat comes from?" He cocked his head, probably only understanding the words "bear meat."

Not wanting to draw this out, I made Baldo vanish and my aether bottomed out. He hadn't resisted much. Raelia exhaled, the sound laced with guilt. I'm not sure why I did it—maybe instinct, maybe something else—but I stepped forward and hugged her.

She didn't pull away. In fact, she leaned into me, resting against my sweat-damp chest. Her hair was silky, the scent oddly familiar—like the worn griffin pillow I favored. Probably because she often used Baldo as one when we camped.

She started to return the embrace, arms just beginning to wrap around me—then stopped. Abruptly, she pulled back and stepped toward the door, ending the moment.

She opened the door slightly and paused. She turned and made eye contact with me. "Thank you. I needed that." She opened the door further and was shocked to see Blaze standing there, probably on his way to the general privy on this floor. Orcs didn't use chamber pots. We all froze, each making eye contact before

Raelia walked past Blaze back to her room, leaving me and Blaze staring at each other.

Amusement was clearly in his eyes, and I knew what he was thinking. I walked forward and closed the door, thinking that no matter what I said, he had already formed his own conclusions. I needed to focus on preparing for the dungeon in a few hours.

Chapter 287: The Vault of the Spirit Arachnid

I was up well before the others and went to check on the horses. Ginger got an extra rubdown while I handed out half-apples to the rest of the mounts. As I brushed her flank, I found myself quietly explaining that I would be gone all day on a dungeon delve and that she shouldn't worry. Of course, she couldn't understand me—but I spoke to her anyway. Ginger wasn't just a mount. She was a companion I trusted.

Leaving the stables, I found most of my companions in the common room sporting hangovers. Even Maveith had his head down to avoid looking at the bright glowstone sconces. I passed out some morning glory stems, but my supply was getting low. Benito, who was not joining us, was missing, and a quick earth pulse confirmed he was asleep alone in his bed upstairs.

Mateo didn't look the least bit regretful about last night—if anything, he seemed energized. He always talked a big game, but now that I thought about it, I couldn't recall him ever actually following through and visiting a brothel. Glasha joined us a moment later, wearing an unmistakable orcish grin. The two of them carefully avoided eye contact, which I found quietly hilarious.

I briefly toyed with the idea of calling them out, just to see their reactions, but thought better of it—especially with Blaze casting sidelong glances between Raelia and me, clearly trying to puzzle out whatever was going on between us.

"We have an hour before sunrise. Do you have any questions?" I asked. The delve group was Raelia, Maveith, Mateo, Glasha, and me. Blaze was just here to see us off.

"What is our share of the loot?" Mateo asked with a smirk, sucking on his morning glory noisily.

"Equal share of the reward chests, and I decide on the distribution of anything else found." My tone indicated I was referring to the essence collector. I was still uncertain whether I would reveal its presence to Glasha, but I would hate to leave so many essences behind. No one else had a question, and they seemed recovered enough from celebrating.

I only knew the entrance was just outside the city. "Glasha, can you lead us to the entrance?"

It was about a mile's walk beyond the western gate. Nearby, large oak trunks— probably cut from inside the dungeon—were stacked neatly to dry. Six tattooed orcs in steel cuirasses stood guard, each with long spears and blades at their hips. They looked like experienced warriors, not just gatekeepers.

Glasha stepped forward to speak, her voice clear and authoritative. "Glasha Mistborn, the Chronicler. Here to delve today."

I half-expected some kind of confrontation from whoever we had displaced, but the guards were the only ones present. Still, I couldn't quite figure out why so many elite-looking sentries were stationed at a single dungeon entrance. There was no immediate sense of danger, but I made a note to stay alert when we emerged—just in case.

The largest of the sextet nodded, his face hidden under a polished steel helm, and motioned for his men to move aside. Blaze took the opportunity to depart. "Good luck, and bring me back a trophy." He clasped wrists with each of us before returning to town.

I was last and said seriously, "Make sure Benito doesn't get into trouble."

"I will do my best, but I am just one man," he said, a warm smile spreading across his face as he released my wrist and stepped back. As he walked away, I felt grateful to have someone so dependable by my side as backup. Maveith, fierce and loyal, was not just a friend but a formidable force in battle. Yet it was Blaze who had a keen eye for details—the subtle ones—often noticing things I missed and, sometimes, things I wasn't quite ready to share.

The entrance to the dungeon was down a short series of black stone steps. We walked past the familiar, black, oily surface. The entry chamber was small, just a rough twenty-foot circular room. On the wall, white chalk writing in Orcish abounded. The graffiti filled the walls from floor to ceiling, and reading it all would take over a day—if you could read it. I was sure there was wisdom in those words on the dangers ahead, but we didn't have time for Raelia to translate.

I unsheathed Boris's dungeon blade, the glossy silver metal gleaming in my grasp as anticipation charged the air. The others fell into formation, Maveith taking a strategic position beside me in the tunnel that led to the next chamber.

The Shimmering Labyrinth had been unlike other dungeons—it offered a myriad of starting areas and a non-linear path among at least three levels. In stark contrast, we stood in the Vault of the Spirit Arachnid, a traditional series of rooms, each one more demanding than the last, designed to test the limits of our combat skill and cooperation.

Above us, luminous moss clung to the ceiling, casting a mesmerizing light throughout the space. Its vibrant hues—a swirling mix of soft yellows and deep blues—imbued the chamber with a twilight glow, creating a fascinating and foreboding atmosphere, as if it were alive and watching our progress.

"Is everyone ready?" I asked. Seeing no objections, I reminded everyone of our opponent. "There should be five myconids in the next room. Each is about as strong as a man, and they will use their arms as clubs. Some myconids can release spores to poison you or force you to sleep, but the ones we are facing do not have that ability. If they do release a cloud of spores, hold your breath or you will experience a violent coughing fit." I waited until everyone nodded, and I led the way.

The moss seemed to be brighter when the tunnel ended. The chamber beyond had a high ceiling with glowing moss that showed ripples of colors, mostly yellow and blue with some lines of green. Large pillars of black stone stood throughout the chamber, with thousands of small mushrooms dotting the floor. A ten-foot myconid walked carefully among the small mushrooms as if he were tending a garden. Although it had two arms and two legs, that was its only resemblance to a human.

Its entire body was a living fungus. I noticed the other four myconids in the chamber. "Mateo, since you are intimately familiar with it, guard the cleric's body." I didn't turn around to see his reaction as I dashed into the room.

I targeted the tallest one first. It was a little comical to me how slow it seemed as I removed its spongy, fibrous arms with forceful slashes. Maveith was having more trouble, as his hammer had gotten embedded in the head of his first target. Raelia circled a blue myconid and cut chunks out of it with her short blade. I moved to intercept a green myconid that was moving toward Mateo and Glasha. It cast a mist of spores into my path, and I held my breath as I engaged. The fungoid men were poor fighters, relying on direct, telegraphed attacks. I quickly cut down my second opponent and stepped well clear of the cloud before inhaling again.

It had only taken a minute for all the myconids to be disabled, and now it was about removing their heads, which didn't take long. They bled slowly, a clear, viscous fluid oozing from their bodies. The blood was useful as a glue, but difficult to harvest and keep fresh. I was more interested in the spongy masses around the head and armpits that had released the spores.

Corvus's runic dagger appeared in my hand as I worked quickly to harvest what I could. Glasha had watched the fight, impressed, and was now standing over me. "I know an alchemist in the city that pays well for myconid flesh."

"I plan to keep these. I dabble in alchemy myself," I replied.

"Since when?" Raelia said in surprise from across the chamber, drawing an interested Mateo. Realizing her mistake, Raelia shut up, and I harvested in silence as the others wandered the chamber and located the reward chest.

Mateo edged closer to me. I thought he was going to ask about Raelia, who had clearly indicated that she knew me before we met in Artiria. "How did you know? Was it because we were so loud?"

I chuckled a little. He seemed slightly embarrassed. I didn't know if they had been loud or not, but if he was going to give me a reason for being aware, I would use it. "Yes. You two were definitely enthusiastic. Glasha doesn't seem a bad sort. How was it?"

Mateo struggled for words, ensuring no one could overhear him as he leaned in. "Bit weird at first with the face and skin and tusks, but everything was normal after I got past it." He grinned. "She has incredibly strong thighs from riding so much ..."

"Never kiss and tell," I interrupted him, not needing to know the details. Or maybe I was slightly jealous, as it had been a few months for me.

Maveith was searching the mushroom carpet but returned frustrated. "I didn't find anything I recognized. I'm not sure if they are edible or not." His statement made me think briefly of Konstantin, who could tell if something was poisonous. I hoped the veteran had made it out too.

"It is fine, Maveith. I am sure there will be other useful harvests. What was in the reward chest?"

"Six silver coins and a potion that Glasha said was a poison cure." I nodded, but thought it was not a great reward. Yes, the dungeon potion was probably worth a few golds since it wouldn't expire until the seal was broken, but I didn't feel that it matched the danger level.

"You can hold onto the potion," I decided. I had my spell form to purge any poison. "Mateo and Raelia can split the silver."

We had cleared and harvested the first room in fifteen minutes, and I ushered my group toward the next chamber. I stood in the tunnel, looking at the large pool of murky green water covered in algae. The green glowing moss lining the ceiling reflected off the surface, making it appear an even deeper shade of green. A few swirls in the water indicated the giant snapping turtles beneath the surface. I didn't think the healer had told me how many there were, but I identified four distinct moving swirls.

"I will handle these. You all can wait here," I said. When one of the swirls got close, I stepped onto the bridge. The water churned, a turtle immediately closing in on me, and I waited. The turtle surfaced in a foamy mess as it surged onto the bridge. Its long neck shot forth and slammed into my stacked air shields, stunning itself momentarily. I moved around them and hacked the head off in a two-handed slash. I was beginning to appreciate Boris's dungeon blade. I was able to isolate the other three turtles and similarly dispatch them all in less than five minutes.

Looking back at the group, I saw Maveith try to muscle the first turtle onto its back. "Leave it, Maveith. I don't feel like turtle soup."

Disappointed, he said with a pleading look, "But it goes extremely well with chicken broth and potatoes. It was one of my favorites growing up."

Maveith needed a win after our slow travel. "Fine, just harvest one. While we wait, Mateo and Glasha can scout the next room. Do not enter," I warned.

Mateo looked confused for just a moment before realizing I planned to use the collector. He ushered Glasha down the corridor. When I was sure they were out of sight, the collector appeared in my hand.

As I worked on collecting the first turtle, Raelia hovered over me. "She is smart and will figure out you are sending her away for a purpose eventually." I ignored her and focused on the essence forming from the weak azure smoke being pulled into the collector. A small, dark-purple sphere formed—a minor strength essence. The dungeon was harvested so often that I doubted I would get anything but minor essences.

"I would have preferred not to have her along at all," I said testily while I consumed the first essence. Moving to the next turtle, I added, "She is planning something. See if you can figure out what it is." I handed the next minor essence to Raelia and the third to Maveith. The fourth I gave to Raelia to hand to Mateo secretly.

We waited while Maveith got some turtle steaks, and I stored them. The meat had a funny scent to it, and I hoped it was safe to eat. The chest was another disappointment: ten silver coins and a vial of thick black oil. The best I could decipher from the dungeon script was that the contents was something called ever-burning oil.

We joined Mateo and Glasha at the end of the corridor. They parted so I could inspect the room. The ceiling had the same glowing moss we saw throughout the dungeon, but it was pulsing slowly. It shifted from a bright blue-green to completely black in a slow, repeating strobe effect. Large sections of the ceiling were also completely free of moss. This was likely where the lurkers should be hiding, but I couldn't see them at all.

"I see four," Glasha offered, seeing me struggle.

I grunted, still trying to find my first one. "How many should there be?" I asked, as I didn't think the orc healer had told me.

"Five," she said definitively.

Seeing that I was not going to admit I couldn't find the creatures, she pointed to the far wall. "There are two there, overlapping."

I blinked rapidly when the chamber was at its brightest and could now see that the black rocks looked too smooth in that area. She quickly pointed out two more nestled in the transition between the wall and ceiling. I was actually impressed she had spotted them. "Have you delved into this dungeon before?" I asked.

"No, but I have been in the Endless Dark and fought lurkers before," she admitted. With Glasha's back turned, I noticed Raelia slipping Mateo the essence, which he consumed immediately.

"Why did you travel into the Endless Dark?" I asked conversationally, content to wait until all threats were identified.

"The Caliphate monitors all access points to the Endless Dark. Sometimes, the Supreme Cleric orders expeditions into the depths to survey the known paths," Glasha responded, still scanning the chamber for the last lurker.

"To what end?" Raelia inquired from behind us.

Glasha directed her focus at my group. "They monitor the wandering creatures. Although we explore all thirteen dungeons in the Caliphate, some entrances remain a mystery. These dungeons become saturated and periodically release their spawn into the Endless Dark. Most perish in the Endless Dark, but a few manage to reach the surface. That is why the Esenhem elves foolishly destroyed most of their dungeons.

"Most forget, but it was the dungeons who trained and equipped my people and your people to fight the Titans. Without the dungeons, we would have stood no chance at victory. The Boutan orcs honor dungeons and what they provide," Glasha said proudly.

Maveith was listening raptly and asked, "Why did the dungeons help fight the Titans?"

Glasha's head tilted left and right as she struggled to come up with a reason. "I am not sure, as it was five thousand years ago. But I think the Titans were trying to destroy the dungeons. It is why most of the great dungeons no longer exist. This"—she indicated around her—"is just an infant dungeon, no more than three thousand years old."

"Dungeons can have babies?" Mateo asked, perplexed.

"This is not the time to discuss lore," I said, halting the conversation. We eventually located the last lurker above our entrance.

I indicated Glasha and Mateo. "Mateo, take Glasha and wait with her in the last chamber."

Glasha was surprised and slightly angry. "Why? I can help. Why don't you trust me?"

"Where did you go and what were you up to after you logged the job as completed in the Adventurers Hall?" I asked pointedly.

Glasha's eyes studied me for a moment like she was trying to peer into me and get all my secrets. Maybe that was exactly what she was doing. "I was sending a message to Cleric Mynasha to get herself to Grila in the next two days if she wanted to contract your services."

"The escort job I already told you I didn't want to take?" I said irritably. "I am still not interested."

Glasha wasn't deterred. "If you help her, she can help you get what you want. Maveith's sister." She had a triumphant, tusky smile on her face.

Damn it, I cursed inwardly. "Who told you that?" I asked harshly. But I didn't really need to ask. Mateo was already slinking away.

"Don't blame Mateo," Glasha said, smirking. "He was quite drunk, and I have been told I am quite persuasive." Mateo was hiding innocuously behind Maveith.

"Did you use magic on him?" Raelia said accusingly.

"No," Glasha stated defiantly, with a quiet snarl. The orc and elf stared each other down under the strobing lights of the dungeon.

"Well, it's done. It is not a dangerous secret unless Glasha plans to use it against us," I said, breaking the tension.

"I have no intention of doing so, even if you do not aid Mynasha."

"How can the cleric Mynasha help me free my sister?" Maveith said in his deep voice. We all turned to face the cleric. Maveith added, "I thought clerics were not allowed to own slaves, and only warlords were afforded that privilege in the Caliphate."

Glasha nodded in agreement. "That is true. But the Supreme has the power to free any slave, even one owned by a warlord."

I frowned, realizing where this was going. "The only way she can help us is if she becomes the Supreme Cleric?"

A wide grin formed across Glasha's face. "Yes."

I groaned. "Let's complete the dungeon, and we will meet with your cleric friend," I said loudly, shelving the discussion for now. I saw Maveith getting excited at the prospect. Maybe he was thinking he was closer to getting his sister back. Or maybe he thought that he could free all the goliath slaves in the Caliphate.

I turned to the chamber. It was dotted with large black stones that made moving within it difficult. The lurkers would most likely attack during the dark phase of the strobing ceiling moss. I tried to recall everything I could from Hearne's lessons and my bestiaries.

Lurkers were nightmarish creatures that resembled hideous manta rays with impressive ten-foot wingspans or larger. They had sacs that they filled with air to float. I only knew this because a skilled alchemist could make levitation potions from those sacs.

Their skin had a camouflage that allowed them to blend seamlessly into their surroundings, making them nearly invisible until it was too late. As they swooped down from above with their massive wings spread wide, they aimed to engulf their unsuspecting victims. If you happened to be alone when one of these monstrous beings descended upon you, becoming ensnared in its constricting wings would spell your doom. The pressure would immobilize you, leaving you utterly helpless as its circular maw of serrated teeth chewed on you.

As I surveyed the dimly lit chamber, I quickly formulated a plan. "Raelia," I called out decisively, "we need your fireball to strike at the pair lurking on the far side of the chamber. Can you reach them?"

Raelia took her eyes off of Glasha. Raelia's trust had been broken after Glasha seduced Mateo to pump him for information. Raelia turned, scanned the chamber, and nodded. "It is within my range, but I cannot charge a fireball until I step into the room."

"Not a problem. We will give you the time you need. Maveith, you will target the one over the entrance, and I will handle the other two. I will toss my glowstone into the room to keep it lit." Mateo looked ready to join us in the fight. "Mateo, if any of us are captured, it is your job to cut us free. But don't enter unless one of us is in danger."

We prepared and Maveith entered first with me directly behind him. I tossed the glowstone to the center of the room at the moss's brightest phase. As the moss dimmed, the lurker above the door dropped toward Maveith. He was prepared, and with a grunt, his hammer connected, folding the large creature like a bedsheet.

With the combat underway, the two figures in the corner of the ceiling glided down toward us. Annoyingly, the pair on the far wall also left their perch to approach. While Raelia's fireball was growing, I focused on the two approaching me. They were silently gliding toward us in a controlled approach. I made the decision to go on the offensive. I used one of the black boulders to leap and meet the closest lurker in the air.

Boris's runic blade removed a large portion of the wing, and a hissing sound from the wound echoed in the chamber while blood sprayed. The creature couldn't control its descent and crashed to my right. Instead of falling to the floor, I landed on an air shield that appeared beneath my feet, allowing me to hack the second lurker as it approached.

I wasn't as successful in this attack, and the lurker's mass managed to knock me off my improvised platform. The impact also wasted my aether shield as a blue flash flared. I landed awkwardly as Raelia yelled, "Fireball!" in warning.

I oriented myself as best I could and established an air shield in the direction of the two uninjured lurkers as her fireball raced toward them. The blinding explosion, heat, and concussive wave deafened and blinded me momentarily. I channeled aether to my eyes, and my vision cleared instantly with my aether sight. I trickled aether to heal my eardrums, which were ringing loudly.

Dry, hot air greeted my lungs. I had been a lot closer than the others. As I stood, I sent aetheric healing to my right knee and sprained ankle from the bad landing. The surviving lurkers were all flailing in their death throes on the ground, their air sacs burst from the rapid heating.

The others were blinking back their sight from the flash and were clearly deaf, yelling to talk. I didn't respond, knowing they couldn't hear me anyway. I dispatched the three injured lurkers who lived through the blast. They were genuinely disgusting creatures in the light, with mouths that reminded me of a lamprey's.

The reward chest appeared on one of the stone boulders in the chamber's center. Raelia recovered first, as she had been smart enough to close her eyes when she launched her attack. "I am sorry, I invested more aether than I should have into the spell."

Glasha was healing Maveith's ears. "It was effective," Maveith bellowed, louder than he needed to.

"There is a safe room ahead. Why don't you all head there and rest. I will clean up here," I said.

"Do you have injuries in need of healing?" Glasha asked, assessing me from a distance. She had seen me in action again and probably had questions about what I had done to stand in midair.

"No, wait with the others. Maveith, prepare lunch," I ordered.

"But it is still morning," Maveith stated. "We have been in the dungeon less than an hour."

"A snack then." I waved him off. I needed them out of the room to use the collector. If I was right, the lurkers might give me an essence with a magic affinity. The group eventually left me to work. At first, I examined where the gas sacs were on the lurkers, trying to figure out how to harvest the organs. Most of them had ruptured in the heat of the fireball, but I did manage to harvest a few of the rubbery sacs. It was more out of curiosity than a desire to try my hand at complex alchemy.

I checked to ensure the corridor was clear before starting work with the collector next. I was right: the five lurkers yielded four minor air affinity essences and one provided a strength essence. The creatures probably used aether to create the gas in their sacs that allowed them to float.

The essences were more valuable than the contents of the reward chest—fifteen silver coins and a lesser dungeon healing potion. I joined the others and found them sitting around a firepit on stone benches. The ceiling moss here glowed a bright yellow, almost a match to daylight. I distributed the coins and gave the healing potion to Mateo.

He immediately apologized. "I am sorry about revealing our purpose in the Caliphate. It just sort of came up. Like she said, she can be persuasive."

I shook my head in disappointment, like Konstantin used to do to me. In a calm voice, I told him, "Don't make excuses. Just don't let it happen again, Mateo. I blame Glasha more than you, anyway." He nodded vigorously and stashed the potion after I told him what it was.

Maveith handed me some jerky and cheese. "The next chamber is the easiest of them all. Two rust monsters. Raelia and Maveith should be able to injure them with their bows; I will go with them while Glasha and Mateo rest here."

"Rest?" Glasha said incredulously. "I haven't done anything!"

"There are just three rooms left. You probably won't have to do anything," I said dismissively.

She studied me. "You should slow down. If you clear the dungeon too fast, it will draw attention."

"And give your cleric more time to reach Grila," I retorted. Her reaction told me I was spot-on in my assumption, but she was right; we were moving too fast. "We can always have lunch in the final room after killing the ghost spider."

I didn't argue further and walked to the next room with Raelia and Maveith. Raelia used a fireball to blind and disorient the two rust monsters before she and Maveith killed them with arrows. The collector yielded two minor earth essences, which I decided to keep for myself. The chest had twenty-four silver coins and a black stone serving dish. The stone matched the abundant black material of the dungeon.

We walked back to the safe room with the dish, hoping Glasha could shed some light on it with her lore spell. Mateo and the orc had been talking around the firepit and looked up. Mateo sported a grin. "We heard the explosion. That was fast! If delving is this easy, I may grow to like it. I bet Blaze and Benito will be upset after hearing how easy it was."

I didn't respond to Mateo to show he wasn't entirely off my shit list just yet. I handed the large black plate to Glasha. "Do you know what this is? It is from the reward chest."

She took the plate and turned it over, looking for markings and finding none. Next, she used her spell on it. "It is a simple preservation plate. It will keep food hot—or cold—and prevent the food from spoiling."

"Is it worth anything?" Mateo asked, looking at the polished black stone plate.

"I think the local warlord has a set of them. He may be interested in purchasing it for a few gold," she said uncertainly.

"Can I have it?" Maveith asked, looking longingly at the stone plate. I nodded and handed him the plate, not having a use for it myself.

I considered Glasha for a moment. I was going to ask her to use her lore spell on Boris's blade and maybe a second artifact after we had left the dungeon, but I was uncertain, now that she had manipulated Mateo—even if Mateo had enjoyed being manipulated.

"I will check the fifth room myself," I announced sternly, leaving no room for argument. I walked to the fifth room alone. The dungeon creature was a single ogre and would only take me a moment to handle. The chamber had a small waterfall and a carpet of grass. The ceiling moss was mostly white in this room with patches of pink. The ogre was splayed out and snoring on the grass.

I had never seen a dungeon creature sleeping before, and it intrigued me for a moment until I realized it was faking. The ogre's eyes kept drifting open in my direction before squinting shut. It would have been comical if not for the smell that had reached me. Ogres had nasty scent glands and preferred to be covered in their own filth. This ogre was likely less than a day old but had already created an eye-watering scent that hung in the air.

With the collector in hand, I walked straight into the chamber as the ogre scrambled to its feet. It reached for a large club it had hidden on the other side of its body. It never got to stand to its full height before it grabbed its chest and coughed up blood. Confused, it went to all fours before collapsing as its lungs filled with blood and it stopped breathing. Its aether resistance wasn't much, but it still bottomed out my aether pool.

I paused in my walk and surveyed the chamber. When I identified the reward chest near the pool at the base of the waterfall, I relaxed. The chest yielded thirty silver and a potion of giant strength. It was not the first such potion I had, and this one was much weaker than the one I got from the owlbear chamber in the Shimmering Labyrinth.

The ogre yielded only a minor strength essence, which was a bit disappointing. I had been hoping for a constitution essence to feed Ginger. I added some wounds to make it look like I had fought the behemoth, then wandered the chamber a bit, looking for any small creature the ogre might have fed on.

The pool at the base of the waterfall had tadpoles and some frogs. I didn't even try to catch them to test the collector. The dungeon was so heavily delved that it was already struggling to produce enough aetheric smoke for the essences I was collecting.

I didn't hesitate to walk to the dungeon's final room. This massive chamber was lit by dark-blue moss, giving it and the large oak trees inside it the appearance of being twilit. Thick webs crossed everywhere among the trunks, leaving no clear path.

The ghost spider was extremely large and probably hiding in the canopy above. With its ability to become invisible, there was no point risking the room by myself. I would prefer for my aether to recover completely as well, and I wanted my companions nearby in case I made a mistake.

When I returned to the safe room, everyone turned to me with anticipation. "The ogre is dead," I announced, my voice steady. Only Glasha looked surprised. I distributed the thirty silver coins among them, choosing not to keep a single piece for myself. "Inside the reward chest, I also found a strength potion," I said, presenting the shimmering vial to Raelia. Her eyes widened in surprise, but she quickly masked her astonishment, accepting the gift with a nod of gratitude.

I sat on one of the benches and drew Boris's blade. If Glasha was going to try and use us, I had no qualms about using her. "Glasha, what can your spell tell me about this ..."

Chapter 289: She Looks Familiar

Glasha didn't object and gently took the dungeon blade as I placed it softly in her hands. Like all the weapons my companions and I carried, the ornate hilt and guard were obscured with tarnish and wrappings to hide their obvious artificed origins. Based on what I had seen among adventurers, this wasn't an uncommon practice.

"Dungeon forged," she said, inspecting the silvery length of the blade and running her finger down it. I watched the orc intently under the moss's light. Her efforts had also drawn the attention of the others. I was sure Mateo would be interested in getting the Primus's blade evaluated. She closed her eyes, and I didn't see any spell forms traced in the air, so the ability must be inscribed on her core as a spell form.

She didn't speak for long moments, and Mateo asked, "Did she start? Is she finished?"

Glasha smirked, her tusks protruding. "Unlike some people, I don't feel the need to rush things." Mateo backed away, flushing. Glasha opened her eyes, blinking them rapidly to adjust to the light. As she handed the blade back to me, she explained, "It is a young blade, about one hundred years old. Found in a reward chest after slaying a monstrous black dungeon troll. The blade is artificed to be nearly indestructible and never lose its edge."

I frowned, as that seemed pretty typical of all blades forged in dungeons. As I sheathed it, Glasha added slyly, "It also imbues the wearer with additional strength when he attacks. It is a minor effect, but you may have noticed your strikes land harder than normal. The blade has tasted the blood of many victims during its existence, some very recently. You killed the previous owner to claim it with malice in your heart."

She was clearly trying to demonstrate her skill. I nodded, but I hadn't noticed any increased strength when I used the blade. Still, I might have missed the effect and just believed it was the adrenaline of combat. "Thank you," I said, nodding.

"My fee is two gold," she said seriously, her grin gone and her hand extended.

The stunned look on my face made the orc cackle a raucous laugh, her benign feminine appearance disappearing. Now she looked like a suitable villain. "I jest with you, human. No charge for a friend." *We were friends now?*

Maveith shuffled forward uncertainly, ready to ask a question, but the orc woman beat him to it. "Yes, it is free for you, too, Maveith." She extended her hand, expecting the goliath to hand her his large hammer. Instead, he pulled the skinning knife from his belt and handed it to her.

Her eyebrow rose in surprise as she took the small blade. The grip was tightly wrapped in leather, and the length was slightly tarnished to hide the runic relief work. She didn't need to take as much time with this artifact. Her eyes flashed open, surprise clearly showing. "Where did you get this? The dungeon that forged this is ancient."

Maveith looked at me before he answered, not wanting to say the wrong thing. "The Shimmering Labyrinth in the Ruins of Caelora." I didn't see any reason to lie. The Esenhem elves and Bartiradians already knew of the dungeon's discovery.

"The artificing is immaculate. Much cleaner than younger dungeons." She handed it back to Maveith. "You have already harvested some interesting creatures with it. The blade responds to your will, cutting easier or dulling as needed. It is not indestructible, though, so treat it with care." She looked over the group, eyebrow raised. "Anyone else?"

I stopped the session, unsure if we were revealing too much. "I think we are done for now. Let's execute the ghost spider and harvest it," I said, standing. I checked my aether shield amulet, making sure it was recharged. Everyone gathered their things, and we walked to the final room.

As we passed through the ogre's room, people held their breath and covered their noses, but curiosity still took them close to the body. I had added a few wounds to the body to make it look like it had put up a fight. An experienced scout examining the body should think I had sliced the ogre's Achilles and then pierced its throat when it fell to its knees. There were other, less severe wounds I had added to the body as well.

Glasha paused and walked around the corpse, causing us to wait for her. "Not a lot of blood," she finally commented.

"It was a quick fight," I replied neutrally. She just grunted and joined us for the final chamber.

The forest chamber, with its massive spiderwebs draped in the trees, had a haunted feeling. It was also completely still and silent. The dark-blue ceiling of glowing moss gave it a late-night feel, but shadows dominated under the leafy canopies. "I can just burn down the trees," Raelia stated after we had all been staring up into the canopy from the safety of the corridor for a few minutes.

"The dungeon wouldn't let your fire spread," Glasha said dismissively.

Maveith voiced from the back, "Do you want me to enter and lure it out?"

"Are you volunteering to be the bait?" Mateo asked incredulously. Then, he muttered, more to himself than anyone else, "As long as it isn't me."

"No one needs to be bait," I stated, stepping into the chamber. "Raelia, fireball it when you can." The others followed me inside the room. I had channeled aether to my eyes, and the grayscale of my aether sight made it much easier to discern movement in the leaves above. Without wind, the only way the branches could move was under the weight of the spider guardian.

"I don't see anything," Mateo hissed nervously.

I tossed three common smoke pellets on the ground in front of me. The rapidly expanding clouds quickly thinned in the chamber, but there was enough remaining smoke to see movement in the disturbed air. "That was kind of clever," Raelia whispered.

I ignored her and pointed to the canopy. "There. It is still invisible but it is descending from that tree. Giant spiders are like eight-legged tables. You just have to remove most of the legs to topple them." A line of webbing spewed from where I indicated. The spider was apparently intelligent enough to understand it had been found. The line enlarged into a huge cloud of netting as it passed through the smoke. "Behind me!" I ordered, and the group scrambled behind me for cover. I could feel the heat on my back from Raelia forming a fireball.

The webbing reached us and completely encapsulated my air shield. I was sure Glasha had an epiphany, judging by her grunt of surprise. With its attack thwarted, the spider dropped the last thirty feet to the ground, and the earth churned into small fountains where it stepped as it raced forward.

Raelia's fireball raced over my shoulder and splashed into the path of the spider. The nearby webbing in the trees went up with the brilliant flash, and the spider was briefly outlined in the inferno. Slowly burning tendrils of webs now lit the room. This chamber was much larger than the lurker room, and Raelia's fireball was smaller, so a wave of heat only passed over us this time, with no concussive blast.

I could make out the spider, and it seemed dazed. "Sweep the legs!" I yelled to the others as I moved to engage. The spider's outline was barely visible after Raelia's fireball had charred its body, ruining its invisibility. I was the first to hack into a leg, getting a satisfying cracking feedback as Boris's blade significantly shortened one leg. Maveith's hammer cracked a second, throwing the dazed monstrosity off-balance.

It gave up its invisibility, revealing a massive arachnid towering over ten feet in the air. It tucked its abdomen under itself and spewed more webbing. I dodged clear, but a rushing Mateo was caught in the blast, quickly becoming entangled and tripping. As he rolled on the ground, he unfortunately cocooned himself.

"Raelia, free Mateo!" I yelled as I dodged a descending leg. After it penetrated deep into the ground where I had stood, I hacked at it, trying to focus on the sword's strength enhancement. I still could not detect a difference, but the blade severed the limb easily enough. Overcoming the fireball effects but unsteady on its five remaining legs, the spider attacked Maveith with a lunging bite. The goliath stood defensively, using his hammer to hold the creature at bay.

With its attention away from me, I took out another leg, bringing the main body to the ground. I thrust my blade into the side of its lowered head and twisted, causing it to spasm in its death throes. I wrenched the blade out, widening the wound, and backed away, letting the creature perish from the loss of its blue ichor. I thought it had been an efficient fight, and more importantly, no one got injured.

Glasha looked impressed as she approached the spider. "You work well together. I felt kind of useless but enjoyed the ride." She cast a sideways glance at Mateo. "If you have any other artifacts you wish me to read, I would be happy to."

Mateo was peeling webbing off his armor, only for it to stick to his arms and hands in a mess, but he asked, "Can you do my sword?"

"Good, Mateo, take Glasha back to the entry room. We will wait a few hours there before exiting. You can have your sword identified." Glasha looked suspiciously at me, since I was clearly trying to get rid of her again.

"My aether has fully recovered. I can do it here," Glasha offered in a friendly tone. Mateo, not understanding my reasoning, was trying to clean the spider webbing from the blade to hand to her.

"No, wait for us in the entry room," I ordered sharply. It was a little out of character for me, but I was anxious to harvest the spider's essence quickly. I was almost positive it would be the illusion affinity. Mateo realized why I wanted Glasha out of the way and started to usher her away. I added, "Take the reward chest with you and divide up the coin."

The chests in this dungeon had all been simple oak chests. Maveith located it among the trees, and I pretended to work on harvesting the spinnerets. After Mateo and Glasha left, I relaxed. "She has probably already figured it out," Raelia said, checking to make sure they were gone.

The collector appeared in my hand. "She hasn't seen me use it, and she can't use her spying spell in the dungeon." Finally, the collector didn't struggle to condense the aetheric smoke into a sphere. Disappointingly, it was still a minor essence, but it was of the illusion affinity. It would improve my aether sight slightly.

Raelia looked bored. Maveith was exploring the flora in the chamber, looking for something useful among the maze of webs. "Do you think we should take the job to escort Glasha's acquaintance?" I asked.

Raelia was indifferent, answering with a shrug, "I don't like that she used Mateo. He may be a Telhian, but I kind of like him." That comment surprised me. "We should also be wary of becoming involved in orc politics. They don't like outsiders meddling, even if it is on behalf of one of their own."

Maveith had an opinion. "It would make it a lot easier to leave the Caliphate with Zorana if she was freed."

"We have other ways," I reminded him. "Can we trust the word of a cleric?" I asked Raelia.

"No," she said, shocking me. "The word of a warlord is their honor, and they will follow it as long as you are honorable yourself. The clerics are less constrained. They won't lie or cheat you, but words can be interpreted many different ways, especially in their language." Having just started to learn their language, I could see the truth of that statement.

"We will hear them out, then. If we tell them no, without listening, they may make our mission more difficult." I cracked open the spider and worked out the spinneret before we left to join Mateo and Glasha in the entry room.

Glasha offered to sell the spinneret for us, so I handed her the slimy capsule. Mateo handed everyone seven silver coins and proudly displayed a silver mirror he had found in the chest.

Glasha explained what the artifact was. "It is a simple messaging device. You channel aether into it and the device will hold your image and sound indefinitely, playing over and over inside the reflection. It can be used again by channeling aether. They are popular heirlooms for parents to give their children and grandchildren advice long after they have died. It can hold one message about an hour long, if used properly."

It was a magical recording device. Mateo handed it to me, and I kept it safe, not wanting seven years of bad luck right now. Mateo was also proud of his weapon, as Glasha had revealed it was a spelled blade capable of deflecting aether constructs, and he was eager to test it. Raelia offered to help him by targeting him with fireballs, but he suddenly became less excited about testing its abilities.

According to Maveith, we exited the dungeon after half a day inside. I went first, half expecting to be assaulted by the guards or a group of irate orcs. Six new guards in plate stood watch. A wrinkly, white-haired orc asked, "Is your delve complete, adventurer?"

"It is," I said as the others joined me. He just grunted as another guard recorded our exit in a logbook. Seeing that we would not be detained or attacked, I led us back to the city.

We celebrated our delve in the Adventurers Hall. The spinneret served as proof of completing the dungeon. The orc adventurers suddenly accepted us and we didn't need to pay for drinks that night. Glasha seemed to think Mynasha would arrive late that evening, so we waited and drank, and waited, and drank.

The cleric who eventually entered the Adventurers Hall well after midnight was struggling to walk. She was clearly an inexperienced rider and had just spent too much time in the saddle rushing to get here. She scanned the room and quickly settled her eyes on Glasha, who had already raised a hand unsteadily.

As she approached our table, something clicked: a familiarity. I recognized this cleric, although I might be mistaken, since orcs tend to look quite similar. However, I was nearly certain I had seen this one mostly nude on the bow of the lead ship of the orc fleet that had attacked Varvao.

Mynasha ignored us and sat heavily in an open seat next to Glasha. She let out a pained grunt and then a relieved sigh as she settled. Her eyes stared defiantly at those in the common room who had been judging her appearance and saddle-worn state. The orc adventurers quickly found their game, food, or drink more interesting, averting their eyes. An elf's and a dwarf's eyes lingered a little longer on her before turning away.

"Heal me," she said quietly to Glasha. Glasha's hand went under the table to rest on Mynasha's thigh. A look of relief and bliss flooded the road-weary orc woman. She appeared younger than Glasha, but I was not the best person to discern the age of an orc. I caught a snicker from the dwarf as he misinterpreted the action.

"Thank you, and I see you were able to keep them here. They don't look that special. I hope my efforts in getting here were not wasted." She was speaking Orcish and probably assumed we could not understand her. Glasha couldn't contain her grin. This was going to be an interesting conversation. Still, it was Mynasha who would have to convince us to help her, and so far, the answer was no.

In Orcish, I replied, "You don't look that special either. What makes you think you can become the Supreme Cleric?" Mynasha winced, realizing I could understand her, but recovered immediately.

Glasha cackled a soft laugh at Mynasha's surprise. "I have been teaching the Telhian our language. He is actually a remarkably quick learner." She winked at Mateo. "The others are quick at other things. The elf already speaks our language passably."

Cleric Mynasha settled back in her chair, appraising us one at a time with fresh eyes. Mateo slouched in his chair, and Benito just looked confused since he couldn't understand anything. Blaze had retired for the evening, thinking the cleric wouldn't show tonight—he would owe Benito a large copper in the morning. Raelia had a shadow of distrust on her face.

Mynasha straightened, a confidence radiating from her. "I am the most powerful cleric of my generation," she said, her voice edged with pride. "But unlike the others who covet the title of Supreme for prestige and influence, I care about the people—their safety, their future." Her words rang with genuine conviction.

Glasha hissed through her teeth, "I've told you time and again—it's about more than power and conviction, girl. You have to win over the Elders, and most of them already have their favorites." She gestured toward me with a sharp tilt of her head. "This one can serve as your First and accompany you to the Choosing. I've watched him closely—he's more than capable. Maybe even more so than the warlords backing the other candidates."

"He is not a warlord; they wouldn't allow him at the Choosing," Mynasha said doubtfully.

Glasha waved her off and said, "There is precedent in the past. An elf served as Cleric Jurasha's First, and Cleric Fernasha brought a human twenty years ago."

Mynasha searched her memory. "And neither of them claimed the Supreme's seat," Mynasha countered astutely.

A lot was being said that I didn't fully understand—some of it likely slipping through the cracks of translation. "Could we speak Telhian," I asked, "so my companions can follow the conversation?"

Glasha smirked. "Mynasha doesn't know Telhian," she said, clearly amused.

Mynasha shot her a glare and replied in Telhian, "If I don't know it, that's your failure as a teacher. I know enough of our enemy's tongue to speak with them on the battlefield."

Her pronunciation was clumsy, the words slurred awkwardly around her tusks, but still understandable. "You still have not explained enough of what this task entails. It seems it is a lot more than just escorting her to the selection of a new Supreme."

I directed my statement at Glasha, as Mynasha appeared to be far younger and a babe at delving into the political arena. So far, she was coming off as overconfident and brash. I already knew she was powerful, since she had been on the lead warship that invaded the Empire.

"Not here," Glasha said, standing and looking at the curious adventurers at the other tables. "We can discuss it in one of your rooms."

We all ended up crammed into Maveith's room minutes later. He had the largest room and enough seating with his oversized bed to hold everyone. Blaze, blurry-eyed from being woken, joined us.

Glasha and Mynasha shared a bench against the wall. Two chairs and Maveith's bed seated my troupe, who faced them. It was Glasha who explained everything to us in Telhian. "The Supreme went missing during the reclamation of lands from the Telhian Empire. His enemies thought the expedition's success would give him too much power with the people."

"I don't understand. A victory was a threat?" I said, confused but interested.

"Although the Caliphate looks unified, it is not, much like many other nations." Glasha took a deep breath. "Among the clerics, there are always those who want more power and control. The warlords always want to rule larger cities and have more prominent slaves to display their prowess, by their very nature."

She held up three fingers. "The Boutan Caliphate consists of three orc clans. The Boutan orcs, the Shagar orcs, and the Molnemoac orcs. The Molnemoac orcs were once a powerful nation before the Telhian Empire took their lands and forced them into exile in the Caliphate. Over centuries, they integrated into our society but always longed to reclaim their lost lands. When the Supreme's expedition succeeded, everyone knew the Molnemoac orcs would be beholden to him, shifting the power among the Caliphate clerics. Others did not want to see that happen, so an…accident was arranged. But that does not leave this room."

Glasha was being very forward with the problems of the Caliphate to earn our trust. Much more than I expected. I would not have trusted strangers with such inner political turmoil after just two weeks in their company. She probably didn't realize Benito and Mateo had trouble with secrets.

"What about the Shagar orcs?" Blaze asked. He sounded tired but was leaning forward, interested in the discourse.

Glasha nodded and explained in a scholarly tone, "I am descended from the Shagar. The Shagar orcs were conquered by the Boutan orcs some two thousand years ago. At first, they were an enslaved people, but Supreme Lazgasha declared slavery of one orc over another orc to be forbidden. Only those of other races can be subjugated and forced to serve the warlords now. The Shagar are now mostly farmers, ranchers, and craftsmen with a few becoming Pathfinders, elites, or warlords."

I noticed the veins and muscles in Maveith's arms bulge as he clenched his fists in anger. He was smart enough not to yell, but talking so casually about slavery had made him angry.

I was surprised that Raelia had stayed quiet during this interview. But I wasn't sure if we were interviewing Mynasha or if she was interviewing us. Raelia asked a little brusquely, "You still have not revealed why you need us and what the danger is."

The two orcs looked at each other. I was not surprised that Glasha was the one who continued to explain. She was a historian and a diplomat. She also kept her emotions in check much better than Mynasha. I would call her mature if not for the mischievousness underlying her subterfuge with Mateo. "Mynasha needs an escort to the Choosing. While no one would dishonor themselves by trying to kill her, I expect they would delay her and prevent her from participating."

"Once the Choosing starts, a candidate can have one First at her side. The Elders will issue challenges to narrow down the candidates. Mynasha can only be assisted by her First during the challenges. Then, if she is chosen to be the Supreme, she still needs to complete the Warlord Dungeon. This is usually just a formality, as the First would be a warlord and would have already completed it."

"I thought the thirteenth dungeon was a solo dungeon?" I interjected.

"No. It is called The Demonic Lair and up to four can enter. A warlord is supposed to defeat the four lairs inside alone, but that has changed with time. Now they just need to defeat two of the lairs. The Supreme limits the access of those who wish to challenge the dungeon to become a warlord, lead the orcs, and own others. If the Supreme favors a warlord, he will allow companions to enter with the warlord challenger." Glasha finished talking and reclined against the wall on the bench.

Mynasha appeared nervous. Either because of the information Glasha was telling us or because she was worried I would say no.

"If there is no Supreme, who controls access to the dungeon now?" I asked.

"The Elders," Mynasha spat angrily as she interjected. "They are some of the eldest of the clerics of the Caliphate, but also some of the weakest in power."

Glasha hissed at her companion, "Don't speak such foolishness aloud." With a little sarcasm and snark, she added, "They were chosen for their *wisdom* and *judiciousness*."

I did not know if Mynasha would be a good leader for her people. But I was not invested in her people. Glasha, on the other hand, could use what she knew about our goals against us, but having gotten to know her over two weeks, I did not think she would. I stated pointedly, "I don't see the benefit in it for us."

Mynasha fidgeted, her face clouding in frustration. "You wasted my time summoning me here. I should have been riding to Warlord Dekish's estate," Mynasha said, with an Orcish curse attached.

"The old bull would have you bedding his son or himself in return for his support. And he is no longer the warrior he once was. He probably has trouble getting his sword up these days," Glasha said contemptuously.

Glasha's harsh assessment of Mynasha's prospects caused a silence. "It is nice to know that orc politics do not differ much from elven or human," Raelia said unexpectedly. "Where and when is the Choosing?"

Mynasha leaned forward, studying the small elf woman as if truly seeing her for the first time. There was a spark of hope on her face. When she spoke, her voice carried a conciliatory tone. Her gaze flicked between Raelia and me, searching for an ally or perhaps influence. Did she believe Raelia could sway my decision?

"The Supreme's estate lies in the northernmost district of Becar," she said, her tone pressing. "Twelve days from now. All the warlords and clerics of consequence will be there."

"The Warlord Rhuuk of Agurtra will be there?" Maveith asked vehemently, after being quiet for the conversation.

"Agurtra is not far from the capital, so yes, he is likely to be there with his entourage—and some of his slaves. He might even be serving as a First for one of the candidates," Glasha said shrewdly. Mateo had likely revealed the warlord we sought. He didn't make eye contact with me when I looked at him.

"It is 350 miles to Becar," Raelia said, thinking aloud. "That is thirty miles a day to get there before they select a new Supreme." I was confused as to why Raelia seemed to be siding with the orcs.

"I know. I was sixty miles closer, two days ago," Mynasha said, looking at Glasha with annoyance.

"It is manageable. I have done more, and I can heal us and the horses. It is also on the main trade road the entire way and closer to 320 miles. Doing forty miles a day or more on the road will not be difficult," Glasha said with her tusky smile.

Satisfied that we had heard enough, I said firmly, "I'll speak with my companions—alone."

I gestured for the orcs to leave. They exchanged a glance, then walked out the door. I had no doubt Glasha would be eavesdropping through whatever spell form she had. I scanned the room, waiting for feedback. Blaze was the first to speak. "It puts us in the right direction, and we'll be traveling with two Caliphate clerics. Riding hard with them will make us look less suspicious."

Mateo chimed in from his spot, sprawled across Maveith's bed. "I think we can trust Glasha," he said softly, eyes fixed on the ceiling. I rolled my eyes at Mateo, but he didn't see it.

"I think Glasha has addled his brain with magic," Raelia said good-humoredly.

"Does that hurt?" Benito asked Mateo seriously, not realizing Raelia was jesting. We didn't need this conversation to hinge on Mateo's sexual exploits.

"What about Mynasha? Impressions?" I asked, turning back to discussing the job.

"I don't think we should get involved in orc politics. Let's use them to reach the capital and then go our own way," Blaze suggested. It made sense, but if we were escorting them there, I doubted we would be free of them so easily. Especially since I appeared to be Mynasha's only hope.

"If she can free Zorana, I say we do it. I can serve as her First for this Choosing," Maveith stated, adamantly in favor of accepting the job. I don't think Glasha had the goliath in mind to stand with Mynasha, but I wouldn't tell him that at the moment.

"Raelia? Benito?" I prompted them for feedback.

Benito had been paying attention and was slightly surprised I was asking for his input. He appeared deep in thought. "If it gets us closer to Maveith's sister, we should do it," he stated simply.

"I don't trust clerics," Raelia said thoughtfully. I guess I was just bad at reading women, because I thought she favored taking the job and helping the clerics. "But I do like Glasha," she said, surprising me again. "It might be good to have a cleric or two owe you favors in the future."

In the end, this was my decision. All eyes looked to me to make the final call. With the weight of leadership on my shoulders, I announced, "Fine. We will escort the clerics to the capital."

It was early morning, but I decided we should leave immediately. The Caliphate had no portals, and time was tight to get the cleric to the Choosing. I also wanted to keep anyone off-balance who might try to stop us from getting Mynasha there. "Saddle the horses; we will ride out of the gates before sunrise." My companions didn't question me and went to pack their things in their rooms.

I found the two orc clerics in the hallway, waiting for our decision. "We will escort you to Becar, but we are not committed to helping you in your bid to become the Supreme. One hundred gold for the job." I announced our fee, thinking it was slightly unreasonable for a 320-mile escort, but I figured they would pay it.

"That is not acceptable!" Mynasha started, but Glasha stopped her, putting her arm on her shoulder.

"It's fine, I will pay. Mynasha doesn't have the means," she said, explaining Mynasha's outrage. "I'm sure once you get to know how charming Mynasha is during the trip, you'll help her in the Choosing." Humor colored her words, but I was not going to be swayed easily like Mateo.

I was already packed and walked outside with the clerics to find a massive, smoky-colored mount. Mynasha's horse almost matched Maveith's in size. She hadn't even unsaddled it when she had arrived some two hours ago, leaving it tied outside the Adventurers Hall without access to water.

As Mynasha approached, the dark-gray stallion snapped its head and bit her shoulder, knocking her to the ground. They clearly did not have a friendly relationship after the mount had been pushed to get here. Mynasha held in a yelp of pain as she got up to strike the mount, but I seized her hand. Her pale-gray eyes burned as she looked at me, not knowing how to react.

I took the reins from her other hand. "You abused this mount getting here, and I can see the saddle sores. We can spare a few minutes to rub him down and have

Glasha heal the injuries." Mynasha narrowed her eyes at me but relented, stepping away. I rubbed the neck of the horse and snuck an apple into my hand. I led it to a fresh trough of water, and while it drank greedily, I unsaddled it. As I rubbed the mount down, the others exited the Hall and went to the stables to prepare our horses.

Mynasha's mount wasn't a warhorse, but he was a fine young riding horse with a strong personality. After I rubbed out his coat, Glasha healed the saddle wounds, and he calmed down. I checked his hooves and shoes before saddling him again. Now hydrated and chewing happily on a second apple, he was ready to go and became friendlier toward Mynasha.

Mynasha had stood back and watched me work the entire time, judging me in some way. Benito walked Ginger to me and handed me her reins. After an apple tax, I was in my saddle. The dim light of the streetlamps was all that lit our way as one pony and seven horses' hooves clattered on the stone pavers, taking my growing party toward the northern gate.

Chapter 291: Strength of Giants

The gatehouse was open, and two orcs in hardened leather armor stood watch. They had long spears and became alert as we passed them, studying us. Our clerics did not hide their natures, Glasha's brilliant red hair on display, and I was sure the guards would report our passing. Glowstones appeared among my companions, giving us a soft halo of light. Blaze and Raelia rode out front, while Benito and Mateo rode in the rear. Maveith rode next to Glasha while I ended up next to Mynasha.

We rode in silence till the sun cracked the horizon. The glowstones vanished into their small black bags, and I ordered an increase in pace. We passed farmers' carts heading toward the city's markets for a while before the road cleared of all traffic.

Mynasha broke our silence—our pair was the only quiet one among the group. "Are you really as capable as Glasha claims, Telhian?"

"You can call me Eryk," I said evenly. "And I'm not Telhian. I was conscripted into their Legion against my will. But yes, I can handle myself. Your magic during the Varvao invasion was impressive."

She shifted, visibly bristling. Her sleek black hair snapped as she turned sharply to face me. "Did Glasha tell you that?" Her voice held a wary edge—was she wondering if I cared because I was in the Legion?

Glasha twisted in her saddle to glance back at us, surprise flickering across her face. "I didn't tell him," she said, studying me with renewed curiosity. "How did you know Mynasha was with the Supreme's Annexation Armada?"

I paused, weighing whether it was worth holding back. But really, what harm was there in a little bragging? "I was scouting the fleet as it passed through Kraken Bay. Saw quite a bit of Mynasha ... and her handiwork."

Mynasha's brow lifted, intrigued. "You were one of the Hounds that harassed our fleet?" she asked, her tone a mix of surprise and curiosity. Either she hadn't noticed my veiled comment about her being nearly naked—or she simply wasn't the type to be embarrassed.

I heard the steady trot of Mateo's and Benito's horses drawing closer—they were listening now, too.

"I was a Hound," I admitted, keeping my voice even. "But I hold no loyalty to the Empire. I did fight a Pathfinder who called himself Rakuh of the Sun Shadow Clan, when they made landfall."

Mynasha's expression shifted—first surprise, then a flicker of grief, quickly buried beneath simmering anger. "Your pack of Hounds killed honorable orcs," she said tersely. "Rakuh was the patriarch of his clan. Well liked among the people and clerics. We didn't even know he had fallen until we reached the walls of Varvao." Mynasha's mind was turning as she recalled the events of the attack. "Was your pack also behind the ambush on the Silent Night Clan?" she added, no longer angry, but sounding curious to solve a mystery.

"I don't know," I said carefully. "Rakuh was the only orc I spoke with."

It was a partial truth. I suspected she was referring to the Pathfinders who had discovered my hiding spot—wedged inside a boulder after the fleet sailed up the Varvao River. But I wasn't ready to give her more. My eagerness to brag might get me in more trouble than it was worth if Rakuh was as popular as she had said.

A silent tension hung thick between us as we continued riding. Eventually, we rotated riding partners. She ended up beside Glasha, and for the next few hours, the two spoke in low, rapid Orcish, too quietly for me to make out their words—but not their mood. Mynasha was clearly troubled. I suspected I had become the subject of that conversation.

Mynasha and Glasha kept casting glances my way as we rode north—measured, quiet looks that felt like pieces of a conversation I wasn't invited to. They were plotting, that much was clear. And with each passing mile, my willingness to help them after reaching Becar eroded.

When we stopped for a midday meal, Mynasha finally gave voice to the question that had clearly been nagging at her. "How did your Hound pack bring down Trakor's roc—Chaostail?"

Aware of Glasha's disdain for Warlord Trakor, she leaned in closely to seek the truth. Both clerics desired to uncover what truly happened amid the chaos surrounding the death of one of the prominent warlords.

I kept my response vague. "He was overconfident. Came in too low and too fast. From what I saw, the roc's wing clipped something during the dive—it spiraled out of control and crashed." I let the words hang in the air. I didn't mention that I was the one who had crippled the beast. Glasha and Mynasha might not seek revenge—but I had no doubt others would if they learned I was party to it.

Glasha's response was cool and introspective. "It was Trakor's death that tipped the balance. With his strongest supporter confirmed dead, it became possible to move against the last Supreme."

"I don't understand," I admitted. "How was the Supreme killed? And why would anyone want to become the Supreme, knowing they're painting a target on their own back?"

Glasha answered for Mynasha again, her Orcish fast, clipped, and sharp-edged. I caught only fragments, but tone gave me clues. "I won't tell you how the Supreme was removed," Glasha said finally, in Telhian. "Even speculation could come back to haunt me. But he was old, arrogant, and blind to how angry he made others when he took credit for their successes. He also blamed others for his failures—much like Warlord Trakor was prone to do."

Mynasha exhaled, her voice composed. "The Supreme isn't just a title. They are the spiritual heart of the Caliphate. The Supreme's word is law. Clerics and warlords alike bow to his judgment. Much like your Telhian Emperor, he believed his authority made him invincible. And like your Emperor, that belief was his downfall."

Glasha addressed me with respect. "I suggest we continue riding. Mynasha can assume your language lessons in exchange for you improving her Telhian." Glasha's obvious ploy was to get me to know Mynasha better. I was fine with additional language lessons, but I did not think I would be swayed by Mynasha. Surprisingly, Mynasha was much less arrogant as a teacher, but she lacked patience. Fortunately, I was a fast learner.

In school, I consistently struggled with learning foreign languages, and even struggled in English classes. Either my consumption of essences or the dreamscape amulet had made the learning process much easier for me than before. I pushed the group until late evening on the first day, making over fifty miles according to Glasha, who was watching road markers.

After consulting with Glasha, I opted to stay in the smaller towns along the road. There was no formal inn in these small farming communities, but older farmers had a few extra rooms that they rented out to travelers. Glasha was very persuasive when dealing with these orcs, and we were never required to pay, but I left a few large coppers behind in my room anyway.

Raelia once again showed her displeasure with me for taking lessons from another orc. I got to see her angry countenance during the daily ride and in the evenings, as she no longer had Baldo to distract her. Maveith did his best to serve as an intermediary, and Blaze became her favorite partner to ride with.

We rode four days without incident before encountering a roadblock with eleven mounted orcs, tattoos covering their necks and the visible parts of their arms. "Warlords?" I asked Glasha as we assessed the situation from afar. They were clearly awaiting us, as evidenced by their intense focus and their horses' restless dancing.

Glasha studied them with her spell form before answering. "Warlord Sutra is the warlord among them. The rest are elites that answer to him. Sutra is aligned with one of the Elders. I don't see any Pathfinders among them, which is a good sign that those clans have not become involved." Glasha let out a long exhale. "We have a history. I will talk with him; maybe he will let us pass uncontested." Doubt laced her tone as she kicked her pony forward.

Before she could ride off, I joined her, urging Ginger to follow but signaling for my companions to remain. Coming alongside, I asked, "If there is a fight, can we kill them without consequences?"

"Only if they initiate it. And they won't," she stated confidently as we rode together. Behind us, Blaze, Maveith, and Raelia readied their bows as the tension started to escalate. Glasha's white pony pulled up in front of the warriors blocking the road. I studied the orcs' stern, seasoned faces. They did not look happy to be here, or to see us.

The largest of the group stepped forward—broad-shouldered and imposing, with a heavy gold chain draped around his neck, each link set with colorful stones. His voice was deep and disappointed. "I expected more from you, Glasha Mistborn. A month ago, you told me you wouldn't get involved. And yet here you are—parading your candidate toward the Choosing." He looked at me disdainfully.

Glasha's jaw tightened. Her response was sharp, immediate. "You used to say my mind shifted with the wind. Well, the wind has changed. What I do with my time is none of your concern."

"Sister," he said, the word weighted with both admonition and familiarity, "you know better than to defy the will of the Elders. All your efforts will come to nothing. You're only making more enemies—something you already have no shortage of." Siblings? I glanced between them but saw no obvious resemblance.

Then he turned his gaze on me, his expression curling into contempt. "And this," he said, gesturing toward me with visible disdain. "This is who you've chosen to stand beside Mynasha?"

Glasha practically laughed. "He can understand you, brother. Perhaps you would be willing to step aside after a contest of honor?"

The large orc laughed thoughtfully, his armor rattling. "Telhians have no honor to contest!"

Glasha gave me an apologetic look before speaking. "He defeated Rakuh of the Sun Shadow Clan," Glasha challenged. I suddenly felt stupid for revealing my duel to Glasha and Mynasha. Now, she was using the information against me. Sutra's men obviously knew Rakuh, and they were a mixture of impressed and discontented, judging by their murmurs.

One of the men barked, "I will fight him to regain Rakuh's honor!" He was the next-largest man after Warlord Sutra.

Warlord Sutra snarled at Glasha and anger flared in his eyes. I could tell he didn't want to fight today and had been manipulated into it by Glasha. I knew how he felt. "No, I will beat down the Telhian for the Sun Shadow. I, Warlord Sutra of the Mistborn Clan, challenge this—"

"Eryk Marko of Fortuna's Chosen," Glasha interjected.

The Warlord growled, "Eryk Marko of Fortuna's Chosen. Do you stake yourself to an honorable contest for passage?"

"I don't understand what is happening," I hissed angrily at Glasha. She would have to answer for this after the fight. "I don't appreciate you volunteering me for this …"

She moved her pony closer. "It is a combat of skill. The first to yield loses. I am *paying* you well for circumstances like these," she reminded me. Damn, she had me there. She explained more softly. "It is a lot less perilous than if our two companies engaged each other." I had to agree on that point, as we were outnumbered two to one, but we did have three spell casters.

"Rules?" I conceded her point that I had asked for a large sum to escort Mynasha safely.

"No spell forms, and the first to yield loses. Try not to kill him, or you will lose honor—and our mother would be upset. Remember, I can heal injuries to the flesh, so you do not need to hold back." She said the last loud enough for the warlord to hear. It didn't rattle Sutra and he dismounted. The warlord was half a head taller than me and much wider at the shoulder.

I looked at the petite Glasha and then at the warlord. He had grown in stature, standing on solid ground, and his muscles flexed under his tattooed neck and arms. "You two came from the same mother?" I questioned incredulously.

"Different fathers, but yes, we share a mother. You still need to accept the challenge." She smiled contentedly as her plan came to fruition.

I suppose this fight was what we were getting paid for. "I accept the honor combat for passage," I stated loudly for the orcs and my companions to hear. If I lost, did that mean the job was over? Not that I planned to lose.

Glasha got serious. "I will monitor the fight and ensure neither warrior uses aether!" Sutra and his elites seemed to accept the pronouncement, and I had a feeling Glasha would not let me cheat even though I was fighting for her.

The warlord did something I did not expect: he pulled a potion from his belt, popped the wax seal with his thumb, and downed it. I recognized the vial and the lingering smell in the air. It was a Pathfinder's stamina and alertness brew. He was obviously preparing for a prolonged fight. The rules did not make sense to me. "We can use potions?"

"Yes, and runic armor is fine, just no spell forms. It would be best if you stored your aether shield amulet. It is a battle of warriors, not magic," Glasha responded. I was impressed that she had realized I had the aether shield amulet from observing me in the dungeon.

I had my own stamina potions, but I also had other potions. I sorted through what I had available in my mind, and only one potion made sense. Warlords were the strongest warriors in the Caliphate, and ending this fight quickly was wise. His greatest strengths were his tattoos, which enhanced his physical prowess, but apparently, he would not be able to use them.

A dungeon potion appeared in my hand, and I broke the seal before the warlord could discern its purpose. I had only read up on its effects, and this was my first time using such a potion. I only knew that you needed to consume the entire potion or you would only get a fraction of its power. I downed the vial and immediately felt my muscles heat and swell under its spreading effects.

My heart thudded as my body suddenly required more blood to fuel my temporarily increased muscle mass. My only miscalculation was that my adventurer's armor suddenly got very tight, forcing me to loosen a few buckles quickly.

It was the giant's strength potion I had gotten from the owlbear reward chest in the Shimmering Labyrinth. The potion lasted about ten minutes and would give me the strength equal to a stone giant for that time. After the potion expired, I would be left in a miserable state, requiring a large amount of food to recover and for my muscles to be healed from the strain. I was not certain if the ring of sustenance would counter this hangover effect, but I guessed I would find out in ten minutes.

My steps felt light, and the dungeon blade felt weightless as I drew it. I removed my shield from Ginger's saddlebag and tapped her rump to return to the others. She looked at me momentarily before trotting to Maveith. The warlord suddenly appeared less confident as I faced him. The potion and my runic weapon had given him pause. His men remained mounted but formed a large, rough circle around us. At Glasha's motion, my own companions came forward to join the circle. Benito was already trying to get one of the orc elites to place a bet, navigating through the language barrier. Blaze and Raelia we talking animatedly about my chances. I had other things to focus on.

The strength potion made me feel invincible as I faced the warlord. His weapon was a two-handed bastard sword with tremendous length, its blade reaching five feet. I recognized it as a runic weapon, just not dungeon-forged. "When do we begin?" I asked my opponent, who was studying my footwork carefully. I had been stepping casually so as not to reveal my skill.

"We already have," he grunted, raising his massive blade in both hands and taking quick, controlled steps forward. I sidestepped to his right, reading his dominant hand as his left. His blade whistled through the air in a horizontal arc at waist height, forcing me to retreat or be bisected. After the blade passed in front of me, I shifted my weight off my back foot and rushed forward.

He only had two choices in my mind. Spin and do a 360-degree turn to bring his heavy blade back around, or retreat himself. Instead, he surprised me, taking one hand off his blade and attempting to block my sword with his bracers. Boris's blade cut into the greaves, but they were only covered in leather and the blade scraped across the metal underneath. The silvery metal I briefly glimpsed told me he was concealing runic armor.

I was surprised only momentarily as I punched out with my shield into his sternum. The blow was solid, thudding loudly on impact, and much stronger than I had anticipated. The warlord stumbled backward to regain his footing. This strength potion almost felt like cheating.

I didn't let him recover, pursuing his retreat as he interposed his massive blade between us to give him time to recover. I used my shield to force the blade away before he could regain his defensive footing for leverage. Boris's dungeon blade stabbed forward as I lunged, pushing power from my hips through the length of the blade, piercing his abdominal armor and penetrating almost all the way through his torso.

I heard Raelia cheer first, some shocked gasps from the orcs following after, but my focus didn't leave the fight as I quickly pivoted the blade's tip inside his body and removed it before stepping back. The warlord was having trouble standing, and blood was leaking rapidly onto his leggings from the wound. He would need to be healed quickly, or the stomach bile would cause extensive damage. The whole engagement had taken about five seconds and it was already over. If he chose to fight on, he would die from internal bleeding. I was probably just as shocked at the brief fight as he was, but I tried not to show it.

Sutra looked at his sister instead of me. I couldn't read his expression through his pain, and Glasha didn't look smug. Instead, she pitied him. Maybe their relationship wasn't as antagonistic as I had perceived. "I concede to Eryk Marko of Fortuna's Chosen," he forced out with difficulty while one hand covered the hole in his armor. Glasha immediately dismounted to heal him. I cleaned my blade in the grass and returned to take Ginger's reins from Maveith.

Raelia looked the most satisfied of my companions. Mynasha had a look of shock on her face at my prowess, her opinion of me elevating. Benito hissed, "You didn't give me enough time to get a bet in place." Blaze, Maveith, and Mateo just congratulated me on my victory.

Glasha's healing was weak, so it took her a long time to heal her brother. They talked quietly while she worked on him. The strength potion wore off, and my incredible feeling of invincibility faded. Every muscle was sore as I directed healing through my spell form. I hadn't exerted myself, so the damage to my muscles was not terrible.

When Glasha finally finished, he mounted his horse, and his warriors left with the warlord. "Will we have to do that again?" I asked as she joined us.

She looked at me, a little annoyed. "You defeated him too quickly in front of his warriors. You took a lot of honor from him today." She sighed. "At least if word spreads, others will be hesitant to challenge our progress."

I didn't understand orc culture. Was Glasha blaming me for winning? As we rode away, I missed the feeling of power the potion had given me. I yearned to feel it again, and I fantasized about returning to the Shimmering Labyrinth to collect more.

Chapter 292: Exiled Elder

Mynasha found herself riding next to me as I devoured some salted candied nuts. It was taking a fair amount of aether to heal from the potion, and my ring of sustenance had not dulled my appetite. I wasn't sure if my convergence spell form to get the most from essences also extended to the strength potion. There might be some truth in that speculation, given how much aether I gathered from dungeon aether restoratives. Maybe it was just dungeon potions, as I don't think the effect carried over from alchemist-brewed potions. I couldn't recall if dungeon-brewed potions worked better on me than alchemist-brewed.

Mynasha interrupted my wandering thoughts. "It was an impressive victory."

"He was too aggressive in his first attack. He should have tested my defenses and speed before committing," I said dismissively. My strength was so ridiculous that it wouldn't have mattered, but I was still used to analyzing the fight and putting myself in my opponent's shoes.

She didn't have a response and we rode in silence. She didn't even offer to continue our Orcish lessons. Before we were about to cycle pairings, she said, "I find you acceptable to serve as my First." She paused for a breath. "I would be honored to have you stand with me through the Trials."

I didn't have time to respond before she cycled back to ride with Benito, who quickly tested her patience with stories of his entertaining exploits. I should have been paired with Blaze next, but Glasha maneuvered her pony to take his spot, and he didn't object, staying where he was at the front.

I didn't have to wait long before she revealed her purpose. I thought it was going to be pressing Mynasha on me after she had just begged me to help her. "I know an old cleric a few miles off the road ahead where we can stay."

I shook my head, thinking that it would give her enemies more time to place obstacles in our path. "I would rather we push through. A few miles would add hours to the journey."

Her jaw clenched a little. "It would be beneficial for Mynasha to talk with Cleric Tarnasha before the Choosing." At least she hadn't made it sound like an order. It was more of a request.

I had apparently earned the respect of both clerics. "Is that how all clerics are named? Adding -asha to the end of their names?" I asked, not committing to the detour.

"When we are recognized, we choose our own name. Usually, it derives from our birth name. 'Asha' means spiritual guardian of the people. Before I was recognized as a cleric, my name was Glorza. It basically means runt of the litter." She laughed to herself at some private joke.

I nodded at the information, as it reminded me of other religious orders that allowed name changes with promotions. I let out a slow breath. "How important to her success is meeting the cleric?"

She looked back to make sure Mynasha was occupied with Benito before continuing. "Tarnasha was an Elder, and also went through a Choosing as a candidate himself, long ago. He can give her wisdom and tell her what to expect of the Elders."

"I am guessing he wasn't chosen to be the Supreme," I said rhetorically.

"No. He was expelled from the Elders as well. Or, I should say, they didn't accept him back. He was not the strongest candidate, but I do believe he was the wisest and had the people's interests at heart, much like Mynasha, so he can be an ally.

"Power and influence will always prevail in the Caliphate. Mynasha has the power but not the influence." She looked back at Mynasha again. "But she will put our people's interests first, as Tarnasha would have. That is why I am helping her. I didn't think she stood a chance until I stumbled upon you." Her grin looked more feral than happy with her tusks.

"I have to consider my companions," I replied dismissively, but I was considering how much I really cared about the orc nation. Glasha looked like she was about to say something to press her case, but stopped.

Before sunset, Glasha directed us to a worn game trail. I didn't like how narrow and overgrown it was, so I handed Ginger's reins to Mateo as I scouted ahead on foot. I pulsed earth speak, only picking up small animals in the dense woodlands. The woods were full of towering evergreens hundreds of years old, their dark-green needles creating a dense canopy overhead. As I ventured deeper along the path, the crisp, invigorating scent of pine needles surrounded me.

As I approached a wide stream a few miles later, I decided to pause and wait for the rest of my group. On the far side of the stream, a well-worn path wound its way up a gentle rise, where wisps of gray smoke curled upward, hinting at the presence of a nearby dwelling. When my companions finally emerged from the dense woods, they allowed the eager horses to drink.

I sensed something and turned to see an older, bald, gray-skinned orc standing on the rise. Two impressive white wolves flanked him. A few of the horses got skittish at the sight of the wolves and pulled on their reins. The trio had appeared almost silently and had been out of range of my earth speak. Glasha yelled up to him over the rushing water, "I wasn't sure you were still alive, Tarnasha."

He spat heavily on the ground, looking over our eight members. In an unpleasant tone, he yelled down at us, "Glasha, is that you? I hope you brought something delicious for dinner. I am not feeding all your friends." He walked away, disappearing over the rise, and the wolves went with him.

"Don't worry, he grows on you in time," Glasha said reassuringly. "He is probably upset I haven't visited him in over two years."

After the horses' thirst was satiated, we led them up the slope. Glasha was first to enter a small clearing with a single-room cabin. A tripod suspended a large, cast-iron pot over smoking coals. The two wolves flanked the firepit, protecting their master's dinner. Log seats surrounded the fire. I signaled for the others to care for the horses while I approached with our charges.

Tarnasha had already sat, and his eyes looked unfocused. He wasn't blind but definitely had difficulty seeing. "Why are you disturbing my rest, Chronicler?" he asked as he stirred the coals.

"Rest? I thought you came here to die," she said with a teasing tone.

"I will when I get around to it," he retorted with a chuckle.

"You always say that when I visit, yet you are still alive when I come back," she joked, and the two orcs had a laugh between themselves. "This one is going to the Choosing as a candidate," Glasha said more seriously. Mynasha straightened her back some, presenting herself to the old orc.

He squinted at Mynasha through furrowed brows, frustration etched across his face. "Damn it! Heal my eyes, Glorza! Why do I even have to ask anymore?" His voice was tinged with impatience. Glasha approached the timeworn orc with a playful snicker, her fingers outstretched as she reached for his head. As her hand rested on his head, his eyes gradually cleared, allowing his appraising gaze to fix on Mynasha.

"Don't waste your time going to the Choosing," he advised, his tone heavy with caution. "It should be called the Already Chosen." A swift slap from Glasha to the back of his head caused the nearby wolves to lift their heads in concern. Their ears perked, but their bodies remained still and watchful, waiting on the pleasure of their master. My hand instinctively moved toward my blade as I prepared to defend the cleric. "Isn't that what you wanted me to say?" he said, rubbing his head.

Glasha chastised the old orc. "No, I changed my mind. That is why I brought her here. Help her prepare!"

"Prepare her?" he asked, baffled.

"Yes, for whatever trials the Elders plan for the candidates. You were one once, after all," Glasha said impatiently.

He growled unhappily at Glasha, "I was part of two Choosings in my lifetime, one as an Elder and one as a candidate. Neither were enjoyable experiences." He stopped talking and stared at me like he was seeing me for the first time. "Is he a human?"

"He will be her First, once we convince him," Glasha said with a wink before I could object.

He laughed aloud, "Oh, I would love to see the Elders' reaction to that! I can see Kytasha breathing fire and Loliasha having a stroke at the arrogance of it."

"It has been done before," Glasha said calmly, trying to give me a reassuring nod.

The old orc laughed, his wrinkles disappearing as he grinned. "That is why a Chronicler can never be the Supreme. How long ago was that? I assume he didn't survive." I looked at Glasha questioningly.

Glasha pursed her lips. "He wasn't killed, he just never exited the Demonic Lair."

"Same difference." The old orc dismissed her with a wave of his hand. He sighed, seeing that he wasn't going to convince the women to abandon their quest. "Fine. I will talk with her and tell her what to expect." He indicated me. "By his dazed expression, you should talk with him and tell him what to expect. I might even come with you just to see what dragon shit you are dropping on the Elders."

The old orc stood, cracked his back, and straightened, and I could see his eyes looking around, acclimating to his improved sight. "Come, child. Let me tell you how to survive the Choosing. Mind you, not how to become the Supreme, just how to survive it." Mynasha looked uncertain for the first time but followed after getting a nod from Glasha.

The wolves looked to their master, but he never gave a command for them to follow, and they lowered their heads between their paws in disappointment. I looked at Glasha for an explanation with an agitated expression.

While she gathered her thoughts, a strip of bear meat I had prepared for Baldo appeared in my hand. The two white wolves immediately perked up, sniffing the air. They didn't leave their spots guarding the kettle, though. I tossed the meat to the one on the left. It landed on the pine needles within reach, and he sniffed it before consuming it greedily. The other wolf looked at me like I had somehow betrayed him by giving it to his brother. I tossed the pleading wolf a second piece, and it snatched the meat out of the air. Both wolves slowly shook their tails in a friendly manner but remained guarding the pot.

Glasha moved to check the pot, and the wolves growled at her. She grunted. "Those beasts never liked me much." She returned to her seat, rebuffed. "While they are talking, we should talk about your duties. The First's duties are to stand by their candidate."

I interrupted her. "I never agreed to be part of the Choosing."

"Well," she said heartily, "consider this information in case you *do* decide to help Mynasha." I shook my head but let her continue. As she talked, I tossed dungeon bear meat to the white wolves, alternating between the two.

"As I was saying, the First stands by their candidate. Usually, it is one of the more popular and powerful warlords who is backing them—to signify the warrior caste is willing to obey. When a candidate cannot find a First, they can always enter the Choosing alone, but will certainly fail."

Maveith interrupted, asking for food to prepare for our group. I gave him some dungeon bacon and potatoes to go with what he had in his pack. The wolves sniffed the air, their eyes following the retreating goliath. I tossed each some cooked bacon, and their tails resumed swaying, showing their happiness. Glasha shook her head, maybe upset that I didn't toss her some bacon, before she continued, "The Elders—there are five currently—will offer challenges to the candidates until two remain."

"You mentioned it before, but what is the nature of these challenges?" I asked, willing to listen.

"They are tailored to eliminate the unwanted candidates." She smiled tuskily. "For instance, if the Elders wanted a candidate with an earth affinity to assume the Supreme seat, they would bury objects in a mountain a few miles away. Only those returning with one of the objects in a predetermined amount of time would advance."

"Do the candidates fight each other? Are candidates killed during these challenges?" I asked.

Glasha chewed her lip. "It does happen. However, violence on another candidate disqualifies them from the Choosing and could see them exiled."

"But no restriction on violence against their Firsts?" I said, filling in what was not said.

"But not against their Firsts," she confirmed seriously. "Do not worry. We are not as petty as the First Citizens of the Empire. It is deeply frowned upon and a great loss of individual honor to kill another without reason. And no, winning the Choosing is not a valid reason to kill."

"Would me being a human be a reason? Or a Telhian?" I asked. Glasha pursed her lips, her jaw tight, but did not answer. I pressed further. "How was the Supreme killed, then? Your principles make no sense to me."

I caught something briefly in her eyes before it disappeared—guilt or something else. Glasha got uncomfortable on her seat. Perhaps it was me questioning her people's ethos. "The Supreme was not attacked directly, but he was guided to his demise. And no, I was not a party to his departure." She inhaled deeply and let out a long breath. "But I could have prevented it and I chose not to."

She was waiting for me to judge her. After some thought, I said, "Everyone is righteous in their own mind. Only those who write the history will determine who was, in fact, righteous."

Glasha looked at me in disbelief and burst into loud laughter. The wolves grew alarmed and finally moved away from the fire, getting behind me. "And because I am a Chronicler, I can determine whether I am, in fact, righteous or not in my own actions."

It was not what I had been going for, but it had broken the mood somewhat. A massive explosion thundered in the woods. The wolf on my right tucked its head under my arm, seeking protection. The other one cowered behind a log. I stood on alert, my companions rushing from where they were preparing dinner.

"There is no danger!" Glasha said, stopping us. "Mynasha is just demonstrating to Tarnasha that she does have the power to become the Supreme." Another explosion rocked the woodlands, and I covered the wolf's large ears as I had done for Oscar during thunderstorms when I was little.

I noticed a flash before the explosion this time. Was she using lightning? More explosions followed, and soon, splinters were raining down around us in the clearing. A shiver ran through me as I comforted the wolf. Mynasha was exploding trees with powerful lightning over a quarter mile away, and the debris was reaching us. How powerful was she?

After more than a dozen explosions had shaken the area, I was covered in pine needles and splinters that had fallen from above. One of the large white wolves looked for comfort with its head in my lap. I remember when Oscar was a puppy, he was afraid of thunder and lightning. I empathized with the wolf. His brother had pushed himself behind me, trying unsuccessfully to hide under the log I was seated on. I figured the pair would have left if not for their master's dinner cooking nearby.

Raelia approached the firepit, irritably cleaning pine needles out of her hair. With a bit of awe, she said, "Fifteen lightning strikes, each with tremendous power. Her aether well must be immense."

Glasha grinned, not hiding her happiness that we were impressed. "It is, but it is because she can channel aether from ley lines. This cabin sits at a minor nexus. But I think she reached her limit trying to impress Tarnasha." I followed Glasha's eyes to a stumbling Mynasha coming down the path. She was only wearing a thin brown shirt that was soaked in sweat, leaving little to the imagination. Tarnasha carried her bundle of clothes.

From a distance away, Mateo was whispering loudly to Benito, and it didn't take much to figure out what it was about. My own curiosity took hold. "She is using a spell form for the convergence affinity? Does she need to be … naked for it?"

Glasha stared at Mynasha, who was struggling to walk. "It helps. If she didn't, channeling that much aether might set her clothes on fire."

"How is she not burnt?" I asked, realizing how much aether she had just channeled in seconds. "Is her aether tolerance that high?"

Glasha chuckled. "No. I understand why you would think so. The aether she pulls up from the ley lines goes directly into her spell forms. It does not pass through her body. It is extremely dangerous and requires a lot of skill in aether shaping to do it this way."

The pair had reached us, and we quieted. "Rest in my bed, child," Tarnasha said tiredly as they approached. "Heal my ears," he said to Glasha as he fished pine needles out of his hair. Glasha rose to obey. The wolves' tails started wagging, and they went to their master, abandoning my protection.

"I am surprised you two didn't run for the hills." He rubbed them both between the ears reassuringly. "These two were scared of their own shadows when I found them after their mother had been killed." Glasha finished her healing and returned to her seat.

Tarnasha sat down in front of the cooking pot and addressed the wolves. "But I suppose you wouldn't abandon your dinner, either." The old orc removed the iron pot's lid and sniffed it before spooning large portions for each wolf into a wooden bowl, then filling a third for himself. He sighed like he had been the one exhausted and not Mynasha.

As he sat to eat, Glasha eyed him impatiently, restraining a smile. "Well?"

The old orc blew on his spoon to cool his thick stew. He ate a few mouthfuls noisily before answering Glasha, who was growing impatient. "She is impressive but rash, young and narrow-sighted. She may make a decent Supreme with a good advisor."

"You are volunteering then. Great! I have places to be and things to do!" Glasha replied merrily, and Tarnasha choked on his food.

"No, woman! Stop putting words in my mouth! I am happy here with these two pups," he indicated the wolves, who looked up longingly at him, begging for seconds, their bowls clean. He sighed and spooned each of the wolves another serving. He moodily returned to eating his own stew.

Glasha waited while he ate, and when he finished his bowl, he added, "But I would perhaps like to see my old friends among the Elders." His words were laced with sarcasm. At least, I thought it was sarcasm, as it was difficult to tell in the Orcish tongue.

Raelia tapped my shoulder and indicated that Maveith was done cooking. Blaze was coming back from checking on the horses, nodding to me that all was well. I left the fire, and the two wolves stood, abandoning their empty bowls to follow me, probably hoping for a second dinner.

Tarnasha whistled, getting the pair's attention. "Where do you two think you are going?" They looked at me and then at Tarnasha before lowering their heads and returning to the old orc's side. Glasha and Tarnasha dove into conversation as she tried to convince the ex-Elder to come with us and support Mynasha's candidacy. I thought maybe he could serve as her First.

Any of those lightning strikes would have blown me up just like those trees, aether shield amulet or not. Maveith handed me a perfectly seasoned bacon, potato, rice, and pepper mash. Tasting it, I nodded appreciatively. Blaze informed me, "Two of the horses will need some healing, but they are all sound."

"Glasha, two of the horses need healing before you sleep tonight," I yelled over to Glasha from twenty yards away, and she acknowledged the request before returning to her discussion.

"What is the plan?" Blaze asked as we ate. All eyes focused on me.

"We finish escorting them to Becar and look for Maveith's sister. If Warlord Rhuuk is in the capital, we will see if she is attending him; if not, we go to his estate south of Agurtra to look for her," I explained.

"You will not help the lightning cleric become the Supreme?" Mateo asked, a little in disbelief. Did I come off as someone who helped every person who asked for it?

"Our priority is finding Maveith's sister. Only if the paths intersect would I consider it." Mateo grunted in disbelief. The camp conversation devolved into how much damage those lightning strikes could have caused an army. Blaze noted that the dungeon pauldrons we had unearthed would be extremely useful against such a foe.

I came back from washing my bowl and checking on the horses. Everyone was lounging about and had not even made an effort to set up camp. We had barely trained the last few days, and it looked like we were getting complacent. "We will train two hours before setting our camp around the cleric's firepit." Benito groaned, as he had eaten three portions and had to loosen his armor to sit. "You need to be able to fight on a full or empty stomach, Benito," I said seriously. Shit, was I turning into Konstantin?

"Can we choose what weapons to train in this session?" Blaze asked hopefully.

I gave him a sideways glance. He was going to choose his bow. But I thought to give the company some leeway. "We will rotate partners. Each pairing can split time choosing weapons. Benito, you are with me first." I was becoming Konstantin. I was thinking of how I would make Benito regurgitate his gluttonous meal. I shook my head in disapproval at myself. As we moved to a clearing, I told him he could decide first.

He furrowed his brow in thought. "My sword to your dagger?" He offered hopefully.

"Do I get a shield?" I asked, pulling Corvus's dagger.

Surprised I had agreed, he paused, his eyes dancing, looking for the trap. "Umm, no shield?" he said unconvincingly. I just nodded, and we both wrapped our blades in tacky cloth.

Benito had chosen to go without a shield as well and quickly regretted his decision. I was a step faster than the short man and made use of my elbow and free hand. After a few exchanges, his lip was bleeding and he had a limp. He had managed to strike my leather cuirass twice, but neither strike would have impeded me in real combat.

Maveith barked that it was time to rotate partners. "Switch weapons!" Maveith had an innate ability to tell time, so twenty minutes should have passed. He was sweating heavily from chasing the nimble Raelia around. It looked like they had chosen only fists. Benito looked pleadingly at me, and I didn't know why. I could have targeted his gut with kicks and punches to bring up his dinner, and I had not.

"Just swords, and we will work on your defenses." Benito tended to overcommit on his attacks, leaving openings for his opponent. We grabbed our shields, and I wrapped Boris's dungeon blade. I went easy on him, having him focus on protecting his right side, his sword arm.

My next pairing was with Blaze, and he suggested I serve as a moving target with my shield. I knew he was not serious, but I agreed. Being able to judge the path of an arrow toward you and interpose your shield was a complex skill. When there was only a single archer, it was more feasible to track the release and trajectory of the arrow. I retrieved my helm and let the fun begin—for Blaze.

As I jogged laterally, he released his arrows in a steady rhythm, aiming for either my torso or thighs. Seven arrows stuck in my shield, while two others missed me by a few inches. I started to vary my jogging speed to make it harder for him, and then I varied my distance. He still managed to strike my shield half the time. I even passed on the opportunity to switch weapons, giving him more archery practice. Two arrows penetrated my shield and pierced into my arm. My aether shield and bracers stopped both strikes from harming me.

When we switched, Mateo groused, "I am not going to serve as your target dummy, Blaze."

"Blaze, you need to practice with your sword," I reminded him. He reluctantly went to retrieve his blade. I was facing off against Maveith, who had a massive grin on his face. "Why are you grinning?" I asked suspiciously.

"I am ready this time," he said while maintaining his grin.

Benito chirped, "I have a large copper on Maveith." He looked around for any takers.

"I will take you up on that," I said, causing Benito to frown. I wasn't sure what game was being played here, but I was up for a challenge this evening. I needed to vent a little from constantly being pressured by the clerics to get involved in their problem.

Maveith squared off with me, both hands on his hammer. His grin was gone, and intense focus remained on his face. I usually bested him by dodging a heavy swing that he couldn't recover from quickly. He had already given away his plan with his fingers dancing up the shaft. Hand placement closer to the head would allow him to recover quickly. He had tried it before without much success, but he might have improved with practice. The others paused their practice to watch us engage. If Benito knew Maveith's plan, then they all knew Maveith's plan.

Maveith stood his ground, forcing me to initiate. As predicted, one hand slid up the shaft to act as a fulcrum to increase his reaction speed. A large clang sounded as his hammerhead batted my strike aside. He recovered quickly enough to intercept my shield bash attempt as well. But he didn't stop there and attempted to rush me and get inside my guard. One hand released the hammer shaft and lanced out in a punch.

Resisting the strong urge to use an air shield, I parried the blow with my shield. I was almost caught off guard as he used my shield, blocking my line of sight to lunge in an attempt to bear hug me. With only one choice, I fell onto my back and kicked off Maveith's knees into a somersault. I came up in one smooth motion, a little surprised that it had actually worked so well.

Maveith had dropped his hammer in the bear hug attempt and looked at me and the hammer, trying to figure out if he could reclaim it before I retaliated. I made the decision for him, rushing to cut him off from his favored weapon …

Maveith limped to Glasha for some healing, and I collected a large bronze from Benito. The others looked a little sullen as well. Were they upset that I had won? I rarely lost to any of them when we practiced, and was more of an instructor. Was I really a pompous ass like Konstantin when it came to our practices?

After he was healed, I observed Maveith handing his runic hammer to Glasha. She pulled back her scarlet hair as she prepared to use her lore spell on the weapon. With intense focus, she examined the hammer, holding it delicately in her hands for what felt like an eternity. As the minutes ticked by, my companions' curiosity grew, and they turned to watch the cleric use her magic. When she finally returned the hammer to Maveith, they engaged in a brief conversation before Maveith made his way back to our group. He had a satisfied look on his face.

Mateo probed him first. "What did Glasha say?"

"It was forged to purify mithril ore," he said, grinning. "It is so old, with such much history, that she cannot see back to its own forging."

"Mithril?" Benito asked, in some awe and confusion at the mention of the mythical ore.

"There were rooms in the dungeon where it could be obtained," I answered. "The smiths of Caelora used to mine, refine, and forge it. Mithril can only be found in dungeons and is extremely difficult for smiths to work."

Raelia interrupted me. "That is not true. The denizens of the Endless Dark mine it, but small deposits only occur near the ley lines." I nodded at her, thinking that it was probably true. I had not delved too deeply into the smithing books in the dreamscape.

The excitement of Maveith's weapon having been revealed, Raelia smirked. "I get Eryk next in the pairings. I want no weapons."

Raelia had been practicing her unarmed combat with the others this entire evening. Was this an attempt to best me in our practice? I cautiously nodded and started to remove my armor. We were equal in speed and nimbleness, but I easily overpowered her. "Why are you taking off your armor?" she said, frowning.

"You already have yours off. I want the match to be even." She scrunched her face in distaste but couldn't argue my point. Mateo and Benito were talking, and I could tell this was another planned spar. They had been preparing as a group to beat me. I could understand their frustration, as I had faced the same feeling with Konstantin. With my last piece of armor off, I faced Raelia.

She was nimble and slippery in combat. She even had a unique spell form that was a danger sense, alerting her to an impending attack. It shouldn't help her in this straightforward contest. We closed and circled, and I tried the oldest trick in the book. "Your boots are untied."

Raelia glanced down as she stepped back, not giving me a chance to take advantage. Her expression turned into a scowl at my poor attempt at trickery. She growled, frustrated, as she circled to my left. Maybe she thought my armor's encumbrance would have given her the slight advantage she needed. Her hair and face were already covered in sweat and dirt from her earlier practices. The others looked on, hoping for the elf's victory.

She finally committed, pushing off a protruding stone to lunge at my leg. I couldn't see the advantage of it but was cautious as I retreated. She went into a dive just to catch my ankle. She used my own leg for leverage to get behind me. I had one chance to attack the top of her head, but I lost it when I hesitated to strike her.

She had a firm grip, and I was not too familiar with Elvish grappling. She leveraged her body weight into my knee to force me to the ground. Raelia weighed 120 pounds at most, but she was using all her body weight on just my knee joint. I complied and went to the ground, but I kicked back hard with my other leg, hitting her squarely in the shoulder. She grunted but didn't let go.

She was fully determined to win this struggle, and Benito's cheer told me I was not the favored one in this contest. She was working her way up my leg like an unwanted parasite, keeping leverage on my ankle so I couldn't get her. I thought this was all ridiculous because I weighed more than twice what she did.

If I let her win, would it be good for the company to see the leader fall? Raelia had clearly endeared herself to the others as they cheered her on. She was covered in dirt, pine needles, and sweat. I locked her head in my free leg and alligator-rolled on the ground to try and break her will, but it only made her filthy.

Raelia was grunting as she strained to get me to submit by forcing my knee joint in the wrong direction. My entire leg was flexed, and she wasn't going to overcome my vastly superior strength. My hubris was my downfall as I repositioned, and she took the opportunity to scramble up my body and get behind me, achieving a chokehold.

With my legs free, I stood immediately, and she was too focused on trying to choke me to figure out my plan as I jumped in the air and twisted my body. I landed with all my body weight on her. It stunned her and she released her grip enough for me to turn into her. I was straddling her hips, pinning her to the ground. She momentarily tried to grab my neck again, but it just smashed both our foreheads together, a contest I won.

I got control of one of her wrists and then the other. She was heaving deep breaths under me, her legs flailing, and I was slightly winded as well. In the somewhat compromising position, I rasped, "Do you concede?"

She squirmed briefly, but my knees kept her hips in place. Instead of getting angry, she slowly smirked. "I almost had you," she said breathlessly. I tightened my grip on her wrists, suspecting it was a trap. She rolled her eyes. "I concede— this time." I stood up and helped Raelia to her feet. My knee was still painful to put weight on, and I patted her shoulder, brushing off debris and showing her she had put forth a good effort.

Blaze looked amused, while the others looked disappointed at Raelia's defeat. It was almost dark, so I called off the last pairing. My knee was a bit strained, and I had to heal it as I walked back to Glasha and Tarnasha. They had also been watching the wrestling match. "Are we set to leave in the morning?"

The two orcs looked me up and down, somewhat amused at my filthy state. Had I embarrassed myself by almost losing to Raelia? I brushed off some debris. Tarnasha spoke for the pair. "I will be joining you, but we will leave midafternoon tomorrow. I must explain to my pups that I will be gone for a while, and Mynasha needs more time to recover."

I wasn't sure if the old cleric meant he could talk to animals or if he was speaking generally about his wolves. I replied neutrally, "Good. We will set up camp around your firepit, as I don't think your cabin can hold all of us."

Much later that night, I felt someone lie quietly behind me in my bedroll, spooning me. Mateo was on watch, so it was someone else in our camp. The body pressed into me, and I thought that it had to be Raelia, as it was the only thing that made sense to me. I had been replaying the wrestling match repeatedly in my mind, unable to get the few hours of sleep I needed. I slowly turned over, only to be greeted by a mass of white fur and a panting wolf. A bit disappointed, I turned away and drifted off to sleep.

I woke a few hours later. Somehow during the night I had rolled back over and was now hugging the large white wolf. The warmth had been welcome, but I needed to relieve Mateo and Maveith on watch. The wolf roused with me, shaking its coat. Its brother was sleeping outside the door of the single-room cabin. I thought this might be the one I comforted during the thunder and lightning display. I rolled up my bedroll and sent the griffin pillow and bedroll to storage.

Mateo stretched his back, seeing that I was awake. Maveith was on the far side of the cabin, and Mateo went to get him. I would be the only one on the second watch, as my earth speak would help me watch a larger area.

Maveith and Mateo found their bedrolls after stirring the coals of Tarnasha's fire. I decided to check on the horses and walked the thirty yards to where they were. The white wolf plodded at my side, and I passed him a chunk of bear meat. Good food was the best way to befriend an animal, as Ginger could attest.

The injured horses had been healed and I gave all the horses half an apple each before I returned for my watch. Maveith had waited for my return before curling into a ball in his bedroll. We hadn't set the tarp tents because Glasha had guaranteed no overnight rain. I was starting to wonder what the extent of her magic was.

I found a comfortable rock roughly shaped like a seat and settled in. I pulsed earth speak, practicing refining my feedback from the pulse. The wolf sat behind me, higher up on the rock. He was hoping for a few snacks throughout the night, which he would receive, as I was apparently a pushover.

I watched my group from a distance as they stirred with the rising sun. Maveith was the first one up and quietly moved to prepare breakfast for everyone. Raelia was up shortly after and walked past me with a self-satisfied grin to check on the horses and tend to her own business. Blaze was next, and he moved to help Maveith prepare breakfast. Mateo had stood the first watch, so I couldn't fault him for sleeping in. I was about to go wake Benito but hesitated. Waking him harshly was something Konstantin would do with a self-satisfied grin.

Benito was probably sore from practice last night and exhausted. He had taken the worst beating and didn't get any healing from Glasha. I reclined in my seat and reached back to rub the wolf's coat. "That one is scared of his own shadow," came a voice from behind the wolf. Startled, I looked back to see the wrinkled orc. I hadn't pulsed earth speak since the sun rose, but I was certain he hadn't exited the cabin. He grinned madly. "I still have some tricks you young ones haven't seen."

In Orcish, he commanded, "Hunt!" The brother wolf by the door stood and looked for his sibling to follow. I had given him over two pounds of meat throughout the watch, and I wasn't sure he would be motivated to hunt. He finally rose after Tarnasha nudged him strongly with his foot, but spent a minute stretching before sauntering off into the woods with his brother. Tarnasha sat down next to me. He smelled like mint and pine needles.

"Are you going to try and convince me to serve as Mynasha's First?" I asked the orc.

He considered his response. "Glasha thinks you will break before we arrive. I told her you are a mercenary and need to be paid your due." He started digging around in his leather hides for something. Coin was not going to sway my decision. He eventually found what he was looking for and handed me a blue sphere.

It wasn't an essence, or at least it wasn't one I was familiar with. It was the size of a major essence, a large marble, but lacked the characteristics of an essence. It emitted no faint glow and it had no visual appearance of movement within. To me, it appeared to be a simple, dark-blue stone. I tried to channel aether into it, but it was slippery and refused to take it. It must have been magical in some way. Confused, I looked up. "I give up, what is it?"

The old cleric smiled. "It is an obfuscation stone. Though the name is a bit of a misnomer. A better name would be a clairvoyance antithesis. It repels any spells with the clairvoyance affinity."

"Seems like it would be valuable to those hiding from mages. Why would you give it up?" I asked, handing it back to him. It was not enough of an incentive for me to help Mynasha.

"Well, since I am leaving here, it no longer serves much purpose for me." He chuckled to himself. "Not that anyone was searching for me. I just didn't want to be found. It is also imperfect. Other affinities have spying and tracking spells, though not over as great a distance as the clairvoyance affinity."

"Why did you think that would convince me to be Mynasha's First?" It was a valuable artifact, and I was mostly certain it would fool a blood compass, but I would need to test it out. If I had such a device, I could have fled the Empire without concern of being tracked.

"Besides its value, if you are planning on absconding with the goliath's sister, it could come in handy," he explained. My jaw tightened and my anger boiled at the fact that Glasha had revealed our purpose in the Caliphate to Tarnasha. She might trust this old cleric, but I had not formed an opinion of him yet.

Realizing something, I narrowed my eyes and stated a bit tersely, "I thought if I helped Mynasha become the Supreme, she would free Maveith's sister? Why would we need to flee in stealth?"

Tarnasha laughed softly. "Most certainly. Her word would be law if she was the Supreme. But that doesn't mean others wouldn't seek revenge against an honorless outsider who interfered with the Choosing."

He stood and addressed me as he pocketed the stone. "It will be dangerous to flee the Caliphate with her," he said gravely. "The warlords and clerics would unite to hunt you. Although outsiders are tolerated, the Caliphate and warrior caste in particular would not take such insults to their honor lightly." I nodded as if I understood, but he wasn't aware that I could simply place a living person in my dimensional space.

The wolves trotted into the clearing, one carrying a small faun in its jaws. Tarnasha addressed me. "I need to explain to them I am going away for a while." He then addressed the two wolves. "Good work, Coryn and Ryshan. Come, and I will harvest your favorite parts and speak with you."

"You can actually talk to them?" I asked, my mind momentarily off the stone.

"It is an imperfect spell form, but they can understand me well enough." He walked down to the stream, and the wolves followed with their prize.

I helped clean up the campsite and ate with the others. Raelia returned from the horses, and it looked like she had spent time washing up at the stream because her hair was wet. We lounged around the fire, waiting on Glasha and Mynasha. Tarnasha returned from the stream, but the wolves were not following him. I guessed my new wolf-friend was temporary, but maybe when I settled down, I would get a dog.

Mynasha emerged at midmorning, fatigue visible on her face, but she seemed more confident now that she had another ally for the Choosing. Maveith prepared an early lunch for all of us, and soon we set off on our horses, heading north. Since Tarnasha didn't have a mount, Mynasha let him use hers. She would be walking until he could buy one. Maveith and Blaze led our group, followed by the trio of orcs.

I trailed further behind, but it was clear the orcs were strategizing about the Choosing. Once, early in the trek, I caught a glimpse of white deep in the woods, but after that, I didn't see any sign of the wolves. It was a relief that the wolves were staying back, as the townsfolk would likely view them as a threat and try to kill them.

We followed the stream rather than retracing our steps on the game trail. Tarnasha assured us it would shave a few miles off our journey—an appealing prospect after a long morning on foot. By midafternoon, we rejoined the main trade road, and not long after, we reached a town where we managed to procure a riding horse for the old orc.

It didn't take long for him to start complaining of saddle sores. Before the sun had dipped too low, he was already asking Glasha for healing. She gave him a sideways smirk. "You need to grow your riding thighs, old one. We've got nearly a week of hard days ahead. If I heal you now, you'll just be in pain again tomorrow." Still, when we made camp that evening, she took pity on the bowlegged orc and eased his aches with a touch of healing magic.

While the others settled in, I consumed one of the minor earth essences and set out to scout the perimeter of the farmstead we were using for the night. I hoped the chaos I had stirred up by unlocking my water affinity had calmed by now. The earth essence settled in more easily—it even sharpened my earth pulse slightly, pushing the range out a little farther. There was some mild discomfort, a churn in my gut, but nothing I couldn't manage. I decided I would take the second minor essence a few days before we reached the capital.

The two minor strength essences had gone to Benito and Mateo. They wouldn't get much from them in terms of power, but the boost to their morale and the reward for their loyalty and friendship were worth it. That left my current stock at three apex water essences and four minor air essences. I wasn't ready to take the apex waters just yet—my body and mind needed more time to settle. As for the air essences, it would be a long while before I could unlock another affinity. Maybe by then, I would have better options available.

I didn't spot any tracks around the farm, and my earth speak didn't detect any threats beneath the surface. With things quiet, I had everyone train for an hour after dinner. It was just light conditioning drills to keep us sharp. Afterward, I allowed them to turn in for the night.

I took first watch with Blaze. The camp had gone quiet, fire crackling low between us. After a stretch of silence, I leaned closer and whispered, "Am I really that bad of a leader?"

Caught off guard, he stammered, confused. "What? Did you hear something?"

"When I sparred with Raelia, you were all hoping she would win. You were rooting against me," I said softly.

Blaze chuckled to himself. "Just the opposite. I think we all aspire to be what you have become. Two years ago, you were a raw recruit joining the company. You couldn't ride a horse and whined daily about your sores. Now you are fearless and running off to fight werewolves and ankhegs alone. Besting you, even in practice, is an accomplishment."

Blaze paused in thought. "You could give us more compliments on our improvements. You are too much like Konstantin, pointing out our shortcomings. But no, you are a good leader. As good as Castile or Adrian, just in a different way."

Feeling assured that I was not screwing up too badly, I grinned. "I didn't whine aloud. Just groaned a lot." Blaze started laughing and I joined him.

We were silent for a long time before Blaze spoke again. "You know Raelia has been trying to get your attention for most of the journey."

"What?" I retorted, surprised and confused. "Is this about her being in my room in Adorechi?"

"No." He laughed a little louder. "I know nothing happened there. For a man who is so perceptive, you tend to miss what is right in front of you. Did you even notice that Mateo stopped trying to gain her attention?" He patted my confused shoulder and went to wake the next watch.

During the next three days of riding, I received some more language lessons from the orcs between their strategy discussions. My focus was more on my group than the passing countryside. I did catch Raelia eyeing me a few times, but didn't sense any underlying meaning in it.

She was an elf, and I was human, after all. She was on this expedition for Maveith, not me. I watched how quickly Mateo and Benito responded to any orders I issued. Maveith was a ball of anxiety as we got closer to the capital and his sister. He would be finding out soon if his sister was alive.

We were just two days from the capital of Becar, according to Glasha, when a thundering cavalry came up behind us. The dust cloud was visible down the road, and with my spyglass, I saw there were more than one hundred mounted warriors in heavy armor. The forerunners of the unit had extensive tattoos. Damn it, just two more days and we would have been done with this. I started giving orders. "Dismount and move to those rocks!" The rocks would prevent them from charging us.

Glasha cut through my orders. "Stop. They are not here for us. Move off the road; they will pass." Everyone was tense as the thundering procession approached, but as predicted, they ignored us and rode past. One of the tattooed leaders peeled off and circled back to us.

He looked over our group, some confusion on his face. He finally decided to address Mynasha, probably because she was riding the biggest mount among the clerics. "Honored Battle Cleric, finding you on the road is fortunate. A force of mountain trolls commanding dark ogres has emerged from the Endless Dark."

"Where?" Glasha interjected, her tone hard.

The orc bowed his head in deference. "Chronicler, the Skull Passage." I must have missed how the clerics were identified. Was it her red hair that marked her as a Chronicler?

Glasha furrowed her brow and said angrily, "What of the passage guardians?"

"All dead from the report I received." He looked over the clerics and then us, expecting something.

"We will meet you there," Mynasha declared with a steely resolve, her eyes locking onto the rider with confidence. Glasha's jaw clenched tightly as rage radiated from her. The rider, acknowledging her words with a subtle nod, spurred his horse forward to rejoin his warriors. Tarnasha shook his head. "The Skull Passage is a day and a half in the wrong direction. We will miss the start of the Choosing."

With determination in her voice, Mynasha declared, "As a war cleric, my duty compels me to go, even if it means missing the Choosing." Her eyes held resolve, embodying the weight of duty.

Glasha hissed, "I know. You would lose honor if you didn't, and word of it would eliminate you from the Choosing after they called you a coward. It is all too convenient of an event to happen on our approach to Becar! One of the Elders or warlords must be behind it!" Glasha was chewing her tongue. "We have no choice but to go."

Tarnasha was skeptical. "How would they force an exodus from the Endless Dark?"

Glasha chewed her cheek and answered obscurely. "There are ways."

I pulled Ginger to join them. "No one asked me if I would agree to another detour."

"We will go with or without your escort," Mynasha declared before spurring her large mount forward, leaving us behind.

I locked eyes with Glasha and then Tarnasha, thinking. I turned and looked at my companions. Raelia had told them what was said. My eyes sought Maveith. He gave me a slow nod of consent. "We will go with you, but we will not fight the trolls or ogres. It is not our fight." Glasha nodded in thanks, and no more words were spoken. We all spurred our mounts into a trot to catch up with Mynasha.

We caught up with the impatient Mynasha. She looked satisfied that we had followed, and she remained riding out front. I settled Ginger between Tarnasha's and Glasha's mounts. "What do you know about the Skull Passage and these trolls and ogres?"

Glasha spoke for the pair in a lecturing tone. "The Caliphate guards all the known entrances to the Endless Dark. The Skull Passage was discovered during …"

I growled irritably. I already knew the orcs guarded their passages and did not need a history lesson at the moment. "Just give me the relevant information so I know what to expect."

Glasha bristled a bit at my harsh words. She took a breath and began again. "The Skull Passage is in a valley, and is called so because when it was discovered, it had a lot of bleached bones from creatures from the Endless Dark that made it to the surface." She eyed me, triumphant that she had imparted a bit of her knowledge. I waited for her to continue.

"If my memory serves, the fort garrison there was over two hundred strong with Warlord Ashanti commanding. The mountain trolls frequently come out in singles or pairs but are rarely organized in numbers. The dark ogres are slightly slimmer and darker-skinned than their surface counterparts. What truly differentiates them are their solid-black eyes. For all their stupidity, they have incredible night vision, making them dangerous foes in the dark."

I thought back to what Hearne had taught me in Hound training. "I know a bit about mountain trolls. They are the largest of all trolls and have an incredible sense of smell for tracking their prey. Although they cannot regenerate severed limbs, they still possess incredible regeneration of the flesh."

Glasha nodded. "All true. Their strength is also unmatched; they could easily wrestle an ogre into submission. Most likely, they bullied the dark ogres into servitude. You are as good as dead if you are struck by one of their blows. It is believed an unknown dungeon in the Endless Dark is releasing them, as most that come to the surface through the Skull Passage are not as large as would be expected of the species."

"Unknown dungeon?" Mateo had sneaked close enough to listen in.

Tarnasha turned slightly in his saddle and addressed Mateo. "Some dungeons only have access gates in the Endless Dark. That is why we watch the entrances to the Endless Dark on the surface so intently."

Glasha added in her scholarly tone, "New dungeons take hundreds of years to create access portals on the surface, but some never do. If these mountain trolls are from a dungeon, it would be an older dungeon due to their size."

I increasingly did not like this the more it was explained. "How far to the passage?" I asked unenthusiastically.

Glasha seemed to consider where we were for a moment. "Fifty miles. Maybe a touch more. But the trolls and ogres have most likely spread out after defeating the garrison. They might be raiding the countryside."

Up ahead, Mynasha turned off the main road, following the fading dust trail of the mounted warriors. We followed her lead, and Glasha and Tarnasha's conversation turned to how they might still reach the Choosing and help Mynasha become a candidate.

I drifted back to the others and advised them of our strategy. "If our charges are threatened, Maveith, Blaze, and Raelia will attack the threat from range. I will stand with Mateo and Benito. You already know what to expect from ogres. Let me tell you about mountain trolls …"

I laid it on heavy about the dangers of facing a mountain troll. The horrific memories of facing a powerful storm giant were in the front of my mind. I didn't want anyone getting foolishly brave and charging one—namely Mateo. If we did encounter a troll, I would be happy to make it brainless rather than risk anyone's life.

In the evening, we began to encounter fleeing orc civilians. Most were carrying very little. The clerics stopped to talk to a few of the people and found one who had worked in the fort at Skull Passage. The news could have been better.

"I was sleeping in one of the towers 'cause I was doing work there. I heard the first ogre bellow in pain in the distance, triggering one of the defenses. The garrison quickly mobilized to the walls, and our cleric lit up the night sky." He shivered at the memory. "Three dozen or more of the foul ogres were crossing the defenses. Monstrous trolls were shepherding them forward from behind."

"How many trolls?" Mynasha asked calmly.

"I didn't count, but half the number of ogres would be my guess. I watched the fight until the first troll reached and climbed the eastern wall. I climbed down the lift I was using to bring stone up the tower I was repairing and ran." Mynasha showed concern at the numbers.

"Are you sure it was that many trolls?" Glasha interjected, also concerned.

"Yes, honored cleric. Like I said, I didn't count, but there were more than twelve." Glasha dismissed him, and he limped to catch up with the group.

Tarnasha furrowed his brow, clearly skeptical. "Sounds too fantastical to be true. A dozen mountain trolls? If it is true, we would be fools not to wait for at least half that number of warlords and their men."

Both Glasha and Mynasha exchanged tense looks. Waiting meant the Choosing would be well underway by the time we arrived—perhaps even decided. To my surprise, Mynasha stepped forward and took control. "We proceed, but with caution. Given time, I can handle six mountain trolls."

Tarnasha, the old cleric, let out a deep, rolling laugh. "Child, you are powerful, yes—but six or twelve, a pack of mountain trolls is an army by itself. There's no shame in delaying. No loss of honor in accepting that the seat of the Supreme is already lost."

"We can still approach carefully," Glasha interjected, more thoughtful than defiant. "We're mounted—we could outrun them if needed. Besides, those warriors who passed us on the road probably weren't the only ones summoned. Reinforcements may be moving behind us."

I wasn't thrilled. Everything I had ever heard about mountain trolls suggested they were solitary brutes. If a dozen had gathered, something was deeply wrong. Hearne once said that facing two that were not actively copulating meant Fortuna herself had cursed you.

"I'll ride ahead and scout every few miles," Glasha said at last, her voice firm. "If they're out there, I'll make sure we're not caught unaware."

We continued along the side road, and before long, the last of the fleeing civilians vanished behind us. The silence settled in with the dusk, heavy and creeping. Facing dark ogres or mountain trolls at night would be close to suicide.

Fortunately, I didn't need to raise my concern, as Glasha had already anticipated it. During one of our pauses for her to scout, she returned and pointed northward. "There's a defensible cave about half a mile through the trees. Big enough for the horses."

We followed her through the thinning woods and came upon it—not quite a cave, more an overhang at the base of a small cliff, sheltered by a massive stone slab that jutted outward like a natural awning. Sparse tree cover gave us a clear thirty-yard perimeter in all directions. Rocky shale littered the ground in front, slippery underfoot. The space was generous, nearly forty feet across, twenty feet deep, and tall enough for the horses to stand comfortably inside.

I gave orders to my company. "Maveith, Raelia—sweep the area for tracks. Blaze, Mateo, Benito—water the horses, then get them secured in the shelter. No fires tonight. Don't even use the thermal stone," I said. "Mountain trolls have a sense of smell sharp enough to smell blood over a mile away."

The group scattered with practiced efficiency. As they worked, I stepped deeper into the cave, placing my palm to the stone and pulsing earth speak. The stone echoed back the images as I searched for any unwelcome surprises.

I shouldn't have been surprised to find a stash of rusty weapons behind a loose rock. This world had a millennia of rich history. I wiggled the rock, moss having grown in the seams over time, making it snug. Tarnasha watched me curiously, and when I freed and dropped the stone, he approached.

I pulled out the blades one at a time, each coated with rust. "Glasha, come look at these," Tarnasha called over to the Chronicler. She had been discussing something with Mynasha but joined us. In the end, there were ten long swords that had been secreted away.

"None of them are runic in nature," I said disappointedly. "Does your lore spell work on non-artificed items?" I asked, handing the last blade extracted to Glasha. She nodded and began studying the blade before focusing inward on her spell.

She eventually leaned the blade against the wall. "They were made in secret by a smith. They were plotting to kill the warlord who ruled over their town. It was some five hundred years ago, and the town no longer exists. It was called Clearmoor." She indicated the forest, "Those woodlands used to be pastures."

"Your gift never fails to amaze me," Tarnasha stated reverently.

Glasha smiled. "Well, I only get flashes of the object's life and purpose. I saw lots of sheep, and I remembered from old maps that this area used to be Clearmoor, a town that raised sheep for wool."

"Still impressive," I said. "These are worthless. The quality isn't great, and the metal is too far gone." I put the swords back in the alcove but didn't waste effort moving the stone back.

When they returned, I helped Benito and Blaze with the horses. Blaze whispered, "I don't like it. It's too quiet by the stream. Even Benito was spooked." Benito was usually blissfully ignorant of most things—especially danger—until it was right on top of him.

"Let's wait for Raelia and Maveith to return," I said, nodding. It wasn't long before they did.

Raelia reported somberly, "Ogre tracks over half a mile south by the stream. Dried blood on the rocks nearby but less than a day old."

"Direction of travel?" I asked, alarmed. If there was an injured ogre, maybe one of the trolls would be following it.

"We tracked it a quarter mile heading away from us." Maveith tried to whisper, but still, his voice traveled in the acoustics of the shallow cave. "The tracks were at least half a day old, so we returned."

"We now know at least one of the ogres from Skull Passage reached this far." I turned to Glasha. "How far is it to Skull Passage from here, and when did the trolls attack?"

"The attack was two nights ago, and the passage is about twenty miles from here," she replied, joining my group. "Did they find anything?"

"Ogre tracks," I replied.

Glasha seemed to consider. "We should tie one the horses out among the trees. That way, if the …"

"No," I snapped at her. I wanted to add that we could tie her out there instead but held back. "I will sleep now and take the watch the rest of the night." Glasha nodded in acceptance and returned to talking with the others.

As night settled over the woods, I struggled to find comfort in sleep, drifting in and out in restless intervals. Eventually, I rose to my feet, the cool, damp air wrapping around me, and told Maveith and Raelia to rest, relieving their watch. A light drizzle was falling outside our cave, creating a fine mist that hung in the air. I hoped the precipitation would work to our advantage, cloaking our presence and masking our scent trail.

I channeled aether to my eyes and periodically used the spyglass. There was not the usual amount of night activity in these woods, another bad sign. One thing was always certain: the smaller animals always knew when to hide.

The drizzle turned into a light rain, and the saturated ground muted my earth speak pulses. At least I still had my night vision. I caught movement in the distance and tracked a deer running at full sprint. From the direction it was running, I had a good guess of what was chasing it. Still, it was over one hundred yards away, meaning that whatever was chasing it wouldn't see us. I waited to rouse the others until I knew for sure.

It was faint, but I could feel the ground tremble—or maybe it was my earth pulses picking up the tremors. Not one, but two ogres plodded along after the deer they would never catch. I sighed in relief as their strides did not slow, and they disappeared to my right. My relief was short-lived, as a lanky giant followed with long strides. I couldn't see the upper torso through the foliage, but I knew this had to be a mountain troll. I prayed to Fortuna under my breath that the troll would continue after the ogres, but when it reached the path we had used to get to the cave, it stopped.

With my spyglass I could see it turning; I guessed it was sniffing the air. I leaned over to wake Maveith but noticed he was already sitting up. "Troll," I whispered. "Wake the others."

At least the ogres were chasing the deer. Fortuna cursed me, as the troll emitted a long, loud howl, and the rain seemed to stop for a heartbeat. Fuck, it was calling the ogres back. "Everyone up now!" I hissed. I just hoped it was not calling its troll friends as well.

Chapter 296: Trolls to the Left of Me, Ogres to the Right ... Here I Am, Stuck in the Middle with You

"Mynasha, get your lightning ready. There is one troll and two ogres—so far," I hissed while keeping my sight trained on the troll's legs.

"There are no ley lines beneath us; I would have to draw mostly on my own aether. I can only form two powerful lightning strikes at the moment." I looked at her incredulously. She couldn't see my exasperation in the dark, so I voiced it.

"What happened to you being able to handle six trolls?" I hissed. I looked to ensure my companions were getting ready, but they were at a disadvantage due to the darkness and needed a plan.

"I can still draw aether from the environment, but it takes longer," she whispered calmly, and started shedding all her clothes as I cursed under my breath. At least I could take one troll out myself if needed.

The troll's calls were answered from both the right, where the ogres went, and from behind it, to our left. The only good news was that the answering calls sounded the same in the rain, so hopefully we were only facing one troll and a few ogres. "Prepare to throw your glowstones if they attack. They should have trouble walking on the shale."

Two of the horses started getting anxious and neighing up a storm, probably smelling the troll or ogres. There was no way we were going undiscovered now. "At least the ogres are bathing before our fight," Mateo said with a soft chuckle, but no one laughed at his joke.

While the cave was good shelter, it also meant we were cornered. We didn't have time to saddle up and escape into the night. Grumpily, Benito muttered about the lack of a body shield as he prepared. I didn't have the heart to tell him that a troll wouldn't have respected the shield anyway. This was going to be a disaster of epic proportions if the clerics couldn't hold their own. To my knowledge, only Mynasha had offensive magic.

"Raelia, alert everyone when you start to form a fireball." It was more so that everyone would be prepared for the flash effects of the explosion. My night vision spell form protected me from the effect, but the others would be blinded.

"I can grease the shale in front of the cave," Tarnasha said suddenly. "It will only last about a minute but it should give them trouble."

"Throw the oil you have over there now. It doesn't matter if the rain washes it away," I said, pointing. I noticed the troll's legs moving toward us. Branches cracked in the canopy as it pushed through the trees, following its nose and the sound of the horses.

"It is a spell," Tarnasha replied indignantly. I just waved at him to do as he wanted. I didn't have time for the old orc. As branches snapped in the canopy, the horses became increasingly agitated. The troll's head appeared to me about one hundred yards away, towering about twenty feet from the ground. I was glad the others couldn't see the hideous creature in the dark, its eyes going wide with surprise at what it had just found, its mouth forming a smile with jagged, crooked teeth.

I could hear ogres returning from the right over the light rain pattering on the stones. "Lightning?" I asked while keeping the spyglass trained on the troll.

"I can't see it clearly," Mynasha hissed irritably.

"Well, it can see you clearly," I spat back. Perhaps I was a bit angry about being in this situation.

Instead of advancing, the troll bellowed into the air again. This time, its call was returned by a matching bellow that echoed across the woods. "Dragon shit, there is another troll," Blaze said despondently.

"It has ogres as well," I said heavily. I looked briefly at Benito. "Benito, cut the horses free if it looks like we will be overrun. It will give them a chance to escape and may distract the enemy. If I order any of you to run, don't question me, just do it."

The ogres that had been chasing the deer returned, their sucking, muddy footfalls echoing ominously. They moved out of the tree line ahead of the troll as a screen. I hated smart monsters. "Throw your glowstones!" I commanded. We could not fight in the dark at such a disadvantage. Five stones appeared from their pouches and arced through the air. One sank into a muddy puddle and another disappeared between two pieces of shale, but the remaining three radiated enough light in the misty rain to see by.

Three glowstones now cast shadows outward, and the outlines of the ogres were visible at the forest edge. I looked over at Mynasha, who had completely disrobed and had motes of blue aether crackling around her as she wove a spell form in her hands. I thought it was my aether-infused sight that let me see the spell workings more clearly. A benefit I would need to explore if we escaped this mess.

"Mateo! Eyes on the enemy!" I hissed at him. He was distracted by Mynasha's silhouette. I knew once the battle started he would be focused, but it felt right to remind him at the moment.

Blaze's and Maveith's bows twanged as arrows streaked the forty yards to the ogres. The ogres bellowed in rage and ignored their troll handler's command to wait. At least, that is what I guessed from the twisted anger on the troll's face when the ogres rushed us.

Mynasha thrust out her hands and thick, ragged lightning shot forth and struck the leading ogre. The lightning briefly connected the two before it detached from the cleric, and her end rushed toward the ogre. A thundering boom deafened me as the ogre exploded in a gory mess. Its fellow ogre stumbled from the concussive blast. Even with my ears ringing, I suddenly felt much better about our odds of winning.

"I need two minutes before I can go again," Mynasha rasped, and I glanced over at her. Her skin was steaming and her knees looked wobbly from the effort. Using her own aether must be more taxing than channeling it from ley lines. The other ogre had stumbled but hadn't stopped its charge, arrows protruding from its chest and belly. The lightning flash had blinded my companions, and their arrows were now missing their marks.

As our ears rang from the thunder, Glasha yelled to us, "Two trolls and two more dark ogres coming—about a mile away."

"Is that all?" I screamed back, my sarcasm lost in the need to yell so everyone could hear.

"So far! I just searched out to two miles," she yelled back.

"Well, three trolls and three ogres means we each get one, right?" I barked at my companions with mock cheerfulness.

Benito didn't seem thrilled. "I really don't want one. You can have mine, Eryk."

I didn't have time to reply, as the ogre had reached the shale slope, the stone crunching and sliding under its massive feet. I moved to the edge, out into the rain. Unlike the others, I had the amulet and could take one fatal strike. A wave of putrid stench washed over me. I thought the rain made the ogres smell worse.

The ogre's foot slid out behind him with a spray of shale, and it crashed down face-first. I rushed out of the overhang and brought my blade down on the back of its head. It sank satisfyingly deep into the skull. The ogre snapped its head back and howled in pain, its spittle coating me but also ripping Boris's blade from my hand. *Really? Shouldn't he be dead?*

"Troll is coming! I will send my fireball when it is in range!" Raelia shouted behind me. She had prepared a large pyrotechnic for the party and was ready to release it. She had woven other spell forms with it to enhance its destructive capability, but her range was only thirty yards.

"Strike the troll!" I yelled as I pulled the black spear into my hands from my space. It was no time for secrets. The howling ogre presented its chin to me as it tried to reach my blade, and I drove the spear through its mouth and out the back of its head. Before it could fall and trap another weapon, I extracted the spear and returned it to my dimensional space. I would answer the curious and amazed gazes from the others later.

I levered my foot against the now-definitely-dead ogre and worked out my sword. Raelia's fireball sped over me toward the approaching troll, who was either reluctant to break the tree line or waiting for its companions. It covered its face as the flaming ball struck it and engulfed it. While everyone else was blinded, my aether sight adapted instantly. I watched the troll reel, but it didn't seem to be fazed as the incendiary device washed over it.

"Lightning?!" I yelled.

"Not yet!" Mynasha yelled back, annoyed. "I need to focus more aether or it won't be strong enough!"

"She has time; the other trolls are still a distance away," Glasha said calmly. I ground my teeth. If we didn't get rid of this troll now, we would be rushed by three trolls and two ogres at once.

"Marvelous fireball, Raelia! How long till your next?" I asked, watching the angry troll consider his options. I could tell he was furious about losing his ogres and being slapped by the fireball. His skin looked cooked, and I knew fire was the one type of injury they did not heal quickly.

"That was most of my aether," Raelia said guiltily. "Maybe one more, half as strong."

"Save it for the ogres then," I told her solemnly as I stepped back out into the rain. Maveith's and Blaze's arrows had barely penetrated the troll's thick hide. "Hold your arrows for the ogres, too. They are having no effect on the troll."

I started to hear the other trolls in the distance when the cleric finally announced, "I am ready." She extended her hands once again, and the lightning flashed and tethered to the troll. Its face formed a hideous look of shock and fear. The lightning snapped to the troll, and its chest exploded. But the creature did not fall. Its flesh was blasted away to reveal ribs and gore leaking from its massive body.

It bellowed in rage and pain, and a howling, angered call answered from the woods. "I hope that isn't his mother," Benito said breathlessly.

I was thinking of asking Raelia to fireball the exposed chest cavity, but the troll went to a knee and crawled back into the woods. "Will that kill it?" I asked uncertainly.

"No, but it will not be able to fight for a few days. It lost a lot of muscle in the explosion and has to be in excruciating pain," Glasha said clinically. "Still no other trolls or ogres out to two miles. We may have gotten lucky."

"Don't tempt Fortuna, please," Benito whined.

The troll let out excruciating, pained cries as it crawled away. The thundering in the woods approached, and it was clear that it had reunited with the other trolls and ogres. Perhaps the injured troll was warning them that we were too tough a fight and they should leave us alone. The troll had acted somewhat intelligently so far.

When the cries ended and the forest went silent, I knew we were screwed. I pulled out the spyglass and saw movement among the trees, but it was not heading away from us. Who knew trolls and ogres could sneak? The rain was picking up, adding to the ambient noise, but still, it was clear that they were spreading out to rush us: the worst-case scenario.

Glasha confirmed to the others, "The two ogres are moving up the center, and the trolls are on the right and left to flank us."

Thinking, I asked, "Can you target the head with your lightning?"

Mynasha shook her head. "No, it is more like lassoing the target. Once I lock onto it, I release the destructive aether down its length and cannot control where it lands."

I laid out my hasty plan. "Well, at least try to explode its head. The troll on the left is yours. I will take the one on the right. Raelia, slow the ogres with your fireball, and everyone else, focus on the ogres as well."

"You are going to fight a mountain troll alone?" Mynasha asked incredulously.

"Yep," I said as I moved out into the rain and crossed the shale, pulsing earth speak. Benito said something, but I didn't catch it over the noise of the falling rain. My earth speak feedback was all blurry with the water-soaked ground, and I had to get to the trees before the ogres spotted me. I thought I was successful and waited behind a large trunk just inside the tree line.

My earth speak picked up the troll first. It crouched as it moved under the trees, plodding in the mud as it moved closer. I had estimated its path well, and it was going to pass close to my position. I just had to hope Glasha was not watching me when I did this.

The ogres roared to draw attention to themselves as they broke from the tree line and rushed my companions. Scared horses and the sound of bowstrings echoed in the night with the rain. Raelia's fireball flashed a distance away.

My troll increased its pace, closing in on me, and I stepped out, my sword held high. It looked surprised and amused at the tiny human facing it. My sword came down in a faux slash, and its eyes widened as its head tumbled from its body, its neck now secured in my dimensional space. I was surprised it had only modest aether resistance, but then again, I had raised my space affinity to over one hundred. Of course, my aether bottomed out, and I lost my aether sight. I could see the glowstones through the trees and stumbled to rejoin the fight.

A flash and a thunderous explosion told me Mynasha had expended her lightning. Breaking from the tree line, I tried to figure out what was going on. I didn't see the troll, just two ten-foot-tall ogres struggling to reach the group. I broke into a run, hoping to hamstring one of the ogres from behind. The ogre never saw me coming. I sliced into its calf as it scrambled on the greasy shale. I couldn't get an angle on the Achilles, and the hamstring looked too fatty to ensure a disabling blow.

I shifted clear just in time as the ogre slammed into the shale, howling in pain. Benito and Mateo confronted the last one while Maveith dropped his bow and pulled out his hammer with practiced ease.

The ogre brought its crude club down hard on Mateo's shield, slamming him backward a good five feet. He hit the ground with a grunt of pain. Benito moved in from the flank, but the ogre caught him with a sideways swipe that connected with his shield. Benito let out more of a squeak than a cry as he tumbled out of range.

Maveith charged, hammer raised. He brought it down in a wide arc, but the ogre caught most of the blow with its thick forearm. The impact still staggered it—but not enough.

I turned back to finish my own opponent, aiming a clean strike at the base of its neck. The ogre twisted with surprising speed and caught me with a brutal backhand. I couldn't dodge on the oily shale—my footing gave way.

My aether shield flared to life, absorbing the worst of the blow, but the force of the blow still made me slide down the slope of shale. I slid several feet and came up disoriented, breath caught in my throat. Still, I forced myself upright, shaking off the stars in my vision. There wasn't time to hesitate. I rejoined the fight.

It looked like Raelia and Blaze had added some arrows to the ogre Maveith was facing down. Maveith was holding his own, so I looked to finish my crippled ogre and get revenge for the bitch slap he just gave me. My ogre was confused and on one knee. I thought he was looking for his troll masters. I could see the clerics preparing spells and facing the ogres, so I assumed the other troll had been killed or incapacitated.

As my ogre tried to defend himself from his knees, I removed three of his fingers. Then he lost his entire hand on his other arm. That broke his will, and he began sliding across the shale to try to make it to the forest. Maveith's hammer came down on the other ogre, the loud crack caving in its head. Blaze and Raelia started targeting the fleeing ogre with arrows. The ogre slowed, fell, and soon stopped moving.

The heavy rain hadn't stopped as I rejoined everyone. "Is the other troll dead?" I asked.

"It fell over there and has not moved. I got a large portion of its neck with the lightning," Mynasha said, grinning. Maybe she was looking for praise, but she was the one who had gotten us into this. I nodded and ran back out into the rain to behead the troll she had injured, Maveith following me. It took a dozen blows before the head was freed from the body. Mountain trolls couldn't regenerate limbs. It was safe to say it was dead.

"How did you kill your troll?" asked Mynasha, still steaming and mostly nude when I returned to the shelter.

"Same way." I indicated the troll's head I had just hacked off. "I will rest for a bit, and then I will hunt down the last troll with Blaze and Maveith," I said tiredly. I rubbed Ginger's neck to soothe her after all the excitement, and it helped me calm, too. The stench was now our biggest enemy. I doubted anyone would be able to sleep. I would need another fifteen minutes for my aether to recover so I could kill the last troll and use the collector on it. I also hoped to get an essence from the troll I had beheaded in the woods.

Mateo had broken ribs and a concussion. Benito had a broken arm—again. Both men, despite their injuries, remained stoically quiet while Glasha did what she could to heal them. She could not heal broken bones but would do what she could. I didn't tell Mynasha to dress, as the distraction helped Mateo and Benito deal with their pain.

I thought I had gotten away with beheading my first troll, as Glasha was not eyeing me suspiciously. I sat and leaned against the wall, inhaling the stench of the ogres and letting my adrenaline fade. We were truly Fortuna's Chosen to have survived that.

373

"Blaze. Maveith. Let's go." I stood tiredly from the wall and stepped out into the steady rain. Neither of the clerics volunteered to come with us, but I could see Mynasha was spent. I addressed Glasha. "Keep your sight focused far afield so we are not surprised. Raelia, you can explode a small fireball in the sky to warn us if she sees a threat." I pulled my cloak around me and nodded to Blaze and Maveith. "Walk behind me with your glowstones," I ordered.

I led them into the woods, and soon, we arrived at the troll I had killed. While they inspected the troll, I walked the surroundings to make sure the missing troll was not going to find us. When I returned, I got the question I was expecting. Blaze indicated the troll. "You cut the troll's head off in one swing? How? It took you a dozen strikes to hack off the other one."

I smirked, and the neck of the troll thudded on the ground between the head and body. The blood from the stump mixed with the muddy rainwater. Blaze gawked for a while as the collector appeared in my hand.

While the essence pooled from the troll's body, Blaze squeaked out, "Really?" I knew he would put it together quickly. A major essence of healing formed, and I cursed under my breath, not at the essence but at my inability to harvest the troll Mynasha had killed.

"Yes. It only works once, and it takes me about half an hour to recover enough aether to do it again." I put the white pearl with silver and gold swirls into my belt. With my core still healing, I needed to space out consumption of any affinities.

Maveith's voice echoed softly. "Eryk is how we survived the Shimmering Labyrinth. Without his magic, there is no way he would ever have rejoined you."

"And the spear?" Blaze asked.

"A reward from the Shimmering Labyrinth," I responded, looking over the bloody corpse. It was wearing rough hides, but the only sack appeared contain body parts for snacking on. "Maveith, anything worth our time?"

"I don't know. Troll's blood?" he replied. "Maybe the hide, I think. I cannot process it, though."

I nodded. "I know troll's blood is an alternate base for advanced healing potions. But it needs to be stabilized when it is collected. I do not have the solution prepared to do so," I said, standing. "Let's find the missing troll."

I could tell Blaze had a dozen questions but wisely kept them for after we finished the last troll. Even with the rain and mud, it didn't take long to find the trail of massive, muddy footfalls leading us to it. It was under a massive pine, leaning against the trunk. I motioned to my companions to wait and circled to approach it from behind and downwind. The troll was struggling with its raspy breath and was oblivious to my presence.

At the last moment, it suddenly became alert, but it was too late; I took most of its neck rather than risk engaging it. It quickly tumbled over, and I hacked away, freeing the head completely to make certain it would not rise again. Spookily, its wide eyes followed my first few sword swings.

I took out two canteens, emptied the elven ambrosia, and filled them both with fresh troll's blood. The blood would be in stasis in my dimensional space, allowing me to utilize it in the future. I hated losing canteens, but healing potions were more valuable than water or even elven whisky.

As I used the collector on the troll, getting another major healing essence. I waited for Blaze to ask his burning questions. "Does Castile know that you can kill that way?" he finally asked.

"Yes, I told her in the Shimmering Labyrinth."

"Can you just do that to anybody?" He gestured at the troll.

"No. I have failed against mages with high aether resistance." He nodded slowly, and I wondered how his mind worked. Was he replaying everything I had done since joining the company?

"Are you like a god? Maybe Janus or Mars in the flesh?" he asked offhandedly, hiding a smile.

"I consider myself more like Mercury. You believe in the gods?" I asked skeptically, arching my eyebrow.

"Well, no. But your power—it is even more impressive than Mynasha's." I shrugged, but something clicked in my head at that moment. Mynasha had a strong affinity for convergence but used it to draw aether from the environment and ley lines. I had a strong convergence affinity, but used my spell form to milk essences. Was Mynasha an otherworlder? Zyna had told me all the races had been brought to Desia from their home worlds, so it seemed plausible.

We searched the body from a distance without delving into its large sack of animal and orc body parts. We all agreed there was nothing worth harvesting. "Let's get back to the others and get the horses saddled. Maybe we can convince the clerics that we have done enough."

We arrived back at the cave to find Raelia standing watch alone. Well, that was not completely true, because Glasha was using her scrying spell. "Anything?" I asked her.

"No," she replied, focusing on me. "Is the other troll dead?"

I studied her for a moment before nodding. She was either a good poker player or she had not been spying on me. "We are moving out now. The stench is too strong for us to sleep and I want to get away from the battle site in case more trolls investigate. We should leave for Becar."

Mynasha struggled to get up. "We can't until the troll horde has been stopped."

"You killed three trolls and four ogres, isn't that enough?" I asked.

"I didn't ..." she started, but I interrupted her.

"*You* killed three trolls and four ogres," I stressed. "The honor is all yours."

Glasha spoke an unfamiliar word in Orcish that silenced Mynasha and nodded at me appreciatively. "Still, we need to scout the fort. We must find out what happened to the warriors who rode ahead of us." I groaned. If these trolls were out hunting, wasn't it obvious those warriors were dead? "I can scout from miles away; there's no need to approach the fort," she conceded at my hard stare.

"Just because the mason only saw a dozen trolls, that doesn't mean there are not more. We could be walking into a large host." Seeing their stubborn gazes, I growled. "Move along the cliff. We leave now." It was in the direction they wanted to go, and I was going to take the opportunity to try and get another essence. Blaze understood what I wanted and helped get everyone moving quickly. Mateo was walking delicately, and hung back with Benito, who had his arm in a splint. They disappeared into the dark morning, their hooves and boots crunching on the shale as they went.

The last troll produced a minor healing essence, and I took two minor strength essences from two of the four ogres. I secretly gave Benito and Mateo the strength essences when I caught up to them. After we cleared the shale, we veered into the woods, moving slowly in the graying morning. The rain hadn't stopped, but I decided to let everyone rest under some dense pines.

I approached Glasha, who was searching through her saddlebags. "How is your aether? Can you continue scouting?"

"It is fine. I have a deep well and can go for a long time yet." She looked at me, and I could tell she had questions, judging by her eyes.

"What did you see?" I asked. We both knew I was talking about me and not trolls or ogres.

After a moment of thought, she answered. "You have a collector? I can see why you wanted to keep that from me. Your crassness in the dungeon makes a little more sense now." She must have just checked on me while I harvested the last troll and ogres.

We studied each other, and I broke the stalemate. "Is it going to be a problem?"

Glasha cracked a tusky smile. "Just don't go showing it off to a warlord. They will find a way to challenge your honor to get it from you," she chuckled.

"My honor?" I questioned.

"They will say you don't have enough honor to possess something so precious. Or that you are too selfish to own it. Or that you are in their lands and haven't declared it. They always think of something if they see something they want. Some of the Caliphate clerics are the same," she explained, laying out her race's convoluted logic.

"Trying to steal from me is honorable?" I said, shaking my head in disgust.

Glasha laughed. "Stealing? You need to spend time among our warlord elite warriors. Only then can you truly understand our sense of honor—doing what is right for the Caliphate and our people is at the forefront of their minds, but I concede that it can be twisted for personal gain as well."

"Do I trust you, then, to put my secret above the needs of the Caliphate?" I said softly, eyeing the other two orcs.

"I will not use the knowledge to threaten you to become Mynasha's First. But I would keep the collector's knowledge from her just the same. She is young and—desperate to help her people." We stared at each other, coming to an unspoken understanding, and she returned to the group. I wasn't certain if I was making a mistake or not, but I was playing the cards I was dealt.

We stayed in the woods off the main road but moved toward the garrison fort. Glasha stopped just before midday to warn us that one troll, three ogres, dozens of horses, and her people's warriors were attracting carrion birds two miles away. A battle had taken place, most likely with the cavalry that had passed us, and they had only managed to kill a single troll.

"It looks like they were ambushed. The terrain features were ideal for an ambush. They fought valiantly for the Caliphate," Glasha reported somberly.

I decided to go and scout alone and covered myself in anti-scent powder. Ginger didn't like me leaving and tried to follow. Raelia rolled her eyes at me but didn't say anything. Maveith just nodded and stood watch in case I called for help.

I was confident that with my earth speak, I would not be surprised, and I was the fastest runner among us. I waited in the woods, studying the carnage with my spyglass.

The scene was horrific. The ogres and trolls had used blunt weapons on the warriors and mounts, and seemed to have torn them apart to harvest their organs. It was also a message to the next group that came down the road. It was a note saying, *We killed dozens of your people, and you only killed one of us.* I didn't leave the woods. Instead, I returned to my group, informing them of what I had found.

Inconceivably, Mynasha was not deterred. "A larger force will be assembled. That warlord was too anxious to gain honor and glory for himself. The next assault will be more organized, with the support of stronger clerics," Mynasha stated firmly. Maybe she felt some guilt for not riding with them. If she had, she would most likely be among the dead.

"If you wait, you will most definitely miss the Choosing," I reminded her.

"Some things are more important. If these trolls break into the country, hundreds of my people will be at risk and it will take many weeks to track them down." She stood straight. I had to admire her conviction. I nodded and agreed that we would continue to scout the fort.

We stuck to the woods and rocky cliff face until Glasha halted us a few hours later. "The garrison fort and passage are just a few miles away. If I am given enough time to prepare, I can scout from here." I waved for her to do it, then ordered the horses watered, rubbed down, and resaddled in case we needed to run.

Glasha examined her pack and started using metallic dust on a rock to carefully draw spell symbols in a large circle. It took her two hours to arrange the complex workings, and I thought a strong breeze would ruin her efforts, but they stayed undisturbed as she prepared to amplify her spell.

She was using ritual magic to enhance her spell form for her scrying spell. She checked her work thoroughly before she called Mynasha over. "Connect a bridge of aether to me, Mynasha. Feed the spell form slowly; do not overwhelm it." Mynasha nodded and disrobed. Blaze and Raelia did what they could to keep the Mateo's and Benito's eyes off the spectacle. I didn't move, wanting to know what Glasha saw in real time.

I waited as the two orcs seemed to sync their aether together, Mynasha feeding Glasha's spell. I activated my own aether sight to watch and saw aether flowing in the air through the runes. It was surreal, almost like a light show overlaying everything they were doing, the ground steadily emitting aether.

Glasha's eyes were closed as she reported. "They have occupied the fort," she said bitterly.

"How many?" a sweating Mynasha asked.

"Six trolls, unless there are more inside. No, seven. There is one sleeping on a roof. Ogres … I count ten, but many look wounded." I could see her face harden at something she was seeing.

"What is it?" I asked.

"They have herded a number of people for food. They killed all the warriors, but there are maybe thirty women and children from the surrounding villages." She blinked rapidly and looked at me. "The trolls and ogres we fought were probably foraging parties, finding those hiding nearby."

"We need to rescue them," Mynasha stated passionately. "They can't wait for days while the warlords gather and form a force to retake the fort. I don't care about killing the trolls; we just need to rescue the people. They are probably eating a dozen or more every day." I actually respected the cleric. She genuinely cared for her people. It was a fucking stupid idea, but at least I could respect her principles. I could now understand why Glasha thought she would also make a good Supreme.

"The only way to rescue the people is to kill the trolls," I said, shaking my head in disagreement.

Mynasha smiled. "I hoped you would say that. We just need to draw the trolls to us. I felt a ley line nexus nearby in the road. I can connect to it and will be able to use my lightning."

"Yeah, who is going to draw them to you?" I asked rhetorically, since I had already guessed it would be me. Having done it so many times, I actually considered myself a master at it.

Chapter 298: Fish in a Barrel

I went with Maveith and Mynasha to scout the nexus, not completely convinced the cleric could deliver as promised. Seven trolls seemed too big a task, especially when she had taken over a minute between lightning attacks in the last battle.

The nexus was three miles from the fort, but centered on the road, and the tree line was a hundred yards from it. When I asked if she could be halfway to the tree line in case we needed to run, she quashed my hope. "I need to be standing closer to the nexus, in the center of the road. It is a small nexus, and the closer I am to where the ley lines intersect, the easier it is and the quicker I can cycle."

I tried to make her see reason with body language and words. "I won't risk my companions. If you fail to deliver, you will be overrun. Can you make twenty attacks before they reach you? What if they throw boulders at you? Will your horse remain with you while you attack?" I bombarded her with questions, hopefully instilling some doubt in her.

"I can," she confirmed confidently. "Remember my demonstration for Tarnasha?" she boasted. Clearly, I hadn't changed her mind.

"That was fourteen? Fifteen?" I responded immediately.

"Fifteen," she confirmed. "But I could have continued." She held her chin high. I doubted her assertion, since she had been practically falling over on her walk back to the cabin.

I sighed, took out my spyglass, and looked up and down the road. The good thing was that the road was clear for twenty paces on both sides, so it would be challenging to create an ambush. "It's muddy from the rain. Should make it easier to outrun them on horseback," I said, more to myself than anyone else.

"You are going to do it?" Mynasha asked, surprised.

"Yes, but these trolls seem somewhat intelligent, and they may not even leave the fort. I also plan to ride past you when I retreat. I am not stopping to protect you, and my companions will not be defending you either." I stated firmly, leaving no room for debate. She would either deliver or be swarmed.

My actions were not wholly selfless. I admitted to myself that there was some gnawing greed in me that knew I could perhaps manage to get more healing affinity essences. They were extremely rare, and increasing my affinity would increase the speed and efficiency with which I could heal using my spell form.

When we returned to our camp, I listened to a tired Glasha report. "There were a few fights between the ogres that the trolls eventually stopped. An eleventh ogre returned with two injured orc children to add to the pens. I didn't see anything else for a mile out, but I think the trolls are worried that their brethren have not returned."

I frowned, knowing it would be harder to draw them out of the fort if they suspected their fellows had been slain. Glasha did have some good news. "There was no activity at Skull Passage to the Endless Dark," she finished. I nodded my thanks.

She looked exhausted from the hours of using her aether. "Rest. I will post Maveith and Raelia to guard the camp."

Mateo was the angriest when I told them my plan. "Eryk, you cannot fight a troll-cursed army by yourself!"

"At least let us support you from range at the tree line. We can have the horses ready to go if we need to flee," Blaze offered as a compromise. Maveith nodded in agreement.

Raelia's eyes challenged me as well. "Why are we following you if you keep trying to get yourself killed?" Was she worried about me?

I dug my heels in. "No, you will not join the fight." Before they could object, I continued, "You can watch from the tree line, but do not reveal yourselves." I knew they would ignore my orders if I got in trouble, but at least I could end this argument now. I wanted to get this over with before night fell and our reconnaissance could change. I let everyone rest for a few hours before we moved toward the road.

We left all our camping gear behind near the cliff to make our loads as light as possible in case we had to flee. It was late evening when I reached the road, with maybe four hours of sunlight remaining. "How far to the fort?" I asked, rubbing Ginger's neck reassuringly.

Glasha entered her scrying trance and spoke while scouting. "Just under three miles to the fort and another mile to Skull Passage beyond. As you get closer, another cliff will emerge on your right. Both cliffs eventually converge in a crevice: Skull Passage. But before that, the fort will be built into the cliff face on your left. A small village used to surround the garrison, but it looks like the ogres destroyed the buildings for fun." She opened her eyes. "I count eight trolls and eleven ogres now."

"Where did the extra troll come from?" I asked, annoyed but not worried. In the grand scheme of things, one more troll would not make a difference.

A bit frustrated, she snapped back, "It might have been nestled comfortably in one of the buildings, wrapped in quiet sleep, or maybe it was scavenging for food nearby." Her voice was tinged with exhaustion. "I did my best."

I nodded, accepting the final tally. "Let's go and see if I can bait them out."

I rode into the road with Mynasha, and she staked her mount to the ground behind a boulder, walking twenty feet away. I frowned. That massive gray would tear free if things got hairy. I added another stake and line to hold him, hoping it would work, but I thought he was too far from the cleric. Would she even have time to get in the saddle before they reached her?

I walked to where Mynasha had situated herself behind a waist-high rock on the side of the road. "Run if you cannot handle it. Don't wait," I advised one last time. I didn't wait to see if she acknowledged me as I continued past her, pulsing earth speak as I went. One of the healing essences appeared in my hand

384

as I walked. I really shouldn't take this, as my core needed more time to settle, but even a tiny advantage would be welcome. Thinking better of it, I exchanged the major healing essence for the minor one and consumed it.

I had been right to be cautious, as the essence indigestion was much worse than a few days ago and I almost vomited. When it settled, I pulsed earth speak and continued walking.

My cautious approach was rewarded a mile later when a crude pit trap with a foul-smelling ogre hiding inside was revealed. Dry grass covered the pit, and the ogre stirred restlessly inside, eager for me to come closer to spring his surprise. I guessed they had tossed the excavated earth into the wide stream nearby. It wasn't a bad attempt, as it would look like trampled grass to the unobservant.

I obliged the ogre and continued my patient approach. I didn't notice any other obvious areas of matted grass, and at the extreme range of my next earth pulse, I confirmed no other pit traps within sixty feet. I removed the ogre's head. Well, most of its head. I had done the action while blending my earth pulse and dimensional space overlay. The ogre collapsed into the pit, and Ginger yanked her reins at the noise, trying to warn me. We had been upwind, and she had not smelled or sensed the ogre.

I gently stroked Ginger's neck, soothing her as I waited for my aether to recharge. My senses were heightened, alert for any signs of danger, and Ginger fidgeted beside me, her unease clear as she tried to understand my ignorance of the danger she sensed. She didn't realize I had already handled it.

As the wind briefly shifted, it carried with it the unmistakable, pungent scent of the ogre, causing me mild nausea. I instinctively reassured Ginger again, feeling her tension under my hand. "I can sense your apprehension, girl," I murmured softly, "and I think you might be right about this."

She didn't talk back, but I imagined her eyes saying, "Get the fuck on, and let's get the hell out of here." I dropped the ogre's head in the pit before continuing to complete the unenviable task of climbing down there to harvest its essence. Getting so close to the bloody, foul giant in the enclosed space was almost not worth the minor strength essence.

It was getting closer to dusk when I finally continued our slow walk. I could see both sides of the ravine narrowing, funneling me toward my target. I spotted the fort from over a mile away. The surrounding countryside had smoldering and flattened buildings. They had left nothing standing.

My appearance caused a stir. With the spyglass, I could see ugly troll heads popping over the wall to look in my direction. The question was whether any of them would rush out of the gates. I sent one last earth pulse before swinging up into Ginger's saddle. Her body language told me she was ready to turn around, but instead, I stubbornly waited. Just when I thought the trolls were too smart to fall for the ploy, seven ogres and four trolls burst out of the damaged gate.

I held Ginger with my knees as I studied the force rushing me. A few of the ogres limped, and one was missing an arm. The trolls were shepherding the ogres forward, one swatting an ogre with a wooden maul that had once been a tree. The ogre stumbled but picked up his pace. I felt flattered that they had sallied forth with such numbers just for me.

I turned Ginger and started her at a trot. She wanted to run, smartly, but I held her back. Her training made her obey, but I suspected I was going to need to give her some apples for putting her through this. We couldn't get too far ahead of the ogres or the trolls might give up. For the next mile, I let them slowly close in on our position.

When I noticed Mynasha's horse tethered in the distance, a boulder crashed to my right, sending up a spray of dirt as it skipped down the road. I turned back and saw that the group had reached the ogre pit and stopped. The trolls were angrily tossing rocks at us, and I kicked Ginger to get her off the road as more boulders crashed down. "I think they are angry," I told Ginger as I scanned the sky for the arching rocks.

The trolls had probably planned to push me into the ogre pit, thinking I had bypassed it. I was fortunate that only two trolls seemed motivated to throw boulders at me. It was easy enough to judge their trajectory and move Ginger in plenty of time. After a dozen or so futile throws, the trolls seemed to start an argument, causing me to wait. One troll eventually punched another, sending it crashing to the ground in a tangle of limbs. Then, at the barking order of the troll, the ogres were unleashed.

The ogres broke into a run. Weirdly, their steps had a single cadence. Seven ogres could create tremors even when running together almost half a mile away. I didn't wait long before retreating. Approaching the stone where Mynasha hid, I could smell the ozone in the air from the aether she had gathered. She was primed and ready, and the question was whether she could recharge fast enough to kill the rushing ogres and trolls.

I trotted past her and stopped at her gray mount, shielded behind the boulder where it was staked. I said I had planned to leave her to her fate, but I was curious about whether she could pull it off. I switched to my aether sight to see her work the aether around her. The ground was oozing wisps that rose and coiled around her in a maelstrom. Her naked body glistened and steamed as it perspired from the effort of controlling the power she was drawing to herself.

I watched as the charging ogres rushed forward, oblivious to the fate that awaited them. Nervousness settled in as the lead ogre closed to within a hundred yards. Their all-black eyes gave them a sinister appearance that was probably not needed in the current circumstances. The ogres were barely staggered in their approach, and I didn't think Mynasha would have enough time to take them all down with them bunched together.

Just before the ogres reached fifty yards, the cleric stepped out, revealing herself, her hand stretched out. Lightning dashed forth and lassoed the leg of the lead ogre. The cleric released her end of the tether, and it recoiled toward the ogre in a flashing explosion. My eyes were not affected, as my aether sight was active, and I saw the ogre's leg blown off its body. The concussive force and sound staggered the others around it. The surprise had slowed them.

A breath later, another lightning bolt lassoed a second ogre, this time around the chest. I could tell by the thickness of the lightning that it was not as powerful as what she had used on the trolls. When she released this time, the strike blew large chunks of flesh away and caused the dark-skinned ogre to stagger and fall. My attention was distracted as the noise and light show spooked Mynasha's mount. The large gray had already freed one of his stakes.

A third and fourth lightning strike flashed and cracked behind me as I tried unsuccessfully to get the horse to calm down from atop Ginger. My attention was split as Mynasha slowed the ogres' rush. I assumed they were blinded, deafened, and confused as well. The trolls were still coming but had slowed at the onslaught of lightning.

She was actually doing what she said she would do. A fifth ogre was lassoed and exploded, its head shooting high into the air. The remaining two ogres were disoriented and blind, tripping over the body parts of their companions. My ears were ringing, so I couldn't hear the ogres howling in pain. Her next lightning strike targeted a troll who had come within her range. If she failed to take it down in one strike, she would have to flee or risk being overrun.

She invested more aether in this lightning and managed to wrap the troll's right leg. The lightning explosion didn't remove the appendage but did expose the bone and destroy the muscle. As the flesh was stripped from its appendage, the twenty-foot, grotesque monstrosity was felled like a tree. As it fell, Mynasha targeted the next troll, getting lucky by wrapping its leg as well.

The remaining two trolls who had been trailing the others reconsidered their decision and turned to run, quickly getting out of Mynasha's range. She shifted her focus to the two disoriented ogres. The repeated lightning strikes had finally spooked her mount enough, and it was racing down the road away from the fight.

Cursing, I went after it while the lightning strikes continued behind me. Ginger trusted me to guide her, as she was also somewhat blinded. I caught the gray's reins at a full run and slowed it, Ginger's body crashing into the gray's as I yanked hard. The thunderous explosions had ended, and I returned with Mynasha's horse.

As aether healed my ears, I could hear a lone moaning ogre. Mynasha was prone on the ground, but no enemies appeared around her. I dismounted to check on her, seeing my companions rushing from the woods. "Get her into the woods and to safety," I ordered. "We will be in trouble if those two trolls stop running and return!"

Benito and Mateo worked to get the cleric across her horse, covering her and then laying her unconscious body across the saddle. "Raelia and Maveith, stay with me for the moment."

Benito led the large gray to Glasha and Tarnasha. Raelia was impressed by the carnage. "The cleric conjured nearly twenty lightning strikes. And you look unwounded." Was there a tinge of relief in her voice at the latter? I nodded like it had happened just like I expected it to.

After I watched the others fade into the trees, it was time to work. "Maveith, make sure they are all dead. Raelia, keep watch while I harvest the essences," I said eagerly. For once, I was reaping the rewards of another.

Maveith silenced the one bellowing ogre and then gave each troll head a few blows. I started with the trolls, getting two major healing essences. With their essences harvested, they would not regenerate. Mynasha had struck each one three times to make sure they were dead. Large sections of their skeletons were exposed. The first two ogres gave minor strength essences, while the third gave a major constitution essence. My boots were coated in bloody mud and gore as I waded through charred flesh and bone. The air smelled so strongly of ozone, I couldn't smell the ogres at the moment.

My harvest was interrupted by Raelia. "Riders coming down the road."

I looked toward the garrison first, seeing nothing. Then, turning the other way, I saw a cloud of dust in the distance. I harvested another minor strength essence before storing the collector and standing with my companions. "Display your adventurer's medallions," I said before they reached us.

A thundering company of over two hundred orc warriors and clerics surrounded us while gaping at the carnage. A dark-green-skinned orc with tattoos appeared to be in charge and rode forward to address us. "I am Warlord Krage. You adventurers have done the Caliphate great honor in battle."

I looked at Raelia and Maveith before speaking. "We were only tasked with guarding Cleric Mynasha. This is all her work. She is resting in the woods with two other clerics and three of my company." I pointed to where they had disappeared in the woods. "We think the fort still has six trolls and four ogres. They have imprisoned over thirty of your people for food if you are seeking honor for yourself."

I just wanted him to leave so I could use the collector on the rest of the ogres. That was not going to happen. He sent some of his warriors into the woods to find the clerics, and then dismounted with his two clerics to inspect the dead ogres and trolls. At least with Warlord Krage here, we might be able to continue on to the capital.

Castile looked over the young mage on the bed that Eryk had left her to deal with. She was probably attractive under the gag and all the grime. She sighed as she pulled out the short knife hidden on her hip and cut the cordage and leather straps binding her ankles, but left her hands tied. Eryk had gone overboard with securing her, and she didn't want to waste time unraveling the knots.

She wondered what he meant when he said he was rough with her, but doubted he had abused the woman. It wasn't in his nature, but then again, she had been wrong about so many men in her lifetime. He also couldn't escape fast enough from the room after depositing her—so maybe he had some guilt about how he had treated her. It was still unfathomable to her that he could store people in his dimensional space. She guessed she was even now underestimating its size.

Next, she checked the bandage wrapped around the woman's thigh. It was still wet with blood and hadn't clotted completely. The mage poison must be new to the Hounds, as she had never heard of it, or perhaps it was a secret that Erk was not supposed to share. Since they frequently hunted rogue mages, it made sense that they would have ways to deal with them. She cleaned the wound and put on a fresh dressing. Eryk had mentioned that healing potions would be less effective until the poison cleared her body, so maybe that could wait until after she awoke and could access her core.

She left the gag on for now and moved to the writing desk with Selene's pack. She started emptying it and laying out its contents. The woman had certainly taken a small fortune: stacks of gold and silver and two modest piles of jewelry. She searched the jewelry, but didn't find anything that excited her aetheric probing.

Returning to the bed, she pulled away the gag. Eryk could have used something a little less soiled. It was best that she didn't wake up with it in her mouth. As she cleaned the woman's face with water from the pitcher in the room, some familiarity struck her. Maybe she had seen a younger version of Selene during her time as a mage commander. Then again, the First Citizens were all related in one way or another, so she could be confusing her with someone else.

A knock came at the door, and she found Lirkin standing there. On seeing the bound woman, he looked over at the bed questioningly. Castile gave him a look. Now was not the time for questions. Distracted, he asked, "I wanted to see if you wanted something to eat. I will need to go to the market." Judging by his expression, he clearly wanted to know who the woman was, and his eyes bulged at the fortune on the writing desk when he noticed it.

"Yes. Prepare something for the three of us." Castile wouldn't give him details, as she didn't have them all herself. "How has the hiring been going?"

Lirkin snapped his attention back to Castile. The two servers who had worked at the inn and cleaned the rooms had left when the establishment was sold, so he was interviewing replacements. He was seeking probably four servers or maids and one barkeep. Lirkin planned to do all the cooking himself. Lirkin found his voice. "I interviewed a dozen this morning. I'm glad Mateo and Benito had already left; some were quite comely and they would have scared them off. I talked to the woodcarver for a new sign as well."

"Oh, have you decided on a name then?" Castile said, still ignoring the identity of the bound woman.

"Yes, Adrian's Rest," Lirkin said.

"Fitting," Castile replied, smiling, her throat getting tight. Castile finally indicated the woman. "She should be up in a few hours. Perhaps while you are out, you can get some simple clothes for our guest. You can use some of her coin." Castile's nose twitched. "Draw her a bath when you have time. I need to keep an eye on her."

Lirkin nodded obediently, took two gold coins from the desk, and left. His mindset was still rooted in not questioning his mage commander. That would change over time if she stayed with him. He was a good man, close to her age, and they might grow closer eventually. She still wanted a family, and maybe when she felt truly safe, she would seek his bed if she didn't find another.

Selene had light auburn hair and a soft, oval face. Castile checked her eyes to make sure she was not faking being asleep; they were a lovely, soft green. She wished she had been blessed with such looks. She found it disconcerting that both Viridia and Selene were so lovely. Did Eryk have some type of heroic disposition for rescuing beautiful women? She smirked to herself, as he had, in a way, rescued her. By that logic, she would be considered beautiful even though she knew it was far from the truth.

Castile closed her eyes and sent out her all-seeing eye, a habit she had developed in the Legion. She checked her surroundings periodically if she didn't have legionnaires on guard. The aether burn had not lessened after the lessons from Elaro, but she could see that their effectiveness would come with more practice.

She searched the building and the stables, finding nothing but the old innkeepers packing a wagon in the small courtyard out back. In three more days, they should have all their belongings moved. Castile searched Selene for weapons, but guessed Eryk had already done so. She did find a thin knife strapped to her inner thigh and smirked, imagining how Eryk would have reacted if he had found it. At least it proved he had not abused her in that way. She also discovered another secret pouch containing twenty more small gold coins, which she added to the desk.

She thought about stripping the mage, as she had pissed her undergarments, but decided to let her wake on her own first. Many hours later, Selene Greco stirred. Castile waited until she opened her eyes groggily and started to panic. "Calm yourself, Selene," Castile soothed. "You are safe and in the company of friends. I will free your wrists once you are fully awake."

Selene's mouth was dry and hoarse as she tried to speak, so Castile gave her water so she could wet her tongue and throat. Her voice was uncertain as she recalled her memories and took in the room. "Where am I?"

"Gramney, the capital of the Grand Duchy of Manch. You are in Adrian's Rest, an inn in the city," Castile said levelly, giving her more water.

"How did I get here?" Selene asked as she regained more alertness.

Castile couldn't help but chuckle a little. "A mutual friend smuggled you out of the Empire. Don't worry, according to him, they are certain you are dead." Selene tried to sit up and Castile helped her. Her eyes focused on the wealth on the table. Castile put her at ease, "It is all yours. Lirkin took some coins to get you some fresh clothes and food. But I have not touched a thing. If anything is missing, it is because he gave it to your legionnaires."

Confusion and realization washed over her face. "Helena and Sylvia live? Are they here as well?" Hope was in her voice.

"I don't know if they still live. Your abductor left them alive, though," Castile replied. "I am Mage Castile Duval, ex–mage commander of the Empire."

Selene's glassy eyes stayed fixed on Castile, seemingly still fighting the effect of the oblivion pills. "Ex–mage commander?"

Castile didn't know how to break the news softly, so she just said it. "The Emperor is dead. Rumor is that Duke Octavian is maneuvering for the throne and is close to seizing it."

"Good! He killed my parents!" Selene said angrily, and the tendons in her neck bulged.

Castile observed her flaring anger for a moment before saying more calmly, "The Emperor was too addled to order the death of your parents. According to the man who rescued you, it was Centurion Sergius of the Western Hounds and Duke Octavian who plotted to gain your family's mines."

Castile studied her reaction for a long time as Selene processed the news. Confusion, disbelief, and then anger passed over the woman's face. "I knew Duke Octavian was involved, but I thought it was only at the direction of the Emperor. The Emperor was furious with my father for rejecting his son's marriage proposal to me."

Seeing that Selene had gained an understanding of the situation, Castile cut the bonds on her wrists. Selene rubbed the red marks on her wrists and Castile watched her carefully, ready to act if she tried to form a spell. "What do you plan to do now? You are far from the Empire, and the Empire is being squeezed from all sides."

Selene was quiet and lost in thought. In a deep, serious voice, Selene responded, "If it wasn't the Emperor, I will do whatever I can to make Octavian suffer for the murder of my parents."

"Then we're of the same mind," Castile said reassuringly. "It's best we keep to the shadows for now and wait for word from the Empire. I still have contacts in a few of the cities." Castile leaned in slightly, lowering her voice. "If we act too soon, Octavian will know we're here. And truthfully, the Empire may tear itself apart without our help."

She paused before adding, "The Bartiradians may be licking their wounds, but from what little I've heard, there's a goblin army stirring in the south, Caliphate orcs pressing from the west, and the Esenhem elves tightening their grip on land they have occupied."

Castile didn't understand why she couldn't let go. She could live quietly in the Grand Duchy, but she owed too many debts. Most of her soldiers had died needlessly because of the First Citizens' whims. She needed time to heal, but it felt good to be on the offensive instead of always on the defensive.

Lirkin's footsteps echoed in the hallway, and he knocked. "A bath is prepared, and food will be ready in an hour. Clean, used clothes are in the bathroom."

"Thank you," Castile said in a dismissive tone. Lirkin walked away. She turned to Selene. "Your abductor saved another woman, Viridia Janus, who is of the same mind as us. Now, Selene, it will take time to build some trust between us, but you must not tell anyone how you arrived in Gramney ..." Castile hoped the impressionable young mage could be molded into an ally.

Castile sat with Viridia Janus in the small apartment behind Adrian's Rest. This was where Castile now lived, as Lirkin had taken one of the inn's rooms and seduced his barkeep. She wasn't a bad woman for him—a widow with two boys who worked at the inn's stables. She was somewhat jealous of how easily he had fallen into the life of an innkeeper. He was even growing a paunch on his belly. Castile struggled to let go of the Empire.

"How is the burn today?" Viridia asked, concerned as she sipped some wine she was evaluating for bulk trade.

"Same. The exercises are working, but it is going to take time. Maybe in a year I will be able to ignore it," Castile said softly. Viridia offered her a sympathetic look. "Did Selene leave?"

Viridia nodded. "She left this morning to hire more guards for the olive orchards. I have faith that Selene will handle the troublemakers." Viridia had been doing everything she could to gain control over her husband's fractured trade empire. The olive orchards were especially important to her, not just for the wealth they would bring but also because they spat in the face of Emperor Octavius, who now controlled the Telhian Empire's monopoly on olives and olive oil.

In just two more years, her orchards would start bearing fruit. Then, she could begin encroaching on the Empire's significant profits. Viridia seemed to believe that damaging the Empire's finances was the best course of action. Selene Greco, the former First Citizen Mage, wanted to confront them directly, but they didn't have an army.

Castile had seen the Empire's corruption from the inside, and now she wanted to hasten its collapse—from a safe distance. Her aim was for it to fall under the weight of its own rot, sparing the people as much suffering as possible.

"I wanted to discuss our agents in the Empire," Castile said, savoring a sip of cold wine. It was crisp, rich, and definitely a product worth pursuing. Viridia rolled her emerald eyes in response. It had taken Castile weeks of persuasion to get her to fund the fledgling spy network. Time was already slipping away. Castile knew they had to move quickly before their connections dried up. There were precious few they could trust with the knowledge that the three women—all presumed dead—were alive and quietly hiding in the Grand Duchy of Manch.

"We can't trust anyone from Telha," Viridia groaned again. Castile thought she hated sending so much gold for possibly no gain.

Castile prepared the same argument again. "Viridia, we need agents in Telha. They only need to keep us apprised of what is happening. They don't need to know who is paying them," Castile said patiently.

"But why a duchess?" Viridia moaned. She had a hatred of all First Citizens and it had taken her some time to warm to Selene.

Castile calmed. She had grown to like Duchess Veronica in her time in Sobral. The Duchess was a good woman and the only one left alive from Antonia Segreto's network that she was aware of. "Duchess Veronica has no love for Emperor Octavius. I am surprised she has not been supplanted, but I suspect it is because Sobral Province has nothing of value besides the people," Castile said patiently.

A little exasperated, Viridia lamented the cost. "Still, two thousand gold?! That is nearly half of our budget."

Castile explained for the umpteenth time, "She needs the gold to stabilize her lands and resist the pressures of Emperor Octavius."

Something caught Castile's eye. The door to the kitchen was pushed open. No one should be in the house. She cursed, the pain of aether burn flaring as her shadow chains extended. If it was just one assassin, she could handle it. Her chains halted the attacker, constricting him. Castile was shocked by the scruffy, gray-bearded face before her. She thought he was dead. Was he here to kill her?

It had been a tough trek across the Bartiradian Kingdom. Konstantin had abandoned everything that marked him as a legionnaire. He kept his two runic blades hidden, wrapping them and using them as stakes in his oversized pack. The kettle of souls was tucked at the bottom of his pack. He had been posing as Gilda's brother and Helena and Sylph's father as the group moved deep into enemy territory, pretending to be refugees. Gilda spoke fluent Bartiradian, and the others were learning rapidly.

Konstantin found the generosity of the Bartiradians off-putting. No one in the Telhian Empire would be so welcoming to strangers. Whenever they told their tale of their farm being swallowed in the war, generous handouts of food and offers of shelter abounded. It didn't hurt that he appeared to be an old man with two daughters in his care. Sylph's charming and disarming smile didn't hurt their cause either.

He wasn't sure how he felt about Gilda inviting herself along. The shapeshifter had chosen her portly-old-woman appearance. She had introduced herself as Konstantin's wife on one occasion, and he had to share a room with her that night. He didn't sleep at all, too on edge in such close proximity to a creature he had been taught to hunt and never trust.

He saw Gilda as a lost puppy looking for a master, and for some unfathomable reason, she had decided Konstantin was it. It still made his skin crawl when he thought about her true nature. He also knew the woman had an odd idea of empathy and morality. It made him hesitant to discard her for fear she would turn on him. Just like Antonia, he had trouble thinking of her as anything other than a tool.

Crossing the border from the Kingdom of Bartiradia to the Grand Duchy of Manch was a lot easier than they had thought it would be. A customs office had recorded their names in the Duchy logbook and made sure they had no merchant goods before an illusionist mage scribed their pictures on parchment for their records. Then they were free to enter.

The capital of the Duchy, Gramney, was only fifty miles from the border. He was betting that Castile had told Eryk to go there before they separated and that Eryk had passed the message to the ex-legionnaire, Helena. He hoped to find whatever was left of the company in the city—if any of them were still alive.

Knights of the Grand Duchy patrolled the streets of the relatively clean capital. The buildings were not as grand as those in the Empire, but the people seemed to be happy as they went about their days.

"Where do we go from here?" Sylph asked with a bright smile, now that they had reached their destination. She unshouldered her pack to roll her shoulders. The shield she had taken from Centurion Sergius was hidden inside.

Konstantin considered the city. "We can walk the trade district and get a room there before exploring the city on our own." Konstantin was eager to get comfortable with the foreign city before trouble inevitably found them.

"I will stay with Sylph," Helena countered. The two women took comfort in each other nightly, and it was hard to separate them.

"I will stay with Konstantin," Gilda added, making him wince internally, but he gave a curt nod of acceptance.

The group ate first, sampling some of the Duchy's cuisine. It was heavy on spices, garlic in particular. It was not to Konstantin's taste, but he figured he would have to get used to it if he was going to settle here. He was already considering what kind of work he could do. He was leaning toward becoming a teacher again. He had enough gold to start a free school for the poor children.

They meandered through the bustling streets of the city for half a day, completely captivated by the vibrant tapestry of cultures intermingling. It was nothing like the Telhian capital, where foreigners walked with guarded steps. The skyline was dotted with a blend of ancient architecture and modern buildings near the mighty Halton River, which stretched two hundred miles to the ocean.

Konstantin recalled teaching histories of when the city thrived right along the riverbanks, but relentless flash floods over the centuries had forced it to retreat to higher ground. Now, a myriad of port towns flourished along the river's banks, feeding the city with constant commerce. This city served as a crucial hub of inland trade for the neutral duchy, where merchants from far-off lands gathered, their voices blending into a multicultural symphony.

Konstantin saw a number of people in the current Telhian popular fashion. Each time he hoped he would recognize someone as they turned, but disappointment followed every time. Gramney was a massive, sprawling city climbing up a slope, and he shouldn't have been surprised when he had no luck locating anyone from the company.

"I'm bored," Gilda pouted theatrically. He had almost completely forgotten about the shape changer following him.

"Go explore on your own then," Konstantin said dismissively. The old woman frowned, but unfortunately, she did not leave his side.

Something caught his eye a few minutes later, and it took him a while to figure out what it was. A large, red, new sign for an inn proudly displayed its name, Adrian's Rest. Adrian was an uncommon name outside of Telha, and the red on the sign almost matched the color of Legion armor. "I need a drink," Konstantin said, not waiting to see if Gilda would follow him inside.

The common room was active, with locals eating an early dinner and young women bouncing between tables to serve and clear dishes under the watchful eye of a matronly barkeep. He found a corner table in the shadows and sat. Gilda sat across from him. Soon, they both had large plates of food and cold ales in front of them.

The fare featured traditional Telhian stew, thankfully not over-spiced, but under-salted—just like Lirkin used to make. As if the very thought had summoned him, he stepped out of the kitchens to talk with the middle-aged barkeep. Konstantin settled into the shadows and watched Lirkin, who was already developing some pudge on his belly, talk to the woman, kiss her on the forehead, and then retreat back into the kitchen.

Eryk had told the truth, and at least someone had done it. He ignored his food as he looked around the room and waited. Soon, his food got cold, so Gilda took it away without asking. The shape changer could eat twice as much as a man. Konstantin was shocked as Castile entered the room wearing a dull-blue dress next to a beautiful woman in an exquisite green dress. The other woman's eyes were an emerald green that darkened quickly in the low light of the room.

Castile overlooked Konstantin, but Gilda sensed his tension and turned to look. "Looks like your mage commander lives," she said, amused.

Castile ordered something from one of the young women and exited out the back toward the stables. "Stay here," Konstantin said, standing to follow.

He walked out the front and around the alley to the stables instead of going through the kitchens. Out back, there was the usual inn stables and what seemed to be a small two-story house. A stable boy came out, and Konstantin went to enter the stables, waving off the stable boy to say he didn't need help. Seven horses were inside. He moved out the back and through the tack room to go around behind the residence.

With a little push and pull of his spell form, he was inside the back of the residence. He was glad he still had his Hound boots. They were worn, but holding together after crossing Bartiradia. He paused, listening to the muffled conversation of the two women in the next room. The melodic voice of the younger woman and Castile's somewhat harsher but wiser voice seeped through the door.

"We can't trust anyone from Telha," the younger woman stated with irritation.

"Viridia, we need agents in Telha. They only need to keep us apprised of what is happening," Castile said patiently.

"But why a duchess?" the woman named Viridia said angrily.

"Duchess Veronica has no love for Emperor Octavius. I am surprised she has not been supplanted, but I suspect it is because Sobral Province has nothing of value besides the people," Castile said patiently.

"Still, two thousand gold? That is nearly half of our budget," the beautiful woman replied. It was clear to Konstantin that the two were plotting something in the Empire. On their way here, he had heard that Octavius had seized control of the throne, changing his name from Octavian to Octavius. The foolish citizens thought it meant there might be a chance for peace, now that the Emperor was dead. But all First Citizens lusted for power, none more so than Octavius.

"She needs the gold to stabilize her lands and resist the pressures of the new Emperor," Castile replied. Konstantin thought he had waited long enough. These two women were clearly up to some foolish things, and it was best to talk sense into them before they brought attention to themselves. Castile was free and didn't need to do anything so foolish.

He opened the door swiftly, and Castile's eyes snapped to him. Immediately, her shadow chains formed around her, and she lashed out to wrap him. He hesitated to speak because of the rage on her face. He had assumed she would be happy to see him. His chest constricted as he was immobilized.

Konstantin rasped out from under the constriction, "I am not here to kill you." The shadows slowly fell away, and he realized her face had not been a mask of rage but pain. "Burnt?" He said the one simple word when he could breathe.

Castile nodded, but still looked at him with suspicion. "I didn't recognize you for a moment. How did you find us? Did Zyna tell you where we were going?"

"Zyna is dead," Konstantin said flatly. He had liked the old fire mage.

"I know. I was there when the Emperor killed her, but she told Ignis to come here. I assumed she might have mentioned it to you as well," Castile said, her voice heavy. Konstantin winced as he rubbed his sore chest, shifting his position to sit down. This allowed him to take in the striking green-eyed beauty who was seated next to Castile.

Her gaze was focused on him with the same intensity he directed toward her, and he couldn't help but notice the way her emerald eyes sparkled with curiosity. For the first time, he felt acutely self-conscious about his disheveled appearance, the weariness of his travels evident in his unkempt hair, beard, and foul commoner's clothes.

"No, I found a pair of legionnaires who knew Eryk, and he hinted that they should come here. It was a bitch getting through Bartiradia, but we arrived this morning," Konstantin said casually.

The green-eyed woman smiled brightly, and her excitement stirred something in the old man. "Sylvia and Helena? Are they here in the city? Selene will be excited to see them."

"Yes." He nodded. "They are searching the city now for signs of other legionnaires. Did you say Selene? Selene Greco?" He had heard the two talk about the First Citizen Mage with fondness on their journey here. "Eryk didn't kill her?" he said, confused.

"Kill her?" Castile laughed, finally relaxing. "He brought her here and dumped her in my lap!"

Konstantin couldn't process what she had said. "What? When? Eryk is dead."

Castile stopped laughing. "Dead? You should know better by now. He arrived in Gramney before us! Took an Adventurers Guild ship to Esenhem and portaled from the elven lands here."

The shock of the news stunned Konstantin. He was only able to whisper one word. "Alive." A tear started to form, and he quickly rubbed it away to hide the weakness.

Konstantin gathered himself, not wanting to show weakness in front of Castile or the woman. "Where is the boy then?"

"I will go and tell Selene her legionnaires have come for her. Maybe they can join the mercenaries we're hiring for the olive orchards. I think it will be fun to see their shock when they see Selene alive," said the woman. She winked at Konstantin, and it sent tickles of electricity through him. "I hope it is as entertaining as seeing this man's reaction to hearing about Eryk."

He needed to get a hold of himself and not lust after a woman he had just met. The sensual woman rose. "We can talk tomorrow after I bring my children to the academy for classes." Konstantin admired her backside as she left.

Of course she was married with children, he scolded himself. He watched her leave, her hips intentionally swaying slightly as she walked. Castile wore a small smirk after the door closed. "Be careful around her. She wears a few artifacts to influence men to her will."

Konstantin shook his head and hissed under his breath, "Knew it had to be something like that."

"It only magnifies their underlying desire. It does not create it," she said, breaking into a full smile. "That is Viridia Janus. Eryk rescued her and her children from Centurion Sergius's blade. But Sergius killed her husband, Merchant Milo Janus, not long after when he sought revenge." A thread of hope rose in Konstantin, but he quickly pushed it down. A beauty like that would not be interested in a grizzled veteran like him.

"I killed that spawn of Cerberus," Konstantin spat.

"Actually, I was the one who killed him," said a voice from the kitchen. Castile jumped, and Konstantin forced himself to remain calm.

"Gilda, you didn't leave our packs unattended, did you?" Konstantin motioned calmly to the now–young woman shapeshifter. "This is Gilda, Antonia Segreto's poisoner."

Castile looked over the young woman in baggy clothes and then back at Konstantin. She was trying to puzzle something out, but gave up. The pain in her body was finally ebbing away with the use of aether. Gilda sat in the chair that Viridia had vacated. "I dropped them behind the bar and asked the keeper to watch them while I pissed," she answered plainly.

Konstantin relaxed a bit. His swords were safe. "Sergius is dead, and I took the kettle of souls from the palace. Octavius will not be able to clear the Ruins of Caelora and claim the Shimmering Labyrinth."

Castile's eyes widened, and she smiled happily. "There are other ways, but your news does brighten my day. Eryk also alerted the Adventurers Guild to the discovery of the Shimmering Labyrinth. I am sure the bureaucracy and the Empire's accord with the Guild will kill any exploration for many months."

Konstantin exhaled slowly, examining the small sitting room. "Where is Eryk? And who else made it?"

Castile's happiness faded instantly. "Linus is working for Duchess Veronica. He was injured before the final battle where the Emperor fell. Firth as well, and we just received word that he and Wylie joined the Hounds."

Konstantin's eyes widened in shock. "Firth sided with Emperor Octavius?" The young Wylie followed that man's every word, so he could see him following Firth. But he had thought better of Firth.

"They are being trained to hunt deserters, from what our agents are telling us," Castile said morosely. Castile shrugged and studied Konstantin as she said her next words. "Blaze, Benito, and Mateo went with Eryk and Maveith to rescue Maveith's sister in the Caliphate."

"They did what? That …" Castile held up her hand to calm Konstantin down.

"They entered the Caliphate as adventurers. If they are careful, they should have a good chance of succeeding," Castile said reassuringly.

Konstantin wasn't buying it. He stood and paced. "Careful!? Eryk?!" he growled as he paced, lost in thought. Why did everything have to be so complicated? How did they even learn Maveith's sister was in the Caliphate? "How long ago?" he finally asked tensely.

"Two weeks and a day," Castile said, watching him. She already knew what he was going to do. All men were the same, thinking they knew better than everyone else.

"Damnable Adventurers Guild. It is a good cover for moving in orc lands. Maybe they would let an old man like me join," Konstantin said, talking more to himself than Castile.

"There should be a portal to the capital of Esenhem in two days. Eryk and the others utilized it to save time," Castile offered helpfully.

"Two days," Konstantin growled, thinking.

Gilda sat straighter, her face blank. "Are we going to join the Adventurers Guild?" Konstantin's head snapped to the shifter. Just what would he have to do to get rid of the creature?

"You can do what you want, Gilda. But it might not be safe for you in the Guild," he warned her. Unfortunately, she didn't look deterred.

"Let's eat and discuss it over dinner. I am sure Lirkin wants to see you." Castile gave him a devilish smile. "Maybe I can convince Viridia to join us."

Two days later, Konstantin extracted himself from Viridia's bed to dress and get to the teleport. Castile had pushed the two together, and Konstantin didn't resist too strongly, either. Viridia was an unattainable Venus, and she probably didn't want to get attached, but they had both needed the physical stress relief of last night—and the night before. He thought he had satisfied her needs well enough. He managed to leave without waking her.

If he was lucky, maybe Gilda would have slept in. When he arrived at the portal, Gilda was already there, still holding her young woman's appearance. A bronze adventurer's medallion hung around her neck. He grunted a greeting and they moved to the courtyard. As they walked, she sniffed him repeatedly, but her face remained blank, and she didn't talk.

Two hours later, a golden-haired elf teleported them to Artiria, the capital city of Esenhem.

Warlord Krage had a formidable constitution. I watched him stride close to the corpses of ogres and trolls, seemingly unfazed by the stench that made my eyes water now that the adrenaline of battle had faded. His boots, along with those of the two clerics flanking him, were soon caked in bloody mud and gore. The dry grass swayed lazily in the still air, causing me to think they had avoided the worst of the odor thanks to a stiff breeze conjured by one of the clerics. I caught fragments of Orcish spoken between them, mostly astonished remarks about the sheer scale of the carnage.

Relief swept over me when Krage's men emerged from the tree line ahead of my companions and charges. For a moment, I had feared they might have retreated when the cavalry arrived, mistaking it for a hostile force.

Mynasha approached, unsteady in her saddle. Krage's gaze flicked to her, but it was Glasha he recognized. Glasha, it seemed, was either widely traveled or well known among the orc ranks.

One of Krage's clerics stepped forward and bowed respectfully. "War Cleric Mynasha," he said, his voice tinged with veneration, "I have heard tales of your prowess—but witnessing your control of lightning with my own eyes is truly an honor."

Mynasha didn't respond, and I think she was using all her energy to remain awake and stay in the saddle. Glasha greeted the orcs with a smile. "Warlord Krage. Cleric Falasha. Cleric Ottasha. You are a long way from your cities."

Warlord Krage addressed Glasha stiffly. I guessed there might be some animosity between the two, judging from his tone. "We were on our way to the Choosing to support Cleric Ottasha when we were informed of the invasion from the Endless Dark."

"As were we with our own candidate," Glasha responded curtly to some hidden accusation. One of the clerics widened his eyes, trying to puzzle out who among Glasha, Tarnasha, and Mynasha sought to be the Supreme. Glasha didn't make him wonder. "Mynasha seeks to become the Supreme." The cleric, who I assumed was Ottasha, eyed his competition and then looked back at the carnage.

Warlord Krage nodded slowly. "Warlord Melkos is two days behind us. He implored us to wait for greater numbers, but …" His hand indicated the carnage.

"Mynasha needs at least two days to rest before casting battle lightning again. Perhaps you could handle the remaining six trolls and four ogres yourself? All the ogres are recovering from severe injuries," Glasha challenged him. It was a smart way to delay one of Mynasha's competitors.

I could see the indecision on Krage's face. He could gain this Caliphate currency called honor or wait. As a leader, he was processing what an attack might cost him in men and what it would gain him in honor. He slowly shook his head negatively. "It is too much. A mountain troll is as good as ten elite warriors."

"Will you not be late to the Choosing then?" I asked. The warlord and his clerics turned irritably to me for intruding. Glasha just smirked, realizing what I was doing.

Cleric Ottasha spoke with icy words. "Adventurer, Caliphate business is not your concern."

Glasha made to speak, and I irritably thought about removing her head, thinking she was going to inform the new arrivals that I was serving as Mynasha's First. Thankfully, she didn't. "The human speaks the truth. The Choosing will begin in two nights under the full moon."

Ottasha growled, showing his tusks. "They will wait for me. Elder Daccasha herself suggested I become a candidate."

Tarnasha laughed loudly from atop his mount. It was clear these orcs didn't know who the old orc cleric was. I guessed he was too long removed from orc politics. "Daccasha scrubs the latrines for the Council of Elders. She is the youngest and least liked among them. Her word is as valuable as the leaves you use in latrines." The old orc said it convincingly, but I was unsure how he could still be in tune with the politics since he had been in seclusion. I guessed that maybe Glasha was not his only visitor.

His words did silence Ottasha, who went into deep contemplation. The warlord's men returned from scouting the garrison fort, and an animated discussion ensued. They were too far away for me to hear, and the rapid speech made it difficult for me to pick up much, other than that they were discussing the wrecked village and the trolls in the fort.

I moved closer to Glasha, who was still mounted. "Has Mynasha done enough? Can we depart for the capital and leave them to finish the job?"

She watched the warlord for a moment before dismounting to talk to me privately in a whisper. "I think we will be leaving in the morning once Mynasha has had a full night to recover. Otherwise, she might not be able to remain in the saddle." She indicated Warlord Krage. "Either they will attack at first light or wait for Warlord Melkos, who should bring at least five hundred warriors.

Either way, Mynasha has earned enough honor to depart. These clerics have witnessed it and can attest to it when they reach the Choosing after us." She didn't sound confident, but it was probably the only course of action open to Mynasha.

I nodded to Benito, Blaze, and Mateo, a signal to retrieve the gear we had secreted along the cliff. From his body language, I guessed that Ottasha was worried by Mynasha's display of power and her fearless confrontation with the trolls. Of course, she had some help drawing them out of the fort, but I didn't need any credit. I did wonder what they would make of the ogre I left in the pit. Most of its head had been cleanly removed, and not by lightning.

The warlord's warriors began setting up defenses and a camp just off the road. I looked to Glasha to see what her plans were. She had been listening in on the conversation between the warlord and two clerics. When they parted ways, she approached me. "Warlord Krage was planning to serve as Ottasha's First, but is now reconsidering." She had a mirthful smile on her face.

"Is he going to serve as Mynasha's First, then?" I asked hopefully.

She hissed in displeasure at me. "Unlikely. There is some turbulent history between us. He does not think Ottasha stands a chance and doesn't want to lose any honor by standing with him as his First." She shook her head. "Warlords are battle-focused, and they only see power in strength. The strongest cleric does not always win the seat, but eliminating Ottasha now is good for Mynasha, so I will not dissuade him." Caliphate politics were beyond my understanding, but at least it sounded like we would be leaving soon.

I turned to find Mynasha seated and Mateo serving her some food, which she ate mechanically. "Will Mynasha be ready to leave in the morning?" I was half worried she would want to see the battle to its conclusion.

"I will make certain of it," Glasha stated confidently. I nodded and went to join my companions.

We made camp in the safety of the tree line. I rewarded Ginger's bravery today with a pair of apples after rubbing her down. Since I was slightly worried about the trolls attacking in the night, I forced myself to sleep early so I could remain on watch through the night. Even a quarter mile away, the ogre's stench reached us. The orcs would burn the bodies in the morning, but if they did it now, the stench would be much worse. Burning ogre fat was a good way to repel insects—and people.

Maveith woke me with a gentle shake a few hours later. He knew best how much sleep I needed with the ring. My large friend hovered, relaying the news of what I had missed. "We are leaving at first light. Mynasha has been convinced to leave and not join the final assault to reclaim the fort."

"That is wonderful news," I acknowledged while working out the kinks in my neck that had formed from sleeping on the hard ground. The warlord's camp had a number of fires a short distance away, but all seemed quiet. Raelia was up and moved to walk with me to the watch. She probably planned to sit with me for the rest of the night. She found a tree on the edge of the camp, and we sat on either side. It was far enough away that we could whisper without disturbing the others.

It wasn't long before she asked, "If we find and free Maveith's sister, will you be going with them to Stone Mountain Island?"

"Most likely," I said. I awkwardly paused before asking, "Are you coming with us?" The small elf woman grew on you after a while, and I didn't mind her company. I thought she was no longer angry with me for my decisions, as well.

"Are you inviting me?" she asked in a slightly mischievous tone. It was odd how well I was getting to know her nuanced speech.

I could tell she wanted me to say something but I was not sure what. "You don't need me to invite you. You are free to travel wherever you want. You are welcome to stay in our company, but I plan to send Blaze, Mateo, and Benito back to Gramney if we are successful in finding Maveith's sister."

Raelia let out a long, vocal sigh. "I should return to Artiria. My aunt granted me leave, albeit reluctantly. I have ... obligations."

I glanced over at her, then back into the night. She definitely wanted something from me. Maybe she wanted me to tell her what to do. "What kind of obligations?" I asked carefully, expecting her to dodge the question.

She surprised me by answering. "I'm meant to be a bridge," she said quietly. "Between the two Glavien branches in Esenhem and Bartiradia. They've grown apart over the last few centuries. The family heads want unity again. A symbol. That's supposed to be me."

"A symbol through marriage?" I speculated.

She nodded. "Eventually. Not soon. Maybe in two decades or so. But yes. The idea is that I'll marry into a family in Esenhem allied with House Glavien to strengthen ties."

I don't know what emotion that stirred in me, maybe jealousy. "Do you get a say in it?" I asked after a stretch of silence.

Raelia gave a soft laugh. "Of course. We are not beasts. I'll have to approve whoever it is. But it is still a duty expected of me."

I was quiet for a moment and looked over at her. "You don't seem angry about it."

She shrugged, her gaze distant. "I made peace with it a long time ago. Being a Glavien means living a long time with choices that sometimes aren't entirely your own. It's not as bad as it sounds. I've seen worse fates. It was one of the reasons I chose to be a Griffin Rider in my youth. I reveled in the freedom." A smile formed on her lips. She shifted her Ranger's cloak around her shoulders and settled against the tree. "I am taking a nap. I leave my safety in your hands tonight."

Raelia didn't say anything else after that. Her eyelids fluttered, and within minutes, her breathing slowed, but a slight smile remained. She had fallen asleep, the tension easing from her shoulders, and was probably dreaming of flying on her griffin.

Before dawn, I worked to prepare the horses, and soon, my entire group was up and preparing to ride. Mynasha was still slightly unsteady on her feet but looked much better and at least seemed self-aware. Raelia looked better this morning too. She seemed almost giddy as she bantered back and forth with Benito and Mateo.

The news from the warlord's camp in the morning was even better than we could have hoped. Two of the trolls had retreated into Skull Passage, returning to the Endless Dark. Maybe it was the two trolls who had seen Mynasha's chain lightning up close, and I couldn't blame them for gaining some sense. The departure of two of the trolls was enough to embolden Warlord Krage to assault the fort. His roughly one hundred men and two clerics rode out at sunrise.

After a quick, cold breakfast of jerky and dried fruit, we set a fast pace early, but there was no way we were going to cover three days of travel in just one day. Glasha's magic extended to knowing relative distances. She assured us that we were nearly 130 miles from the capital, a difficult distance to cover in two days, but she would keep the horses healthy.

At one point, I was riding next to Tarnasha, and he explained what was going to happen. "The candidates will be presenting themselves at sunset to the Elders in a ceremony. It is unlikely we will be able to attend." He continued gruffly, "The Choosing doesn't truly begin until the first test, which is usually the day after the candidates are recognized, but it can be delayed under certain circumstances. There are those among the Elders who might wish to start early."

His hand extended to me, the obfuscation stone in his palm. "I am not going to serve as her First," I reiterated.

"That is your choice. This is mine. You have done enough for my people to earn this. You are a match for any warlord of the Caliphate. It was an honor to travel with you," Tarnasha said respectfully.

I took the stone with a nod of thanks. I managed to find a way to secure it inside my armor. If I stored it in my dimensional space, its ability to prevent clairvoyant magic wouldn't be effective.

We rode through the following day, passing villages and farms, only stopping briefly to water the horses. In the early evening, we encountered Warlord Melkos's army. Orderly columns of riders approached, and Glasha happily went to talk with the tattooed warlord at the front. I watched from a short distance as the impressive orc grew angry. I figured it was because Warlord Krage was about to finish off the remaining ogres and trolls, making all of Melkos's effort pointless. His troops stormed off to try and join the assault.

As the sun set, we continued into the night again. The horses were feeling the fatigue, but Glasha said we were still nearly forty miles from Becar. She was doing her best to keep them healthy.

By midmorning, our exhausted party reached the outskirts of Becar. The city sprawl was immense, and I knew it was one of the largest cities on the continent. While Telha was more densely populated with taller structures, Becar was a sprawl of buildings.

A steady stream of carts flowed down the roads, laden with food and goods to supply the city. The road switched from packed earth to stone as we caught sight of the impressive walls in the distance. "The primary Adventurers Hall is near the center of the city's main square, but there is a lesser Hall on the outskirts," Glasha informed me. "We will head there and settle our accounts." I was suspicious that she was not pressing me to be Mynasha's First now that we were here.

The lesser Adventurers Guild Hall was a cavernous structure, reminding me of a church. It smelled of sweat and ale. Dozens of adventurers, mostly orcs, lounged in the large chamber. These guild members didn't remind me of the hardened fighters I had seen elsewhere, and I guessed this branch catered to easier tasks.

Glasha didn't waste time, quickly confirming our task was completed and releasing funds from her personal accounts to us. She handed me the heavy pouch of gold as soon as it was handed to her. "The Elder compound is north of the city if you are looking for us. Use Mynasha's name to gain entrance." She walked briskly outside to Mynasha and Tarnasha, and I followed. The trio of orcs rode away, circling the city with a sense of urgency.

My companions looked at me expectantly. Maveith's green eyes were heavy with anticipation. It wouldn't be long now before we either found his sister or found out what fate had befallen her. Warlord Rhuuk had purchased her more than ten years ago. The city he administered was a day's ride from the capital, but there was a chance Rhuuk was at the Choosing.

"Let's find the main Adventurers Guild and put a plan together," I said, taking the lead. We guided the horses toward the flow of orcs moving through the inner city gates. The port capital reeked of salt and fish, though the ocean itself remained blocked from view by the looming sixty-foot wall that rose before us.

"Don't look so anxious, Maveith. We are close and will have news soon." I patted my friend on the back. He was studying every goliath that we passed with an eager hope on his face, only to be disappointed. If the goliath appeared mistreated, the tendons in his neck bulged, but he restrained himself.

Maveith nodded slowly. "She might be close. We should start looking immediately."

"We are all saddle-worn. In the morning, we will spread through the city in pairs." Maveith nodded at my words.

Despite the city's size, traffic moved easily through the wide gates. A few orc guards in weathered metal cuirasses stood by, watching the crowd without much interest. Navigating the city streets with horses was slow going, even this early. We made frequent stops to ask for directions. It became clear why Glasha had been reluctant to enter. The city was a maze, and each minute inside chipped away at the time they had left to reach the Choosing.

The inner city was no longer dominated by orcs and increasingly turned into a melting pot of different races as we made our way to the center. A river split the city down the middle, and docks lined both sides, filled with dozens upon dozens of ships. The water had an oily appearance, and it was clear by the smell that the sewers flowed directly into it.

From there, it was easy to find the Guild symbol proudly displayed above the press of people. The Adventurers Hall was a grand stone building on the banks. It appeared to have a private dock with a few Guild ships tethered there. I noted that the *Shorebreaker* was not among them. After we stabled the horses, we entered.

Entering the common room replaced the foul smell of the city with alcohol and tobacco. A few curious eyes looked us over but quickly returned to whatever they had been doing. It was clear that these adventurers were much better equipped than the ones at the outer city Hall. I paid for rooms and was about to lead my companions up the stairs when I paused.

A fat old woman sat in the corner of the room. She looked vaguely familiar. Something clicked, and I placed her. She was the eastern Legion Hall cook in Telha. One of Antonia's agents. Konstantin had warned me that she was an assassin, and a chill went down my spine. There was no way she could be here for us. She was clearly wearing her guild medallion around her neck, and when we made eye contact, she smiled. It seemed like a friendly smile, but the idea that someone from the Telhian Empire recognized me was unwelcome.

Gilda. Gilda was her name. I remembered it from the one time we met. We locked eyes across the room, her smile persistent but her motivations unreadable. A dozen possibilities flickered through my mind. I had paused too long and my companions noticed.

"Do you know her?" Raelia asked from just over my right shoulder.

I figured if there was potential danger, I should make them aware. "She is a Telhian," I said, a frown creasing my brow. "She works for one of the Praetorian Guards, but Castile was under the impression that her handler, Antonia, had been killed." My mind raced, trying to identify her possible motives with the most plausible explanation I could come up with. "She might be here to disrupt the Choosing for her new master. Or maybe she is looking for deserters." I looked at my companions to make sure they heard me. "We should head to one of our rooms."

As we turned to head up the stairs, Gilda stood up and headed for the back door. The sound of clashing blades echoed from the practice yard where she was going. Damn it, she wasn't alone. The tension tightened in my stomach as I considered our options.

I hurried with my companions up the stairs and into the nearest of the rented rooms. The air hit me first. A pungent mix of sweat and stale sex. The sheets were clearly unchanged, and I doubted anyone had bothered to clean since the last guests. The orcs might tolerate humans, but that didn't mean they had to be hospitable. "Mateo, bar the door. Blaze, take the window," I said sharply, already scanning the room for anything that looked remotely clean.

I was tense, and it bled over to my companions. "What are we going to do?" Maveith's voice rumbled in the room.

"Don't worry, I will deal with her." I would make it look like an accident, maybe a heart attack. She was old and fat and it shouldn't be too hard. "While I am doing that, Raelia and Mateo will find out if Warlord Rhuuk is in the city. Then we will see if he brought Myra or Zorana with him."

"What should I do?" Maveith asked anxiously.

Maveith needed something to do to ease his anxiety and keep him from doing something foolish. "Walk the outer city with Benito. Ask some of the captains at the docks about where they are going and when they lift anchor. Start looking for the best way to escape unseen. And stay out of trouble." Maveith nodded sharply.

An abrupt knock at the door made everyone lapse into silence. I looked at Blaze, who indicated that the window was clear. I walked to the door and pulsed earth speak. The floor had stone tiles, but the building was mostly made of large timbers, and I got a fuzzy image of two people on the other side—one likely a woman and the other a man. The knock came again. "Who's there?" I asked in an annoyed voice.

"Open the cursed door," a familiar voice said in Telhian. Blaze's head snapped to me, and Mateo's jaw slackened.

Benito was the only one of us who hadn't lost his tongue, and he whispered in disbelief, "Konstantin?"

I thought it could be a trick, so I motioned Mateo back and everyone to draw their blades. I lifted the bar and carefully opened the door, prepared with my blade and my dimensional space. Konstantin stood on the other side, a satisfied look on his face. A young woman who resembled Gilda stood behind him—maybe her daughter.

"Well, are you going to let me in?" he asked smugly, but his eyes were dancing in merriment at our disbelief. His eyes studied everyone in the room with their blades readied, and he nodded in approval and acknowledgement.

"What are you doing here?" I asked. His clothes were still sweaty from practice, but he looked fit, and I could see the outline of an adventurer's medallion under his shirt.

His happiness faded, and he growled, "I came to make sure you didn't do something stupid and get yourselves killed." His eyes had settled on Raelia, and I could see the curiosity in them, trying to figure out why an elf was traveling with us.

"Well, we are all fine. Thanks for stopping by." I made to close the door. Shock appeared on his face, and he almost didn't react in time to stick his foot in the door. I let a smile crack my face, as I hadn't been serious. For some reason, with Konstantin here, it felt like things would go more smoothly.

I let him force open the door and step into the room. He caught my smile but shook his head like he was disappointed with my attempt at humor. His hand rested on my shoulder, ignoring the blade in my other hand, trusting I wouldn't skewer him. He patted me and withdrew his hand as he walked past me. I suspected that was all the joyfulness from seeing me I was going to get from the man.

The young woman followed him. She had a weird cinnamon smell that almost made me sneeze. Konstantin ignored me and clasped wrists with Mateo, Blaze, Maveith, and then Benito. He then faced Raelia, studying her, which caused her to step back. A cold chill went through me. Did he recognize her?

"Are these boys holding you against your will?" He asked half-seriously. Clearly, he was trying to get back at me for trying to shut the door on him.

Unspoken words passed between them, and Raelia smirked a little. "And what if I said yes?"

"I would do everything in my power to free you, of course," he said in terrible Elvish. I was hoping Raelia would rebuke him for his brutalization of her language, but she just laughed.

"I am here for my goliath friend." She motioned to Maveith. "I have not been kidnapped or abused—much." She added the last little bit while her eyes roamed to me. Konstantin followed her eyes to me, a bit of surprise on his face.

Irritated that the game of words was turning to his favor, I countered. "Her name is Raelia, and she came of her own free will." My tone turned to suspicion. "How did you get here?"

Konstantin spun on his heel, and I noticed he wore two swords now. He explained conversationally, "I ran into some friends of yours in the Imperial palace. They had gotten themselves imprisoned. I released them, and they said you told them to seek sanctuary in the city of Gramney."

"I helped free them as well," the young woman interjected from the doorway. Mateo was already focused on her.

My mind worked quickly, with only one name coming to the forefront. "Helena?" I said, surprised.

"And her partner, Sylph," Konstantin noted. "We traveled together to Gramney." His lips curled into a genuine smile of happiness. Not something I expected to see on the old man. It vanished as he realized what he was doing. "Seems you've been a busy man since you left my care at pup school. Helena and Sylph say they owe you a debt for saving Selene. I've already collected on the debt Viridia owed you." My face twisted in confusion, and that just made another unnatural smile form on Konstantin's face.

"But how did you get here ahead of us, Konstantin?" Blaze asked pointedly.

Konstantin motioned his companion inside, and Mateo rushed to get her a chair. Konstantin took the seat, forcing the woman to remain standing, but she did not look upset. There were no other chairs for the despondent Mateo to offer the young woman. "We caught a portal to Esenhem from Gramney. We were a little over two weeks behind you. We knew you were going to Agurtra, as that was where you thought Maveith's sister was." I nodded. His story sounded plausible so far.

"Gilda got us passage on a courier ship from Artiria to the orc city of Darchret. From there, we traveled across the Caliphate to Agurtra," Konstantin said, like it was just another normal afternoon for him.

Maveith tensed. "Did you find Zorana in Agurtra?" he bellowed, louder than it needed to be.

Konstantin shook his head slowly, causing Maveith to deflate. Konstantin's companion spoke. "I infiltrated the estate and talked to a number of slaves and staff. Zorana was not there presently, but she is alive." Maveith's hope quickly renewed on his face. "Warlord Rhuuk took her to Becar, but we have not been able to locate her in the three days we have been here."

"We were also awaiting your arrival. I assured Gilda you would eventually join us," Konstantin added haughtily.

Gilda continued as if Konstantin hadn't interrupted her. "We think the warlord has her on an estate north of here, but elites and Pathfinders heavily guard it, and several clerics are also on the grounds. We were turned back both times when we wandered close, and I don't care to try again. There are mastiffs that patrol the grounds who can sniff out anything." I looked at the woman. That might explain why she smelled like cinnamon. Something to avoid the scenting of the dogs.

"We did learn that the sprawling estate is where the Elder clerics who advise the Supreme reside," Konstantin said. That was just like Konstantin, getting more done in less time. Now that he was here, I supposed he would take over.

I hadn't liked being in charge anyway. Being responsible for the lives of others was a heavy burden. "We used our adventurer's medallions to travel freely in the Caliphate under the auspices of doing jobs." I pointed to his medallion. "How did you manage to accept job postings without registering?" I had been under the assumption that adventurers from outside the Caliphate needed to register in one of three cities: Khoura, Becar, or Imararal. Konstantin had clearly not visited any of these cities before arriving in Becar.

Konstantin shrugged. "We never took any job postings. No one ever checked if we were registered."

I ground my teeth a little and was slightly shamed. Maveith had recovered from the good news of his sister being alive. An energetic exuberance and eagerness showed on his face. "Is Myra alive as well?" Myra was Zorana's friend and had been captured at the same time.

Gilda nodded. "She is. We think she is also here, but have not seen either goliath. We have not been able to get inside the compound, with so many guards about. The warlords are meeting for some reason."

"They are selecting a new Supreme. The last Supreme is presumed dead, and word has not been spread," Raelia revealed with some bluster. I had been about to say the same thing, but she beat me to it. She smirked at me.

Konstantin's eyes widened, and he slowly nodded as the pieces fit together in his head. "Now that does make sense." His mind churned before he spoke directly to me. "I suggest we wait until a new Supreme is selected and Warlord Rhuuk returns to his estate. It will be easier to rescue the goliaths then." I was a little shocked Konstantin was deferring to me in this decision.

Maveith looked anxiously at me, and I could tell he didn't want to wait. If I didn't do it, he would probably offer his services as Mynasha's First. "I have a way to get in and check on Zorana and Myra."

Konstantin cocked his head, waiting for an explanation. I tried to make it sound like it was just another day for me. "We escorted one of the candidates to the Choosing. I was asked to be her First, but turned her down."

"I have heard of the Choosing, but what is a First?" Konstantin asked, leaning forward in his chair.

"It is usually a warlord who stands by the cleric during the Elders' selection trials. A Chronicler thinks I would make a good First for her candidate," I explained succinctly.

"Really?!" He leaned back in his chair, disbelief on his face. "Now, just what did you do to make them think that?"

Konstantin waited for me to answer. Under his scrutinizing gaze, I hesitated, as I felt he was going to judge my response. Benito broke the tension with a grin. "Eryk wiped out a whole pack of werewolves, uncovered Titan relics, killed an ankheg solo, and took down two mountain trolls on his own."

Konstantin's eyebrow rose slowly, though his eyes never left mine. "Did he now?"

Mateo jumped in, eager to add more. "Don't forget about finding a necromancer and his army of skeletons." I didn't know how two skeletons made an army.

Raelia crossed her arms and lifted her chin slightly. "He also defeated a warlord in honor combat," she said, a thread of pride in her voice. I turned to her, caught off guard by the support.

"The Hounds trained me well," I said, deflecting the credit. The lack of surprise in Konstantin's steely blue eyes made me think that Castile had shared a fair bit of information with him. I was more curious about the blank stare of the woman with Konstantin. She did not appear impressed with any of my feats. "How many more people are with you?" I indicated the woman.

Konstantin followed my gaze to the woman. "Just Gilda. She's a changeling. Antonia's father raised her from infancy, and she served their family for decades. Now she's my persistent headache that never quite goes away." Despite the sharpness in his words, there was a flicker of respect there and maybe even a hint of fondness. Knowing Konstantin, the latter was probably not intended.

"Changeling?" Mateo asked, taking a step back. His overtures to the woman were quickly being retracted. He had sheathed his sword but made to draw it again. Gilda's eyes traveled over everyone in the room, judging their reactions to her nature being so casually revealed. She didn't seem upset, just curious.

I was shocked that Konstantin was traveling with such a creature. Changelings were inferior to doppelgangers, lacking many of the qualities of true doppelgangers. While they could change their appearance, they were limited to a mostly humanoid form. They also lacked the superhuman strength of a doppelganger. I had fought powerful doppelgangers in the Shimmering Labyrinth, and they were formidable opponents. I remained calm and waited for Konstantin to explain.

He shrugged and talked about her like she wasn't in the room. "She has attached herself to me and is mostly harmless. Changelings are intelligent and have the same desires as people. But any emotions or facial expressions they express are just an act, as their true form lacks facial musculature." He gestured at the young woman.

She studied Konstantin blankly for a moment before her body changed, and Mateo tripped and fell backward to get away. The woman grew a few inches and her hair receded into her scalp. Her face went from pale to gray, and her teeth yellowed some. Her limbs elongated somewhat before the transformation finished after a dozen heartbeats. Unlike a doppelganger, the changeling still looked mostly humanoid in its natural form. I knew they had a sexual identity, unlike a doppelganger. They were still hunted in the Empire, which made Konstantin's travel companion all the more curious.

Konstantin waved his hand, signaling she could revert, and she regained the young, not unattractive woman's appearance. Mateo's blade was half drawn, and I motioned for him to sheathe it. "Fascinating!" Raelia exclaimed. "I know there are small enclaves of changelings, but I have never met one." The woman tilted her head at Raelia's words; perhaps that was her way of showing interest.

Konstantin shifted the conversation and said, "Tell me about the cleric who wants you to be her First."

Raelia was the first to reply. "She's just using him to gain the seat of the Supreme."

Konstantin studied Raelia for a long moment, then shifted his gaze to me. When he spoke again, his voice was calm but edged with steel. "I learned long ago not to trust elves. Or orcs. Or humans," he said, looking back at Raelia. "Trust yourself. Protect your family and your friends. Now, tell me about the cleric who wants you to stand with her."

I noticed Gilda moving to a corner and Mateo circling to the other side of the room to distance himself. I nodded to Konstantin, welcoming his advice. "We helped a Chronicler, Glasha, find some artifacts. She was aware of a cleric, Mynasha, who was aspiring to become a candidate for the Choosing. She thought I could help, since no warlord would stand with her without a heavy payment."

"Eryk found the artifacts with his magic earth-talking ability, but I dug them up," Benito piped up, trying to be helpful and get some credit for his work.

Konstantin arched his eyebrow again, forcing me to explain. I was unsure why I didn't like Konstantin knowing my secrets, and Benito had revealed another one. Maybe it was because I wanted to surprise him when he least expected it. "I can use my earth affinity spell form to see into earth and stone," I admitted to the veteran.

He slowly nodded, probably replaying everything he had seen me do since we met. I liked to think he was impressed. "Good. What is the danger of becoming Mynasha's First?"

From his tone, I knew what Konstantin was doing. He was trying to get me to think out all possibilities before jumping in. "According to the orcs, I would face resentment from the other candidates and Firsts, since I am not an orc. They might find a reason to accidently kill me during the trials."

Konstantin nodded, seemingly unconcerned that my life might be in jeopardy. "How long does the Choosing take?"

No one seemed to know, but I guessed. "It can't be more than a few weeks."

Maveith stirred, anxious to be included. "Mynasha promised to free my sister and Myra if she became the Supreme."

I tempered his enthusiasm, no matter how much confidence my friend had in me. When there were politics involved, nothing was certain. "There is no guarantee that I could help her become the Supreme. More than likely, I would make an enemy of the cleric who does become the Supreme."

"Well, at least you are thinking it through," Konstantin said, satisfied with my response. "Still, if they are inviting you among them, you could confirm Maveith's sister is there. It could save us time and help prepare."

"You think I should do it?" I said, slightly surprised. It would be counter to what I was taught in the Hounds—operating in the open among the enemy.

"It is your decision." Konstantin relaxed into his seat. "Either that or we wait till the Choosing is complete and follow Warlord Rhuuk when he leaves, if he leaves." Maveith got a little uncomfortable.

My mind turned to the possibilities, and I nodded. "We will go in the morning. Since we arrived late, she might have missed her chance anyway."

"We were delayed because Mynasha exploded some ogres and trolls with her lightning," Benito offered helpfully.

"I am sure there is a good story behind that. I haven't finished my training for the evening. Eryk, why don't you show me how much you have learned since we last practiced against one another." Konstantin stood, not waiting for my response, and I followed him out of the room.

The others looked ready to follow, but I waved for them to stay. I nodded reassuringly to Maveith. "Rest up." From his demeanor, I knew Konstantin wanted to talk with me alone. We descended the stairs and walked out into the practice yard. A dozen adventurers, mostly orcs, practiced as Konstantin moved to a corner. A few eyes followed us, but no one seemed overtly interested.

Konstantin whispered, "Be careful when you go. Store the goliaths in your bag and leave." He was letting me know that he was aware of my spatial powers, confirming to me that Castile had informed him.

"It might not be that easy. I need to be close, and I will be the first one they suspect if she goes missing," I said, wrapping my blade with the tacky cloth.

"Where did you get that blade?" Konstantin asked, impressed.

"I killed Boris Angella and took it. He was trying to loot Caelora when we crossed paths again," I replied casually.

Konstantin looked surprised for a moment but then grunted in approval. "You have been busy. Did you kill Centurion Sergius's son as well?"

I nodded. "I killed Corvus and destroyed the secondary Archives as you told me to." My casual tone mimicked Konstantin's usual nonchalance at accomplishing something monumental, which made Konstantin chuckle.

We faced off, borrowing the wooden practice shields in the yard. We engaged three times as we tested each other. "It looks like you lost a step or two, old man," I said, smirking.

It riled him up, and he pressed into me again. I parried his snap kick, which he used his shield to conceal, and I slapped the edge of my blade on his kicking knee, giving him a limp as he retreated.

I almost felt guilty as Konstantin's mind churned to find an advantage. I was faster, stronger, and with the dreamscape amulet, I had an equal—if not greater—amount of combat experience. The stubborn man did not give in and came at me repeatedly. I noticed my companions standing on the second-floor balcony, watching us. We were drawing the attention of the other adventurers as well.

After nearly half an hour, we were both soaked in sweat. Konstantin sported three bruises for every one he gave me. I could have healed them instantly, but I felt that would be cheating. Konstantin suddenly stopped the sparring. "Enough practice with a shield. Let's switch to two weapons." It was clear he had exhausted every trick he could think of and was left wanting.

While Konstantin wrapped his new runic blade out of sight of the others in the yard, I asked him curiously, "Where did you get that?" It looked to be a dungeon blade, but had veins that, when they reflected the sun, looked like lightning.

Konstantin snorted with a note of pleasure. "Took it off Centurion Sergius's corpse." It was clear he was not going to add anything. I went and got a weighted practice sword. There were too many eyes for me to pull a second blade from my dimensional space. I rarely practiced with two weapons and only did so in the dreamscape, so I was out of practice, which was probably why Konstantin suggested it.

We returned to our dance of blades, with Konstantin briefly getting the advantage. I quickly got accustomed to the two-weapon styles again. I did need to practice this style more, as it required split focus in my thinking. I enjoyed Konstantin's frustration more than I should have as we practiced. Then he snuck a light touch past my guard. I parried it well enough, but it brushed my thigh lightly, and small arcs of lightning raced into me, causing my leg to spasm.

Konstantin was a bloody cheater, but I quickly recovered, putting my weight on my other leg and using his flurry of blows to balance myself. My entire leg was numb and barely responding to my will. "Why did you reveal your sword's ability in a public place?" I asked to distract him. If I had shown such an ace, Konstantin would have laid into me.

"Two of the adventurers over there already know," he said, annoyed as he stepped toward my good leg. Since my back leg wouldn't respond, I couldn't pivot to defend. I laid an air shield on the ground and two in his path. As soon as he felt them, he tried to reverse his momentum, but I was too quick, slapping his hamstring and deflecting his blade.

"Your victory," he finally conceded, his tone heavy with resignation. He gestured toward a shaded spot beside one of the weathered water barrels. Konstantin swore darkly at half of the Telhian gods, his voice strained as he limped across the dusty yard. Beads of sweat dripped from his forehead, matting his graying hair. He shook his head in frustration, a look of deep disappointment etched onto his weathered face.

The area sheltered us from prying eyes and ears. The spectators drifted back to their own training, their conversations fading into the background. My companions stepped back from the balcony, but Gilda lingered, her intense gaze fixed on us for a few moments before she, too, chose to withdraw. We settled into silence as we both drank our fill of water.

"You didn't need me," he finally said.

"What?" I replied, confused.

"You can handle yourself, and the men respect you. Leadership is a burden, one you are much more suited for than me," he said considerately. I didn't know if I believed him, so I remained quiet while I thought about it. "Be careful, Eryk. Always hide what you can do."

"While I am at the Choosing, I need someone to keep Mateo and Benito out of trouble," I finally said. "Blaze could do it, but I would appreciate you helping him. We also need to find the best way to flee the Caliphate once we have Zorana and Myra. I cannot think of a better man for the job than you."

"Huh," he grunted noncommittally. "Okay. Just make sure I don't have to avenge your death. I am too old to fight half the warlords of the Caliphate." We both chucked, but I sensed he might have been serious.

We talked for a while as Konstantin gathered my stories of all our encounters on the way to Becar. He made me retell the sahuagin boarding attempt in detail and pointed out a few mistakes I had made. He was concerned about the mountain trolls from the Endless Dark, especially when I told him that Glasha thought they were summoned by a cleric. If one of the Elders or other candidates could control a dozen trolls from the Endless Dark to delay a lone cleric, they were truly dangerous.

We both moved gingerly, as I hadn't healed my injuries yet. We ate a large meal with the others in a private room, and the atmosphere was different with Konstantin here. Gilda did dampen the mood some, but it almost felt like we were back in the company as Benito embellished story after story with Mateo contributing details. Raelia was even smiling.

As the night deepened, I found myself retiring to my room, the warmth of the drinks still coursing through me. The glowstone cast dancing shadows on the walls as I settled in, my mind restless.

I reached out with my earth speak ability to keep aware of my companions. Raelia passed by my door twice, her footsteps silent on the wooden floor, yet she never stopped to knock, leaving me wondering about her thoughts.

In another room, I could sense Maveith's agitation; he was pacing, the soft thudding of his footsteps echoing through the floor. Meanwhile, Gilda had quietly slipped out of her room and found a perch on the roof of the Adventurers Hall, where she stood watch in the cool night air.

Just before dawn, the sky began to lighten, brushed with hues of purple and gold. I left the Hall and stepped through the city gates, the cobblestone road stretching out before me. The chill of the morning air energized me as I walked toward the Choosing.

The massive wall wrapped all the way around the city and encompassed the river that ran through it. On the other side of the river, north of the city's walls, the plains extended with no farms in sight. I felt out of place as I walked on the desolate road. My only weapon was my runic dagger, but I had worn my adventurer's armor. There was no one in sight as I crested a hill. Below me, in a long valley, numerous structures were dotted among black stone paths.

Large pairs of dogs walked the sprawl's perimeter under a handler's care. I was only standing there a moment before a pair of mounted orcs thundered upon me from the right. I remained calm and waited for them. Maybe I should have ridden on Ginger, as I was forced to look up at the agitated riders as they reined in their mounts.

The pair were both tattooed, and I identified them as Pathfinders by their armor and weapons. "Human, you need to turn around and go back to the city. You will only be warned once." The orc's tone was flat and threatening.

"I am here at the request of Chronicler Glasha to serve as Cleric Mynasha's First," I said confidently. The two orcs looked at each other, confused, clearly at a loss for words. They had a brief, harsh conversation, uncertain of a course of action regarding the impudent human standing before them.

The older of the two finally ordered the other, "Bring the Chronicler here. She can resolve this." He turned to me. "If you are wasting the Chronicler's time, your honor is forfeit and your life ends here, human." His voice was harder now. I nodded and waited as the other rider kicked his heels, his horse thundering down into the valley.

It got awkward, so I pulled out an apple and started crunching it. All horses were apparently the same. The Pathfinder's mount kept trying to dance closer in hopes of getting some. I could tell the Pathfinder was not a skilled horseman from his poor control over the spirited horse. I tossed the core in the grass, and the horse eagerly took it, to the consternation of the Pathfinder.

It was almost an hour before I saw Glasha's pony riding up from the valley, escorted by the Pathfinder who had gone to find her. When she arrived, she was a bit breathless but wearing a massive grin. "You have come," she said.

"Am I too late to accept your offer?" I asked, somewhat amused by the Pathfinder's disbelief that I had been speaking the truth.

"Demons, no! The Choosing has been suspended until Warlord Melkos and Krage arrive to confirm Mynasha's claim of besting five mountain trolls," she said, smiling with the knowledge that it would be confirmed. "Cleric Anatasha is about to be severely disappointed that he challenged her honor on that fact."

The Pathfinder interrupted the banter. "The human is allowed to descend to the valley, Chronicler?"

"Yes," she hissed impatiently. "He is with me. Return to watching the grass grow!" She turned her pony and walked it as I caught up with her. I gave the Pathfinders an *I told you so* look before settling in beside her.

Glasha was walking her pony at a sedate pace, and I took the opportunity to ask, "How are things going?"

Glasha groaned comically, "I don't know if it's going better or worse than expected. Tarnasha has been in six shouting matches since yesterday with the Elders about protocols. Your appearance will cause another round of quarrels, I'm sure." She grinned madly. I could tell she was having fun, even with the Caliphate's future hanging in the balance.

"What of the competition?" I asked the red-haired orc.

"Five other candidates for Supreme. The sixth and seventh have already pulled themselves out of consideration. There will be a sixth if Cleric Ottasha presses his candidacy when he arrives," she said mildly. "Three are favored more heavily than Mynasha, though. It is not going to be an easy road."

I wasn't concerned about their politics. Glasha knew why I had come, so I asked directly, "Is Warlord Rhuuk here?"

She looked over at me, her tone serious. "He is. He is serving as Cleric Jhuarkasha's First. He has four goliaths with him, but I am unsure if any are the ones you seek."

I nodded, happy but also cautious. "Is there any way you can get me close enough to confirm?"

"Unlikely. Each paired candidate and First have their own compound in the valley. The slaves do not leave the compounds." My dissatisfied look made Glasha sigh and roll her eyes. "Fine, we can stop at Jhuarkasha's compound under the pretense of arbitration."

We reached the bottom of the valley, and the mastiffs there were the size of Glasha's pony. The dogs had rich brown leather vests that matched their coats. One trotted close to me as I walked next to Glasha's pony. It sniffed the air tentatively and growled, massive canines showing in its snarl. His partner started barking, a deep rumbling threat. Other mastiffs nearby joined the chorus.

Glasha looked irritated at the handler, who rushed forward, scolding the dogs and pulling them out of our path. "They are trained to uncover anyone who is not of our blood. You can expect more such encounters." I turned and could see a half dozen pairs of slowly quieting hounds in this area of the valley. It would not be easy to sneak around unseen—or un-smelled.

We walked past a number of large longhouses as we made our way deeper into the valley. Each large building had smaller support buildings surrounding it. Some of the structures had open windows and doors and looked abandoned. Others had a myriad of activity as people flowed around the primary structures and smaller support buildings. Some had elite guards standing watch outside, while others looked to only have civilians.

Seeing me studying the structures, Glasha explained, "The compounds are assigned by the Elders. Most of the year, they are empty. Warlords and clerics from across the Caliphate descend on the valley when an important gathering occurs. The higher your importance, the closer your temporary residence is to the valley's center."

The large structures were spaced about a hundred yards apart, divided by dense thickets for privacy. They continued far into the valley. As the number of occupied structures increased, I studied the orcs moving about their business of serving the leaders of the Caliphate. Most walked with purpose and were laden with goods. Some appeared to be running messages between the buildings, judging by the haste in their steps.

We had passed a lot of buildings and were approaching the center of the valley when Glasha abruptly turned her pony down a path. I turned off the primary dark stone path to follow Glasha. Two elite orc warriors flanked the wide entrance to a longhouse. The tattooed guards stepped to block her approach even before she reached the door. Even Glasha's title was not going to gain her quick entrance.

Glasha, in a sharply irritated tone, barked, "Tell Jhuarkasha that Chronicler Glasha is here to discuss the Choosing." A graying orc exited the building at her words and studied Glasha before retreating inside without a word. Glasha growled quietly so only I could hear. "I hope you appreciate me supplicating. Once you identify your goliath, let me know and I will extract us."

We didn't wait long before a tall, lean orc exited the structure. He had a feral grin on his face at seeing Glasha. I assumed this was the cleric candidate from his loose clothing and lack of musculature. "Glasha! Have you discarded your poor choice of a candidate and come to support me instead?" His tone was slightly mocking, and I was a bit concerned we would not gain access.

Glasha sighed. "I came to discuss an alliance for the first Trial. This is Mynasha's First." She waved her hand in my direction, and the orc seemed to notice me for the first time. His eyes widened, and he started laughing.

"Seriously, Glasha? A human? How desperate is your candidate? She might as well concede and retain what honor she can." Jhuarkasha chuckled to himself. Even though orc culture was different, I would say this orc had what I would call a punchable face.

"If you don't want an alliance, that is fine. I know what the first Trial is, though." His mocking visage faded instantly.

"That would be duplicitous and lessen Mynasha's honor," he said angrily. Glasha sported her own orcish grin now. "Fine. Let's discuss a partnership for the first Trial only." We followed the disgruntled cleric inside, one of the guards taking the pony's reins.

The room beyond was massive, with dozens of orcs, humans, and five goliaths moving about. One more than Glasha had said. Furniture was scattered across the chamber, and a single cooking stove was lit in the center. As my eyes adjusted to the darker room, I sent aether to my eyes to see better. The room was divided into areas for sleeping, eating, sitting, and combat practice. Four elite warriors fought a monstrous, bare-chested, tattooed orc. He twirled his sword in a blinding display of skill, speed, and power. His two-handed sword connected over and over again against his opponents' weapons, forcing them back.

As I focused my gaze, it became clear that he was channeling aether through his tattoos, which had a soft, luminous glow in my aether sight. The sight of his lightning-fast movements deserved my admiration. A wave of uncertainty washed over me, making me question my ability to confront such a dangerous warrior. Yet I took solace in the fact that I had other tactics to turn a battle in my favor.

I tore my eyes from the impressive display to focus on the face of the first goliath we approached. This goliath was clearly a female and was helping two human women prepare food at a long table. Curiosity made all three look up at us as we approached. I only knew Zorana from the dreamscape, but this goliath was not Zorana. Her eyes looked devoid of energy. She was broken, with no spark of will there. The two other women working with her were the same. I pitied them and feared what I was going to find.

It was clear the cleric was guiding us toward the fighting orcs, which was fine because I would be able to get close to the other goliaths in the chamber.

Three other goliaths were also feminine in their curves. One was working on mending some clothes, and the other two were among the spectators watching the combat, their backs turned to us as we approached. The goliath working on the leather stitching was not Zorana either. We were being led to the fighting practice when the orc warlord paused, seeing Cleric Jhuarkasha approaching. The combatants retreated, and all eyes turned to us.

My heart raced as the goliaths turned, and I immediately recognized Zorana. The joy she displayed in the illusory space was not there. Here, in reality, her expression was blank, but at least her eyes were not dead like the first goliath's as she studied me with curiosity.

The large warrior wiped the sweat from his face and took us in. Cleric Jhuarkasha was excited to speak. "Warlord Rhuuk, Chronicler Glasha has come to bargain. She brings Cleric Mynasha's First!" I knew Cleric Jhuarkasha was expecting a stronger reaction from the warlord, but his eyes just settled on me as he studied me. "A human!" the cleric emphasized to get a reaction, but none was coming. There was a cold, calculating nature to this warrior that I returned. We were two alphas staring each other down.

"What bargain does she bring to us?" he asked, finally focusing on Glasha. It was clear who was in charge of this partnership and making the decisions.

Glasha spoke to Warlord Rhuuk, ignoring the cleric, sensing it too. "I know what the first Trial is. It heavily favors Cleric Fioasha."

The warlord waved his hand dismissively. "Not unexpected. We will not be one of the two eliminated in the first Trial. We do not require your assistance, and I do not want to owe you any favors, Chronicler. Mynasha has not even been recognized as a candidate yet."

With a little anger tainting her voice, Glasha replied, "She will be by tomorrow, and Cleric Anatasha will be forced to withdraw after challenging Mynasha's word!"

The warlord bellowed a deep, wicked laugh that made some of the slaves cringe. "You hope for too much, Chronicler! Cleric Anatasha will lay the blame on someone else for supplying terrible information. You can leave." He turned his muscled, tattooed back on us to return to his practice. I looked one last time at the side of Zorana's face. She was much older and thinner than her manifestation, but it was definitely her. I wanted to reveal myself and reassure her, but that would be beyond foolish. Maveith would be exhilarated when I told him she was alive.

Cleric Jhuarkasha was a bit flummoxed as he walked with us to the exit. He wasn't deterred and almost pleaded, "What is the Trial? I can promise we will not hinder Mynasha in the first Trial."

Glasha seemed to consider as we walked the length of the chamber. A little distastefully, she finally spoke. "The first Trial is to return with a pixie. It must be presented alive. The last two to return will be eliminated."

The cleric growled. "What a foolish Trial. But you are correct; it does favor Fioasha heavily." He stopped his escorting and eagerly returned to the combat that had ensued again behind us. He was going to use the information whether Rhuuk liked it or not.

"A pixie? The annoying woodland fairies? Are they common around here?" I asked.

"There are untouched groves a dozen miles northeast of the city. They are rare but can be found there," Glasha replied. "Tarnasha learned of the Trial from one of the Elders. Mynasha is going to have difficulty with it, so my hope is that you can aid her now that you are here. Your abilities were unknown to the Elders when they were selecting the trials." Glasha formed a mischievous grin.

Pixies were tricksters and not overtly dangerous unless they or their home were threatened. They would not be happy with having one or more of their number abducted. "I should be able to help. I will come back tomorrow morning, and we can formulate a strategy."

Glasha stopped walking and turned to me. "Didn't I tell you? Unless it is part of a Trial, no one who enters the valley can leave until a Supreme is selected," Glasha said innocently.

I stopped walking. "No. You definitely failed to mention that," I said, annoyed.

Chapter 304: How to Win Friends and Influence Warlords

I was seething internally, walking next to Glasha as she led her pony. Orc attendants rushed along the path with packs of goods, looking at me curiously. "Did you find the goliath you were looking for?" she asked calmly.

I bit down an angry retort and answered evenly. "She was among them, yes."

Glasha nodded slowly and said more somberly, "While most warlords treat their slaves with veneration, Warlord Rhuuk is known for his proclivities with his slaves."

My knuckles cracked as I made a fist. "What type of proclivities?" I was glad Maveith was not in my place. I assumed he would not have been able to restrain himself.

Sensing my anger, Glasha tempered her response. "He seeks to assert his dominance over them in a number of ways." She paused as she considered her next words carefully, trying not to make me angry, but I had heard enough.

"Not for much longer. Can my companions join us?" I asked tersely.

"I have given it thought. The answer would be no …" I tensed before Glasha continued, "… but warlords are allowed their attendant slaves. With you being a First, you should qualify as well. Tarnasha can announce you as Mynasha's First and then we can summon your companions."

I hesitated. Would bringing Maveith here complicate things? It was his sister and he should be here. "They wouldn't be able to leave either," Glasha said, seeing my contemplation.

"I will write them a note and explain it to them then," I said, coming to a decision.

"I can have it delivered when it is ready," Glasha said. She motioned me down a narrow, winding path that led to a modest longhouse, its weathered wooden structure standing alone, devoid of any surrounding outbuildings. Unlike the bustling estates I had witnessed before, there were no slaves or orcs scurrying about outside.

"Is there a way to free Zorana without helping Mynasha?" I asked as we approached the longhouse.

Glasha stopped. I was not sure if she would tell me the truth or not. "If you had honor, you could challenge Rhuuk."

I rolled my eyes. "How do I get honor?" I asked.

Glasha chewed her lip, her tusks showing. She snorted, in thought about how to explain it. She had tried many times during the journey, but in the end, it seemed that honor was reserved for warlords, clerics, and elites in orc culture. "Honor is earned and bestowed by others with honor. It is extremely difficult for an outsider to accumulate honor. In the short time we have, I do not see that as a feasible path," Glasha said as she opened the squeaky door of the longhouse.

"My only recourse is to help Mynasha become the Supreme," I said discontentedly. I was having thoughts of Warlord Rhuuk experiencing an unfortunate brain aneurysm. It was smoky inside from the wet wood burning in the center of the longhouse. Mynasha and Tarnasha were trying to cook dinner in the haze. I suspected they had been given only wet wood on purpose because I did not see a single attendant anywhere in the cavernous building.

Tarnasha stood, a bright, tusky smile on the old orc's face. "Eryk! You have come to join us. We don't have much to offer, but please sit." There were no chairs, just dirty blankets spread around the fire. I folded my legs under me and sat. Mynasha was studying me, some disbelief on her face that I had come.

"Well, I am here. Catch me up," I said, motioning to everyone. Glasha tied her pony to a rail inside with the other two horses before coming to sit with us.

Tarnasha spoke for the group. "The five Elders are waiting for Cleric Ottasha. If he confirms Mynasha's slaying of the trolls, she will be allowed to be the sixth candidate. Ottasha may be the seventh, but he may have lost Warlord Krage's support."

"Of the other five candidates for the Supreme, the favored is Fioasha, and he has the support of three of the five Elders," Glasha explained. "He is a powerful cleric with strong affinities in nature and earth. That is why the Elders chose capturing a pixie to be the first Trial."

It made sense that the competition was rigged. "And his First?" I asked.

"Warlord Etus. He is the admiral of the northern fleet and well liked among the populace," Glasha stated while turning over the wood. "You have already met Cleric Jhuarkasha and his First, Rhuuk. Jhuarkasha's strongest affinity is protection. I think Rhuuk hopes to be able to control Jhuarkasha from the shadows. His spine bends with the wind." I nodded. I had not gotten a favorable impression of either of them, and Rhuuk was destined to die if what Glasha had insinuated was true.

Tarnasha stirred his pot on the coals. Whatever type of soup he was making, it was sparse. Maybe they planned to starve Mynasha into failing. I pulled out candied nuts and handed the bags around. I had purchased them in Telha long ago, but they were still warm from the vendor I had purchased them from. My orc sponsors greedily consumed the salty-sweet treat.

"Cleric Anatasha challenged Mynasha's claim of slaying the mountain trolls. It is likely he will be forced to withdraw his candidacy, but he does have one supporter among the Elders. The other two candidates are Cleric Nalgrasha and Cleric Sarkasha. Both are unknown factors and neither has support among the Elders," Tarnasha supplied.

Glasha had finished her nuts and took a bowl of soup before saying, "Nalgrasha is a powerful weather mage, and Sarkasha is a skilled illusionist. The only concern I have about them is that they appear to be conspiring together."

"And their Firsts?" I asked, crumpling up my empty bag and tossing it on the fire.

"Newly raised Warlord Batale stands with Nalgrasha, and Warlord Thaill stands with Sarkasha. Neither has earned much honor among the warlords," Tarnasha supplied helpfully.

"Will I even be recognized if I stand as Mynasha's First?" I asked. This seemed to be a point of contention between Tarnasha and Glasha. The three orcs looked at each other, with Mynasha looking the most uncertain.

"We will find out tomorrow evening," Glasha finally said. "Warlord Melkos has purged the trolls and ogres. I expect Cleric Ottasha and Warlord Krage are racing here as we speak." Glasha stood and nodded respectfully to me. "I will get your message to the Adventurers Hall."

I nodded, pulled out some paper and a quill, and began to write. I tried to keep my words as obscure as possible so the message would not give anything away if it was intercepted. I told Maveith his sister was safe and alive. He could come only if he could restrain himself and stay unarmed. Slaves were not allowed to carry weapons.

I told Konstantin to take command of the others and start looking for passage on a ship for all of us, including two "future friends." I rewrote the letter twice before folding it and giving it to Glasha. She left immediately to find a runner.

Seeing that I was finished, the old man whispered to me, asking wistfully, "Do you have any more food?" I chuckled and produced some elven bread and apple-berry dungeon jam. I looked at Mynasha, who looked apprehensive and hadn't spoken much since I had arrived. I offered her a steaming meat bun.

"What is this remarkable spread?" Tarnasha gasped, tasting it.

"Apple-berry dungeon jam," I replied, amused by the noises he made while eating it. He must be feeling the aether-bleed effect of the dungeon food, and it was also an excellent jam. The meat bun I gave Mynasha had dungeon bear meat and potatoes in it, but she didn't seem to realize the benefits as she ate mechanically.

Tarnasha praised me. "Your talents are wasted on the battlefield, Eryk." I handed him one of the hot meat buns in appreciation of his praise, even though Maveith had made the jam.

I stood and started to make a place to sleep on the worn wooden floor. My earth pulse told me a massive rat nest resided under our shelter—at least thirty that I could count. I assumed it was going to be a fun night. As we all settled in, Tarnasha used his magic, weaving a complex spell form that caused all the rats and nearby creatures I could detect with my earth pulse to flee. He let out a soft chuckle, and I couldn't shake the feeling that the rats had not been there naturally.

When Glasha finally returned, it was late and unhappiness was etched clearly on her face. My heart sank at the sight, and my mind raced with concern—had she been unable to contact my companions? "Your message was sent to the Guild Hall," she assured me, her voice steady yet tinged with exhaustion. "I'm confident your companions will receive it shortly."

"What is the problem now?" Mynasha asked, sitting up. She had been trying to sleep, but it was clear her adrenaline wasn't letting her.

"Nothing," Glasha said a little too tersely. Eventually, she conceded, "It is him." She pointed at me. "Apparently, the Elders just passed a rule that only warlords can serve as Firsts for this Choosing! That is itself against the rules, as any change requires one year to take effect!" She growled, then calmed. "I have been arguing with Elder Daccasha and Kytasha for the last three hours!"

I handed her a meat pie and a skin of elven ambrosia. Hopefully, the elven whisky would help her calm down and sleep. This was mildly good news for me, as it meant I wouldn't have to serve as Mynasha's First. Glasha spent an hour venting her rage aloud until the ambrosia finally knocked her out.

I remained awake most of the night, lying there prone and sending out earth pulses. A few patrols with mastiffs walked by our longhouse, but there was no excitement to be had. As dawn approached, I took the opportunity to get my few hours of rest. Glasha stormed off when she woke, and Tarnasha followed her to play politics.

That left me and the young cleric. "Where were you born?" I asked to break the silence of midmorning.

"Why do you care?" she asked calmly, giving me her attention. She looked to have fully recovered from her lightning display and the long ride.

"Curiosity. You look a little different than most of the orcs I have seen." I was trying to gently start a conversation to see if the powerful cleric was an otherworlder like me.

"A small settlement that you have never heard of," she said, getting comfortable on the blanket. She seemed open to talking.

"Were your parents powerful clerics as well?" I asked while stirring the coals.

"No," she said slowly, studying me. "Neither of my parents could use aether."

"Isn't that unusual? With you being so powerful?" I probed.

"I was adopted when I was a babe. I was found in a field of cabbage," she admitted.

My mind was racing. Were infants also pulled into this world? I genuinely believed Mynasha was an otherworlder because of her rare convergence affinity. I kept the conversation going, asking about her childhood and how she had discovered her magic. She probably thought I was just trying to get to know her and was very open. In reality, I was searching for clues.

I gave her lunch from my dimensional space, and before I knew it, I was also answering her questions, albeit with more obscurity. Mynasha was very interested in my own magic, but I didn't reveal anything that she hadn't already seen.

It was late afternoon when a thundering procession could be heard outside. We both went see the source of the commotion, and dozens of riders were headed to the center of the valley. "I have to go and meet with the Elders," Mynasha said. I made to join her, but she shook her head. "No, you need to remain here until you are recognized as my First." Mynasha grabbed her small pack and raced down the path to join the others.

Left to my own devices, I took care of the three horses, cleaning the floor and walking them around the building for a little exercise before watering them and staking them to graze. Even though I was fairly confident I was not being spied on with the help of the obfuscation sphere and my earth speak, I only took magebane from my space to practice. It was well past sunset when my trio of orcs returned.

They were not alone. A smiling but anxious Maveith was leading his large black horse and Ginger. His smile creased his face, but he kept turning and searching as if his sister was about to jump out and surprise him. He looked odd to me without his unstrung bow on his back or the heavy hammer swinging from his hip.

We shook wrists, but Maveith pulled me in for a hug that squeezed the air from my lungs. "Don't kill me or this will be harder than it needs to be."

Maveith released me, beaming. "I thought you were tougher than that."

"Let's not test the limits of my body. You came, so I am assuming you understand." Maveith nodded, but I hoped he would not forget when he saw Zorana.

I looked at the orcs. From the smiles on their faces, I assumed it had gone well. I didn't even have to ask before Mynasha barked happily, "You are to be my First!"

This was no time for jokes or innuendos, so I just nodded. "How did it happen?" I asked while handing out food.

"It was a master display of guile and deceit!" Tarnasha said happily.

"Not so!" Glasha joked. "They were just ignorant of our human friend's prowess." She saluted me with her waterskin. "Warlord Krage spoke to Mynasha's killing of the trolls. He then offered his support to serve as her First!"

"What? I am confused. I thought he was supporting Ottasha, and if he offered, why am I still Mynasha's First?" I felt I wasn't going to like the answer.

"Ottasha withdrew his candidacy. I think it was because Krage didn't want to risk his honor supporting him," Mynasha said excitedly.

"Eryk is a much better option," Maveith said in support. I frowned.

"Cleric Anatasha also withdrew after his challenge to Mynasha's honor was proven to be without merit!" Tarnasha added jovially. "Two candidates have already fallen from consideration!"

"You still haven't answered my question," I said, my voice tinged with irritation. I leaned forward, my voice tense. "Why isn't Warlord Krage standing as Mynasha's First?" My eyes narrowed. I was eager for clarification as the weight of the title hung on me, unwanted.

Glasha's excitement dimmed as she explained, "When Warlord Krage offered to stand with Mynasha, the Elders panicked. He is a highly respected warrior and his support would have lent her candidacy far too much legitimacy. They pivoted. Fast. Suddenly, the human being as her First was no longer controversial, and they formalized the decision on the spot." She gave me a wicked smile. "Little do they know just how dangerous this human really is."

Maveith laughed with them. I was glad to see my friend could at least see the humor in this. "Great," I offered with sarcasm.

"The first Trial begins at first light tomorrow. You two must be seen by the Elders leaving the grounds so they know you did not depart earlier. With five candidates, only the first three to return with a live pixie will be allowed to continue," Glasha said excitedly.

"Can Maveith come with us?" I asked, drawing the goliath's attention.

The two orcs looked at Tarnasha, who was the expert, having once been a member of the Elders. "It would be frowned upon but permitted, as long as he does not assist."

"I wish to remain here," Maveith said resolutely.

"Can you two keep him out of trouble?" I asked Glasha and Tarnasha seriously.

They both looked over at the towering goliath, who tried to look as innocent as possible. I knew he was going to try to see his sister. I was having doubts about the wisdom of bringing him here.

Glasha slowly smiled. "I can come up with a few things to keep him busy. He can carry my things while we spend the day gathering support for Mynasha among the warlords and clerics."

One thing was for sure: I hated orc politics.

I joined the orcs as they discussed the first Trial. "There is only one forest a half-day's ride from here that is known to have a sizable population of pixies," Glasha announced, her eyes glinting with anticipation. "All the candidates will be racing there at dawn, but they must pass the Elders' longhouse."

Maveith had finished with the horses and was making himself a place to sleep. I was frustrated, as I could have been replaced by a competent warlord, and they had chosen me. They didn't notice my displeasure, and Glasha continued, "Pixies are tricksters and difficult to catch, especially alive. They can use their magic to transform their bodies into small animals. Some of the more powerful ones can push thoughts into your mind."

I looked at Maveith and reminded myself of why we were here. My feelings were secondary. "They can also make themselves invisible and disrupt magic," I added, knowing they could unweave spell forms like Castile.

"True, but some can only blend into their surroundings and do not have true invisibility," Tarnasha said, contributing his knowledge. "Most of their magic comes from innate spells inscribed on their core, but some pixies can weave spell forms."

I was apprehensive about going after the fey creatures, not knowing what I was getting into. "They have true mages? Do they have offensive magic?" I asked with some disbelief.

Tarnasha smiled at my bewilderment. "I have never heard of pixies throwing lightning or exploding their enemies with fireballs. But their magic can scramble your mind, make things appear that are not really there, and cause mesmerizing dancing lights to hover in the air for hours. Even though pixies are known for being carefree and mischievous creatures, they are intelligent beings. I know of one instance where they compelled a group of Pathfinders to dance until they died from exhaustion. Never underestimate your foe."

That was a sobering statement, but I smirked to myself, thinking that after the pixies saw me dance, they would probably be so offended that they would let me go.

"In my training, I was told that if you had no thoughts of harming them, they would leave you alone," Mynasha said, apparently the only one in our group who was not well educated in pixie lore.

Tarnasha was eager to share his knowledge. "They are not malicious beings. Quite the opposite, as they have been known to help as much as tease with their magic. They can ascertain your intentions, and if you do not intend to harm them, they might play a few tricks on you, but generally will leave you be. Since you intend to abduct one of their number, I doubt they will be very welcoming."

"Well, good thing I am not the one trying to capture one," I said in mock seriousness, glancing at Mynasha. She could be burdened with the pixie's ire. Ginger was antsy because I had not given her much attention since Maveith had brought her. I went to deliver her an apple, as it was going to be a hard ride tomorrow.

We continued talking about pixies for the next two hours before Mynasha tried to get a few hours of sleep. I was too worked up to sleep at all. Tarnasha expected the other candidates and their warlords to do what they could to hinder us. Mynasha was the most powerful mage among the candidates, and therefore the largest threat to the favored candidate, Fioasha.

As the orcs tried to get some rest, I pulled a small pack from my dimensional space and packed it with food and gear, unconcerned about those in the room seeing my efforts. Magebane was also on my hip now, the hilt still carefully wrapped to conceal its runic nature. If I had to draw it, there would be no way to hide it as a powerful artifact, but being among powerful mages, it was the best weapon to have at the ready.

Maveith sat with me in silence. No words were needed tonight. Our objective was close and we just needed to be patient until we could act. He took out a leather pouch to stitch. "Do you think she will recognize me?" Maveith said unexpectedly.

"You are kind of hard to forget," I replied jokingly.

Maveith sighed. "When I fled, I wasn't much bigger than you are now."

"I cannot imagine you ever being that small, Maveith." I chuckled and he laughed a little as well before falling into silence again.

An unhappy neigh echoed from the horses, and I went to check on them. I could imagine the other candidates' allies causing problems by messing with our mounts. According to Glasha, such an act wouldn't tarnish the honor of the candidate.

Ginger was dancing on a train of ants crawling around her. I think it was a devious plan to exhaust our mounts by keeping them awake all night. I had some alchemist's salve that could double as an insect repellent, so I rubbed all the horses' legs with it and sprinkled the remainder on the ground.

Ginger's head pushed me hard from behind, but I think it was in gratitude. I rubbed the horses down again, finding a few ants I had missed. I checked with an earth speak pulse and found that at least the rats had not returned. After giving an apple to each horse, I started to pack our saddlebags for tomorrow. I found a note from Konstantin in my saddlebags. It read, "Don't get yourself killed." I could imagine him saying it as an order and not a suggestion.

I could tell the sun was coming soon, and the orcs were stirring and getting ready. It wasn't long before I led Ginger alongside Mynasha, who was leading her large gray. Tarnasha and Glasha flanked us as we moved toward one of the larger structures in the valley.

Maveith walked behind us, his head on a swivel. There were a number of goliaths out gathering large buckets of water from wells. It was a stone building, the only two-story one I had seen. "It looks like we are the first ones here," Mynasha said excitedly.

Glasha was stomping mad as she stared down the old cleric ahead of us. "No, the others have already left." I looked up and guessed it was nearly an hour before sunrise, based on the blue moon's position and the gray sky.

A line of old, weathered orcs stood outside the stone building, their skin patchworks of grays and greens, each face etched with the lines of time. They appeared to be patiently waiting for us, their eyes glinting with a mix of curiosity and smugness. In front of them, a wrinkled old woman stood with a light smile. Her smile wasn't a greeting; instead, it seemed to reflect a profound sense of self-satisfaction.

"When did the other candidates leave?" Glasha growled at the Elder.

The Elder eyed me disdainfully, and I knew my presence here was not wanted. They would have been better off taking the warlord's offer. She then looked at Glasha. "I said you could leave at the start of the new day," the Elder said, grinning.

"That was not how you phrased it," Tarnasha hissed. "You said …"

Glasha cut him off angrily and barked at Mynasha, "It doesn't matter, go! You are behind the others by hours!" Glasha motioned at us to hurry. I sensed a confrontation coming between the clerics and I was happy not to be there for it. I swung up into Ginger's saddle, gave Maveith a nod, and kicked Ginger to follow Mynasha. We passed a few watch posts before we reached a road.

The rising sun made it easier to increase our pace. Ginger was happy for the run, but I soon had to rein in Mynasha's anxiousness. We couldn't run all the way there. Still, we made excellent time, covering about fifteen miles before majestic trees rose in the distance, easily over three hundred feet in height.

The grassy plains appeared to stop just at the forest edge, like a line had been drawn there. It was going to be dark in those woods under such a dense canopy of leaves. The most serious threats we had discussed last night were treants, pixies, and of course, my favorite: spiders. It didn't mean that those were the only threats, just the ones that we would most likely encounter as we searched for our prey.

As we approached the tree line, two horses bolted from the trunks far to our left. Mynasha hissed as she recognized the riders. "Cleric Fioasha has already succeeded. Now, the pixies will also be alerted to our intentions." From a distance, it did look like a warrior and a cleric were on the horses, a covered crate bouncing behind one of them. They looked our way but didn't stop as they raced back to Becar to be the first to complete the first Trial.

"We should walk," I said, dismounting as we entered the forest. My feet needed to be in contact with the ground for my earth pulse to be effective, which Mynasha knew. The horses needed the rest anyway, their sweat steaming from their bodies. I walked in first boldly, as my earth speak highlighted dangers at a distance.

We passed a few bedded-down deer, a deep tunnel network of normal-sized forest weasels, and then a nest of giant wasps, who took exception to our proximity. Mynasha created a lightning shield that cooked the fist-sized wasps before they could sting us or the horses. She killed dozens before we distanced ourselves from the nest and moved deeper into the darkening woods.

"I wonder if we will find a house made out of candy," I whispered as we walked.

"Why would a house be made out of candy?" Mynasha asked, confused.

"So the witch can attract children and then cook them, of course," I replied matter-of-factly.

"We would never allow a hag to remain alive in the Caliphate to eat children," Mynasha said seriously. I just sighed and kept pulsing my earth speak. We stumbled upon some saddlebags, and the Mynasha searched through them as I remained on watch.

"It belongs to one of the warlords," Mynasha said after a moment. "He didn't drop it; the straps were cut." I looked up into the trees and past the massive trunks.

"Pixies?" I asked, looking for any sign.

"Most likely," she confirmed, holding the cut leather for me to inspect. It was not one clean cut. Instead, the broken end showed lots of smaller cuts. "The pixies are probably taking out their anger on the other candidates."

I noticed a squirrel racing along the ground. It was circling our position. *This might be a lot easier than I thought.* The pixies were coming to us. The squirrel was acting curious and unnatural.

When I pulsed earth speak, the squirrel froze. It locked eyes with me and I cursed, "Dragon shit." Mynasha looked at me, and I explained, "The pixies were able to sense my earth speak pulse." They were highly magical creatures, and I now had doubts that I could store one in my dimensional space if needed.

I took one step toward the squirrel, and it didn't move. However, when I got about thirty feet away, it bolted up the far side of a tree. It paused fifty feet in the air and spied on us from its perch. "Is that a pixie?" Glasha asked, studying the squirrel doubtfully.

"I don't know, but it is definitely not a squirrel." A thought brushed my mind, telling me it was most definitely a squirrel; there was nothing to see here, and I should be on my way. The thought was unnatural, and I easily pushed it aside.

"Yes, it is definitely a pixie." The squirrel chittered at us angrily, as if it was my fault for not succumbing to its mental suggestion. It was good to know I could resist the pixie's mind games.

"Watch the squirrel," I requested as I scanned the woods around us for more. I sent out three more earth pulses, but it didn't pick up anything unusual. It looked like we only had to contend with one pixie. A boom echoed among the trees, and Mynasha and the squirrel looked in that direction. I studied the squirrel, not getting distracted. It soon raced off toward the explosion, jumping through the branches. I guessed one of the other clerics was getting impatient.

"Do we follow?" I asked Mynasha. I already knew she would say yes, as only two more candidates could pass this trial after Fioasha.

"That explosion was likely from Cleric Sarkasha. He has powerful spells that can deafen and stun opponents." As if to highlight her guess, more thunderous booms echoed in the woods. The canopy suddenly became alive with the sound of raindrops. It hadn't looked ready to rain when we entered the forest.

"Nalgrasha," Mynasha hissed. I nodded in agreement, as he was a weather cleric and was supposed to be working with Sarkasha. It was clear they were battling something in the woods.

We moved cautiously forward, leading the horses. Thick drops of water splattered on and around us. The water was less of an issue than the noise it was creating, which fuzzed the feedback of my earth pulses. We paused when we could see lights dancing, flitting in the dark woods through the thick trunks.

I remarked on the scene playing out. "If the clerics keep this up, they will wake the treants." I didn't know if that was true, but the clerics were definitely stirring the shit with the noise, weather, and lights. Treants were dangerous foes, as they could animate other trees, creating a woodland army in moments.

I grabbed Mynasha's arm to stop her. I leaned into her and indicated to her with a nod. "That tree hollow to our right." We were still a distance away from the action, but I caught a brief glow from the tree's hollow. It was twenty feet off the ground, but I thought it might contain a pixie in hiding. Mynasha nodded, and we moved to the tree. I leaned against it, pretending to discern what was happening in the distance.

My earth pulse worked poorly through the wood, and all I could sort out was that a dozen different small figures huddled inside, no more than six inches in height. Pixies were generally about a foot, so perhaps this was their young hiding. "Juvenile pixies," I told her in Telhian, and she was immediately excited. The hollow was small, just large enough to reach into, but I had second thoughts, as taking one of their children might stir their anger even more.

I thought Mynasha would ask me to climb and inspect the hollow, but she handed me her reins and started climbing the wet bark. She had a crude butterfly net tucked into her belt. There were plenty of handholds in the rugged bark, and she reached the hollow quickly while I watched from below. As she peeked inside, the hollow lit up with a blinding light, and small, winged creatures dashed out in the rain. Mynasha swung wildly with her net, but unable to see, she missed the pixies as they flew away.

With my aether sight, they looked like streaks of light as they dispersed. The tiny humanoids with shimmering wings sought new cover in the tree canopy. Two smaller pixies tumbled from rain strikes on their gossamer wings and dashed toward the ground to hide in a rocky crevice a hundred feet away. I kept my eye on the opening in the earth as a blind and cursing Mynasha descended.

The orc cleric's face was burned, and her eyes looked damaged and unfocused. Apparently, a dozen pixies could create a damaging flash. My spell form had protected me well enough, and I had been a distance away. Mynasha fumbled for a health potion. "Why did the Elders want these foul creatures alive?!"

I shrugged, knowing pixie parts could be used in higher-tier potions. "Maybe because their wings can be used in potions of flying, and their blood can be used in aether-restorative brews." My focus was on the crevice as we approached the split rock they were hiding in. I was hesitant to pulse my earth speak for fear they would feel it and flee.

As Mynasha's vision cleared, I held out my hand for the net. I dropped Ginger's reins and walked to the split rock. Standing close, I pulsed earth speak and sensed the two tiny creatures hiding deep inside. Maybe these younger ones couldn't feel my earth pulse, as they remained still. Or maybe they were petrified, as the forest still boomed with combat. These were definitely two of the smaller specimens that had been hiding in the hollow.

I felt bad for what I was about to do. I couldn't move one of the pixies to my dimensional space because they were entwined, hugging each other. Their aether resistance would be multiplicative. I pulled a large cask of whisky from my dimensional space and cracked it open. I then poured the alcohol into the crevice. If the pixies didn't come out, they would drown.

I wasn't disappointed. The two pixies crawled out rather than drown in alcohol. They looked like miniature elves, one with pale skin and the other with soft, blue-hued skin. The net flashed in my hand, and both pixies were captured. They were sputtering from having inhaled the booze. I grabbed the first one entangled in the net, carefully folding its wings back as I wrapped it. It bit viciously into my spider-silk glove, but its tiny teeth couldn't penetrate the material. I repeated the procedure with the second.

Both pixies were cocooned in clean bandage wraps, their mouths covered. Both had a feminine appearance; maybe the pixies were all feminine. Mynasha was staring at the two tiny, captured prisoners, intrigued.

Their eyes were red and slightly swollen, probably from the alcohol. I felt cruel as I handed the two swaddled bundles to the war cleric. Sadly, I said, "We should go before they realize we captured two of their children. We were fortunate that whatever that is has continued." I pointed at the light and sound show in the distance.

Mynasha seemed shocked that the task was already done, and she nodded dumbly. We had only been in the woodland for a little more than an hour. She carefully packed the two pixies in a small cage she had come with, but left them bound. We both mounted, oriented ourselves, and started to ride. It wasn't long before I noticed fluttering in the trees around us. It was clear the other young pixies had seen what we had done and would not let their siblings go without a challenge …

Chapter 306: The Pixie Gambit

Ginger moved rhythmically beneath me as I scanned for obstacles. She sensed the urgency of my need to escape the woods. If it was only the young pixies following us, perhaps they couldn't hinder our travel. I assumed their magic would be weaker and less refined than the adults. Sparkling lights accompanied by buzzing sounds started to appear to our left and right as we raced to leave the woods. The pixies were getting closer, trying to distract and possibly slow us.

Mynasha didn't seem worried about their efforts. "There is nothing they can do to stop us."

"Don't jinx us like that," I retorted.

"What is a jinx?" she asked. I had used the word from Earth without realizing it.

As if in response, an echoing, earsplitting thunder spread across the woodlands. "That is a jinx," I said, annoyed. "The pixies were not trying to stop us but call for help."

The noise was directly in our path, and I assumed it was a treant being awoken by the pixies. I turned Ginger to the right, and Mynasha turned her mount, and the forest started to come alive to our right. At least we had left the region where it had been raining, but we needed to make sure we didn't get turned around in the forest and go deeper by mistake.

If I had been in this situation before coming to Desia, I might have panicked. Now, I was clearheaded and focused on surviving. My heart was racing and I was weighing options as they presented themselves. Mynasha was not as calm, and I guessed it was because she was usually surrounded by elite orcs when she went into battle. Here, we were very much exposed.

"Left! Turn left when we are clear of the awakening trees!" That was an understatement of the situation, as the entire forest seemed to be animated, though moving ponderously slow.

"Maybe it's an illusion of pixies," Mynasha yelled over the horses' hooves pounding the ground as we wove between the trunks. I wished it was, but the scope and the fact that I didn't feel any pressure on my mind made me think we were facing the real thing. The treant must have been powerful to awaken so many—unless there was more than one.

"Just focus on escaping!" I barked at her. We turned again, away from the churning ground as roots came alive beneath Ginger like snakes moving in the earth. Fortunately, the treant was too slow and didn't have enough range, and we soon left the living woods behind us. My aether sight could still clearly see the streaks in the canopy above as the pixies followed us.

Thoughts of releasing the prisoners came to me, but that wouldn't guarantee our freedom, and I doubted Mynasha would give them up now that she had them. Lines of daylight appeared through the trees. Maybe we were getting close to the grassy plains. It also made sense that Cleric Fioasha and his warlord were racing away when we saw them. It wasn't because they wanted to get back quickly. They were likely fleeing for their lives.

I thought we were getting close and our escape was assured. That was when a roar echoed in the woods, and I pulled Ginger up. Mynasha followed suit, and the horses danced as they snorted to catch their breath.

The roar came again and I couldn't place the direction. It sounded like King Kong was wandering the woods. "What is that?" Mynasha asked, her voice unsteady as she checked on her package. I gave her an annoyed look, as these woods were in her kingdom, not mine.

I caught a streak of light zipping down behind us. Most likely, the pixie was invisible, but my vision could see the aether. I placed an air shield in its path, as it was targeting the cage on Mynasha's horse, trying to free its brethren.

The pixie thudded full speed into the shield and fell to the ground. It remained invisible, and Mynasha was oblivious to its presence. It must have survived because it was still invisible. I swung from my saddle to the ground as the roars got louder. I scooped up the invisible pixie and stuffed it into one of my pouches that held my copper and silver coins.

We didn't need a third pixie, but we might need the leverage if things went downhill—not that they were not already going that way. Also, truth be told, I didn't want the pixie stepped on by the horses as we prepared to take on whatever was charging at us.

"Maybe it is time to break out the lightning," I hissed at Mynasha as I drew the magebane. The next bestial roar was closer and sounded angry. It was also definitely coming from our escape path. The pixies above danced in anticipation, seeming to say, "You're in trouble now!"

"I need a moment; there are aether lines here I can draw from," Mynasha said, now standing beside me. Behind us, the treants were still stirring up the forest. In front of us was the beast, and the other direction would take us deeper into the woods and back to the other clerics battling the pixies. Why did everything always have to be so complicated?

A large shadow thundered through the woods, and I relaxed. It was just a big-ass bear. I could remove its head and ... The bear stood on its hind legs and pulled a massive axe from behind it. "What the ..." I whispered as the bipedal bear broke into a run.

"Werebear!" Mynasha said, shocked. It clicked in my mind. There were rare lycanthropes that could transform into bears. They were supposedly more friendly than werewolves, but this one seemed particularly unhappy with us. Probably because we were kidnapping his friends.

The roaring bear man's charge spooked Mynasha's gray stallion, and she lost control of the reins. The horse bolted into the woods. Our hard-earned cargo was going with it. The distraction also caused the cleric to interrupt her casting as she cursed. At least Ginger didn't bolt, but she did backpedal to stand behind me. I imagined Ginger saying, "You can have this one." I rapidly layered some air shields in front of me as I prepared to take on the nine-foot monstrosity.

Three of the four air shields were destroyed on impact, but did their job as the upright bear was halted in his tracks and the wind knocked from his lungs. He was stunned, and I stepped forward to slash into his shoulder. Magebane was a short blade and its aether-infused edge cut like a razor, parting the werebear's matted fur.

He took a moment to acknowledge the injury, and as he bellowed in pain and rage, I attacked his hamstring from the side. My slash didn't get good depth, and I was forced to retreat as the beast's axe came down. If the creature used aether, he would find it hard to control now. More importantly, he was slightly hobbled, and I glanced at Mynasha, who was indecisive about going after her horse or fighting the werebear. "Lightning!" I said, aggravated. Did she think I could handle a thousand-pound bear-man alone!? "The pixies are lost!"

"You are too close!" she barked back.

"Just do it!" I yelled. The werebear's large, black, predatory eyes were locked onto me, and I didn't want to bottom out my aether to kill him. There were just too many unknowns ahead of us. The living forest, for one, was probably creeping closer as we were delayed here.

A lasso of lightning lashed around the werebear's torso. He looked down, perplexed, but then his eyes widened in realization and fear. The chain lightning detached from Mynasha and snapped to the werebear.

I felt the concussive lightning explosion as the air became superheated and expanded just a few feet from me. My ears rang with pain and my nostrils inhaled ozone and the scent of burnt hair. A line of charred flesh circled the bear-man's waist. His fur was burned away, and he was disoriented. I channeled my healing spell form as magebane repeatedly cut into his thick, muscled limbs. The werebear collapsed, one leg and one arm useless.

"Let's go!" I yelled at Mynasha. I didn't have time to kill the werebear and collect his essence. The hide was too thick and resistant, even to the runic weapon. The awakened forest was also moving closer. Mynasha hadn't removed her clothes and was steaming something fierce from the large amount of aether she had pulled. I whistled and Ginger came, somewhat reluctant after the cacophony of battle and magic.

I swung up into the saddle and pulled Mynasha behind me. "We have to go get the pixies," she said, looking in the direction her horse had fled.

"No, we don't!" I reached into my pouch and my hand grappled with the struggling pixie. I pulled it out as its tiny arms flailed against my fingers' superior strength.

"You caught another one!" she exclaimed as her arms wrapped around my waist to help keep her balance. I kicked Ginger into a gallop. This was the brave pixie who had tried to save the others, which I admired. One of its wings was creased like paper, probably from crashing into my air disc. Its small, feminine features were scowling in rage and anger.

I brushed aside its weak attempts to penetrate my mind. It was the same height as the others we had captured, maybe six inches in height, with shimmering wings that folded behind its back, currently trapped by my gloved fingers.

Bouncing along, I carefully wrapped the pixie's wings back, as I had with the others. It only struggled momentarily before it relaxed, resigned to its fate. The human expression did make me feel guilty. Some quick bandage wrappings secured it in a cocoon; then I stuffed the pixie back in the belt pouch so I wouldn't have to look at it.

I didn't see any streaks or flashes above us, so the other pixies must be chasing down Mynasha's gray stallion. We finally reached the edge of the woods, the grassy plains spreading before us. Gray skies dominated the late afternoon with a light drizzle, and my mood matched the landscape.

"We should race back to the Elders. The others could overtake us at any time," Mynasha encouraged me.

"Ginger cannot run that distance carrying two people," I stated flatly. I realized it was likely that I was going to be walking back alone in a moment.

"Someone is coming from the forest," Mynasha warned me a few minutes later. I craned my neck to see two large black steeds thundering across the grass. We had just reached the road, and they overtook us not long after. Instead of riding past us, they slowed, most likely to gloat.

The cleric had dark-gray skin, and his leather clothing looked wet and coated in something sticky. They had not had a good time, but they still had two horses to our one. "Mynasha! I am surprised to see you heading back. Giving up already!" Smugness oozed off the cleric. He had a crate on the back of his mount, which probably contained his prize.

I hoped Mynasha would navigate this situation with intelligence, and she did. "Sarkasha, I must admit I'm surprised you left your dog Nalgrasha behind. We had a harrowing encounter with a werebear that sent my mount into a panic before it bolted away. The crate and net I had secured to my saddlebags are now gone." Her voice carried a blend of remorse and frustration—a good acting job on her part.

I pulled up Ginger to get the pair to stop as well. They complied, stopping to keep the gloating going. I just needed them to stop moving so I wouldn't kill the pixie I was trying to steal. "It is a pity you will not have a chance to lead us. But now you need to be more diplomatic in your future dealings, and know when to get on your knees." Mynasha's arms tightened around my waist in anger. My aether bottomed out, and the crate looked undisturbed from my vantage point— a successful theft. Hopefully the pixie was intact.

Mynasha spat on the ground, her tone getting slightly hostile. "If you are elevated to Supreme, I will leave the Caliphate permanently!"

Sarkasha laughed boisterously. "Please, you enjoyed our time together. Well, you should hurry along so you can watch me in the second Trial. I believe Nalgrasha isn't far behind me." He turned his horse, and his warlord fell in beside him as they thundered down the road.

"History?" I asked as I slid out of the saddle. Mynasha looked at me questioningly.

"An old lover," she hissed. Old was right, as Sarkasha had to be at least twice her age. I shrugged, as it was not my place to judge.

"You need to get back quickly. Ginger is fast and will get you there before the others." I took the time to feed Ginger a pair of apples and explain her duty to her. My priority wasn't talking to my horse, but instead giving myself time to recover my aether.

Just as Mynasha was getting impatient, I produced the pixie. She looked confused, as it was wrapped in cordage and not bandages. It was also closer to twelve inches, rather than six. Confusion was etched on her face. I didn't wait for her to sort it out, emptying one of the saddlebags. "Secure the pixie so they don't know you have it until you need to present it to the Elders." I didn't make eye contact with the new pixie to avoid more guilt.

Ginger was soon racing down the road after Sarkasha. I watched them disappear and realized I had a long, fourteen-mile walk back. But first, I would make a quick detour back to the woods to ease my guilty conscience …

Chapter 307: Catch and Release

I didn't approach the tree line; instead, I sank to one knee a short distance away. I pulsed my earth speak, but I was far enough away that it couldn't reach the woods. I pulled the irate fairy out of my belt pouch, her tiny eyes full of malice toward me. She had found her fight again and was trying to chew through my gloves with her tiny teeth.

"I don't know if you can understand me or not, but this was not my idea. I am letting you go." Her tiny expression of hate didn't change, so I assumed she didn't understand.

I unwrapped her quickly, stood, and stepped back. I waved my hand, indicating she was free to leave. She looked up at me defiantly and didn't move, probably thinking it was a trick. "Go, Tinker Bell!" I shooed her away with a different gesture. The pixie's wings unfolded, but the damaged one fluttered oddly. She hissed at me like a snake and took to the air. She veered off immediately to the left as she tried to fly and crashed to the ground, tumbling through the grass and dirt in a tumble of tiny limbs and distressed shrieks. Of course my act of conscience would go badly.

The little fairy only needed to walk fifty yards to the trees, but instead, she tried twice more to fly and crashed both times. It was hard to watch, like watching a lame bird, so after the third crash, I moved to pick her up. As I stepped toward the pixie, a stiff, ominous breeze carried a metallic scent from the forest.

The smart thing to do would be to walk away and let the pixie make her own way to the forest. I felt something watching from inside the woods, judging me. If it was another pixie, hopefully it would read my good intentions. I took another step and knelt, holding out my hand toward the wounded pixie. The injured pixie seemed to consider my offered hand, the scowl on her face relaxing. With my other hand, a Pathfinder healing potion appeared. I was reasonably confident it would work on pixies and used my thumb to break the seal.

The foul odor of spoiled milk hung in the air. The pixie sneezed and then covered her face, as if about to wretch. She was not going to drink it. Hell, I would only drink one if I was going to die. Then, I noticed a squirrel high in the branches watching us. It might be the one we encountered when we first entered the woods, but I could not be sure. My pixie looked into the woods at the squirrel and then back to the potion, a disgusted look on her face. She came forward and reluctantly stepped onto my hand, her scowl returning.

I saw the pixie clearly and up close in the fading evening light. With her pointed ears and pale skin, she really did look like a miniature elf. Her silky red-brown hair was disheveled from her rough treatment and from crashing into the ground. She was wearing clothes woven from thin blades of dried grass. Her translucent wings shimmered, then suddenly folded behind her and seemed to disappear.

With my other hand, I slowly tilted the healing potion. Her tiny hands unenthusiastically grasped the opening as the brew spilled slowly out. She sputtered, coughed, and hissed as she tried to drink the smelly concoction. She pushed away from the vial when she had her fill and fell backward onto her rump in my hand, coughing.

I hid a smirk as I stood slowly, holding my hand up toward the woods. The fairy vomited onto my hand in one last act of revenge before her wings splayed out, and she took to the air, this time zipping around my head once and spitting at me before darting into the woods. I guess I was not going to get a thank you.

I looked for the squirrel, but it was already gone. My act of kindness done, I stepped away from the woods and started to walk back toward the road. I hadn't walked long before I noticed two mounted orcs bolting from the woods further down the road. I quickly held up my spyglass to see which cleric and warlord they were. It was Warlord Rhuuk and Cleric Jhuarkasha. This angered me, since they had Zorana, but it looked like they would be the final pair to pass the first Trial unless someone else had snuck past us.

But were they the last ones, or were Warlord Batale and Cleric Nalgrasha still in the woods? I kept checking over my shoulder, wondering. I didn't have to wait much longer, as the last two orcs came thundering down the road less than ten minutes later. I stepped to the side, content to let them pass.

They didn't slow, and the warlord's horse veered into my path. I could have made his life miserable with layered air shields, but I moved further from the road to avoid being *accidentally* run down. They looked at me disdainfully as they passed. I couldn't affect the Trial outcome any more than I already had, and let the smug and haughty orcs go without taking any action.

I was over two miles down the road when Mynasha's gray stallion caught up to me. I had missed its approach and was shocked when it arrived. Its saddle and packs were missing, but the bridle remained. I wondered if the pixies had sent the horse to me or if it had wandered to me alone. The stallion nudged me, and I understood that he wanted an apple for being so loyal.

After he consumed the delicious apple, I checked his bridle to find that it was cut in a number of places, ready to break with a hard pull. His bare back was slick like oil, even though it looked clean. The pixies had been eager to get some revenge. At least his shoes seemed in good condition and had not been tampered with.

It took some time to wipe off the invisible oil. I hoped the pixies were watching from somewhere, frustrated that their tricks hadn't worked. I pulled out some cordage from my dimensional space and fashioned a temporary bridle, tossing the damaged one on the side of the road. I climbed onto the horse and rode bareback to the valley. I realized that I hadn't done as good a job as I had thought in cleaning off the oil. It was a challenge to stay on the gray horse.

My thighs burned from holding myself on the gray, and I couldn't spur him into anything more than a fast walk as night descended on us. I reached the entrance to the valley well past sunset. The orcs at the outposts looked at me, seeming amused in the light of a glowstone, probably thinking I had been ditched and was coming back in disgrace. I ignored them as I went into the valley to find out the first Trial's results.

The stone building where we met the Elders in the morning was closed, with two Pathfinders standing guard. Rather than try to gain entry, I returned to our longhouse to see if Maveith, Glasha, Tarnasha, and Mynasha were there.

As soon as I dismounted, I healed my screaming thighs and walked the gray into the longhouse. The three clerics were around the fire with Maveith cooking something. They all looked up, and Maveith had a huge grin on his face. "You are back." He abandoned his cooking efforts and walked over to me, embracing me. "I saw her."

I looked irately at Glasha and Tanasha. "Maveith, you didn't …"

Glasha grunted. "He wouldn't sit still until he saw her. I let him see through my spell sight. Uncomfortable for both of us. They are not aware of the connection between the goliaths."

I nodded and hoped that was the case. If they found out we were here for Zorana, it would give them leverage. "Well, good then. Thanks for coming to look for me," I replied tersely. After Ginger got her apple reward for carrying Mynasha back, I made to rub down the gray.

"We could not leave the valley. The Choosing is still going on," Glasha reminded me. I just grunted.

Maveith joined me and helped. He whispered loudly, "I saw Myra too. She looks defeated, Eryk. We need to save her as well."

I nodded and I patted the big man's shoulder. "Don't worry. We will not leave without them. They are never out of the sight of others, so I think our best course right now is to make Mynasha the Supreme. If I fail in that, we can try something more drastic."

"Thank you. I do not doubt you are capable of changing the cleric's fate," Maveith intoned.

"Fate?" I asked, confused.

"The Supreme is able to decide the fate of the other candidates, according to Glasha. Otherwise, there would be too many candidates to count. It is how

Tarnasha was exiled and cut off from his allies." Maveith's words gave some weight to this competition. It made me respect Mynasha more, knowing the cleric was betting on herself. Knowing orc honor, she wouldn't be killed, but I suspected the new Supreme would give her undesirable tasks.

"Is Mynasha still among the candidates? Not eliminated?" I asked the orcs. They had not told me if the pixie had been successfully delivered.

With his orcish grin splitting his face, Tarnasha happily informed me, "She is. Cleric Fioasha and Cleric Jhuarkasha were the other two successful candidates. Although Cleric Sarkasha accused Mynasha of cheating and stealing their pixie."

"It took an hour before we convinced the Elders that even if it was Sarkasha's pixie, it was within the rules. Some of my *favorite* Elders were foaming at the mouth by the end." Tarnasha's joy got a slight grin from me.

"How did you do it?" Mynasha asked interestedly, bringing me some of the food Maveith had prepared. "How did you steal their pixie?" she asked, more pointedly.

All three looked interested in my reply, but I ignored the three orcs' questioning gazes. "What happened to the five pixies?"

"It is just four. They are caged in the Elders' residence. Their wings have already been removed," Glasha stated dismissively.

I winced at the cruel treatment, even though I knew how valuable the wings were to alchemists. I hoped they didn't plan to exsanguinate them for their blood as well. "Well, if you win the Choosing, release them," I said firmly, locking eyes with Mynasha.

"Pixies are a nuisance ..." Mynasha started.

"She will release them if they have not been harvested," Glasha said, interrupting Mynasha and nodding to me. I think the Chronicler understood my compassion. "Most likely, they will not go to the alchemists until after the Choosing is completed. Did you make a pact with the pixies for their freedom?" she added curiously.

"No. I just feel bad that we abducted them from their homes for a stupid contest," I said truthfully.

"The other candidates likely killed a number of pixies," Tarnasha said offhandedly. "The pixies will not leave the woods for vengeance, if that is what you fear. A sizable ley line runs underneath those woods. They are much weaker the further they are from it." The horrific thought of what essence a pixie might yield to increase my own power occurred to me. I discarded the idea. They were not my enemies, and killing a sentient creature that didn't intend me harm was malicious.

"What about the next Trial?" I asked, finishing with the horses and taking the steaming onion and potato soup from Mynasha.

"It will be announced tomorrow at midday. The Elders need time to find a proper task that only Fioasha can succeed at," Tarnasha said sardonically.

"Will the Supreme will be chosen after the next task?" I asked. The soup was salty but otherwise good. I nodded my thanks to Maveith who was distracting himself once again with stitching.

Tarnasha let out a tired sigh. "Unlikely. Most likely, they will only choose to eliminate one candidate, just in case something unforeseen happens. Then, there will be a final Trial for the seat of the Supreme. Probably something that will pit the candidates and their warlords against each other."

I rested peacefully for a few hours, and at dawn, Mynasha was summoned alone. I recognized the warlord who came to retrieve her; it was Warlord Krage, the one who had withdrawn his support for Cleric Ottasha and whom Mynasha had rejected when he offered to be her First.

The warlord did not seem angry or smug, at least. "Only the three remaining candidates are allowed to meet with the Elders. They will be assessed on a tablet reader before the second Trial is announced," he informed Glasha patiently for the third time.

"Her First should be allowed to accompany her!" Tarnasha barked angrily at the warlord, who just shook his head helplessly.

"I am just delivering the message," Krage said. I suspected why they wanted to assess the candidates. The Elders didn't want any more surprises. They were also probably trying to figure out how Mynasha had stolen the pixie. As long as they didn't try to assess me, I didn't care.

The warlord exhaled a low, slow breath. "You have done well stirring the hornet's nest, Mynasha. I learned last night that Cleric Nalgrasha and Sarkasha were working with Fioasha and the Elders. They planned to be the other candidates arriving with the pixies and were going to step down from consideration after the first Trial. The Choosing might have ended yesterday if they were successful. Now, there are three remaining candidates who all want to assume the Supreme's mantle."

That news shocked my three clerics, and they began to interrogate Warlord Krage for more information. He didn't know much, but the thirty-plus warlords in the valley talked to each other as they awaited the new Supreme's coronation.

Eventually, Mynasha was escorted to the Elders by the warlord. I did note that he studied me for a time. Probably trying to figure out what I had that he didn't. From experience, I knew it was never fun being the last one picked on the playground. Glasha and Tarnasha were anxious while they waited. I tuned out their conversation. To distract myself, I cleaned up the open stalls and walked the horses outside to water them.

This farce of a Choosing should be over soon enough, and I needed to start planning how to abduct Zorana. From what I had overheard, it was clear that the Elders were not going to allow Mynasha to ascend to the Supreme's seat.

It was well past midday when Mynasha returned. She looked a little haggard. We all sat around the fire while she talked. "They tested us on a tablet reader, and then we were asked to demonstrate our spell forms for them. I was the only one tested so thoroughly that I drained my aether core." That got an angry glare from Glasha.

"When do they announce the second Trial?" Glasha asked, steel in her voice.

"Tonight. At sunset. It will likely begin right after they announce it," she replied tiredly.

Glasha hissed, "You won't have time to recover! Foulness! I hope a lustful ogre invades their beds tonight!" I had to listen to the orcs lament the unfairness of it all, but what did they really expect? From what I had seen, this was how orc politics worked.

When we led the horses to the Elders' central stone building, dozens of tattooed orcs and clerics formed a ring around the six Elders. I had missed the announcement of the first Trial, so I assumed it had looked similar to this. Warlord Rhuuk stood next to Cleric Jhuarkasha, facing the Elders in the large circle. We joined them, and soon, Cleric Fioasha and Warlord Etus joined us, completing the list of candidates.

I was surprised at how quiet it was with all these powerful warriors and clerics of the Caliphate around us. I could feel their eyes on my back. Was it respect or anticipation? After last night, they clearly knew that Cleric Fioasha was destined to lead them soon, and they were here to pay their respects and see how events played out in his favor.

I felt something brush my mind briefly, though it retreated when I focused on it. Was that one of the Elders or a cleric in the crowd? I scanned the alien faces, but there were too many. I saw curiosity, disdain, anger, and a myriad of other emotions as I met their eyes. The same Elder who had taken such joy in tricking us stepped forward. She was more reserved this evening.

"Esteemed warlords and clerics of the Caliphate!" the weathered and aged orc bellowed, her voice booming across the vast assembly with the obvious aid of magic. Her deep-set eyes scanned the gathering, ensuring that her message reached every powerful figure present. "The second Trial will rigorously test the candidates' fortitude, intelligence, mastery of the aetheric arts, and even their diplomacy!"

A tense silence enveloped the group of formidable leaders, their expressions stoic and contemplative. The faint rustle of leather and the muffled sounds of restless horses outside the circle hung in the air. "They must climb the Spire and claim an artifact of one of the inhabitants! Only the first two candidates to return successful will be allowed in the third and final Trial of the Choosing!"

This announcement broke the silence and caused the circle to erupt into a chorus of soft, harsh whispers. The Elder wore a smug smile, probably knowing that the Elders could always dismiss whatever was brought back as counterfeit.

"What is the Spire and what lives there?" I asked quietly.

"It is a lone mountain on the northernmost point of the continent," she whispered. "The last of the ancient storm giants live there. But the Caliphate has a pact to never disturb them. It makes no sense to upset the accord." Judging by the confident looks on the Elders, I was sure it made perfect sense to them.

"Cleric Fioasha comes from a village at its base," Mynasha added with realization and a little anger.

"Of course he does," I said sarcastically. "Don't worry, I have fought a storm giant before. Granted, I wouldn't say the encounter went well, and I think our best option when we see one is to run as fast and far away as we can." Mynasha gawked at me, not knowing if I was being serious.

Horses were already being led into the circle, and the others were mounting and riding away. I noted irritably that their saddlebags were bursting with supplies, so they had been forewarned of the long trek. "How far is it to this Spire?" I asked as I swung up into Ginger's saddle.

"Four days hard ride from here. We don't have supplies, and I have never been there myself," Mynasha said tersely. I translated four days hard ride into two hundred miles away in my head.

Maveith parted the crowd so Glasha and Tarnasha could reach us. "Clerics and Supremes have climbed the Spire before," Glasha said as she joined us in hushed conversation. "They sought the Titans' wisdom. Be respectful and deferential if you meet one and they will likely not kill you."

"Why do we have to meet them?" I asked, frowning.

"Because all the easily retrieved artifacts are long gone," she said assertively. "I've reviewed the records from past expeditions myself. If the Elders made a pact with the Titans to allow only their chosen candidate to leave ... you will need to be cautious."

I had a few sarcastic retorts ready, but bit my tongue. Now wasn't the time. "Maveith," I said, meeting his eyes, "don't do anything until I return." Maveith was my biggest concern as I his anxiety was evident. He nodded slowly but I was not reassured.

"We only have enough supplies for a day," Mynasha pointed out.

"I've got it handled." I nudged Ginger forward. The crowd parted as we moved to catch the others.

We raced out of the valley, and Ginger was the only one happy about the urgency. Mynasha was eager to overtake the others, but it would be four long days in the saddle. Maybe it was my cynicism about the Trials, but I was confident that Fioasha would probably just have to walk into his old village, be handed an artifact, and ride back.

"We can stop in a village this evening and get supplies," Mynasha said as she galloped beside me.

I suspected the nearest villages might have been warned about Mynasha and would not offer timely aid. "There is no need. I have enough food for us and the horses to get us to the mountain." She looked surprised, but I didn't want her to dwell on my dimensional space. "I was prepared for this eventuality," I said dismissively. Thinking ahead to possible problems, I asked, "Is there a trail going up the Spire for the horses?"

The lightning cleric bounced beside me in her saddle, assessing me again before replying, "I believe the summit is only accessible on foot, but I have never been there. Some of the past Supremes used to make a pilgrimage to seek the wisdom of the giants. I know not all of them returned." That was not what I wanted to hear.

If there was lore about dealing with the storm giants, perhaps we should have spent some time talking with Glasha before we left. The road was familiar as we headed north, but we soon turned off the main road to follow a lesser road that paralleled the coast. It should be easy to find the Spire, as it was on the northernmost tip of the continent.

When we took our first break at a spring to water the horses, I pulled out meat buns for us and grain to go with the grass the horses were eating. Of course, Ginger also needed an apple for her hard work. Mynasha's appetite was satiated with a second meat bun.

"We have rested long enough," Mynasha said anxiously after just a third of an hour had passed.

"There is no point in rushing and risking injury to the horses," I said, not moving. She studied me a moment before reluctantly retaking her seat on a log. I nodded to her. "What else do you know about the Spire and the residents?"

"It is the last known enclave of storm giants on Desia. They are thousands of years old if the stories are true. Sometimes, a Supreme will visit them, seeking wisdom or lost knowledge," she replied, offering the same knowledge she had before.

She had also mentioned that sometimes the Supremes wouldn't return. "What type of knowledge would cause a Supreme to risk their lives?"

Mynasha bit her lip in thought. "I don't know. I think the art of tattooing was passed down from the storm giants."

"That is fascinating. How do the tattoos work?" I asked conversationally.

"It is a secret of the Caliphate," she stated. She seemed to reconsider. "The elves have appropriated the knowledge but have not utilized it, to our understanding. For your loyalty, you have earned the right to know the secret as well."

Mynasha moved in front of me and sat on the grass, much closer than she needed to be. I think she was afraid of being overheard while revealing the tattoos' secrets. "The tattoos are a blessing and a curse for those marked with them. You cannot imprint spells on your aether core if you are tattooed. Instead, you wear your spell forms on your skin."

I interrupted with a question. "What if you already have a spell form on your core before you are tattooed?"

She frowned at being interrupted. "It will be blocked and unusable, permanently lost, the tattoos draw your aether from your core in a chaotic current."

"Then why get tattoos at all? Spell forms are much more flexible," I replied, drinking from my canteen.

Mynasha looked a little indecisive for a moment. But eventually, she revealed the truth. "There are benefits. For instance, the spell forms that can be tattooed can be of any affinity, not just affinities you are strong enough to create a spell form for."

That was interesting, since affinities were rare. "How does that work?"

Mynasha inhaled deeply and exhaled slowly as she revealed the secret of the Caliphate warriors. "The ink the tattoos are made of holds the affinity of the spell form, transmuting the raw aether. It is common knowledge that we use essences for the ink, but I will not reveal the other ingredients required to make the ink. Another benefit is that the warrior does not need to master controlling their aether. They just—squeeze their aether core to release the aether. Their saturated body naturally pulls it to the tattoos, activating the spell forms."

Something occurred to me. "The warriors must activate all their tattoos at once then?"

She looked a little uncertain. "For most, that is the case—empower all or none. It is rare for a warrior to be able to focus their aether into just one tattoo, but it is not unheard of. The tattooist must also be highly skilled in aether shaping to keep them separated with the turbulent aether."

"What do the tattoos do?" I already knew what they did from my Hound training, but I was curious about what Mynasha would tell me.

Once again, she looked hesitant to tell me but eventually answered my question. "A Pathfinder will have two or three tattoos focused on stealth, while one of our elite warriors typically just has one that is focused on either strength or speed." She grudgingly explained a little further when I waited for her to continue. "Our elites usually have tiny aether cores, so they cannot sustain more than one tattoo for long. Giving them two just shortens their combat effectiveness."

"And the warlords?" I asked, already guessing her answer.

"Three or four, and rarely five. There is only so much space on the body, and the skill of the tattoo artist comes into play to avoid overlapping with other tattoos. A warlord always has the three tattoos: speed, strength, and endurance. Beyond that, it varies depending on what the tattooist has mastered," Mynasha explained.

Something occurred to me. "What ingredient in the ink is found in the Warlord Dungeon?"

Her jaw dropped open like I had uncovered one of the Caliphate's greatest secrets. Her jaw moved, but no words came. It made sense in my mind that if a warlord needed to complete the dungeon, then it had to be a secret to their power. "Demon horn," she said after a long pause. "How did you know?"

I shrugged. "It was obvious. It is the only dungeon in the Caliphate that outsiders and adventurers are not allowed into."

"I ask that you do not spread this even if you think it is—obvious," Mynasha said tersely. "My people have feeble aether shaping skills. We have a tenth of the number of clerics that the elves have mages and a quarter of that of humans. Raising our best warriors with the tattoos is the only way to defend our lands. If others started tattooing their weaker warriors ..." She left the rest unspoken.

I was not going to make any guarantees about that, but I nodded slowly in understanding. "We can leave now," I said, standing.

We were soon back on the coastal road, passing small fishing settlements. When night encroached, we dismounted and walked the horses rather than divert to rest in a town. By morning, Mynasha was stumbling, and I offered her the pea-green Pathfinder potions of stamina. I had ten left and didn't need them, as I also had four elven stamina potions that tasted much better.

Each vomit-tasting concoction worked for about eight hours, increasing alertness and invigorating you with a powerful stimulant. I was surprised when Mynasha immediately downed the potion and belched a foul air. She seemed to like the taste and my opinion of orc gastronomy suddenly plummeted. Soon, she was alert again, and we continued our ride.

We had short conversations over the next two days. I learned Warlord Rhuuk had five tattoos: strength, speed, stamina, self-healing, and toughness. The toughness tattoo fortified his organs and skin against attacks. He was also one of the few warlords skilled enough to activate individual tattoos.

Warlord Etus, who was the First of Fioasha, had five as well: strength, speed, stamina, water breathing, and a gust of wind. Since he was an admiral of the northern fleet, it made sense that he had chosen the latter two. He was also capable of activating specific tattoos.

It was good to know your enemy's strengths, but Mynasha seemed to think there would not be a direct confrontation between our groups. I doubted that orc honor would hold when so much was at stake.

By the third day, even Ginger was eager for a rest. "How are you still going? I never observed you consuming a potion," Mynasha asked me during one of our spells of walking the horses. She was stumbling from both fatigue and soreness.

"Human constitution," I replied to the cleric, who once again reassessed me. "But we do need to rest, at least for a time. The horses are beginning to stumble, and we don't want them to come up lame." Reluctantly, Mynasha agreed.

We took refuge in a small, isolated farm, where we gave the old farmer a large silver coin in exchange for staying in his hay shed. The farmer and cleric asserted that payment was unnecessary, but I insisted. Even I needed rest. We all bedded down after a meal, and I found myself drifting off to sleep.

My dreams were not pleasant, as I confronted ancient storm giants who somehow pulled the truth from me about my role in killing one of their number. I ended up flattened underfoot and woke in a sweat. I returned to sleep and used my experience in the dreamscape to try and twist the nightmare into something more palatable. The best I could do was grow myself to match the size of the storm giants and wrestle them into submission.

Mynasha shook me awake. "It has been almost half a day."

My hand was on my blade. I couldn't believe I had slept for so long, but it was already morning. Even the horses had been so exhausted that they hadn't stirred during the night. We unbarred the door, and I spent some time mucking out the shed, as it was not intended to stable horses. Mynasha didn't understand my insistence on cleaning up after us, but explaining how a guest should act was useless, as she was used to being venerated by the common people.

The rest of the ride to the Spire was strenuous for the horses and Mynasha, but the only environmental issue was a warm, steady rain on the third day. When the Spire came into view, it was awe-inspiring, jutting out of the distant landscape into the sky. It looked to be an isolated, narrow mountain with a ring of clouds around it. Faint flashes of lightning in the clouds could be seen even in the brightness of day.

We paused to admire the odd sight. It felt ominous and uninviting. "Having second thoughts?" I asked, turning to the cleric.

Mynasha stared for a moment, maybe reconsidering. "No. My people need me. I will continue on this path."

We continued, and the rocky grasslands started to show flocks of sheep as we approached the Spire. A town began to emerge in the distance, and Mynasha indicated it. "That is Rosenrock. That is where Fioasha grew up." It was still a few miles from the Spire and didn't have even a wooden wall surrounding the twenty-odd stone buildings with thatched roofs.

We walked our horses into town and were greeted by someone I recognized as a cleric. The orc wore worn leathers and wore a tusky smile while he greeted us. "Cleric Mynasha. It is an honor to meet you. I am Cleric Woolasha." He bowed his head in respect. "Cleric Glasha sent word to meet you and help you. Cleric Fioasha and Cleric Jhuarkasha have already started the climb with their Firsts."

In disbelief, Mynasha exploded, "How did they get here ahead of us!" I was still hung up on the fact that their Firsts had accompanied them. I had thought, or maybe hoped, that Mynasha would climb the Spire alone.

Woolasha smiled conciliatorily as he relayed the bad news. "Cleric Fioasha grew up here. I know he can wash away fatigue for himself and others. Cleric Jhuarkasha can do something similar, holding fatigue at bay, but only for himself." I could see the frustration boiling over in Mynasha. "Cleric Jhuarkasha is only a few hours ahead of you. Fioasha is half a day ahead. If you wish, I will take care of your horses. The ascent is too treacherous and narrow for them."

I really didn't want to trust this stranger with the care of Ginger. If they were lying about being on our side and something happened to Ginger, I wouldn't be able to restrain my vengeance.

"Your mount will be safe with me," he said, as if reading my mind. "On my honor, your horses will be well cared for even if you do not return. It is just three miles to the start of the trail." He indicated behind him. "If you want to rest, I will have my acolytes prepare something for you."

"Yes," I answered before Mynasha could. "We will rest for an hour before starting out. We would appreciate it if you could tell us whatever you can about the Spire." Selfishly, I had hoped the other two candidates would have already returned before our ascent, and we could turn around, avoiding the risk of facing the storm giants altogether. Mynasha slowly nodded. Another hour to possibly gain valuable knowledge would be wise.

Mynasha was impatient as we sat and were served by young orc attendants in drab, gray robes. The local cleric's house was humble but cozy.

Woolasha sipped some pungent tea. "I will tell you what I can. It is a challenging climb, and the task the Elders have set forth is difficult. I suspect Fioasha might know a few places where he might find an artifact without summiting the Spire and confronting the Ancients."

"Ancients?" I asked, puzzled.

The cleric nodded ardently. "That is what we call the oldest of the storm giants. They come here to live out their last days, even though that may be centuries. We do not know how long they actually live, though there is one storm giant that has been around since the founding of the Caliphate," Woolasha replied instructively.

I interjected with a pertinent question. "What is the name of that storm giant?" If it became a FUBAR situation, maybe knowing the name would be useful.

"Khrusos," the cleric replied earnestly.

That sounded familiar. "Kronos?" I questioned.

"No. Khrusos," he said patiently, sounding out the name a few times for me. Perhaps the translation or passage of time had altered the giant's name. Kronos was Latin, after all. He waited till I was satisfied before continuing.

"Now, the Spire has been called many things over the years: The Crown, due to the persistent lightning storms surrounding the summit; Death's Holme, since that is where the storm giants go to die and most who venture to climb it never return; and Wisdom Peak by Supreme Annalasha, who centuries ago visited the Titans on more than five occasions. But the Titans call it Olympia, and you should use that name if you plan to converse with them." My blood chilled. There were just too many similarities to Greek legends to be a coincidence.

Mynasha didn't see or sense my unease. "Can't we find an artifact without confronting the Titans?" Mynasha asked, a little distressed. At least she was smart in not wanting to risk an encounter with the giants.

Woolasha nodded. "That is probably wisest. You may come across some relics during your climb, but most will be too large to carry back with you. Fioasha used to climb the Spire as a youth. Not to the summit, but it was considered brave among the young men and women to explore the lower paths. Like I said, he most likely knows where artifacts are easily accessible on the lower slopes."

Mynasha clenched her fists in frustration. What did she expect? The Elders probably consulted Fioasha before assigning the task. They likely required something sufficiently dangerous to announce to the assembled warlords and clerics. It was either admirable or naive that she still thought she had a chance to come out on top of the Choosing.

She regained her composure. "What do you suggest we do if we have to climb to the summit?" I clenched my jaw. She had used the word "we." I did not want to climb to the summit. I could accompany her partway, but it was her task to convince the Titans to relinquish an artifact, not mine. I wondered if we could have cheated and just used one of the buttons we had uncovered in the plains. I wished I had thought about it before we left, but Glasha did say she registered them with her superiors.

"If you do summit, announce yourselves. Do not be foolish and try to sneak in and steal something. The last of the storm giants wield powerful magic, the likes of which can erase cities from maps." I could attest to that, having seen a single storm giant excavate a massive crater in a swamp.

"We should go," Mynasha said, standing determinedly. She was done waiting.

I stood slowly and handed the cleric a handful of silver and a bag of apples. "For my mare. One apple a day. If I don't return, explain my fate to her." He looked at me, perplexed, but took the coin and apples.

The walk to the Spire was a lightly worn path through the rocky grassland. A number of sheep paused in their meal to watch us, and I could read their minds. They were thinking we were idiots for heading toward the ominous tower of stone in the distance.

After trekking a few miles through rocky terrain, we finally arrived at the base of the Spire. The mountain loomed above us, its colossal form becoming more imposing with each step we took. When we stood at its base, we were met with an astonishingly sheer cliff that seemed to extend impossibly into the sky. It was an awe-inspiring sight that defied nature.

"This feels—artificial," I breathed softly in the cold but humid air. Around us, massive blocks of stone were partially buried in the ground like ancient, fallen sentinels. The entire sight was reminiscent of Devil's Tower back on Earth.

My companion dismissed my remark and veered onto the worn path to the right, each step echoing on the damp stone. A gentle mist drizzled down from the swirling clouds overhead. After a few moments of following the cliff, we found ourselves standing before magnificent stone towers that loomed on either side of the wide path. The ancient giants had clearly crafted these colossal structures themselves. The tower surfaces were adorned with faded pictographs—timeworn symbols that hinted at a long-lost language. The sheer size of the towers made me feel tiny in comparison. They were living testaments to a bygone era where the Titans ruled.

We paused briefly, taking in the breathtaking view. The uneven stone path before us wound upward, curling around the massive Spire that loomed overhead. Mynasha, determined, stepped forward, passing between the two tall structures. As we moved past them, the extent of the towers' damage became obvious. Their once-imposing facades bore the marks of a fierce attack; large chunks of stone had fallen away, leaving gaping holes.

I sent a few earth pulses out, hoping that perhaps an artifact would be buried within easy access to end this expedition early, but there was nothing. The abandoned towers appeared to be made primarily of solid stone, with space for defenders on just the top floor. I continued to pulse my earth speak as we climbed the path, hoping to find something.

At first, I was confused as to why we had been told to leave our mounts. But after we had ascended a few hundred feet, we saw that a large portion of the path had fallen away, and a fresh, narrow path had been carved into the cliff at specific points. I needed to turn sideways to walk the ledge, and the horses would have stood no chance of making it past. I guessed that the Titans had done this on purpose to prevent large forces from scaling the Spire en masse.

When we reached the far side of the Spire, the ocean was hundreds of feet below us. It felt surreal, as the clouds that circled the tower were still so far above us, making a persistent mist that made the stone slippery. It would take hours to reach the top of the tower, judging by the gradual grade of the spiraling path.

An hour later, we encountered a second portion of the path that had fallen away. The carved-out walkway was even narrower this time. I briefly wondered if the storm giants could just leap the twenty-foot span of the missing path. Shortly after passing this section, we encountered another tower centered in the path. This tower had mostly crumbled with time or from an attack, and we had to scramble over the rubble.

On the other side was water runoff from above, and the muddy sediment on the path clearly showed four sets of footprints. "Why don't we just wait here and take whatever artifact one of the others recovers?" I asked Mynasha.

"That would not be honorable," she said dismissively. I wasn't joking, though. We had stolen a pixie. What was different about an artifact?

I suddenly got a little angry at the convoluted orc honor. I might have yelled a little in my retort. "And setting up this Trial so Fioasha has all the advantages is honorable? You must realize that you have no chance of assuming the mantle of the Supreme and leading your people. This is all just a dog and pony show to make it look like there was a selection process."

Mynasha winced at my verbal assault but didn't back down, showing some spine. "I understand what you think." She pointed to the prints in the mud. "But that is proof Fioasha is ascending the Spire. That alone tells me he has honor. He may be better prepared for this Trial, but he is not dishonorable. If you do not want to stand by my side, just return to town and feed your horse apples while you wait for me to return!"

"Okay." I spun and started to scramble back over the rubble. I slowed when I reached the top of the pile and looked back. Mynasha was gone. She had continued without me. *Did I feel guilty?* Maybe a little bit, but following her seemed foolish. Adrian had once told me: "You cannot save everyone, Eryk," which felt applicable now. Then why did I turn around after fifteen minutes and follow the cleric? Mynasha was the best way to get Maveith's sister back without a fight.

I walked slower than I needed to, hoping to come to my senses, but it never happened. I climbed over two more ruined towers before entering the misty clouds that contained crackling lightning. With my earth speak, I could walk forward confidently without having to worry about falling to my death if I encountered a portion of collapsed trail. That was probably why I caught up to Mynasha, who was hugging the cliff face and testing the path carefully with each step as she traversed the mist.

I stayed fifty feet back, not announcing myself. When the mist cleared for her, she resumed walking. I waited in the mist to let her get ahead again before following. The halo of clouds was now below me as I circled the tower, and it looked like I was not far from the top. At least, it didn't look like the cliff went on forever above me. The air was definitely a lot colder, and my manticore cloak was soon draped on my shoulders.

My earth pulses picked up the coming summit before my eyes did. Mynasha had stopped at the end of the winding path. It had taken most of the day to climb, and Neptune's Tear was coming out with the fading sun. It was a little disconcerting that neither of the other candidates had passed us, returning with their artifacts. I had seen other signs that they were ahead of us: piss and shit on the path, scraps of discarded food, a discarded empty waterskin, and footprints in soft mud.

Mynasha was frozen and didn't move around the bend for a long time. I was curious about what had made her pause. I silently edged forward until I could see her. She stood between two smaller pillars, gazing out at the summit. I walked slowly to stand by her side. She didn't acknowledge me, as if she had expected me to join her. She was still mesmerized by what she was seeing.

"Thought you might be hungry," I said, handing her a meat pie. Mynasha took the offered food, as she had not been carrying any supplies. I handed her a canteen next, as it had been a strenuous climb and she had to be dehydrated.

I finally got to see what had given her pause. A shallow green valley extended across the caldera. It was maybe three miles across to the far side, but a few white buildings could be seen among the colossal trees. It didn't look like paradise, but it definitely felt out of place in its surroundings. Even the cold air that had dominated the last hour of the climb was gone, replaced with warm, moist air coming from the valley below. Mynasha was obviously hungry. By the time I had taken in the view, she had finished the bun and drunk the entire canteen.

"I saw two of the storm giants in that clearing there not too long ago." She pointed to an open space in front of one of the white buildings.

"Did you see either of the other candidates?" I asked.

"No, but Woolasha said we shouldn't try to sneak in. I was waiting for one of the storm giants to come to me." I didn't have a response, as he had indeed advised that. I pulled my spyglass to my hand and scanned the valley slowly. At least four clearings had four large white stone structures that reminded me of Greek architecture. "Do you see anything?" she asked.

"Just a few aurochs in the far field," I replied after scanning again to make sure.

"Maybe we need to announce ourselves," Mynasha said.

"Don't go doing anything drastic …" I started to say, but she had already extended her hands toward the sky. Two thick bolts of lightning extended into the sky, followed by a crack of rolling thunder. Well, she certainly knew how to announce herself. It didn't take long before a giant emerged from one of the buildings, paused, turned toward us, and then started to walk in our direction. I doubted it would take him long to cover the distance…

The storm giant didn't seem to be moving with haste to meet us, but his long strides quickly carried him through the trees and along a path that wound down into the valley from where we stood. The giant paused, looking up at us before beginning the climb. Maybe he thought we had smartened up and fled.

I was expecting an ancient-looking storm giant, but as he approached, he was barely over ten feet tall and lacked the time-worn beard and blue-gray skin tones I anticipated from my first encounter with his race. His pale-gray face would have seemed youthful if I didn't have to crane my neck to make eye contact. The giant was dressed in leather and wool garments, all of which were dyed a deep blue. His gray eyes watched us, waiting.

"Do you speak storm giant?" I asked Mynasha, who stood confidently.

"No," she replied, and bowed to the giant. In Orcish, she spoke to the giant. "We come as friends and to request an audience and a blessing."

The skin of the giant reminded me of Maveith's, though the giant was much leaner of build than the goliath. "Are you with the others?" his coarse voice grumbled out in rough Orcish. I relaxed a little, thinking that perhaps this interaction might be cordial rather than a life-or-death encounter.

Mynasha considered her response carefully. "No, but we are here for the same thing. We request the gift of an inconsequential artifact."

The giant's gray eyes studied us before he spoke. "You can still depart and descend Olympia, or you may follow me to stand before Khrusos for judgment." His tone was flat and uncaring, making the situation all the more ominous. We were a curiosity to him, but he did not care if we lived or died.

Pessimistically, I thought if we entered the valley and they decided we might make a good snack, escape was going to be nearly impossible. "Is our safety guaranteed?" I asked.

"No," the giant said with a slight smirk that faded immediately. "But you will be allowed to speak," he grumbled out. Then he chose to add a little snide comment. "How much depends on what you say." I was not liking giant humor.

"We will meet with Khrusos," Mynasha affirmed. I was not so confident about the "we" part. Still, I fell in beside Mynasha as we followed the short giant.

The gravel path to the caldera was steep and would have been easier with steps, in my opinion. Old, long-abandoned fortifications lined the path as we descended. From what I observed, I thought that the storm giants didn't seem worried about being attacked in this refuge. That didn't make much sense to me, but it would be difficult for an army to scale the Spire. Maybe they would be warned if a threat approached.

"When did you know we were climbing the Spire?" I asked our escort.

The giant looked down at me, his foot briefly slipping on gravel. He was not at risk of losing his footing, however, because he had remarkable balance even for his size. "Ephemeris was aware as soon as you passed the gatehouse." That sent a chill up my spine. They had probably been watching us ascend. They didn't think us a threat or they would have intercepted us on the climb. *Why chase the lambs when they can come to you for slaughter?*

As we reached the valley, a thick grass carpet with scattered, large hardwood trees appeared ahead of us. I could see a foraging auroch in the trees. This close, I could tell that it was larger than the specimens I had seen in my travels. Its shoulders matched our escort in height. "How many storm giants live on Olympia?" I asked, not expecting an answer. Logistically, I was wondering how many giants this relatively small valley could support.

The escort looked at me as we walked and answered, "Five storm giants reside here. But the stone giants tend Olympia. There are eleven of us." He said the last pointedly, clearly wanting credit for maintaining this vale above the clouds.

It made sense that our escort was not a storm giant. I didn't get an imposing, ancient-aura feeling from him. Mynasha was surprisingly calm, and asked politely, "And what is your name? I am Mynasha, and my companion is Eryk."

"I am Lampter, son of Hesper and Lethargia," he proudly replied. "I tend the vegetable gardens and fill the reservoir there." He pointed up across the valley. I couldn't see the reservoir, but I nodded like I was impressed anyway.

We soon found ourselves among the trees on a heavily traveled path, and I felt like we were being watched—not by the creatures in the woods but by powerful magic. Whoever was doing it was not being subtle and wanted us to know. Even Mynasha suddenly seemed worried, as she began searching the towering canopy and looking deep into the woods.

My obfuscation sphere burned where it touched my chest as it feebly tried to ward off the powerful intrusive mage's sight. The heat forced me to send the sphere to my dimensional space, and the oppressive feeling slowly faded.

Whoever had been watching us wanted us to know that we couldn't hide, even with an artifact. It made me doubt that they had been aware of us when we started our climb, as the sphere had not reacted at the time. Also, we had not been met at the edge of the caldera, and Mynasha had to announce us with her lightning. The Titans were not all-seeing and all-powerful.

The aurochs appeared to wander the valley freely. Large cow pies were often visible along the path, and the grazing animals could be seen through the trees. We passed another stone giant, much larger than Lampter, who seemed to be milking one in a clearing. The giant looked at us curiously before returning to her task of squeezing the udder's teats to fill a stone bucket. Her thick fingers worked methodically, coaxing heavy streams of milk from the massive udder. Each jet landed with a wet *whoosh*, rhythmic and loud, like someone drumming.

Lampter led us to a large, grassy clearing with a white marble building on the far side. Large Greek pillars circled the structure, reminiscent of the Temple of Athena Nike. We started to cross the grassy expanse, and I noticed the flowers among the grass were familiar to me and shouldn't be growing at this altitude.

Many of them were used in alchemy, but a number of them were also rare. Our guide trampled a patch of blue velvet flowers. They were one of the necessary ingredients for invisibility potions, but needed to be harvested under Neptune's Tear when the petals became translucent. I couldn't even fathom the riches we were casually crushing.

My wandering thoughts ended when we reached the structure. It was much larger up close and looked like an open-air pavilion. I hesitated to enter as our guide walked away, leaving without announcing us. Before stepping in, I noted the best escape routes and the general direction we had come from. The shortest way into the trees was to our left, and that is where I planned to go.

Mynasha waited for me, probably not wanting to enter alone, although she wore confidence on her face. Passing between the majestic, ribbed pillars made me feel small. I entered a large open-air auditorium with Mynasha. Three epic thrones were at the far end. A giant of monumental proportions occupied each.

The central throne dwarfed the other two and had a flared backrest, but that chair's storm giant looked younger than the other two. My instincts told me it was Khrusos, or more likely Kronos, of myth and legend. I shouldn't have been surprised. I had a spell form to slow my aging. He could probably do the same if he was the fabled god of time.

My eyes had passed over the other two candidates, who were before the assembled giants. Fioasha was on his knees, isolated and alone to the left. It took me a moment to figure out that he was not paying respect but was injured, as his leg was bandaged and at an odd angle. His First was not at his side, or anywhere in sight. Cleric Jhuarkasha and Warlord Rhuuk stood to the right, both healthy and watching us. Their faces didn't reveal what we were walking into. Something about the scene didn't feel right.

Mynasha whispered, concerned. "Where is Warlord Etus?" I didn't reply, but I thought he was probably dead judging by Fioasha's condition. Fioasha's eyes revealed his immense pain from his injuries.

As we slowly walked forward, the giants' three sets of eyes watched us approach. The two giants flanking the central throne appeared to be aged females in pearl-white togas. The central figure, whose eyes were focused on us, wore a black smock secured to his waist by a thick leather belt. He reclined on his throne, his face impassive but his eyes judging.

Just what were we walking into? As we moved to stand between the other candidates, I could feel the energy of the assembled trio of storm giants. If gods had auras, then I was being pressured by it. I felt awe and hopelessness battling inside my head.

"Another orc pest brought a human pet with her." The giant's deep voice echoed in the chamber. The other orcs now had their eyes fixed forward, acknowledging the storm giant and offering us no help. "Offer your case so I may decide your fate," Khrusos said with finality.

Mynasha gave me an apologetic look. This was not the reception we had been expecting. Khrusos appeared to be annoyed, and I guessed it was because of Fioasha. Mynasha gathered herself. "Lord Khrusos …"

"Lord?!" He bellowed a laugh. "Do not presume to call me a lord, king, emperor, or any other title you insignificant beings use to describe your leaders. I am Khrusos." His name was a title unto itself.

"I apologize," Mynasha said, bowing low. "Khrusos, we have come to seek your generosity. We …"

With grinding anger, Khrusos interrupted Mynasha. "What makes you think I am generous?" His voice grew to a roar. "Your people revolted against our magnanimous rule!" He stood from his throne, rising to over twenty-five feet in height. Veins bulged on his arms, and his jaw was tight. He was not in a great mood and navigating this audience was feeling more and more perilous.

The aged storm giant woman to his right spoke for the first time. Her tone was tempered by her commanding voice. "Khrusos, sit!"

The ancient storm giant turned on the aged woman; their eyes met in silent communication. His anger slowly faded, and he resumed his seat. His temper cooling, he gestured. "What have you brought me in tribute? These fools brought nothing of interest. I hope you don't disappoint me as well," he added with a note of warning.

I knew Mynasha had nothing to satisfy the storm giants. I wasn't sure what to offer from my space. We looked at each other and she looked apologetic for getting me into this.

I sighed, stepping forward. "We have brought you a cauldron of apple-berry jam," I said. My thoughts switched to my escape plan. Could I call forth the black spear and pierce his eye when he came forward to collect the cauldron? The two elderly giants flanking him made killing Khrusos risky.

The cauldron appeared on the floor between me and Khrusos. His large eyebrow arched in surprise, and I could hear Rhuuk and Jhuarkasha shuffling movements behind me to my right. The cauldron was only half full of jam. Maveith had made it in the Shimmering Labyrinth, and it had been three-quarters full then. I had used it slowly, but since I didn't need to eat much with the ring of sustenance, a significant amount remained.

Khrusos leaned forward in his seat, his massive nostrils sniffing the air. Instead of coming to the cauldron, the cauldron came to him. A spell form flashed in front of his hands and the cauldron sped toward his outstretched hand.

His smallest finger was almost as big as the cauldron opening as he stuffed it inside. His finger was covered in jam, and he sucked on it. His face lit up in surprise, clearly enjoying the sweet treat. He took three more dips of jam before he handed the cauldron to the giantess to his left.

Khrusos appeared much less agitated. His voice echoed as he said, "You have earned my favor to leave." He waved his hand dismissively, signaling only to Mynasha and me. The other candidates still awaited their fates. Although Fioasha had the advantage of growing up in the Spire's shadow, he had somehow angered the Titans. We had also not achieved our goal of acquiring an artifact from the Spire.

Meeting Mynasha's eyes, I knew she would not leave without an artifact. "Do you like bear meat?" I asked the ancient storm giant.

In a mocking tone, Khrusos addressed me. "Would you hunt a bear to prove your prowess to me, human? I gave you leave to keep your lives, yet you persist in annoying me."

This wasn't going well. My artifacts would only be dollhouse toys for the storm giant. I poured all the remaining bear meat onto the floor in front of me. The floor was glossy marble, so maybe it wasn't that unsanitary. Hundreds of pounds of bear meat appeared, blood soon spreading from the large pile. "I already hunted a few bears ..." I began to say with a smirk, but I immediately realized that I had misstepped. Khrusos's eyes flicked between me and the pile of meat. The appearance of the cauldron hadn't surprised him, but clearly, the volume of meat did.

The old storm giant on his left spoke to Khrusos with a lisp. "He was not born on Desia."

A sudden weight pressed down on me as if someone had just increased gravity tenfold. I was not the only one. I heard Fioasha cry out in pain, and Mynasha went hard to her knees, using her hands to brace herself. Khrusos was too far away for me to use my dimensional space on him, not that I thought I could overcome his defenses. I remained standing, as did Rhuuk and Jhuarkasha. My leg muscles trembled as I resisted, and I had no chance of running.

The old female stood and walked to me. She bent over to study me like I was a curiosity. Her pale-gray eyes looked past me. She spoke for the other giants, not me. "He is a recent arrival. The aether engines are still functioning and bringing others here."

"I DO NOT CARE!" Khrusos yelled in restrained rage. "I acknowledged my defeat and the folly of Hephaestus. The child races can have the planet and the universe for all I care!"

They ignored me as I strained to remain standing. "This one is also a recent arrival." The storm giantess's gaze had fallen with a lecherous hunger on Mynasha, who was sweating and trying not to be flattened to the floor.

"Ephemeris, no," Khrusos said, addressing the storm giantess. "They have not violated the guest's sanctity." His piercing gaze made her sit back down, but it was obvious she wanted us. I suspected her intention was to invite us to dinner as the main course.

The third storm giant tapped her wrinkled hand on the arm of her marble seat. "I am curious what else the human has, guest or not." Suddenly, the giants' language changed from Orcish to what I assumed was the language of the Titans. Their rapid speech showed only tiny hints of Latin as they discussed our fate. I assumed that they were discussing whether to turn us into essences, but that was probably just my pessimism. We were all held helpless by the intense gravity.

Khrusos yelled a few minutes later, and Lampter arrived shortly afterward. I believed Khrusos didn't want to waste my gift, as the juvenile stone giant quickly gathered the meat onto an auroch hide. Although the stone giant was within range of my dimensional space, killing him would not help us escape from this. When he left, Khrusos turned his gaze on me. His lips curled into a smile. "Now, human. Let's see what else you are carrying hidden from my eyes."

Chapter 311: Humbled Hoarder

I was cursing both my life decisions and Mynasha. "I know where Atlantium is!" I forced out, trying to find leverage. Khrusos studied me, some curiosity in his eyes. I could rush him and try and take his brain, but I hesitated. If it didn't work, I would be flattened.

"So do I, human. I lived there for centuries," he said with a mischievous sneer.

Shit, what else can I offer? "You look good for being six thousand years old," I quipped, and I imagined being consumed by the massive head in front of me, my bones ground by his teeth.

Khrusos smiled. "Ha!" He laughed from his gut, the air reverberating from his voice. "I do, don't I? It is closer to eight thousand, but I tend to lose track of time. Now let's see what you are hiding." Khrusos's eyes glowed with aether as his smile remained. I felt like my aether core was being torn apart. I think I screamed, but I couldn't be sure. My legs gave out and I face-planted into the floor, cracking my jaw and chipping multiple teeth. I now knew what it felt like to be manhandled by someone with magic far beyond me.

A young griffin's wail of pain sounded. I forced my head to turn, only to see a large pile of goods with Baldo sitting on top. I had certainly collected a lot of shit over the last two years. One of the female giants complimented me. "This human is impressively large." Had I not been in excruciating pain, I might have quipped some innuendos in response to try to gain some goodwill.

Baldo squawked in protest as Khrusos walked toward him and scooped him up. "I haven't tasted griffin in ages," the storm giant's voice boomed.

Shit, I was helpless. "Please leave the griffin alone!" I yelled. "He is a companion and friend." The agony passed and left vertigo in its place as I felt the weight lift. I fought back bile as I got to my knees. Baldo was trapped in the cage that was Khrusos's hand, only his head protruding and clearly in distress. Mynasha was still flattened on the floor, eyes transfixed by the pile of goods before her. She was astonished, her lips parted in awe. I didn't need to turn to know that Rhuuk and Jhuarkasha were just as speechless behind me.

Khrusos considered the griffin. I thought he was going to bite off Baldo's head, but instead he dropped the young griffin unceremoniously. It was a good sign that he didn't eat him, but Baldo slammed hard into the marble floor, succumbing to the oppressive force on all of us. His wings were splayed and he was twitching as he tried to move.

I searched for my dimensional space. It was still there and didn't seem shattered. My aether core was full, but it felt like I had been kicked in the balls. I made my decision. Baldo disappeared, draining my aether. Khrusos looked at me, some curiosity on his face. Was he going to rip open my dimensional pocket again? Our eyes met, and he seemed to see me differently this time. He gave me the slightest of nods. Was that respect?

The two giantesses left their seats and walked toward the treasure hoard. As they stepped, they slowly shrank in size to that of a human. Khrusos tittered at his companions but followed suit, also deflating to appear no bigger than I. This caused the orcs to gasp in shock, which only made the Titans amused. One of the females commented, "Yes, we have walked among you since you overthrew us." Khrusos gave the female an annoyed look that silenced her. Of course their reduced size made it easier for them to go through my things.

I was helpless as they sifted through my mess. One of the females took one of the ginseng roots, sniffed it, and nibbled on it. Soon, the entire stock of two-thousand-year-old ginseng was being handed out and munched on like a snack. I had planned some high-tier alchemy for those roots. The candied nuts were the next victims of the giants as they ignored the artifacts and focused on the culinary treats.

Potion vials were cracked and leaking onto the floor. When the liquids mixed, they produced a slight smoke. My alchemy glassware was mostly shattered. Pieces of armor were tossed aside as they dug through the pile like children on Christmas, looking for the best presents. The giants still appeared to have retained their strength, and they cared nothing for being gentle as they searched. I wasn't sure if they were searching for something specific or just being curious.

My essences were soon found in the manticore pouch. Khrusos upended the supple bag into his hand, and the other two crowded around to see what he had found. I took advantage of the distraction to return the dreamscape amulet and essence collector to my dimensional pocket. I would have salvaged more, but it was all I had the aether for at the moment. The giants didn't appear to notice as they were focused on dividing up the essences among themselves.

The loss of the four major healing essences was painful. One of the females—Ephemeris, I think—took one of the many apples on the floor and bit into it, her weathered face lighting up in pleasure. Khrusos had picked up the black spear and was twirling it admiringly. I was waiting for another opportunity to salvage precious items.

The third giantess was sniffing the bottle of elven ambrosia. She took a long pull before speaking. "Father, has he not paid enough tribute for his due?" Father? By a human standard, she looked to be over a hundred, while Khrusos only looked to be in his forties. Ephemeris was taking the opportunity to gather up Ginger's apples in a sack she had found among my things.

Khrusos sighed and dropped the black spear. As it clattered on the floor, he faced us. In a much more deferential tone, he addressed us. "Very well. For the nourishment and amusement you have provided, you have earned a boon. What do you seek?" I craned my neck to make eye contact with Mynasha, indicating that she should speak.

She had fought to get to her knees. "Any inconsequential artifact that is easily portable," she said, breathing heavily from the strain. I took the opportunity to check on the others. Fioasha was face down and wheezing heavily. Warlord Rhuuk was still standing, but from the hollow look in his eyes, I guessed he had drained his aether into his tattoos, enhancing his strength to do so. His eyes met mine with a cold, calculating stare. He had seen too many of my secrets. Jhuarkasha was huddled into a ball, and I was unsure if I had observed everything that had happened.

Khrusos was growing again, releasing the magic that had compacted his body. Ephemeris had taken her apples and was also rising to her original height. The third giantess who had aided in stopping the plundering picked up the last paper cone of candied nuts. She gave me a wink before returning to her seat. An odd ally; I didn't even know her name.

As the three storm giants seated themselves again, the weight slowly lifted off of me. Fioasha gasped the loudest in relief. I was urgently feeling out my aether recovery. How much aether did I need to reclaim the most valuable of treasures?

A metal object clattered to the floor in front of us. "An inconsequential artifact," Khrusos barked. "A key to nothing but made of precious metals in thanks for your *thoughtful offerings*." He chuckled to himself at his unwelcome humor.

The key was rectangular and made of silvery metal that reflected the light. Odd, unfamiliar runes adorned its length. Mynasha edged forward to retrieve the key and looked surprised at its weight. "You two may leave," he said, dismissing us.

I looked at my worldly possessions: the overturned assessment table, scattered clothes, a small armory, and a few books now soaked in the liquid of various potions. An array of alchemy ingredients among the broken glass. The troll's blood would spoil if I didn't return it to my dimensional space.

"You can take what you will," the giant said, amused at my longing stare. I had to tell myself not to be angry. I wore magebane and had recovered the collector and the dreamscape amulet, my two most precious artifacts. I needed to stall for some time to recover more aether to collect more things.

"Is there a way for me to go home? Return to Earth?" I asked, stepping closer to the pile, my eyes searching for valuable artifacts.

It was not Khrusos who replied, but my odd ally among the three. "Earth? Is that what you call the origin planet of the humans and half-men?" I think the half-men she mentioned were halflings. "A strange thing to call a planet: Earth."

I nodded, giving her my attention for the moment. "There is a way for me to go home?"

Her gray eyes brushed over me with a penetrating gaze. It was more than a stare. I felt like I was being undressed. "No. The World Gates are no more."

"Gates? Then how was I brought here? How was Mynasha brought here?" I pointed back at my companion.

Khrusos spat. "Ignorant human. The aether engines are still active. That fool Hephaestus built the machines on the ley lines deep in the earth. He gave the engines sentience to power the gates. It allowed my people to conquer your world and many others," Khrusos growled out threateningly.

"Until the demons," the unnamed giantess said with a tight jaw.

Khrusos growled. "Until the demons," he agreed reluctantly. "We destroyed all the gates to end the demon horde. We tried to destroy the aether engines, but Hephestus had changed them and they allied with you lesser species to turn on us!"

Khrusos was stewing and his anger rising from his memories. He did not appear willing to continue and I thought it was time to leave.

Ephemeris took up the narrative though. "I was not yet born." She looked at Khrusos. "But I was told what happened. The aether engines became known as dungeons. They fought for their survival. First, they created creatures and sent them to fight my ancestors. Then, they got more devious when they realized they were not going to succeed. They trained your people to fight us. Gave them artifacts. Gave them magic. Gave them alchemy." She indicated my pile of loot.

Khrusos angrily interceded. "It was not the pitiful smallfolk that doomed us. It was our own bickering among the clans. The infighting weakened us and made us susceptible to your tricks. You are trapped here, human; you cannot return to your planet. The dungeons can only pull people here and all knowledge of the World Gates is destroyed. Now, my patience has run out. Leave."

It was clear the storm giant did not like his history revealed. I bowed slowly. "Thank you for your time. I am Eryk Marko." I bowed low toward Khrusos. "Khrusos." I bowed low toward Ephemeris. "Ephemeris." I bowed low toward the final giantess. "I did not overhear your name. May I have it before we depart?" I wanted to know, but I was also stalling for as much time as possible to replenish my aether for one last grab.

"You have manners, human. I am Anemae, daughter of Khrusos." She nodded at me with a contemplative smile on her dark-blue lips. I turned to the pile and began picking up items, quickly sending them to my space. There were a number of grotesque things mixed in that I had long forgotten about: a cockatrice head, organs of man and beast, a large stack of earth drake hide, and chunks of myconid flesh.

I left all the food for the Titans, lamenting the lost dungeon harvest that I thought would last a decade. The black spear vanished first, then Boris's dungeon blade. I slowed, trying to judge what I could take with the amount of aether I had left.

I took all the artifacts in quick succession, digging them out as I went. The black jade chalice, the brooch, my blood compass, the ring of influence, the dungeon spellbook, an orcish hand axe, my sole remaining glowstone, Orc's Torment, and finally, the tablet reader. I had waited on the tablet reader because its mass took a decent amount of aether to store. I avoided making eye contact with the giants for fear they would grow impatient.

The griffin pillow and weasel pelts were next, followed by an assortment of easily accessible clothes. Then I took what jewelry, silver, and gold I could find easily among the mess, tossing it into the chest I had liberated from the werewolf before storing it. I would have to replace my alchemy kit and supplies. Fortunately, most of my remaining pellets and healing salves were in my dimensional belt.

One of the jars of oblivion pills hadn't shattered, so I grabbed it next. There were still many weapons and an equally large amount of equipment remaining. I stored the three bows before Mynasha grabbed my arm, whispering harshly, "We should leave *now*." I didn't look back at the seated Titans, but I sensed their amusement at my humbling was over. I bent down and tucked the two massive fire bear pelts under my arms, then started walking toward the exit with Mynasha.

There was still so much I was leaving behind. I hoped at least that the Titans would enjoy the food. When we exited the temple, it was still night, and I felt like running. We entered the woods and soon reached the edge of the caldera, where we began to climb. We had been the first to succeed. As we reached the lip of the Spire, Mynasha bared her canines. Her face was a mix of happiness and anxiety. The clouds below were illuminated with flashes of lightning as we hastened down the spiraling path.

Chapter 312: Changing Fortunes

The blue moon shone brightly as we hurried down the Spire. We felt safer after passing through the misty lightning clouds. I held Mynasha's hand and guided us with earth speak. Once we cleared the clouds, it grew much darker, the clouds obscuring the moon's light.

Mynasha kept glancing up as if she feared the Titans might change their minds about letting us go. After we climbed over the rubble of an old guard post, she asked seriously, "You're not from Desia. Are you an outlander?"

"We called them otherworlders in Telha. Besides, I think outlander is copyrighted," I said dismissively. I was distracted, angry, and trying to figure out a way to keep my secrets. Although, outside of Telha, my secrets mattered less.

"Copyrighted?" Mynasha asked, confused at the word.

"What?" I said, preoccupied. My mind was a jumble of thoughts. Maybe the Titans had fished around and scrambled my brain a bit, as it was difficult to focus. I shook my head, trying to clear it. "Never mind. If you believe Khrusos, you are one as well, but not from where I came from." I paused in thought. "At least not from the same time as me. You aren't a murloc, are you?"

"A murloc?" The war cleric tried another unfamiliar word on her tongue. She was still in some shock herself. The Titans were essentially powerful enough to be considered gods, and thought of themselves as such.

I waved my hand, revealing the truth. "Forget it. It was a bad joke. Otherworlders from my planet, Earth, founded the Telhian Empire two thousand years ago. I was pulled here two years ago. Otherworlders have stronger affinities when they arrive, allowing them to become powerful quickly. In the Telhian Empire, they are hunted to prevent them from threatening the First Citizens' rule." I started walking again, thinking the best place to ambush the other clerics would be at the base of the Spire. They would be tired and unsuspecting.

"Stop!" Mynasha spat, exasperated. "I am not an otherworlder!"

I sighed and turned to her. I had felt violated and humbled by the storm giants. I lost a lot for her Trial, and so far, I haven't gained anything except promises that depended on whether she was raised to lead the Caliphate.

I bit down on my anger. "I don't know if you are or not. Do you remember anything before you were adopted as an infant? Otherworlders arrive in groups." She gave me a blank stare, clearly unable to recall her early years. I sighed. "Well, your ability to pull aether from ley lines means you have a strong affinity for convergence. How many other rare affinities are you strong in?"

We stared at each other for long moments in the dark. "You have a strong affinity for space?" she finally asked. I nodded slowly. It was obvious after my dimensional space had vomited out everything I had secreted away over the last two years. She exhaled and spoke. "Of the rare magics, I have strong affinities for convergence and worlds. I have some affinity although weaker in the other rare magics," she admitted. I gave her an *I told you so* look, which she may not have been able to see in the dark. Orc dark vision was not as good as my aether sight.

"Are there other otherworlders in the Caliphate?" I asked hopefully. It was a mystery I had been too busy to investigate. But there had to be others. Maybe others from Earth. I had feared looking too hard would draw attention to me and reveal my origins.

Mynasha looked to be slowly accepting the truth of it. "Glasha would know better than I. I recall that about forty years ago, there were some elves, but it is said that the Supreme ransomed them to Esenhem. I was not alive, so I don't know any details, but Glasha would," she responded numbly.

Knowing how powerful otherworlders were, I had my doubts that they were ransomed. Giving your rival neighbor powerful mages didn't seem wise. "From what I know and from what the Titans just confirmed, otherworlders come from multiple other worlds. My planet was Earth," I reiterated. I looked up nervously, but I hadn't felt anyone scrying us. "Let's get down to the base of the mountain in case the Titans change their minds about letting us go."

In the dark, we made good time, but the effort was draining. We didn't have any water, as my stock was all left on the audience chamber floor. I was dehydrated and my mouth was gummy. The ring of sustenance still required me to drink, and I had been sweating profusely. Mynasha was feeling it too, and she stumbled in relief at finally seeing the towers that flanked the base of the Spire. Sunrise was not far off, and I stopped looking for a way to climb the tower.

"Why are we stopping?" Mynasha asked with a cracked voice.

I wasn't sure if I should tell her my plan. "Go to town and ride back with your prize. I will wait here for the others." I could see the confusion on her face slowly crystallize to realization.

"You are planning to kill them." She didn't seem upset. She was just stating the facts. "That is not honorable and would cause me to forfeit as a candidate."

"I cannot let them know about my powers," I said firmly.

In the darkness, I could see the incredulous look on her face. "Powers? You mean your dimensional pocket? You think you are special?"

I felt that was unfair, given how much I had supported her through the Trials. "Yes."

"You are not. There are a dozen clerics with pocket spaces," she said.

"As big as mine and capable of storing living beings?" I retorted. I could see her suddenly recalling the griffin. My dimensional space had only been about two-thirds full when Khrusos had torn it open, but even at that level, it demonstrated the immense space affinity I possessed. They would probably figure out I had stolen the pixie. I made a mental note to find out how Khrusos had managed to force open my space.

Mynasha was still processing. I gave her time as I looked for a way to climb up the tower. She drew my attention when she spoke. "No. I believe yours is bigger. But it is just one spell form and not a threat to the Caliphate." *Oh, how little this one knew.*

"There are many more powerful mages than you. There are clerics that can change the weather and bring a blizzard at the height of summer. Clerics who can summon a Kraken to sink a fleet. Clerics who can bring the dead back to life. Your own Emperor was the most feared void mage in a millennium. I can call down lightning to destroy cities from a mile away."

My opinion of her decreased. I didn't think she was connecting the dots that I could store people—and parts of people. "Still, I plan to wait for them." I turned and quickly climbed up thirty feet to a ledge with an entrance to the empty tower. Mynasha, surprisingly, climbed up after me. I looked at her questioningly.

She looked a little smug about my surprise as she sat on a large stone in the tower across from me. "I will wait with you. I owe you too much honor, so if this is the path we must walk, I will stand with you as you stood with me. Do you have anything to eat?" she asked, arching an eyebrow.

I was a little shocked that she chose to stay with me and was setting aside her quest to become the leader of her people. I fished around in my belt pouches and found a number of potions, coins, and pellets that I already knew were there. In one pouch, I discovered a small pile of apples—just five that I had made easily accessible for Ginger and forgotten about. I handed her one and ate one myself. Ginger would be very upset that I only had three apples remaining.

The shadow of the Spire was cast on the landscape by the rising sun. As it moved in front of us, we waited for the fate of the other candidates. After a few hours, all but one of the apples were gone, and Mynasha had fallen into an exhausted sleep. Many things that Khrusos had said were playing through my head.

In my first few months on Desia, I longed to return to Earth. After Macha, that yearning had slowly subsided, and I had accepted my fate. Deep down, I had always believed there would be a way to return.

My life here was definitely more exciting, and I was someone important. Well, relatively speaking. At least to my friends. Yes, I was happy with my life here, but maybe one day I would search for others from Earth. Perhaps I could send a message to my family on Earth to let them know I was alive and doing well. It was probably a fanciful thought.

Around midday, Mynasha's stomach growled in protest, causing her to wake. She moved to empty her bowels in the far corner of the tower. She wasn't shy about it at all, talking while she did so. "What if they don't come down?"

"What?" I hadn't considered that. How long would we wait? "We will wait till sundown."

"We don't have food. We could return to the town and come back," she offered, returning to me at the ledge. "We can tell Woolasha we don't have an artifact yet."

My mind went to another possibility. "What if you are the only one to return? Will you become the Supreme?" I asked, thinking that if I killed the others without Mynasha knowing, perhaps her ignorance would allow her to take the seat.

"The Elders will divine the fate of the others," she answered, reading my unspoken thoughts. "Your deeds will be seen as mine."

Magic was always the wildcard factor. I made a decision. "Let's return to Becar." Mynasha looked surprised, so I explained, "The best way forward is for you to become the Supreme. I will leave the Caliphate with my companions and the goliaths before anything can come of it if you become the Supreme."

"If that is what you want," she said, but I could tell she was relieved. We scrambled down the rocks, and she gasped when she thought I had jumped the last ten feet. Instead, I used air discs to create steps for a quicker descent. We were soon walking on the rocky terrain back to the town.

"What is your world like? Is it different from Desia?" Mynasha asked with curiosity.

I slowed a little. I hadn't talked to anyone about Earth in all my time on Desia. "There is no magic, but technology that is far superior to what mages can do with spells. There are a lot more people, too. We have myths of the Titans and some of the creatures on Desia. Somewhere in the past, people from Desia must have traveled to Earth."

We walked in silence for a while. Mynasha was deep in thought as the town came into view. A few black sheep trotted over to greet us. Mynasha shared her troubled thoughts with me. "If I am not from Desia, I wonder what the planet I came from is like. Do I have family there? Would my life have been different if I had never been brought here?" I finally understood why she had been willing to give up the Supreme's seat. She was questioning everything. I was not the best person to give her guidance, so I remained silent.

We reached the town, and Cleric Woolasha greeted us while others from the town looked on. "You were the last to leave, but are the first to return! Did you meet with success?"

Mynasha appeared impassive. "The Titans were challenging to deal with, but my First bartered for an artifact."

Woolasha's eyes lit up and his face bore a tusky smile. "That is fabulous. I can send word to Glasha that you are returning! I will let her know if anyone follows you. Your mounts have been well cared for and will be saddled shortly." As if they had been summoned, two young boys came forward, leading the gray and Ginger. Ginger was excited but restrained herself from dragging the young orc to greet me. It was nice that she had been worried.

Ginger's head pushed into me for attention and an apple. Maybe she wasn't worried about me, but her supply of apples. I didn't have the heart to tell her I only had one left. I didn't even have any grain to supplement her diet of grass. As she munched on the very last dungeon apple, we mounted and turned to the road.

I took one last look at the Spire in the distance, the peak hidden behind the lightning clouds, and couldn't help but wonder what was happening up there.

We didn't rush back to Becar, but maintained a safe pace for the horses. My conversations with Mynasha mostly entailed answering her questions about Earth. Reflecting on my old home was starting to make me feel homesick. I wondered what my parents and sisters thought when I disappeared. Did they try and find me?

Glasha and Tarnasha met us at the guard post when we arrived at the entrance to the Elders' valley. Glasha was finely dressed and grinning at us. Both looked like they had been waiting for some time. Glasha practically shouted, "You found success and are the first to return!"

"Is there any word of the others?" Mynasha asked, sliding out of her saddle. Her legs were unsteady, and Glasha moved to heal her.

"Fioasha is dead," Glasha said, sounding unremorseful. "Cleric Jhuarkasha and Warlord Rhuuk left Rosenrock two days after you. They also were successful in obtaining an artifact from the Titans." I didn't like hearing that Rhuuk still lived. When we had stood in judgment before the Titans, there was something in his eyes that had worried me, a predatory intelligence.

Tarnasha was delighted as well. "The Elders are fighting among themselves about what to do now that Fioasha is no longer a viable candidate. We don't believe Jhuarkasha currently has enough support among the Elders to be named Supreme."

"Neither does Mynasha. But our position is tenable, and the Elders will have to announce the final Trial when Jhuarkasha returns," Glasha added optimistically.

When we reached our longhouse, I was stunned. A dozen orcs and a few human slaves were inside, along with furniture and crates of supplies. Glasha was a bit smug. "Some of the warlords are hedging their bets in case Mynasha becomes the next Supreme. Over a dozen wish to take a meal with her or seek an audience for advice."

Mynasha's jaw was slack at how quickly her fortune had turned. My mind processed what was missing. "Where is Maveith?"

"Ah, yes. Our goliath friend got into a little bit of trouble," Tarnasha said with a bit of wariness.

Chapter 313: The Third Trial

A chill ran through me. "What kind of trouble?"

"He was caught consorting with another goliath," Tarnasha said, sounding unconcerned.

"It was not his sister," Glasha added, not helping my angst.

"Where is he then?" My anger and concern started to rise. These clerics should have kept Maveith from getting into trouble.

"The warlord he offended has co-opted his labor until the end of the Trials. Do not worry. Harming Maveith in any way would allow you to take his life," Glasha said indifferently.

"Where do I find this warlord and my friend?" I said icily, not caring about orc honor.

"You should let it be," Tarnasha started to say, but Glasha interrupted him with a slight smile.

Glasha stood. "I will bring you to him. We can resolve this tonight if you wish." I was exhausted, but I was not going to let Maveith toil away for a warlord. Glasha rose, and I followed her out. As we walked, she talked.

"It is Warlord Korth. He was a supporter of Fioasha and will not be happy that his chosen candidate is dead while Mynasha remains," Glasha explained.

"Tell me what I need to know. I thought Maveith was considered my attendant since I was Mynasha's First. If all of this is happening through your machinations to make me confront one of Mynasha's enemies, you will also feel my ire," I said heatedly.

Glasha paused and looked at me. "Maveith was trying to get word to his sister that he was here. He was lingering at the stream where goliath slaves fill large buckets. A human slave reported the interaction. Warlord Korth came to our camp and demanded his honor be restored. I negotiated the payment down to labor." It sounded like something Maveith would do, and think safe, but I was still blaming the clerics for letting it happen.

"And are you trying to force me to confront Korth?" I said heatedly, since Mynasha appeared almost giddy the closer we got.

Glasha considered her words. "Korth is a lost pup looking for purpose. It wouldn't hurt for you to show him Mynasha's strength. But no, I did not orchestrate a confrontation. You could let this play out, and Maveith will be back with us soon." I still felt like my strings were being pulled and what little trust I had with the clerics was wanning.

I was silent as Glasha led us to a longhouse closer to the center of the valley, which told me that Warlord Korth was important in the Caliphate. Orc attendants rushed inside as we approached, and two elite tattooed warriors guarded the entrance. They moved to block my path.

"I am here for my goliath," I stated loudly as I approached. I could hear voices and the sound of scrambling inside. The two orc elites gripped the pommels of their swords but did not draw them.

"Patience, he will come to greet you," Glasha whispered. The door to the longhouse opened, releasing the scent of cooking meat and incense.

Warlord Korth was only slightly taller than me but much wider at the shoulder. Heavy hand axes hung on both hips. He was shirtless and had a sheen of sweat on his torso, which was covered in tattoos. He sneered slightly. "The human comes to beg for his slave back."

"I don't beg," I replied flatly. "You took my goliath while I was guiding your next Supreme on the second Trial. You besmirch my honor and I demand satisfaction." I didn't know if that was a correct challenge, but it sounded good.

A growing grin appeared on Korth's face, and I guessed this was perhaps the outcome he had been hoping for. "Humans are not entitled to slaves in the Caliphate and your position as a First is temporary." His sneer grew.

I didn't know how to navigate the interaction. I looked at Glasha for help. "Warlord Korth, the Elders have recognized this man as a First. During the Trials, all Firsts have the same status as warlords. If you wish, you can petition the Elders since there is no Supreme to pass judgment. Or you can release the goliath."

Korth scoffed. "The goliath was caught trying to convince my slave that escape was possible."

"I do not believe you. Bring my goliath here to speak for himself," I said, grinding my teeth. Maveith was not stupid enough to trust a goliath he had just met.

Warlord Korth finally looked uncertain. Glasha erupted into a massive grin, seeing the uncertainty. "Yes, let's question the goliath. If I recall, I think Cleric Hynasha can see the truth of words."

It was finally Warlord Korth's turn to grind his teeth. The cleric and Maveith were both summoned. Maveith, for his part, did not look upset and only nodded at me with a small grin. I let Glasha do the talking, as I would probably escalate without need. "Cleric Hynasha, you have been asked to confirm if the goliath's words are true." The cleric nodded. His body language told me he was familiar with Glasha and was perhaps even an ally. The warlord started to look even more uncomfortable.

Maveith was questioned in Elvish by Glasha. "Maveith, please retell the events."

Maveith nodded knowingly to Glasha and I suddenly got angrier. Maveith was clearly in on this! Maveith's deep voice rumbled. "I was getting water and struck up a conversation with another goliath, Jolan. I asked him if there was a goliath called Zorana in the valley. And if he did, to pass a message to her."

"And what was the message?" Glasha asked.

"Her brother Maveith is here," Maveith said.

The warlord interrupted in terrible Elvish. "Did you tell Jolan that you were here for her?"

"Zorana is not even your slave, Korth," Glasha snapped.

Maveith answered the question anyway. "I told her I was here. Not here for her."

"Truth," Cleric Hynasha confirmed, in better Elvish than the warlord.

"Since you have taken Eryk's goliath without cause, it is only fair that he take yours," Glasha announced. The warlord's hands went to his axes and squeezed the grips while we all waited. Instead of pulling his axes, he stormed off into his longhouse. A confused goliath soon exited and Maveith beamed.

As we walked back to our longhouse, Glasha explained. "Sorry, we needed you sufficiently angry to confront Warlord Korth."

"You didn't tell Eryk the plan?" Maveith rumbled.

"It was a dragon shit of a plan! What if I never returned from the Trial, Maveith? What if I had attacked the warlord before it was resolved?" I said angrily.

"Blame me," Glasha said. "Maveith wanted to get word to his sister, and I came up with the plan."

Maveith tried to calm me. "Eryk, this is Jolan from a village not far from mine. He got word to Zorana that I am here."

"What does it matter? He is going to back to the warlord at the end of the Trials," I retorted.

Glasha shook her head. "No. It was established that Maveith was taken without cause. Jolan is now yours. I could try to explain it but it would only give you a headache."

I didn't know how to express my anger at Maveith and Glasha for manipulating me. Maveith clearly looked guilty, but he had achieved his goal of sending a message to his sister, and we were here for her. I hope this subterfuge did not interfere with our efforts to save her. He could have made things worse, but voicing my anger would only make him more anxious and potentially do something else stupid.

We returned to our longhouse. Maveith gave me a quiet apology before heading off to talk with Jolan. Glasha went into deep discussion with Tarnasha and Mynasha. I rubbed down the horses, trying to calm myself, and eyed the new slaves and orcs working in the longhouse. There were four humans in drab brown smocks. They looked well fed, but wouldn't make eye contact with me as they helped prepare a meal.

Ginger's head lowered into my back, causing me to stumble from the unexpected shove. "Damn it Ginger, I don't have any more apples," I said angrily, turning on her. She took the hint and turned away, abashed. I had forgotten that I had left three dozen apples with Woolasha, but it was too late to get them now. I wasn't angry at Ginger, but at being manipulated and seeing the human slaves. It didn't feel right and reminded me of how I had been forced to serve as a legionnaire, essentially a slave to the Telhian Empire.

Among the slaves were two old men, one bald and the other with closely cut gray hair. An older, pudgy woman with streaks of silver in her black hair seemed to be directing both the orcs and humans. The fourth human was a younger woman who was hauling buckets of water with two younger orcs. They were using yokes on their shoulders to carry two heavy buckets at a time. My protective instincts made me want to free her.

I almost missed a divine sight as I was focused on the food being prepared on several tables. Then I noticed the buckets filling a large brass tub that seemed to have a system of pipes for heating water. That could only mean one thing—a bath. I approached the older human woman and asked in Telhian, "How long have you been a slave?" She looked at me, confused. I repeated in Orcish.

In a thick, sharp accent, she replied, "I was taken as a child from across the sea by slavers."

"Are you treated well?" I asked seriously.

"I am fed, clothed, and given time for leisure," she said cautiously. "Do you need something from me, warrior?" My eyes unintentionally drifted to the bath briefly. She tsked at me. "That bath is for Cleric Mynasha. She is to present her artifact before the Elders in the morning." I sighed, as a hot soak would have been nice to soothe not just my body but my mind.

I looked over at the younger woman again as she entered, carrying two more buckets. She was closer to my age. "What about her? How long has she been a slave?"

The older woman looked at the younger one as I studied her. She had a tangled mess of auburn hair pulled back. Her face was marked with soot and faint freckles. The woman pursed her lips. "Nolona has been with us since her teens, maybe twelve years." The old woman warned me seriously, "Don't get any ideas. She belongs to Warlord Rakkim and is only here to make Cleric Mynasha comfortable. She is not here for your comfort. He has killed others for defiling his property."

"That is not what I was thinking," I said indignantly. But anger simmered that the warlords treated people in such a manner.

I could see I had made a poor impression on the woman, and the others were starting to stare. I was still unhappy with Maveith, so I let him talk to the new goliath in the corner. I moved to join the conversation Mynasha was having. Glasha had the Titan key in her hands and was using her lore ability on it. I joined them, waiting for her to finish and reveal its lore.

Glasha's eyes opened, her face marked by perspiration, and she exhaled a long, slow breath. "It is a key to a vault high in a forgotten mountain city. The Titan was right, it is useless. My final images were of the vault being looted by elves thousands of years ago when the city fell."

"Then why did he keep it? It seems odd to carry around a key for thousands of years if it is useless," I said, annoyed.

Glasha agreed with a nod. "The Titan used it as a focus for light magic. The enchantments on the long side are for magnifying spells. They were also what allowed the key to open the massive vault doors."

There was another issue that needed to be aired. "Did you tell them?" I asked, making eye contact with Mynasha.

Tarnasha chuckled. "That you are concerned about others finding out you can store a griffin in your dimensional space?" He was clearly enjoying the fact that I was uncomfortable with the secrets I guarded for long. "Don't worry, boy. If Warlord Rhuuk wants what you hold, he will challenge your honor. Even though he is one of the best warriors in the Caliphate, I think you can handle yourself."

Glasha nodded in agreement. "Mynasha said you had a number of intriguing…items. If you want me to delve into their histories, I will. I just need time to replenish my aether stores. The key took a lot from me."

I nodded, but I was upset that Mynasha had so easily revealed my secrets to her allies. At least the door was open for me to have more of my curiosities examined by Glasha. "What is the plan? What will the final Trial be?"

"Mynasha and Jhuarkasha will present their Titan artifacts in the morning to the Elders. I am sure they will be debating all night about who they prefer as the Supreme and will design the final Trial to accomplish that end result," Tarnasha said spitefully.

"Mynasha needs to look presentable before the Elders, warlords, and clerics. We are hoping for someone to donate something suitable for her to wear." Glasha indicated the array of supplies now littering the longhouse.

"I don't need …" Mynasha started to say.

Glasha hissed at her, stopping her objection. "You do. If you are to become the Supreme, you need to start looking the part. Not like some backwater village cleric."

A brief argument broke out among the three, and I kept glancing at the slaves as they worked. "Were you given ownership of those slaves?" I interrupted, pausing their conversation.

"They are on loan. They are just here to help, like the others," Glasha answered. "You can do what you like with them." She gestured at the group. Why did everyone think I had an ulterior motive? The old woman had already warned me off, but maybe she was just protecting the younger woman in her group.

The orcs continued their heated argument about what Mynasha needed to wear to impress the warlords. "I have these," I said, producing the massive fire bear pelts. The pelts shimmered in the firelight from the cooking fire. They were marvelously soft, and with the proper lighting, almost seemed to be on fire themselves.

"Where on Desia did you hunt fire bears?" Tarnasha said, stroking the fur appreciatively. "I think this is a fabulous idea. We can make a cloak for Mynasha and you. It will certainly draw the attention of the warlords. Not one in ten would be brave enough to take on such a beast this size."

While they were ogling the pelts, I asked, "Do you mind if I use the bath first, then?"

"I wasn't planning to use it at all," Mynasha said. I took that as my cue and walked over to the large brass tub.

"I heard," the old woman hissed irritably. I smiled at her as I undressed and slid unabashedly into the hot water. It had been too long. An attendant handed me a bar of abrasive soap. As I scrubbed, I noticed something odd—not exactly noticed, but felt. My thoughts seemed muddled and harder to grasp. I closed my eyes and reached out with my healing and purify self spell forms. Damn, the orcs were sneaky bastards. The water was poisoned. Well, maybe not poison, but it definitely contained some drug that was absorbed through the skin.

I carefully let it work and pretended not to notice its effects, but I also tried to identify what it was supposed to do to me. It appeared to be a powerful muscle relaxant that fogged my brain. After I confirmed the effects, I eliminated the toxin from my body. It should not take a lot of effort for me to appear slow-witted. Let them think they had succeeded.

Of course, the toxin was planned for Mynasha and not me. From the angry stare of the old woman and two of the orcs hovering near her, I assumed they were responsible. If Mynasha had bathed first, she would have succumbed to the drug. I don't think Glasha's healing would have cured Mynasha before the third Trial in the morning. I don't even think her healing could have affected it. My purify self spell form was eliminating it, but my healing spell form had no effect on it.

Knowing the old human woman was in on the deception made me less willing to care about her fate. She had been targeting Mynasha, but her efforts had snared me. I took pleasure in the heat and her dismay for the next two hours in the tub. Across the room, the fire bear pelts were being attacked by a score of workers as they tried to make them into presentable cloaks before morning.

The old woman slammed a mallet into the side of the tub. I had been pretending to sleep in the hot water. "Get up or Cleric Mynasha will not have time to clean herself."

I pretended to have difficulty standing when I exited and looked around, seeming confused as I slowly dressed. I walked in a daze to Glasha, who was overseeing the fabrication of the fire cloaks. I leaned into her and told her about the dangers of the water, then went to get some rest myself. I was sure Mynasha would not be taking a bath tonight.

I slept heavily and woke up when Maveith shook me. My hand was already on my hilt as my mind went into overdrive. I quickly reeled it in, remembering I had to appear drugged. Getting to my feet slowly, I saw that the activity in the longhouse had only increased in the few hours I had slept.

"Your new cloak is ready. I admit it is more opulent than the manticore cloak I made for you. I helped with some of the stitching. You will look regal, Eryk. Better than any of the warlords," Maveith said cautiously. He could probably read my body language, which indicated that I was not happy with him.

The cloak draped well across my shoulders, and it was large enough to wear over heavier armor as well. Glasha nodded approvingly. "You only need a crown to look like a king."

"I think I will pass. I have enough trouble being responsible for just a handful of men. Is …" I indicated a sleeping Mynasha with my chin.

"She decided she didn't want a bath, even though I told her she smelled like an ogre's ass." Glasha exhaled theatrically for the audience. "Well, she might not smell like one, but at least she will look like a Supreme."

The black spear appeared in my hands. If Warlord Rhuuk was returning, hiding the size of my dimensional space seemed like a moot point. "Can you read this?" I indicated the impressive spear. The spiraling black wood grain of an ancient treant made up the shaft. The leaf tip looked just like an actual leaf, and the black metal added to the spear's mystique. Glasha's eyes widened, and she spun the shaft so the blade was on the floor. She pressed the blade between a crack in the floorboards.

"Don't show this to the warlords," she whispered, and looked at the slaves, who hadn't noticed the spear yet. "The dull black spearhead is dark mithril. It is indestructible and will always keep an edge."

Her excitement rose as she stroked the length of the shaft. "It is a replica—made by a dungeon, but there are echoes of the original." Her eyes closed as her hands caressed the wood. "Its name was Heartseeker. The favored weapon of the King of Caelora. The enchantments allow the dark mithril to cut through anything, even dragon scales if there is enough force behind the strike." She exhaled, her eyes remaining closed. "The original still remains, and this weapon has a connection to it." Her eyes shot open and she coughed.

"Are you all right?" I steadied her.

"I … I … I tried to follow the connection back to the source but was rebuked. That … that shouldn't be possible." She pushed the spear into my hand. "Put it away and only take it out if you truly need it. Something else can sense this weapon. Something powerful. I think it might be the King of Caelora or whatever is left of him." Great, one of my strongest weapons needed to be kept hidden from the original owner and envious warriors.

"It is time to wake Mynasha," Glasha said, collecting herself. I wondered if Mynasha had told Glasha that she was an otherworlder. Soon, there was a lot of activity as we made to get ready. I kept up my act of being a dullard from the drug. I hoped it would give us a small advantage when we entered the third Trial.

We walked to the Elders' residence, both Mynasha and I wearing our hastily made fire bear cloaks. I had to admit that we did look good. The consortium of warlords and clerics had circled the area outside the stone residence of the Elders. There were over three hundred people, by my estimate. Envious stares and whispers about our attire hung in the air. Even the assembled Elders looked shocked at our dress as the sun rose and illuminated the fire bear pelts.

Warlord Rhuuk had a long black cloak made of fine fur, while Cleric Jhuarkasha had a dress made of yellow and red feathers. Both looked impressive, but they didn't equal us. When things calmed, there was a ceremony to present the artifacts. The key was given first by Mynasha. Jhuarkasha presented a six-inch pick for cleaning underneath a Titan's nails. The Elders declared their veracity to the assembled crowd.

The leader then addressed the assemblage. "Cleric Fioasha fell during the second Trial. It has been determined that neither Cleric Jhuarkasha or Cleric Mynasha played a role. Instead, it was Warlord Etus who angered the Titans by demanding an artifact from them instead of paying homage to them." That solved the mystery of what had occurred before we arrived.

The Elder took a deep, unhappy breath. "The Choosing has but two remaining candidates." I could see the anger and disappointment on the faces of the Elders standing behind her and Warlords in the crowd. "We have deliberated long and hard to decide on a suitable task for the final Trial that will enable us to find a Supreme to lead the Caliphate in the new era."

The air was thick with anticipation as she paused dramatically. "The candidates and their Firsts will enter the Warlord Dungeon together! The first to return with two sets of greater demon horns will assume the mantle of our next Supreme!"

I grinned. *Dungeons. Something I was good at.*

Chapter 314: The Demonic Depths

A throaty roar of approval echoed among the circle of Boutan orcs. They would have a new Supreme shortly, but Mynasha was not happy. "They have chosen Jhuarkasha to be their next Supreme," she whispered to me.

"I don't understand. We go in, cut some horns off some demons, and come out." I thought we had all the advantages here.

"No. Warlord Rhuuk trained for years to fight the four demons laired within. I never even studied them or how to fight them. We will need to consult with Glasha," she said worriedly.

We had missed part of the next announcement as we had talked. The Elder finished addressing the assemblage, saying, "They can enter anytime they wish, after sunset."

"Where is the dungeon entrance?" I asked, leaning in.

"We are standing before it. That stone building was built over it. I believe there is a long set of stairs descending to it, but it takes an hour to descend," she said as she scanned the crowd for Glasha.

"Wouldn't that mean the entrance is in the Endless Dark?" I asked.

"Yes, there are sealed passages to the Endless Dark near the dungeon entrance from what I know." Mynasha found Glasha, and the crowd parted for us as we moved to her. Glasha's face was unreadable, and we secluded ourselves farther away with Tarnasha. It looked like Rhuuk and Jhuarkasha were heading back to their longhouse to get supplies and prepare. They did not appear shocked at the announcement of the Third trial.

"What do we need to know?" I asked when we were clear of the mass of orcs.

Glasha did not have the same indecision on her face that Mynasha had. "On entering the dungeon, you will exit into the center of a massive chamber. Red glowstones embedded in the ceiling light it. Lesser creatures from the demon realm wander the main chamber. You will be fine if you do not draw too many to you."

"I thought demons didn't exist on Desia," I said. I remembered that Khrusos had said the Titans had sealed the gates when they encountered a planet populated by demons.

Glasha nodded and responded in a serious tone. "True—to an extent. This is one of three dungeons on Desia that spawn demons that I am aware of. Even if they do escape the dungeons, they are sterile. Few ever reach the surface, as the denizens of the Endless Dark wisely hunt them with a fervor."

"Why don't you destroy the dungeon?" I asked. If the demons were a threat, then it would make sense. Then I recalled that the Caliphate harvested the horns to make the ink for their tattoos.

"It is complicated," Glasha said slowly. I eyed Mynasha, who looked away guiltily. Glasha continued, not explaining. "The four demons are in four caves on the perimeter of the central chamber. Each cave glows with a different light: yellow, green, blue, and violet. Each of those chambers holds a different greater demon and will seal you in when you enter." Glasha caught her breath, and I could tell she was anxious for us.

Mynasha still looked unsure of herself and the Trial. "What of the demons? Do you know how to fight them? Will my lightning work on them?"

Glasha spoke slowly as she recalled the knowledge. "Unfortunately, the walls are lined with colored glowstones that will draw your lightning to them—and any powerful spells, actually. You can use it, but connecting to your target will be much harder. One of the greater demons is completely immune to lightning: the shadow demon. It is the most dangerous of the four. The other three are the ice demon, snake demon, and greater hellhound. All of them have horns, so any two will satisfy the Elders' Trial."

None of those options sounded appealing, and I had not been educated about demons in Hound training. Demons were a myth in the Telhian Empire, but some demons like hell hounds could be summoned. Glasha did her best to prepare us, lecturing us on how to fight the demons and what dangers to expect in the large cavern. We spent our hours before sunset gathering as much helpful information as possible from the Chronicler and Tarnasha.

As we talked, the warlords and clerics started to break into groups and set up camps around the central building. Their slaves and attendants rushed in with tents and tables, as if they were throwing a tailgate party. They clearly planned to wait here for the victor to exit in triumph.

The hours seemed to disappear quickly, and evening came. "You should go," Glasha suddenly said as the sky turned to dusk. "The hellhound and snake demon are your best choices." Glasha was indicating a procession coming down the primary path. Warlord Rhuuk and Cleric Jhuarkasha were returning. I felt mildly prepared as I removed my fire bear cloak and handed it to Glasha.

Mynasha handed hers to Tarnasha, and we walked side by side to the stone building to enter first.

One of the Elders, a gray-skinned orc with a hunched back and pruned features, held open the door on the side of the structure for us. Beyond the door were steep stairs with worn steps. Blue glowstone sconces illuminated the stairs. I hadn't known that glowstones came in different colors. The stairs were barely wide enough for us to descend side by side, and each step dropped over a foot. As our boots scraped on the stone with each step, a slight echo traveled ahead and behind us.

"It is 2,323 steps to the bottom," Mynasha said softly. "I heard the descent is not so bad; it is the climb after exiting the dungeon that is the killer." She smiled weakly at her attempt at humor. I just nodded in return, more focused on the task ahead of us. The walls became a patchwork of different stones the deeper we went. Ominously, a few stones had ancient claw marks torn in them. The massive size of the hand that made them caused some trepidation, but they were clearly ancient.

The descent went much quicker than I thought, and soon, we stepped onto a large oval landing with a familiar massive, flat, oily wall on the far side. Two iron doors dominated the right wall. Blue glowstones lined the wall to our left, casting a bright, eerie blue light throughout the chamber. "I have never been down here," Mynasha stated in awe. "Those doors continue to the Endless Dark, but I was unaware there was more than one."

I was focused on the entrance to the dungeon. "I have never seen a dungeon entrance that size before. It is large enough for a giant—or Titan—to enter easily." Mynasha didn't respond, but looked apprehensive. Learning that she was an otherworlder while being forced along in the Choosing had rattled her, leaving her no time to process. Maybe she didn't even want this anymore but was too overwhelmed to realize it. I was not a therapist, and we were too close to finishing.

The echoing footsteps above us indicated that we didn't have much time before the others caught up with us. I drew magebane and stepped into the oily surface of the dungeon entrance.

Glasha hadn't done the chamber justice. The vast ceiling loomed high above, with large patches of red glowstones scattered sporadically across it. A humid heat enveloped us, carrying the smell of a gym locker room. The terrain was moderately rocky, with patches of black lichen and yellow mushrooms.

Glasha had warned us about the mushroom spores that could affect you if you got too close. The spores would create a thick mucus in your lungs, and in minutes you would suffocate. The lichen was edible but didn't have alchemy uses, or at least, it didn't have any that Mynasha knew of when I asked her.

Lesser demons dominated the red-bathed, rocky landscape around us. A bulbous pig-man that Glasha had called a dretch was closest to us, just a dozen yards away. They were hideous creatures, shorter than me by a head with ugly, bulging veins along their rubbery flesh. Sporadic patches of bristly hair placed them high on the fugly scale. One of them turned their pig-like face to us, but we knew we were safe near the only dungeon exit. According to Glasha, there was a halo around the portal that the demons could not encroach on.

My vision caught a movement, and I prepared myself as Cleric Jhuarkasha stepped through. Warlord Rhuuk appeared behind him as the oily surface released him. My eyes locked with Rhuuk's. I could end this all now. His eyes betrayed his opinion of me. He might have been curious before, but now I was standing in his way, an obstacle to overcome.

I half-expected them to initiate something, but instead, Rhuuk pushed Jhuarkasha and irritably ordered him, "Go to the yellow chamber!" That cave held the snake demon, one of our preferred targets. We watched them move away from the oily door. Rhuuk led the way, cutting down two dretches with powerful swings of his large blade. The heinous creatures squealed in pain but were quickly silenced. We had been warned they could summon more of their kind with such displays.

"The hellhound then?" I asked Mynasha. We had planned to kill the snake demon in the yellow chamber as well, but would have had to target a different demon or steal the horns from the others.

Mynasha oriented herself toward the distant violet glow on the wall—the opposite direction from where the other pair was headed. The purple cave was where the hellhound could be found. She disrobed to just a halter top and leather skirt.

Dungeons fed off ley lines, granting Mynasha almost unlimited aether during this delve. While her offensive spells might be hard to control, she had several defensive spells that would speed up our journey. I led the way and killed my first dretch.

They appeared threatening with four-inch claws, but were clumsy and surprisingly slow. With two quick swings, I opened its belly and then its throat. As its black lifeblood spilled out, I kneeled and retrieved the collector. At least I could gain something from this expedition. Soon, blue aetheric wisps started rising from the corpse.

I was shocked to see that the essence that formed had spiraling white and blue smoke within. It was just a minor essence, but it was the charm affinity. I looked at the disgusting creature and thought nothing was charming about it.

"You got an essence?" Mynasha asked as I pocketed it.

"I did. I will not slow us down, but it would be a pity to waste the opportunity," I said, standing. She didn't object, but looked surprised. She didn't need to know how special my collector was.

A humming sound echoed overhead. It was another threat from the large chamber: blood stirges. They were large, red, furry, bat-like creatures with a long, sharp proboscis. They were not dangerous to us, but if they did pierce your flesh, you would bleed for hours. We quickly tracked a trio of them descending on us. Mynasha's lightning shield cooked them when they dove. The three smoking bodies thudded onto the ground, and she looked pleased with herself.

As I moved to use the collector, she advised, "You won't get anything from them. They have so little essence it would be futile."

I shrugged. "It couldn't hurt to try." The minor essence that formed was dark green and felt extremely satisfying. Quickness was very useful and made the pain of losing the healing essences to the Titans slightly easier to bear. When I had three of the minor dark green essences in hand, I stood. Mynasha's skin was already coated in a sheen of sweat, and disbelief was etched on her face. "Guess Fortuna is smiling on me today," I said dismissively.

I walked past her and soon found more dretches to cut down. It was like practicing against a training dummy; the creatures moved so poorly. They only had one unique attack: expelling a cloud of noxious gas that made you wretch uncontrollably. As long as you held your breath, it wasn't even that great a threat. Six dretches and six charm essences later, we encountered the third and final type of creature we had been warned about in the primary chamber.

The small green demon was incredibly fast and more of a nuisance than an actual threat in the dungeon. It had a tail with a stinger that could inject painful poison, but they were opportunistic attackers, according to Glasha. If you got into a fight with several dretches, the green imp would turn invisible and try to stab you from behind before retreating. Their tiny claws couldn't do much unless you were incapacitated. They would also steal from you if you were not observant.

She called them quasits, and this one was so intimidated by my stare that it disappeared. I immediately activated my aether sight. The quasit appeared as a shimmering echo of aether as it moved away. I didn't give away that I could see it, not tracking it with my eyes. Seeing the invisible was apparently another useful benefit of this spell form. "I will watch our backs when we are attacked," Mynasha stated, looking for signs of the tiny demon.

"Not needed. Just keep a lookout for the blood stirges and we will be fine. We are getting closer to the cave." I indicated the violet glow emanating from the wall ahead of us.

When I engaged a pair of dretches a few minutes later, the little invisible demon made its move. As I was cutting down the pig-men, it attempted to rush in and stab me in the calf. I caught the creature fully in the chest with magebane on a back swing, cutting it almost in half and sending its broken body away in a heap.

"How did you do that?" Mynasha asked, staring at the tiny, broken body oozing dark blood.

I didn't answer immediately; instead, I made sure the dretches were dead and knelt over the quasit with the collector. As the collector worked, I explained, "Its invisibility was imperfect. Also, Glasha said they would attack when we were engaged, so I was ready."

"How come I didn't notice anything, then?" the cleric protested.

"I don't know, but you should try using your lightning to see how it is affected by the glowstones," I replied, taking a minor essence from the collector. It was unique and looked like a whirlpool of dark blood. It was slightly mesmerizing, and I almost felt like I was being pulled into the tiny sphere.

"What is it?"

"I think it is an abyssal essence," I answered her. At least, that was what I recalled. The abyssal affinity was less demonic and more about spell forms that cursed or hindered a target. I stared a moment longer before pocketing the essence. "Drink some water, and then we will continue." We were both sweating in the hot, humid chamber, and I pulled a canteen to my hand. I used it to wash down one of the quickness essences, enjoying the tingly feeling spreading through my nerves.

I could tell Mynasha had a thousand questions. Her constant glances at the collector showed that she was smart enough to realize that the collector was more than it seemed. By the time we had reached the violet wall, I had killed three more dretches, Mynasha had killed five blood stirges, and I had surprised a second quasit.

I was giddy at the essence harvest. All the dretches gave charm essences, and I thought I had figured out why. They could communicate with each other through telepathy. At least when they attacked in pairs or trios, I noticed that they were coordinated but didn't communicate vocally.

One of the stirges produced a lesser healing essence instead of a quickness essence. But the real prize was the second quasit. It produced a minor essence, but this lesser essence was milky gray. An extremely rare essence of aether shaping. This could improve my control over aether, and with enough of them, I could eventually trace spell forms in the air with my aether.

It was too precious to consume at the moment. I would consume it by itself after this was over. "What affinity does that affect?" Mynasha asked over my shoulder. She wasn't being coy; her face was clearly showing bewilderment.

"One of the magic attributes, I believe," I answered as I pocketed it. I brought her attention to the archway a few yards away.

The archway was formed with blocks of deep-purple glowstones. Deep inside the entrance, a monstrous black canine beast with fiery glowing eyes paced back and forth, waiting for us. I walked closer but did not enter. Ignoring the hellhound, my hand brushed the purple glowstones; the red ones in the ceiling chamber were too far away to reach, but maybe I could mine some of these …

The violet glowstone beneath my hand had multiple facets. Upon closer inspection, it seemed to contain a crystalline matrix inside, as if it had grown from crystals and then been sheared off. My earth pulses indicated that my guess was likely correct.

There were two types of glowstones: those that were mined and those that were artificed. Artificed glowstones were mined glowstones with runes embedded in them and were much more valuable, as the artificer could enhance their brightness. However, they needed to be recharged more often, as they quickly depleted their aether.

Mined glowstones, which I had thought could only emit a white light before now, absorbed aether from the environment. Their intensity faded over time, but they could be recharged as well. They also tended not to be as bright as artificed glowstones.

"What are you doing?" Mynasha asked as I stroked the stone in thought.

"Mining glowstones," I responded as I overlaid my dimensional space to encompass a large cube.

"They are very brittle and difficult ..." She stopped talking as a large void appeared in the archway. "Guess that works too," she said, impressed.

A large block of unique glowstone could be valuable. I could also use it as a weapon or shield. It had taken more aether than I expected, indicating some aether resistance in the stone, but nothing significant. My aether reserves were now about half—primarily due to the mass of the stone I had collected.

My sight turned to the impatient hellhound. The violet glowstones lined the short tunnel leading to its chamber. It meant Mynasha's lightning would be useless inside. "Are you ready?" I asked her.

She nodded and started to draw aether to herself. For this creature, our strategy was for her to provide defensive aid. She had lightning shields and a lightning aura that slowed everyone but her. The black hound's shoulder was taller than me. Glasha said the typical strategy was to net or entangle the creature's legs, restricting its movement. Aside from its powerful jaws, the beast could regurgitate a fiery napalm that stuck to you while flash-burning. I had been burned in the heat of a fireball before and didn't want to go through that again.

"I am ready," she said steadily. Her clothes steamed as the dense aether surrounded her. Together, we stepped into the short corridor of the hellhound's chamber. It didn't attack, and I could see intelligence in its glowing red eyes. Was this creature allowed to keep its memories like the doppelgangers in the Shimmering Labyrinth?

"The exit is sealed," Mynasha stated. I took a quick glance behind us. A wall of violet glowstone had sealed us in. The hellhound began to circle to our right—toward Mynasha. Like dogs, hellhounds were pack hunters and targeted the weakest first. I was armored and armed, and it had assumed I was stronger than Mynasha.

The beast's throat began to glow as it prepared its fiery breath weapon. As per our plan, I stood behind Mynasha and waited. Its long maw had dangerous-looking, yellowed fangs. A rumbling grew as it readied itself to attack. When its mouth opened, a wide, rolling flame erupted.

The wave of red-yellow fire caused blue sparks to burst from Mynasha's lightning shield protecting us. Just a heartbeat later, a wall of flame stood before us, blocked by Mynasha's spell wall. We were not wholly spared as the heat washed over us, making breathing difficult as the hot air entered our lungs. I coughed once and held my breath. Then our plan went to shit.

Neither of us was prepared as the hellhound slammed into her lightning shield, shattering it but slowing considerably. Glasha had told us its tactics would be to wash us in fire, and while we burned, it would flank us, trying to crush one of our legs in its fearsome jaws, and shake its victim. Instead, it had used the wall of flame to hide its rapid approach.

I stepped into Mynasha, wrapped her up, and spun her away with my shield arm to get her out of danger. With my other hand, magebane slashed down on the beast, catching its muzzle and opening a long gash. It yelped so loudly my ears rang. I didn't stop its momentum, though. It was too large for me to dodge, and it barreled into me, forcing me to the ground. My aether shield flashed blue as its claws tried to rake across my chest.

Damn it, I didn't want to use my instant kill, but I also didn't want to risk an injury in a prolonged fight. I was currently very vulnerable to a potential injury. I took a large portion of the beast's neck around the spine. It didn't have as strong an aether resistance as I expected, but my aether still bottomed out.

The beast collapsed on top of me as a lightning strike shattered one of the violet glowstones in the wall. A second glowstone shattered overhead, showering me in violet crystal rocks. "It's dead!" I yelled at Mynasha. "I'm fine!" My ears were ringing from the thunder following the lightning.

I had to yell two more times before she stopped the onslaught. The cleric was breathing heavily, with steam rising from her body. Since I had bottomed out my aether, I couldn't use my aether-infused vision, but I could imagine the aether swirling around her. She also had her long, curved knife in her hand and was ready to stab the beast.

Mynasha sheathed her long dagger and helped push the hellhound off me. I worked the magebane out of its shoulder. I hadn't been able to interpose the blade in time to stab it through its heart. This encounter might have gone a lot differently if I hadn't had the aether shield amulet. Glasha's advice had almost doomed us, but I couldn't blame her. I should have added my air shield to Mynasha's lightning shield, but I was too focused on reacting to being flanked.

I was covered in hellhound blood, which was soaking my spider silk undershirt. It burned and would probably cause a rash, but I knew it was not dangerous. The hellhound's body was self-immolating, consuming itself. Soon, only a thick ash would be left behind, which was useful in alchemy. Mynasha released her hold on the aether. Her halter top looked ragged. Even her leather skirt had dried and cracked in the short time that she was pulling aether from the environment.

I knelt as the body of the beast was destroying itself and used the collector. The stream of blue wisps diminished quickly. I hadn't thought to harvest the creature right after killing it—a minor fire affinity formed on the collector's plate. Maybe I could have gotten a major essence if I had acted quicker.

We both watched the hellhound shrivel, combust, and turn to ash over the next minute. All that was left was a black skeleton and its two nubby horns. I shook the ash off the skull and handed it to Mynasha. "I was useless," she stated despondently.

"We just weren't well prepared enough," I said, blaming Glasha. Having almost died multiple times over the past two years, I could easily dismiss it. "See if you can find the reward chest while I gather some of this ash."

The ash was almost sticky and would need to be dried to be useful. I would need to replace my alchemy equipment, but this ash was utilized to make napalm pellets. My spider-silk gloves were coated in ash when Mynasha returned with a bone chest, hundreds of tiny bones fused together to make up the walls and lid. It might have been attractive if not for the fact that the lid was made from tiny skulls.

I opened the chest to find a bed of silver and gold coins supporting a book. Taking the book out of the chest, I opened it under Mynasha's watch. "You can read that?" she asked, a little surprised.

"Just because I swing a big sword doesn't mean I haven't studied magic," I replied as I worked through the pages and spell forms within. It was a very complex spell, but I could piece it together a little bit. "It is definitely a fire affinity spell. Maybe halo—or ring of fire. Do you have the fire affinity?" I asked, closing the book.

"No," she replied. "Anything we find in the dungeon is yours," she asserted. I nodded and the book disappeared into my dimensional space. Maybe Raelia would want it, or I could sell it if I ever needed coin.

"I need about fifteen minutes to recover aether and recharge my amulet. Then we can head to the ice demon room." I sat on the floor and pulled out a waterskin, taking in the chamber in detail for the first time. Mynasha sat next to me, and I handed her a second waterskin. The skull thudded on the stone as she dropped it.

"I need to recover, too," she said. After taking a long pull, she closed her eyes and rested her head against the wall in meditation.

The chamber was almost entirely stone, with some black lichen growing in patches. I wondered what the dungeon fed the hellhound. My experience was that each room had some type of ecosystem in it. Veins of water with a violet tinge from the glowstone light drizzled down the walls. It almost looked like the walls were crying.

The mystery of what the hellhound ate would have to remain a mystery. When my aether had sufficiently recovered, I elbowed Mynasha gently. She was instantly awake from her trance. Her lack of urgency to complete the Trial told me that becoming the Supreme was no longer a priority for her. We drank some more before venturing into the large cavern and heading toward the blue glow in the distance.

I paused to harvest some of the yellow mushrooms, not getting close enough to set them off before sending them to my space. I noticed tiny bites from some of the mushrooms, so I guessed that was what the quasits were eating. I hoped to come across more of the green imps. So far they had yielded unique and rare essences.

As we followed the outer wall, we found the blood stirges nested high above. Three to five would launch at us when we passed under one of the nesting crevices. Mynasha was grateful to be of use, as her lightning shield made quick work of them.

The dretches didn't seem to wander near the walls, as the blood stirges appeared to feast on them. We disturbed one such feeding. The bloated corpse of one of the dretches had a half dozen stirges draining it of fluids. We could have passed it without disturbing the feeding, but the stirges yielded their own treasure.

When we finally did attract the attention of a green imp, we acted ignorant of its presence, pretended to rest, and left a bag of nuts just out of arm's reach. The quasit took the bait, thinking itself invisible, and tried to steal it. Magebane took one of its legs and it squealed in pain as it rolled on the ground. Its bulbous eyes looked at me for mercy. Its small, needle-like teeth didn't help its cause, and I ended its life.

I took the collector out quickly, and my eagerness was easy to read. A small, shiny, black sphere formed. A third quasit, a third different essence. It was one of the most valuable of the magic attributes—channeling. There were so many burnt mages in the world that the price for such essences was astronomical. This minor essence would be just a drop in the bucket for Castile. Still, I planned to save it for her.

Concerned, Mynasha advised me, "Make sure you hide that." She indicated the collector. "If Jhuarkasha or Rhuuk see it, they might find an excuse to take it. I've never heard of a collector being so—efficient." I had gained trust with Mynasha over the past month, but I wasn't going to confirm her suspicions. She owed me, since I had guided her through the entire Choosing.

I nodded to her and stood. We only encountered one dretch before we came in sight of the blue-ringed entrance. I had collected twenty-two quickness essences and two more minor healing essences from the blood stirges. In addition, I added one more minor charm for the single dretch we slew.

As we approached the entrance to the ice demon cave, we were not surprised to see Cleric Jhuarkasha and Warlord Rhuuk coming from the other direction. I was surprised we had beaten them here. The shadow demon was a difficult opponent, and it was inevitable that they would come here next. They were still over fifty yards away, with a few wandering dretches between us. They hadn't noticed us, as they were engaged in a fight. The cleric stood behind Rhuuk as he managed to fight three dretches while being dive-bombed by two stirges.

We observed one of the stirges bouncing off an invisible shield. Jhuarkasha focused on protection magic while Rhuuk handled all the combat. Despite that, he appeared exhausted and was covered in dretch blood, moving much slower than when he had entered. "We should quickly eliminate the ice demon before they arrive," I said, interrupting Mynasha's focus on the pair. She nodded, and we stepped into the blue cave.

Chapter 316: Caught Between a Rock and a Hard Place

Rhuuk must have been fatigued from his relentless combat, as he was carrying the pair. His swings lacked their usual ferocity, and I assumed he had depleted much of his aether; he wasn't using his tattoos at the moment. Even though the dungeon enhanced the recovery of aether, he could not charge forward recklessly.

We paused in the short corridor to the ice demon chamber to watch the other two progress. Mynasha observed, "They both look to be conserving aether, probably for the fight with the ice demon."

I was not as certain. "Will they try to steal the horns when we come out?" I asked.

"No," she said, then hedged, "Possibly. Maybe they are conserving aether to confront us after we fight the demon and are weakened." At least she was admitting to herself that honor was secondary to the prize of being the Supreme.

My hand brushed the blue glowstone to my right. I took a modest block of it into my space. I needed to conserve my own aether, as I had only recovered about two-thirds of my capacity. While Rhuuk fought, I spared a glance into the ice demon chamber. Frost coated the blue glowstones within, and a thin layer of snow covered the icy floor. It was a treacherous environment to fight in, and we had been warned that the longer we fought, the colder the chamber would become. Since we would be sealed inside the freezer, it would be a death sentence if we couldn't slay the demon quickly. Of course, Maveith had the ring of warmth that would have helped.

I tried to find the demon. We had been told the ice demon blended into the floor to look like a snow-covered stone, but from my vantage point, I could see a dozen or more large stones. I was slightly concerned that the demon might resist my dimensional space, resulting in a desperate fight. From Glasha, I knew it was a highly magical creature, capable of creating a frozen aura around itself.

It was also covered in a white, bony, plate exoskeleton, making it difficult—even with a runic weapon—to locate flesh. Maveith's bludgeoning hammer would have been handy for this encounter.

"Are we going?" Mynasha asked, seeing my uncertainty as the competition drew closer.

"I say we let them fight the demon and take the horns when they exit." Mynasha looked uncertain at the suggestion. She had followed my lead so far and I had carried her.

"We cannot kill them," she stated resolutely, but didn't say we couldn't rob them. I nodded, sheathed magebane, and the black spear appeared in my hand. Having watched Rhuuk practice, I thought the spear was a better weapon to keep him at a distance since his broadsword had longer reach than magebane.

We watched the pair work slowly through the dretches and blood stirges to reach the corridor where we were waiting. They came up short, not expecting to see us there. Jhuarkasha barked mockingly at us. "Too afraid to fight the demon?" It was a weak taunt, clearly crafted to lure us into killing the ice demon. The cleric lacked cunning, among other things. I could see him being a puppet of the warlords, but I didn't know if Mynasha had the fortitude to stand up to them either. Not that I cared for the fate of the Caliphate.

My eyes slid to Rhuuk, and I tried to read his intentions. Rhuuk was covered in dretch and stirge blood but showed no signs of fatigue. Even though Jhuarkasha was the candidate, Rhuuk was clearly the one in charge. Mynasha was waiting for me to answer the insult. Apparently, I was the one who spoke for our team. "How do you know we have not already defeated the ice demon?"

The cleric peered into the snow-blanketed, icy chamber beyond, his face betraying panic. If we had both sets of horns, we could complete the third Trial. The snow lay undisturbed, making it evident that we had not crossed the threshold into the demon's domain, but uncertainty was on the cleric's face. "They have not," Rhuuk voiced aloud, figuring it out, not breaking eye contact with me. His eyes drifted to the spear for a split second and then moved back.

"The demon is all yours." I gestured slightly with the spearhead to let them pass, but they didn't move. It was a standoff. I think they planned to take the horns from us when we exited—but that was also our plan. I assumed they had intentionally slowed to let us enter first. They had been acting more fatigued than they actually were, as well.

Jhuarkasha tried not to give away their intentions, but turned to Rhuuk for orders. The tendons in Rhuuk's hand flexed, and I watched the tip of his blade for movement. His eyes held an eagerness to test his skill against mine, but he was also intelligent. He had studied me on numerous occasions and had seen what my dimensional space held.

"You can have the goliaths if you give us the hellhound skull." The warlord's statement threw me off. He laughed darkly at my surprise. "You thought we wouldn't find out why a human would help a candidate in the Choosing?" *Damn it, Maveith!* I assumed that his actions had revealed why we were here.

"We didn't tell anyone," Mynasha said quietly from my side.

"I know," I said while maintaining eye contact with the warlord.

I tried to regain my mental footing, thinking out the implications. There had to be spying and divination magic, but Maveith's attempt to contact his sister was likely the reason they knew. I shook my head slowly. It didn't matter. I was certain the bulky pack Jhuarkasha carried had the snake demon horns. If we left the dungeon, he would have leverage over me, as Zorana and Myra were his slaves. Maybe he wanted something more—something he had seen in my dimensional items? A slight anxiety stirred in me. I couldn't let him live.

I grinned, showing confidence. "How about a friendly wager? We will put up our hellhound skull for the snake demon horns. The winner walks out of here with both. Just me and you, no need to get the clerics involved." If Mynasha was involved and we moved to the large chamber away from the walls, she could probably end this quickly. But I was worried that Jhuarkasha could shield Rhuuk and prevent my attacks.

I was going this route because I had doubts about fighting the ice demon, and then having to fight Rhuuk right after. Glasha had indicated the ice demon was not much weaker than the shadow demon, and we had hoped not to fight either.

The warlord didn't take long to answer. Rhuuk looked at the spear and my sheathed blade, clearly wanting both artifacts on his face. That was why I was surprised when he answered, "No, human. You have no honor."

Really? We were talking about honor now!? I ground my teeth, but I had learned enough about warlord honor in our months in the Caliphate to twist it to my advantage. "I killed Warlord Trakor; it was I who brought down his roc, Chaostail, north of Varvao," I said. "I claim his honor as mine."

"You lie, human," Cleric Jhuarkasha yelled at me, spittle flying from his mouth. Stealing a dead man's honor was dishonorable and had to be met with an honor challenge, so I thought I would force a fight either way. Mynasha had taken a step back from me, also stunned by my claim.

Warlord Trakor had led the expedition to conquer western Telha; his unexpected death nearly doomed it, causing infighting among the remaining warlords and clerics. From Glasha and Tarnasha's conversations, I knew Trakor had been an ally of Rhuuk, but I did not know how deep the alliance went.

War Cleric Mynasha had been at the head of that fleet as the strongest cleric, and I had just stunned her by admitting that I was the pain-in-the-ass Hound who had killed Pathfinders and warlords alike, nearly thwarting the annexation.

I could also claim Pathfinder Rakuh as my victim and claim his honor, but I thought I wouldn't need to, given Rhuuk's reaction. I had killed Rakuh in an honor duel when I freed the goliath slaves in Kraken Bay. That Pathfinder was the patriarch of the Sun Shadow Clan and was respected throughout the Caliphate. Glasha had warned me that several warlords and clans would seek to avenge his death.

My eyes had not broken their contact with Rhuuk's. Some people didn't need a Truthseeker to read the truth in another. "No, I believe he tells it true." Rhuuk's breathing had slowed as he prepared mentally and physically. "Death or surrender?" he asked, setting the terms.

"Death," I didn't hesitate to respond.

"No!" Jhuarkasha barked, gathering his wits. "Surrender!"

"Not your decision, cleric. It is my honor to barter," Rhuuk said dismissively. I caught something in their exchange. Was this an act? I had only recently learned the orc language so the nuances were still a little lost on me, but reading body language was something I had gotten good at from all my weapons practice. They had been expecting this outcome—maybe they even desired it. *Don't doubt yourself, Eryk*, I told myself. I could beat Rhuuk.

"We should move out to the large cavern." I gestured with my spear, not liking the ice demon at my back.

"I am comfortable here," Rhuuk said, motioning Jhuarkasha away. At least Jhuarkasha didn't cast any spells on him—or at least none that I noticed with my aether-infused sight active.

Rhuuk was an imposing warrior, built like Maveith and more agile than Benito. With his tattoos, he was probably faster and stronger than me, and on top of that, he had more combat experience. But what he didn't have was a dimensional space.

The blue-lit corridor we were standing in was twenty feet wide with a ceiling to match. Rhuuk's stance changed as he gracefully circled my right. Mynasha backed away from me, and I think Rhuuk knew she couldn't use her lightning in proximity to the glowstones.

His footwork was some of the best I had ever observed. It gave away nothing of his intentions, and he glided like a feather, barely disturbing the ground. I almost felt embarrassed watching him, knowing my own footwork paled in comparison. I would have liked to cross blades with him for no reason other than to add him to the dreamscape, but I was not risking my life.

I circled him, watching closely while the two clerics looked on for a minute, before he narrowed his eyes and moved in closer. When he came within ten feet, I attempted to move a portion of his chest to my dimensional space. Instead, thunder rocked the area, and I was thrown backward, tumbling in a daze across the ground. I barely had enough awareness to realize I was heading in a very bad direction—toward the ice demon room. I laid out my body and skidded to a stop. I was conscious, but my head hurt and my aether was depleted. I fumbled in my pouch for a lesser healing potion.

The healing potion worked too slowly, my vision crystallizing. At least it looked like Rhuuk hadn't been spared. He was picking himself up off the floor of the main chamber, Jhuarkasha hovering over him but reluctant to help and interrupt the honor duel.

I realized what had happened slowly. This had happened to me once before when I had tried to place the belt with small dimensional pouches into my dimensional space. Another dimension could not exist inside another and was forcibly expelled. Did that mean that Rhuuk had an artifact on him—or had his own dimensional space? My hearing returned as I stood, and Mynasha was hovering, uncertain if she should help. I probably should have gotten more clarity on the rules before we started.

Rhuuk looked angrily at Jhuarkasha from the ground. Jhuarkasha stepped back. "I didn't know you would be affected too!" The cleric said apologetically, some fear in his voice. I had been set up. They had figured out the extent of my abilities and prepared a counter. I was stupid for not realizing it. Rhuuk struggled to his feet, clearly suffering from the concussive blast. He fumbled for his own healing potion, and I looked for my spear. Fuck, it had rolled into the demon's chamber behind me. Shit—one of the snow-covered rocks was creeping closer to it.

I drew magebane and started to advance on Rhuuk, who still seemed disoriented, but it wouldn't last. And it didn't. He retrieved his blade before I closed in on him. He parried my first attack and regained his footing as his mind cleared from the healing potion. I pressed as best I could, but he was clearly channeling aether to his tattoos, as he was faster than me. I didn't think that was fair, as my aether pool had been drained in the explosive feedback.

I was forced back as Rhuuk regained himself. My hope was that he would expend his aether on his tattoos, and the fight would be even once again. I was tracking my own aether, which was recovering painfully slowly. Realizing he had the advantage, Rhuuk pressed the attack. I grunted when I blocked a heavy swing, my shoulder aching from the force behind it. I told myself to just parry or dodge in the future. So much for consuming essences like candy for the last two years. I was physically outmatched.

Rhuuk was deft with his broadsword and difficult to read. I was soon sporting a deep cut on my right thigh and bicep. The leg wound hadn't reached the muscle, but the wound on the arm had. If my shield hadn't been in my dimensional space, this might have been more of a fair fight, but as it was, I was at a disadvantage. The exchanges got more and more violent as I went on the defensive, retreating. I took another cut to my same injured arm; this time, he reached the bone, making that arm useless.

He paused, finally drawing in heavy breaths, and the emptiness in his eyes told me he had exhausted his aether. Only a few minutes had passed, and I began to retreat toward the ice demon room. In a prolonged fight, I realized I would lose. Maybe I could lure him into the demon chamber and turn the demon against him. Rhuuk wasn't stupid and didn't move, allowing me to step back. He was content to recover his aether so he could recharge his tattoos. After gaining some distance, I took the chance to drink a lesser healing potion from my belt. He frowned, clearly displeased. He might have thought the Titans had destroyed all my potions.

Most importantly, as the potion worked, my wounds closed, and the potion mitigated my blood loss. I was feeling some weakness from the blood loss, just another sign that things were not going well for me. I was at the entrance to ice demon room, but Rhuuk did not follow, clearly understanding my intention to lock us inside. "You cower like a human," he berated me. "You are not fit to be a First, or to be allowed in this dungeon."

I wanted to laugh. He somehow thought his insults would make me come to him. Minutes passed as we continued to stare at each other with thirty feet separating us. Rhuuk was forced to cut down a dretch that had wandered too close. I was content to let my aether recover. With the channeling ring and my attribute, I think Rhuuk would be shocked how fast I could replenish my aether.

I was now able to cast a few air shields or retrieve items from my dimensional space. I used some aether to boost my blood. Perhaps Rhuuk thought I poorly channeled aether or believed the backlash had damaged my dimensional space.

I dissuaded him from thinking that as the black blade appeared in my other hand. His eyes narrowed at the weapon, but he clearly did not realize it was Orc's Torment—at least not yet. The clerics watched from opposite sides of the entrance. Mynasha looked worried and frustrated at the same time. Rhuuk took a moment to reach under his armor and toss aside metal fragments. Was that what had repelled my dimensional space? Or was he trying to deceive me? I hated clever opponents.

I looked back at the black spear. The ice demon disguised as a rock had crowded close to it, hovering near it. That irked me, as I didn't want to lose the powerful weapon. I checked on my aether and walked out to the corridor to confront Rhuuk. He changed his posture very slightly. Maybe he was not ready to receive me, recovering himself.

With magebane in one hand and Orc's Torment in the other, I pressed my attack. He started to backpedal, on the defensive now that I had the advantage with two blades and he could not use all his tattoos. He still enhanced his speed and strength for quick exchanges, but I was now focused on wearing him down, rather than being baited by openings. One thing I did have was bottomless endurance.

He was very deft with the broadsword and it took time before Orc's Torment finally cut through his gauntlet and sliced the back of his hand. His hissed but didn't cry out as he retreated further into the open cavern. Jhuarkasha was confused and nervous at the turn of events.

Rhuuk's eyes were locked on the black blade. "You have no honor to bring such a vile blade into the Caliphate." I didn't respond, but a smile crept over my face. I could tell he was desperate. I circled and made him kill a dretch while he sought an advantage.

Minutes passed as we played a game of cat and mouse. Konstantin would be mad that I was playing with my food, but I had a plan. An effect of wounds from Orc's Torment was that magical healing would be ineffective; Rhuuk learned that after I cut his hip with magebane. He swiftly drank another healing potion and growled in frustration as it failed to heal his wounds.

That poison now flowed through his body, but frustratingly, he was still able to command his aether enough to activate his tattoos. I almost lost my arm trying to take advantage of an opening. I could have used an air shield to pressure him, but I had another fate in mind for him.

I asked as haughtily as I could, "Violet or blue?"

His confusion was evident on his face. "Violet or blue?" he echoed.

"Yeah, what is your favorite color?" I asked, gaining confidence as I closed.

"It does not factor into the contest," he retorted angrily.

I had stopped a dozen feet away. "Actually, it does," I stated. "I wanted to know …" I paused dramatically as a cubic yard of violet glowstone appeared above his head. He had no chance of seeing it with his helm's visor. As the stone fell, too slowly for my liking, I finished, "…what color to make your tombstone."

Panic appeared briefly on his face as the pressure settled on him. He made the mistake of trying to resist instead of getting out of the way. The stone crushed Rhuuk, and a squirt of his bodily fluids splattered on me. Some of his limbs still stuck out from under the glowing violet stone, but he was most certainly dead. Technically, I could say that I hadn't killed him if questioned by the Elders.

"Guess I won. I believe that is ours," I stated tiredly, looking over at the astonished Jhuarkasha, indicating his pack with the snake demon horns.

Chapter 317: Why Do They Always Run?

Jhuarkasha was momentarily in shock at Rhuuk's demise. He looked from the large violet glowstone to me and back, then started running toward the exit in the center of the massive chamber. In my best Tommy Lee Jones voice, I mused to myself, "Why do they always run?" I was not in good shape to chase the orc cleric, with my injuries only partially healed. He could have at least been polite and given me half an hour to self-heal.

A rope of lightning wrapped his waist and promptly exploded in a thundering flash. He stumbled and stood, uninjured, and began to run again once he regained his feet. Mynasha repeated her attack, and this time the cleric fell, moderately wounded. It appeared he hadn't reestablished all his defenses. Her third attack was diverted to the ceiling, exploding a red crystal forty feet off the ground in a brilliant shower of red sparkles.

I shielded my eyes as I was covered in chips and flakes of glowing red crystals. "Stop!" I shouted at her. Regaining my sight, I saw the air around her heat as she pulled more aether to herself. She looked at me questioningly and I approached her, talking while I walked. "The dretches will get him. You said we couldn't kill them." I wasn't sure how good the Elder Truthseekers were, but plausible deniability was always best. My bone inscriptions might protect me, but Mynasha didn't have my advantages against truth magics.

"You killed Rhuuk, and Jhuarkasha has no honor," she rebuked me. She looked a little angry that the cleric hadn't relinquished the snake demon horns.

"I didn't kill Rhuuk. He was just standing in the wrong place at the wrong time," I said, smirking. Her forehead creased before she mirrored my grin in realization. Jhuarkasha screamed for help as the first dretch reached him, but this just caused a buzzing of stirges to gather overhead. I stood next to Mynasha and watched him try to consume potions to maintain his defenses.

He was surprisingly successful as the minutes dragged on. It was clear he had a lot of aether and was practiced in shielding, even though I judged him a lackey. The problem was that he wasn't moving, and the dretches were slowly calling in support from their brethren. Four dretches now circled him and four stirges buzzed above him. He lasted much longer than I gave him credit for—almost twenty minutes—and he even managed to kill two stirges, although four took their place.

Mynasha relaxed as the dretches tore the body apart and consumed the flesh greedily. They didn't stop with the flesh, and their jaws soon splintered and ground the bones noisily. It was one of the most gruesome displays I had seen on Desia. I lamented the loss of the essence, but I was not in any shape to fight the four dretches and the six stirges now circling.

I decided to use the collector on Rhuuk before he stopped producing an essence. I wasn't sure if I needed to remove the glowstone grave marker to get the collector closer, so I activated it near his exposed shoulder. The aetheric essence was just thin wisps, so I definitely needed to move it closer to the heart. The major essence that formed was pale yellow, reminding me of a large lemon drop—an insight essence. An odd essence for a warrior.

I looked toward Juarkasha's corpse, where now seven dretches were feasting, and lamented the loss of the cleric's essence again. There would be nothing left to use the collector on. I turned away to approach the ice demon entrance.

"We don't need the ice demon if we can recover the snake demon horns," Mynasha said logically. I ignored her as my eyes locked on my black spear. The demonic rock was practically touching it, waiting for me to try and reclaim it.

"I want to reclaim my spear. Will you help?" I asked, not taking my eyes off it.

To her credit, Mynasha nodded and joined me in support. "I can be ready in a few minutes," she said as she started drawing aether again. I nodded and remained standing, my eyes fixed on the spear while drinking water to restore my fluids. I strapped on bands of small metal spikes that would allow me to move on the ice.

I waited until Mynasha stood beside me, her own ice spikes attached to her boots. We stepped across the threshold, me with magebane in one hand and a shield in the other. The other end of the short corridor sealed us in, a wall of blue glowstone now blocking our exit. The wash of cold air caused goosebumps to rise on my skin, as the temperature was already below freezing. Our breath formed clouds in front of us. Inhaling deeply hurt my lungs.

When we talked with Glasha, we had already developed plans for each demon. Unfortunately, the hellhound had not cooperated, and now the ice demon was doing the same. The rock unfolded to a standing posture, powdered snow falling off its bony exoskeleton. A nine-foot golem-looking demon stood before us, holding my damn spear!

"I am going to need that back," I said heatedly. Instead of cooperating, the ice demon crouched and launched itself at us. Lightning and air shields hindered its movement as we circled on the icy ground, our spikes gouging the ice as we moved. The demon was not skilled with the spear and swung it wildly. Normally, the creature fought with its impressive claws, but it seemed to like my weapon.

Its massive hind legs could launch it forward at an impressive speed, but the bony plates made it slow to turn, so as long as we kept circling, we could stay out of its reach. One mistake and the thousand-pound demon would grapple us, and it would be the end.

Our plan, and the plan of most warlords who fought this demon, was to get a blade in its knee joint. If we succeeded in that, its movement would be greatly hindered. The problem was getting close enough. It was swinging my spear in a massive arc like a fly swatter. The floor was treacherous, and we could slip on an ice patch at the worst possible moment, even with the metal spikes we wore.

As the temperature dropped rapidly, I began to worry. "Do you want me to?" Mynasha asked. Our plan B was for her to spray her lightning and hope she hit the monster. She was already channeling so much aether for her shields that her halter top was gone and her leather skirt was not far behind. On the positive side, the aetheric aura around her seemed to be holding off the cold for her. She was actually glistening with sweat.

"No, I will try to disable it," I responded. I had studied the ice demon's movements, and it was mostly predictable, but the last thing I wanted to do was test the black spear against my armor. I had seen the spear in action too many times and had watched it easily part armor and flesh. I closed in on the demon, going into a slide as it swept the spear in an arc. It passed a few feet over my head as my body slammed into the bony leg. Magebane sought the joint and I forced it between two bony plates.

I planted both my feet on its shin and pushed off, sliding backward in plenty of time before the spear came crashing down in a spray of ice chunks. Its movements reminded me of a clumsy robot. With magebane embedded in its knee, it could no longer bend the joint or turn rapidly. Boris's sword appeared in my hand, replacing magebane. I had been hoping magebane would disrupt its ability to keep dropping the temperature, but the air did not feel any different. I couldn't wait to find out, as my sweat was crystallizing to ice as soon as it formed on my skin.

"I will circle and attack it from behind," I yelled to Mynasha. Her lightning shields had effectively restricted its movements, but my time was running out, and Mynasha had some difficulty moving on the ice while pulling aether from the environment. If cold incapacitated me, we would lose.

I quickly got behind the demon and hacked away at the bony plates. Splinters of frozen bone peppered my face as I focused my swings. The progress was too slow, so I risked trying to remove the creature's head. Glasha had been right; it was a highly magical creature with strong aether resistance. Just not strong enough to resist me. The demon's body froze and slowly toppled over.

The exit was no longer barred, but the temperature was still well below freezing. Mynasha was already heading for the exit. As she stopped gathering aether, the cold she had been shielded from suddenly rushed to her.

I reclaimed my black spear, noting the reward chest near the wall of the chamber. It looked like a solid, square block of ice, and it could wait. Some things couldn't. As the cold air stole my body heat through my sweat, I shivered uncontrollably, waiting for enough aether to retrieve the collector. I managed to work magebane out of the demon's knee and sheathe it while a thin layer of frost slowly formed on my body.

When the time came, I was numb and my mind was foggy. The collector yielded an apex water essence. Just what I had been hoping for. I stumbled out of the demon room into the hot, humid air of the main chamber. Mynasha had been watching me and gave me a mother's disapproving look. "It could have waited," she chastised. I just shivered in response. Maybe, but I had guessed that I might have gotten only a major essence if I waited longer.

Mynasha allowed me to warm up slowly while she guarded us. The area was clear and the dretches had finally finished with Jhuarkasha's corpse, having dispersed and returned to wandering again. We needed to see about claiming what was left of Rhuuk and Jhuarkasha's gear, and I also wanted to go on a quasit hunt now that we were not rushed.

I returned to claim the block of ice when I was mostly healed and somewhat thawed out. I stored it and brought it to the main chamber to thaw out. I could see silver coins contained in what looked like a large porcelain serving bowl with runic writing on it. While the ice melted, I reclaimed most of the large violet glowstone so I could sort through the disgusting mess that was Warlord Rhuuk.

All that I was able to claim from the human pancake was his runic broadsword and a silver runic ring. Everything else was damaged beyond salvaging and covered with his bodily fluids.

"Do you have the ice demon horns?" Mynasha asked. After I nodded, she asked, "Are we returning to the surface?"

"Not yet. I want to see if we can catch more of the quasits." She nodded slowly in understanding. "We will see what remains of Jhuarkasha soon," I said, tapping on the icy prison I sat on. It took nearly two hours for the block to melt, releasing three dozen large silver coins and the large bowl, which was decorated with scenes of demons fighting. The scenes, featuring a wide array of demons, required careful observation, as the runes blended into the images.

"Glasha will use her lore spell on it for you," Mynasha said after I had spent half an hour studying it. I was trying to piece together the runes I could see but was having difficulty. When I thought I was on the right track, I would find minuscule runes on a demon's sword or boots. I was skeptical about giving it aether since I did not know the bowl's purpose.

We walked to where Jhuarkasha had met his end, cutting down a pair of dretches and harvesting them before reaching him. A pair of stirges were trying to suck blood from the stony cracks in the floor. I cut them down and harvested them as well. There was nothing left of the cleric besides bloody, shredded robes. We didn't need the snake demon horns, so we did not search for them. The dretches might have eaten them.

We searched the area, finding some non-runic gear that was now ruined. "Did he have any artifacts?" I asked Mynasha after searching for a time.

"A talisman and bracer ..." She paused, thinking. "That is all I remember."

We expanded our search and looked for those items, not finding anything after cutting down four more pig-men. I theorized, "Maybe the dretches ate them?" Did I really want to cut open the stomachs of the foul creatures? In the end, I tried searching the stomachs of four dretches near the kill site. While I found some partially digested orc flesh during the nauseating work, I didn't find any artifacts.

We turned our attention to attracting the quasits. The chamber was less than half a mile across, but the wandering dretches would attack you if you got within twenty yards of them. I took the opportunity to add blocks of yellow, red, and green glowstone to my space.

The shadow demon chamber appeared ominous, with only a faint green glow emanating from within. We were not going to tempt fate by challenging the strongest demon. That was why our progress was slow as we searched for the elusive green imps. Seven dretches and four stirges later, I finally spotted one. It was sitting on a small boulder, nibbling on a yellow mushroom.

The tiny creature eyed us suspiciously as we approached. If Mynasha used her lightning, there would be nothing left to use the collector on. I hoped it would turn invisible and try to hide. Instead, the bastard dashed away with its mushroom prize. "Why is the little shit running away?" I cussed.

The pursuit became a tedious and frustrating game of endless cat and mouse as the quasit kept out of range, always stopping to sit and watch us while eating its mushroom. I tried to leave nuts on the ground to lure it, but it didn't seem interested—maybe it was aware I was trying to trick it. When I left one of my few remaining apples for it, another quasit snagged it while I was focused on the first.

When I got upset, Mynasha warned me to calm down, but she was clearly amused. "They are tricksters and thieves. It is their nature, and they will use your frustration to make you make a mistake." I grunted in response, not liking that a small green demon was besting me. The second quasit was invisible and hiding between two rocks with its prize apple. I moved within range and stored the entire creature inside my dimensional space. I wasn't surprised by its strong resistance to my space magic—but I still overcame it.

The original quasit immediately became upset, chittering at us in an unfamiliar language as it frantically searched for its missing companion. I just grinned at its dismay in triumph. "Let's go, Mynasha."

She was surprised as I started heading back to the chamber's center. The quasit was not done with us, trying to get revenge by luring dretches and stirges to us. I welcomed the easy kills and essences. I was just waiting till the creature made a mistake and got close enough to snag.

Its thirst for vengeance overcame its caution. With my back turned, it rushed me while it was invisible. My earth speak told me exactly where it was, and it joined its companion in my dimensional space. Mynasha was not even aware I had taken the second imp.

The exit portal loomed in front of us. I had gathered almost fifty lesser quickness essences and half that number of lesser charm essences. Only a few dretches roamed in the distance now.

We left and started ascending the numerous steps to the surface. Mynasha was correct; these stairs were exhausting after a day of intense fighting in the dungeon. When we finally reached the top and stepped outdoors, the bright, early-morning sun shone directly in our faces and blinded us. A field of tents encircled the stone building, and an unusual horn sounded to notify everyone of our emergence.

The warlords, clerics, and Elders rushed to see who had emerged first. Mynasha had a bag in each hand, one with a hellhound skull and the other with an ice demon head. I could tell the Elders were not happy that we had emerged first. Mynasha was shuffled off to be questioned by the Elders, and I was left standing alone under the intense glare of warlords and clerics.

Glasha approached and saved me. She pulled me aside to talk privately. "What happened to Jhuarkasha? Is he coming?"

"The dretches got him," I stated simply, in case we were being spied on. She looked shocked.

"What about Warlord Rhuuk? Didn't he protect him?" she asked as she came to terms with the good news.

With a flat tone, I informed her of his fate: "He got stuck between a rock and a hard place."

Glasha was confused, but I didn't care. I was tired and wanted this over with. "What happens now?" I asked impatiently. Glasha brought her attention back to me as Tarnasha joined us.

"The Elders will confirm the demons' horns are fresh from the dungeon and that Mynasha completed the Trial honorably," Tarnasha said. "Are the others coming?"

"I don't think they will be exiting the dungeon," Glasha answered for me. I just gave a short nod to confirm. Tarnasha's jaw fell open but no words came out.

"Will I be questioned? Can I depart? When will Mynasha free the goliaths?" I asked a little impatiently.

Tarnasha found his voice, a tusky smile forming. "It is unlikely that you will be called before the Elders to answer questions. You can go wait in the longhouse. I suspect the Elders are trying to find some way not to confirm Mynasha as the next Supreme. We need to make sure that does not happen."

I shook my head. I didn't care for Caliphate politics. Would Mynasha be a good ruler or just a figurehead? She was better than the other candidates and probably better for the people, but probably not for the warlords, even though she was a war cleric. I didn't care. I just needed her to hold up her end of our agreement and free Zorana and Myra.

Under the scrutinizing eyes of the warlords, I walked back to the longhouse. My armor was ruined, soaked in foul demon blood and other fluids. The demon blood had not only stained the leather, but also caused it to rot. It was destined for the fire.

The longhouse was quieter, but the slaves and orc attendants were still present. I was about to go to Ginger when Maveith stood, suddenly towering over the others in the chamber. His expectant face begged for the answer to his unspoken question. "Mynasha is the new Supreme," I informed him.

Maveith crossed the room and slammed into me, embracing me. My vertebrae popped as he squeezed. I was expecting the hug, but not that it would be so long. "Maveith, I need a bath," I said breathlessly.

"Can I go to Zorana?" he asked, finally releasing me. Eagerness lined the big man's face.

I smiled reassuringly but tempered his enthusiasm. "Wait until the clerics come back. We delivered on our end, so the clerics will have to deliver." The other goliath was standing behind Maveith, but we were speaking in Elvish. Maveith was deflated but nodded in understanding.

I scanned the room. The old woman's mouth was agape in shock. "A hot bath for me," I ordered. She narrowed her eyes at me. Since she had poisoned me before, I gloated a little hotly, "Mynasha completed the third Trial first. She is the new Supreme." I didn't know if that was true yet, but I sounded confident.

The old woman looked shocked, but eventually, the buckets started to flow. I took the opportunity to remove all my armor and clothes to inspect myself. I had an angry, red rash on my skin that was resistant to my healing spell form. It was also hot to the touch. I was certain it was from the hellhound blood, but it only bothered me when I fixated on it.

Another irritating thing was that the injuries from Rhuuk's blade to my thigh and arm had healed, but there were fine white scars where the skin had closed. My healing spell form told me the area was completely healed, and that there was no scar to heal.

I wrapped myself in a blanket and went to greet an impatient Ginger while I waited for my bath. She shied away from me. "Come on, girl, I have smelled worse." She didn't seem to agree. Some animals just knew something was terrible when they smelled it. I recalled the myths of Earth, where demons were considered evil and unnatural. To me, they just seemed like any other monstrosity among the many I had encountered, with the exception of ogres— they could kill with their stench.

The young human with freckles approached me with a bucket. "Do you wish to be scrubbed down before you enter the bath?" she asked subserviently, her head lowered.

"Nolona?" I asked, recalling her name.

"How do you ..." she trailed off, confused.

"The old woman told me. Do you want to be free?" I asked. She had straightened her auburn hair and was mostly clean now. Her pale skin now highlighted her freckles. Not pretty, but attractive.

She bowed her head. "You honor me for remembering my name. I ... I ... I ..." She didn't know how to answer my question, maybe thinking it was a trap.

"Were you taken from across the sea as well?" I questioned, taking the bucket from her. I didn't need someone to scrub me down.

She did not make eye contact. "I believe so. I am not educated. Orc sailors boarded our ship and I was taken with my sister. She did not survive …" She trailed off sorrowfully.

"I will see what I can do for you with the new Supreme," I offered. She looked up at my statement, trying to hide her hope.

"You can continue your duties. I can wash myself," I dismissed her.

As she left, I realized I was probably being petty. Freeing the young woman was the right thing to do, but I only wanted to free her and not the old woman because she had attempted to poison Mynasha with the bathwater. As I cleaned myself, I noticed my hair had clumps of things I did not care to identify. I scrubbed my skin raw with the brush and wiped myself with a cloth, removing the worst of the filth before moving to the heated bath.

The water had a floral scent to it, and before stepping in, I wondered if the old woman had poisoned it again. It would be an audacious move by the old slave. The water was much hotter than last time. Maybe it was pettiness, but I enjoyed the heat. I focused on my body, looking for changes as it settled. The heat was the only thing penetrating my body; there were no signs of toxins or poison. I sighed and closed my eyes, fighting off sleep.

Humans and orcs alike interrupted me with offers of food and assistance in washing. I declined them all, just wanting to wallow in the hot water being circulated through the fire by pipes. I dried myself twice, making them scrub the tub and fill it again. Now, the water remained clear as I pruned. Maveith was pacing and talking to the other goliath in their native tongue.

It was hours before Glasha and Tarnasha entered the longhouse with triumphant energy. "Things went well, I take it," I yelled as they looked for me in longhouse. Maveith was already moving to intercept them. They moved to stand over the tub with tusky smiles.

Glasha yelled like a child. "She was confirmed! The coronation will be with the rising sun tomorrow."

"That is great," I said, truly happy and slapping the water. "And the goliaths?"

Tarnasha spoke. "With Rhuuk dead, they will be freed and set into your care. Mynasha has promised that. There is just one thing …"

I cocked my eyebrow, expecting some sort of betrayal. "You are not allowed to attend the coronation," Glasha finished for him.

This was not a big deal, but their expressions suggested that they thought I would be upset. I acted like I was, asking hotly, "Why?"

Glasha went from jubilant to angry, mirroring me. "The Elders are upset that a human boy succeeded in helping Mynasha. They are trying to needle the new Supreme with obscure laws."

Slightly more cynically, I questioned their motives. "Do you think they are trying to keep me away from the coronation so they can move against Mynasha?"

"No," Tarnasha said tersely. "That breach would cause a civil war. They will try to remove her in other, more subtle ways after she has had time to acclimate. But acting so quickly would tarnish their honor."

"Mynasha has asked me to extend an offer to you." I looked expectantly at Glasha. "She wishes to elevate you to a warlord of the Boutan Caliphate. She will bestow Warlord Rhuuk's city upon you to rule." The thought of power over so many others might be appealing to others, but I didn't welcome it. I slowly shook my head no. "She was certain you would say no. Ask anything else of her, and she will see it fulfilled for all that you have done."

I indicated the young human woman. "Free all the goliaths in the Caliphate. Free the woman," I indicated Nolona. "Hell, free all the slaves! I will take any others that can get here before I sail."

The two orcs looked a little stunned at my request. "Her time as Supreme would be short if she fulfilled such a request. There are more than a thousand goliaths, perhaps as many as two thousand in all of the Caliphate. Would you settle for all the goliaths in the city? She could pass this off as a reward for your assistance and homage owed by the warlords to her authority—freeing the goliaths and the woman," Tarnasha said judiciously, indicating Nolona.

I thought on it for a moment before nodding, more so because of the logistics involved in getting thousands of goliaths halfway around the world. Just feeding them would be a nightmare. "How many, and when can I leave?" Maveith was closing in on me in the tub. "Maveith, now is not the time for another hug," I warned him.

"You may leave now to return to your companions. Your request will be fulfilled as soon as she is ordained. New Supremes often present numerous edicts when first coronated," Glasha said, her voice tinged with a hint of relief that I didn't press my request to end slavery in the Caliphate. A quick exchange between the two orcs resulted in an estimation that perhaps fifty goliaths resided in the city. My head throbbed at the thought—fifty Maveiths?

527

"When can I see Zorana?" Maveith's voice rumbled earnestly.

The two orcs looked at each other before Glasha spoke with a slight smile. "With Rhuuk dead, I can arrange it now." She nodded to me and left the longhouse.

I dressed in simple clothes, amused that the slaves had tried to clean my armor and clothes. Demon blood just never comes out. I told them to burn the soiled items while we waited for Glasha to return. Maveith couldn't sit still or be calmed. He paced and left the longhouse multiple times to check the path.

It was early morning, the sun not far from rising, when the door opened. Maveith stood abruptly. Four goliaths scuffed their feet on the floor as they ducked to enter. There was a lot of confusion on their faces as they looked around the longhouse, all eyes turning to them. Glasha was right behind them, a stern expression on her face as she winked at me.

"Zorana!" Maveith finally bellowed, causing all the attention to focus on him. I recognized Zorana, and recognition slowly formed on the goliath's face. Tears were pouring down Maveith's cheeks. No one had moved. Did he think his sister was angry with him? Rejecting him?

Maveith took a tentative step toward the group. "Maveith?" Zorana said in a hoarse whisper. She separated from the others but did not rush toward her brother. If this was not a happy reunion, I was going to turn in my Fortuna-favored card.

Maveith approached, standing in front of Zorana, just a few feet apart. I held my breath. Then Zorana lunged at him, wrapping him in a hug, and started bawling. Her voice was hard to understand as she spoke Orcish, but it sounded like: "I didn't believe them. You came for me." Watching, I may have shed a tear or two myself.

As the goliath reunion proceeded, Glasha approached. "The new Supreme is busy and will not be returning here—perhaps if you can wait a few days, she could find the time to meet with you." I shrugged, guessing that she no longer needed her lowly human.

"We are all going to head back to the Adventurers Hall in the city then," I said. "Can I take the woman?" I indicated Nolona.

Tarnasha tried to dissuade me. "There will be parties celebrating the new Supreme's honor. You cannot show yourself at the coronation, but you would be honored by many of the warlords at those gatherings who wish to curry favor with Mynasha."

"I have all the friends and allies I need," I said dismissively. I hoped I would never have to return to the Caliphate.

I saddled Ginger and headed back to the city with my goliath entourage and Nolona. We arrived at the Adventurers Hall in the afternoon. I found my companions playing cards around one of the tables. A young Gilda was sitting in the corner of the room on watch. Benito jumped up on his chair, pointing at me. "Told you! He even looks like he just bathed!" Well, he had me there. He turned on Konstantin. "You owe me a gold!"

Then Benito's jaw fell as the stream of goliaths entered after me. The common room went silent at the unusual sight. It was Mateo who broke the awkwardness. "Maveith! Are you going to introduce me to your sister?"

Maveith's bright smile was showing. "I already warned her about you, Mateo! She is not your type," he added a little more strongly in warning.

Mateo briefly looked hurt before he beamed with Benito, while Raelia looked relieved to see me. We had been gone a few days—it was no big deal and Baldo was safe and mostly uninjured. I moved to sit with them, Blaze clapping me on the back. Maveith led his shell-shocked group of goliaths to the desk, getting them rooms.

"What does he owe you a gold for?" I asked Benito. Konstantin handed his mug to me.

"I bet you would fail and come crawling back to us," Konstantin said half-seriously.

Benito corrected him, thinking about the exact wording Konstantin had used. "No, you said he was going to get himself killed messing in orc politics." Benito was too loud, and the orc adventurers in the hall turned to him. He shut up and sat down.

Konstantin winked at me, and I liked to think the bet was more to distract Benito and less about my prospects. A gold coin flipped through the air and clattered on the table before Benito. He took it and pocketed it in a flash with a satisfied grin. Konstantin said gruffly, "There were rumors aplenty of what was going on. None of them good." Okay, maybe Konstantin did have his doubts about my prospects. After seeing the lengths the Elders had gone to rig the trials, I couldn't blame him.

There was no time to harp on it, as Maveith's large frame was standing over me. "Eryk, they need to be registered as adventurers to get rooms."

Maveith had the coin and badges for the rooms, but I had to argue with the clerk for twenty minutes to convince him the goliaths had been freed. It was a frustrating affair, and I had to leave my guild token with him in case I was proven wrong. The goliaths took food and drink up to their rooms to rest, as most of them were still stunned at the whirlwind of events. I told Nolona to go with them to keep her away from Mateo.

I sighed, taking a long sip of ale, and sat back with the others. It was slightly bitter but not bad. I nodded conspiratorially. "Did you get a ship, Konstantin?" He nodded. "Can it hold fifty goliaths?" I said seriously. Blaze's eyes widened in worry.

Konstantin's face soured, his whisper harsh as he guessed my intentions. "We cannot free and escape with fifty! Be happy with those you have."

I waved my hand, unconcerned. "No need," I said, finally breaking into a grin. "I freed them all. As long as I am not betrayed, they will be released to me soon." The table was awash with disbelief.

Konstantin seemed to be the only one thinking ahead as he wrestled with the news. He hadn't shown any shock, which irritated me. "Fifty? I think we can manage that. We would need to charter a ship instead, but it is going to cost a fair amount of gold." It looked like I was footing the bill; maybe I would have to part with an artifact.

I looked over my companions. "I want Benito, Blaze, and Mateo to return to Gramney." They looked ready to object, but Konstantin supported my decision.

"Castile needs to be informed and needs protection herself. There are traders headed south all the time. Since I am going with Maveith and Eryk, it makes sense for you three to return," Konstantin said conversationally.

"You're what?" I said, stunned. I locked eyes with Konstantin.

His eyes danced in pleasure at my surprise. "I always wanted to see the other continent." He let a half-smile slip and winked. "Besides, Emperor Octavius is hunting me. Best to get some distance."

My stunned look made him indicate Gilda. "She killed a pair of Hounds in the city two days ago. I am pretty sure they were here to get some revenge for

Centurion Sergius. They were not the first sent after me in the last month, either. We should take this to a more private setting." I scanned the crowd. The other adventurers were taking some interest in our table conversation.

We moved to a large, private suite in the Adventurers Hall that I paid for at the counter. It came with a clean, plush bed that I was looking forward to utilizing. My companions pressed me for details of the Choosing and my role in it.

I told a very bland tale of how I helped Mynasha become the next Supreme of the Caliphate. They scoffed in disbelief at the pixie hunt. They laughed with me when I said we confronted three storm giants, thinking I was exaggerating. They outright called me a liar when I described the demon dungeon, so I gave each of them one quickness essence to consume as proof. A lesser man might have released one of the quasits to prove his truth. Even though I was well lubed with alcohol, I was smart enough not to.

I felt that telling my companions my final revelation was necessary as well. Maybe it was because I had been drinking too much with them. They had shown me loyalty and risked their lives. "Also, I should tell you: I am an otherworlder."

Konstantin, Raelia, and Gilda did not look surprised. Benito's face twisted into confusion. Blaze seemed contemplative. Mateo was the one who spoke first. "Are you one of the First Legion. From the other world? A spy?" His words were slurred and his mind was not functioning. It was probably not a great idea to tell Benito and Mateo this secret. But I wanted them to know in case I never saw them again.

"Something like that. But I think you know I am not a spy. I was just a normal man with a shitty job and little purpose in life," I replied as I used my purify self to eliminate all the alcohol in my system and sober up.

We explained to Benito what an otherworlder was, but I was not sure he understood in his drunken state. It was very late when everyone headed to their rooms. Raelia lingered behind, and I thought I knew why. "You want me to release Baldo? The Titans slightly injured him, but we can heal him."

Worry was suddenly etched on her face. "What?!"

"He is fine!" I reassured her. "He was just slapped into the floor by powerful magic. If he needs healing, we can get it for him." I had to go into more detail about the encounter before she calmed down about her griffin. She was obviously more concerned about Baldo than me.

I started to escort her out because I wanted to get a few hours of sleep before the action started tomorrow, but she resisted, slapping away my hand guiding her.

"No! Wait." She suddenly looked uncertain, but gained her courage back. "I wanted to let you know I changed my mind."

"You don't want to be a Griffin Rider again?" I asked, confused about what she was talking about.

"No," she said angrily, stepping into me and looking up at me like I was an idiot. I couldn't figure out what I was doing to make her mad. "I changed my mind about coming with you," she said heatedly.

I relaxed. She just wanted permission to come with us. "Oh, I am sure Maveith won't mind you joining us," I said, addressing her fear.

"No." She pushed me backward, forcing me to sit on the bed. Standing over me, she seemed angry. "I am going for you! Not Maveith." I didn't understand until she pushed me onto my back and climbed on top of me locking her lips to mine…

A loud knock on the door woke us. I stretched away from the sleepy elf, seeing that the sun was barely rising through the window. Konstantin's voice barked over the knocking, "Your goliaths are here, Eryk. You and Raelia should dress." I wasn't surprised that he was aware Raelia was in bed with me. "The clerics dropped off a chest for you too." A thud could be heard in the hallway as Konstantin dropped and I heard his boots walking away.

Raelia's naked body untangled from mine when she cracked her eyes open to stare at me. I didn't know who had a bigger morning-after grin, me or her. It was probably the wrong time to offer her some mouthwash. As she dressed, I dragged the chest inside the room and opened it.

I was a bit shocked by what it contained. Raelia gasped as inside were finger-sized gold trader bars and three shields. There was a note from Glasha on top.

You found these Titan artifacts, so I thought it fitting they remained with you. The runes are damaged and warped but perhaps you can find a master artificer to repair them. There should be enough gold here to get all the goliaths home. - Glasha

Raelia looked into the chest, not surprised by what she saw. "Should have been more gold," she scoffed. I moved the entire chest into my space.

"Are you sure you still want to come with us?" I asked after we finished dressing. She looked different to me this morning, more feminine, more beautiful, and happier. She had always struck me as focused, secretive, and defensive before. Now she couldn't stop grinning.

She gave me a cross look, and I guessed I had said the wrong thing. "Because if you decided not to come, I might decide to stay instead," I said, course-correcting. She reached up and patted my cheek, gave me a quick kiss, and left the room. She had some sway to her hips as she left, successfully drawing my attention to them. I sighed, not regretting last night, but worrying about where this might lead us. I followed her out of the room to the street.

The street was crowded with dozens of uncertain goliaths of various skin tones and sizes. Blaze was walking among them, trying to find someone who spoke Telhian. Mateo and Benito were discussing something privately and kept glancing at me, then at Raelia. It was challenging to keep secrets in a small group. But where was Maveith?

"That is a lot of goliaths," Gilda said in a detached observation. I hadn't even noticed the shape changer move to stand next to me.

Konstantin walked out of the confusion of bodies, holding two large, covered cages. "Seventy-seven goliaths, one human, and four pixies," he reported, handing me the cages with an unreadable expression. "You're going to need a bigger boat."

Renna's sweat was drying as she stood on the balcony of the Mage College, looking over the city of Telha. She had just finished practicing with the short blade Eryk had given her. The intense exercise was a welcome distraction from her situation.

She was in the suite for the chancellor of the Mage College. She had stood here with Eryk many times, watching the sunrise. Now he was dead, and any thoughts of him coming to rescue her were shattered. Even the small bed they had shared was losing his scent. Everything had fallen apart so fast in the last few months.

First, Eryk had left for the Hounds. Then Zyna took her to serve on the war front alongside her. She saw firsthand the destruction an avenging mage could bring to bear on his enemies. The Emperor was turning the fortunes of every battle with his incredible power. The aftermath of the battlefields turned her stomach, but she could tell Zyna was trying to harden her, to season her for what she was to become. A tool for the Empire.

Then Zyna turned against the Emperor just as she was about to defeat the fleeing Bartiradians. Renna had been paralyzed with shock as mages and legionnaires began fighting each other. The brutal battle and ensuing chaos still haunted her nightmares. At first, she didn't understand what was happening, thinking Zyna was being controlled and that the Bartiradians had set a trap. But no, it was a bloody coup.

Initially, in the battle, she had just defended herself, but eventually she sided with Zyna. When a void attack from the Emperor pierced Zyna's head, she went into shock. Zyna was a pillar of strength for her, a mentor. When Renna came to control her power, she imagined Zyna as a colleague and friend. Dozens of the Empire's best legionnaires and mages had fallen on the field that day. She was swept up by Duke Octavian's men and held prisoner.

She had been questioned extensively by the Truthseekers and had managed to satisfy them that she had not been privy to the treason, nor had she attacked anyone during the coup. She had been mostly forgotten for weeks in Duke Octavian's camp as he treated with the Esenhem elves for peace and pressed the Bartiradians back to the border by force. She might have fled—if she had anywhere or anyone to flee to.

When Duke Octavian's entourage returned to the capital, a triumphant parade was held for him. He professed that he had avenged the Emperor's death at the hands of his Bartiradian killers and reestablished the treaty with the Esenhem elves, effectively ending the war on the eastern front. The great victory for the Telhian Empire had rung through the streets.

No word of Zyna's or the others' betrayal had circulated, nor had the identity of who actually killed the Emperor—Renna recalled that it was some legionnaire with a bow. She assumed all those who could speak the truth were now long dead or allied with Octavian. The value of her life if she didn't cooperate was made known to her by subtle threats from those around her.

It was clear that Renna's value as a powerful mage was the only thing keeping her alive. Too many mages had been lost in the war and the insurrection led by Zyna. Renna had been stashed here in these apartments, supplied with food and spell books brought to her by legionnaires who guarded her door. The spell books on the table were for powerful spells: immolate and tornado.

Immolate was a spell that targeted a small area, rapidly increasing the temperature and igniting everything inside. It was a painful way to execute enemies of the Empire in a public setting. The tornado spell created a swirling vortex of air that continued to grow as long as it was fed aether. It could be directed at armies if the mage was given enough time. Being forced to learn these spells was a way to make sure she was helpful in the Empire.

They thought she would be comfortable in these suites, but instead, they reminded her painfully of wonderful memories and a more carefree time. Eryk's presence had briefly rescued her from her fate as a brood mare for one of the Emperor's sons. Eryk had made the days bearable for her, and she had looked forward to spending time with him. Now he was dead, and so was any fantasy of Eryk rescuing her.

After being sequestered in the tower, Renna had befriended the quartet of legionnaires who guarded her. She learned Eryk's fate from them. One of the legionnaires even got the official report. Eryk had died fighting the Boutan orcs in the western Empire. She read it nearly a dozen times, unable to believe it. Eryk had always seemed invincible to her, like Fortuna was actually protecting him.

She needed to harden herself to her reality if she wanted to survive. She watched the city below as it prepared to welcome its new Emperor. The door to the common room banged open with authority, sending a chill through her. She rarely had any visitors, but guessed her presence would be required at the parade.

She straightened her spine to face the intruder. She froze in place; it was Mage Ona. Her sleek black hair was pulled back tightly, and her piercing blue eyes scrutinized Renna. "I'm surprised they haven't already hanged you," she said mockingly. Zyna had warned Renna that Ona had acquired a potent amulet that amplified her charm abilities. Since that time, Renna had trained in both mental and magical defenses.

She was surprised that Ona was alone and couldn't help retorting with a stinging comment. "Where is your brother? Doesn't he hold your leash?"

Ona wove a spell form with one hand, and a dagger of ice condensed in her fingers. Anger was clear on her face as her veins bulged and the tendons in her neck strained. It was no secret that her twin brother, Cashius, abused her. Her treated his own sister like he treated all women. "I am no longer tied to him," Ona said icily.

Renna didn't back down, and they stared at each other for a long minute. Ona and Cashius had tormented Renna since she had arrived at the Mage College, but now Renna was more powerful than both of them combined. They couldn't accept that someone outside of the First Citizens had more raw power. A realization washed over Renna: Ona was a First Citizen! She wore the ceremonial brooch that indicated she had been raised. Ona smirked in victory. The condensed ice blade clattered onto the floor, but it didn't shatter.

Renna wiped the shock off her face. "Why are you here?"

A malicious smirk formed on Ona's face. "I am to ensure you cooperate during the coronation and walk diligently by Emperor Octavius's side."

"What? Why would I do that?" Renna's mind raced. Why would she be given such a position of honor?

"Because you are to be my uncle's next wife," Ona said gleefully. Renna felt the threads starting to invade her mind and she began the fight for control.

Renna fought back and forced out, "Duke Octavian is married."

"Not any longer. Calvia is dead," Ona said neutrally as she split her focus. "Calvia died by an assassin's blade ten days past," Ona added without remorse for her aunt.

"Why me? Why not you?" Renna said as she started to sweat and considered taking drastic action. Her sword was not far away, but two unfamiliar legionnaires stood by the door, probably Ona's guards. She could just run and jump off the balcony and try to fly to freedom.

"Me?" Ona laughed a little too maniacally. Maybe the offer had already been made or suggested. "No." She fingered her First Citizen brooch. "I am tired of being told what to do. You, however, do not have a choice!"

Ona pressed her will upon Renna, and she was much stronger than she remembered. Still, Renna kept her wits about her and focused. Her hand slid down to her thigh as her entire body perspired, soaking the thin fabric of her exercise clothes. She had one of the blades Eryk had given her strapped to the inside of her thigh. She wouldn't become a mindless puppet. She would kill Ona—or herself.

"Enough!" An authoritative voice echoed, coming from the stairs. Duke Octavian strode into the room, his authority emanating from him. No, not from him, but some artifact Renna couldn't place. She had met him a few times and had never been impressed before. Something was enhancing his aura. Three Imperial legionnaires in their shiny breastplates stood guard and were silent as their future Emperor approached Renna. His heavy red and gold robes flowed around his regal stature. Maybe it was the robes …

Her heart raced as he approached and stood before her. Ona's tendrils retreated from her mind, allowing her to breathe more easily. "Do you love your Empire?" he asked, studying her.

Renna stumbled over her words. "I … I love the people of the Empire, yes."

A wide smile spread across Octavian's lips. "Good. The Empire has need of your services." Renna was wise enough to remain silent as Octavian paced in the common room of the apartment, pretending to inspect things. She was sure this encounter was orchestrated. Maybe this was the alternate plan after Ona had failed to control her.

"The Empire is besieged, Mage Renna. It will fall without a strong hand to guide it through these troubling times. I am that hand, Renna." He made eye contact with her. His black hair and beard framed his angled face. To her, there was nothing attractive in his features, but some influence made her respect his visage.

"Did you know the goblinkin have surged from the Endless Dark and established two cities at the base of the Dragon Spine Mountains?" he said softly.

Renna stumbled for the right words. "I did not. I have been locked in the tower since we returned to the capital."

He manufactured a sympathetic look on his face. "Not locked away, my child. You were being guarded from assassins and the influence of traitors. Now that I am sure they have been dealt with, you can leave the Mage College whenever you want. Your guards, of course, will accompany you for your safety." He gestured in a circle. "The goblinkin are not the only threat. Varvao has fallen to the orcs and they fortify their gains in the Western Empire. The Adventurers Guild has sent envoys and warned that the accord has been broken with them, and they are demanding concessions. Agents from the Mitzra Brotherhood have been plaguing my attempts at peace and interfering with the excavation of Atlantium."

Renna couldn't help but show anger at the mention of the orcs, as they had killed Eryk. Octavian smirked and nodded at her evident anger. "Yes, the Empire faces many challenges and is sick, and I am the man to heal it. But I need your help to return the Telhian Empire to its glory." His eyes drifted to the two spell books. "How is your progress?" he said, cocking an eyebrow in her direction.

Renna had never felt so alone before, so isolated. She knew her life might be hanging on a single poor decision. "I have almost learned the immolate spell. I can trace their patterns in the air, just not fast enough to sustain them."

Duke Octavian smiled. "Very good! I was told you were a remarkable young woman!" He turned on Ona. "My niece may have been too hasty in announcing my intentions to you. I have suffered a great loss recently." He held his head in sorrow. "I need time to grieve. You need time to decide if I will be a good husband." His poorly honeyed words caused her to feel ill, but she didn't show it. She gave him a slight, placating nod.

He made eye contact with her again. "But in the interim, I need to show power tomorrow at the coronation in front of the First Citizens and Esenhem ambassadors." Renna's eyes shot open in surprise.

Octavian looked displeased. "Yes, the elves will be there. I had to make numerous concessions to secure the border with Esenhem. All I ask is that you walk by my side." He offered a manufactured smile.

Renna had no choice but to notice the malevolent smile on Ona's face. She knew there was something else going on here. "I ... I ... I ... can walk by your side." Octavian smiled happily, and Ona smirked triumphantly.

"I knew you loved your Empire," he said as he took his leave.

The following eight hours felt endless as attendants fitted her for clothes and prepared her for the following day. Some used magic while others relied on mundane means to get her ready as quickly as possible. It was unnerving because none of them spoke to her, no matter how much she tried to converse.

At noon the next day, she was escorted to the Imperial palace. She had never been inside the walls and was shocked at the exorbitant luxury throughout the structure. She was brought to a massive chamber, easily a hundred paces across. In its grandeur, it was barely a quarter filled. She knew several challengers to the throne had been dealt with, but this gathering felt—sparse.

A delegation of nine elves stood off to the side and appeared to be there as observers only. They all wore blank expressions, but their body language told Renna they would rather be elsewhere. As the ceremony began, Renna did as she was instructed and stood on Octavian's right. When he was crowned, he became Emperor Octavius, the Justice Bearer—a pompous title for a pretentious man.

Renna tuned out the ceremonies as they proceeded slowly and tortuously. There were dozens of mages in attendance mixed in with the First Citizens. She assumed everyone here was an ally of the newly crowned Emperor Octavius.

When the crown finally rested on Octavius's head, moderate applause erupted from the gallery. Renna was just glad this was over. Though he had promised to give her time, she was expecting an engagement announcement from the acolyte of Juno standing before them.

Instead, the acolyte of Juno began a wedding ceremony. Anger flared in her, but should she have expected anything less from Emperor Octavius? There was a brief ceremony raising Renna to First Citizen status, as an Emperor could not marry too far beneath himself.

Renna clenched her teeth to get through this. She could give in and become subservient to Octavius's whims, or she could wait and accumulate as much power as possible to herself. Then she could break free and maybe seek her revenge against those who had injured her. Certain First Citizens and the Boutan orcs who had killed Eryk were at the top of her list.

END OF BOOK FIVE

The winner of the fan fiction contest has chosen not to have his story included in this book. Details on how to join the next contest are available on my Patreon, and entry is free.

Eryk's Adventures Continue …

DRAFT OF BOOK SIX, TITLED *GODOK*

IS ON MY PATREON: PATREON.COM/ALWAYSROLLSAONE

BOOK SIX ESTIMATED RELEASE ON KINDLE: SEPTEMBER 2026
I KNOW THAT IS FAR OUT, BUT BOOK 6 IS BEING SPLIT INTO BOOKS
6 AND 7

BOTH BOOKS 6 AND 7 REQUIRE ADDING CHAPTERS TO KEEP THE
BOOKS OVER 150k WORDS

BOOK SEVEN WILL BE TITLED: THE OTHERWOLRDERS

BOOK EIGHT DRAFT IS FINISHED AND TITLED: ISLE OF THE DEAD
ON PATREON

BOOK 9 HAS BEEN STARTED AS OF SEPTEMBER 21st 2025!!

LOOKING FOR THE LITRPG COMMUNITY?

Join LITPRG BOOKS on Facebook

Or

r/litrpg on Reddit

Special thanks to my patrons for supporting my writing on Patreon. You keep the words flowing and give excellent feedback. As a self-published, independent author, I rely on you to spread the word of my stories.

Seraphim Tier Supporters (as of 10/3/25):

1536539, 1decimal7725 ., 1Sayto, 314resqi, 50hp, 9crimes, A Nani Muss, A. Mak, Aaron , Aaron, Aaron, Aaron Coote, Aaron edison, Aaron Flowers, Aaron Guhin, Aaron Murad, Aaron Offenberger, Aaron Spielman, AB, abcd, abdellah Jamad, Abdulaziz Adam, Abraham Madsen, Absentheresiarch, AbyssalMage, AccidentalReader, Acid, Adam, Adam B, Adam Crawford, Adam Gray, Adam Irgens, Adam K, Adam Spring, Adamant, Ade Adeshoye, Ades Limbo, Aeryn Connerley, Afonya, agoblinsgoblet, Agoons , Agustin Dornelles, Aharon morgenstern, ahgans, Ahmad Abdulfattah, Aidan, Aidan Tremeer, Aiden Johnson, Aiden Ruiz, Aiden Wilker, Aiste Zukauskiene, AK, aka Valr, al lun, ALDGD, Aldon Aquarian, Alec Ruth, Alec Young, Aleck Girard, Alessandro, Alex, Alex, Alex, Alex, Alex, Alex Clevenger, Alex Dread, Alex Galaitsis, Alex Hoffman, Alex Landon, Alex Staub, Alex Zajfal, Alexander , Alexander Child, Alexander Dalton, Alexander Galyen, Alexander George, Alexander Jacobsen, Alexander Jesus, Alexander Strothe, Alexander the Tall, Alexander Van Oyen, Alexis Parks, Alfred Dunn, Ali, Alianok , Alias, aliasbeauchamp, Allan Greenwood, Allen, Allen Walker, AlmightyTurnip, Alpenmann, Althion, AM, Amon, Amos, Andre Belanger, Andrea, Andreas Kristensen, Andreas Vaage, Andrei Sima, Andrei Stoica, Andrew , Andrew, andrew allred, Andrew Crawford, Andrew Crews, Andrew G., Andrew Glass, Andrew Gonzalez, Andrew Hernandez, Andrew Kroll, Andrew Mcafee, Andrew McIntosh, Andrew Nevius, Andrew Omeara, Andrew Ratchford, Andrew Volz, Andrew Wieland, Andrew Yamamoto, Andrieu Pierrick, Andriy Karpus, Andy Baker, Andy Panuska, Andy65pr, Anel Alic, Angad Chawla, Angel Mongeotti, Angela Findley, Angus, Anne Limoge, Anonymouse, Anthiaris, Anthony, Anthony E Perkins, Anthony Fackenthall, Anthony Glenn, Anthony Vieira, Antigerio , AntonF, Antonio, Antonio Bosonetto, Antonio Harris, Antonio Mihai, Antti Väisänen, Anttkk01, Aoth the Arcane, Apelila Paresa, Apinsig, Apophixas, Aram Proudman, Arc4203, Archmage, AreGee, ARF, Arget, Arkell Henry, Arnoud, Arockwell919, Arron Hardiman, Art , Arthur Ibanda, Arun Aruljothi , Aryan Eimermacher, Asadbek Abduxoshimov, asdsa fasfas, ASeaInStorm, AshTek, Aspiring Sage, Aspluve, AstroMyrkat, Audrius Smaginas, Austin , Austin Lee, Austin M, Austin Smith, Auzterify, Avery Duval, Avery Elliott, Awople, Axel Karlsson, Aymane Bakkar, Aymeric Le Tiec-Gimbert, azume, Azwrix, B , B P, B-K, B0X3R0CK, B3CKMANN, Babtain, Bacon, BadgerHound, Bananaboat, Barbara, Barrett Spearman, Barry Carr, Barry Weaver, bart rijnhart, Bart92, Basil Legg, bbjace, Bearded Bastard, bee dubs, Beldin53, Beli, Ben, Ben, ben, Ben, Ben, Ben Bailey, Ben C, Ben Dolbec, Ben Dover, Ben Enz, Ben Hixon-Fisher, Ben Maes, Ben Mauk, ben poore, Ben Schmidt, Ben Waschuk, BenGruesome, Benjamin, Benjamin , Benjamin Berndt, Benjamin fell, Benjamin

Tran, Benni, BenniBent , Benny Hernandez, Bernard Faust, Bernardino Campa IV, Bertram Wilberforce, Big Al, billwanchalo, Billy Hogan, Binu, bioticisbasic , Birchowl, Bjorgy , Blake Stagni, Blankdust, BLead Irish ambassador, Blopingoper, Bluesquared, Bo Tran, Bob , BoB, Bob , Bob, Bob, Bob Hiler, Bob Smith, Bobbuttons, Bobby, Bobby Hartley, Bobby Schmidt, BobbyMcDilan, Bobyrkjedal, Bog Sagget, Bogdan Ezaru, Bohto, Booleans, Boomer, Booz Dowg, Borindak, Boris Mak, Brad D, Braden Moody, Braden Wills, bradley murphy, Bradly Feller, Brandan Skeen, Brandon , Brandon Baier, Brandon Ginn, Brandon Moore, Brandon Terry, Brandon Travers, Brayden Bell, Bree, Brett F, Brett S., Brett Ulakovic, Brian T, brig head the hug, Brinoch, Brodie, Brody L, BroLord211, Bruce Monnett, Bruce Weeks, Bryan , Bryan Foster, Bryan Hill, Bryan Leggett, Bryan Swanson, Bryce, BrycenBeans, Bryn, BubblyGhost , Bulldops, Bumblebeepotato, Byte core, Bücherwurm, Cade Tendick, caeven, cairo191, Cakeboss , Cal, Cale Roberts, Caleb, Caleb Clinkscales, callum joyce, Callum Peters, camelDetective, cameron, Cameron Earl, Cameron Richardson, Capt Zig04, Carl, Carl buck, Carl Creighton, Carlo , carlos espana, Carlos Guzman, Carlos Montojo, Carlos Solis, Carly Couch, Carlye Hawkins, Carnaza, Carson Mengerink, Carugh, Casey, Casey Dearing, Casey Gillespie, castleton03, Catherine, Catherine Gray, CCBlazes , Ceagle, Cedric Petri, ch0zo, Chachi, Chad cline, Chaddaï Fouché, Chai Chang, Champ13316, chance ahlberg, Chance Atkinson, Charles Anderson, Charles Thompson, Charlie King, Charlie Shakles, Chase Schulte, Chaz Baz, Chelsea Edens, Chevin, Chris, chris, Chris, Chris, Chris, Chris, Chris, Chris Atkinson , Chris Bailey, Chris Bradshaw, Chris Carew, Chris Chung, Chris Frase, chris hill, Chris O'Connor, Chris Spangler, Chris6, christian, Christian, Christian, Christian Meek, Christian Mordal, Christian Pettersen, Christian Twedt, Christoph, Christopher Alaniz, Christopher Bonsall, Christopher Catania, Christopher Frederick, christopher fryhover, Christopher Killian, Christopher MacDonald, Christopher Miller, Christopher Sears, Christopher Streat, Christopher Swan, Chriszy , Chuck Snipes, Church, Ciaran Madden, Ciaran O'Collins, CJ , Claire Sarsam, Clint V, Clockwork, Cloudly lofi, Clox, CluelessTurtle95, Cody, Cody, Cody Bryson, Cody Harlow, Cody Hollibaugh, Cody Sherwood, Colden Dostal, Cole, Cole, Cole Bailey, Cole Cressman , Cole Nyquist, Coleman Smith, Colin, Colin Flynn, Colin Heaning, Collector of Stories, colton , Colton, Commander Lobster, Conan Wilks, Connor, Connor Butler, Connor Eulberg, connor uttley, Conor Donahue, Conor O'Kelly, Conste, Corb, corefish665, corey wu, Cornelius Van Swol, Cory Casassa, Cory Crowell, Cory Durban, Cory Harris, Cosmo Kramer, Costin Berbecaru, CozyGoblin, Craig Claussen, Crasher, cRoMaToR, Crookie Gram, CRW, Cryin Daily, CryptoBird, CTQ, Curly Cloud, CurseOfNineTales, Curtbro, Curtis, Cutler1812, Cyanin, Cyko, Czahr, D Akiva, D Y, D.P, Da Worst John, DaDude, DaisyShirt, Dajiinn, Dale lee, Dalton Trent, Damien Hinkle, Damz, Dan , Dan Ethwer, Dan Patchin, Dan Weiss, Daniel, Daniel , Daniel Billings, Daniel Burghardt, Daniel Cabrera, Daniel Cox, daniel dantas, Daniel Diaz, Daniel Elliot, Daniel Foster, Daniel Kennerly, Daniel Kerrick, Daniel Marzan, Daniel

McConville, Daniel Mclean, Daniel Simchuk, Daniel Smith, Daniel Taller, Daniel Tran, Daniel Velasco, Daniel Wilkinson, Daniel Willard, daniello baucicaut, Danny Callinan, Dante , Dar-Angol, Darek Jarosik, Dariel Sosa, Dark Chaos, Dark Messiah, Dark Steel 04, Darnon, Darrell, Darrell Legler, Darryl Peltier, Dave , Dave Rocker, Daviculus, David , David Blackman, David H, David Kloiber, David Kordys, David Mclellan , David North, David Pooser, David Rainford, David Takace, David terry, David Weller, Davide Gris, Davis Unruh, Davram Bashere, DaWykitat, Dax, daz kenzie, dbdlion, dbohomolov, DD, DDose , Deadmoo53, decimus, Delakar , Deliver roo, Delta , Dennis Burke, DenverDrew , denym123, Der J, Der Toti, Derek M Baron, Derek Paterson, Derpy Nation, Derrick Long, Derrick McDowell, derrick oil, Desmond Montague, Detlefas, Devin Hanson, DH, DIACONU BOGDAN, Dib Ismael, DicedOnions, diego, Diggs, dillman , Dima , DLJD, Dmitry , DOCORK, doddib, Dominic Carattini, Dominic French, Dominic Passalacqua, Dominik Keresi, Dominik Kolak, DominusIgnis , Don, Donald , DonMc, Donny Blue, Donovan Slosberg, Doops Doop, Doritoscrunch, Doug, Doug, Douglas Bevil, Douglas Brackett Jr, Douglas Lilley, Douglas Lucas, Douglas Park Jnr, Douglas Sauve, Douglas Sokolowski, dqmj7vmn6t, Dragon , Draken, Dreaming Author, Drew Dalgleish, Drew Roberts, Druen Dorn, duckeggs, Durzo, Dustin Kelley, Dustin McClure, Dusty Stone, Dutt Awsome, Dvd, Dwayne Taylor, Dylan, Dylan Alexander, Dylan Andrezeski, Dylan Sully, Dynnu, E Brown, Eb, eddy miot, Edison, Edoardo Caletti, Edvinas , Edward Battaglino, Edward Covell, Eich8noe, El Camino 82, El_Dominicano, Eli Butler, Elias, Elijah Garner, Elmar Jürgens, emacsuser, Emil, Emma, Emma1997, emmanuel akala, Emo Used HM01, Endre Myrvang, Enjoyer_Of_Books, Enoch Chong, Er Morales, Eriach, Eric, Eric Fry, Eric Fuller, Eric Kane, Eric mats, Erik Houk, Erik McFetters, Erik Ruehl, Eriks vitolins, Erkki Parkkulainen, eroth, Errannz, Estacado, Ethan Halm, Ethan Hensel, Ethan Rosenberger, Etrius, Evie Freylap, Evil_Rises, ExMemoria, ExRys, ExternalChaos, Ezekiel_Elated, Faa Diallo, Fabian , Fahnir, Falconer, Fallacha, Farm Boyaf, FartMother, Faruk Hussein, Fast Lance, FastFoodNation, fbolt55, FeelingsandFoibles, Felipe E Montes, Felix Chin, Fennil, Fenris, Fethryn, Fias, figaro1010, FightingJoe, Filin, Filip, Filip, FinalSmile, Finn, fkwtflol, Fl0dis, FLaMe, flame5333 jef, Flameskull 04, FlamingWombat3, flitter, FloopyMuffin, Florijan Ratajc, Flormph, Flusspferd, Folregg, fondlec, Forty Forty, Francis Abair, Francisco Rosa Leal, FranciscoDirect, Frank , Frank, Frank Meads, Frankie, Franklin , Fred Fontenot, FreeForAll, Frog Joe, FryHandler, Fríði Friðmundsson, Fullblack , Furkan Arslan, G, G, gab papigabi, Gabe Canada, Gabe S, Gabriel Albino, gabriel Armieux, Gabryel, Gafall, GameJuris, gappy, Garnt , Garrett, Garviel Geist, Gary Dunderdale, Gary Haynes, Gary R. Hovatter, Gary Skellington, Gavin, Gaétan Fairy, General Mustard, Geof Brown, Geoff R., George Aspi, George Dashner, George Kramer, George mathis, Gerin, Germano, ghladheon, Ghost, GhostStep, Giantorange , Gilles , gingerbeard, Girge, glare31337, Glassdios, glen perry, Glenn S, Glibbernox, Gokufix Murphy, Goldarch, Golden, Goldenman128, Gonzalo Cordova, Goose, Got Heem 11, Grant lee merrifield, Grant Ruhoff, Grantland Case, Grave-of-Orion, Greatish44, Greed, Greenboy676, Greg310, Gregory Crane, gregory pfister, Gres, Griffin bube, Grosbilljunior, Gruesome_Garry, Gummie, Guuldan, Gwalmeich, H, Halfpint, Halmerbauer, Hanif Badirou, Hans-Henning Vogt, Hao Li, Hao Meng, Happybirthday 213, HappyNoms, HappyTrails, Harrison Brown, Harry Sapien, Hasmuffin, hasrul naim, Hassan Masroor, Haven Kardel, Hayden Futch, Heather Goff, Heddall, Henry Keegan, Henry Uguala, Hi, HideousGrain, HiLander, Hiliwan, Hilly, hjemme, Hms, Hoang Le Minh, Hollowlce, Hons, HoodleWoodle, Hornblower, Howard Feld, Howard McCallen, Howard Smith, hrs, Hugh Jass, Hugo, Hugsenuef, Hunter L, HyperS, Hypnotical, Håkon, I Is Patron, Ianjack101, ibrins, Icaro Souza, iCe, Ichigo Kurosaki, IG, Igor Chmurski, Igor Twardowski, il, Ilya Katz, Imagination, ImBaroqe, Imgpk, Incraze, InfernalDrake, inkaral, Inner peace, Insomnia, Instep, Inter, Invalid Entry, isaac maxwell, ISB, Ishozar, Ittnir, iuvius, Ivan Kanewske, Ivo Lieberam, izzy xl, J Whit, Jabama, Jack, jack axe, Jack Dallman, Jack Gomersall, Jack J. Lee, Jackdaw, Jackel13, Jackson Hazeltine, Jackson P, Jackson Ragland, Jacob , Jacob, Jacob Andrews, Jacob Bullock, Jacob Devine, Jacob Diver, Jacob Garza, jacob james, Jacob Jimenez, Jacob Kendall, Jacob King, Jacob Lawlor, Jacob Smith, Jacob Theis, Jacques, Jade BONNET, Jaimenz, Jaishel, Jake, Jake Dramose, Jake Farmer, Jake88, Jakob, James, James, james, James Adams, James B, James Brookman, James Crutchley, James Dalton, James Dellorso, James Hanson, James Irwin, James Klatt, James Mason, James Mitchell, james nunn, James Phillips, James R, James Reese, James Wright, James1, Jan Flammer, Jan Kingsly, Japon, Jared, Jarl, Jarred Allen, Jason , jason, jason ashford, Jason Baines, Jason Jaca, Jason Pierce, Jason Quinn, Jason Thiroux, Jason Weathers, Jasper Cooke, Javaie davis, Jay, Jay B., jay gamble, Jayden Gibbs, JC, JCoe, Jeanny, Jeff, Jeff Astor, Jeff G, Jeff G., Jeff Gelb, Jeff Hall, Jeff James, Jeff Kollada, Jeff Maiden, Jeffery Cantrall, Jeffrey whitworth, Jeffrey Worrall, Jelani Willock, jens petersen, Jentry Lange, Jeremiah Ramirez, Jeremy Loffredo, jeremy macquart, Jeremy McMahon, Jeremy Miers, Jeremy Neumann, Jeremy Stohl, Jeremy Terral, Jerkface, Jerremy Chancey, jerry dickerson, Jerry Holman, Jesper Hansen, Jesse, Jesse Murray, Jesus De Guzman, Jethro, Jim, Jim Baumann, Jim Clay, Jim D, jim jaco, Jimmy, Jlan, Joaquim, Joe, joe, Joe Broussard, joe kimball, Joe Mathis, Joe V, Joel, Joey New, Johannes, Johannes, john, John, John, John, John b, John Bruehler, John Doe, John Doe, John Gabriel Regier, John Horan, John Howard, John Hurley, John Hyland, John Jimenez, John L., John Marcus, John McCarter, John McClenaghan, John Mockert, John Moses, John O'Connor, John Pendt, John Queen, John Ryan, John Schroeder, John Smith, John Van Lennep, John Wickham, John Zupke, johnathan stewart, Johnny Lewellen, JoKit, JollyRodger, Jon, Jon, jon, Jon H., Jona, Jonah Thomas-Morris, Jonas, Jonas Sorgalla, Jonathan Boustani, Jonathan Gleeson, Jonathan Mitchell-Donnelly, Jonathan Parkin, Jonathan Walker, JonO, Joost Boere, Joppest , Jordan , Jordan, Jordan A, Jordan Brewer, Jordan Long, Joseph, joseph beaufait, Joseph Dye, Joseph Gambs, Joseph Sutherland, Joseph Wade, Joseph *wade Miller III, Joseph Whang, Josh, Josh Fryza, Josh James, Josh Lewis, josh s, Josh Turple, Joshau , Joshua, Joshua, Joshua Davies, Joshua Fletcher, Joshua Hall, Joshua Hutton, Joshua Mclemore, Joshua Morris, Josiah, JP, JR Jones, Jravid, JS , Jsdorris, Jswcp, Juan Almagro, Juan Diego, Juan Duran, Juan Magallon, Jude, Juha Laaksonen, Jules Pearce, Julian Godfrey, Julian Lockwood, Juliana, Julien , Julius, Julius Bolin, Julius Gutierrez, Julkur, Juninho Santos, Junior, Just a dude, Justin Barnett, Justin Biebow, Justin Elliss, Justin Garrett, Justin Golenbock, Justin Gray, Justin Jumper, justin snowden, Jye Bell, JZP, Ka Bo, kaalveiten , Kai, Kairê Leão, Kaladin12, Kallen23, Kananiio, Kapitoshka, Kaptain Blauebär, Karkas, Karlo Braceros, Karma-mojo, karmaslap , Karnnie , Kasim Charles-Walcott, KatarnK , Kavi Fullerton, Kavi Kottege, Kawaii Potatoe , Kaze , Keepcookin', Kegan, Keith Keogh, Keith Turner, kelvin Lamar riley, Ken Goretzki, Ken Jones, Ken Q, Ken Richmond, Ken Williams , Ken WoTCom, kendall taylor, Kenevil Blackhart, Kenneth Burns, Kenneth c King, Kenneth Fazzone, Kenny, Kent Malizia, Kentucky Fried Children, Kerene Horsford-Nero, Kevan Benson, Kevenalex , Kevin, Kevin , kevin B, Kevin Bulington, Kevin Green, Kevin Robertson, Kevin Spock, Key, Khalyos, Khress , Killean, Kilobravo777, Kim Simpson, king hero, KingMike , kingZ, KipBR, Kirby Rheiner, KIRK CHANG, Kirk Morgan, Kirk White, Kirvin, Kit, Kjc, KJS, Klatue, Ko-Ray, Kolja Strohm, Kompass , Konge, Konstantin Eckert, Koral, Korriberg, Korv Stroganoff, Koryna Diaz, kovi 17, Koyze222, Kraahk Torenstahl, Krensr, Kristof Dohrmann, Kristoffer Persson, Kspires999, kutetsu Kutetsu, Kwonk, Ky Theriault, Kyle, Kyle Barber, kyle hirshson, Kyrre Göran, Kévin, L, Labruta146, Ladyhotcomb, Lars Himmelberg, Lars Nyland, latus , Lauta, Lavos, lawda199, Lawrence Loo, Lazarius, lazarus, LBHammers, leafs, LeapoldJKLOL , Lee Cravey, Lee Mccartney, Lee Powell, Lee S Rosen, Lee Singleton, Leherion, Lemes , Leo Grassilli, Leo Hartmann, Leon Rolf, Leshawn Mackey, Levi J Barella, Liam Andrews, Light, LillysHeart, Lindasm, LIndy, Lintharas, Lloyd William Brydie, LM W, Logan, Logan Petersen, Logan Vandermause, LogicalGay, Lonly Alex, LoquaciousT , Lorax, Lord Rahl, Lordberty , Lordberty, LordDark , lordsenju, Lorenzo Campbell, Lost1nCarcosa, lowbar squat, Loweti , LQ, lspd, LT, Luca van der Ster, Lucas Jakobsen, Lucas Sevenants, luir mor, luis angel jimenez rubio, luis dellinger, Luis E H Basulto, Luis Rubio, LuisC, Lukas Pribil, Luke Ganny, luke whitsell, Lunchtime, LundeFool, Lupercal, Luqman, lusR, lxllxl592, Lycantinu , Lyle Parr, Lynia, m h, M Schweibold, M van Dongen, M- F, M.R N, M.S.McGowan , m0000se, M4 Milli, M4AD, Mach Laveiilan, MacMahon Wenzl, Mads Jørgensen, Mae, Magda , MagicWafflez , Mait, Malachi Taylor, Malcolm Nicholson, Mandrell Thompson, Manni, Mantiqore, Manuel , Marc Arft, Marcel Mengdehl, Marcellus, Marcos Subervi, Marin MNA, marjorie_brown59@Yahoo.com, Mark, Mark, Mark, Mark Chandler, Mark Corwin, Mark Mersman, Mark Newton, Marnie , Marten Byl, Martin Ljungberg, Marvin Amann, Marvin Rodriguez, MAS, Mason, Matej Pavin, Matheus Pozzobon, Mathias Gebhart, Mathias Iversen, Mathias Richard, Mathieu Fortin, Matt, Matt Dewit, Matt DiMeo, Matt Funk, Matt Hidayat, Matt Miller,*

Matt Suhre, Matt Walters, Matt Weber, Matthew, Matthew, Matthew Barker, Matthew Bernardin, Matthew Crooks, matthew dooley, Matthew Harris, Matthew Konishi, Matthew Montevideo, Matthew Murphy, Matthew Parikka, matthew young, Mattole Whitaker, Max, max George, Max Moraw, Max Wolf, Maxamud Ciise, Maxcrazy7, Maxime Lequain, Maximus, Maximus Terror, Mazid Alkhaldi, McPatreon, mcross72, Mdog, Mediko, MeepGod, Megan M, MelchY2797, Melissa, Mers, Mgs, Michael, Michael, Michael, Michael, Michael B, Michael Basso, Michael Behrens, Michael Buckbee, Michael Byrne, Michael Esparza, Michael Harris, Michael Hurtt, Michael Kemp, Michael Mayfield, Michael Nau, Michael Pate, Michael Richter, Michael Ryan, Michael S, Michael Salamon, Michael Santry, Michael Shearer, Michael Steed, michael wolff, Michal Vašiček, Michelle H, Mick Gormley, MidhetC, Miguel Ochoa, Mikael Ayoul, Mike, Mike, Mike, Mike, Mike, Mike Cyr, Mike Dabrowski, Mike Martin, Mike Mike, Mike Smith, Mike suders, Mike Uchiha, Mike Weiser, Mikey Wilburn, Mikeyg1999, Mikhail Brenning, Mikiru189, Mikkel Hansen, Milo Bundervoet, Mina She, Minocho, Mitchell Heilman, MJ, MN, mojosilver82, momo, momo2009, Mongkon Srinoi, Monsi, Montana weatherly, moon, Moresleepneeded, MoritzM, Mortamir, MountainFoundation, Mr. Bro, MrFixit, MrPerikles, MrPrince, MrRobonator, MrWolfy, MrYahikoM, Ms. Link, Mubarak Sulaiman, Mueller, Mugatu9, Myke Sh, Myro, Mysani, N, N Holifield, Nabeel Javed, Naira, Nairolf90, NaKd hermit, Name, Name, Name1, nameless_anonymous, Naomi France, Nasir Mahmmud, Natan Jacobs, Nate, Nate, Nate, Nate Kaufman, Nathan, Nathan Gallagher, Nathan Lassiter, Nathan Mayes, Nathan Starke, Nathan Terv, Nathan Tran, Nathan Zhang, Nathaniel Chan, Nelson Francis, Nelson Hayes, Nelttab, neo, Nerosol, Nervous Man, Neutron_Bomb, nfi42, Niceandunaware, Nicholas Buchanan, Nicholas Carter, Nicholas Chew, Nicholas Eden-Smith, Nicholas Harris, Nicholas Kelly, nicholas lay, Nicholas Livingston, Nick, Nick Ceriani, Nick Nicholson, Nick Somich, Nick Swenson, Nicolas BOUCHON, NightRider, Nightworm, Nijex, Nik Dunlap, Niklas Mauksch, niklas strack, Niko, Nikolai Rose, Nikolas Lachinski, Nikos Riggos, Nimbus, Nina Speicher, Noah Löfgren, Noah Roberts, Noah Slatkin, Nobody, noel meehan, Nolan, Nolan Nivison, nonyabiz2, Noobokhin, Norm, Nova, NovaZero, Novus, Npad11111, NPCMasterRace, Null Null, numberwho, nymaxilian, OccasionalNewb, Oetti, Oguz Kilcan, Oh Snap, Oires, Olatubosun Korede, Old Silver, Olka Porebska, Olu Akano, Omar Fajardo, Omoz Osadebaima, OnlyBoops, Oranje, Oscar, Oscar Arrowsmith, Oscar Heiberg, Oskar Hamberg, Oskari Ponkala, OSLeaf, Osman, Osman Hussein, Otter Pops, Otto Kovar, OutlawOC, Owen Jones, P.R. Bakker, PA-JO, Pablo, Page, Pal. ie, PandaDeus, PapaSmurf1K, Parzival, Pascal L, Pat Schwertel, patato man, Patrick, Patrick Benham, Patrick Camp, Patrick Dziak, Patrick Lodge, Patrick M. Nagel, Patrick Norris, PatronTurtle, Patt, Paul, Paul Bleakley, Paul pepping, Paul Rauner, paulo pereira, Pavante, Paxi, Paym, Peevara Kheereemek, Pere, person1357, Person8, Pete, Pete Vogel, Peter Palma, Peter Pan, Peter Stawiarski, Peter Taliaferro, Phil, Philip Ross, Philipp Duckwitz, Philipp Rüger, Philippe Lafreniere, Philippe Millot, Phillip Ingram,

Phillip Simons, Phillipp Zschiedrich, Pierre-jean Samaran, Pijeon, PitterPat, pizzaranger, Polar Bear, Poldarn, Pontus Allansson, Poon Yee, Poon Yee, Potato, PotatoFry, prateek choudhary, Prinny Knight, procrastinator1000, pseudonym, PTW, pugstg, Pulse, Puri Iresan, Putrick, Quasiwani , Quez, Quinn Hill, Quinstin, Quintox Talos, R, R. Maxwell Steele, R4wlo, Rachael Heal, Rachel, Rachel Clark, Raelik, Rah, Rahul Sanku, Randall Kemper, Randy, Ranthorn, Rasmus, Ravonsword Aceicer, Raymond handy, Rd Zg, ReadAthon45, Reader reading, Readreadread, Reaper22, RebelRitch, Red Goblin, Red NCS, Reece Grimshaw, Reece Raphael, Reece Uberuaga , Regnar Jordan, Reid, reindeer wrestler, Reiner, Rejdan, Remi, Rene Sabathier, Rene Schweitzer, Revan, Rex Martin, Rgirlgreen, Rhett White, Rhys Jones, Ricardo Fusano, Ricardo Jose Sandoval Matos, Ricardo Miranda, Richard, Richard Acedia, Richard Allred, Richard Barboza, Richard Brown, Richard Ramage, Richard Thorn, Rick, Rick, Rick, Rick Martinez, Ricky Yaple, Rico, Riley C, Rion Smith, Rise, Rishav Giri, rizen, Rob Read, Rob Travis, Robert , Robert, robert , Robert, Robert, Robert, Robert Biederman , Robert Butterfield, Robert Crawford, Robert D. Brannan, robert devoe, Robert Gill, Robert Gzivna, Robert Hinshaw, Robert Miln, Robert Robinson, Robert Ruyle, Robert Wagner, robert wojcik, Roberto Dias, Robin Düwel, Rocking-Redman, Rodney Lervold, Rokuro 74, Rol, Rolands B, Roll 2 Seduce, Roman II, Romel Gelin, Ross, Rossi Nuttall, RottenTangerine, Roxanne, Roy Karros, ruben flores, Rubeno, Ruby Whirlwind, Rugger , Russell Housby, RW, Ryan, Ryan, Ryan Banks, Ryan Bennett, Ryan Carbary, Ryan Cooke, Ryan Cowan, ryan guthrie, Ryan Lamb, Ryan Lee, Ryan Lyle, ryan nowell, Ryan Wisdom, Ríkarður Schmidt, Rönïn, S, S33K3R, SaltyPepper, Sam , Sam, Sam, sam, Sam , Sam, Sam, Sam, Sam, Sam Brunette, sam derek chavez chauvin floyd, Sam Driessen, Sam Lilly, Sam Miller, Sam Shiflett, Sambiguous, Sambor P, Samer Kafawain, Samuel Arbon, Samuel Brodt, Samuel Kovanen, Samuel Richardson, Samuel Sever, Samuel Wagner, sanjay prabhakar, Santakat , Santiago Pinedo, Santos Montalvo, Sarah, Sarah Anderson, Sarah Sheldon, Sareg, Sarganne, Satanael, sauna24, Schmiddy, Scot Thomas, Scott Coston, Scott Dawson, Scott Flem, scott girvan, Scott Marshall, Scott Zabokrtsky, Sean, Sean Flood, Sean Hall, Sean Johns, Sean Kauffman, sean m., Secret Squirrel, SENLI, Senna, senses, Septimus , sessoran -san, Seth Bunger, Seth Knutson, Shade, Shadowm, ShadowOfHavoc , Shadowsarescary, Shahar Soel, Shain Oleson, Shandlar , Shane Granger, Shane Hill, Shane Ring, Sharkmanwolf , Sharon Esserine, Shaun, Shaun Delaney, Shaun Mitchell, Shawn McCurry, Shay Stokes, Shaybae , Sherman, Shogun, Sidekick, siim orav, silder, Silent Rain, Silver, Silver Beard, SilverbladeTE, Simogolf, Simon Hill, Simão Wiborg de Carvalho, Sindre, Sir_Kardis, SirReality, SirViver, sithrebel, Sixcatsina Trenchcoat, skati5, SkippyARC, Skyra, Skúli Baldvinsson, Slambo, Slapjack, SleepingNight, Sleepy_Kiwi, Sm8thShadow, Smartfolk, SMILL3Y, smpx, Snakee, Snehil, Snowmad, Snowtree, Snugglebadger, Sooraj Nair, Soulslayer, Sp4ceBacon21, Spaniel Armada, Sparks, Spencer Foreman, spencer w, Squire, Stahl, Stanisław Nędza, Starter_guy, SteelCavalier, steffen stefansen, Stephan , Stephan Brinker, Stephen , Stephen, Stephen Iken, Steve, Steve, Steve

B, steve H, Steve Verdusco, Steven, Steven, steven, Steven B, Steven Savage, Steven Wood, SteveP, stijn eloot, Story Seeker, Strategist One, Streettrash303, Stretchheart, striderfighter, Stryker, SUlex, Sunto, Superposhposh, Suvan, Swanie, Swen, SwiftFate, Sye, Sébastien Kingsbury, Sébastien Piller, T, TallyOne, Tamati Mccallum, Tandom44, Tanner, Tanner Andrew, Tate Norris, Taylor Bouchard, Tazz D Sichmeller, TechMagic, TechX, Ted, Ted mend, Ted889, TeDureShi, Telclivo, temm99, Tempest, Tenro, TerjoR, Terry Guardia, Terry McMillan, Tetsu-nii, TG, THA LE, Tha Le, Thaabit Rivertree, Tharineish Jeyaraj, That guy, Thatguy, The Agent Colson, The Bard, The Cobra Den, The Dude2540, The Elabama, The Fool, The g, The Immortal Orange, The Madman, The Raccon Federation, The1Jeff, TheBum, TheEarlofBronze, Thefreddygamer, TheIronChoad, Theo Tomss, thermal, TheSilentGiant, Thiago Pacheco, ThisIsSquare, Thomas, Thomas Alexander, Thomas Reynolds, Thomas Shaw, Thomas Sloan, Thor Gotschal, Thug Cola, Thundermike00, Tim, Tim Christensen, Tim Dony, Tim Qunell, Tim Reekmans, tim Tuite, Timm Zöllner, Timothy Freeman, Timothy McGrady, Timothy Turba, TinySri, tishane Imperial MageKiller, Tj, TkleonM, Tobias Evighoej Laursen, Todd Kibler, Todd Weightman, Tom, Tom, Tom Dyster, Tom Lambert, Tom R, Tomasz Pieniak, Tomcat, Tomer Erez Ketzev, Tony, Tony B, Tony Selvaggio, Tork, Torphin, Torran Herbert, tory vancleef, TOUZOT Michael, tpearson54, Trace_Of_The_Ghost, Tracie Travoli, Trako, Travis, Travis Shaw, Trenton Scott, Trenton Towers, Trey Zyvoloski, Tristan Oelkers, Troy Muenzenberger, Tty, Tuqueque, Turin, Turora, Tyler, Tyler Buchanan, Tyler Giarratano, Tyler Itri, Tyler Lainer, Tyler Lanza, TyrTheFallen, UkrainianEgg, Ulises, UMCDaEMON pp, UncagedSplash0, Unchosen, Uo, Uğur Karaşar, Valcry, Valter Anunciação, Varkath, vazey125, Vellgander, VeryTiredLeaf, Viceroy Tilton VI, Victor Berland, Victor Metzler, Victor Radivchev, Vincent Ngai, Vincent_IV, Vinnie, Vinny Fontanez, Virgil Washington, Viriath, visigoth, Volkan Elitok, Vsauce 9001, Vu Nguyen, Waffle Bacon, Wafflin, WaitingRoom, Walead Abdelhalim, walla blyet, Warm Hand-Off, Wellington, Weritax, Wes, Wes, Whatever Works, Wheels42, Wilhelm, Will, William Allison, William Bevers, William Blumig, William C, william farmer, william fruchterman, William Horn, William Littrell, William Parkhurst, William S., William Spiva, william wallace, William Ward, willydasilva, Win, Winslet Di Caprio, woleves, WolfeBot, Wouter de Groot, Wren Ao, ws, Wtfergu, Wurger, Wurli Baer, Wxavy, wy, Wyatt, Wyatt Bramel, Wyatt Eggert, Xeno morph, XiraelAcaron, XLegio, Xonian, Xrfwiz, xyphion, Yewbow, Yo, Yotenheim, Youssef Alaoui, Z, Z, Z Zeng, Z934, Zabuza Momochi, Zac Crow, Zach, Zach Christianson, Zach Courchaine, Zach Ellis, Zach Johnson, Zach Kelley, Zach LaPointe, Zach Zivalich, Zachary Atwood, Zachary Ebbinghaus, Zachary Parrish, Zack Countler, Zander mcneill, Zane, Zbigniew Lopato, zee, ziciiskq, Zolltann, zombo bombo, zsell, Zseta, ZXCVB, Álmos Juhász, Ángel Agüero Samudio, Émile Dufresne, Егор Клинов, максим Попов, あひやひや,

www.ingramcontent.com/pod-product-compliance
Lightning Source LLC
Chambersburg PA
CBHW052346020726
47503CB00001B/132